The Theatre of the World

with all Best wishes Butla

The Theatre of the World

A Novel of Tudor Southampton but also of love and war, Armada and Counter Armada, of pirates and privateers, exploration and discovery, of imprisonment and freedom, of poetry and death, of families and children

C.B. Butler

Matador
9 Priory Business Park,
Wistow Road, Kibworth Beauchamp,
Leicestershire. LE8 0RX
Tel: 0116 279 2299
Email: books@troubador.co.uk
Web: www.troubador.co.uk/matador
Twitter: @matadorbooks

ISBN 978 1788036 580

British Library Cataloguing in Publication Data.
A catalogue record for this book is available from the British Library.

Printed and bound by CPI Group (UK) Ltd, Croydon, CR0 4YY
Typeset in 11pt Baskerville by Troubador Publishing Ltd, Leicester, UK

Matador is an imprint of Troubador Publishing Ltd

To my historical friends
Mary South & Gloria Tack

Remember that the theatre of the world is wider than the realm of England

Mary, Queen of Scots, on the day before her execution

Theatrum orbis terrarium

Published in Antwerp in 1570

Southampton at the time of Elizabeth I

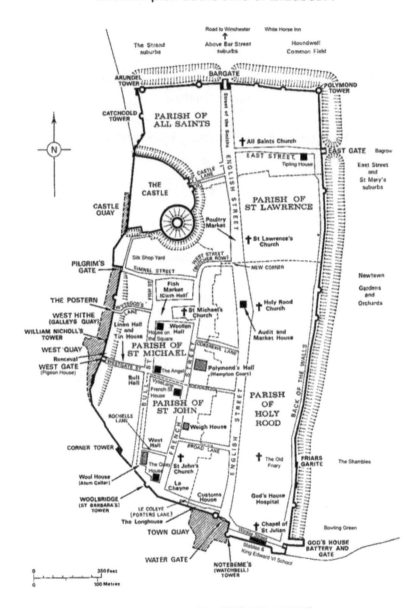

Cast of Characters

Richard Mudford, town sergeant, known as Diccon
Jack Mudford, brother of Richard
William Mudford, father of Richard

Joan Mudford, daughter of Jack, also known as Joannie
John Dypere, town billman, friend of Richard
Alice Dypere, sister-in-law of John
William Dypere, late husband of Alice
Will & Christian Dypere, children of Alice & William
Mark Dypere & George Parker, cousins of John
Old Mother Dypere, John's mother
Tamsin Cooper, common woman
Luisa, Lawrence, Little John, Philip, her children

Alderman Crooke, former mayor and master of Richard
Margery Crooke, the Alderman's wife
Margaret, their daughter married to Alderman Biston
Alderman Biston, mayor and long time enemy of Richard
Dick, Bart, & William Biston, sons of Alderman Biston

Manual Diaz, Portuguese merchant
Luis de la Castro, Portuguese merchant
Jacinta Gomez, half sister of Luis
Antonio Gomez, son of Jacinta
Father Ricardo, a priest
Senor Lopez, a doctor
Dom Antonio, pretender to the Portuguese throne

Walerland Sohier, member of the French Church
Wauldure Sohier, his wife
Jeannot Sohier, his daughter
Elizabeth & Jeanne, his granddaughters

Lawrence Prowse, sea captain and privateer
Edward Alleyn, an actor
Edward Cotton, a merchant

Robert Deveraux, Earl of Essex
Henry Wriothesley, Earl of Southampton
Robert Cecil, Secretary to the Queen
Queen Elizabeth I
General John Norreys

Francis Drake, privateer
John Hawkins, privateer
Lord Admiral Howard, Lord High Admiral of England

William Foxe, town sergeant
Mrs Lister, wet nurse
Annie & Dowsabelle, Mrs Lister's daughters
Mary Smith, a silk weaver

Berta, a former slave
Sam, her son
Saskatan, a native of the New World

Jacket Hall, an orphan
Tom, a foundling
Elizabeth, a ladies maid
Peter, a servant
Peg, a maidservant

Ned Dible, sailor & Ferryman
Captain Jurd, ship's captain
Mr Darvolle, a goldsmith
John Jervice, an apothecary

Mr Dutton, a school teacher
Mr Bathe, a headmaster
Mr Davison, a headmaster
Mr Pett, a preacher

Various mayors, sheriffs, privateers, courtiers, & townspeople

Part One

1586

Chapter One

He was 27 years old and if he didn't die of plague, an accident or at the point of a Spanish sword, he was, he estimated, halfway through his life. He was as old as the reign. He smiled, remembering that his mother had convinced him the annual celebrations for Elizabeth's coronation were in fact to honour his own birthday. It was a day of wonder, each year a public holiday with singing and dancing, feasting, free beer – and all for him! Perhaps he had known deep-down that his mother had just woven the tale to make him feel special but it still hurt when his younger brother Jack had spoilt the illusion, mocking him for being taken in. Richard thought Jack had probably been jealous that he had no special day for their mother had loved her first-born more. If he concentrated very hard he could still remember the smell of her, the toss of her hair, the way she brushed and mended his clothes so he would look well on his birthday, a credit to her. She had died so long ago now. To his left he could see the tower of St Mary's Church outside the walls. His mother was buried somewhere in the cemetery, along with so many past inhabitants of Southampton. He idly wondered where his brother Jack was now, probably in the White Horse inn playing at dice and drinking beer bought by others. He was their father's son: charming, sly, handsome, a wastrel.

From the top of the town's Bargate he could gaze over the house tops and see Southampton Water calm and beckoning. Far in the distance lay the Isle of Wight, protecting the harbour, giving it the natural advantage of double tides on which the town's wealth and prominence had been for so long founded. Wight would make a good base for any invasion, provide deep water ports, access to the Low Countries, and control of the Channel and was close enough for Parma to march on London. He needed to start work on the survey and make plans for defence. No one knew how soon it would be but everyone believed the Spanish would come as relentlessly as the tide itself. Still, he was also thirsty and he had to go to Alice's to pick up John to make the circuit of the walls.

He padded down the rough stone steps to street level. The stench from the Bargate jakes was almost overpowering and he made a mental note to speak to the Mayor about monies to have it cleansed. The prisoners at the counter howled at him as he passed. The prison was filling up with the usual hotheads who had let too much drink convince them that arguments were best dealt with by using their fists; a couple of queens had been too free with their favours in the sight of disapproving citizens; some foreigners looked too Spanish; a pirate had preyed on his countrymen rather than the French and not thought to pay off the Mayor; and the usual thieves and vagabonds, the latter causing more offence than the former.

"Quiet down!" he shouted. "You'll be fed when I get back, and if you don't want your fines doubled tomorrow you'll behave yourselves whilst I am away."

This only led to more jeering, spitting and gesturing and he didn't really blame them. The stagnant water in the bottom of the moat which ran outside the gate was likely to cause an outbreak of fever in the unsanitary conditions of the prison.

Still, prison wasn't supposed to be pleasant, it was meant as an incentive for the quick and speedy payment of fines to gain release.

"Mudford!" Richard turned and saw the Sheriff Robert Russell hurrying up the street. He was a big burly man, one of the town brewers, but his face looked grey and greasy and he breathed with a rattle, and he was always in a hurry, as if he knew he didn't have much time left. "Have you started the audit yet?"

"Just going to make my rounds."

"You talk as if you are off for a stroll around the Marland's fields. You heard what was said at the town council, the Queen has received intelligence, all coastal defences must be strengthened, full alert." Richard said nothing, after all talk would only delay the task further.

"Well don't stand there, do you think the Spanish will sail idly by whilst we piss about? Get on with your task; I need a report by the end of the day."

"I'll write up my findings and recommendations and deliver them to the council chamber before the sun goes down."

Russell's cheeks flushed, which only made the grey pallor of the rest of his face look like a mess of pottage. Richard allowed himself a grin as he strode out down English Street, Russell couldn't read. As he was about to turn left into East Street he saw a small movement out of the corner of his eye behind a buttress of All Saints Church. It was a barefoot scrap of a girl, in clothes too small, matted hair and snotty nose.

"Joannie, what are you doing hiding there? Where is your mother?" The child said nothing, just glared sulkily. "Are you hungry?" Joannie was always hungry, her mother invariably forgot to feed her and her father didn't care. The child begrudgingly fell into step beside him like she was doing him a favour. There was a baker's shop a little down East Street. Richard pushed the door and went in.

"Sergeant Mudford, what can I do for you? Not come to check the assize I hope, it was only done yesterday."

"I don't need an assize to know who has been making light bread, Pearce. I need some food for the child."

"Are you going to pay for it, the brat normally steals it."

"Well so would you if you were hungry enough."

"That's as maybe, but not when you are just trying to make an honest crust." Richard gave him an incredulous stare as he paid for a 1d loaf. "You haven't see Joannie's mother, have you?"

"Heard she'd run off," he said as he banged the loaf on the counter. Richard gave him another look, "I know it's a bit stale but it's all I have left. Today's not my day for baking, which reminds me I need to get to the mill. All right, all right, I'll let you have it for half price, seeing as how you are a town official."

"Run off where?"

"Lord knows. She got into a fight with the wantcatcher's wife, who thought she'd been, you know, with her husband." Pearce gave a nod and wink, bearing his blackened teeth and furry tongue. "Anyway, heard she had linked-up with a soldier who had a passport for Bath."

"Not likely to be back then."

"Looks like your brother is going to have to start paying for his mistakes."

Robert gave Joannie the loaf and told the child to go and wait for him outside the Bargate. He'd track Jack down later and tell him he would have to look towards the child.

He carried on down East Street. It was the old route back to St Mary's the town's mother church, and the least salubrious part of the town within the walls, but at least it was within the walls. Living was worse on the other side in Bagrow and the Shambles. A brush of twigs above Alice's door indicated she was open for business. The small front room of the cottage formed the ale house, with scarce enough room for a dozen men, though often twice that crammed in. Alice was popular and her ale was good.

There was never much trouble at her place as her brother-in-law, one of the town billmen, lived there, and it was a favoured recreation space for the rest of the men of the watch. Today only three men sat on the wooden benches. They nodded at Richard he recognised them as ferrymen, George Parker, Ned Dible and young Mark Dypere.

Alice came out from the back with a jug of ale and three odd cups, which she set down on the uneven table. She wiped her brow with the back of her hand and grinned at Richard.

"Would you like a mug, Richard?" He nodded. "Come through to the back.... Are you after John?"

"Is he here?"

"Still asleep, I'll call him."

They went behind the cloth that formed the doorway. The children were eating bread and milk sitting on the steps that led up to the upper chamber, Alice's two and the orphan she was fostering, Thomasina Hall's boy.

"Can you afford to keep him, Alice?"

"Promised Thomasina. I get a few pennies from the Mayor, and a share of a cow, he don't take up much room and barely eats a thing."

Richard knew that wasn't true but Alice's options were few. She'd been a widow these six months since the death of John's brother William, who had taken ill with the sweating sickness and died. Richard had liked William, he had been a friend. They were of an age and had been in the muster together. William had been of strong fishing stock, and his mother still lived across the river at Itchen Ferry. John and William had grown up rowing passengers across the river till they had settled in the town in search of better opportunities.

Alice pushed her hair back under her cap from where it had escaped, fair brown tendrils, looking a little dull now but Richard remembered how it had looked when she took a bucket of water into the yard and washed it with the Italian soap given to her by an amorous sailor. The water had run down her neck and between her breasts, and soaked the cotton of her shirt.

"Johnny, are you up? Richard's here."

There was a clatter as if John had woken with a start and tumbled out of his truckle bed. Alice poured Richard his ale and he fumbled in his purse for a coin. She reached out and touched his hand saying, "You are a guest." Her hand was still soft but in parts the skin had roughened from work.

"For the children." He put the coin in the little yellow and green painted Flemish pot, an heirloom from Alice's mother that stood in pride of place on the shelf, the home of rainy day money.

John appeared yawning, with sleepy eyes, pulling on his shirt and lacing his breeches, carrying his boots and jerkin. "Give us a pot of ale, love." He plumped down on a three-legged stool, rubbing his short hair in lieu of a comb. He was wiry and compared to Richard, slight of build. His hair was dark, as were his eyes, and he was not tall but he was full of energy – usually. He was tough, an experienced sailor to whom many came for his opinion on tides and where to find the best fish. Richard drained his ale.

"Hungry?" asked Alice.

"Yes, but I need to check..." he let the sentence drift away. "Later, when we get back."

John got to his feet and stomped his boots till they sat comfortably. He grabbed his bill staff from the corner. "Right, let's see what the buggers are up to."

They went out and carried on down to the end of the street and the East Gate. Richard always thought the East Gate to be the least impressive of the town's five main gateways and assumed that it was because it led out, not to a major thoroughfare, but just a well travelled path back to old Hampton. His former master Alderman Crooke told him it had been a great town back in the times of Alfred, but like much of England in those dark days it had been harried by the Danes, so the townspeople had moved to higher ground and founded Southampton. Richard wondered whether the town would survive an even greater onslaught.

They greeted the guard at the gate and another of the town sergeants, William Foxe. He was a competent enough fellow but had a slightly walled-eye, which made it disconcerting to hold a conversation with him.

"Bloody shambles," muttered Foxe. "Don't think these ditches have been cleared for ten years. We're going to have to get a gang up and it will take a good few weeks to clear them properly. We ought to get another gang on cutting furze to line it afterward, furze with good long thorns like Jesus' crown to stick in those bloody Papists where it hurts. Look at the bloody walls here, fart at them and they'd tumble down. You spoken to the lime burner yet? We need fresh mortar to make some repairs. Shame Moore the mason died, should have known better, master mason falling off his own bloody scaffold, bloody good mason too. Reckon his wife will end up in Bedlam the way she's carrying on, I know she's got five kids and one more on the way but all that screaming and wailing isn't going to change things. Twice I got called to her house by the neighbours. I told her she's gonna have to go onto the poor relief."

"I'm going to speak to the new mason tomorrow, he's doing his own recce round the walls," said Richard.

"Well, keep an eye on the bills. With all this bloody invasion nonsense it's a licence to mint money for all these craftsmen. Hi John, how you doing? How's that sister-in-law of yours? Bloody lovely girl, when she going to get wed again? If I could get rid of my missus I'd marry her myself."

"Don't let Edie hear you talk that way or she'll strap you to the cucking stool and dowse you in the ditches and you'll get stuck in places you won't want to talk about," John laughed.

"Speaking of which," Foxe dropped his voice, "some fella at

the Grave Maurice told me that bloody pine needles, or was it pine cones, were good for stopping your stuff getting the missus pregnant. Have you heard if that works?"

"Sound painful to me," said John.

"Bloody painful," said Foxe. "Mind you, stones aren't much better. Missus tried beeswax once."

"My Ma mixes up a potion for the girls of the Ferry village, rue, savin, mint, but you have to go careful," muttered John.

"John!" spat Richard. He could arrest them for speaking of such things. As officers of the court they should know that.

Foxe winked his one good eye. "Best stick to the leather I got from a Dutchman I guess."

"We should get going," said Richard, moving off.

"Well I hope the rest of the defences aren't as bloody terrible as this, it's a weak point, you mark my words." Foxe spat into the ditch, shaking his head in exaggerated despair.

Richard and John carried on along the eastern walls till they reached the site of the old friary. The few remaining friars had left nearly fifty years before after the last abbot had tried to stand up to the old King. They stopped off to relieve themselves at the friars' benches where the friars had built their reredorter out over the town moat.

"So don't you use anything?" asked John as he shook his cock.

Richard didn't answer. He knew common women used wool soaked in vinegar and, if he wanted to protect himself from disease and ward off infections, that linen soaked in potions held on with a ribbon was a trick he had learned from Italians visiting the port.

Richard gazed over at the old friary dovecot. It had been turned into a half round tower to boost the eastern defences but someone had forgotten to tell the doves and pigeons, which still made nests in the surviving nooks. Yet the eggs and fresh meat were a bonus when the harvest was poor. Pigeon droppings were also full of nitre. Extraction was a foul process but the black powder produced, saltpetre, was worth a fortune as gunpowder for weapons. Suddenly there was an almighty bang from God's house tower. As the town's main guns were stored there Richard and John ran towards the tower stuffing their shirts back in as they went.

"What the hell? It can't be the Spanish, there would have been a warning, a beacon, a rider," John said almost to himself.

"The smoke is coming from inside the tower, the gunner must have fired," Richard answered.

As if he had heard them Peter Breme came spluttering out of the wooden door at the foot of the stairs that ran up to the long gallery which held the town cannon.

"Peter, is that you?" John called.

Peter's face was covered in black soot and he was patting down his clothes putting out the embers that were making scorch marks all over the front of his doublet.

"Hello lads!" He started to cough and splutter again and John patted him soundly on the back.

"What's going on?" asked Richard.

"Just been doing a bit of test firing. Some of those guns haven't been fired in a while and I was trying out a new powder mix."

"Not very successful were you?" John laughed.

"It's not a funny matter, young John. I don't know if we will be able to withstand an assault by a trained up army with eighty year old ordnance, and when all's said and done, I'm a glazier."

"Do your best," said Richard. "Do you need a hand clearing up?"

"No you're all right, Diccon, I'll just wait till the smoke clears. I'll go to the friary tap and clean myself up a bit."

"Will you report to the Mayor tomorrow, on the guns and what we have in the way of powder and saltpetre? Oh, and the Mayor wants you to play the drum for the muster on Friday."

"Yes, don't worry I'll be there, and I'll be up and see the Mayor after court tomorrow. Do you think I will be able to claim for my clothes? This is my second best doublet."

Richard just smiled and the two men left Breme, heading towards the friary. They walked along to the Water Gate at the bottom of the High Street and cut along Porters Lane and through the warehouses that dotted the quay, past St Barbara's tower and alongside the Earl of Southampton's townhouse, past the site of the old mangonel catapult and through the West Gate. Richard made notes and they discussed the weakest points, where repairs were required and the sites that needed to be cleared, where little cottages and other illegal shelters had been made in the dark corners around the walls. They went out onto West Quay and made their way past the Postern Gate to Biddlesgate. The gate was filthy and the air was putrid. For some reason it was a favourite dumping ground for sewage and other waste, being near as it was to the little house of sighs, one of the town's public latrines. Richard told John to get the carters onto clearing the mess but John thought they should leave it as the smell would probably overcome any invaders, or at the very least they would slip on the shit and ruin their fine uniforms.

They went up onto the walls and when they reached Catchcold tower, found an old couple squatting there. The woman was sick and Richard thought likely to die. He gave them a few pence, which he noted in his account book and told them they would have to move on in a few days. The men climbed the spiral steps to the next tower. The top of Arundel tower poked into the sky near 60 feet high. It was windy at the summit but gave a magnificent view over the harbour, walls and quays and down the water to Wight. The Mayor had stationed one of the watch there to keep look out.

"Who goes there, friend or foe?"

"What?" said John. "Who goes there? I am a foe, and even if I understand English, am I going to admit it?"

"Well what am I supposed to say?" mumbled Arthur. "I've been up here hours, I'm cold, I'm hungry, I'm bored, I don't think anyone is coming any time soon. Can't I go home to my bed?"

"I'll send someone to relieve you when we get back to the Bargate," said Richard, as he peered through the crenelations. "Look, the Mayor is trying to get us in readiness, just in case. There are so many rumours flying about but the Queen has had intelligence that King Philip is now committed to trying to invade."

"But it's going to take him a bit of time to organise something like that, even with his empire and his silver." John was gazing out over the water too.

"Let's hope so, as we damn well aren't ready."

"Oh great, thanks you two, I feel lots better now."

The two men left Arthur staring out and jogged along the top of the north wall back to the Bargate.

"John, will you see to the prisoners' food while I write up my report?" He glanced down as he went to go inside to the courtroom over the gate and saw the small figure of Joannie, kicking the dirt with her bare feet. "Christ!"

"What?" asked John.

"Joannie, I forgot I told her to wait for me here. Look, give her some of the prisoners' food and then bring her upstairs. When I have finished I'll try and find Jack."

"Will do." John disappeared down the wooden staircase, leaping down the last six steps and headed to the lock-ups grabbing Joannie on the way.

Richard went into the Town Hall. A couple of burgesses were chatting to the town steward in the corner. Richard went to where he knew the town clerk kept a hidden stash of parchment and tore off a strip. He noticed the reverse was covered in Latin with illuminated letters and assumed it must have been a book plundered from the priory. He took a quill and ink,plumped down on one of the benches and started to scratch away at his findings. He had struggled with his letters at first as he had been twelve before he had had a chance to start learning them. Even today they roamed across the page with abandon, not like the practised court hands of the town's official record keepers. When he had finished he used the clerk's sand to dry the ink and left his report on the Mayor's table, inside the coffer, where he had collected his other reports and papers for the next day, asking the steward to lock them away when he was done. He had just finished when John and Joannie appeared at the doorway, the little girl refusing to enter the grand room, a place associated with summary justice and to be avoided.

"Finished?"

Richard nodded.

"Right I'm off to get some supper myself, are you coming to join us?"

"Thanks, yes, once I catch up with Jack. Ask Watkin to go relieve Arthur will you."

"Sure." John disappeared.

Richard glanced about him to make sure there was nothing else that needed his attention and then followed John down the stairs whistling at Joannie to follow. They went under the gateway and across the bridge that spanned the moat. The watchman called out to remind Richard to be back before curfew when the gate would be closed. They passed the pound where a couple of errant pigs and a horse that had been taken from a suspected thief were corralled and soon reached the town mill and the White Horse inn adjacent to it. There were a couple of benches outside, where a few packers and workers from Gubbyns Farm were idling. Parking the child next to old Father Fryer, who let her have a sip of his ale, Richard went inside the inn.

It was gloomy and dimly lit with poor quality candles that gave off a watery yellow light. A greasy smell of mutton and cabbage lingered in the air. A group of men were crowded into a corner and the whoops and applause made Richard feel that Jack was probably in the centre. He pushed his way through the small crowd, whose personal hygiene left something to be desired. One man was emptying his bowels into the piss pot whilst still trying to keep any eye on what was going on. Jack was playing 'Find the Lady' and from the crowd's reaction Richard assumed he had reached the part where he was letting some poor fool win a few rounds before he fleeced him. The action was being egged on by the Biston Boys, Jack's usual cronies and plants in the crowd. Richard never ceased to marvel at how gullible people were. He caught Jack's eye, it was just a flicker but he knew Jack had seen him. He and his brother shared the same piercing blue eyes and dirty fair hair. They both were broad shouldered, Jack slightly less so but he was a little taller. He was also much more handsome. Richard raised a brow and he saw Jack gnaw his lip in annoyance.

"Gentleman, if you will just excuse me for a minute, nature calls – now don't run off I want a chance to win back my hard earned wages." Jack had never earned a wage in his life. He got up grabbed his brother around the shoulder and staggered with him into the backyard.

"Are you trying to ruin my business?"

"By rights I ought to arrest you for gambling and giving ill example to the youth of the town."

Jack spat and stood hands on hips waiting to know what Richard wanted.

"I've got Joannie outside."

"Who?"

"Your daughter Joan."

Jack's expression and bearing didn't change.

"Her mother's run off."

"She'll be back."

"Not this time, at least not for a while, she's gone to Bath with a soldier."

Jack laughed, "Good riddance, she was a foul-tempered whore."

"She's left Joannie behind."

"And that's my problem?"

"You're her father."

"So you say. We have already established her mother was a whore who would sleep with anyone for a farthing."

"Including you."

"Excuse me, I never have to pay for it."

"Jack!"

"She's not my kid, Diccon, for Christ sake, she looks nothing like me. She looks nothing like her mother who for all her faults, which were many, was a good-looking whore."

"Well, her mother thought you the father, the Mayor has given you handouts for the child as he thought you the father, even the child thinks you're her father."

"So I am in a minority. She's an ugly brat, sulky and has a nasty streak – and before you make any cheap remark – she does not get that from me."

"Well you are going to have to take her."

"Why?"

"Because if you don't I will arrest you and I will tell your pals in there how you are duping them."

"Well, perhaps we are related as I can see where Joannie gets her traits. Are you sure you didn't sleep with her mother?"

Richard just stared at him till Jack sighed, flung open the side door of the inn and stomped back inside and marched through to the front entrance.

"Joannie, get in here. Mary, my sweet," he grabbed inn's maidservant round the waist and kissed her on the neck, she struggled but not much, "Can you find a corner for my little girl, just for tonight? I'll make it worth your while." He kissed her again, pushed Joannie into her arms, winked at Richard and rejoined his friends all in one graceful movement.

Richard had to run to get back through the gate. The watch took great pleasure in jeering at him, starting to bring the portcullis down to make him run harder. In the end he had to spring and roll underneath the pointed wooden stakes. The men had the grace to cheer. He brushed himself down not too sure what he had rolled across, and carried on jogging down the street and back towards Alice's. Alice had taken down the brush of twigs but there were still men lolling good naturedly on the stools and benches. The family were in the corner squeezed onto a settle, John, little William and baby Christian with Jacket Hall on the end. Richard slid onto the bench opposite as Alice came out from the back room with steaming bowls in her hands.

"Perfect timing, as ever."

She put down a big bowl of oysters and another of fish stew, and went out again to bring back trenchers of bread. The men took out their knives and Alice fished out spoons from her apron pocket. She looked about her to make sure there were enough mugs before she poured the ale.

"Smells wonderful, sister," said John.

"I see you were out fishing last night, explains why you were still a-bed this morning." Richard drank a large draft of ale. John just smiled, he had been using illegal nets so thought it best to keep quiet, as Richard could sometimes take his position as town sergeant too seriously.

"Nucle Diccon," squealed Christian, and wouldn't be comforted until she got to sit on Richard's lap. Richard tried to feed her oysters but she turned up her nose. "Mamalady, mamalady."

Alice sighed. "You are not having any more marmalade until you have eaten some stew young lady." She pulled the toddler onto her own lap. "You should never have impounded that marmalade, Richard, I can't get the children to eat anything else."

"What was the man to do? Two foreign merchants trading

outside the market, it's against the law, and I love marmalade too," said John.

"I've got some lemons – a few left over from the Bishop of Winchester's New Year's gift," said Richard, "perk of the job."

"Jacket, why aren't you eating?" asked Alice. "Is something wrong?"

"S-Sorry Aunt Alice, I'm really full." He glanced across at Richard. Richard thought the boy looked like a human rat, sunken cheeks, mousy hair, protruding front teeth.

"Don't be silly, you have hardly had a thing today."

"You shouldn't turn up your nose at good food," said Richard, "you should always eat while you can. You never know when there will be famine."

The boy looked terrified but picked up his spoon and started to gulp down the stew.

Richard helped to clear the last of Alice's customers out of the house and then stepped himself into the clear night.

"Do you have to rush off? Stay and talk awhile." Alice leaned on the door jamb.

"Thanks for the offer but I have court tomorrow, big day." He leaned across and kissed her gently on the cheek. "Thanks love, it was a great meal."

Alice put out her hand to stop him leaving, "Richard, the things they are saying, that the Spanish are going to invade, bring the inquisition, march their armies into London like they have done in the Low Countries..."

Richard looked down into her soft grey eyes and decided not to lie. "There seems to be good intelligence that there is a plan to invade, but it's a long way from happening. They need more ships, more men, even more money, Drake and the others are doing a good job disrupting the Spanish treasure fleets. Even now the Queen is reluctant and is trying to negotiate, according to what I heard my Lord Marquis of Winchester say to General Norreys, trying to buy us time, the seas are the key. Hawkins knows that. I've seen some of the new ships, they're fast, Alice. They carry more guns."

"But Spain, it's so big, so powerful."

"Try not to worry, there will be time for that but not yet, not yet, I promise."

Richard smiled and kissed her cheek again. "Goodnight."

Chapter Two

The courtroom was beginning to fill up. There were a few people paying burgess fees and other craft fines, making their presentations to the Mayor, who accepted their fines. The steward duly noted it was received and the Mayor added the tally to his mayoral fine book. It would soon be time for the main business of the day and so Richard went down to the ground floor taking the keys for the lock-ups with him. John and a couple of other watchmen were chatting outside waiting for the sign to bring the prisoners up. Mostly they were the flotsam and jetsam that turned up in any town, looking for work, looking for trouble, or just looking. Richard unlocked the iron doors and pulled them open.

"Come on, the Mayor's waiting," he kicked a couple that were still sleeping to give them some encouragement. The prisoners filed out under the harsh eyes of the watch and made their way up to the courtroom.

Mayor Erington looked pleased with himself. "The owner of that horse turned up, made a nice profit for the animal's board and lodging." He rubbed his hands with glee. He was a greedy man and hardly an example of an honest lawgiver having been up in front of previous mayors on several occasions for bad language, serving short measures at his inn, getting into arguments, leaving rubble on the street and other infractions. He farted loudly and often, due to eating too much rich food at most meals. "So what have we here?"

Richard led the miscreants forward one by one, and gave report of their sins. Most just hung their head, gave no defence and hoped to get away with the lightest fine; four pence for dry frays and sixpence for wet being the norm. If they could scrape the money together they could walk free, if they had to wait for friends and family to gather up the cash it was back to the lock-up.

"And what have we here?" said Erington letting off a raucous bout of wind.

The young man was obviously foreign, of Mediterranean extraction. He had a head of soft brown curls hanging in ringlets around a boyish face. His brows were thick and expressive, his nose large but well-shaped, he had deep brown eyes, thickly lashed and one was nearly closed where it had obviously met a fist. His cheek was heavily bruised and the knuckles on his olive skinned hands scrapped where he had fought back his attackers. The boy said nothing but looked contemptuous.

"Mudford?" asked the Mayor.

"A fight broke out at the Crown—"

"The Crown!" Erington was incredulous; the Crown was his own inn.

"—at the Crown," continued Richard. "When the watch arrived to break up the fray, they were also attacked by the prisoner."

"I did not know who these peoples were," the boy spoke in perfect but heavily accented English. "I am doing nothing, and am attacked, my clothes, torn, look, see."

"Stand back!" The Mayor drew away, "Attacking the watch is a very serious offence."

"And what of the offence done to me? Men beat me for no reason."

The Mayor looked around him as if to suggest that there was always a reason.

"How do we know you are not a Spanish spy?" The Mayor looked triumphant at his own logic.

"I am Portuguese," the boy's voice was heavy with scorn.

"Spanish, Portuguese, it's all as one now."

"You know nothing, you are ignorant."

Richard gave the boy a shove and grasped his collar, "Be quiet or it will be the worse for you." The boy started to open his mouth but something in Richard's look made him think the better of giving another retort. Instead he glowered at Richard and the Mayor.

"Mr Mayor," the Portuguese merchant Manuel Diaz had slipped in the hall, he had been a regular in the town in recent years being a leading trader in woad. "I am sorry to interrupt your deliberations on this most serious case but wonder if I might say a few words on behalf of my young compatriot. The young man fixed his one-eyed glare on his countryman. The Mayor grunted but waved Diaz to continue, he traded in woad himself and had conducted business with him.

"Thank you, Mr Mayor, for your indulgence. The young man before you is a relative of mine, Luis de la Castro, I promised his parents that I would do what I could to train him in the ways of a merchant and to that end they sent him here to Southampton so that he might begin his education." Most of the audience were listening intently to what Diaz had to say, his voice was soft and lyrical, almost hypnotic. Richard directed his gaze to Castro, who was looking oddly at his benefactor as if he was interested to hear what he had to say, or could not quite believe it.

"My mistake, my error, for which I can only apologise, was to give the boy some freedom after his long journey, to explore this wonderful town. I did not explain to him the townspeople's natural reluctance to associate with a stranger, and a stranger

22

from the lands ruled by the King of Spain. That he needed to have a burgess to intercede for him. It was not his intention to provoke but nevertheless that was the outcome. I am hoping if Luis gives his heartfelt apologies and I make just reparations and promise to take more control of him during his stay here, that you, Master Mayor, with whom I have had the honour to do business these many years, would on this occasion...?" Diaz left the question hanging.

Castro looked furious and was barely containing himself. The mayor's attention hung on the word 'reparations' and the hint of preferential business opportunities in the future. Richard whispered to John, "There is something else going on here, if the Mayor lets him go we need to keep an eye on young señor de la Castro." John nodded.

The Mayor pretended to consider, set an outrageous fine that Diaz accepted and looked to Luis to play his part and make an apology. The young man considered his options and decided to swallow his pride.

"Mister Mayor, gentlemen of the watch, burgesses of Southampton, I confess my ignorance. I apologise for provoking the situation which led to the shedding of blood." He didn't say 'most of which was mine' but he wanted to, "I promise that I will be of no further cause of trouble or disturbance to you, Mr Mayor." The fine was paid and Diaz hurried the young man out of the hall, both hissing at each other in Portuguese. John slipped out after them.

There was only one more prisoner, a girl of indeterminate age, barefoot, in old fashioned patched clothes. She wasn't pretty but her face was interesting, lively, a shrewd intelligence in her blue eyes. Her fair hair was filthy but showed an attempt at styling. She stood her ground proudly, most miscreants would not have done so, especially as she was in trouble for begging and offering her body in the hope of food. She looked as if a meal was a stranger.

"Well, what have we here? A young queen by the look of

it, not much to recommend her. Would you give her a poke, Mudford?" Richard didn't answer. Erington liked to take the moral high ground with women who sold their favours. "Corrupting young men, putting desire in their path, you are shameless, a harlot, a common whore."

"I am poor and I am hungry, my options are few."

"Work not an option? Rather take it easy lying on your back? You are a disgrace to the good honest women of the town."

"We are all daughters of Eve."

"Don't talk back to me!"

"Give me work, I am willing."

"What are you good for? Nothing but filth and degradation! You are not from this town?"

The girl didn't answer at first and Richard gave her a shove. "No."

"Where is your home?"

"I'm not going back there."

"Oh really?"

The girl folded her arms against her mean chest.

"Mudford, the charges."

"She was found in Bagrow, pleasuring Gilbert Smith against a wall."

Erington feigned outrage and disgust, "We must put a stop to such bawdry – girl do you have money for a fine?"

The girl shook her head incredulous. "If I had money do you think I would let fat, old, disgusting men touch me." She made it sound as if she was describing Erington.

"Carting," spat Erington. "Double lashing and then make sure she is expelled from the town".

Richard took the girl's arm and started to pull her towards the door. She began to struggle and scream demanding to know the punishment for her customer. She kicked and scratched and spat, she was obviously used to street fighting and had probably lived in the gutters for years.

"Stop struggling, or you will fall." She scratched his face and kicked his shin. He clamped her arms, tossed her over his shoulder and pitched down the stairs. Bevis the carter was already hanging around outside, he was pretty sure he would always get some work from the court. Richard bound the girl to the back of the cart and paid the carter 8d. for his trouble, the town crier was rolling up his sleeves and flexing his muscles.

"Let me guess, double rations," Simms said. "Bet he's touching himself up now with the thought of it." Both men glanced up to the windows of the guildhall where Erington could be seen gazing down. Simms ripped off the girl's shirt exposing her narrow back and small dirty breasts.

"Bastard, these are all the clothes I have, what am I to do?"

"Not my problem," said Simms pulling back his arm and bringing the lash down onto her back leaving a deep wheal as the girl cried out in pain. Richard ran back up the stairs. When he got back to the hall, he saw Simms had been right, Erington had his hand down his breeches.

"Mr Mayor, is there anything else?"

"Mmm? No, no we are done." Richard could still hear the girl's screams as the lashes continued.

"Mr Mayor, did you not think the incident with the Portuguese strange?"

"Strange? In what way?"

"I'm not really sure, it's just a feeling."

"A feeling?" The Mayor gave a deep sigh of satisfaction and withdrew his hand, the carting must have been over. "Well when you have worked out what the feeling is, please feel free to let me know. You are expected at the Dolphin." Richard looked blank. "Alderman Crooke wants you to meet him there."

"What for?"

"I don't know and I don't care, I'm not your clerk."

Richard went down the stairs again and headed towards the largest inn on English Street, a grand establishment with courtyard and gallery and many well-presented bedrooms. Crooke had got control of the premises as part of a shady deal done by his son-in-law Biston whilst the latter had held the Mayoralty a few years earlier. Richard was about to enter the inn when he saw John loping back up the road.

"John, over here." John crossed the street.

"Anything?"

"Like you said, just a bit odd. Once they got outside they started to really go hammer and tongs, couldn't understand what they were saying but it was clear that young Luis was in control, calling the shots. I followed them back to Diaz's lodgings in French Street and hung about a bit but it looks like they are there for the night."

"Right," Richard was thoughtful. "I'm just going to see Mr Crooke, I'll sound him out, he's done business with Diaz. Can you go back and see to the changeover of the watch for me and I'll meet you back there later." John nodded and moved off.

As Richard entered the inn and looked around. He heard Crooke call out to him, "Richard, my boy, over here!" He was sat in the corner by the best window, richly dressed with the remains of a fine meal in front of him. "Do you want something to eat? Boy, more wine here and bring some more stew."

"Its fine, I'm not hungry."

"You should eat when it's offered; you never know when famine might strike."

Richard smiled as he slipped onto the bench opposite his old master and benefactor, he knew Crooke was a rogue but he was fond of him. His hair was greying now and a little bald patch was forming on top, making him look like a monk which, as a staunch Protestant, would not have pleased him. He was the wealthiest man in town and lived well; his nose was becoming bulbous and his cheeks ruddy but his small, dark eyes, though pouched were still sharp and sparkling.

"How are you my boy? You look well, except for the scratch."

26

Richard dabbed his cheek. "Unruly prisoner who objected to their sentence."

The food and drink arrived and Richard tucked in.

"How's Mayor Erington?"

"Not as good as you." Crooke had been mayor for the second time the previous year, which had led to Richard's promotion to senior sergeant.

"'Course not!"

"How is Mistress Crooke?"

"Margery is well, thank you Richard, she misses seeing you, you must come round, make a proper visit."

"And Margaret?" Margaret was Crooke's daughter and briefly Richard thought he might try for her hand, but she had married the then recently widowed Biston, whose prospects and wealth were well above Richard's.

"Well, she's well, quite the lady now. I won't ask after that scapegrace brother of yours. Had to throw him out of here a couple of weeks ago for trying to gull some visiting merchants."

"I'm sorry, Master Crooke."

"Not your fault, Richard, not at all, you have been all an elder brother should. Still I have not brought you here to gossip, but to talk some business, money to be made—"

"—like before?" Crooke had bent the law whilst mayor to justify the impounding of foreign ships, taking payments from others that had been forced into harbour whilst outrunning pirates, sea-beggars and other enemies. Richard had been his strong arm. Their activities had brought them into conflict with the Lord High Admiral, who did not object to their activities but did believe such profits should come to his office.

"Going on the offensive shall we say? Prowse, over here!" He was gesturing to a dashing young man who had come down from one of the rooms above. "Captain Prowse, I'd like you to meet my one time apprentice Richard Mudford." The two younger men shook hands. Prowse was something of a dandy with pearls in his ear, a fine ruff, well cut doublet and clean white hose.

"Lawrence Prowse, late of London."

"London? What has attracted you from the capital, down to our quiet little town?" asked Richard.

"Profit, Richard, profit." Richard thought him somewhat familiar with the use of his Christian name but he had a winning manner that was hard to resist.

"Captain Prowse has been lured from London by the thought of prize money, Richard, we are going into the privateering business," Crooke explained.

"Risky," said Richard.

"Indeed, indeed," replied Crooke, "But the bigger the risk the bigger the gain." He moved closer and lowered his voice, "Captain Prowse has a fine reputation," Prowse merely smiled accepting the compliment as given, "but he is unfamiliar with the tides and the ways of the waters here. That's where you come in Richard. We need to recruit a crew, knowledgeable men, like your friend Dypere and set up a network to dispose of the goods and make sure that the Lord Admiral is as little aware of our activities as possible. Also we don't want to be cheated by victuallers and trades people. If they know what we are about they will put up their prices. It will be worth your while my boy, you know that."

Richard didn't consider too long, it was typical of Crooke's way of working, but no one in Southampton were friends of the admiralty and felt their ancient rights to pirate goods were being challenged by the Admiral and his shark-like lawyer Dr Caesar.

"Whatever I can do, Master Crooke."

"Good man." Crooke called for more wine and the conversation took a casual turn as Richard tried to find out more about Prowse the man. As far as he could ascertain Prowse seemed, for a man on the make, a relatively upright fellow and Richard found his personality warm and open and felt they could work well together. When Prowse excused himself to use the privy Richard took his chance to ask Crooke about Diaz and the other Portuguese merchants.

"Sir, I wanted to ask you about Senor Diaz."

"Diaz?" Crooke looked puzzled, "I've done business with him for about ten years now and have no cause for complaint." He settled himself back in his chair and waited for Richard to explain.

"Maybe I'm imagining things. It was just there was a young Portuguese fellow up in court, got into a fight, usual stuff. Normally it would just be a cooling off in the lock-up, fines paid and that's that. But Diaz turns up in court to plead for him with some tale of him being a relative and then pays far too much in fines without a murmur."

Crooke thought for a while. "Well perhaps the community is being a bit more protective of one another. With all this invasion fever running around the town any small incident can be blown up if you are in the wrong place."

"Maybe you're right, I must be getting as edgy as everyone else."

"My connections in Spain tell me that though the King Philip is finally decided on invasion, he can't decide on the best method. He's reading up on every attempt on these shores since the Romans! No one believes anything will happen for another twelve months at least."

Richard thought Crooke's knowledge would be sound as he had traded with Spain for years and had many contacts.

"There is one thing I've noticed," Richard was all attention. "There's been a lot more trading activity, particularly around woad. I didn't think much of it, was just glad of it. Oh and Diaz has no family."

Richard thanked Crooke, he stayed a while longer to be polite then excused himself and made his way back to the Bargate to check all was well for the night watch before going home to sleep. He became aware of a scuffle going on against the wall as it ran eastwards away from the Bargate. He wondered where the watch was, cursed and ran towards the figures. He was furious as he drew near and saw it was the watch. A couple of the men were just standing around, a couple were jeering and John was squaring up to Walter.

"What the fuck is going on?!" yelled Richard, the rest of the men jumped guiltily and stood aside but John still had Walter round the neck and was thumping him in the stomach. "John! Let him go." Richard pulled John off and pushed Walter back, who once free tried to counter-attack John.

"Explain or I'll chuck you both in gaol right now."

John breathed deeply. "I found him trying to get the girl to screw him."

Richard wondered what girl he meant and looked around him. Crouched in the shadows beside the wall, staring vacantly ahead and holding the shreds of her shirt against her chest was the girl who had been carted earlier that day. There were a few coppers on the ground near her. He looked back at Walter whose breeches were unlaced and who was displaying his private parts.

"For Christ's sake man, tidy yourself up. What in God's name do you think you are doing?"

Walter was still breathing heavily and looking murderously at John, he licked his lips and with difficulty pulled his eyes back to Richard. "I just wanted a bit of fun. If we're all going to die soon, what's wrong with that? She's a whore, it's her job. She was just pretending not to want it, to get more money."

Richard punched him in the stomach. "You're a disgrace, you are an officer of the court and you're worse than half the men we lock up. You two take him to the lock-up." Walter started to complain. "Say one more word and I will have your job and fine you till you squeal." He turned on John. "And you're lucky not to be in there with him."

"What? What did I do?"

"It's what you didn't do; control your men, for one. Get off home and clean yourself up."

John spat blood-coloured spittle onto the ground and walked off. Richard sighed.

"Right unless the rest of you want to be up on a charge, get on your rounds."

He turned back to the girl who seemed to be in some sort of shock. He picked up the coins off the ground and pushed them into her hand, she tried to throw them away, "Don't be a fool, take the money and tomorrow leave town." He straightened up.

"I want to die."

He didn't think he had heard right, "What?"

"I want to die."

"Don't be an idiot, no one wants to die."

As he started to walk away the girl let out a noise, something between a cry and a wail. He told himself not to stop but he turned around and walked back anyway. He stood over her for a while. The faraway look had returned to her eyes. He looked around him and saw Bevis's cart, his boy asleep underneath wrapped in sacking. He went over and fished another sack out of the cart. He took his knife and made slits to create a hole for a head and arms and then went back to the girl. He tossed the sack at her.

"Put that on."

She stared at him not quite understanding his words, but then looked at the sack. She took it and pulled it over her head.

"Come with me." She didn't move. "Fine stay where you are then."

He started to walk away again. He heard a rustle behind him but didn't look back. He went down English Street and turned right up the narrow Castle Lane. He skirted the bailey wall and cut down the side of St Michael's Church. He heard the patter of bare feet behind him. He crossed the square and Bull Street and made his way to one of the old courts off Simnel Street,

Silkshop Yard, in the corner of which was his tiny thatched cottage.

He was always happy to come home, the two room cottage had been his home since the age of twelve. When he and Jack had first come to live here they had shared the upper room with a sailor and an itinerant cutler. The cutler had frightened them as he sat in the corner slowly sharpening knives but the sailor was worse, covered in tattoos, with no front teeth. Yet having found some amusement terrifying the two young boys, they turned out to be good companions and fantastic storytellers. The sailor had given both boys a small dagger-shaped tattoo on the inside of their forearms, Jack had cried himself silly. The sailor had also pierced their ears which made Jack cry even more, though he always sported the most extravagant earrings since. The cutler had moved away to Bristol but left the boys two fancy knives and Richard still had his. By this time Richard was apprenticed to Alderman Crooke and lived mostly in his establishment but he managed to maintain a share in the lodgings for Jack. When the sailor did not return from a voyage, Richard was doing well enough to rent the whole room. Downstairs had been the home of the Basill family, but the whole family had perished of plague. The boys had been terrified that they would die next but they never got as much as a fever. They took advantage of others being reluctant to move into the lodgings to strike a good deal on the whole cottage. Eventually Jack moved on but Richard couldn't quite manage to leave, even though he could afford somewhere better, and despite getting into regular trouble at Court Leet for having a thatched house inside the walls – an incitement for fire – carried on living there.

Richard unlocked the door and walked into the small kitchen and living room, he left the door open as he got a fire going in the fireplace. He heard the girl come in.

"Sit down." He pointed to the small table with two stools

against the wall opposite the fire. "I'll get some water and see if there is something I can do for your back."

He picked up a leather bucket and went back into the yard where there was a standpipe. The town was lucky to have a fresh water supply that had been set up by the friars hundreds of years before. There were taps all around the town for local people to access the water supply. He filled the bucket and went back inside. The girl was examining his room and was about to reach for one of his books on the shelf above the table.

"Don't touch that. It's valuable."

"I can't read anyway." She said bitterly and sat on one of the stools. Richard added a bit of water to yesterday's stew and hung the pot over the fire. He went to the cupboard and got out some vinegar and a salve the local apothecary made up for him to help heal the many cuts and bruises that were part and parcel of his job. He took a cloth and put everything on the table.

"It will sting," he said. "Lean over the table."

He lit a candle, he only bought or acquired the finest wax candles. He rolled up the sack to reveal the many wheels. The marks were livid and red but few had split the skin and drawn blood. Simms must have held back. Richard dabbed the cuts with vinegar to stop them becoming infected and rubbed on the ointment, the girl whimpered as he worked. When he was finished he climbed up the wooden ladder to his bedchamber and in the linen press dug out an old shirt. He went back downstairs and told the girl to put it on in place of the sack. While she changed he spooned the meat and vegetables onto a mazer and put it on the table with a spoon. He also poured ale into two wood mugs.

"Not giving me the fancy glassware then?" the girl asked.

"That's Venetian glass, don't–"

"–I know don't touch it". The girl started to eat greedily but stopped hooking a piece of vegetable out of her bowl with suspicion, "What's that?"

"Potato."

"What?"

"It's something new, usually eaten by princes and nobles put it in your mouth it's too good to waste." She didn't look too sure but did as she was bid. She was too often hungry to be choosy.

"You can sleep, in the corner on the settle; there is a piss pot over there. If you steal anything I will hunt you down and cut off your hands."

Richard took the candle and went up to his bedchamber. He sighed with anticipation at his bed. He had a good bed, Alderman Crooke told him it was a sign of respectability and position to have a good sturdy bed, with pillows instead of a straw bolster. He had a crewel work blanket and a tester over the top to stop mice and other creatures dropping onto the bed below. On the wall opposite was a small hanging depicting the Battle of Ronceval and the plasterwork was painted with images of fish and boats. John had drawn them; he was a talented artist and had worked from time to time with the town painter on civic projects around the public buildings of the town. Richard peeled off his clothes and folded them. He splashed water over his face, and scraped off the worst of the day's dirt and grime, he used the piss pot under the bed before clambering into it, falling asleep immediately.

Chapter Three

He woke with a start and for a moment wasn't sure why then became aware that the girl had slipped into his bed.

"What are you doing?"

"Paying my debts," she said as her hand slipped onto his cock.

"Debt? Stop that."

"Why? You're as hard as iron."

"I was having a very pleasant dream."

She went to slip on top of him.

"Get off." He shoved her away.

"Don't you like women?"

"I like them well enough."

"Well it's a shame to waste—" She went to move onto him again. Her body was bony and thin.

"Get off! I don't know where you have been." He shoved her away again.

"Look, I have nothing else to pay with."

"You don't have to pay me at all."

She was silent for a minute as if considering what he had said and then she dived beneath the covers and took his cock into her mouth. Richard was worried for a moment that she would bite it off, but she was very practised and he started to lose his power of thought.

"Jesus!" He forced himself to focus. "Just get off." As he tried to work out what to do, his body got more excited, he suddenly lost control and could feel himself coming. He shoved her again and this time she ended up on the floor as he released. He swore loudly and leapt out of the bed, looking for something to clean himself with. He was aware of her staring up at him.

"Better than most," she said appreciatively.

"Get back downstairs, tomorrow you're out of here."

She stood up slowly, her body was boyish and almost hairless, but she swayed her narrow hips as she walked back to the trapdoor and lowered herself down the ladder. Richard sat on the bed and rubbed his forehead, this would be the last time he took in a waif and stray. Still it had been a while since he had had a woman. He thought he would never get back to sleep now, but he was wrong.

The sound of the local cockerel and the pealing of St Michael's church bells woke him. He pondered a minute wondering if he had dreamt the events of last night. He could hear the girl moving about downstairs, so presumed not. He got up and washed the sleep from his eyes, dressed quickly and slid down the ladder. The girl had tidied away the debris from last night's meal and had set the table for breakfast, she was toasting bread by the fire.

"I hope I did not wake you."

He didn't answer, got some marmalade and cheese from the cupboard and apples from the barrel. He poured himself some ale. She put the toast on his plate and he started to spread it with the marmalade.

"You certainly have exotic food."

He still said nothing and she sat down and began to eat.

"I was thinking, that maybe I could look after the house for you, a busy man like you can't have time—"

"I have a char woman and you're leaving."

"I don't have anywhere to go."

He just kept eating.

"You might as well have left me to die."

He banged down his cup, "I'm beginning to think that myself."

"Why did you help me?"

He didn't answer for a long while; he cut off some cheese and sliced an apple. "Because once someone helped me when I had nothing."

"Yes, yes, see and look how well you have done, I just want a chance."

"I gave you a chance but Walter was right, you are just another whore."

The girl looked utterly miserable and pushed away the remains of her food.

"It really annoys me when people waste good food."

She looked grimly at him but pulled back the plate and began to eat again as if every morsel was poisoned and about to choke her. He cleared the table and prepared to leave.

"Do you want your shirt back?"

"Keep it."

She picked up the sack from the night before and pulled it over the shirt for extra warmth, everything had a value when you had nothing. Richard opened the door for her. Reluctantly she went out and he followed locking the door behind him. She trailed after him along the streets and alleys; he led her not to the Bargate but down to the East Gate. He stopped in front of a cottage and knocked on the door. It was opened by the man who had stopped the guard from raping her. Richard entered and the girl followed. Alice and the children were at breakfast. John went and stood against the fireplace, he looked grumpy.

"Richard?" Alice looked surprised to see him and even more surprised to see his companion. Richard cleared his throat uneasily.

"Alice, I was wondering if you could do something for me?"

"If I can, Richard."

He pointed to the girl, "She needs somewhere to stay till she gets on her feet. I thought maybe she could help out, serve the ale, and watch the children or something."

"I don't know, Richard. I can't afford to pay anything."

"Bed and board, maybe a few tips, she can sleep on the floor."

"Where did she come from?"

"She was up in court yesterday."

Alice looked at John. "Is this the girl you were telling me about?" John nodded. Alice dropped her voice as she said to Richard, "She was in court for prostitution, Richard, and I have children in the house."

Richard looked sheepish, "I don't know what to do with her."

Alice looked at the girl, "What's your name?"

"Tamsin, Tamsin Cooper."

"How old are you, Tamsin?"

"Fourteen."

Richard swore inside his head.

"Where is your family?"

"I have no one."

Alice looked quizzical

"I didn't know my Pa, my Ma had worked on the streets, and she made me take her place. Men like young girls, she could get more money from me."

Alice looked shocked and then considered Richard and John as if they represented the depraved nature of men.

"I didn't want to do it anymore, so I ran off and then I found I was good for nothing else."

Alice rubbed her forehead and then her neck as she struggled to make the right decision for her family. "Listen to me. Tamsin you can stay here, for a few days till we can work out what to do, but no funny business, do you understand me?"

"Yes, missus."

"Right go into the yard and take off those filthy clothes, and scrub yourself down, till your skin is red and your hair squeaks. I'll find you a skirt."

"My shirt is clean, he gave it me."

Alice glanced at Richard, "Oh did he? Well you can keep that. Go on, I'll be out in a minute."

John showed her the way.

"Richard, you didn't?"

"No I didn't!" but he blushed and thought Alice must have assumed he lied. John came back in.

"Are we all right?" said Richard.

John shrugged and smiled. "Sure we are."

"Good, I'll see you at the muster then." Richard went out into the fresh air and breathed deeply.

Chapter Four

As the threat of immediate invasion started to fade the atmosphere in the town returned to normal. The extra watches were stood down, but quietly behind the scenes the town fathers made repairs to the defences and stockpiled gunpowder. The Queen ordered more new ships to be built, dreadnoughts, swift and fast with guns that were cast from just one mould; it was said they could fire over longer distances and with more accuracy than any previous guns. Musters were still held regularly and a system of beacons and messengers were set up along the coast. Richard kept an eye on the Portuguese traders in the town, he spoke to the bailiff and water bailiff but apart from an increase in trade nothing untoward seemed to be happening. Luis de la Castro appeared to be as Señor Diaz presented him, a young man learning the trade of a merchant.

Richard soon found his attention taken elsewhere as he helped Alderman Crooke with his new enterprise. Crooke had persuaded a few other burgesses to take shares in the *God's Speed*, the ship he and Prowse had acquired to undertake their foray into privateering. Richard helped with the provisioning; a pound of biscuit and a gallon of beer per day, per man, a pound of salt beef or pork per man on flesh days, one dried codfish for every four men on fast days with oatmeal and rice if the fish gave out, a quarter pound of butter and half a pound of cheese, with honey for sweetening. The ship would have an oven for baking bread. He found, with John's help, a competent crew. He also purchased gifts that might smooth the way with any natives they might encounter: caps, stockings, gloves. Richard steered clear of Alice's, he did feel guilty and he hoped the problem of Tamsin would go away. From the comments John made it didn't seem as if the girl was settling in too well, she did not seem to appreciate the opportunity she had been given and John said Alice thought she was more trouble than she was worth. John was more sanguine; he liked her confidence and bravado and thought she would settle down once she felt she was safe.

Richard was dressing with care. He had been invited to a formal dinner at Alderman Crooke's. He washed, he combed his hair, he even rubbed some unguents onto his body, and he wore his best doublet. Alderman Crooke lived in a fine house on the High Street, one of many properties he held in the town. A servant ushered him into the large open hall, double height with a gallery at one end on which the town minstrel was perched to entertain the visitors. A large stone fireplace dominated the room and as a testament to the wealth of the owners, a large glass window dominated the far end. Fine oak panels were affixed to the walls and Flemish tapestries adorned the room, dozens of church candles burnt in Spanish candelabra. A large table was weighed down with silver plate and bowls, on the side cupboard were dishes of meat and fish, sculptures made of sugar, pies, and sweetmeats.

"Richard." Margery Crooke enveloped him a crushing hug. She was dressed like a courtier in a lavishly embroidered gown, strings of pearls and a large starched ruff. Her hair had been teased into curls and coloured to make them appear red, a little cap pinned on the top. "I am so glad to see you, you have been neglecting us." None of Margery's male babies had lived more than a few weeks, so she had adopted Crooke's apprentices to fill the void.

"You are looking very handsome, Mistress Crooke. If it would not seem impolite I would ask you to run away with me."

Margery laughed and pinched his cheeks and kissed his mouth. Alderman Crooke appeared at his wife's side, "Do I have something to be jealous of Margery?"

"Of course, Richard and I are planning to elope."

"But not before dinner." They laughed at their little pretence.

"Richard, my boy, let me introduce you to my other guests."

Crooke drew Richard across the room where a tall, well-built man of middle age stood, with an equally tall woman of sharp features who Richard assumed was his wife. Their clothes were well cut but sombre and Richard identified them as Walloons, French speaking Protestants who had fled from persecution in the Low Countries. Their homeland formed part of Philip of Spain's empire but had disappointed their overlord by embracing the new religion and using it as a tool for revolt and independence. That of course did not sit well with Philip who flooded the country with Spanish troops.

"Richard, meet my friends Walerland and Wauldure Sohier, they have recently arrived in Southampton and have joined the Communion at St Julien's Chapel. This is Richard Mudford, the best apprentice I ever had, clever and hardworking, he will make something of himself, mark my words." To Richard it seemed a strange introduction. He bowed and made polite noises.

Margery joined the group. "And here is Jeannot."

Jeannot was the Sohier's daughter, and their only child. She had the palest skin Richard had ever seen, her hair was hidden away under a demure white cap but Richard could see it was a

42

fashionable red and, unlike Margery's, natural. Her eyes were very pale green and she had an unnerving stare. She didn't speak a word.

The Sohiers were leaders in the immigrant community that had an enclave down around Winkle Street and the little church that the Queen had granted them for their particular form of Protestant worship. They were involved with trade of course, everyone who lived in the town was, but it became clear that they also supported the sea beggars, their countrymen who were both freedom fighters and privateers, usually both at the same time.

They were soon joined by the final guests, Crooke's son-in-law Alderman Biston and his wife, the Crookes' daughter Margaret. Margaret greeted Richard warmly, Biston did not. He did not approve of Richard's place in his father-in-law's affections, he thought Richard common and that he was pushing himself into the company of his betters. He hated Jack of course, who he blamed for the corruption of his sons Bartholomew and Dick who spent their time drinking and gaming. Richard thought they were quite capable of ruining themselves but could understand why any parent would take against his brother. They had brought their younger son William with them. He was still a child but old for his years, a dull boy, prim and prissy and of course his father's favourite.

Crooke made a fuss of them all and ushered them to the table. Biston did not seem very impressed with the other guests either, he was very conservative in his religious views having publicly fallen out with the vicar at his Parish Church of Holy Rood. Margery engineered the seating arrangements so that Richard was next to Jeannot; he thought he was being led into some kind of trap. Margery tried her best to engage the young woman in conversation, to draw her out, but Jeannot would not be drawn. She looked often at her mother who also tried to encourage her but Jeannot was more interested in picking at a thread on her sleeve with her long, slim fingers. Richard idly wondered what she would look like naked and found himself blushing when Walerland Sohier asked him how the fitting out of the *God's Speed* was going. Richard hesitated to reply, not sure how much Sohier knew.

"It's all right, Richard, Walerland is coming in with our enterprise," Crooke said as he tucked into pigeon pie.

"The fitting out is nearly complete. She's a fine ship, she has such an ease about her you almost feel her eagerness to be at sea."

"Is it appropriate to imbibe a vessel with feelings as if it were one of God's creatures?" asked Madame Sohier.

"I have spent too much time with sailors, Madame. They love their ships more than their wives."

Madame Sohier sucked in her cheeks and pursed her very thin lips.

"We hope to be at sea within the next few weeks," Crooke added, "in good time for the treasure fleets."

Walerland nodded his head with his lion's mane of silver hair, "That is good."

Richard was feeling rather hot, the heavy wine and rich food was making his head swim a bit.

"You should give us a song, Richard," said Margery just as he was draining his glass; the wine went down the wrong way and made him cough and splutter embarrassingly. "He has a fine voice, he would sing away as he worked, always singing."

"That was a long time ago," said Richard, praying silently that Margery would get distracted and move onto another subject.

God wasn't listening. In the end Richard could do nothing, although he longed to punch Biston's smirking face. He made a good fist of 'Pastime with Good Company', an old tune written by the Queen's father, and managed to avoid an encore after William threw up from eating too much sugar and pudding. He did notice Jeannot looking at him with more interest. As the party broke up Crooke took him aside.

"What did you think of Sohier's daughter?"

"Quiet."

"Well that can be a blessing in a wife."

"A wife?"

"I'm suggesting nothing, but you should be thinking of your future, you have done well for yourself but you need to cement it with an advantageous match. The Sohiers managed to leave with most of their fortune intact. She is their only child and they need to make contacts, establish networks in the town. Think about it, my boy that is all I say." Margery had joined her husband and was nodding in agreement.

"The girl is past her first blush and her mother is keen to see her married. It would make me so happy to see you settled. A good marriage could make your career. You might follow Crooke and be mayor one of these years."

Richard knew they were right, "I don't think she is interested in me."

"Nonsense," said Marjory, "you're a good looking boy, well-built, hard working. How could she not be interested?"

"I'll think about it."

"Put yourself in her way. Cultivate the family."

"All right, I will do my best."

Richard wasn't sure he wanted to marry Jeannot. He wanted to be married but he thought she might be a cold fish, and he needed someone to warm him at night as well as bring him money and position. He decided he ought to go and see Alice the next day. He had a surprise for the children and thought that might get him back into Alice's favour.

Chapter Five

When he entered the cottage he heard the sound of raised voices and the shattering of a pot on the ground, followed by the noise of someone getting slapped around the head. Alice stormed out from the back room and when she saw Richard she gave him a murderous look.

"'Bout time you showed your face. You dump your problems on me and disappear."

Richard looked sheepish. Alice brought herself under control.

"She doesn't know how to behave herself. She is either rude to customers, or flirts outrageously and some people think I have gone into the brothel business. Old Father Fryer turned up with tales of how he lost his virginity as a boy in the stews the town ran just across the road and that he dreamed of another such adventure before he died! And she's clumsy, I can't afford the breakages, and she's not clean."

"Alice, I'm so sorry. I'll get the watch to put her out of the town; she can take her chances on the road."

"How is that going to help? I'll just feel guilty that she might die in a ditch." She sank down on a stool, "I don't know how to reach her."

Richard sat down beside her, "its early days, love, she's been abused since birth, she doesn't know how to react to kindness, she thinks there must be something behind it, that she will have to pay."

"I'll try a bit longer, but if she doesn't get better..."

"I know. Listen, I want to give you and the children a treat!"

Alice looked suspicious.

"Really, I am going to take you all out for the day, it is a holiday and I know of something special that is going on."

Alice thought for a moment, "I'll get the children ready."

"Good girl."

The children were running around in a high state of excitement, encouraged by John. Alice had disappeared to put on her best gown and tidy her hair. Tamsin appeared from the back room, loitering in the doorway and pretending not to be interested in all the activity. Alice came down the stairs.

"You look very pretty, sister," said John, "doesn't she, Diccon?" Richard nodded.

"Are we all ready?" he said and they started to move towards the door.

"Will you be long?" They all looked at Tamsin and then at one another.

"Mmm, a few hours," said Richard.

"Should I open up?"

"No," said Alice, "not today, we're having a holiday." She sighed deeply and against her better judgement added, "Why don't you get ready and come with us?"

"I don't know."

"Well, if you are too busy" said Richard.

"No, it's all right, I'm ready now as it happens."

"Not before I do something to that hair," said Alice rushing to get a brush and ribbon.

Ten minutes later they were walking up the street, others were moving in the same direction. Alice looked enquiringly at Richard but he said nothing. They went into the Dolphin's yard, it was crushed with people. Richard gathered his little group and guided them into the inn, upstairs and into an upper room that looked over the courtyard. It was already set out with chairs and a servant was putting some food on a side table. Alice looked about her as the boys whooped and ran to the window, Christian twisted in John's arms trying to break free and join her brother.

"You have connections, Mr Mudford."

Richard helped Alice to be seated, he and John sat either side, the children in front of them, and Tamsin hovered in the corner of the window. The courtyard had been cordoned off with straw bales and fencing, guards tried to keep the crowds back. Banks of seating had been set up but there was not enough for all the people who crowded in. At the far end of the courtyard there was a tent and covered wagons painted with fantastic figures. Richard's eyes swept over the crowd. He saw many people he knew, from the watch and from Silkshop Yard. The Portuguese merchants were there with Luis de la Castro. He looked up at John and stared for a long time. Dark figured Walloons were stationed opposite and Richard raised a hand to the Sohiers, indicating they should join his party. Mr Sohier signed they were fine, but his wife muttered something to him which made Richard think she was telling him he should have accepted.

Alice was giggling as much as the children; she saw the little exchange and asked who the people were.

"A Walloon family, lately arrived, Alderman Crooke has some business dealings with the father."

Alice looked thoughtful.

A trumpet blared out. Mayor Erington came into the circle. Tamsin took in a sharp breathe and tucked herself away behind the curtain.

"Good people of Southampton, welcome on this wonderfully

sunny holiday to our feast of entertainment supplied free, for your benefit by me, your Mayor. You will see wonders today that no one has ever seen before!" The crowd sighed collectively. "Still you don't want to hear more, from me, enjoy."

The Mayor bowed and the crowd mainly cheered. The town waits stepped into the circle and started to play. The tension was really starting to build. Richard gazed about the room to make sure everyone was enjoying themselves. Jacket was just reaching out to take an apple off the table; he saw Richard looking at him and quickly withdrew his hand. Richard stared at him harder, what was wrong with the boy? He reached over and grabbed an apple and took a large bite out of it. The boy's face fell. Richard grabbed another apple, tossed it at him and turned away.

"Are we all having fun?" yelled John. "Tamsin come out from behind that arras. You won't see a thing, here take my chair, come on, I'll sit on the sill, come on, sit." Gingerly Tamsin came out looked down into the crowd searching for Erington but the Mayor had disappeared. She sat down nervously as if she thought she was going to be found out.

The trumpets blared again; the crier stepped forward and called everyone to attention.

"My lords, ladies and gentlemen," the crowd whistled and clapped, there were no lords and ladies in evidence. "May I present," there was a dramatic pause, "the Queen's bearward." Cheers were heard all around.

"Oh Richard," said Alice, "not bear-baiting, I don't like it and I'm not sure if the children—"

"Wait, just wait."

The Queen's bearward looked the part, big and bulky, his muscles stretching his clothes, his beard bushy as were his eyebrows and his hair. He swept of his hat and bowed low.

"Ladies and gentlemen, at the kind bequest of Her Majesty," the crowd murmured 'God Save the Queen and Long Live Her Majesty', "I have been tasked to travel Her Majesty's lands and display for the wonder and awe of her subjects the fantastical creatures that live in her majesty's great tower in London."

People started to jostle to get a better view. "Firstly from Her Majesty's colonies in the New World: the porcupine!"

A cloth was drawn back from a cart at the back of the circle. The bearward's helpers ushered out the strangest of creatures. It was not large, perhaps the size of a badger but its body was covered in long prickly spines.

"Look, Christian, look, William." Alice pointed.

"Pig," said Christian, which was what she called any animal.

"A prickly pig," said William. Jacket was leaning out over the window ledge. John grabbed his shirt to stop him stumbling over.

"Is it dangerous?" said Tamsin. "Are those prickles poisonous?"

"I don't think so, or those fellows wouldn't be so close." said John.

The bearward delighted the crowds with the tales of how the creature had been captured, brought back and presented to the Queen. Richard thought the story lost nothing in the telling. The porcupine was oblivious to it all, scrabbling away in the dirt, rummaging for food. The helpers encouraged the creature to make a circuit of the stage by leaving a trail of titbits. Everyone agreed it was a truly marvellous sight. Eventually the porcupine was returned to its cage, the bearward promised that at the end of the performance, those who wanted to could visit the cage and see the creature at close quarters.

"My lords, ladies and gentlemen, if the porcupine is strange and exotic my next creature is mythological, the king of beasts."

The audience tried to guess what it must be. The helpers asked the crowd to stand well back and not lean over the barricades, then they positioned themselves around the arena and made a show of their arms and weaponry.

Alice glanced nervously at Richard and held Christian close, the little girl bellowed her dissatisfaction. "Hush, hush or I will take you home."

A covered cart was wheeled into the centre of the arena. The trumpets blared again and there was a drum roll. Slowly the cover was pulled back from a barred cage. Right on cue there was an almighty roar, women screamed, children cried. The majestic and terrible creature was a lion. He shook his mane and padded around his cell looking down on his subjects. The bearward had a long stick and whip and prodded at the lion to make it roar again and show its claws.

"My God, I don't believe what I'm seeing," said John.

"Don't blaspheme!" said Alice.

The bearward moved forward and opened the cage. More women screamed. More children cried.

"Hush, hush, do not excite the lion!" A quiet descended.

"It looks like the lions in front of the Bargate," said Jacket.

Two great carved wooden lions sat on their haunches either side of the entrance to the Bargate, behind them were two paintings, one of Sir Bevis and the other his squire Ascupart. The town was justly proud of its founding by Sir Bevis great knight from the Age of Chivalry who easily conquered lions and Saracens and dastardly relatives who tried to steal his inheritance. The real lion did not look very inclined to leave his cage, but got up grudgingly at the insistent prodding of the bearward and lazily plodded down the steps to the ground whereupon he promptly sat down.

"Is it safe?" asked Alice as she grabbed Richard's arm.

"It's a wild beast, used to running down its prey and tearing it limb from limb," Alice moved closer. Richard saw that in the cage was the remains of a cow's carcass and though it unlikely the lion would be looking for a pudding. The lion was a bit disappointing, it didn't attack anyone or try to leap over the barricades but the audience were well pleased.

"God, that lion stinks," said John.

"What have I told you about swearing?" muttered Alice.

The bearward was talking again. "Ladies and gentlemen we will take a few minutes to settle the creatures and move the straw bales into position for the next part of our presentation. Ladies and gentlemen, we shall be presenting a play with puppets!" This aroused great excitement and clapping.

As the helpers got to work, Richard stood and passed food around. The children declared themselves too excited to eat and begged to be taken down to get a closer look, except for Christian who had fallen asleep. John agreed to take the boys down and hoisted William onto his shoulders.

"I'll come too," said Tamsin. "I'll help out with the boys, if that's all right, missus?"

"Yes, of course," said Alice, surprised at her volunteering, "John, don't let them get too close."

They went out and Alice attacked the food with gusto. "This is marvellous, Richard, so clever." Richard allowed himself a feeling of smugness, but the moment was spoiled when the door opened and Alderman Crooke came in with Captain Prowse. Prowse's practised eye sought out Alice immediately.

"Madam." He bowed low

"Sorry to intrude, Richard, just wanted to check you were all enjoying yourselves."

"Yes, thank you." Richard's reply was almost curt.

"Thank you, Alderman Crooke, the rest of our party has gone to inspect the lion and porcupine, the town has never seen such wonders." Alice almost gushed.

"Madam, should you ever visit London, you must allow me to escort you to the Tower of London where the Queen has a whole menagerie of beasts."

"Forgive me," said Crooke, "this is Captain Prowse, he is going to take command of my newest ship. In fact, if you would not mind could I possibly borrow Richard for a moment?"

Before anyone could make an answer Prowse replied, "I will keep the young lady company if you like, you don't need me do you?"

Without waiting for a response he picked up a chicken leg and started to nibble making sure not to drip grease on his starched ruff. Richard and Crooke stepped outside the door.

"Won't keep you a moment, Richard, just wanted to know if all is well with the *God's Speed*?" He started to walk down the stairs and Richard had no choice but to follow.

"Yes, I have had her all checked over, she is seaworthy. We are doing another trial next week. I have gathered together stores, they are waiting in the warehouse, except for the perishables, which again I will get at the end of next week. The crew is signed on so just another ten days and all will be ready."

"I'd like you to accompany Prowse, and that fellow Dypere."

"I have duties—"

"I have spoken to Erington and the other burgesses who have invested, they want someone to keep an eye on things, someone they can trust."

"Don't you trust Prowse?"

"I think he is a fine fellow, but he is a Londoner when all is said and done, so you will be a bit of an insurance policy. I'll make it worth your while."

I hope so thought Richard, who suffered greatly from sea sickness. They had reached the hall and found themselves in the company of the Sohiers, though not by chance Richard was sure. They bowed and exchanged pleasantries and then Crooke managed to detach himself. Monsieur and Madame Sohier drifted idly to the window as if to see if the puppets were ready to appear.

"And M'zelle, you are well?" began Richard.

The girl, no woman, she was past her first youth, took a while to reply as if she was considering his question from all angles and was still not sure of her reply. In the end she nodded slowly.

"Excellent, and do you enjoy the entertainment?"

"Lions are wild beasts, they enjoy nothing more than tearing other creatures, limb from limb." Her voice was soft and breathy.

"Yes, there is that, the fellow outside though seemed subdued enough. And what of the porcupine?"

She looked perplexed. "What of him?" Her eyes flicked over to her mother asking to be rescued. Her mother looked away.

"What indeed. Still I'm looking forward to the puppet play."

"I am not, it is an excuse for idleness."

"Oh I thought it more an excuse for happiness."

She looked shocked, walked over to her mother and whispered in her ear. The older woman frowned. Richard excused himself as the other men returned and took the stairs two at a time. He could hear laughter coming from the room. Prowse had made himself comfortable on a chair. He and Alice were bent in close conversation over the din from outside. Then Alice stood and leaned out over the balcony to call the boys back in. Richard noticed Prowse admiring her breasts.

"Alderman Crooke asks that you join him down below," lied Richard.

"Ah Madam, it seems I must drag myself from your company, enjoy the rest of the day, Mudford." He bowed again in a way that Richard found irritating. A few minutes later the children burst back into the room.

"The lion's breathe was really foul," gasped Jacket, and William giggled. "And you should see his pooh." They discovered they were ravenous and fell onto the food.

Their shouting and general jumping around woke Christian, who started to cry until John gave her a spiced biscuit.

"Mama, can we go and sit at the front for the puppets?" asked William. Alice thought for a while.

"Stay where I can see you, don't talk to any strangers and wait for me at the end, perhaps Tamsin – where is Tamsin?"

John looked around him as if he had misplaced a knife. "She was with us."

Richard peered out of the window. "There she is, over the far side."

She was standing dreamily leaning up against the timber frame of the other wing of the inn that ran down the side of the courtyard. Richard's attention was drawn away to the group of men stood next to her, the Portuguese merchants, turned inward and talking to themselves intently as if all the colour and activity in the yard was not there. The ringleted head of Luis de la Castro turned slowly and he stared back at Richard for a long while before turning back to join the discussion.

"Come on children, I'll come down with you."

"John, you don't have to do that, I should take them."

"It's all right, Alice, I don't mind. Christian, do you want to come and see the puppets?" Her mouth and cheeks were full of biscuits but she managed to nod.

"Let's all go," said Alice and they gathered themselves up and made for the door. "Richard, are you coming?"

"In a moment," he said and the door closed behind them.

He sat down on the window seat picking at the remains of the feast as the crier announced the return of Her Majesty's bearward who in turn introduced the puppet play. He paid little attention to the content of the play, some moralistic tale, mixed with politics and slapstick. Towards the end the yard started to grow gloomy and torches were lit. Finally, with a long sigh he made himself get up and go down to join the throng of people pushing their way back under the arch that led onto English Street. He gave up trying to fight his way through and waited till Alice, John and the children found him.

"It was so much fun, Richard, you should have come down," said Alice. She didn't notice that he made no reply as she was distracted by Christian pulling at her skirt asking to be carried.

"I think I could make a life on the stage," said John.

"Being a lion tamer?" asked Jacket.

"Or moving puppets?" said William.

"As an acrobat," said John he did a couple of cartwheels and a back flip and then walked down most of East Street on his hands. Passers-by clapped and cheered and a merchant tossed a penny into his path. John flipped onto his feet and picked it up.

"I'm going to go home," said Richard.

"Don't you want a drink?" asked Alice.

"No, I'm full." He pulled John aside, "Alderman Crooke wants us to ship out on the *God's Speed*".

"Great! I long to be at sea." Richard pulled a face and shook his head.

"I'll see you tomorrow," called John as Richard strode away.

Chapter Six

The next few days were all business. The *God's Speed* was a fine vessel and Richard forgave Prowse his arrogance as he clearly knew his business, he had the best navigational instruments made by Humphrey Cole. They would be needed as navigation was often not more than guesswork. Prowse had a copy of William Bourne's *A Regiment of the Sea*, Hakluyt's *Divers Voyages Touching the Discovery of America* and a translation of Medina's *Arte de Naviguar* as well as a copy of the Bishop's Bible with its portrait of the Queen on the title page. He also had maps, in the form of parchment crossed and re-crossed with rhumb lines, dubbed in with the British Isles, Norway and other lands that those who had gone before had found. Richard was impressed. The men took to Prowse also, considering him firm but fair, they sang as they worked dreaming of riches ahead.

"God send, God send, fair weather, fair weather, many prizes, many prizes." Richard wondered if they would still be singing after weeks of eating wormy biscuit and maggoty porridge.

John was in his element, scooting up the rigging, talking maps and charts, tides and shallows. There were also the secret discussions on weapons, cannon and gunpowder. Richard was more at home with that part of the project, he had made it his business to know all about the guns held by the town, from the culverin to callivers. He had bought and studied a copy of 'The Art of Shooting' from an itinerant bookseller. Crooke, like most of the burgesses had his own store of weapons as well. Richard was as good a shot as it was possible to be with such imprecise equipment. The ship carried small canon, lombards, and a falconet which swivelled from its mount on the bulwarks, they also carried javelins, crossbows and pikes which were better to use for hunting fresh meat. It wouldn't be long now till the adventure began.

Richard was on his way home, his body ached from helping to load the vessel and he was looking forward to a long draft of ale and a good night's sleep. As he unlocked the door he saw a movement in the shadows. He turned quickly and a man had stepped up behind him, Richard grabbed him round the neck and slammed him into the wall.

"Ow!" Richard loosened his grip. "Jack, what are you going skulking about? You're lucky I didn't use my dagger." A child whimpered.

"And good evening to you too. Don't start crying Joannie for God's sake."

Richard hoisted the child up, "It's all right Joannie, no harm done, your pa just took me by surprise." Jack made an unpleasant noise at the word Pa.

"So, what are you doing here, Jack?"

"I need somewhere to stay for a few days, my options are limited with the girl."

Richard opened the door and let them in, "I don't know, Jack, I've a lot on at the moment." He put Joannie down and found her a dry biscuit to suck.

"Look, it's just temporary, I need to keep my head down."

"Are you in trouble again?"

"Nothing I can't handle but the kid is cramping my style. Look, how about you take her for a bit and...?"

"No."

"Why not?"

"She steals things."

"Well there is that but blood is meant to be thicker than water."

"No."

"Well at least let us stay tonight."

Richard wasn't happy but agreed. He went up into the bedchamber and pulled a truckle bed out from underneath his bed. He opened a chest which held spare blankets and a sailor's hammock. He hooked the hammock between the roof beams. Jack's head appeared at the trapdoor.

"Blimey, you still have the sailor's hammock." He climbed into the room and sat himself on the hammock, swinging back and forth, "Takes me back this does, wonder what happened to the old boy."

"Bottom of the ocean I suppose."

"Look, Diccon, I need to find somewhere more permanent for Joannie."

"Couldn't you rent a room?"

Jack looked appalled, "Don't be daft. How about that Alice woman? She takes in foundlings."

"Joannie isn't a foundling, and Alice has enough on her plate. Look I'm tired, do you want something to eat?"

"Of course."

"Right." He put mutton, bread and ale on the table. They ate almost in silence, Jack irritably telling Joannie to stop slurping and close her mouth. When they finished Jack told Joannie to go up to bed.

"Goodnight Joannie," said Richard. The child looked over her shoulder for a moment before continuing to climb the ladder.

"I can't take her, Jack, I am shipping out on the *God's Speed* soon."

"I heard Crooke had a venture."

"What have you heard?"

"You don't have to be a mathematician, Diccon. We could hide out here whilst you're away."

"Hide out?"

"Some ruffians are eager for blood, you know how it is." Unfortunately Richard knew exactly how it was.

"No. I don't want people breaking up the place, or you selling off my possessions."

"I wouldn't do that to you, Diccon, not unless I had to."

"Look, you could go across to Itchen Ferry, I'll ask John's mother to put you up."

Jack looked as if he was being sent to Muscovy.

"I need somewhere I can put Joannie. Perhaps she could go to the alms-house."

"She's not sick, Jack, can't one of your girlfriends look after her?"

Jack gave him a long suffering look, he thought for a minute, "I suppose there is always Pa."

"What!"

"He's back."

"Back! He's dead, I thought he was dead."

"So did I, but it seems we were mistaken. He tapped me up for a drink in The Rose, gave me the fright of my life."

"Did you give him one?"

"What?"

"A drink."

"No, yes − well he took me by surprise. Anyway he said he was staying in Bagrow."

"Not interested."

"He asked after you."

"Not interested."

"He is still our Pa." Richard just looked at his brother and then began to clear away the remains of the meal. "I'm going to bed."

"He's changed, he's an old man."

"People don't stop being mean, just because they are old. You can't leave Joannie with him."

"She'll be all right, he wants to see his granddaughter, she'll be fine if you give me some money to pay him." Richard disappeared up the stairs. When he reached his chamber he saw Joannie was fast asleep in his bed. He blasphemed and apologised to God as he threw himself onto the truckle bed.

★

Jack and Joannie left the next morning. As Richard carefully locked the door to his house Jack looked over his shoulder.

"You know I can pick that don't you?"

"If you get stuck come back."

"I'll sort something out."

Jack didn't reappear that evening and Richard decided to go to Alice's for a drink. The little tippling house was full, a group of fishermen from the Ferry village, Parkers and Dyperes and many of the men who would be sailing with them were there muttering about the voyage and the booty they hoped to share. One of the growing number of itinerant booksellers and pamphleteers was hawking his booklets round the tables, there were few that could read but they hung on his descriptions of the cruelty and depravity of the Spanish. Richard glanced at the poorly printed matter. The *Most Excellent method of Curing Wounds* seemed the most interesting and he tossed the man a coin, which was accepted most eagerly. Not having done much trade that evening the man tried to draw Richard into his discourse but Richard tucked the book into his jerkin and went to find a quieter spot.

Richard sat in a corner drinking quietly watching Alice and Tamsin dashing around keeping their customers well furnished with drink. Alice smiled over to him occasionally. She was strong and could carry several jugs and pitchers at once. She could give a man a hefty clip around the ear if he became too familiar, and her smile was wide, her teeth still good. Her high forehead glistened with dewy sweat. Tamsin's behaviour had improved but not much, if the men were ugly she was rude and if they were pretty boys she would let them take liberties. Alice had only once found her out in the alley, knelt down in front of one of the Biston boys. Tamsin had screamed and shouted that she needed to have some money of her own, 'in case she needed to run'. Alice boxed her ears and locked her in the store room. There followed an uneasy truce. Alice said she thought Tamsin had something on her mind of late as she had become quiet and moody instead of loud and belligerent. Richard thought that an improvement. Someone slid onto the bench next to him, it was Luis de la Castro.

"Out alone? That's not very sensible," said Richard.

"I was looking for you. Señor Diaz would not approve."

"Why not?"

"He thinks I should leave well enough alone."

"Good advice."

"You have me followed."

"Only every now and again."

"Why?"

"You're up to something. That's not necessarily a problem as everyone in the town is doing things they shouldn't. I just need to make sure that what you are up to will not harm the town or England."

"I'm just a merchant."

"If you are just a merchant, I am King of Spain."

Luis laughed but it wasn't from mirth, "You think I'm a spy."

"Are you?"

"No, not in the way you think."

"And what would you know about how I think?"

"You think I am in the employ of Philip of Spain."

"Are you?"

The young man spat on the ground.

"Well that's all right then," said Richard, heavy with irony.

"I am Portuguese."

"So you have said before."

"Philip took over my country."

"I am not one to speak well of the King of Spain but he did have a legitimate claim."

"He is a foreigner, he cares nothing about my country only what it can do to shore up his empire. He wants to rule the world."

"Well he's made a good start."

The boy signalled Tamsin to bring him a drink, "You want more?" he asked of Richard who nodded. Tamsin stood close to Luis, he was very pretty. He squeezed her buttock and thanked her for her service.

"If you have something to say get on with it. People are beginning to notice the company I am keeping and this house is not the best one for you to be in tonight."

"It is true that the main line of the royal house of Portugal has died out but there are other claimants that those who are true Portuguese would prefer." said de la Castro.

"Such as?"

"Dom Antonio."

"He's a bastard."

"Some say the same of your Queen."

Richard leaned over and hissed into the boy's ear, "You speak like that again and I will cut out your tongue."

"I am just saying, Dom Antonio's father was of the Blood Royal."

"And his mother was his Jewish mistress."

"Dom Antonio is a good Christian."

"His revolt failed."

"It was ill prepared, Philip is strong, has much money and

many soldiers. But he is overextending himself, he is tied up in the Netherlands, his ships are harried by their sea beggars as well as your Queen's privateers. France is not his friend."

"France has troubles of its own."

"The King of France keeps promising support to Dom Antonio but does nothing. But perhaps your Queen will think differently."

"I doubt if Elizabeth will want to get caught up in a European conflict."

"So she says to the ambassadors but always behind the scenes she is meddling, and if Philip carries through his threat to launch an Armada perhaps it would suit the Queen to deflect him by supporting a revolt in Portugal."

"Perhaps, but it is not certain the Armada will be coming."

"It is coming, believe me, I have seen the ships being built, the King takes a long time to make up his mind but once it is set there will be no deflecting him."

"Well much as I like discussing politics with you, what has all this got to do with you being in my town?"

The boy drew in a long breath, made a decision and lowered his voice.

"Señor Diaz and others support Dom Antonio. They are using their resources to turn woad into a treasury for Dom Antonio and he will soon have monies to make an attempt on Portugal. I am acting as an agent for Dom Antonio, His Highness also hopes soon to have a warrant to travel safely to England. So I want to reassure you I am doing nothing that might bring down the English crown. On the contrary I want to see England strong, to be part of an alliance against Philip."

"And?"

"I ask you to stop having me followed, I do not want to draw attention to myself, I am not a spy for the Spanish King but doubtless there are others who are. I swear to you on my honour I do nothing to undermine Her Majesty, all I am about is trade and making money. Believe me, the Queen may find it useful for Dom Antonio to be a distraction."

"I cannot promise anything but to be more discreet. But take my advice, soon England will get too hot for you, too many people here think the Spanish and Portuguese are all the same and if the rumours of invasion flare up again you won't be safe. If you want to get a message to Her Majesty I suggest you seek out Mr Fowler when he comes to town. He is an agent for the Earl of Leicester and is due to visit to pay the rent the Earl gives to the town for the farm of sweet wines. The Earl of Leicester has the ear of the Queen. He will decide if your proposal has merit."

"Thank you for the information."

De la Castro put a silver coin down on the table and left. The men in the bar eyed his departure with suspicion and wondered about his business with the town sergeant. George Parker even had the nerve to ask him what he was doing consorting with a Spaniard. Richard did not deign to answer but left the inn soon after and he could hear them muttering as he went. Richard did not feel himself enough of an expert in intrigue, politics was a dangerous business. There might be something in what de la Castro had said, but his betters could decide on that.

The next day was a Sunday and Richard decided to take himself down to St Julien's and join the communion of the French speaking Protestants. They had started using the old chapel some twenty years earlier after they received sanctuary in England thanks to Her Majesty. Richard believed in God, of course, he was a Protestant as the Queen demanded. He had no memory of the old religion, it had been swept away before he was born, but he was not a fanatic. He didn't argue about what really happened during communion, he didn't pore over pamphlets and published sermons, he had a terror of the Inquisition but more often than not when he was in church his mind wandered. He liked the music and singing but didn't care to be hectored from the pulpit. He made sure he went to service often enough not to get fined, he prayed to God to help him be better, to protect those he loved, to be spared from disease and famine.

The Walloons who used St Julien's were a different set of Protestants, Calvinists. They were stern, they disapproved of many things he liked, cards and bowls, plays and dancing but they had a strong work ethic and had prospered in the town. If he was to make a match he would have to show himself to be a man of religious conviction. He had enough French to be able to take part in the service. He had dressed soberly and slipped quietly into the back of the tiny chapel in the grounds of the Maison Dieu. He drew no attention to himself, he focused on the pastor, he knew people were snatching looks at him but he showed himself to be oblivious. At the end of the service he made to slip quietly away but was stopped by Monsieur Sohier.

"Richard, it is good to see you at our communion. Have you been before?"

"No, sir, I have not, but having made the acquaintance of your family, wished to find out more."

"That is good, that is good."

"I also felt the need to ask that God look upon us kindly for our voyage."

"He is on our side, Richard, fear not."

Richard bowed and made to leave. Sohier made a decision, "Before you sail, come dine with us."

"Thank you, sir that is most kind of you." Richard bowed again. He walked down Winkle Street and out of God's House Gate. On the bowling green a few men were playing, they stopped for a while, they knew Richard was a town sergeant and that they should not be doing so on a Sunday. Richard merely waved and they started to bowl again. Richard watched for a few minutes but thought it would not be appropriate to join them, not until he knew his future was secured.

Chapter Seven

The *God's Speed* was about to sail. Prowse was calling out orders, all was activity. He inspected the bilge pumps making sure they would be fit for the task ahead. The elm cylinders were still covered in bark so that the wood would not dry out, the pumps had been caulked with pitch and the iron plungers flanged with leather washers were ready to rise and fall to send the spurts of filthy bilge water spewing over the sides. An empty hogshead was chained to the rails on either side of the ship ready to collect urine, which could then be used to quench any fires. Folded nearby were two or three pieces of old sail, ready to wet in the piss. Richard sat on the deck and tried to focus.

"Diccon, we haven't even cast off yet!" John was laughing.

"I think I want to die."

John laughed again. There was a shout from the key and a figure ran up the gangplank just before it was drawn up.

"What the—" said Prowse.

"Reporting for duty, Captain."

"Who are you? I have checked the complement and everyone is accounted for."

"It's my brother," said Richard. "Why are you here Jack?"

"Sea air, a voyage for my constitution."

"You have to get out of town."

"No freeloaders," said Prowse.

"I'm a much better sailor than my brother," said Jack, "I'm a better fighter too."

"Richard?" said Prowse.

"It's true, and he's good on the drum. Jack, no causing mischief with the crew, no gambling on board. Any trouble and Captain Prowse will hang you and I will help him."

"Sounds like an excellent deal to me. Well let's get this anchor hauled up the sooner we are at sea the better." The musicians struck up a shanty to help the men work in time.

Richard groaned and lay on the deck, "Where's Joannie?"

"She's fine, she is, she's fine."

"You left her with Pa, didn't you?"

"Well if she's going to keep stealing things, she needs to get better at it," said Jack as he started to help pull up the anchor. Richard didn't think he was joking.

Richard was sick for three days even though the sea was obligingly calm. Gradually he started to get used to the rise of the ship and its roll and managed to stay upright. He didn't think he would eat till they returned to port.

"Glad you are feeling better, Richard," said Prowse. "It's a bit grim for the rest of us sharing such a small space with a vomiter." He put down his cross staff, he had been taking longitudes. "Log, lead and lookout," he muttered under his breath. Richard looked quizzically. "My own little shanty, taught to me by John Davis, the finest seaman I know, the three Ls, lead, log and lookout will help you through fog, ice and an iron-bound coast."

Prowse packed away his compass, cross-staff and chart and made notes in his traverse book. It had five columns, one for courses, with the time spent of each, the second containing the distance travelled in each watch, the third for observations of the sun and the fourth for the wind and the last for remarks.

"I've never seen a book like that, or some of the instruments you use," said Richard.

"Well, in making voyages such as ours, you have to make some of it up as you go along."

"That's a comfort," said Richard, wryly.

Prowse had called the crew of thirty men, plus the musicians and soldiers, onto deck. He had discussed with Richard and John the problem of keeping discipline and maintaining control over the crew, this could be the difference between the success or failure of their venture. Several of the men were quite green. Most of the experienced ferrymen like George Parker had turned down John's offer of crewing the *God's Speed*; they liked to keep themselves to themselves and not get involved with the town's business if it could be avoided. Prowse's hero was Drake, though Richard had found him something of an arrogant braggart when he had met him. He knew Drake had fallen out with John Hawkins, who had thought he had looked only to save himself when they were betrayed in the Caribbean by the duplicitous Don Martin. But for all his faults Drake knew how to keep his men in line in a profession which engendered loose liberty and encouraged an undisciplined life. Prowse felt he needed to show the men he was tough and wanted them to be in no doubt of the punishment for acts of indiscipline.

"Men we all hope to be made by this voyage, we mean to send a message to the papists and bring honour to England. We will need courage and we need discipline to ensure the success of our voyage. I will brook no mutiny, no insolence. Do well by me and I will do well by you, if not the punishment will be fierce. Draw a knife on an officer and I will strike off your hand, assault a shipmate and you will be ducked from the yardarm, steal from your fellows and I will shave your head". Some erupted laughter here, for Tom Cavendish was bald as a coot. "I will shave your head and smear it with feathers and boiling oil. We are on a Christian mission. If you fall asleep on duty or blaspheme I will have you flogged. Do I make myself clear?" There were murmurs of assent, the younger members of the crew looked fearful, the older ones smirked, if Prowse did not deliver no amount of rules would save him. The men had signed up on the promise of booty, a third of captured prizes would be shared amongst them, plus anything they could grab that was not part of the raided ship's fittings and cargo.

They made for the Caribbean over two thousand miles in one direction from west to east and nearly a thousand from north to south at its widest point. There were hundreds of islands, with little government and wide open for trespassers. Portobello was now the point of landing for the treasure of Peru and Chile, and was turning into a sleazy, brutal place into which piled gold, silver, pearls and gems. The *God's Speed* was not large but it was swift and well gunned, unlike the galleons that would be carrying bullion back to Spain, but the Spanish would rely on numbers, they had to hope that the weather or other acts of God would split the fleet up.

"There are merchant men to be had as well," said Prowse, "Spanish, Portuguese, maybe even French. Gentlemen, let us offer up Drake's prayer 'O Lord, make us rich, for we must have gold before we see England'."

They knew the fleets from Spain carried taffeta, silks, wine and swords but those coming back from the West Indies carried hides, cocoa and tobacco. Gold and silver bullion came from Peru, Mexico and Chile, emeralds came from New Granada, pearls from Margarita and Rio de la Hacha. Spices, jewels and gold from the Orient were unloaded in Acapulco and then taken by mule to Vera Cruz to travel onwards to Spain. From the Portuguese colonies of Brazil came sugar, hides, indigo, cotton and timber. Richard was happy when he had a chance to liberate a barrel of oranges. Jack turned up his nose at food not suitable for a red-blooded English man but when the sun got hot both he and Lawrence were happy to dip into the barrel and suck on the golden fruit.

The men made a raid on Pernambuco in Brazil. They suffered from the curse of yellow fever. A number of Portuguese cargoes were seized in the Malacca Straits and they kept a captured a merchantman, *Our Lady of Guide*, as prize to help them carry their booty. They took a smaller prize that had been carrying hides, but with the illnesses that had swept the crew they barely had enough men to sail the ships. They had to set fire to another galleon off the coast of California as they could not hold the prize and so dealt a blow on behalf of the Queen. Richard did not like to think too much on the men they had sent to the bottom.

Prowse kept tight control and discipline was paramount if they were to return home safely but Richard sensed the men knew they had a strong hand, there were so few of them and so the harshness, as they saw it, of the regime began to bridle. Most of the men were not hardened seafarers but had run away from a tough life in the country. True sailors like John generally tried to avoid voyages such as these which, in truth, more often failed than were successful. On land the men were lucky if they earned forty shillings in a year and believed this could be made in a week at sea. The possibility of death was high not only from tropical diseases but from dysentery, scurvy and gangrene. At the beginning of the voyage the *God's Speed* had been cramped and overcrowded as Prowse had calculated how many men he was likely to lose in the expedition. Things came to a head when some of the crew tried to break bulk, pilfering from the cargo before it was officially inventoried and divided. There had been arguments earlier about pillaged goods. The crew had the right of course to claim goods and valuables not part of the cargo proper, items found above deck and the personal effects of any crew or passengers. But there were rules, all men were supposed to bring what they had found to the mainmast, where it was shared according to rank.

Chapter Eight

Richard surveyed the crew. Most of them looked shifty and uneasy about the turn of events but would fall in with whoever gained the upper hand. Dick Biston looked cocky and sure of himself, as well he might with a gun in his hand and his three or four co-conspirators egging him on.

"Get back to your duties, Biston, or I will see you swing from the yardarm," demanded Prowse.

Biston laughed in his face. "Who made you the King of Spain?" His companions guffawed at this turn of wit. "We want what is our due!"

"We all agreed on how the shares would be divided before we left Southampton."

"You decided and now we are re-deciding. Why should you and the fat cats lying back in port get the lion's share when we have taken all the risks?"

"I have taken as many risks as you, and on to top of that I've invested in the voyage, none of you have gambled your life savings."

"Because we are poor men!"

"Actually, Dick, your father is the richest man in Southampton," called out Jack from somewhere amongst the rest of the mottled crew, gun in hand.

"Stay out of this, Jack." Dick spat at his old drinking pal, "We have drunk together and made riot together. For that I will spare your brother and you if you come over to us now."

"Now, Dick, you know blood is thicker than water for anyone not called Biston."

"I am warning you," said Dick as he turned to face his tormentor.

"No, Dick, I am warning you." Jack shot him straight between the eyes and he crashed to the deck like a felled oak. "Now you toss those empty barrels over the side."

Jack waved a second gun at Dick's lieutenants as they gazed in shock at their dead leader. He shot one of them in the foot, dropping the smoking gun to pull another from his waistband. The man yelped and his fellows grabbed the barrels and threw them over not sure what was going to happen next.

"Now you, over the side!"

They started to complain and looked at Prowse to save them. Lawrence opened his mouth and then shut it again.

"Over the side or I will shoot you where you stand."

"You can't kill us all, you only have one shot left," said a man called Paulie.

"True," replied Jack, "but I will kill you, my brother will kill Harry. The rest know what happens to mutineers and will stand back for they will either swing or without the Captain never get back to England." Richard had retrieved his caliver and was pointing it at Harry Peasgood."

"Come on Jack," Paulie pleaded, "we meant no harm, it was all Dick, we didn't know what he was about. Massie is hurt, you have taken his foot near off."

"Sorry, Massie, I was aiming for your balls. Now over the side."

"We'll drown!"

"Not if you make it to the barrels, but you had better be quick the tide is taking them away. If you kick strong enough you will make that island yonder. If you don't well you are right it's a watery grave ..." Jack raised his pistol and pulled back the hammer. Paulie and Harry picked up Massie, threw the struggling man overboard, and climbed onto the side after him and jumped into the sea.

"You there, get rid of that body, the rest of you get back to your duties if you want to see your families again and receive any booty," shouted Lawrence.

The men melted away. Jack picked up his discarded weapons. "Where did you get those guns Mudford?" snapped Lawrence.

"I overheard the men talking and thought I ought to take some precautions."

"That's my pistol!" Lawrence grabbed it off him.

"And a serviceable enough weapon, pulls slightly to the left. I had meant to nick Dick's ear, still that's the way it goes." Dick's body splashed into the sea.

"Who will tell the Alderman?" asked Richard.

"No one," said Jack. "They would have to admit to mutiny. I suggest that the log merely records an accident at sea."

Richard looked over the side to where the three remaining plotters were striking for the island.

"Do you think they will make it?" he asked.

"Don't know, don't care," said Jack.

"Do you think I should pick them up?" Lawrence wavered.

"No," said Richard, "you need to be strong, ruthless even if we are all to get home safely."

"He is right," said John. Lawrence slowly nodded his head.

John was on top of the rigging. He called out that he could see the pilot ship approaching. The boatswain on the *God's Speed* signalled back to John that he had seen the pilot ship too. It would not be long now and they would be back in Southampton. They passed the mouth of the River Hamble and a swell rocked the vessels. As the ships slipped passed the guns of Netley Castle there were salutes from both sides. Onwards they went, past the ruins of Netley Abbey and the new mansion of Mr Paulet rising from the old stones, at the mouth of the River Itchen. The tower of God's House loomed standing over the marshes, oyster beds, and bowling green. They sailed under the tower gun battery and reached the town quay with its myriad of warehouses. George Parker came alongside in the pilot boat, John called to him and told him he should have shipped out, that it had been a successful voyage. Parker nodded but did not seem convinced. There were people standing on the quay, not just the porters, carters, bearers, customs officials and other dock workers but townspeople also. News of their progress had preceded them. People were cheering and waving. Richard strained his eyes, he could see members of the French Church and thought he could make out Alderman Crooke and other burgesses, but there was no sign of Alice. Jack clasped his brother around the shoulders.

"Look at them, Diccon, they think we are heroes."

Richard didn't answer, he was reflecting uneasily on some of their actions.

"I think I have found myself, Diccon."

"I didn't know you were lost."

"Yes you did. I have been lost for a long time. But I think I have found the life I was born for."

"Jack, you do understand the difference between a privateer and being a pirate don't you?"

"Don't shit in your own backyard."

Richard shook his head.

"Diccon, I need you to buy me a share."

"What?"

"A share in a ship of my own, maybe the smaller of the prizes. What do you say, The Mudford brothers together again? I'll make you rich, Diccon. Don't look like that."

"Is this just one of your schemes?"

"No I swear, I have been thinking about it almost since we first sailed. We have tough sailors here on the Itchen, we have a town that welcomes privateers, we have treasure ships passing every year, sailed by enemies of England, so not only would we be helping ourselves, we would also be helping the Queen." Jack was obviously convincing himself with his own arguments.

"You've done well for yourself, Diccon, and you have always looked out for me, this way I could do something for you. You're clever, and unlike me you work hard, but it will take you years to make your way without real money."

"What makes you think I have enough money to buy a share in a ship?"

"If I know you, you will have enough to be able to get a loan, you will get something from our booty as will I, come on, Diccon."

Richard looked into his brother's blue eyes. He wanted to believe him, he was his brother. Jack knew he had him.

"Thanks, Diccon. You know I love you best in all the world don't you?"

"More than Joannie?"

"Of course!" Jack laughed. He hadn't given his daughter a thought since he had palmed her off on their father.

"Don't let me down, Jack, it will take £150 to keep even a small ship, with a crew of say fifty, at sea for three months."

Jack just winked. "Here's to lose liberty and undisciplined life."

It took some time to moor the ships. Richard and Prowse disembarked first, leaving the men to fully secure the ships, they wanted to speak to their backers before the booty was off-loaded. Crooke embraced them like prodigal sons.

"A prize ship, you took two prize ships on our first outing. She looks a grand ship," he pointed to the larger vessel. "Did she have a good cargo?"

"Sir, we have made an excellent return on the investment."

Prowse leaned in close, "We have of course put something aside for the Queen but feel the best rewards should come to those who gambled most."

Crooke clasped the pair to him again, slapping them on their backs, "Well done my boys, well done." There were tears in his eyes.

Richard noticed Crooke's son-in-law Biston standing by, looking sour with rage and disappointment. He had chosen not to invest unwilling to risk his ill-gotten gains. Biston preferred to swindle fellow townspeople and enrich himself via legal loopholes and the small print in contracts, but he hated to think he had missed out on grasping more money. Richard wondered if Biston knew one of his sons had sailed, they had been estranged for so long. He was unsure if the man would even care to know his boy was dead.

"There are repairs to be done on all the ships," said Prowse. "We managed what we could at sea, and the *God's Speed* did well for us."

"What of the men?"

"They served soundly," replied Richard. "We lost more through sickness than in fighting, some injuries." He almost winced as he remembered the blows suffered.

"I will make sure their families receive their share and speak to the Mayor." Crooke nodded to himself.

"Sir, there is something else…"

"Yes?"

"Dick, Dick Biston shipped with us," said Richard in a rush. "He was lost sir, I'm sorry."

Crooke sucked in his cheeks and shook his head, "A wasted life, I had hoped…he was not of my flesh but I did what I could to reconcile him with his father." Dick had been the child of Biston's first marriage. At his mother's early death Biston had fostered him out and he had not re-joined the family for some seven years until after Biston married Margaret.

"Would you tell the Alderman?"

"Ah Richard, are those youthful jealousies and rivalries not mended?"

"I was never jealous of him, sir, and do not know why he should have been jealous of me."

"I know he was your elder, with money, connections and cunning but not your intelligence and bravery my boy."

"Thank you, sir, but you will tell him?"

"I will, but today we celebrate, Sohier, come, come and congratulate our boys! I hear young Mistress Sohier has been missing you, Richard." Richard hardly thought that to be likely.

Sohier pushed through the crowds to greet them. The pair got slapped on the back again and Richard wondered if he would end up with as many bruises as he had sustained during the voyage.

"What's it like to be back on dry land?" Sohier boomed.

"I thank God, dearly, though I am still finding it difficult to walk straight."

"I need to get back to the ship," said Prowse, "I must to see to the cargo, secure the ships, pay off the crew who will be desperate to be home, finish my log – I wish I were back at sea already." He laughed, bowed and moved away back in the direction of the *God's Speed*.

"Did he do well, Diccon?" asked Crooke.

"He did marvellously well sir, he is a good man, a good captain, has a good sea head. You did well to appoint him."

"Glad to hear it, thank you, my boy!"

"Mudford!" It was Mayor Erington, "Good to see you back, Foxe has been driving me into insanity. And I can't get used to not being able to look him in the eye. How soon will we have you back at the Bargate?"

"Soon, Mr Mayor, soon. I just have to assist Captain Prowse with the prizes."

Erington rubbed his hands. "A great day for Southampton, Crooke."

"Indeed it is. I feel the town will rise again in wealth and glory."

"What news of Spain?" asked Richard.

"Much as before. The King of Spain sits like a great spider weaving his webs, but God has not favoured his enterprise for he has been beset with setbacks. The Queen of Scots still plots away, prisoner or no."

"The King of Spain has nothing to gain from rescuing her," said Crooke. "At heart she is a French princess. He wouldn't want her on the English throne, he'd rather stick with Elizabeth."

"It's the Queen's meddling in the Netherlands that has brought us to this," muttered Erington.

"Hush," said Crooke, "that is treasonous talk."

Erington went pale, "I assure you I meant nothing against Her Majesty and her support to the Protestant cause, I just meant it's a bit close to home – you know I would never, did not –"

"It's all right, old friend, I understand, but in these times you don't know who is standing under the eaves listening. Let's talk of it no further, we need to celebrate. Richard, we are holding you from your duties. We will meet up to discuss the business of the voyage tomorrow."

"Yes, sir, thank you." He turned to leave.

"Mudford, did your brother ship with you?" asked Erington.

"He didn't sign up, sir."

"He seems to have disappeared leaving a whole barrel of trouble behind him and I have had to pay support to some old fellow that took pity on his daughter. You'll have to sort something; I can't keep on supporting your brother's bastard."

"No, I am sorry, sir, I will look into the matter once I have finished with this business."

"And please come back to work soon, I can't keep track

of the guns, discipline has gone down with the watch and not enough men are turning up for the muster."

Richard smiled, "I'll be back in a couple of days."

★

Richard was exhausted. He had supervised the storing of the cargo into Crooke's great warehouse, employed carpenters and shipwrights to work on the ships, calculated pay and bonuses with Prowse for the crew, helped Alderman Crooke to divide booty amongst the sharers and worked out how little they could get away with giving to the Crown. Richard had met up with Sergeant Foxe and received a report on what had occurred during his absence and was soon back at work. He had dined with Crooke, Prowse and the backers and talked till he was hoarse about their adventures.

He had had a more sober dinner at the Sohiers seated next to the strange, quiet girl everyone seemed to want him to marry. After the dinner he was even permitted to sit alone with her in an alcove away from the rest of the guests, although her maid Elizabeth stayed close. She had the same staring eyes as her mistress, pale watery blue instead of pale watery green. It put Richard off his courtly talk, they made him feel uncomfortable and he was almost happy to be rescued by the Pastor of St Julien's wanting to talk to him about how he might go about becoming worthy enough to join the Communion.

He was glad to be back on land and once again in his little cottage. He hid away, in the coffer beneath the floorboards, his booty money, and placed the other little treasures he had accumulated around the house. Jack had disappeared for a while, giving himself over to debauchery, but Richard kept to his promise and had spoken to Alderman Crooke about a loan to take a share in a ship. Crooke wasn't enamoured of taking a risk on Jack but Richard spoke up for him and

Prowse also put in a word. Although Crooke considered him a bloodthirsty knave, he also thought he could bring success to their privateering concern. In the end Crooke agreed and went in with them. Richard became partner in a small 60 ton ship that his brother renamed the *Magpie*. Richard was pleased when Jack then affixed himself to Prowse in order to learn as much about captaincy as possible. It was the first time Jack had applied himself to anything. John had agreed to help find a crew and it seemed Jack would be away again soon sailing in convoy with Prowse on the *God's Speed*. This time Richard and John would remain at home.

Chapter Nine

He had barely seen Alice or visited the tippling house but his neighbour told him he had received a message to go there that evening. He wondered what could be so urgent. He washed and tidied himself and turned out again reluctantly. A few of the crew were in the house spending their pay, some had even brought their wives and girlfriends. It seemed the celebrations would go on for many weeks yet till all the money was drunk away and the men would sign up for the next voyage, forgetting the misery of the first.

"So you're here." Alice seemed less than pleased to see him.

"I thought you had sent for me."

"I did, come through to the back." She finished serving some of the customers and asked Jacket to look after the bar. Richard wondered where Tamsin was, perhaps she had run off and this was why Alice was angry. He went out into the back room. Tamsin was sat at the small table; John was sat on the stairs. Alice signalled Richard to sit down. She put out beer for him, banging down the pot, John grimaced. She poured some for herself and sat down. She did not give any to Tamsin.

"Alice, what is it?"

"Tell him." She almost spat at Tamsin, but the girl clamped her mouth tightly shut.

"She's pregnant."

"What? How?"

Alice raised her eyebrows at this.

"Of course I know how, I mean who? When?"

"She won't say a word. Don't you know?"

"Of course not." Richard couldn't believe that Alice might have thought he was responsible.

"It's not him," said Tamsin and clamped her mouth shut again.

"Shut up, you little whore." Alice reached across the table and boxed her ears.

"You've been beating me 'cos I wouldn't speak and now you beat me when I do."

Alice went to hit the girl again. "Don't, Alice, it won't help," said John.

"It makes me feel better," Alice threatened. Then she seemed to deflate before Richard's eyes and she welled up with tears, "What am I to do with her? People will think I did not look after her properly; she will bring disgrace into my home. How can I feed another mouth?"

She suddenly reached out and slapped the girl across the face. "You stupid, foolish, idiot child. Don't you know what you have done? You are ruined, people might have forgotten what happened before. I didn't realise, she hadn't bled since she came to me, she said she had not really started. I thought that with what had happened she had not yet become a woman, when she began to struggle to do up her skirt I thought she was just getting fuller because of eating properly, I am as much a fool as she is."

"I'm sorry, Alice, if I had known I would never–"

"Never what? Brought a whore into my house?"

"I've not been a-whoring since I was here."

"Was it Bart Biston? You were happy enough to suck him."

"Alice! You sound like a fishwife," said John.

"No, no." The girl began to cry, "He told me he loved me, he called me pretty, I thought we would go away together and I would live in a grand house like a princess."

"Have you learnt nothing of men from all your time on the streets?"

The girl just sobbed.

"She will have to leave the town. The Mayor will not allow strangers to Southampton to stay here and have children that might become a burden. I can probably get her into the alms-house till she drops, unless you want her on her way before that," said Richard.

"No, I don't know."

"There is another answer," said John. They all looked at him. "We could find her a husband."

"Who? Who would take her, a pregnant slut with no money, no family, no housewifely skills? Richard, do you want her?"

"God no!"

"All right then, I'll marry her."

"Don't be ridiculous, John." Alice was stunned. "Why would you want to throw yourself away?"

"I'm not much of a catch myself, Alice."

"You have steady work, you can fish and sail, you wouldn't beat your wife, you have your booty money."

"That's right, I have enough to get married on and still help provide for you and the children. Besides, I like Tamsin."

"You do?" sobbed Tamsin.

"Yes I do, you make me laugh. You had the strength of character to run away from that monster who called herself your mother. You are trying to learn to work and fit in – Alice, don't look so haughty, she has tried her best. Would you like to marry me, Tamsin?"

The girl stopped crying and thought for a while; she wiped her face and nodded.

"And what of the baby?" asked Alice.

"It's just a baby, sister. It just needs someone to love it. It's no different to you taking in Jacket."

"Of course it's different. Thomasina was my best friend and I knew Jacket's father. You would be giving some unknown man's bastard your name."

"Well that's my choice. If Tamsin wants to tell me who the father is that's fine, if she doesn't that's fine too, I don't actually care." He stood up and held out his hand. "Come on, let's go for a walk by the river."

Tamsin hesitated for a moment and then, making a wide berth around Alice, took his hand and they went out. Alice gazed after them for a long while.

"This is your fault."

"Possibly, probably."

"I know him, he won't change his mind, he is too kind-hearted."

"He is."

"She will make him unhappy, and probably run off with some other man once the baby is born."

"You don't know that."

"What about the father? He might come back; she obviously was in love with him."

"He's not coming back. He spun her a line, got what he wanted. He's long gone."

"Are you speaking from experience?"

"I have done my fair share of promising anything to get my fun."

"Fun, is that what you call it?"

"Men are different to women, Alice, but we do fall in love as well and can be as silly as any young girl."

Alice poured out more beer.

Chapter Ten

The marriage took place quickly; Alice thought it better they were wed before the baby appeared. The ceremony was held at the mother church of St Mary, which was the parish church for Itchen Ferry village even though it was on the opposite side of the river. The church was in a very poor state of repair and the cemetery was overcrowded. The chantry had been sold off at the time of the old King's reforms and was now a farm. There were few guests. John's mother had made the trip across the river with one of her many nephews. Alice was there with the children, Richard of course, and some of the men from the watch with their wives. Others had said they would come to the merrymaking in the village later.

Tamsin wore an old dress that had belonged to Alice. Alice had repaired and altered it, and it disguised the obvious bump. The vicar did look once or twice but he was used to couples having their wedding night before the wedding, especially parishioners from the Ferry village who couldn't always make the river crossing to come to church. Tamsin had flowers and leaves in her hair and almost looked pretty. George Parker and his brothers rowed the wedding party across the river to the inn that John's mother ran. Outside were benches piled with food, nothing too fancy but plenty of bread and fish, meat and vegetables supplied by John's numerous relatives who farmed round and about. There was music and dancing and jugs of ale and beer. It was a warm September day and by mid-afternoon most people began to doze, taking a nap before the festivities resumed again in the evening. John and Tamsin retired to a room in the inn and Alice put the children to bed.

"I have eaten so much," she said when she came back outside. "Let's go for a walk up onto the green."

Richard yawned and stretched but fell into step with her. They took the path that meandered up the small cliff to the green, which opened up and gave a wonderful view over the river and back to the butter coloured walls of Southampton. Lots of little boats bobbed on the water, sailed by ants. Alice sat down and Richard sat beside her.

"I think they might be happy," she said. "John is so easy-going, and perhaps all Tamsin needs is someone to look after her and love her."

Richard didn't answer. Alice laid back on the grass, stretching so her back arched. Richard lay down beside her.

"It's so warm; I love to feel the sun on my skin."

He just murmured in reply. He could feel his eyes getting heavy and he started to drift away just as Alice's hand reached across and felt for his cock. Suddenly he was wide awake.

"Alice, what?"

"Just seeing if you were feeling the same as me. God, I have such an itch."

She leaned up on one elbow and started to unlace his breeches. Richard was in a state of shock and just lay there as she exposed him. She was unlacing her bodice and freeing her breasts.

"Oh that feels good." She loosened her hair so it fell over her shoulders. She looked down at him, her pupils dilated.

"Alice, are you drunk?"

"A little, but don't worry I know what I am doing and what I want." She hauled up her skirts revealing her creamy thighs as she straddled him. Richard pushed her skirts up further so he could see her bush.

"Sweet Jesus, hurry up, Alice, I am getting too excited." She lowered herself onto him, she was moist and he slipped easily inside her. She threw back her head as she moved up and down on him. "Please God, don't let this be a dream, don't let me wake up and find I have imagined this," prayed Richard.

It was fast but it was beautiful. She rolled back off him onto the grass, her arms thrown above her head, her skirts still thrust up revealing her limbs and so much more, she looked gloriously wanton. Richard kissed her and then slipped down between her thighs; he knew he was good with his tongue. She soon was writhing with pleasure.

"William never did that," she breathed. He made love to her again. The sun started to cool and the shadows grew longer. He was resting on top of her, his head between her beautiful pendulous breasts. He could not believe he had sucked and twisted her nipples. He was smiling.

"We need to dress," she said. He disagreed but she won.

They plucked grass from each other's hair and wiped the stains with a kerchief. They walked back down to the village. The sleepy wedding guests were beginning to stir as other friends and family arrived for the evening. No one noticed them slip back, no one had even known they had gone.

It was dark and the night was starry. The muscles on George Parker's arms strained as he rowed them back across the river. Jacket was sat next to him, Parker pretending to let him row. Christian was asleep in her mother's arms and William was curled up in Richard's. John and Tamsin were spending a few days in the village, then Tamsin would stay there with John's mother till her confinement. The row boat scrunched onto the gravel shore. Parker helped Alice alight and held William while

Richard jumped out of the boat and fished for a coin to pay for their passage. They said goodnight and walked up the road to East Gate carrying the two younger children with Jacket trailing behind. The cottages and lean-tos were quiet, they got bigger as East Gate became nearer. There was an occasional bark from a dog, a whinny from a horse, a candle blown out. When they got to the Gate Richard called out to the watchman. They shouldn't really let them in but it was Richard and he pulled rank. They went through to the East Street and to the door of Alice's house. She unlocked it.

"Go on to bed, Jacket, I'll be up soon." She lay Christian on table and took William from Richard.

"Can I stay?"

She looked at him strangely, "Of course not."

"You're right, I'm sorry. I'll see you tomorrow." He kissed her on the cheek and she shut the door behind him. He stood staring at the wood for a long time. He rested his forehead against the door. He slowly turned away and then ran all the way back to Silkshop Yard to try and diffuse the energy he had wanted to be spent in pleasuring Alice. He knew he wouldn't sleep. Richard and Alice. Alice and Richard. That's what it would be from now on.

Chapter Eleven

The next day he kept smiling at inappropriate times, he found his attention wandering; he was even pleasant to the prisoners. The hours crawled by but at last he was free. He wanted to go straight to Alice's cottage but forced himself to head home and change. He had a small glass mirror and he peered and squinted at it trying to get a view of his whole body. His heart was pounding and he felt short of breath, he hardly acknowledged the people he passed on the way because he never saw them. He was disappointed when he arrived, there were customers and Alice was busy. She gave a brief nod, he should have asked her to close this evening. He could have taken her for a meal, they could have smiled secret smiles, he was an idiot. At last the stragglers left, Richard leapt up and bolted the door. The children were already abed. It was just them, he grabbed Alice to him.

"What are you doing?" she said and pushed him away. He was confused.

"I just wanted to kiss you, I have been waiting all day."

"Waiting all day? I don't understand what you mean." She smoothed her skirts and started to clear tables. This was not right. This was not how he imagined it would be.

He cleared his throat. "After yesterday, after what happened, I thought..."

"What happened?" A red flush curled round her neck. "We rolled about in the grass, we had, what did you call it? Fun–" She wiped the table furiously.

"No, no it wasn't like that, it was more."

"Not for me." Her voice was light but she would not look at him.

"What? I don't understand?" He grabbed the polishing cloth and tossed it aside.

Alice sighed deeply, her eyes darting everywhere but his face, she looked longingly at the discarded cloth. "I have been a widow for more than a year, I'm still young, what with the wedding and everything, I just wanted to be with a man again." In lieu of polishing the table she rubbed her neck as if to get rid of the blush.

The room was tipping at a strange angle.

"But you can be, you can be with me, we can get married–"

"–married? I don't want to get married again."

Now she looked at him, was that horror in her glance? He studied her face; it looked like Alice, the same strong features, the same intense eyes, the same wide mouth.

"But I, I don't know what is going on, if it's too soon then we can be lovers–"

"–lovers! Are you mad? All I have is my reputation. I am a respectable widow. I have a place."

"You could have a place as my wife!"

"Don't shout at me!" She breathed heavily, controlling her anger. Her tone became measured. "I am not ready to be another man's wife. I'm not sure I am ever going to be ready. I loved William, he was a good, steady man but I was so young when we wed, I didn't know what life was about, and then there were pregnancies, five in five years."

"You are talking nonsense. I don't know what you are saying."

"All my life I have been some man's daughter, some man's wife, someone's mother, only since I was a widow did I begin to exist. I know I don't have much but its mine. Please don't mistake what we did for love or a relationship. I chose you because I didn't think you would care."

"Chose me? Didn't think I cared? I have loved you for years." Was she stupid? Or was that him?

"I'm sorry, I didn't know, you hide your feelings so well."

"And you have no feelings at all."

He slammed the door so hard the whole cottage shook and flakes of white paint fell to the ground, Christian woke and started to cry. He could hear Alice calling his name but he didn't go back. He wasn't sure where he was going but found himself outside the Grave Maurice and went inside. He drank a lot but didn't get drunk. He stood and walked purposely to the door and out on to the street. He made his way down to the house of Monsieur and Madame Sohier and knocked on the door.

Chapter Twelve

It was a very different ceremony to that of John and Tamsin. The tiny chapel of St Julien was packed, it seemed all the Walloon community were there sitting on the bride's side. Richard had thought that he would have no one. Jack was at sea and he certainly wouldn't have wanted his father turning up, but the burgesses of the town and their wives were present in all their finery, the other town sergeants with their spouses, the men of the watch, and the people from Silkshop Yard had crowded around the doorway. Tamsin had been safely delivered of a daughter but was still living over in the Ferry village. Richard had manipulated the watch to make sure he and John did not work on the same shift. He hadn't seen Alice since that night. His bride was making her way down the aisle on the arm of her father. She was walking very slowly. Richard didn't think they had spoken more than a dozen words in the last two months.

He had got to know Monsieur Sohier, who was god-fearing, sober but kind and devoted to his daughter. He was also over-protective of her, but then she was the only survivor from a dozen siblings. Madame Sohier he thought rigid and unbending, icy eyed and cold-blooded, but she was equally protective of Jeannot. Jeannot was tall like her parents but fragile, her eyes flittered around the chapel like a butterfly trying to escape into the sunshine. Richard turned to the wooden altar and read the names of the saints written in French, the four writers of the gospels. He was under no illusion, he did not love Jeannot, she did not love him. If he was asked to place a bet he would even say she hated him. He didn't care. He was making his way in the world. He owned part of a ship, his future in-laws had leased them a fine house on French Street, they had servants even if one of them was the reptilian Elizabeth. He would do his duty and God willing the Sohiers would have some grandchildren, he would become a burgess and start to take up the various offices that led to the Mayoralty: steward, water bailiff, bailiff, and then sheriff. Jeannot reached his side. The service began, she mumbled and he spoke out too loudly. She curled her finger so it was difficult for him to place the ring, in the end he rammed it on and she winced and snatched her hand away. Too late, they were man and wife.

As they came out of the church a figure broke away from the crowd. It was John. He clasped Richard to him.

"I wish you well."

"Thanks." Richard felt sheepish.

"What happened? Did you and Alice have a falling out?"

"What makes you say that?"

"She's been more in a fury than usual, bites everyone's head off."

"I didn't fall out with her."

"Then why haven't we seen you, you haven't even seen the baby."

"I'm sorry, there's just been so much... How is Tamsin?"

"Well, she is very well, my mother said the baby practically leapt out."

"Good...that's good. What are you calling her?"

John looked around and then at his feet, "Luisa."

"Luisa? You don't mean—"

"–that bloody Portuguese prick you had me following all around town, he's lucky I didn't catch him at it. They met up in the bloody prison. Can you believe it?"

Richard shook his head. De la Castro had disappeared from the town whilst they were at sea, "Least you know he won't be back."

"Unless he arrives with the bloody Armada, I still think he was a spy."

"Come and join us for the wedding breakfast, we are going to the Dolphin."

"No, you're all right, I wouldn't fit in with this lot. I'm going over to the village, I'm going to bring Tamsin and the baby back with me."

"I'll see you then."

"Of course."

The wedding feast droned on interminably, Richard didn't eat much and just drank enough to give himself some Dutch courage for the night ahead. At last they were seen on their way and they walked back to their new home, Elizabeth following three steps behind. When they got in Richard sat down stairs and had a glass of wine whilst the two women went upstairs. After what he thought was sufficient time he went up to the bedchamber, he could hear them whispering on the other side of the door. He made a noise so they knew he was there. Elizabeth came to the door, gave him an insolent stare and barely bobbed a curtsey. Richard went inside. He eyes widened at the sight of his bride. She was sat bolt upright in the bed trussed up like a chicken with a nightshirt that reached her neck and a hideous cotton nightcap hiding her hair.

"Do you have to wear all that?"

She ignored him and stared straight ahead. He undressed

carefully and went to the bed. She glanced at him and recoiled at his nakedness and his erection. He slipped under the covers and tried to caress her. She was rigid, her knees clamped firmly shut and she rolled onto her side into the foetal position. He rolled her back and pushed her knees down and tried to spread her legs. She started to scream and kick and punch. He leapt out of the bed.

"For Christ sake, shut up. I'm not trying to murder you."

She started to pray, the door of the bed chamber flew open and Elizabeth ran in. She also screamed when she saw Richard. "Get out!" he shouted. He spun her around and kicked her on the backside and out of the door. Jeannot was swaying as she prayed like she was in a trance.

"Jeannot! Jeannot!" He shook her till she stopped. "I know you must be nervous, this is your first time, I am not going to force you, we can wait. But we are man and wife and you will have to do your duty." She started praying again.

Richard had gone limp, his reluctant ardour thoroughly quashed. He grabbed his clothes and went out of the room almost tripping over Elizabeth who was lying across the door. She ran into her mistress, throwing herself on the bed and gathering Jeannot into her arms to comfort her. Richard went to one of the other bedrooms in search of sleep. His marriage was a disaster.

Part Two

1587

Chapter Thirteen

It was almost two months after the wedding. They were still sleeping in separate rooms and Richard wished he was living back in Silkshop Yard. He taken up the playing of tennis on the vacant plot south of their house on French Street, so that he might rid himself of pent-up frustration and it gave him an excuse not to go home. Jeannot did not approve either as she thought games were of the Devil, Richard took some pleasure in that. That evening they were to dine out at the home of the new Mayor Andrew Studley. They got ready in silence, walked in silence and at the dinner Richard contrived to sit as far from his wife as possible. They had just finished the savoury course when they were aware of a loud knocking on the door. A pursuivant had arrived from the Queen. Studley hurried out and returned a few minutes later looking very grave.

"The Queen of Scots has been executed at Fotheringhay."

Chapter Fourteen

"Jeannot, things could become difficult now, with the execution you understand. It has cleared the way for Philip, the Queen of Scots has left her claim to England to him." Jeannot said nothing and just concentrated on the cloth she was hemming.

"It is likely I will be called upon to defend England, I need to know what I am fighting for, I need you to be my wife, to properly be my wife." Richard did not do long speeches, he was finding this hard. "I have tried to be a good husband, to look after you and provide for you. You have ensured our house has run, er, smoothly."

His home was a miserable space, most of the servants had left, a couple of women came in to char but mainly it was just him and Jeannot and Elizabeth. There was a lot of kneeling and praying, the food was colourless, there was no conversation, no laughter. Their only visitors were Jeannot's parents, others felt the atmosphere chilly. Richard decided this would be his last attempt at normal married life.

They took their meals in silence except for the scraping of knives against pewter. He wondered about an annulment. In a country where the church was founded on divorce, the concept was not easy. Jeannot concentrated on cutting her food, and chewing on it what seemed like hundreds of times before swallowing. The way she ate her food irritated him and he wanted to push the plate into her face. He shook the image out of his head.

★

Richard was in room, his private space where he had his small treasures around him. He was miserable caused by his own anger and folly. He got out his account book and tried to concentrate. He didn't notice the door open and was surprised as a silk bandage was tied around his eyes, a woman's voice whispered in his ear.

"Come, you will have your wish."

Richard felt a small thrill run down his spine. His hand was taken and he was guided of the room, he could tell he was being led to his wife's bedchamber.

"You don't have to be shy, sweetheart."

"Ssh."

"If this is what you want."

Richard considered, his wife had most likely heard tales of what a wedding night could be, probably in her religion it was not seen as something to be enjoyed. She was shy at showing her body, even to her husband. He wondered if she had some deformity but he lost his thoughts as he was pushed onto the bed. Her hands undid his clothes and he let himself be undressed. He complained a little as his hands were tied with other pieces of silk to the head of the bed. So she did not want his hands stroking her, well one thing at a time.

His sense of excitement was growing and he felt blood rush to his nether regions. In a mockery of his first time with Alice, his wife mounted him. Richard was shocked, she was not a virgin. Was this the reason she had resisted him for so long? She did not want him to know that she had been with other men? Had she been forced at some time? His power of reasoning vanished as his wife pumped up and down, moaning and clawing at this chest. As soon as he lost control she dismounted him and loosened the ribbons. He heard the door close and was alone, he managed to free his hands and remove the blindfold. Jeannot did not reappear and Richard went back to his own room.

He was bemused and the next day it was if nothing had happened. The same performance continued for some time until Richard was starting to find it tiresome, the initial excitement beginning to pale. He tried to talk, suggest that now they had made the step they should normalise their relations. A hand went across his mouth signalling him to be silent. He felt an idiot, blindfolded and tied up.

He felt the silken rope on his right hand slip and he started to work it free. He heard a sharp intake of breath but it was not from the woman on top of him. Someone else was in the room. He wrenched his hand free out and tore off the blindfold, losing control at the same time and releasing into his wife. Except it was not his wife, it was Elizabeth. His wife was in the corner her long fingered hands over her mouth trying to take back that breathe. Elizabeth began to laugh. Richard pushed her off him and loosed his other hand.

"What is this? You are sick and twisted," he screamed at Jeannot.

Elizabeth ran to her and clutched her to her naked breasts as Jeannot cowered. For the second time Richard grabbed Elizabeth and thrust her from his bedroom, he pulled Jeannot off the chair and rammed it against the door. He grabbed his wife by the hair and threw her onto the bed. She was screaming and Elizabeth was hammering on the door. Richard lay on top of Jeannot and began pulling up her nightshirt. He put his hand

102

over her mouth to stop the noise and forced her legs apart. She was as dry as a desert. Richard didn't care, he just kept thrusting. It was over in a minute and he was suddenly overcome with horror and repulsion. He got up and threw water upon himself from the jug on the table near the bed. Jeannot was screaming at him in French; obscenities and hatred. Still Elizabeth banged the door, Richard removed the chair and it flew open. Jeannot held out her arms and Elizabeth rushed to her side. Richard left the room.

Chapter Fifteen

If the atmosphere in the house had been cold and uninviting before, it was now heavy and oppressive. The two women were almost joined at the hip, moving around as one body and whispering to one another so he could not hear or understand. Richard threw himself into his work and there was plenty to occupy him. There seemed to be more poor people than ever coming into the town. Poor harvests and bad weather always drew people to leave the countryside and try their luck in the town, but they found that wheat prices had tripled and the townspeople were not permitted to take in lodgers. Richard wondered if they also wanted to feel safer. If the Spanish did arrive and succeeded in their invasion they were likely to scour the countryside and lay it waste, but they were just as likely to put a town like Southampton to the sword as well.

Richard was making his way to the Church of St Lawrence, the smallest of the town's churches. There were three on English Street, each on the east side. All Hallows was on the corner of English and East Street and St Lawrence was next, with Holy Rood being the last. He could see the column of poor people going into the church. Fifty would receive a handout from the bequest of the Sendy family if they managed to sit through a pious sermon at St Lawrence. Richard couldn't remember the older Sendy but his son had been embarrassed that his father had been notorious in the town as a fornicator, he lived a riotous life but at the end recanted his earlier ways and left a large sum to the poor, his son added to the bequest to be given annually to the poor. In days gone by there were only thirteen official beggars allowed or acknowledged by the town that could don a tin badge and ask for alms, but now the town was almost overcome with poor folk and many were thankful that Sendy had led such a dissolute life. Richard had £2 10s in his purse to be given out, it was paid out each quarter day. He saw people looking at him as he took his place in the church. He had to listen to the sermon as well as the paupers, which was a bit unfair as it tended to be interminably long, the vicar wanting to make sure that the poor really earned their pennies. Richard started to feel a bit nauseous towards the end of the service and barely made it through the prayers to protect Her Majesty before he had to run outside and be sick next to one of the church's buttresses. He felt a bit better but was getting cramps in his stomach. He became aware of a hand on his arm and saw the kindly face of the churchwarden.

"Are you all right, my boy?"

"Yes, sorry sir, I must have eaten some bad meat. I'm fine now."

"Our poor folk are getting a bit restless; they think they might not get their money."

Richard gave a short smile as a pain gripped his guts. "Best get on with it then."

He just managed to distribute the money, beads of sweat were on his forehead but he felt icy cold. Once the last pennies were placed into dirty, rough hands he managed to run to the Bargate jakes before his bowels forced themselves empty. He sat for a while, hardly noticing the foetid smell until someone started to hammer on the stall. He recognised one of the poor from the church as he staggered out. The man gave him a strange look and then had the nerve to wave the air in front of his pock-marked nose as he went into the jakes.

Richard started to feel a bit better. He entered his little office, washed his face and neck and then went up into the courtroom where he found Mayor Studley in discussion with Martin the goldsmith. They were looking at the silver seal recently given to the town by the merchant Richard Eature and Studley was explaining to the goldsmith what he wanted to be engraved on the seal to make it unique to the town. They were so engrossed in their deliberations they didn't notice Richard, for which he was glad as he thought he did not look as well as he should and there were a few stains on his doublet. He tried to rub them off. He heard someone coming up the stone stairs and Symon Reston popped his head around the courtroom door. He spotted Richard and ambled over to him.

"Are you all right? You look as if you met with death on the way to work."

Richard rubbed his belly, "Bit of an upset stomach, it's nothing."

"I heard you had some work for me."

"That's right, come through to the tower room." They walked through to one of the great drum towers that stood either side of the main gate. Richard unlocked the heavy wooden and metal door and the two men went into the armaments store.

"I want you to have a look at the corslettes, they need trimming."

"Mmmm." Reston scratched his head and then rummaged through the thirty leather and steel jackets that hung about the room. "There is quite a bit of repair work needing to be done and some of the leather is pretty hard and cracked."

"How much?"

More sucking of teeth and shaking of his head. "Twenty shilling I would say."

"Fifteen," said Richard.

"With a shilling extra for the oil I will need to lay over them."

The men shook on the deal

"Getting prepared then?" Richard didn't answer. Reston picked up one of the calivers stacked against the wall, putting it up to his shoulder as if to fire it.

"Don't play with that, it's not a toy."

Reston put it back down. "Fair few guns here but hardly enough to scare off the whole Spanish army."

"Well perhaps it won't come to that."

Richard secured the room behind them. Reston left promising to return the next day to begin his task. Richard wanted to go home and lie down but there was a young man waiting for him back in the courtroom. He made an extravagant bow as Richard came in. Richard recognised him as an actor.

"I'm not the Mayor, he's over there."

"Ah right."

"What company are you from?"

"Lord Admiral's." The young man puffed out his chest.

"Oh dear," said Richard.

"What is your meaning? We are the leading acting company in the land."

"Better than Her Majesty's Players?"

"We think so."

"Well I wouldn't boast too much in front of the Mayor."

"Is he a Puritan?"

"Far from it."

The young man looked a bit exasperated and frowned at Richard who took pity on him.

"The Mayor is in dispute with the Lord Admiral at the moment, concerning pirates' goods."

The young man nodded as if he understood what Richard was talking about.

"It's a quarrel over money."

"Ah, do you think he will stop us playing?"

"Maybe."

Richard sighed, but in the end he liked play acting and the boy was right, the Admiral's company was one of the best, with fine London actors. He told the youth to wait and went over to the Mayor who was still talking with the goldsmith.

"Sorry to interrupt, Mr Mayor, but I have a player, his company have a licence to perform and they request permission."

"I'm busy at present, Mudford, you can see that. Look, look at this fine seal, the quality of the silver, I can't afford a mistake in the cutting of it."

"Of course not, Mr Mayor, I merely wanted to suggest that I deal with the players. I'm sure you want them to perform, to take people's minds off things."

Studley thought for a while, "Yes, you are right, thank you, please take care of it for me."

Richard took the key to the Mayor's coffer and went back to the young man.

"Is it the full touring company?"

"Twelve players, Sergeant."

"The first performance will be for the Mayor, here in the Guildhall, your fee will be 20s. You then can perform in the town where you will, the yards of the Dolphin and the Crown are often used. Some have used the bear-baiting ring and several of our burgesses like to give private shows to impress their friends and business associates."

"Thank you, Sergeant. Here is our licence."

Richard copied down the details and then gave the licence back to the young man with a note. "Present this after your performance and you will receive your fee."

"Any chance of an advance?"

"None."

"Can you recommend a good inn?"

"For a company such as the Admiral's, the Dolphin would

suit you well. Carry on down English Street past the first two churches and it sits on the main street before you reach the third church, it has a large yard where you can store your properties."

"Can we perform tomorrow or the next day?"

The latter was agreed upon.

"We will produce some notices. I assume we can announce our arrival?"

"Yes."

"And will we see you at the performance?"

"Of course."

They shook hands and the young man disappeared. A few minutes later Richard could hear the rattling of tambourines, playing of tabors and banging of a drum. He went to the window and watched the boys from the company cartwheel and tumble. The fool did a funny jig and the leading actors stood astride their cart, bowing and nodding at the townspeople who ran to line the road as they progressed down the street. Richard packed up his papers and pen, and bid good day to the Mayor who was looking at sketch drawings that Martin was roughing out on pieces of paper and parchment.

The strangest thing happened that night. Jeannot came to his bed. She slipped in beside him and rolled her nightshirt up to her waist. Richard considered for a moment and then pushed it up further to reveal her breasts. He thought them a bit mean and she was also too thin for his taste, he didn't know why but he was surprised that the hair between her legs was as red as that on her head. He had to rub himself to encourage his cock to harden and eventually it agreed, he moved Jeannot's legs wider so he could enter her. He tried without much success to turn her dryness into a slippery welcome but in the end had to spit on his fingers and transfer that between her legs. Once inside he bent to kiss her. She pursed her lips and wouldn't part them to let his tongue explore her mouth. He didn't mind, he didn't really want to kiss her, it seemed too intimate an act. When they finished they both rolled away from each other, lying on their sides and staring into the darkness, marvelling at the desperate state of their marriage.

Chapter Sixteen

Another silent meal to be prayed over. Richard picked at the stew.

"You are not eating, Husband?" Her voice irritated him.

"My stomach has not been what it should." He spooned the food into his mouth; he hesitated and looked at the spoon as if he expected it to talk to him.

"Is something amiss?"

"No, the food is just spicier than you usually prepare."

"I thought it would please you, I thought it how you liked it. I will take it away and get something else." Now she was irritated with him.

"No, no, it's good. It was kind of you to take the trouble."

She sat back down and pecked at her own small meal.

"You should eat more yourself, there is nothing of you."

She didn't answer.

"Jeannot, there is to be a play this evening at the Guildhall, if you would like to go?"

"I do not care for plays, they breed idleness. I believe they are the work of the Devil, the only words that people should study are those of God."

She caressed the little book of sermons that was fixed by a chain to her waist.

"Right of course. You understand I have to go, don't you? It would not be thought well if I did not."

"It is your soul husband."

"Indeed it is."

The company were good, their star actors were the Alleyn brothers, John and Edward, and they were, presenting a new work by their latest playwright Kit Marlowe called *Tamburlaine the Great*, which had only just been produced in London. Richard thought they would probably perform a cut down version but he was excited nevertheless. The play was epic and bloody, telling the story of how a poor shepherd rose to conquer the world. The younger Alleyn took the role. Richard judged him to be only around twenty years of age, he had the most beautiful voice Richard had ever heard and held the audience from the first syllable to the last. He stalked and roared across the makeshift stage. Richard found himself entranced at the verse, it was different from what he had seen and heard in the past, the verse was blank and although it was English, it was re-imagined into a language of such beauty.

With the rest of the audience he leapt to his feet at the end of the performance, clapping and cheering till his hands were raw. It was a good idea that Jeannot had not attended, she would not have approved of the play or its morality, that someone so cruel and bloody had triumphed. How had the writer expressed it? 'Millions of souls sit on the banks of Styx' were sent there by Tamburlaine and God had not in the end punished him. Perhaps God would not punish Philip's need to conquer either. Richard had so lost himself in the performance he had even forgotten the gnawing at his guts, yet as the audience filed out still talking animatedly about what they had seen and the actors packed Tamburlaine's victories and empire away, he became aware again of the twisting inside him. He should visit the apothecary tomorrow. The young man he had met two days before, that he now knew to be Edward Alleyn sought him out.

He was still in his exotic costume with his face was made up into the vision of a Scythian as imagined by the company.

"So have we earned our 20s?"

"If it was my money to give I would pay twice that much."

"Thank you, Sergeant. And how did you find my performance?"

'Actors' thought Richard, always after praise. "It was magnificent. I am only a country bumpkin but I have been privileged to see many of the travelling players and if my opinion is worth anything I would say that you will be a great actor Mr Alleyn."

"'Mr Alleyn!' I like the sound of that." Richard went and got the company their pay, promising if he could, to attend a new comedy they were to show at the Bullring the next day as a public performance.

Despite feeling ill he was in a merry mood when he reached home. Jeannot was in his bed again, she seemed to have decided that they must make a show of married life. Richard still had to give himself some encouragement to fulfil his part.

The next day he went to John Jervice's apothecary's shop. Jervice's windows were open, indicating he was available for business. Richard entered. It was full of bottles, and dusty jars, there were conserves and confections, pills, trochisks, powders and syrups, plasters and ointments. On the shelves were glister pipes, pots and bags of herbs and spices. On the counter lay lozenge knives, mortars and pestles. Jervice was grinding some herbs into powder as his apprentice looked on with fierce concentration.

"The powder must be very fine, very fine, here you try." He handed the pestle to the boy and glanced up at Richard. "You look terrible."

"That's why I'm here."

"What's the trouble?" Richard explained his symptoms.

"Mmm, some Armenian clay should sort you out and perhaps some sirupus de bizantijs, good for the liver. I will make you up a trochiscus, a lozenge of aloe-wood, musk and a few ingredients of my own, it is a wonderful restorative. Raymond, write this down and watch what I do." The apothecary mixed up Richard's medicines and made notes for him on dosage and when he should take it. "Try to fast for a couple of days."

"That should be easy. I don't feel much like food, I'm only eating to stop the wife complaining about wasting her efforts." The apothecary nodded sympathetically.

"Get yourself some watercress at the market, chew on that, it will do you a world of good."

"Thank you, Mr Jervice."

Richard left the shop and headed to the market around the Buttercross. As he was purchasing the green plant which grew so plentifully in the countryside around the town he felt a tug on his sleeve.

"Hello Diccon, I thought I might have seen you long before now."

Richard took one brief look at the man and walked away. The older man scurried after him.

"Don't be like that, Diccon, let's talk." He grabbed again at Richard's sleeve, Richard pulled his arm away. "Diccon, Diccon," the older man called after him as Richard quickened his stride and marched off. He ducked into the Crown inn, ordered a drink he didn't really want and sat nursing it, trying to force back into the depths of his mind the memories that had started to surface.

"Don't you want that?" The older man sat down opposite and without waiting for an answer sank the pot of ale in one swallow.

"What do you want, Pa?"

"To catch up with my boy."

Richard looked away.

"It's been ten years, aren't you pleased to see your old man?" Richard didn't answer. "Bet you thought your old Pa was dead, but I'm a hard bastard." Richard still said nothing. "Your brother

114

was pleased to see me. I've been looking after his kid, lovely little girl." He signalled for the pot boy to bring more drink.

"Your step-ma has passed on. Drank herself to death, that's why we lost the tipple house." He scratched his crotch, "We drank more than we made, but it was great while it lasted. So I went a-roaming. And now am back. Do you want to know where I have been?"

"No."

"I'm staying with Dorothy, down in Bagrow."

That surprised Richard, Dorothy was the sister of his first stepmother Jane. Jane had been a placid woman, Richard couldn't remember her features but she had been kind enough to him and Jack. His father had married her because he had needed a mother for his two sons but for some reason Jane had annoyed him and he beat her regularly, especially when he was in his cups. One day she just died, worn out with her life and his Pa had moved onto the blowsy and slovenly Olive.

"What do you want, Pa?"

"To catch up with my boy, I told you."

"Don't Pa, just don't."

His father hung his head. He was going thin on top and his hair was more grey than blond now, his left cheek was hollow where he had lost the teeth on that side and his steely blue eyes were rheumy, his nose enlarged. "If you could just see yourself to let me have a small loan, till Jack gets back, I need money for the kid."

Richard snorted, Jack left more than enough money for Joannie's needs. What did you do, Pa, drink it? Gamble it? Whore it?"

His father gave his lopsided grin that had served him so well in his youth. "All of the above."

Richard banged some coins down to pay for the drink and a tip for the pot boy, which he knew his father would steal, and left the inn.

Chapter Seventeen

He almost turned back. Alice, John, and the children were making their way to the Bullring. John turned and saw him and it was too late. He missed their past friendship, he hadn't realised till he cut himself off that John was his friend, his only one in fact. Much to his surprise John was beckoning.

"Diccon, Diccon, over here."

John was smiling, Richard never knew anyone smile so much. He drew up alongside them, Alice was pretending to very interested in something William was saying. John clasped Richard close, "You should not be a stranger, just because you are married, I'm a married man myself."

"Where is Tamsin?"

"She decided to stay in with the baby; it's a bit young to bring to see a play. How are you? You look like you have lost weight, don't you think so, Alice?"

Alice had to face him now; he saw a flicker of shock as she looked at him. He must look worse than he thought. She looked quite pale herself.

"I'm fine just been a bit sick, upset stomach."

"Alice had that at Christmas."

"Are you well now?" asked Richard.

"I think so." She pulled her cloak around her though it wasn't really cold. The children were asking for toffee apples and John took them off. The silence was uneasy.

"How are you all doing?"

"If you visited once and a while you would know." She said. She wouldn't look him in the eye. He traced her profile, that wide forehead and nose just short of being too large, the mouth that had kissed his most intimate parts, into which his tongue had slipped and explored. Her breasts seemed even larger and fuller than he remembered but perhaps it was just the contrast between them and Jeannot's pathetic protuberances.

"Alice, I..."

"What?"

"Nothing, nothing."

"Is your wife here?"

"She doesn't care for theatre."

"Oh." She turned on him angrily. "Are you happy?"

Richard shrugged.

"Was it worth it?"

"What do you mean?"

"Your sensible marriage, you are a man of property now."

"I owe all to my wife's family if that is what you mean."

"You sold yourself cheap."

"Why are you so angry?"

"You wouldn't understand." snapped Alice. Richard fumed.

"Then tell me. You pushed me a way, you didn't want me."

"Why didn't you fight for me?"

"What?"

"You heard me."

"Fight for you? I opened my heart up to you and you tore it out and threw it away."

"How poetic."

"Don't mock me."

"I just don't understand if your feelings were so strong, why didn't you try harder?"

"Are you telling me that if I had asked you again you would have given yourself to me?"

"Well you will never know, you were too busy nursing your wounded pride."

"Alice!"

She started to call the boys. "Come on we are going home. I have a headache." The boys argued but Alice would not change her mind.

"Alice, you stay, I will go."

"Yes, you are good at running away."

"That's not fair."

She started tugging the boys down the road, John shrugged, "I don't know what's got into her."

Richard struggled with himself and then called "I'll come to the tippling house tomorrow."

"Don't bother," Alice called back, "I am going over to the Ferry village tomorrow, John's mother isn't well and I'm to look after her."

"When will you be back?"

She didn't answer. He watched her hips swaying away from him till she turned down East Street.

He couldn't concentrate on the play, the audience laughed loudly so it must have been funny, cuckolded husbands and sour-faced wives featured, but he had enough of that at home.

Chapter Eighteen

Weeks dragged by, he still felt ill but then half the population seemed to be sick, the fever had spread quickly through the town. The old, the very young and the poor suffered most. Richard had to arrange for mass graves to be dug and the alms-house was overcrowded. Still the threat of invasion grew closer and closer. Rumours were rife and everywhere people were searching for signs and remembering old prophesies about England being conquered by men with snow on their helmets. The number of fleas collected together on a window in the Queen's presence chamber was seen as a portent. It was reported that thirty porpoises had been seen swimming up the Thames. Drake had sailed with secret instructions in April and the country held its breath willing their hero to strike at Spain's heart.

Richard was at the council meeting when a dispatch was received sent by Walsingham himself, the Queen's chief spymaster. Studley read the contents and began to laugh and cry all at once.

"Drake, Drake, he took the fight to the heart of Spain. He has caught the Spanish ships at harbour in Cadiz, some 60 ships and 30 were sent to the bottom according to his count, though Mr Secretary believes it was perhaps 20. Great news gentlemen, great news."

"Is there more?" asked Alderman Crooke.

"Drake has not contented himself with the destruction of the Cadiz fleet, he is still harrying the coast. Here, here Mr Secretary quotes directly from Drake. He says that never has there been before the preparation the King of Spain is now making for his enterprise of England. He warns us to prepare strongly, mostly by sea."

A quiet descended in the Audit House.

Richard hardly spent a moment at home in the next few weeks as the defences were checked once again and work commissioned on repairs. The town took Drake at his word and many burgesses prepared their merchant ships, expecting they might be called into service. The hard work seemed to do Richard good and his health improved markedly. He was down at the Water Gate when a cry went up that sails had been sighted. The lookout was puzzled he had never seen the like, but it wasn't the Spanish, it was the *God's Speed* and the *Magpie*. Or it was if the ships had been imagined by Kit Marlowe. The bows were shining with gilt, the topmasts seemed to be wrapped in cloth of gold, the sails were of multi coloured silk and as the ships grew nearer the crew were doing acrobatics in the rigging dressed in silk and brocade. People had run down to the shore and lined the walls to see the sight. Richard could hear people calling and shouting.

"It's Captain Prowse and Black Jack Mudford! Huzzah Captain Mudford."

Jack had done much to burnish his tender legend before he had set sail. Richard carried on with his work and waited for his brother to find him.

"Diccon, where were you, did you see that? I was hoisted up on the shoulders of men who would have run me out of town a few months since."

"Was it a successful voyage, Jack?"

"And it's nice to see you too, Diccon. Thanks for your concern, I am unscathed by my battles."

"I can see you are well."

Jack's skin was tanned and his hair bleached fair, it made Richard feel even paler than he was. Jewels glistened in his ears and he wore a Spanish doublet.

"We did pretty well, a few baubles but no chests of gold."

Richard groaned, "I'm in debt up to my neck Jack financing your adventures."

"Don't worry, I might not have gold but I have the next best thing – sugar."

"Sugar!"

"Tonnes of it, Diccon." They laughed and clapped one another on the back. "I need you to do the paperwork brother, see all receive their due."

"I will, I will."

"I must get the ship ready."

"Ready for what?"

"To go after the treasure fleet of course. Look, we have enough now to pay off our backers and finance the next trip ourselves."

"It's too big a risk, Jack. If you fail, we will all end up as paupers."

"You're a lousy gambler, Diccon."

"No, you are, Jack. Look we can be full sharers but we should offset some of the risk with other partners, my father-in-law, Crooke—"

"–whoa, wait a minute, did you say father-in-law?"

"Yes, I got married."

"Don't tell me you married that French bitch?"

"I married Jeannot and she is my wife, so watch you language."

"Marriage doesn't seem to be suiting you. Is she any good in bed? I can't imagine it."

"That's not everything."

"It's a lot. Jesu, Diccon, I thought I was the one with terrible taste in women."

"Its fine, come dine with us."

"No thanks."

"Pa caught up with me."

"And?"

"And nothing he was after money."

"I left him enough."

"It's never enough, you know that, Jack. You should find someone else to look after Joannie."

"Well as you're married now—"

"I don't think that will be a good idea."

"Wife wouldn't like it?"

"She doesn't like much, if truth be told."

The brothers went and got drunk.

Jack didn't stay around long and Richard missed him. They had rekindled their friendship, which had been lost for a long while. He was having supper at his in-laws but he couldn't face much dinner, his guts were playing him up again.

"Jeannot seems happier," said her father.

They were having a glass of watered wine after the meal and the women were sat doing some needlework. Elizabeth had accompanied them, she hadn't sat at the table of course but close by in case her mistress had need of her. Richard wondered how Sohier could tell his daughter was happier her expression never seemed to change.

"She was always a strange little girl, sometimes she used to cut herself."

Richard looked shocked.

"Don't worry my boy, since we found Elizabeth to look

after her she has been calm. I think she struggled with her faith."

"She has always appeared very devout to me."

"Yes, but she felt she was failing her own high standards of piety. I think if we had been of the old religion she would have been a nun, scourging herself, fasting, probably an anchorite, bricked in to serve God without distraction."

Richard was even more horrified. He wished he could be free of his marriage but he was trapped.

"Still, my boy, we are pleased with the news." Richard had no idea what he meant.

"Sorry, I was sworn to secrecy but we are so happy. You may trust us not to say a word, we will leave it to you to decide when to tell the Communion that we will have a new member."

Richard thought he was going to faint. He took a long draft of his wine and stared at his wife's belly. "Thank you, sir. We are very pleased."

Later that night he examined his wife's body and wondered why he had not noticed before. She had rolled up her nightshirt and was waiting for him to climb on top of her.

"Perhaps we had better not if you are pregnant."

She pulled the shirt down and turned on her side and went to sleep.

Chapter Nineteen

He was sat on the chamber pot. His stools were bloody and he was worried.

"Jeannot!" His wife stirred and raised herself she was getting bigger and was even less graceful than she had been. "I think you should call the apothecary."

"Are you sick again?"

"It's worse."

"I will nurse you," she said.

"I think you should get Jervice."

She ignored him, helping him back into bed and carrying away the chamber pot with its foul-smelling contents. He lost sense of the days. He was hot, he was cold. Jeannot and Elizabeth barely left his side. One or the other sat by the bed watching him with watery stares. Washing him down, helping him to eat, which he mostly threw up again. He was as weak as a kitten. He thought he should make his will and asked Jeannot to send for an attorney but she would not hear talk of death. She brought him some broth, he didn't want it.

"You must eat," she said fiercely. "You must."

"Leave it on the side love, I'll have it shortly, I promise."

She did not look happy but put the bowl on the little side

table. Richard rolled over gazing at the broth. Jeannot left the room. Richard glanced up and thought he saw his wife on the other side of the room but realised it was just a reflection in a glass. Jeannot was stood behind the door looking at him through the crack. She must be desperate to see him eat. He propped himself on one elbow and shakily took the spoon and scooped a bit of the broth. He glanced up. Jeannot was still there a strange look in her eye, like a saint having a vision. Richard didn't know why he did it but he only pretended to put the broth into his mouth. She was smiled cruelly, she slipped away. Richard poured the contents of the broth into the chamber pot and lay back in the bed. His nightshirt was wringing with sweat at his small exertion. Against his will he drifted off to sleep. When he woke she was sat at his side.

"How do you feel?"

"I feel worse."

"Did you eat all the broth?"

"Yes, my love, but I threw most of it up again, I'm sorry."

"Do not worry yourself, I will fetch you some more."

Richard managed a faint smile. "Perhaps you should get a lawyer."

"Do not worry, there, there, there will be time enough."

She picked up the bowl. Richard half closed his eyes and rolled so that he could watch the glass Jeannot was showing the bowl to Elizabeth. The women embraced. They pulled apart and both smoothed down the front of their dresses. Elizabeth had a bump that mirrored Jeannot's own. Richard threw up again. The next time they came with food he pretended to be in fever and lashed out knocking the bowl so its content went over the floor. He felt a little stronger but he knew he was too weak to escape the clutches of the two women. If he could just get them to bring a lawyer or a priest. He slept again. A noise awoke him. He tried to think what it might have been. It was the door, he held his breath, the house seemed quiet. Had they both gone? He heard some voices under the eaves. He thought one his neighbour, one was definitely Jeannot, another voice spoke, Elizabeth! She was encouraging her mistress to their tasks, footsteps hurried away.

Richard hauled himself from the bed, and across the floor. He grabbed some breeches and it seemed to take hours to dress. Boots, where were his boots? He found some fancy slippers and put them on instead. He heard a noise and his heart almost gave out. It was the tinkle of breaking glass. By clinging to the furniture he dragged himself onto the gallery. Someone was below.

"Joannie!" The girl looked up with a start and dropped the silver cup in her hand and made to run.

"Joannie, wait for God's sake wait, I'll give you a dozen cups."

"Swear!"

"On my own life I swear. Just come up and help me. I need to get to Alice Dypere's."

"The tippling house?"

"That's right, Joannie."

"A dozen cups."

"And a gold florin."

It sealed the deal and the child scooted up the back stairs to his side.

"I'm going to have to lean on you, Joannie."

They struggled to the hall, Richard falling down the stairs as Joannie could not hold him. She tried to pull him to his feet. He was too heavy. She ran off and left him.

"Joannie, Joannie, please come back."

She couldn't open the door as it was locked from the outside. She climbed onto a sideboard and opened a side window and whistled. Richard was heaving. A face appeared at the window, it was his father. He had obviously been playing lookout.

"Help me, Pa, please help me."

126

His father disappeared and a moment later there was a crash as a rock smashed through the glass. He clambered through the main window and dropped down to his son's side.

"What's wrong, what's happened to you, boy?"

"You have to get me out of here. I will die if you don't get me out of here."

"Joannie, clear the glass and open the window wide, then climb out." The girl did as she was bid. The old man heaved his son onto his shoulder and then passed him out of the window. Joannie did her best to support him as he sank to the pavement. His father dropped down beside him. The old man and the young girl managed to get him onto his feet. The few passers-by looked and scurried on. Richard didn't know how long it took them to get to the High Street. They propped him up against a shop door.

"I need to get a cart or something."

"The boy," said Joannie pointing at a young boy who was pulling a sled down the road. "He's from the tippling house. He gave me a biscuit."

Richard had closed his eyes. He forced them back open and tried to focus, "It's Jacket," he said hoarsely.

They called out to the boy who had stopped suspiciously, but he clearly recognised Richard because he came across with his sled. He must have been going to the brewers as he had some empty casks on the sled.

"Boy," said Richard's father. "We need your sled, my son is sick—"

"He wants to go to the tippling house," said Joannie.

Jacket thought for a moment and then lifted the barrels off the sled. The three of them pulled Richard on and Jacket, mindful not to lose his charges, fitted the barrels around him. Richard's father pulled and the two children pushed. Richard saw the familiar rooftops slip by; he'd never studied them at this angle before. They turned the corner and the road started

127

to slope down, they were in East Street. Joannie ran on and banged the door.

"We're not open." John's head appeared, he took in the scene not quite able to believe what he saw. "God and his saints!"

"Help us get him inside."

He was aware of a couple of men grasping him, John and he thought the other George Parker, who muttered some query as to why Richard had come here. Richard passed out. He slipped in and out of consciousness he had no sense of time. Jervice came and prescribed theriac, an antidote to poison. A cool hand was on his forehead. He opened his eyes.

"Alice, is that you Alice?"

"Yes, Richard."

"You came back."

"I came back. Sleep now."

He was aware of comings and goings. There were shouts and banging at the door. He thought he heard Monsieur Sohier. He didn't know. A baby was crying. Richard opened his eyes, he focused quite well. "Hello Tamsin, is that your baby?"

The little girl had dark curly hair. She was crying because Tamsin was moving her from one breast to another. Once she reached the new nipple she surrounded it with her rosebud lips and tapped her mother's bosom with her fat little hand.

"You scared us," said Tamsin.

"I scared myself."

"The apothecary reckons that if you have survived this long you will probably live."

"That's good to know."

"He's left an elixir," Tamsin moved the baby in her arms as she got up and reached for a bottle, she eased out the stopper with one hand and poured the dark liquid into a cup and passed that to Richard. He grimaced at its bitterness.

"It has to taste bad if it's going to do you good, everyone knows that."

"I feel so weak."

"Well you haven't eaten for two weeks."

"Two weeks!"

"We are to start feeding you now that you are awake but not too much at one time."

The baby burped.

"She's a beautiful baby."

"I know, I thought at first it was just because I was her mother but I know now she really is beautiful. I didn't think I could make something so perfect. Here you hold her. I'll go and tell the others you are awake and get you some food."

She laid the baby on the bed, it kicked up its fat little legs and grabbed its own toes. Richard thought a minute about the baby in Jeannot's belly. And did he dream that Elizabeth was swollen with a child as well? Was it the fruit of those horrible nights?

Chapter Twenty

As each day passed he got stronger and stronger. He had tried to walk across the room but could only do it leaning on John. His father called in most days to see he was well. It had taken him a lifetime to do a paternal act and Richard could almost forgive him his miserable childhood. Joannie came too, she wanted to know when she would get her silver cups. 'Soon', Richard had said, 'soon'. Alice fussed over him, making his favourite dishes, combing his hair and reading to him. She was a slow reader and often stumbled but it was as beautiful as any poetry of Kit Marlowe. She was neglecting her duties in the tippling house. When he heard Parker and other regulars complain she told them to mind their business.

Then finally one day his in-laws came up the stairs to the loft where he lay.

"I see you are looking better. It is a terrible the shame you have brought onto our house," said Monsieur Sohier.

Richard was stunned.

"We have put out the story that you have removed yourself from your home as you were afraid your sickness might put your pregnant wife in danger. We have said you are in the care of your father. Disreputable character though he is, it is better people think that, than that you ran away to be with your whore."

"What? What are you saying?"

"As soon as you are strong enough, you will be removed back to Jeannot's care."

"You will go through me first," announced Richard's father. "Believe me I have taken many men's lives, yours is as nothing to me."

"What is this, what is this?" Sohier blustered.

His wife put a hand out to calm him. "Leave me both of you, I wish to speak to Richard." The two older men left, Pa with bad grace and Monsieur Sohier sheepishly.

Madame Sohier carefully smoothed the sheet on Richard's bed and sat herself down. For a long while she said nothing.

"Will you go back to her?"

"Never."

"If I arrange for my own trusted servants to watch over her."

"What, like Elizabeth?"

"I never cared for Elizabeth." She thought for a while remembering. "She calmed Jeannot, but she exercises too much control. Whatever wrongs you imagine come from her."

"Imagined? They tried to poison me."

Madame Sohier covered her ears for a moment. There was a long silence that Richard forced himself to break.

"They seem to live in their own world, it's not natural," said Richard.

"I thought once she was married things would change, and then she was with child."

"I think it was part of their plan."

"What do you mean?" said Madame Sohier.

"She did not like me touching her, it made her flesh creep to have me near her. She forced herself to lay with me, once she knew she was pregnant I was not needed." Richard paused, talking was wearing him out. "With me gone she could remain a respectable widow living alone with the child and with Elizabeth. She could avoid further marriage."

"I cannot believe her capable of such a thing."

"Can't you?" Madame Sohier looked uneasy.

"What is to be done?" She tried to sound matter-of-fact.

"You must have a proposal." Richard was too tired for games.

She looked at him.

"Why ask to be alone with me?"

"It won't be long till Jeannot's confinement. I will stay with her till then. I will not remove Elizabeth until after the child is born. It would upset my daughter too much and would not be good for the child. We will maintain the fiction of your illness and removal."

"And after the birth?"

"Elizabeth will be taken care of. Jeannot will be confined and we will raise our grandchild. You will be recompensed."

Richard was not going to agree to this arrangement. No child of his would be raised in a house that had produced Jeannot. Madame Sohier took his silence for assent.

"I will speak to my husband. He will understand it is for the best. He never saw Jeannot for what she was, she is sick but she is my only child."

Richard almost felt sorry for the woman. Almost.

Chapter Twenty-One

He was getting much better, he could spend time out of bed do a few chores to help out. He still tired easily. He thanked God for the money raised from the sale of the sugar, there was enough after settling with creditors and refitting the *Magpie* to keep him and pay Alice for looking after him. The money had been lodged with the lawyer they had engaged to set up their stock company and only he could access it. There was much sickness in the town so few people had time to think of his strange domestic arrangements.

He was sat by the empty hearth wondering when he might be well enough to go back to his duties as sergeant. He missed it and he didn't have enough riches to call himself a merchant adventurer yet. Besides, the war was getting closer. Drake had done much damage and the privateers had drawn the Spanish Admiral away from his plans for Armada to protect the treasure fleets but it was a rearguard action. Most people thought the King of Spain would delay no more and that the invasion was planned for the next year.

There was a knock on the door. Richard was alone. John was on watch duty, Alice, Tamsin and the children at the market. His Pa was in the ale house. Richard called for whoever it was to come in. A girl Richard recognised as a servant of the Sohiers stepped into the cottage.

"Monsieur, you are to come, Madame Mudford is delivered of a child, but alas–"

"–the child is dead?" Richard felt a terrible sadness.

"–no Monsieur, Madame Mudford, she is dead."

It took some moments to understand what the girl had said. Richard looked for the stick that was acting as a crutch and followed the girl out of the house back to the home he had shared with Jeannot. He had not set foot outside for more than a month. Their progress was slow. When they reached the house Richard noticed the window broken when he fled was still boarded up. Weeping women filled the hall, dabbing their eyes with their white aprons. He went slowly up the stairs to the bedchamber he had shared with Jeannot. His wife was laid in the bed. White sheets were drawn up to her chin and her waxy face. Richard wondered if she was at peace. Her mother stood at the end of the bed, her eyes shut in silent prayer. Another servant was cradling the tiny swaddled figure of his child. He went close and looked at the little red face.

"You have a daughter."

He turned to Madame Sohier. "I'm sorry."

"Perhaps it is for the best."

Richard was suddenly aware of screaming coming from somewhere else in the house.

Madame Sohier sighed, "Elizabeth, she became hysterical, trying to cling to my daughter's body."

There was something strange about the screams. Richard left the room and followed the noise to a small antechamber. He pushed open the door. Elizabeth was lying on the floor, a pool of blood between her legs. Richard realised she was in labour. He dropped his crutch and knelt on the floor. He peered down, "The baby is crowning, Elizabeth, you need to concentrate, you need to push."

"Get it out of me, get it out of me," she screamed.

The baby's head was appearing. Richard put his hand beneath its head to stop it banging on the floor and helped guide the small thing into the world. A little girl slipped into his hands. He tried to think what to do next, he needed a knife. He reached into his pocket and pulled his little pocket knife out and cut the cord. He breathed deeply. This was the most exertion he had undertaken in a long time. The baby was silent. He dropped the knife onto the floor, lifted the child by the ankles and slapped its backside. Still it made no sound. He lay the baby on the floor and put his little finger in its tiny mouth, trying to clear its airway. He lifted the baby again and slapped, still nothing. He was beginning to panic as he bent over the tiny body and blew gently into its little mouth. He slapped again. This time the baby squealed and cried. Richard started to cry. He rummaged in a drawer and found a shirt and an apron. He used one to wipe the baby and the other to wrap her, she clutched at his finger and he smiled. He turned back to Elizabeth.

"You have a daughter – no, no stop!"

She had the knife at her throat as he called out she drew it across her neck. A spray of blood soared into the air and splattered against the whitewashed walls. Richard put the baby down and slithered across the room, he cried for help and clamped his hands onto the wound but he had no strength. He couldn't stop the bleeding there was blood everywhere. He could hear people running. John appeared at the door, behind him was Madame Sohier.

"John, thank God. She cut her throat and I can't stop the bleeding, I can't stop the bleeding."

He saw John glance down at the knife in Elizabeth's hand. He took in the detritus of the birth and the crying baby in the corner. He knelt down by his friend.

"Diccon, Diccon listen to me, she's gone. Do you understand? Let go, she's dead." Richard gazed around him he thought he was in a butcher's yard. He looked at his bloodstained hands, his shirt, everything was covered in blood.

"Take him out of here, get him cleaned up." Madame Sohier said calmly.

"I should call the watch, there has been a violent death," said John.

"What good would that do? The court, the shame, the gossip, a suicide."

"What's to be done?" asked John. Richard felt like he was watching a play.

"I will have the room cleaned, I'll have the body sewn into a shroud. She's just a servant, she had no family, no one to ask questions."

"There's a baby."

"We can leave it somewhere, a foundling."

"No," said Richard. He gathered the baby to his chest. "No, no."

"Richard, calm yourself. We can't let it be known Elizabeth had a baby. How would it be explained?" She looked at Richard, her lip curled. "This is your bastard, I presume?"

"You would presume that wouldn't you? Do you want to know how your daughter connived to send her maid to take her place in my bed?"

"How could she achieve such a thing? You must have been a willing participant."

"Do you really want me to tell you what she did?"

The baby let out a cry.

"How can this be explained without bringing shame onto all our heads?" Madame looked as if she would gladly have stamped the life out of the tiny body sucking on Richard's finger.

"I don't know, you think of something, you have everything else worked out." He said grimly

Richard could see her brain working as she thought through

various scenarios. Eventually she took a deep breath, "We'll let people think my daughter gave birth to twins."

"There are witnesses," said John

"They are my servants, they are of the Communion. They will say nothing and I take it you will both keep your mouths shut."

John looked nonplussed but he grabbed Richard by the arm and took him back to the bedchamber. He stripped him of his clothes and put them in the fire and burnt them. He fetched Richard new clothes. Richard laid his two daughters in the same basket. He wanted to get out of the room, he couldn't bear staring at his wife's corpse.

"I'm going back to Silkshop Yard."

"What?" said John.

"I never got around to giving it up. I'm taking my daughters and going to Silkshop Yard."

"Did you father Elizabeth's child?"

"I don't know. They tricked me, blindfolded me and I thought it was Jeannot who came to my bed. I don't know, maybe I imagined it all, it doesn't matter. You heard the old woman. I am the father of twins."

"You're in shock, you should come back to the tippling house till we can figure this out."

"It wouldn't look right and I can't stay here. I never want to be here again."

"The babies will need feeding. How are you going to do that?"

"Take me to Silkshop Yard and then find me a wet nurse." Richard was implacable.

John gave up the unequal fight, "All right, all right."

Richard lent on John's shoulder and John picked up the basket.

"What are you doing? Where are you going?" Madame Sohier had appeared at the doorway.

"Get out of my way."

She thought for a moment and stood aside.

They made it to the Yard. Richard realised he had no key. It didn't matter, someone had broken the lock. They went into the tiny front room.

"Hello son. What have you there?"

"My babies. Jeannot is dead. I have two daughters." John put the basket on the table where Richard's father was sat. They started to cry.

"Hush there, I'm your Grandpa."

"Pa, don't stand too close, I don't want them to catch anything."

The old man laughed. He went upstairs and came back with a clean kerchief. He tore it in two and dunked it into the milk pudding he had been eating. He put the sopping cloth into the girls' mouths and they sucked it dry.

"I'll go fetch Mrs Lister, she's just had a baby," said John and went out.

Richard and his father carried on with the makeshift nipples. About ten minutes later a big fat woman waddled in. There was barely enough room for her to turn around. Even her back was fat.

"Oh let's have a look lovely," she peered at the babies. "Take those cloths away these are what they want." She squeezed her fat breasts.

"That's a lovely pair of paps," said Pa.

"You better believe it." She plopped herself onto a stool which creaked under the strain. She started to unlace her bodice. "You can pay?"

"I'll pay you double what you normally get for each baby, you will wet nurse them alone."

"Sounds good to me. I love babies, come here my lovelies." She placed a baby at each of her enormous breasts. "That's it my pretties, drink up."

Pa burst out laughing.

Part Three

1588

Chapter Twenty-Two

Richard's recovery was almost complete. It was as if he knew he had to get well for the babies, he had no time to worry about himself any more. The women around the Yard took pity on him. They had little enough themselves but they would bring food or clothes that their children no longer needed. They would look at him with their heads cocked, hug him and offer to sit for him when he needed to work. Mistress Lister seemed to have a never-ending supply of milk. She would sit by the side of the fire and laugh and joke with Pa, who had not thought of moving on and she brought round her daughter Annie to help out. Richard thought they resembled a family of farmyard animals. Mistress Lister a big pink sow, with dozens of teats, Annie was bovine featured, big dozy-eyed, not very bright but good natured. Mr Lister never appeared except in his wife's stories but sounded like a little weasel of a man squashed to almost nothingness by his larger than life wife.

Richard was back working. Mayor Studley had decided that he needed to improve the look of the town, remind people it was an impressive place. Richard thought perhaps the money could be better spent on gunpowder but he nevertheless put the painter to work, painting the two lions that stood rampant at either side of the Bargate and arranging for the lion and dragon that loomed over the walking place to be gilded.

Richard's babies were not the only children to find themselves without a parent after the sickness in town and Richard found himself helping to find likely candidates who would take children of the right age on as apprentices. He tried his best to arrange a good match but some just agreed to take the orphans because of the payment they received and then used the children as unpaid skivvies. The right master could be the making of a boy, Richard knew that from his own experience. Persuading Alderman Crooke to take him on, the dirty, ragged and uneducated boy that he was, had changed his life and prospects. Babies were placed with nurses and the Mayor paid for their keep and clothing until they were old enough to be apprenticed. Richard knew he had to make sure his babies were cared for especially if something happened to him. He prayed Jack would do well in their enterprise.

The Sohiers tried to see him but he wouldn't meet with them. They wanted Jeannot's child to be taken into the Communion. Richard's response was to march across to St Michael's Church in the square and ask the vicar to christen the girls. The Crookes stood as godparents and when the vicar asked for their names Richard was momentarily struck dumb, in his head he just kept referring to them as Jeannot's baby and Elizabeth's baby. He stuttered and looked wildly around the old stone walls of the church looking for inspiration. All the paintings of saints had been whitewashed away, the chapels taken down. The vicar stood impatiently by the black marble font, engraved with fantastical beasts except at the place for the cleric where St Michael, wings spread to ward off evil spirits, was carved.

"The eldest girl, Richard, I am sure you would want to name her for Jeannot," said Margery nodding to encourage him.

"Yes, er perhaps, yes, maybe...maybe Jeanne, so she is not quite all her mother."

The vicar dowsed the child who looked surprised but not unhappy. He handed her back to Margery and took the other baby from Alderman Crooke. "And the younger?"

"What about for the Queen, Richard?" suggested Margery again.

The vicar didn't wait for Richard's response but wetted the child and christened her, "Elizabeth."

The baby screamed and bellowed. "But she must be known as Lizzie, Lizzie," Richard insisted as he took the baby back and bounced her in his arms till she quietened.

"Of course Richard, Jeanne and Lizzie." Margery looked as if her heart would break.

Chapter Twenty-Three

"The council met yesterday," said Mayor Studley.

Richard raised his brows waiting for the Mayor to go on.

"They have decided to expel all the Spanish and Portuguese from the town."

Richard wasn't surprised. The antipathy to foreigners was growing, there were more fights breaking out, more accusations of unfair trading practices levelled at anyone who was not of the town.

"It's a shame in many ways, the Spanish trade has been significant to the town since the Italians stopped coming." The Italian galley fleets hadn't visited for years, not since the days of the old King. The town must have been really alive back then, wealth pouring in along with the spices, silks, satins and wine and all the wool traded in exchange. Loaded carts and pack horses from the Cotswolds would have pushed their way through the Bargate. Now they preferred to pay a penance to land in London, but the burgesses always held onto the vain hope that one day the Italian vessels would reappear, three state galleys from Venice, argosies from Florence and Genoa.

"Anyway that's what has been decided and I am to help

them on their way with a small payment, I have put aside 12s and 10d."

"Yes, Mr Mayor."

"Has the work at the sluice at God's House Gate been completed?"

"Yes, Mr Mayor, I have George Ecton's account and I have inspected the work, if we need to flood the moat we can do so. I also have Hugh Mychenor's bill for the repairs to the walls."

"What with all the work being done at the Audit House, I don't know how I will balance my account this year. That's why we can't afford to lose this case against the Admiralty."

The lawsuit was weighing heavily on the Mayor's mind. Why the Admiralty had to pursue it at such a critical time Richard didn't know, unless they needed the money for the war effort as much as anyone else.

"Oh and I paid out 2d for the new leather bag to put the town seal in, sir."

"It's a beautiful seal, Mudford, Martin did well. Why did I agree to take on a second year in office? It's too much responsibility. My own business suffers. Has Alderman Crooke been in to pay the interest on the loan he took from the town?"

"No, sir, not as yet." The Alderman seemed to be risking more and more on his privateering enterprises, Richard knew from the accounts he had borrowed a £100, Richard always thought he had plenty of money but perhaps it was all invested. "But I have William Markett's 10s, he was most grateful that you managed to get him released from being impressed into Her Majesty's ships."

"I should think so, still, Platterer was happy to go in his place."

Richard helped the Mayor count up the money received from the carters he had allowed to work on holy days, poundage from the sale of ships and money from the sale of flotsam and jetsam, which came to him due to his position of Admiral of the port."

"Widow Chinerton has died, sir, I have arranged for her shroud and Read's wife asked for some assistance, he's on his death bed apparently."

"She's that Saracen isn't she? Never understood that marriage. What will she do when he's gone?"

"Don't know, sir, she is a long way from home."

"2s. 6d. Give her 2s. 6d."

"The water pump at St Michael's is broken by the way—"

"You live round there don't you?"

"Yes, sir, and it's a pain in the arse having to go down to Holy Rood."

"All right, all right get it fixed. Damn, the bill's come in for the Bishop's New Year's gift. I thought old Diaz had forgotten, or perhaps he's heard about the council ruling. By all the saints! £2 10s for a barrel of figs, a barrel of olives and some raisins."

"It was thirty pound in weight, Mr Mayor."

"Well that's as maybe, it still seems a bit steep and I don't notice the Bishop doing much good on behalf of the town. At least the Earl of Hertford makes an attempt to support the town for his sugar and raisins. By the bye, Captain Dawtrey will be arriving tomorrow with his men, can you arrange for them to stay at the Dolphin? He's been given charge of the muster by the Queen."

"Sending a professional, things must be getting worse."

"Rumours are rife that the Armada has put out from Lisbon. Well if Dawtrey is going to put the muster through their paces we had better get the drum re-headed, it sounded pathetic last time."

"I'll have Preston the drummer get onto it. I think we ought to get some gambions made for the Water Gate, and I need some brass to make ladles for the ordinance, Wharton the tinker is a good man. And whilst I'm about it I should get some sheepskins for the sponges, I can buy them from Hoskins the glover, he's just had a shipment."

The Mayor nodded, "We should take on some more men I think."

"It wouldn't be a bad idea. I need staves cut and worked to handles for the ladles. There are barrels of pitch and tar that must be moved and we need faggots to heat it. I'll have to buy some barrows, shovels and scoops – the gunner said we need a new gun carriage as well. I also suggest we bring the guns off the *Marigold* into the town."

"What of ammunition?"

"I have 260 pounds of iron round shot, and I have cross bars but I need to get more homen wood for shot for the fowlers. I have asked the cutler to look at the swords and daggers stored at the Audit House; most of them need new scabbards. And of course there will be beer for the men!"

"Of course, and is there anything else?"

"The drummers and the fife player have been asking about liveries."

"Liveries?"

"Well they reckon as they are representing the town and they are part of the defence force."

"Go on, we'll probably all be dead before the bill comes in, stammel cloth only mind."

"And–"

"–What more?"

"They want to have the drums painted with the town arms."

"Right I think we are done here. How are those girls of yours, Richard?"

"Doing well, thanks be to God."

"I have a daughter myself you know, Lidea, apple of my eye. Before you know it they will be pestering you for silk ribbons and pretty dresses."

"If they live, sir, they may have all the dresses they desire."

Chapter Twenty-Four

Richard was sat dozing by the fire, he was rocking the baby's cradle with his foot. Pa was out drinking and he said he might stop at Dorothy's that night and spend some time with Joannie, who had been staying with his former sister-in-law. Or rather Pa had left her there one day and had never gone back. There was a soft knocking at his door. It was very late, Richard thought he might ignore it but whoever was on the other side wasn't planning to go away. He got up, glancing in at the girls sleeping top to toe, and opened the door a crack.

"Alice!"

"Can I come in?"

"Yes, yes of course, sorry, come in please." Alice brushed past him, she smelt of lavender.

"It's very cosy in here."

Richard had asked John to rescue his treasures from the French Street house and the little cottage was almost back to how he wanted it.

"Sit; please let me get you some wine."

Alice sat on the settle, she leaned over the cradle and cooed at the babies.

"They are adorable, Richard, I see one has red hair like her mother and the other is blond like her father."

"Yes, they're not identical twins."

Richard hoped Alice hadn't noticed the red blush on his neck. He poured the wine and lit some candles. He sat back down on the other side of the fire and leaned forward.

"You look well, Richard. You have your colour back and have gained weight."

"I never thanked you."

"For what?"

"Taking me in, caring for me, I didn't know where else to go. No, that's not true, I never even thought about going anywhere else."

"I'm glad you came to us, we missed you."

"Did *you* miss me, Alice?"

She looked down at her hands which twisted in her lap, "Yes, I missed you."

"I'm sorry I behaved so badly."

"We neither of us behaved very well."

Alice gazed into the fire. The candlelight made her face look softer, and picked out the colours in her hair.

"Alice."

She looked up at him but he couldn't say any more. She arose slowly and came and took his face in her hands, "My poor Richard, you have suffered so much, I am sorry for my part in it. I just reacted badly, I did have powerful feelings for you but they frightened me."

"Did? Do you feel nothing for me now?" He circled her with his arms and buried his face in her skirts, she softly stroked his hair.

"I still have feelings, Richard, if you still want me."

"Want you? I ache for you, Alice."

She leant down and kissed him.

"The children are sleeping." His voice sounded hoarse.

She stepped away from him. He swallowed. He stood though his legs felt unsteady, and took her hand. He kissed her again. "Stay with me."

He went to lead her to the ladder and started to climb up, but she pulled her hand away. She looked uneasy.

"Sorry I thought..."

"I want to," she said, "but it would not be seemly. People saw me come here. Besides, it's not fair to leave all the children with John and Tamsin."

Richard sighed, "Then there is no other course. Alice, please say you will marry me."

"You have stolen my virtue, I have no choice."

"Let's make it soon." He thought he would explode if he could not hold her. He held out his hand and she took it.

"You've not been long a widower, won't people talk?"

"Let them, besides Jeannot had hardly turned cold before people were urging me to marry again. A man is not capable of looking after two babies alone."

She wrapped her arms around his neck and he squeezed her buttocks. When he went to fondle her breasts she twisted away.

"We'll certainly begin with a houseful of children. What are your girls called?"

"Jeanne and Lizzie."

"Jeanne and Lizzie, William, Christian, Jacket of course and Tommy."

"Tommy? Who's Tommy?"

"A foundling, from the Ferry village."

"Alice!"

"He is so sweet, Richard, he reminded me of you. He has blue eyes and almost white blond hair."

"Mmm, well we can't carry on living at the tippling house, or here, there's not nearly enough room."

"A bigger house will cost more money."

"I'll ask Alderman Crooke if he can help out with a loan, I'll be able to repay it once Jack gets back."

"If Jack does get back." She lay her head on his shoulder.

"Don't worry, love, I'll work something out. Perhaps we ought to look to open a proper tavern."

"A tavern?" She lifted her head and studied him, "A tavern. I like the sound of that, we could offer food as well as drink; even take in the odd traveller."

"I want to make sure that you will be taken care of in case the worst should happen."

"Worst? What do you mean?"

"Alice, I promised you once I would tell you if I thought there might be an invasion."

"Oh," she looked frightened, "will you have to fight?"

"Yes."

She clasped him to her as close as she could get, "But you mustn't die, I invested too much time in helping you to live."

"I promise. Can we stop talking and make love?"

She kissed him more passionately now as if she was scared that time was already running out. "Soon, we will be joined soon, I promise." And with that she was gone and Richard thought that perhaps he had fallen asleep by the fire and imagined the whole thing.

He ate breakfast quickly. When Mrs Lister arrived he said he had to go out, she was obviously overcome with curiosity but said nothing. He left her feeding the babies and walked to the tippling house. John and Tamsin were trying to feed the children who were being noisy and naughty. They calmed a bit when their mother came out from the kitchen. She smiled at Richard.

"Alice, Tommy is screaming to be fed," said Tamsin.

"Well I'm here now, you can go and feed him." Tamsin gave her an odd look but went out.

Luisa was sat on John's lap, her head was covered in soft curls and Tamsin had tied a red ribbon in her hair. Christian was no longer a baby and William was now a boy. Tamsin came back in suckling the child called Tommy. Richard was surprised that Alice had taken in a baby, he had assumed she meant a child that was old enough to do some chores around the house and help pay for their keep.

Alice came and stood by Richard, taking his hand. "Richard and I are getting...married!"

The room erupted with shouts and whoops, except for Jacket who sat quietly munching his bread and milk with a thoughtful look on his face.

Chapter Twenty-Five

Richard went to see Alderman Crooke. He didn't like asking the older man for money. He had done so much for him already but he knew he had to swallow his pride, it was more than enough to be getting married to a woman with no money and no connections but add to that six young children. Many would think it madness.

"It's madness, Richard." said Crooke, "Look, I know your first marriage did not end well, I won't ask what went on but I know you weren't happy, and that nonsense about you moving out to spare your wife your sickness and I can understand a widower with two small babies. But Alice Dypere? You could do better for yourself my boy, I'm sure Margery could make a few introductions."

"No, sir, thank you. I love Alice and I want to be with her, especially now. Who knows how long we will have. Sir, I hate to ask for your help."

Crooke waved his hand to indicate it was nothing.

"I need a loan, sir, I need to lease a bigger property. I have had my eye on the old beer house, I thought we could decorate it, bring it back to life."

The beer house stood on the corner of Bull Street and Vyse

Lane and had once been an important property lived in by former mayors. A hundred years since a Flemish brewer had turned it into a place to make a new drink – beer, it had been a great success. Of late it had fallen on hard times but it was still a substantial property with more than enough room for Richard's new family.

"I have all my ready money tied up in the *Magpie* but I hope that when Jack gets back I will be able to repay with interest any money you lend me."

"I'm a bit short of hard cash myself my boy, the *God's Speed* should have been back long since."

"Ah, of course, sorry, think nothing of it."

"What of the Sohiers? Surely you had a dowry for Jeannot and they have no one to leave their money to except the girls."

"Perhaps, sir, but we are estranged at the moment. I have asked they put money aside for Jeanne for when she is grown."

"And Lizzie too, I hope."

"Er...yes of course, I meant both of course."

"Look I am sure I can sort something out. I am well known in the town and have a solid reputation. Don't worry, Richard, we will get you the beer house."

"Thank you, sir, you won't regret it."

The lease was soon arranged and Richard urged Alice to fix on an early date for the wedding. Apart from anything else Alice continued to remember her reputation and refused to sleep with Richard again until their wedding night. Alderman Crooke soon came to regret his generosity when a few weeks later the *God's Speed* limped into harbour. Richard hurried to the Dolphin where Crooke was meeting with Prowse, he was desperate to know what had happened to his brother and the *Magpie.*

Prowse still had the privateer swagger and was sporting a trimmed pointed beard in homage to his hero Drake.

"Richard! Good to see you." Prowse clasped his hand.

Closer to, Richard could see his face was tired and drawn and he had lost weight.

"What happened, where's Jack?"

"Don't worry, Richard, as far as I am aware Jack is alive and well, he was when I last saw him anyhow."

"How far behind you is he?"

Prowse looked shifty, he poured himself some wine and indicated to Richard to sit. Richard sat down next to Alderman Crooke who was gazing into the Dolphin's blazing fire.

"He's coming back, but not straight away, he's...he's sailed for the Americas."

"He's done what?"

"We had a troubled voyage, not much booty, we got caught up with part of the Spanish fleet—"

Richard started to speak but Prowse quieted him, "Jack thought the best way to make a return was to head for the coast of the Americas. He thought he might get both the chance of a treasure ship and trade with the Indians."

Richard held his head in his hand. He was relying on Jack, fool that he was.

Crooke put his arm around Richard's shoulder, "Don't worry, Richard, the voyage was not the success of our previous venture but the ship has been preserved and there was a little luck upon the way, we are nowhere near ruined, your home is safe, fear not. But listen to what Lawrence has to say of the Spanish."

Prowse drank deeply, "We got news of the fleet and thought it opportune that we should see what they were about. There were sixty or more men of war holed up in Lisbon harbour, drawn from all over the Empire, they had twenty hulks just for their supplies. We shadowed them as they made their way up the coast. It was awe-inspiring, Richard, I have never seen anything like it. Then they spotted us, I thought we were done for I can tell you. It was only the tempest that spared us it was so fierce. By the time things had calmed down the Spanish fleet had scattered and we made a run for it. We put into a sea beggar port and made repairs, took on provisions. Jack decided to head for the Americas and I came back here. I leave tonight to report to Admiral Hawkins, I think it will be good news for him and the Lord Admiral that the Armada is for the moment dispersed. It's going to take a month or more to regroup I would say, perhaps the Navy should make a strike."

"It's really happening this time." Richard felt sick.

"It's really happening," Crooke raised his glass, "to England."

"To England".

Within the hour Prowse had left. Richard went to report to Mayor Studley and then returned to Silkshop Yard. Pa was dishing up food for himself and Joannie. Mrs Lister was putting down the babies for the night.

"That Lizzie's a greedy little tyke Master Mudford, sucked me dry." Richard counted coins into the woman's hand.

"Will you take some food with us Martha?" asked Pa.

"I cannot stay, Mr Lister will be sat at the table banging his knife, wanting to be fed. It's a pity I can't suckle him as well." Pa and Mrs Lister roared with laughter. Joannie looked sulky and spooned pottage into her mouth.

"See you on the morrow." Mrs Lister swept out, almost gutting the candles in her wake. Richard pulled up a stool to the table.

"How are you doing, Joannie?"

"You still owe me twelve silver cups."

"That I do Joannie and as soon as your Pa returns with my money you shall have them."

Joannie wasn't impressed.

"Actually, Joannie, there is something I need to tell you, your Pa will be away longer than we thought." The girl seemed unconcerned. "He's sailed for the Americas."

"Is that far?"

"Yes it's far."

"So I won't be seeing my silver cups any time soon?"

"Probably not."

"Eat up, Joannie, and then get yourself back to Aunt Dorothy's" said Pa.

"Can't I stay here?"

"No room, Joannie, with the babies and all."

Joannie scraped her plate, "I don't like Aunt Dorothy, she makes me say prayers and wash my face and she tugs my hair with a comb."

"She's a good woman, now be off with you," said Pa with no sympathy.

"Pa, it's a bit dark for Joannie to be on the street."

"Well you take her then, my bunions are drawing." Pa pulled off his boots and an uncompromising stink wafted around the tiny living room. Richard pushed Joannie to the door and they went out into the yard.

"Don't get worrying about your Pa, he knows how to take care of himself."

"I'm not worried."

They walked up Simnel Street, Richard wished he had put on a cloak. He decided to call into the tippling house. At the East Gate he watched as Joannie ran through down to a rickety skelling in Bagrow. She gave him a wave before she went through what passed for a door. He knocked at the cottage. Jacket answered and let him into the cosy room. John was feeding Luisa as Tamsin looked on.

"Hello Diccon."

"You're not doing it right, she's not getting enough," Tamsin poked John.

"Ow. We're trying to wean Luisa, we want to try for a baby ourselves," John smiled

"Aren't you still wet nursing the foundling, Tamsin?" asked

157

Richard. It was well known that the longer women breast fed, the longer it would be before they fell for another baby. "I don't know why Alice took in another child. Perhaps she can find someone else to take him on. We could do without another mouth to feed."

"God, Richard, you're a stupid prick."

"Tamsin!" said John

"What did I say?" said Richard.

"Come with me."

"Tamsin, no!"

"He should know."

"Know what?"

Tamsin looked skyward as if asking for divine intervention. She got up and signalled for Richard to follow. John left holding the baby looked on helplessly. She walked him to the curtain and pulled it back with a flourish. Richard stepped through. Alice was sat on the stairs and was offering her nipple to the foundling.

"Alice, what are you doing?" Richard was confused, Alice would have no milk, should have no milk but liquid was dribbling from her teat. "What is going on?"

"Tamsin, what do you think you are doing? You had no right." Tamsin let the curtain fall and her footsteps went away.

"Don't blame Tamsin," said Richard, "it's you who needs to explain."

"I? I?" Alice looked amazed and then angry, "How dare you!"

"How dare I? I am the man who you have just promised to marry and now I see you suckling a baby. Whose is it? Is it that Parker fellow he is always sniffing around here! Is that why you suddenly found you wanted to marry me? Need a father for your bastard?"

A pot barely missed Richard's head.

"That's right this bastard needs a father."

"I've enough babies I don't need another."

A plate zinged past his nose.

"You should have thought of that before you undid your codpiece."

The baby started to cry and Alice grabbed him to her and marched up the stairs. Richard was furious, she had played him for a fool again. He needed to get out. He wrenched open the back door and walked into the yard. He sucked in the cool spring air, trying to calm himself. Slowly, very slowly his brain began to work. He ran back into the house and up the staircase. The upper chamber was laid out with bedding. William and Christian were on pallets in the corner. A painted cloth provided privacy for where John and Tamsin would lay. Alice was lying on a trestle bed leaning over the boy child so it could reach her breast and suck.

"Alice?"

She ignored him.

"Alice, is Tommy my son?"

"No, the Angel Gabriel came and visited me and the next minute, immaculate conception."

"Why didn't you tell me?"

"You ran off and married someone else."

Well that was certainly true, "Yes but why all this pretence now?"

"You never understood how important my reputation was for me did you? Would you like to see me carted around the town as a whore? Would you like to see me branded in the face?"

"Of course not, but now, now we can make it right."

"Just because we are to marry, doesn't change anything."

Good, it seemed they were still to marry, he hadn't completely ruined everything.

He lay down on the trestle beside her, peering over her shoulder at his son, feeling a little jealous of his baby who had taken what he believed to be his place at Alice's breast.

"God, I feel horny." Alice elbowed him in the ribs.

"Are you sure we can't claim him as our own?"

"No, not now, maybe some time. Once we are married we can adopt him."

"Whatever you say, Alice."

"I'm not sleeping with you."

Richard groaned.

"And I'm not doing anything else either."

"You are a heartless woman."

"Go home."

"I forgot what I came for. Don't be alarmed but I have heard news, the Armada did sail but it has had a setback. The fleet has been scattered but it will be here by summer, so I want us to marry now."

Alice said nothing for the longest while as if she had not heard him at all. She stroked the silvery gold hair on the infant's head and gently kissed it.

"Well the banns have been read, and I have bought the boys new boots and ribbons for Christian's hair."

"And I have a son!" Alice let him nuzzle her neck. He walked back down the staircase. Tamsin and John looked at him warily.

"Tamsin was right, I'm a stupid prick." They had a drink to wet the baby's head. Tamsin went to put Luisa down.

"John, why didn't you say something? You must have known."

"She swore me to secrecy, the same as you did with that business over Lizzie. I tell you I don't like all these secrets, it plagues my conscience. I think I am going to blurt something out."

"You must never say anything about Elizabeth. No one will believe what really happened. They will think me to be some infidel sultan impregnating any woman that takes my fancy."

"You couldn't blame them, three women, three babies."

Richard groaned, "I don't understand it, I'm not Jack."

"Here have another drink, keep your strength up."

160

Chapter Twenty-Six

The date for the wedding was set. It would not be a big affair, minds were on other things.

Mayor Studley had called all the senior burgesses together.

"The Queen is asking the town to supply two ships."

There was a lot of grumbling. The town was not as wealthy as it once was, much money had already been spent on the walls and armaments. Richard felt the burgesses complained too much as they seemed to find money easily enough to equip ships for privateering.

"We must write to Her Majesty and explain our situation," said Biston. "Why should we be expected to shoulder the burden of providing for the Royal Navy. The Royal Navy mind. We are being bled by taxes as it is, the defence should come out of the subsidy monies."

"Christ's blood man, the Queen is asking us to rally to the defence of England," exclaimed Alderman Goddard.

"War is bad for trade," countered Biston. "You have traded with Spain for years, Master Goddard."

"I have many friends in Spain it is true, but their masters are trying to crush this country, they are sending the Armada against us," retorted Goddard.

"And let us not forget the Protestant cause," said Crooke, "do we want the Inquisition here?"

The burgesses agreed they did not. It was well known someone said that all men betwixt the ages of seven and seventy would be put to death and younger children would be branded on their faces to show they were the children of a conquered nation. A pamphlet was passed around.

"It says here," said Crooke, "that their ships are loaded with instruments of torture. I am not sure I believe what is writ here but they say they are bringing pox-ridden queens as well!"

"Children will be tossed on pikes, or have their brains dashed out." The Mayor was ashen.

In the end they decided they could equip one ship and Alderman Goddard offered his vessel the *Angel*. Alderman Crooke proposed that Lawrence Prowse be appointed her captain and Richard was charged with the victualling and arming of the ship. The Mayor took it upon himself to write to Her Majesty to explain that the disability and poverty of the town prevented them from fully responding to her request. His hand shook.

Richard sucked the end of his quill, he must be sure he had forgotten nothing. Food, he ran his finger down the list: veal, mutton, bread, biscuit, cheese, powdered beef, beer. Extra canvas, thread and needles for repairs, nails, baskets, leather pumps, okam, spears – damn tools for the surgeon, he must talk to the smith. He needed to hire a boatman as well to carry out the mariners and soldiers, he'd have a word with George Parker. He should check the guns over again and then there were the general repairs to the town's defences, most of the gates needed new locks. Cap paper, the soldiers would need cap paper for their guns. He would get Lawrence Prowse to double-check the list, he wouldn't want to be responsible for forgetting the one thing that could save England from defeat.

As if he knew he was needed Prowse appeared.

"I was just thinking of you," said Richard.

Prowse raised his brows, "How so?"

"I wanted you to check the list of stores and provisions, make sure nothing is left out." He passed it over to the other man. Lawrence put down a book he had been carrying and took the list, running a finger down the items. Richard picked up the book and turned it over.

"You write like a drunkard!" Prowse laughed, "What does this say?"

"Surgeon's tools." Richard gave him a black look.

"It's a good list, Richard, we will be well provisioned but I worry we are just an armed merchant man. A ship needs to be a fighting unit–"

"–is that Drake talking?"

"The Admiral is right, a ship should carry at least thirty pieces of heavy artillery, firearms, ammunition, lead and a hundred men."

"The *Angel* will be well armed, the town has plenty of guns as do most of the merchants. The men here are good sailors."

"True, true." Prowse returned the list.

"What's this?" asked Richard as he passed back the book.

"All the captains have been issued with it, they call it a Waggoner. It's a book of charts that some Dutchman produced a couple of years ago, it's just been translated into English."

"Any good?" asked Richard.

"I think so, from what I know of the coast and waters around the Channel. Just hope the Spanish don't have copies. We've been given another book as well."

Richard raised his brows.

"Foxe's *Book of Martyrs*," explained Prowse.

"How will that help you sail better?"

163

"I have to read out a martyr's death each day, to encourage the men to fight harder against the papists."

"Good luck with that."

"Anyway, I was looking for Alderman Goddard, I was told he might be here."

"You've missed him, you should try the Audit House," said Richard. Lawrence thanked him and hurried on his way. Richard picked up the list and went through the items again.

"Richard," a woman's voice was whispering his name. He looked up, "Alice? What are you doing here?" He beckoned her into his office, she had never visited his place of work before and seemed uncomfortable. She pushed a stray tendril of hair back under her cap.

"What's wrong, love? You look worried."

"It's Jacket."

Richard frowned, "What's he done?"

"He's gone."

"What do you mean gone?"

"He's run away."

"Good riddance."

"Richard!"

"Sorry, but he's a bit odd, and he hangs about."

"He's a little boy and he tries to be helpful, he just tries too hard."

"So he's run away, when, where?"

"If I knew that I wouldn't be here." Alice sighed and became fretful, "I promised Thomasina."

"What makes you think he's run away?"

"His bed was empty this morning, I can't find him anywhere, and he never roams far. William told me Jacket said he was going away to see the Queen and get a job in her service or some such nonsense."

"Why now?"

"I think he may be scared of you."

"Me! What have I ever done? I've barely spoken to him."

Alice gave him one of her looks.

"Oh I see so it's my fault."

"You have to find him."

"I have to? It may have escaped your notice but there is a war on, and I have a job of work, we are getting married in two days and I still have to organise the house."

"Well I can solve at least two of those problems, I can't possibly get married and move house with Jacket out there lost."

It was Richard's turn to stare but she wouldn't be moved, so thirty minutes later Richard was striding down to the town stables in Winkle Street to borrow a horse. He wasn't the world's best rider, he didn't get enough practice but he managed. He nudged the beast out of the stable, back onto English Street and trotted to the Bargate, over the bridge into Above Bar. He gently dug his heels in and the horse started to canter. Soon the houses fell away. He travelled by outlying farms and started to pass through the wooded common. He stopped at a clearing where the town's cowherd had a cottage, the man was driving a few cows into a pound. Richard called out and asked him if he had seen a small boy come that way but the man shook his head and shrugged.

Richard could only assume Jacket was making for London. It was a well-worn highway with plenty of traffic but there were highway men and other thieves and vagabonds as well as the daily passage of carters, bearers, pack horses and pilgrims. Richard passed the cutted thorn, the ancient meeting place of the town, and opposite the town gallows near the crossroads he left the boundaries of Southampton behind and made for Winchester. Along the way he stopped to ask other travellers and merchants if they had seen the skinny boy with slightly protruding teeth but received the same shake of the head and shrug of the shoulders. Richard convinced himself that the child was probably hiding out somewhere back in town, trying to gain attention but Alice had looked far and wide and Southampton was a small town where most people knew one another. No one had seen Jacket.

About a mile from Winchester Richard saw a carter by the side of the road, his wheel had got damaged and he and his boy were making repairs.

"Do you need a hand, sir?"

"No thank you, young man, we are almost done, unless you can get the ruts in this road repaired of course!" They had a chuckle to themselves about the terrible state of England's thoroughfares.

"Sir, I am looking for a small boy, my wife-to-be's ward. He has taken it in to his head to run off to see the Queen and my Alice is beside herself."

The man looked thoughtful and was sizing Richard up, "And what did he look like, this ward of your wife-to-be, you say?"

"He's about so high, small for his age, a bit nondescript to be truthful, light brown short hair, pale eyes, slightly bulbous, would have on a russet jerkin–"

"We found him!"

"What?"

"He was in the ditch here, if the cart hadn't turned over we would never have seen him, he'd been beaten badly."

Richard's mouth went dry, "What? Is he dead?"

"He was breathing brother but if we hadn't found him when we did–"

"Where is he now?"

"One of the other carters took him to St Cross. We figured the brothers there might know what to do."

"Thank you sir, thank you."

Richard shook the man's hand and vaulted back onto his horse, this time digging in his heels hard so the beast leapt forward into a gallop. It did not take many minutes to reach St Cross though it felt like hours. Richard's heart was pounding as heavily as his fist on the oak door of the hospital. The foundation was ancient and now mainly operated as alms houses but still looked after the poor and took in travellers.

A voice called out for him to desist and a wrinkled old man opened a viewing window. "Who are you? What is the meaning of this?"

"Sorry, sir, I am overwrought. I was told by a carter that my ward has been brought here, badly attacked, a young boy by the name of Jacket Hall."

"Yes he is here, there is no need to beat down the door." The old man banged shut the window and a few minutes later opened up and beckoned Richard in.

"What were you thinking of letting a small boy wander the highways alone? He was set upon you know."

Richard said nothing, he felt he was being unfairly judged. The brother took Richard to his superior. The Warden looked at Richard coolly.

"You are enquiring after the boy. He has been robbed and beaten. But I am more concerned about his mental state. He is clearly distressed at the loss of his boots, a gift I believe from the woman who cares for him. I can get no sense from him as to why he has run away from what appears to be a loving home, but neither can I get him to eat or say anything that might calm him. Are you the new husband?"

Richard was a bit unsure whether to admit to this, he felt somehow that might be a mistake. "I am to marry Mistress Dypere the day after tomorrow – that is if I can restore Jacket to her. Is his life in danger?"

"He is very bruised and shaken but no bones appear to be broken, he was out most of the night but as I say my main concern is his mental well-being. He seems to have no desire to get better and in this state might wish himself to death. You had better come this way, maybe seeing you will improve his state." The Warden spoke as if he felt this outcome to be unlikely.

They walked across the courtyard past the alms-houses set aside for the residents to the communal hospital, which served not only the brothers but also itinerant poor and sick. Several of the beds were taken by elderly men, probably sick inmates or servants. In the far corner was the small figure of Jacket curled up and facing the wall. Richard and the Warden reached the end of the bed.

"Jacket, Jacket," cooed the Warden, "someone has come to take you home."

The shaking of his shoulders showed Jacket was still sobbing although he had no tears left. He turned slowly and horror filled his eyes as he saw Richard towering above him. Richard felt impatient.

"Jacket, I have been riding for a long time, searching for you. What do you think you are doing scaring us all like this?"

The boy was distraught and looked around him as if for some means of escape.

"Jacket," said the Warden slowly, "why did you run away? Did this man beat you?"

Richard was furious, "I did no such thing, Jacket, tell him! And for that matter tell me why you ran off. If you wanted to find somewhere else to live you just had to say!"

The boy looked so utterly miserable Richard felt a bit guilty, "I'm not angry Jacket, but Alice is beside herself with worry."

Jacket raised himself up and addressing himself to the Warden said, "Sir, we are too many, Aunt Alice has all the babies to feed and clothe, I eat too much, I tried to find some work but no one would have me. I thought I could go and fight for the Queen. But...but..." his lip began to tremble again, "they stole my boots, they stole my new boots that Aunt Alice gave me, the first boots I ever had, they stole my boots, they stole my boots."

"There now, there now," said the Warden. "I'll leave you to talk alone, I will just be visiting Brother Michael."

Richard sat down on the bed, he was not good at this and for a moment did not know what to say. "Jacket, is it because of me that you ran away?"

The boy nodded.

"At times, I am poor at thinking about the effects of my words. Jacket, Alice loves you like her own son and when we marry you will be part of our family. I want that too," Richard lied.

Jacket wiped his eyes with his sleeve, "Really?"

"Really."

"Will you be my father?"

There was such a look of longing and desperation in his voice, Richard felt cornered. "Yes, Jacket, if you will allow me I would like to be your father." So few words yet they wrought such a transformation. Jacket's eyes glowed, his chest seemed to puff out, he even pinched himself to check he was awake and then he threw his arms around Richard. "Father, Father."

The Warden came back, "So we have reconciliation?"

"I am sorry, sir, that we have given you such trouble. Is Jacket well enough to travel?"

"I am, I am!" said Jacket.

"I would suggest you both spend the night, the boy is so bruised and I think he needs a good night's sleep."

"Sir, is there anyone here travelling onto Southampton this evening, with whom I might send a message?"

Luckily there was a messenger from the Lord Admiral about to leave after taking some supper. Richard arranged for a note to be sent to Alice. When he went back to the hospital Jacket was fast asleep. Richard was given a bed in the communal guest quarters and had to share the space with a heavy snorer and a tooth grinder, it didn't make him feel any better. The next day he put Jacket on the horse in front of him and encouraged the animal into a spirited trot.

"Father, will Aunt Alice be my mother? I know I had a real

mother I can almost remember her, but if Aunt Alice is to marry you...?"

"Seems sensible."

"Will Aunt Alice be angry about my boots? I fought them but there were three of them and they were older than me."

"Alice is more concerned with your well-being than boots. If you ever find yourself in that situation again let them have the boots."

"Yes, Father. When I get a job I will buy some new boots."

"Yes, you do that."

They got back to Southampton by late morning, Richard stabled the horse first and they walked back to the tippling house, Jacket unconcerned about his bare feet. When they entered the cottage Jacket ran to Alice throwing his arms around her waist.

"I'm sorry, Mother, for making you sad, I will do extra chores."

Alice looked quizzically at Richard over the boy's head.

"I lost my new boots, Mother, they were stolen."

"Don't worry about that, we will find you a pair of John's to wear. But look at your face." Alice lifted his jerkin and squealed at the sight of all his bruises. "They don't hurt too much, Mother, really. I'm so glad to be home."

"I'm glad you are back, go through the kitchen and get something to eat, I'll be there in a moment." She looked over her shoulder till Jacket was out of sight, "What did you say?"

"I was cornered! What does it matter, we have a patchwork family."

Alice took him into her arms, "Are you going soft?"

"No love, I am very, very hard."

Chapter Twenty-Seven

It was the day of his second wedding, scarce a year and a half after his first. This time he waited in All Saints. The guests were few, his Pa, Aunt Dorothy and Joannie, John and Tamsin, Mrs Lister and Annie holding the babies. He twisted the ring he had had made for Alice between his fingers, the goldsmith had engraved the gilt hoop with the words 'my heart is yours'. When Alice arrived in her best dress Pa went and led her to the altar. Richard was smiling like an idiot. Alice was cool and calm till she came to take her vows when she stumbled over the words and laughed, her eyes dancing. They walked from the church to the tippling house where benches had been set outside. Neighbours, work mates, and extended family from Itchen Ferry lolled around them. George Parker looked surly, Richard thought he was jealous and felt pleased. There was food and drink aplenty. Peter Breme brought his tabor and drum and there was singing and dancing. Richard joined the lads from the Ferry in a rendition of 'Poll of Itchen Ferry', an old ballad about Poll and her various suitors. Alice kept admiring her ring and showing all the inscription.

"I have a present for you, Richard."

"Do you?" he felt pleased and excited. She pulled a little

packet from her pocket, tied with a ribbon and decorated with a sprig of lavender. Richard undid the knot to reveal a brooch. It too had an inscription, 'I pray God make Richard Mudford a good man'.

"I will do my utmost, Alice. I will do my utmost."

When it got dark the guests drifted home. John and Tamsin took the children into the tippling house and Richard and Alice walked to the beer house.

"It's a lovely evening, Mrs Mudford."

"Warm and starlit, Mr Mudford."

"I love you, Mrs Mudford."

"And I love you, Mr Mudford.

The beer house was in a poor state, John gave him a hand with the worst of the repairs and Tamsin helped Alice with the mountain-of cleaning. They got the bedrooms ready first so the family could move in. John and Tamsin would take over the cottage but no longer run it as a tippling house, instead Tamsin would come and work with Alice at the tavern. John decorated all the main rooms, painting images on the lime washed walls and timbers to create the illusion that the rooms were decorated with rich tapestries. John primed the wattle and daub walls first with a thin skim of lime and hair plaster before he painted onto them. Richard asked for strawberries and roses. Many strawberries were grown locally, they denoted perfect righteousness and their flowers innocence and purity. The Queen favoured strawberries and roses on the decorations of her gowns. Richard remembered the gown she had worn on her visit to the town when he had seen her as a child. Roses meant love, beauty and joy. Alice asked for grapes, as the symbol of the blood of Christ. John said it would also encourage patrons to think of wine. He added gilly flowers to represent maternal love, given the number of children they had they needed a large supply. Richard remarked that gilly flowers also meant poverty and he hoped that wasn't an omen. John said that as flowers with many petals were also associated with fertility, poverty was a very likely outcome. They decided on daisies for humility, as Alice was afraid they were getting above themselves.

John used dark blue to create the background, the strapwork was woven under and over in a repeating design like a knot garden. Each of the quatrefoils contained the leaves, fruit and flowers painted in white, yellow and red ochre, copper blue, lime white, earth green, and raw umber. Alice worried that it was too grandiose and in the end insisted on some suitable religious texts which ran around the top of the design. The bottom half of the walls John painted to mimic wooden panels etched with diamond shapes and diaper work. Richard gave him a knowing look as he understood the symbol was also a homage to the artist. John just smiled and winked. Richard thought the effect was like having a turkey work carpet hung on the wall, such as he had seen at Alderman Crooke's house. John painted quickly, which was useful as Richard's time was limited.

"Love, I'm sorry I can't help much at the moment. There is so much activity around the council, daily messages from the Admiral, Captain Dawtry and the muster and General Norreys is on his way here."

"Richard, I understand, we have our whole lives to get the house ready. I think by the end of the week we will be able to start trading – if there are soldiers in the town there will be money to be made."

"That's why I love you, such a business woman," Richard kissed her deeply, his hands started to roam.

"I thought you had to go to the council house?"

He was edging up her skirt, "A few minutes won't make much difference."

"I want more that a quick poke thank you! Off you go."

She pushed him out of the door.

The tension was almost palpable as he entered the courtroom. Alderman Crooke pulled him aside,

"We have had news. The Spanish fleet has been sighted, some 127 ships have left Corunna. All ships are to be mobilised, the Lord Admiral wants to have the fleet shadowed up the Channel, harassed. We think they will try for Wight."

The Mayor was speaking, "I have arranged for post horses to be kept at Mr Yonge's stables and I have already dispatched Arthur Ramsden to my Lord of Sussex with a letter touching the Spanish fleet. John Gregorie, I need you to ride post to Portsmouth and take on the messages that have come from Weymouth and Ryde." Gregorie took the dispatches and left the hall.

"Gentlemen, Drake and the Lord Admiral have successfully left Plymouth ahead of the Spanish Fleet. Her Majesty has some 80 ships at sea and they have already engaged the enemy. The enemy however, maintains its discipline and is moving up the Channel towards us. Henry Foster, you are to maintain the ordnance until the threat passes, gentlemen I have asked Bookes the drummer to remain in the town and William Foster is employed to play the fife for us. Mr Steward, can you alert the brewers we need extra beer and see if the Smith has hay that we can purchase for the post horses. Warders of the gates, you know your duties!" There were nods about the hall and a smell of fear.

"We need to prepare the alms-houses and inns, there will be wounded and people could flee here from the country," explained Alderman Crooke.

"We must look to ourselves alone, the town can't sustain an influx of poor and sick soldiers," Biston retorted. Some of the burgesses agreed with him, others looked uncomfortable.

"We need to all pull together, we can't turn our backs on the men going out to defend us, or let their families starve

174

should they not return," countered Studley, he looked tired and careworn. "Richard, the Admiral requests more powder and shot. See that it is dispatched and I think we need more bullets, purchase more lead for them."

"It's all in hand, Mr Mayor, the powder and shot are stored in the Woolhouse ready to be loaded and I have bought lead, castings and canvas. Clement the smith is working on the bullets."

"Well done, my boy. Now we have also a request for victuals from the Lord Admiral, John Holford is ready with his boat and men."

"I'll deal with that, Mr Mayor," said Alderman Crooke.

"And what of the *Angel*, Mr Goddard?"

"Just waiting for the tide, Mr Mayor." There was a scuffle at the back of the hall as someone pushed their way through the crush of burgesses in their cloaks and hats, the urgency of the situation having thrown protocol aside.

"Richard!" it was Lawrence Prowse, "I need to put to sea but I am a couple of men down with sickness. Will you and John sail with me? No one knows guns like you or tides like John."

A silence had descended over the hall, all eyes were upon him.

"Of course, Captain." There was a spontaneous cheer. "I will send a watchman to ask John to meet us at the quay, I will go home and get my things."

"Richard." Alderman Crooke took him aside, "Here take these." He gave Richard his prize caliver and a beautifully tooled sword, ironically it was Spanish made.

"Thank you, sir, I will inflict damage with these."

He hurried out of the hall and ran home. Alice looked surprised to see him and her eyes took in the weapons. She ran to him and kissed him with passion, "Now, now."

He hoisted her up and she wrapped her legs around him, it was urgent and desperate. He let her go and ran to the room they shared. He threw a few things into a sack, flew down the stairs and past Alice as she quietly sobbed in the corner. He went out of the door without looking back and didn't stop till he arrived breathless at the quay.

Chapter Twenty-Eight

He was trying to focus on not being sick as they slipped down Southampton Water and out into the Channel. The Isle of Wight was behind them and the English Fleet all around. Prowse went over to the flagship to get his orders. When he returned he called his officers together.

"The Spanish are sailing in tight formation." He traced the shape of a crescent onto the chart table, "It will be difficult to break them, like a siege at sea. We are commanded to stay out of range of their guns if we can and certainly not let ourselves be grappled, but we must to try and hole them or dis-mast them, cause a nuisance, make them break but not at the cost of our fleet. We will sail in line formation, loose off our cannon and guns, then retreat and re-load. If they aim for Wight, then we are to take them on." All nodded.

Prowse gathered his men around the main mast and led them in prayers for the safety of their loved ones and victory in the battles to come. He knelt on a cushion at a table and the crew chanted their responses. Richard thought about King Philip. Was he in Spain praying for the same victory? Alderman Crooke had told Richard that Philip had arrived in England exactly thirty-four years ago, landing at Southampton en route to marry the Queen's sister, the Queen Mary. Richard tried to imagine Philip walking the streets of the town, taking Mass at Holy Rood. Prowse decided to do a drill for the gunners, though he muttered to Richard that the Queen would not be happy at the waste of gunpowder.

"How can that be?" asked Richard, "If the men are not to practice how can we make the most of our one advantage?"

"We are lucky, we are well provisioned with gunpowder thanks to the Mayor and aldermen."

The men hauled in the cannon and sponged the barrels, worming them clean of any powder residue. Cartridges of black powder wrapped in cloth were rammed home and the barrel sponged again to remove any spilt powder. The cannonball was wiped clean of dirt, inserted into the cannon and rammed home. It was secured with hemp wadding and the gun was run out and lashed into place. The master gunner checked the aim and adjusted the elevation with wooden wedges, his assistant poured a trail of priming powder into the touch hole. On the master gunner's command, the assistant took a piece of smouldering match cord gripped in the jaws of a linstock and put it to the touch hole to fire. Richard was counting in a measured rhythm until he reached a hundred and twenty.

They saw them the next day, twenty galleons, four galleasses, forty-four armed merchant men, thirty-eight auxiliaries and twenty-one supply ships. The ships looked like floating castles, mile upon mile of them, bedecked with flags and pennants escorted with galleasses painted scarlet and gold, the crews protected with decorated shields, the oars all red, sails burnished with the image of a bloody sword. Richard could see the men, like multi-coloured ants, crimson, blue, mulberry. The English looked so dull in comparison dressed in their wool shirts, long breeches and woollen hats, their jerkins dyed brown and green, many cracked and brittle from the weather. Only the English flagship could compete with its 46 streamers and the royal standard of the Tudor Rose on the mainmast. The other English ships simply flew the cross of St George. One of the youngest in the crew started to cry.

"No tears, boy, you are an Englishman!" commanded Prowse.

He barked orders, they ran out the guns, they gritted their teeth and attacked. Hawkins had done well to improve the English guns, they had a further reach and were more accurate but the Spanish formation made it almost impossible to get close enough to inflict real damage. Richard learned to tell the success of a shot by the sound it made. A dull bass thud meant the ball had struck a hull, a rending crash meant the upper works had been ripped through. A whipcrack meant a severed stay, the sound like a dry cough meant shot had punched a hole through a sail. When canvas was ripped it was like hail drumming on a tile roof. Still the great war machine moved inexorably onward. The *Angel*, along with all the other English ships, was driven back towards Wight.

"We are not going to win taking them on one-to-one," said Prowse as they tacked and ran again for the umpteenth time.

"Then we should use guile," Richard looked at John.

"Richard's right, we have one thing in our favour, they won't know the tides, and they won't know the shallows, they won't know how the winds swing round 180 degrees. We need to lure them in, give ourselves some advantage."

Prowse signalled Hawkins. The Admiral's ship drew close, Richard and John joined Prowse as he went across to the flagship.

The Admiral was calm but there was a tightness about him; he knew their chances were few.

"Sir," Prowse doffed his cap, "if I might make a suggestion."

"I am open to any useful intelligence, Captain Prowse."

"These men are local, sir, they know the tides and the shallows. We have a suggestion about how to use that knowledge to give us some advantage."

The Admiral looked from man to man. "Come to my cabin."

John was marking up the Admiral's charts. He looked incredibly youthful next to the sea hardened Hawkins but the older man recognised straight away that John knew the waters around Wight like no other.

"A life of illegal fishing put to some use, my boy."

John looked nervous until Hawkins clapped him on the back and laughed. Hawkins sent messages to the Lord Admiral and the other squadrons commanded by Drake and Frobisher. The Lord Admiral called his captains together to assess Hawkins' proposals. John, Richard and Captain Prowse waited with growing agitation on Hawkins ship. Eventually Hawkins returned and with a smile gave them their orders.

"I believe we have a fighting chance, gentlemen. Good luck and may God be on our side."

They all returned to their ships and soon battle commenced. The smaller swifter English ships taunted their larger adversaries, pretending to flee then drawing them onward. The Spanish could see their prize, the Isle of Wight. Here they could make their bridgehead and wait in a safe haven for the arrival of the Duke of Parma and the mighty Spanish army of the Netherlands. It was the 3rd of August and everyone knew the dice had been thrown. This engagement could be end or the saving of England.

John was calling out the position of the sails, his eyes darting everywhere. He could tell by the colour of the water what lay below. He saw Richard and waved, "Stay Alive." Richard waved back. Richard was loading weapons in readiness for closer encounters with the Spanish ships. He had the crying youth with him and was showing him how to load the calivers and fowlers. "Speed boy but don't waste the powder." The better of the English fighting ships were swooping down on the enemy getting off five shots to the Spaniard's one, Hawkins' effort was working. The English fleet was taking damage but inflicting more, yet it was difficult to know who was winning. The *San Mateo* hove into view. Hawkins engaged and the little *Angel* followed in support.

Richard started to pick his shots, the officers. He fired and passed the emptied gun for the boy to reload and took up another. He was breathing heavier and he knew his heart was still working because he could hear it pounding. The noise around him was a cacophony but his concentration was such that he just blotted it out. Raise, fire, reload. Raise, fire, reload. He felt like one of the mechanical toys that performed at the Guildhall. There was so much smoke, it was burning his eyes and he could not tell if he was getting his mark. He caught a glint of metal on the other ship, a raised sword, he fired and thought he must have got his man as the silver spun in the air. Suddenly there was a tremendous crack to his left as a Spanish cannonade found its mark, a splinter of wood plunged into his arm like a dagger. He sank to the deck pulling out the splinter and ripping the sleeve of his shirt to bind up the wound. He looked around for the boy to help him but saw him lying dead on the deck, the boy's staring eyes looking at nothing. He cleared a bit of the debris and rescued his weapons, the fowler was useless but the calivers were unscathed. He couldn't load so quickly with his wounded arm and by the time he stood back up the *San Mateo* had moved away out of range.

Drake made a reckless attack but the gods loved their hero and his force had started to drive the Spanish away from the eastern Solent, they looked as if they were heading towards Calais. The closeness of the English fleet was making the Spanish Admirals think again about landing on Wight. The fleet started to move away with the English is pursuit. Although the main Spanish fleet managed to stay together, a few of the slowest ships fell behind, the *Santa Ana* and *Doncella* and a Portuguese galleon. Richard and John watched as the *Ark Royal* and *Golden*

Lion moved in to attack and cheered them on with the rest of the surviving *Angel* crew. The artillery barrage was intense and Richard thought the prizes would be won but the Spanish sent in galleasses and they managed to tow their ships away.

★

They had been fighting for two days and Richard was so tired he felt light-headed. His arm was sore from his wound. He had stitched the flesh together using his stitching quill, it didn't look pretty and would scar but the wound was clean. He suddenly was aware of a calmness, the wind had dropped. Without the wind all the ships fell motionless. Seamen were scattering sawdust on the decks to soak up blood. Richard's ears were still ringing from the noise of the battle. He could taste the sulphurous air and his lungs felt full of smoke. He was grateful for the beer ration when it came around.

The Lord Admiral regrouped and again called his captains together, Richard travelled with Prowse and Hawkins to the flagship. He managed to secrete himself quietly into a corner where he could see all the great men of the sea as they planned their next move.

"Gentlemen, we have fought well, my congratulations to your men. I have sent for more supplies and gunpowder and my Lord Seymour is on his way with re-enforcements, 36 ships including 5 galleons and he has the *Rainbow* and the *Vanguard* with him."

There were murmurs of approval. These were the two newest and most modern vessels in the Navy.

"Better late than never," muttered Drake, "We have taken the sting out of the tail for them!"

"The Duke of Medina Sidonia is being prevented from making harbour by our allies," continued the Lord Admiral.

"Who does he mean?" whispered Richard to Prowse.

"Justin of Nassau." Prowse whispered back. "The Dutch have a fleet of about thirty ships blocking the harbour, it also means Parma can't get his troops out to meet up with the Spanish fleet." This was good news indeed, Richard wondered how close Parma's army was. He had imagined they would have seen thousands of Spanish troops on the shoreline, straining to cross the small ribbon of water that was England's best defence.

"So, gentlemen, I estimate that even with the damage we have sustained we will have about 160 sail and that the Spanish are contained for the moment."

"Do you think they might still run the gauntlet past the Dutch? They only have flyboats after all."

"That's Frobisher," said Prowse in a hushed voice, nodding at the dour Yorkshireman, known for his strong language and blunt speaking but idolised by his men.

"If I was them," said Howard, "I would put the army on flat-boats and run them across. If I was them I would have brought some of the army with me from Corunna. Our intelligence tells us that the commanders are hamstrung by their orders from Madrid, no one can make a move without King Philip's say."

"That's no way to run a battle," Drake commented, who was Second in Command of the English fleet.

"Yes, Sir Francis, but there is something to say for discipline within a fleet."

Drake had almost caused the High Admiral and his flagship the *Ark Royal* to come within firing range of the Spanish by disobeying orders at the start of the engagement. It was only his capture of the *Nuestra Senora del Rosario* that had preserved his position. Rumour had it the ship was carrying 50,000 ducats. Drake was shameless and the barb meant nothing to him.

The Lord Admiral knighted John Hawkins, Martin Frobisher and George Beeston on the deck of the *Ark Royal*. Beeston was an elderly man but Richard was amazed to learn the commander of the *Dreadnought* was actually eighty-nine years old. The fleet had fought three major engagements and the leaders had earned their reward but everyone knew the fighting was far from over. They needed to get closer to the Spanish to inflict more damage than their carpenters and divers could easily repair, but such a venture would put their own ships in greater danger.

At sunset on the Friday the wind rose and the Armada moved off heading for Calais Roads, only twenty miles from Dunkirk where they would doubtless rendezvous with the Duke of Parma and his mighty army. The English fleet had continued to track the Spanish and now rode the swell only a long gun range from the enemy. Richard's skill as a swimmer saw him going over the side of the *Angel* helping with repairs. They used anything to hand to fix the leaks, timber of course, but also hides, sailcloth and oakum. Lawrence worked alongside his men, like all the captains, hauling ropes hand over hand with the best of them. Richard could see the local French and Flemish hurrying to get a vantage point on the Calais shore. Far away on the cliffs of Dover English spectators strained to see the next expected battle.

On Sunday Richard took communion on board ship with the rest of the crew and again travelled with Lawrence Prowse over to the Lord Admiral's flagship, where another council of war had been called.

"Gentlemen, we have to assume the Spanish fleet is in contact with the Duke of Parma," said Howard.

"One tide away from England," muttered Hawkins.

"Our own ships are in danger in this anchorage – tangling together – it is only the favour of God that preserves us." The captains and admirals nodded, they knew they had to somehow break up the Armada and drive the ships out from their anchorage, now before King Philip's two forces could join together.

"If I may make a suggestion?" said Drake. All eyes were on him just as he liked, "Fire ships."

The word hung in the air, all sailors feared fire. "Their strength is also their weakness. They stick so close together and, bottled up the way they are, if we can spread fear, they will break and that will give us a chance to pick them off, one by one."

"I agree." said Howard.

The other captains also acquiesced and they set about choosing the ships to sacrifice. The smaller vessels of 90-200 tons were decided upon, and those that had sustained most damage. "I don't have enough spare gunpowder to pack them with explosives like Giambelli's hellburners used back in '85 at Antwerp." Howard puffed out his cheeks.

"They don't know that," said Hawkins.

"Very true, very true."

"I offer you my vessel *Thomas,*" said Drake. It was a two hundred ton merchantman.

"I will match that with a ship of my own!" said Hawkins.

Prowse was distraught and Richard, saddened. The *Angel* had been one of the eight ships selected. They were to go back and put the crew off onto other ships along with the remaining munitions and victuals, then set the sails, pour tar about the decks, set it on fire and send their ship on course to drift into the Spanish fleet.

A pinnace was waiting to take them off. The rest of the crew had gone, they were as despairing as the Captain, as if they had lost a loved one. Prowse had been all business, playing at un-sentimentality till he remained with just Richard and John.

"I've never lost a ship before."

"And you didn't lose this one, it's a noble sacrifice," said John.

"I hope Mr Goddard sees it that way," muttered Richard and they all laughed uneasily.

"Sails set, Mr Dypere?"

"Aye Captain."

"Tar set."

"Aye Captain"

"Then abandon ship."

"We'll wait for you," said John.

"No, I need to do this, off you go."

They scrambled over the side and into the waiting pinnace leaving Prowse a dark shadow on the deck. He stood motionless for a few moments before bending to light the torch. He threw it front of him and leapt over the side as the bright orange flames roared. The pinnace towed the *Angel* into position so the tide and wind started to take her and she joined her fellows, burning pyres thrusting onwards to the massed Spanish fleet. Sparks shot up in the sky and showered the men in the pinnace as they cast the *Angel* free. It was midnight. The pinnace made its way to the *Ark Royal* and Richard, John and Prowse climbed up the nets onto the deck to watch their brave little ship take down the might of Spain. The Spanish broke formation, most cut their anchors to escape the fire ships. They avoided the fire but then had no hope of regaining their anchorage. As dawn broke only the Spanish admiral's flagship was left with four galleons, like bridesmaids clutching a bride's skirts. The Admiral ordered the English fleet to attack.

"The wind is turning, Richard, we have both the tide and the wind." Prowse's face was smeared with soot and something that could have been tears. John looked no better and Richard guessed he must be the same. "Now we have them, well done my *Angel*."

"Look, its Drake, he's after the flagship!" John cried and all the men on deck started to yell, willing their hero on. Again and again Drake pounded the *San Martin* but still the Spanish fought. Frobisher joined in the battle and Hawkins came up on the *Victory*.

"Drake's moving off? Why? He has him, he has him," yelled Prowse over the din.

"Other fish to catch." Richard pointed to the Spanish galleons dashing to the aid of their Admiral.

The *Ark Royal* was moving off, Howard was baring down on the *San Lorenzo*, which had run aground in Calais harbour.

"I'm going to do something useful," said Richard as he took up his caliver and climbed up the rigging.

The Spanish ship was sinking in the sand, a sitting duck, her guns facing skyward. Richard scanned the ship identifying the officers. One man was marching up and down yelling orders trying to get the some of the guns righted. Richard took aim and loosed his shot. The man cried out and fell down heavily, the round had hit him in the head.

Howard had his glass to his eye and he looked up at Richard, "If I am not mistaken, you have shot the commander of the *San Lorenzo.*"

Soon they were alongside and the English set about pillaging the ship. Richard hesitated but in the end joined them, he needed the money. Howard was signalling, he wanted to get back to the fray. Still the Spanish were fighting like terriers, no matter how much the English pounded their ships, they patched them up and they fought on.

Chapter Twenty-Nine

Richard realised they had been fighting for nearly a week when there began a concerted movement among the Spanish ships. They were going to run for it.

Howard called his commanders together. They compared notes on provisions and ammunition, both were dangerously low.

"We have to follow them, we have bloodied their noses but they are still a formidable force, if they think we have given up and gone home they could still try to land further up the coast. Gentlemen, harry them, force them up, they have nowhere to go but round Scotland, God help them."

"To Scotland!" the cry went up.

They pursued the Spanish Fleet right up to the borders. By this time food and munitions had shrunk to almost nothing.

"There's precious little money either," said Prowse. "The order has gone to Lord Seymour to hold the line, the Lord Admiral is making for Margate to try and do what he can for the wounded."

"Is it wrong for me to say I'm glad?" said Richard, "I'm so tired, I can't think straight anymore."

"No, we are all weary, but we have done a great thing here."

"Are they beaten?"

"They will be." Prowse nodded to the lowering skies. Richard looked at the gathering storm clouds, "Here's to Margate."

No heroes' welcome awaited them. Richard could not believe it, men who had fought so bravely were left lying in the street, minor wounds began to fester, fever and sickness was sweeping through the pitiful wasted sailors and soldiers.

"How is it, Diccon, that this can be allowed?" John was shocked, he was pushing coins that he had pillaged from the Spanish ship into the hands of comrades who were begging for help.

Richard went and bought what bread and beer he could lay his hands on to give out. He asked around but there seemed no beds to be had. He found a run-down stable and he, John and Captain Prowse and a few other fellows from the *Angel* helped to move the most in need there. A few poor women promised to look after the men, or shroud them if they died.

"So much for our booty money," said Richard as he handed out a few more coins.

"There are too many, we can't help them all." John felt crushed.

"No we can't but at least we did something for these poor fellows."

"Do you think the women will run off once we leave?"

"Probably."

"Boys," Prowse put his head around the door of the stables. "We have passage on a ship back to Southampton." John and Richard exchanged a glance and dashed for the door.

They all slept most of the voyage. Even Richard didn't care about the bad weather and rolling waves, he was dead to the world. Something inside them seemed to recognise when the movement of the waves changed and they awoke to find themselves sailing up the water to Southampton. They were travelling on a small merchant man so no one gave them much heed as they pulled in to West Quay. They must have been a strange sight, looking more like vagabonds then men who had followed Drake's drum.

"Oh God," said Prowse, "I've got to tell Alderman Goddard his ship's been burnt to a crisp."

"Once he gets over it, he will wear it as a badge of honour," remarked John.

Prowse and Richard looked at one another and both said, "No."

"My one hope is that the Lord Admiral said the Queen will pay compensation."

"Really?" Richard was amazed, Her Majesty was renowned for her parsimony. They walked through the West Gate. People gave them strange looks and whispered as they half recognised them.

"Good day to you, Captain, you are always welcome in my tavern."

The beer house was straight ahead at the top of Westgate Street.

"Will you call me Lawrence? After what we have been through I hope you will count me a friend."

"Thank you...Lawrence."

Prowse strode off and Richard and John went through the door of the tavern, it was heaving, Tamsin was serving behind the bar. She looked up, screamed and slide over the top of the bar into John's arms. They were kissing and cuddling and talking all at once. The customers were annoyed that their drinking had been interrupted. Alice came out to see what all the fuss was about. She stopped dead when she saw Richard and put her hands to her face.

"Hello love."

She punched him on the chest, none to softly as if to assure herself he was real and not an apparition. She started to cry.

"Ssh, love, it's fine. I'm all right, just a few scratches and bruises."

She pulled herself together and began throwing out the drinkers telling them the tavern was shut. They complained but not loudly, Alice was not to be crossed in this mood. Tamsin had gone to pick up Luisa from the family quarters.

"She's pregnant," cooed John, "I'm going to be a father!"

"Congratulations, John." Tamsin swept back and they bustled off to their cottage.

"Where are the children?" Richard asked.

"The babies are at Mrs Lister's, it was easier for me to take them there whilst I got the tavern going, and for the same reason Jacket, William and Christian are over at the Ferry village. We need to find some help but I was minding the pennies till I knew you were coming home."

"Oh love, I'm so sorry for deserting you, just married, just taken on this place, dumping my children."

"They are our children now." Alice stood on tiptoe and kissed him.

"So we are alone and all I can think of is food, getting clean and sleeping again."

"Well that's easy to sort, go and get out of those filthy clothes and wash, there is hot water out back and I will put food on the table. Then we can go to bed and you can sleep in my arms. I'll go and ask Mrs Lister to keep the babies overnight."

"You are a saint."

Once he was clean and fed, Richard's spirits rose. He slipped between the sheets of his own bed with a sigh. Alice took off her clothes and Richard drank in her body.

"God you are so beautiful."

"I have had a fistful of children, my stomach is covered in stretch marks and I'm not sure my breasts are as high as they once were."

"Well you inspire me."

She slipped in beside him.

"I find I am not sleepy after all."

"I'm so pleased."

Richard lent over her and rummaged for a linen sheath on the bedside table.

"Do you really want to wear that?"

"You are the one who doesn't want to get pregnant again, and we have three children still in swaddling clothes."

"Shall I give you a little present first?" She slipped down under the sheets.

"You said you would never do that."

"You have just vanquished the whole might of Spain, so just this once."

Part Four

1589

Chapter Thirty

Jack was back. He sailed into Southampton harbour one bright February morning as if he had only been away for a cruise over to Hythe. In the six months following the battles off the Isle of Wight and Gravelines, time had sped by. The Spanish fleet had eventually been felled by the weather and as the Queen had had engraved on the victory medal "God blew". Those who made it to shore from their wrecked vessels found death awaiting them from the Scots and the Irish, which Richard thought a bit ironic given Philip of Spain's efforts to bring those countries into his enterprise against England. For himself he had found it difficult to settle easily back into the routine of life. Many poor soldiers and sailors travelled home via Southampton, and mindful of all the distress he had seen at Margate, Richard did what he could to persuade the Mayor to be generous in making ex gracia payments to help them on their homeward journey.

The tavern was doing well and but they were struggling to keep up payments on the loan from Alderman Crooke. In their spare moments he and John decorated and repaired the beer house. Richard renamed it the Angel inn and got John to paint a sign in memory of the brave little ship. The government had said 197 English ships had taken part in the Armada campaign, from the *Dreadnought* to the little pinnace, the *Pippen*. Not one ship had been lost except those that were sacrificed. Alderman Goddard got over the news about his ship, especially when the Queen was true to her word and paid over £450 in compensation, according to Lawrence Prowse. However, what was given with one hand was taken away with the other. Mayor Studley spent the last part of his mayoralty in prison for defying the Lord Admiral over the question of pirate's goods. It was only for a couple of weeks but the humiliation was keenly felt but the new Mayor was being just as stubborn.

More and more people were moving to Southampton to try their hands at privateering, including the Earl of Cumberland, Walter Raleigh and Fernando Gorges, as well as a host of lesser-known buccaneers who were closer to thieves and pirates. Even the Queen's own cousin Sir George Carey used his position as Captain of the Isle of Wight to engage in privateering.

The children continued to thrive, for which Richard and Alice gave thanks each Sunday in St Michael's Church. Tommy was a delight, happy and smiling, he loved to hear his parents sing. Lizzie was very bony, pink cheeked with curly blond hair, and as much as Tommy smiled Lizzie laughed. Jeanne was more fretful and gave her father endless cause for concern as she constantly picked up coughs and colds. Christian would soon be five, no longer a toddler but a clever and sweet little girl. William was not quite so clever and struggled with his studies. He preferred going down to the river or visiting his Ferry relations so he could learn to fish, make nets and sail. Jacket still reminded Richard of a human rat but he applied himself dutifully whether to his studies or helping at the inn and each night would embrace his adoptive parents before he went to bed as if he was afraid they would be gone in the morning. Alice had employed Annie Lister to help out looking after the children and Mrs Lister was still wet nursing the girls. Pa continued to live in Silkshop Yard, borrowing money and cadging free drinks at the inn, Joannie stayed there with him until he got fed up with her and set her back to Aunt Dorothy. In this fashion they passed the autumn and winter began.

At Christmas, Madame Sohier had come to the side door of the tavern and asked for Richard. Her features were more pointed and her elbows seemed sharper, which made her look taller.

"Are we never to see our granddaughter?" She demanded as soon as Richard stepped out into the cold night air. When he didn't reply she thrust a wrapped present at him, "for Jeanne."

"I can't take this."

"Why not, why are you being so cruel denying your daughter the benefits we can give her?"

"And if I take the gift, Madame, and my wife asks me where Lizzie's present is, what do I say?"

"It is enough we acknowledged your bastard at her birth rather than letting the world know what you had done!"

"What I had done? Your daughter tricked and then tried to kill me."

"Don't speak so loudly. We only have your word for what occurred."

Richard started to go back inside, she caught his sleeve, "Wait, wait."

Richard turned, "We all connived at this pretence to save our reputations. I am as bad as you in that regard. I tried to be a good husband but we weren't…suited…and I find myself with two children to look after, two. What would you have me do? If anyone should have the right to turn away from the girls it's me, but it's not their fault. If you can bring yourself to favour Jeanne and Lizzie equally then I will consider your request, if not…"

The words drifted off into the still night. Madame Sohier was struggling within herself.

"My husband, is not well, he has not been the same since Jeannot left us."

"You have my terms."

She drew herself up to her full height, she was as tall as Richard. Her mouth was shut in a tight, thin line. She turned slowly and walked away.

Richard waited on the quay as the *Magpie* dropped anchor. She looked in a terrible state and it amazed Richard she had managed to stay afloat. Jack, however, was as ebullient as ever, even though his appearance was more like that of a beggar than a sea captain.

"Where the hell have you been, Jack?"

"Everywhere but there, and I'm not too sure about that."

"We need to talk."

"Get straight to the point, you never think about the niceties of life and manners."

"Shut up, Jack, we have taken on the old beer house."

"Excellent, I could do with a drink."

They walked back to the tavern, Jack waving and embracing people they passed on the way. When they reached the tavern Pa was sat in the corner and raised his cup but didn't let his prodigal son's return eat into his drinking time. Jack kissed Alice and Tamsin, too familiarly. Tamsin had just given birth to a new baby, Lawrence, and pushed Jack away complaining about the soreness of her breasts and tender stomach. She declined Jack's offer of a back rub. Alice shook her head and glared at Richard. Richard pulled Jack to a table and Alice brought over ale.

"So?"

Jack leaned in close, "I've seen the future!"

"I'm more concerned with the present, did we make any money?"

"Some."

"Some? I have a family to support, part of it yours, and loans to repay."

"I know but it's not as if the Spanish just offer up their gold."

"They do to Drake."

Jack pulled a face. "Look, I have had a hard time, we were almost got taken by the Spanish, we've been battered with storms. The headwinds and currents around the Hudson Strait are baffling, one minute I'm trying to anchor in more than a hundred fathoms – had to bend two cables together – next minute we're sailing over rocky reefs with only six inches to spare. We did take a prize but had to throw much of the booty overboard to keep the *Magpie* afloat. I've been up and down the Spanish Main and to Newfoundland and that's what I want to talk to you about. The country's ripe for colonies, it's there for the taking."

"Any gold? Silver?"

"Not like the lands of the southern Americas." It was Richard's turn to pull a face.

"But there is other stuff worth the effort."

"So what have you brought back?"

"Furs, I traded with the natives, they were frightening I can tell you, you never know if they are going to do business or slit your throat. I have some tobacco leaves, the natives swear by their health-giving properties – at least I think that's what they said, makes you light-headed anyway. And I have a hold full of fish."

"Fish?"

"I'm telling you, if we could get a fleet together there is a fortune to be made."

"What about the ice?"

"Well, you need luck–" Richard raised his eyes, "–don't look like that. We did strike ice before the anchor could be catted and it drove one fluke right through the bows, under the water. We had to pump and bail all night till we could heel her over and get the hole out of the water to cover it with a sheet of lead."

"Sorry, Jack, you have had quite a time of it."

"Yes, but the Lord looked down from Heaven and decided us sinners were worth saving. At least if we go for fish and furs in the north we won't have to fight the Spanish for it."

"Well I've done my fill of fighting ... for the present," said Richard unable to keep the weariness and disappointment out of his voice.

"The present?" asked Jack.

Richard shook his head, he hardly knew how to explain himself, the debts, so many children, Alice either too tired or too busy, sometimes he felt you should be wary what you wish for.

Jack poured some more ale, "Tell me."

They did clear a sizeable amount of money but by the time they had made repairs to the *Magpie* there was not enough to fully pay off the loan for the beer house. Thankfully Alderman Crooke was happy on the return on his investment in the expedition. Jack wanted to lease a small house for himself and Richard did not think he could refuse. Jack settled on Quay House, small property close to the water. Richard managed to persuade Jack that he ought to have Joannie live with him. He wasn't very keen but he gave Alice some money and asked her to tidy Joannie up so she would not be an embarrassment. They leased a small warehouse, the Pigeon House above the West Gate, as a focus for their businesses.

Jack was keen to get back to sea and do a bit of privateering. England was still at war with Spain and any Spanish or Portuguese vessel was fair game, especially as the Queen's advisers were sure that Philip would try to invade again. The remains of the Armada fleet had finally limped home and the hawks on the Queen's Council were pressing her to launch a counter-offensive and to destroy the fleet in its home ports. There was even talk of supporting Dom Antonio in his attempt to regain Portugal. Drake was especially keen on this proposal and was entertaining Dom Antonio at his home in Devon.

Chapter Thirty-One

It was a warm spring day and Richard and Alice sat on a bench outside the tavern. Alice had her eyes closed and her face turned to the sun, her lips were slightly turned up at the corners as if she was thinking pleasant thoughts.

"Peace and quiet, Richard, you don't realise the din and crowded life we live still it stops for a moment."

"You don't regret anything do you love?" He tried not to let the worry show in his voice, did she have the same doubts as he? She opened her eyes, turned her head and shook it silently.

"Do you think I'm a good mother?"

"What kind of question is that?"

"To tell the truth, Richard, sometimes I find I am happier running the tavern than suckling babies and chasing after toddlers."

"You were always a woman who was more than a mother or a wife, Alice, I know that and love you for it." He took her hand and raised it to his lips, "Do you need more help?"

"Annie is good with the children, she is endlessly patient and I know she is slow in her work but there is a calm about her. She's still young herself and will improve I think. But there is so much more I want to do with the tavern. I know you help

when you can and so does Tamsin, but with the new baby..."
She closed her eyes again. He could see them moving beneath the lids and knew she was plotting and planning.

"So tell me what you want to do?"

Her eyes flashed open and she slid closer to him.

"I've been looking in the skelling and it still has the old beer making tools inside. Perhaps we could brew our own beer instead of having to buy it in from others. I thought you could talk to the Mayor and get us a licence."

"That will cost more money–"

"–So ask Alderman Crooke to extend the loan, he will do that for you."

"I don't know, Alice, he has helped so much already."

She moved away and slouched back leaning on the whitened wall.

"Can't we wait till after our next venture with the *Magpie*?"

"We can't rely on your brother, he sails off and does what he will, who knows if he will come back, he could just as easily decide to live with the savages."

"I know." Richard thought for a while, "All right I will ask the Alderman, but it will mean taking on more help as well."

Alice slipped onto his lap and wrapt her arms about this neck, "Thank you, husband."

"We are sat on the street, Wife." She squirmed on his lap. "Stop that, Alice." She chuckled and lay her head on his shoulder.

"I am going to speak to your Pa, Richard."

"And say what?"

"That I am fed up with giving him free ale he will have to earn his keep, he can be our pot boy and help in the bar. Didn't you say he used to run a tippling house?"

"Yes, but he drank most of the profits, and the rest went down the throat of the slattern he married."

"He won't get away with that again." She moved her hand down and started to massage Richard's crotch.

"Alice, we are outside."

"You are such a Puritan," she said but she didn't stop and he sighed in pleasure, "Jacket is coming up twelve he can be formally an apprentice."

"You have got everything worked out haven't you?" he asked, she squeezed him hard.

"I thought I could give some shifts to Bart Biston as well."

"Bart Biston? Why would the son of a wealthy merchant, one of the richest is the town, want to work for pennies in the bar?" He nuzzled her neck.

"He was in here with Jack the other day looking for work, his father cut him off, he said he was a wastrel."

"So he is, but I can hardly blame him with a father like his. Poor Margaret, she must be upset."

"I think she slips Bart money when she can. Jack said Alderman Biston is determined to leave everything to young William."

"He's destined to be a chip off the old block." Richard paused, "Is the house empty?"

"You know it isn't, that's why we came out here."

"I can't take you up against the wall!"

"Let's go and have a closer look inside the skelling, I can show you the equipment." They ran like naughty children round to the back yard.

The new mayor was John Bullackre. He was not as wealthy as many of the senior burgesses and merchants of the town and fretted constantly that he would not be able to meet the obligations of his office. As Mayor he had to take major responsibility for the town finances and subsidise his office till the end of his term at Michaelmas. Then he had to wait until the auditors had signed off his account and hope there was money in the coffers to pay any deficit owed to him.

"Ah Mudford, I have just received this letter from the

Council." His eyes were not good and he was squinting at the paper held an inch from his nose.

"Do you want me to look at it for you, Mr Mayor?"

"These court scribes, they cram too much onto a sheet and their writing is too close." He passed the document to Richard who scanned it quickly, "It's about the sweet wine grant." The Earl of Leicester had died shortly after the defeat of the Armada and it was said the Queen had locked herself away for days overcome with grief.

"Who has been awarded it?"

"The Earl's stepson, my Lord of Essex."

"I hear he is the new young favourite of the Queen."

"No doubt then why he has been given the grant."

"I had offered it to the Lord Admiral. I thought it might deflect him from the court case he is promoting against us but I suppose it was politic of him to step aside. I just hope my Lord of Essex pays the rent swiftly to the town. The new young bucks at court think of nothing but spending money, playing at being knights and poets. My Lord of Southampton is a case in point."

Richard picked up another missive, "General Norreys is to come here with an army."

"What! This is terrible, terrible, think of the expense. Soldiers are nothing but trouble. Why? Why are they coming here?"

"It seems there is to be an offensive against Spain and in favour of the King of Portugal."

"I thought Philip of Spain was the King of Portugal?"

"So he is, Mr Mayor, but the fellow I refer to is a Portuguese claimant to the throne, whose cause is being promoted by Drake."

"By Drake you say?"

"And he is coming here."

"Who is, Drake?"

"Drake and his puppet King."

"And am I to put them up? Am I to entertain them?"

"It would seem likely, Mr Mayor."

"Why did I take this office? It is giving me pains in my stomach. The worry is turning my hair grey."

As Mr Bullackre had scarcely a hair on his head, Richard thought this to be the least of his worries.

★

Richard was rubbing goose fat onto Jeanne's chest, "Are you sure this will work, Alice?"

Alice looked up with a frown. She was changing Tommy and Lizzie's napkins and had them lying side by side on the table. "My mother-in-law swears by it, she said William and John never had any colds when they were young."

"There are some that might say old Mother Dypere is a witch."

"Richard! Don't say such things, you know what happens if talk like that gets about."

"Sorry. This stuff stinks. Sorry Jeanne, your Pa is just doing as he is told."

"Tommy!" screamed Alice, the little boy had not waited for a clean napkin and sprayed his mother with piss. "Annie, Annie! Come here girl!"

Annie appeared from the kitchen where she had been having her supper, she had Christian in her arms, "Oh missus, look at you."

"That's enough, come and finish up here, I need to get ready for the tavern. Tommy, you are a naughty boy." Tommy gurgled and waved his legs in the air as Alice dashed off into the tavern. Annie put Christian down and gave her a ragdoll to play with.

"What have you done to your Ma, after she took you in, foundlings should learn to behave themselves."

Annie was not being unkind, she was just murmuring as she wrapped Tommy up and started on Lizzie. It cut Richard to the quick that he could not acknowledge his boy as his own, but Alice would not have it. Richard thought that most people must have their suspicions but Alice said they could talk and gossip as much as they liked, that was not the same as knowing.

"Here Annie, can you see to Jeanne? Give me Tommy." He sat and rocked Tommy to sleep. Jacket came in from the tavern, he looked tired and weary.

"Have you had supper, Jacket?"

"No Father, I've not had time, I'm awfully tired. Perhaps I won't have supper tonight."

"Come and sit at my feet, Annie, get some warm milk with cinnamon." Annie put the girls into their cradle and went into the kitchen. When she came back Richard gave the drink to Jacket, "It would make me happy if you at least drink this and then you may go to bed. You must stay strong, your mother relies on you."

Jacket's eyes kept closing as he struggled to stay awake but he took the milk and sipped, "I know, Father, I think I am getting bigger and I promise to work harder."

"I know you will."

Jacket drained his drink and stood wearily, he embraced Richard, "Goodnight Father, goodnight Tommy." He went over and kissed Christian who pushed him away and then to the baby girls, and finally said goodnight to Annie. "Here, Master Jacket, let me help you up those old stairs and tuck you in with Master William." "Thank you, Annie, I would like that."

Richard laid Tommy into his cradle and pulled out a truckle bed for Christian that she shared with Annie. "Time for bed, Christian." Christian disagreed.

"Don't worry, sir, I'll deal with the young Madam," said Annie as she came back down.

Richard left her to it and went into the bar. Alice was in

her element bossing around Bart Biston and making sure his Pa didn't skive too much. John was in the bar singing a few songs, folk tunes from the village and sea shanties. Richard served a couple of sailors and a visiting trader and then went and joined him. Most of the men in the bar were by now singing along. Alice smiled, their throats would soon be demanding more ale.

Richard was awake. The house was quiet, everyone was sleeping, Alice was breathing deeply and occasionally snoring, which she always vehemently denied afterwards. He was thinking about the soldiers and sailors that were arriving in the town and the ships that were filling the harbour. He had arranged for new rushes to be laid in the Audit House in readiness for the arrival of the King of Portugal. It was really going to happen there was going to be a Counter Armada, a chance to give Philip a taste of his own medicine, well that was John's view. They talked about it often. Why was it playing so much on his mind? Things were going well enough for him here, he had Alice, his business ventures, his work for the Mayor. Alice turned onto her side and Richard snuggled close to her, she still scented her hair with lavender.

He traced his hand down her body, the dip of her waist, the swell of her hips, her strong thighs that clamped around him in her passion, her warm dark place. And yet he knew he was planning to leave her to go on another adventure, to revenge the crying boy whose name he never knew but who's dead eyes he saw most nights, to have a chance at booty and make his fortune so he would never have to go cap in hand again, and perhaps if he was truthful to find some excitement. Alice opened her legs and he slipped his hand between them. Was he wrong to desert his young family? Annie was more use to them than he was. If he had greater riches they could buy the cottage next door and extend into it, the girls would need a room soon, and maybe he could have a little space for himself and his treasures.

Alice rolled onto her stomach and Richard moved on top of her. They were still practising contraception as best they could, including using rhythm and lemon halves though Alice would not go as far as taking wild carrot seeds afterwards. What if they had more children? The tavern was doing well but they would do better if they could clear their debts. He wanted the younger boys to go to the grammar school. He was thrusting quicker, although his excitement was not entirely due to his wife moaning beneath him. He rolled away to a cool spot in the bed and Alice slipped back into sleep. His mind was made up. He would sign up with Drake and Norreys, he would go to Spain, he would make his fortune.

Chapter Thirty-Two

"Joannie, stay still!" Alice was dragging a comb through her knotted hair. Alice had just washed it in the yard and given the girl the first decent scrub of her life. "You have a beautiful new dress to wear, a fine pair of shoes, and a pretty bonnet. You can't put new clothes on a dirty body."

"I don't want to wear shoes, they feel funny."

"Joannie, don't you want to be a lady?"

The girl seemed unconvinced that being a lady would be an improvement to her life. "Your Pa is rebuilding his reputation and establishing his fortune. It could be Joannie that you might be end up an heiress."

"He wouldn't leave anything to me, he says I'm a bastard."

"Joannie, language! You are Jack's only child and he has bought a house for you both to live in. You will be the lady of the house."

"Will I be able to look down on other people, and spit at beggars?"

"Certainly not. There! Lovely shiny hair, now come get into your dress."

Jack came in, "Blimey, Alice, how much did you spend on that!"

"Do you want people to think you are mean Jack? If you are to be a successful businessman you must look to your reputation. Do you want people to look at your daughter and see a mean, poor little thing?"

"One, her parentage is as you know questionable and secondly an expensive dress won't improve what's underneath."

"Jack, you will undermine the child."

They were interrupted by a row in the tavern.

"I'll go," said Richard.

Alderman Biston was stood in the middle of the inn, hands on hips, feet astride, berating young Bart who slinked behind the counter.

"When I was told you were debasing yourself, waiting on those who are beneath you, I could not believe it. I had to come see for myself. Look, look William how far your brother has fallen!"

The youngest Biston aped his father's stance, which was ridiculous in one so young. "Father, you were right to cast him off, he's disgraced our name!"

"Shut up you little cocksucker," yelled Bart. His father struck him across the face.

"Alderman Biston, if you are going to indulge in a family quarrel I would ask you to take it to your own property and not disport yourself in my inn." Richard's tone was even but firm.

"How dare you speak to me like that! You have corrupted my boy–"

"–I did nothing but take pity on him and offer him the chance to earn an honest wage and roof over his head."

"So he sleeps amongst the sawdust and piss pots, my eldest boy, who should have been my joy and my prop."

"Don't worry you still have me, Papa," whined William.

"I told you to shut up, you arse licker," spat Bart.

Alderman Biston cuffed his elder son about the head.

"I have asked you to take this outside."

"Do you need a hand brother?" Jack was at the door with Alice and Joannie behind him.

"You!" spluttered the elder Biston. "You are the one who corrupted my boys, keeping them out haunting taverns, drinking, dicing and whoring."

"Guilty as charged," said Jack.

"Don't think you will get your brewing licence after this, Mudford!"

"You have no right to threaten us like that, your son asked me for work and I thought to give him a chance," retorted Alice.

"Mudford, control your wife, we don't need her Bagrow manners here."

Richard lifted Biston up by the collar, "Don't you ever talk about my wife like that."

"Surely you as a sergeant know the fine for striking a burgess!" Biston's eyes were narrowed, for a moment Richard was back in Alderman Crooke's cellar nursing yet another beating from the older boy when they were both in Crooke's employ.

"If I struck you it would be worth paying double."

"Richard, don't give him the satisfaction, let me hit him," offered Jack.

"Leave my father alone!" said William and ducked behind his father as Jack flicked his ear.

"Ah Richard, is this why you fought for Queen and country, to protect men like him? What did you do in the war Biston?" taunted Jack.

"How dare you ask me what I did, you are nothing but a pirate. How Her Majesty can support scum like you, I wonder if age has addled her brain!"

There was a deathly quiet in the inn. Biston went pale, wishing the words back into his mouth.

"I'll be sure to pass on your thoughts to Her Majesty," said Richard.

"You would not dare." Biston looked about him as if the

walls had ears, "Come, William." He marched out, the boy behind him.

"Are you all right, Bart?" Alice asked. He nodded. "Well you look a bit shaken, go and ask Annie to put something cool on your face, bring out the bruise."

"Who was that fine young boy in the velvet doublet, Pa?"

"That, Joannie, was William Biston. He is not fine, a velvet doublet does not make a mealy-mouthed weasel something to be admired."

"Well I thought him fine."

"Then you are no daughter of mine and if you say such a thing again I will take away that dress and give it to a pauper in the alms-house."

Chapter Thirty-Three

The town was full of soldiers. They loitered on street corners, whistled at girls, drank in taverns and got into fights, and ate the town's store of bread. General Norreys kept them in pretty good order, there was no rioting and not many rapes reported. The Mayor entertained Norreys and his brother at his house for three days, the avuncular host in public, wailing and gnashing his teeth in private. Drake was expected imminently with Dom Antonio.

"I'm mindful to go on the expedition," Richard confided in John.

"Are you mad?"

"No, I can't explain, it feels like something that I should do. It's the chance to destroy the Spanish fleet once and for all, relieve the threat." Richard did not want to admit money was his main motive.

"Well there are enough men here to do that without you joining up."

"You're not interested in going then?"

"For one, Tamsin is pregnant again."

"Again?" Lawrence was only a few of months old.

"We want a big family."

"How do you manage?"

"We don't need much. I earn, Tamsin gets a bit, I fish and I had a little booty left to set us up."

"Think how much booty you might get if you sailed with Drake."

"I'm fine, I don't need to risk everything for more money and I don't understand why you need to either."

"I'm running two houses, the children are growing and they need things. Alice wants to expand the business, the *Magpie* is high risk."

"It seems to me you need to simplify your life."

"I didn't realise it would be so hard. I was on my own for a long time and then suddenly I am living with all these people, I can't think, I can't read, there is no quiet." Richard did not mean to confess so much.

"Surely you wouldn't want to give up your children?"

"No, but I wouldn't mind giving up other people's. Sorry, John, I didn't mean that. I know William was your brother and I love William and Christian, I do, but it's hard, all I wanted was to be with Alice but we get so few moments just the two of us. When we're in bed she's often so tired and we have a quick fumble and that's it, or we have to sneak away into a corner but its five minutes between customers or changing nappies."

"God, I didn't know you felt like that Richard. Look, we could take the children, or we come and run the inn for a couple of days. You could go off to a fair or take a boat down to the Isle of Wight or something."

"Thanks John, that's good of you but I can't help thinking if I made some real money, we could have servants, a bigger house, more time, more space."

"Would Alice be happy just being a burgess wife, she loves that tavern, she likes having the hustle and bustle around her. Have you talked to her?" Richard shrugged. "Have you told her what you plan to do?" Richard shook his head.

"You need to say something, you know you do. God, tell her soon, I can't bear any more of your secrets."

★

The streets were lined with people trying to get a glimpse of their hero Drake. He was travelling with an entourage because of the King of Portugal. Dom Antonio was unprepossessing, a receding chin and thinning hair, pigeon-chested and sallow of skin, not exactly the figurehead anyone would choose. However, there was someone else in the group that fitted all those ideals. He was tall and well formed, youthful with curling brown hair and a charming smile, he was much more richly dressed than either the King or Drake. He was the young, dashing Earl of Essex.

Richard had managed to get himself an invitation to the corporate banquet to be held in the Audit House, the premier civic building situated next to Holy Rood Church in the middle of English Street. He was sat well below the salt but luckily the guests of honour were better performers than most actors, their movements were extravagant, their voices booming. The only person who struggled to follow the conversation and discussion was Dom Antonio who's English was not very practised. The difference in accents from Drake's Devon burr, Essex's courtly drawl, the Mayor who was pure Hampshire Hog, and Alderman Crooke who hailed from Dorset caused him to sport a puzzled frown for most of the dinner. Every now and then someone would raise a cup in toast and Dom Antonio would enthusiastically join in, oblivious as to what he was celebrating.

"Her Majesty," said Essex with a knowing nod, "understands that it was only the bravery of her Navy and by God's good grace that England was spared, but the Queen is also aware that many Spanish ships managed to return to Spain."

"There are perhaps forty sitting in northern ports alone,"

215

put in Drake, not wanting his knowledge to be outdone, "These are the first objective of Her Majesty."

There was much clapping and banging of cups on the table.

"Her Majesty's second objective is a land offensive in support of Dom Antonio and the enslaved people of Portugal," added General Norreys. Dom Antonio sat up straight at the mention of his name and several cups were raised in his direction. Norreys was feeling more than a little put out that the inexperienced Earl of Essex had joined the campaign and was acting like its natural leader.

"Indeed," said the Earl, "a great opportunity of glory for us all."

"A great opportunity to tie up King Philip's forces and prevent him from planning a second Armada," muttered Norreys.

"To fund the expedition Her Majesty has set up a joint stock company to spread the opportunity for rewards amongst as many of her people as possible. I myself am a leading partner," said Drake.

Richard thought this a weakness in Her Majesty's plan but would never had voiced this opinion out loud. Drake may be a hero but he was also self-serving. Dom Antonio and the enslaved people of Portugal would be quickly forgotten if a Spanish treasure ship hove into view.

"What is the size of the fleet and army?" asked Alderman Crooke.

"We have 180 sail, including our Dutch allies. Our forces number 23,000, 19,000 being soldiers," said Norreys.

All were impressed with that, there were more toasts, cheers, jokes at the expense of the Spanish and general bravado. Richard reflected that the force was similar to the one sent against England, and the Armada had failed. His resolve momentarily wavered.

"The main fleet will sail from Plymouth," said Drake. "A

second group will leave from Southampton to escort Dom Antonio."

"Dom Antonio!" yelled the Mayor who was already the worse for drink.

The banquet was interrupted shortly afterwards by entrance of officers from the Queen's Council. Essex looked surprised and uncomfortable at their arrival and their Captain was equally not expecting to see the Earl.

"My Mayor—"

"—come and join us, take some refreshment."

"No thank you, Mr Mayor, we are here for Alderman Biston." All eyes swivelled to where Biston sat. Having identified his quarry, who was by now looking a little green, the Captain said, "You are to accompany us to London."

"Why? You have no right to order me around I am a citizen of Southampton," blustered Biston. Crooke put a calming hand on his arm.

"You are a subject of Her Majesty and you are to come and explain the words you spoke against Her."

Biston was white-faced now, a vein throbbed in his forehead. There was a complete hush in the hall, "I have no idea what you are talking about, it is a foul calumny, I am a loyal subject—"

" —Then you won't mind coming and explaining that to the council...in person." The Captain indicated now was the time for Biston to rise. "You need to go with them Biston," said Crooke in a low voice. "I will arrange for a lawyer. Stay calm and admit nothing but your devotion to the Queen."

Biston swallowed and rose unsteadily. The Captain went to assist him but Biston motioned him away and walked in stately fashion down the hall. The Captain bowed to the assembly, gave a long look at the young Earl and followed his prisoner. As Biston passed Richard he paused briefly to hiss, "You! You did this and by God you will pay, you will rue the day you made me your enemy!" Richard opened his mouth to protest but decided it wasn't worth the breath.

"Well gentlemen, what entertainment you supply!" cried the Earl downing his wine, but Richard could see he was unnerved by the events of the evening. "Sir Francis, General Norreys, I believe we should tarry no longer. We have pressing matters to attend." He rose to indicate the evening was over. The older men looked peeved but followed his lead, Richard wondered if the Queen knew her favourite was here.

Richard knew he had to tell Alice, there was no time left. He helped to serve in the tavern that night, gave the older children supper and read their stories. When the last drinker had departed he emptied the piss pots and cleared down the bar. He made a drink for Alice and rubbed her neck and shoulders that ached from moving casks and waiting on tables. When at last they went to bed he did all the things he knew she liked. She lay back now on the pillow, a smile on her lips and breathed contentedly.

"You must have done something very bad."

"What do you mean?" He hoped she would mistake his flush for afterglow.

"All this attention, you must have something to confess or otherwise you want a great favour."

"I just want you to know how much I love you that is all."

There was a noise and she sat up getting half out of bed. "Is that one of the babies?"

"No, no it's just a cat, lie back down. You're right in a way, I do need to speak to you."

"So speak." She kissed his shoulder and looked up at him through her lashes.

"I have to go away for a while."

"What do you mean go away? On business for the council."

"No." It was no good, he would just have to come out and say it, "I am going with Drake and Norreys."

"Going? Going where?" The truth began to dawn, "Do you mean to Spain?"

"Yes."

"Then tell the Mayor it is impossible. You did your bit, you have a family. People need you, he must choose someone else."

"It's nothing to do with the Mayor."

"Then what?"

"It's me, I want to go."

She sat up again and looked down incredulously, the moonlight made her body glow eerily.

"You, you have volunteered?"

"I'm going to."

"So it's not too late?"

"I've made up my mind."

"You've made up your mind! Without talking it over with me, your wife?"

"I'm talking now."

"No you're not, you're telling me. You tell me you love me so much, yet you are going to leave me and probably get killed. You are deserting your children, you are leaving us to cope with a new house and new business without your help, without your wage. Why? Why?"

"I don't know I-"

"You don't know!" Alice was beyond anger.

"All I do know is that I need to get away for a while. I am so hemmed in, I have no time to think, I didn't know it would be like this."

"And how did you think it would be? When you marry you take on responsibilities, you work for your family and if you are lucky you will have a partner to share things with you. We are building our family home here, our future! Do you think it's easy for me looking after your children as well as my own? Don't you think I want some time to myself occasionally?"

"We are in debt, I could earn enough booty to set us up

for life, you could be a fine lady, the children would want for nothing—"

"I don't want to be a fine lady. I like this life, honest work, knowing we are building something. The children want for nothing now – except a father. Do you think so little of them you prefer adventuring than staying put? Did Jack put you up to this?"

"No."

"John?"

"John does not want to go, he wants to stay here."

"It's a pity I didn't marry him then."

"Alice, listen, you don't understand. I hate going cap in hand asking favours, I hate the shadow of poverty hanging over us—"

"We are not poor. Compared to how it was when I grew up, how I lived with William this is like paradise."

Richard retorted, "You did not know poverty like I knew it, you did not grow up as I did, it has made me as I am—"

"You are talking like a child. You are so self-indulgent. I see you with your little box of treasures like some miser or greedy priest—"

"They are the markers of my life that is all, they are my anchor."

"Well I wish them all on the fire. In fact I will burn them myself."

She went to pull the box from under the bed but he grabbed her and pinned her down.

"Is this what you did to Jeannot? No wonder she didn't want you to touch her."

He raised his hand. "So will you strike me now, go on, pretend I'm a Spanish soldier. Beat me why don't you?"

He rolled back off her.

"You are a coward. You are afraid of life. Go on, go on, be off on your adventure, we don't need you." She was kicking and punching him now. "Get out my bed, get out of my bed."

He tumbled to the floor. Slowly he picked himself up and

grabbed a shirt and breeches. She was kneeling on the bed, her hair cascading down her back and her chest heaving. She was glorious in her nakedness, like an ancient Briton warrior queen waiting to be coated in woad and blood. He left the room and went downstairs, pulling on his shirt and tiptoeing through the living room where the little ones slept oblivious of their parents combat. He slipped through the door into the bar. Bart Biston stirred on his straw mattress. Richard sat down on a settle, staring at the empty fireplace.

"Missus thrown you out then?"

"Go back to sleep." Bart shrugged and rolled over. After a long while Richard stretched out on the settle and tried to sleep himself.

The next day it was as if a hoar frost had crept up the window panes and eased its way inside, covering the pounded dirt floor with a blanket of misery. Alice would not look at him, speak to him, or even stay in the same room as him. Richard started to pack the things that he would need and then went to find the Mayor. He was in the Audit House, holding his head and clucking about the mess and the costs of the banquet. Richard wondered if he had gone home or had been drinking all night.

"Mudford, I was looking for you."

"I am here, Mr Mayor, and I need to speak to you."

"I take precedence, Mudford. Drake was talking of your exploits last year. General Norreys is most keen that you join his campaign."

Richard saw an opportunity to protect his interests and countered, "Ah, but I have my family, business commitments, my service to you and the council."

"Yes, there is all that but it would look well on the town to put more into the venture, so worry not about your family I will make sure they are well looked after and I will struggle on as best I may."

"That is most generous of you, Mr Mayor."

The Mayor hesitated, trying to calculate how much money he might have inadvertently committed.

"I will do your bidding," said Richard.

Chapter Thirty-Four

Richard was at the quayside. The place was chaotic but he assumed there was some underlying organisation enabling the loading of stores, armaments and men. He would have to go aboard soon but he was hoping against hope that Alice would relent and come to say goodbye. The number of men still on shore was thinning out and he would not be able to wait much longer, he had refused passage on two lighters already. He could hear raised voices, a Captain was trying to hold back women, wives and mothers of some of those departing. Then he heard his name, he offered up a prayer in thanks. It was Alice, she was near hysterical and had Tommy clamped to her hip. Behind her was Annie with Lizzie in a shawl tied to her back and Jeanne in her arms, Jacket was pulling along William and Christian. They were all crying, the babies howled, even Annie was blubbing. The Captain was at his wit's end.

"Madam, you can go no further, this is a military operation."

Alice kicked him in the shin, she was crying so much her words were incomprehensible. Richard ran towards them, "It's fine, they are my family, give me a moment!" The Captain limped off rubbing his shin and cursing. Alice threw herself into her husband's arms.

"I'm sorry, I love you, I don't want you to leave but but if you must go, tell me it's not because of me." Seeing her in such distress overwhelmed him.

"Oh Alice, I love you, I love the children. I don't know what was wrong with me, but the things I saw at sea affected me greatly. Oh God I am so sorry, so sorry, I love you, I will always love you. I won't go, I'll buy myself out, don't worry, please don't cry, don't cry."

They were kissing and crying and the children were crowded round, holding his legs. Then all at once they were laughing.

"Oh Alice, can you forgive your stupid, stupid husband?"

"I can if you forgive your headstrong wife. I have thought there is a little space off the skelling, that can be your space, you can think there and we will all be forbidden from entering."

"Love, I never want to be parted from you there will never be a place that would not be for us both."

Suddenly they heard another woman's voice hailing him. The Captain came into view again.

"Is she your wife also?"

"No, but she is the wife of my best friend. Let her through please, we will just be a moment and not cause you any more trouble."

Tamsin was like a galleon herself, so huge was she in her pregnancy. She clutched baby Lawrence and Luisa held her skirt, tugged along like a skiff.

"Richard, you must help us."

"What is it? What's the matter? Where's John?"

"He's been pressed!"

"What?"

"I don't know how it happened. I searched everywhere then the ostler at the Crown told me he had seen him in a group of pressed men."

"He must already be aboard, I saw nothing all the while I was waiting here." He kissed Alice, "Stay here, I will get the lighter over to the flagship, I'll find him and buy him out or get someone to take his place."

"Be careful," cried Alice as he ran and jumped into the lighter that was just pushing off. George Parker was in charge of the boat and Richard made his way forward.

"George!"

"Diccon."

"Have you seen anything of John Dypere? It seems he's been pressed."

"No, not him, if they had taken anyone from the Ferry we'd have slipped them over. I did hear tell some men had gone over earlier though, to the flagship."

"Can you take me there?"

Richard scrabbled up the rope net and over the side. He searched the ship but could find so sign of John. He went in search of General Norreys and found him in converse with Dom Antonio.

"Sir, I am sorry but may I speak?"

"Ah the sniper! I am glad you are to join us."

"No, sir, you mistake me, I have come to find someone who has been pressed. His wife is just about to give birth and cannot be without him. There is money to release him and another can be found to go in his place."

Dom Antonio snorted, "So General your soldiers pick and choose when to serve their Queen."

"It's immaterial."

"Sir—"

"Enough, the anchor is weighed and we are to sea. Neither you or your friend will be able to return until the mission is over."

Richard ran onto deck, he had not noticed the increase in the ship's roll any movement was as one to his delicate stomach. It could not be true. The quay was already some way in the distance. He went back down to the General.

"Sir, my wife and my six children await me on the quay."

"Six children you say, well perhaps your wife will be glad of the break." He smiled and Dom Antonio smirked.

"What have I done? What have I done?"

Chapter Thirty-Five

"The first priority of Her Majesty is the destruction of the Spanish Fleet, she has made that clear." Norreys was getting exasperated. "There are forty ships in Santander according to Her Majesty's intelligence."

"The Queen also desires that I attack the Spanish treasure fleet," insisted Drake, "I am to station myself off the Azores."

"Her Majesty also wishes that we support Dom Antonio so we should make as soon as we can for Lisbon." Essex was determined.

Richard had somehow found himself attached to Norreys' staff. He thought the General had felt some compassion for his predicament and finding Richard to be literate as well as knowledgeable around armaments had adopted him, and for his part, despite his unhappiness at his own folly in being in the invasion force, Richard had a growing respect for Norreys. When the staff meeting broke up the General poured them both wine.

"So Richard, what a mess we find ourselves in. The three commanders are all pulling in different directions."

"Surely, sir, we can achieve all the Queen's aims if we take them one at a time, destroy the fleet, land the force in Portugal and then intercept the treasure fleet."

"Simple and straightforward, but you have forgotten Drakes avarice and Essex's lust for glory. You know he did not get the Queen's permission to sail, he needs to return the hero to avoid her fury."

"Whatever we do we must do as quickly as possible, before King Philip has time to prepare."

Richard took some of the food left from the Captain's table and went to find John. Once they had been safely out to sea the pressed men had been released from their imprisonment and put to work. John had got over his initial fury and as he loved to be at sea he had soon thrown himself into improving the running of the ship. With Richard having Norreys' ear, John got himself promoted out of the common crew. They chewed on the salt beef and bread.

"Trouble amongst the top men then?"

"They are only thinking of themselves no that is unfair the General serves the Queen first but Drake wants silver and Essex is so full of himself – he knows nothing of war but what he has seen in plays."

Soon after the leaders reached a compromise. Drake took some of the fleet to La Corunna, he had apparently received knowledge of some Armada ships in that port. It was to be a fool's errand, they lost a fortnight and did not destroy any Armada ships. In fact the only one that was lost by the Spanish was scuppered by their own crew. Norreys was furious, unable to do anything but at least he managed to persuade Drake to land the army at Peniche, north of Lisbon.

"So Dom Antonio, where are your forces, where is the rebellion in support of your claim?"

Dom Antonio looked uneasy, "General, I do not understand, my intelligence was that my supporters would rally to me. They must have been terrorized by the Spanish."

Essex snorted at what he considered their cowardice.

"You should not mock my Lord, it is little different than when the English turned and ran at Villa Franca!" Dom Antonio pumped out his mean chest and there was a dangerous tension in the air.

"Sometimes it is better to live to fight another day," said Norreys. Dom Antonio pursed his lips. Back in '82 he had nearly won his kingdom. He had forty French ships and eleven English privateers in his fleet but the English had fled when they saw the Spanish taking the battle.

"We must press onto Lisbon, it is what the Queen would want." Essex was agitated, walking up and down trying to burn off his excess energy.

Norreys could see no other course so with a heavy heart the army set off in the heat and dust towards the Portuguese capital. John and Richard accompanied them.

"I'd rather be with Drake," said John, "I'm not fond of marching."

It was long and the heat was taking its toll on the men, some died every day. Richard was worried, the Spanish knew they were coming, they would have fortified Lisbon, the English lines of communications were getting strung out, and there were no welcoming locals to support them. The men tried to keep their spirits up by talking about how the battle would go, how brave they would be. Richard knew that if and when they faced the enemy with swords in hand and pressed close together they would be overcome with fear. It was a disaster. Richard could not see how anything was going to be gained from this invasion. They were losing too many men. There was no glory, no great battle to win, just endless marching, dust, heat, sickness.

They attacked Lisbon but they did not have the men and supplies for a long siege. The Earl of Essex was becoming increasingly frustrated. He had donned his armour, he was going to make a grand gesture to be a chivalrous knight but the men thought him an idiot. Norreys had given up trying to argue with him and was content to leave him to his fate, except knowing the Queen's partiality he ordered Richard to cover him with his gun.

"Let us hope your marksmanship was not a fluke."

"Yes, sir," said Richard. He was annoyed. He didn't want to throw his life away, he wasn't a knight, he wasn't chivalrous and he wasn't brave.

There was a light shining in the eyes of the Earl of Essex. Richard was made to think of early saints in their ecstasy.

"Why so glum, Mudford?" Richard's eyes were scanning the battlements looking for snipers.

"Not fond of grand gestures, my Lord."

Essex laughed, "You don't understand what it is like to be born under a star, to be marked out for greatness. I know fame awaits me, I will outshine my stepfather."

"I have never known such certainty, my Lord."

"You are but a common man."

"That is most certainly true, my Lord. And my concerns are that of a common man, to stay alive and return to my family."

"There is something else inside you that I recognise. You have stepped out of the walls that encircled you. Will you find contentment again?"

Richard didn't answer, this was no time for philosophising, they were sitting targets with several thousand people wanting them dead.

The Earl hurled his ceremonial sword at the gates of Lisbon. The inhabitants were too shocked to do anything but gape. English honour it seemed had been was restored. Then there was nothing to do but retreat. Richard and John were in the rearguard. They finally managed to rendezvous with the beleaguered fleet but by the time they got into the last boat the Spanish were upon them. They had artillery. All at once they were in the water. Richard looked around him. Many men were dead, others were floundering. Some were striking out for the ship. Richard considered his options. He thought he would probably be able to make the ship if it didn't move off any further. He saw the glint of the Captain's perspective glass. He looked around for John, John who could not swim. He saw him clinging to a spar of wood. He had a cut on his head and looked as if he was in trouble. Richard struck out and reached him just as he loosened his grip and was about to go under.

"John! John!" Richard grabbed him under the arms. "It's Diccon. I can keep you afloat if you don't struggle." Richard knew he had no chance of making the ship with John in his arms. He would have to head for the shore.

"Save yourself," John rasped before he lost consciousness.

It would have been easy to let him sink under the waves and swim to freedom, but Richard did not consider that for long, instead he kicked and pulling John along, headed towards land.

Part Five

1590

Chapter Thirty-Six

Richard tore strips from his shirt and did his best to bind John's wounds. John cried out.

"Sorry John, my hands are so battered, I'm all fingers and thumbs." He chuckled. "That doesn't make sense."

"Thanks, Diccon."

"Though I'm not sure this is doing much good."

"No, I mean for saving me. You only ended up here trying to get me off the press gang and now by saving me from drowning, you're a prisoner." They had been marched deep into Spain by their captors. Lucky not to have been slaughtered, lucky Richard had enough Spanish to talk of ransom. They had finally ended up in Cadiz.

"You are my friend, John, and to be truthful, the only one I have. What would you have me do?"

"Well thank you all the same. Do you really not have any friends? What of Foxe...Captain Prowse" John struggled to think of others.

"I have people I will take a drink with, and others I won't. There are people I look up to and people I put up with. I know many people but not many know me."

"I'm not sure even I truly I know you, Diccon, although we

have been acquainted since we were boys. You are very closed, Diccon, very closed." What did he mean? That Richard was private? Reticent? Secretive?

"I have had to look after myself since I was nine and was out in the world by twelve, I knew to make myself quiet and not to take up too much room, to look and listen and learn. What I don't know is how to be open."

"Try living in amongst a raggle taggle of relations in a small cottage, you have to shout to make yourself heard, make a show to get noticed. And my Ma, she has a heart as big as a ferry boat and she spread it over us all."

Richard had a bad pain in his chest, he wondered if he had a broken rib. John was dozing, his face a mottled mess. Richard tried to make himself more comfortable but was overcome by a wave of pain that made him cry out.

"Diccon, what is it?" John tried to stir himself.

"It's nothing, cramp, sorry to wake you."

"I'm tired but I don't want to sleep, especially as we don't know how long we might have."

"What are you saying?"

"They are going to kill us aren't they?"

"I need to believe they will not," said Richard. He thought about Alice, his girls, Tom.

"Do you think they believe we don't know anything?"

"Well we don't, not the sort of intelligence they want. We are just pressed men, who don't want to be here."

"If you say so."

"I say it and you need to say it, and we need to say nothing else."

"Won't they kill us if they don't think we can help them?"

"We are prisoners of war and I keep telling them we have families who will ransom us."

"I don't, my family doesn't have a penny," said John.

"Listen, the Mayor said he would look after my family if I went on the Armada. He will look after Alice, and Alice will look after Tamsin. We have connections, Alderman Crooke, the Sohiers."

"The Sohiers are not going to help you surely?"

Richard considered, "Maybe, maybe not, but they won't let Jeanne starve and whilst they think little enough of me, I am still Jeanne's father." Richard winced again.

"Do you ever think about it?" said John after a while, he had obviously been pondering.

"About what?" asked Richard though he knew very well John's train of thought.

"Jeannot, Elizabeth. What did you do to make them want to poison you?"

"What makes you think I did anything?"

John tried to shrug and groaned at the effort.

"I thought," began Richard, "I thought that most people marry for practical reasons and they rub on pretty well. We didn't love one another, but it was mistake not to realise that we didn't even like one another."

"I don't think my Ma liked my Pa most of the time but she didn't try to kill him, not that anyone would have blamed her if she had."

"I was not unkind to her, except after she tried to trick me...I don't know what made them think it would succeed."

"What happened?"

"I'm too embarrassed to say."

"Diccon, we are in a cell, we are being interrogated and beaten by our captors and will likely be hung or worse. What is embarrassment set against that?" John was right, Richard cleared his throat.

"On our wedding night, she wouldn't...you know."

"Oh."

"I was patient, John, I was, but I told her that I wanted our marriage to be a proper union between man and wife."

"Oh."

"They played a game, blindfolded me...I thought it was a bit exciting."

"Oh."

"John, stop saying 'Oh' in that way, like you are a great philosopher about to pronounce."

"Sorry, go on, I'm interested, makes me forget how I can barely see out of my eyes."

"There's not much else to tell. I discovered I was being ridden by Elizabeth, not my wife. After that I was in such a fury, I took my rights. I'm not proud of what I did...I should not have used force even if it was my entitlement. But they made me pay."

"Oh."

Richard began to laugh, even though it hurt.

Richard was trying to sleep because he thought it must be night and it would help his body to heal if he gave it rest. He could not get Jeannot and Elizabeth out of his head. That was John's fault. If he had sat down with Jeannot and talked maybe they would have found a way to resolve how they lived together. Perhaps if he had been content that they lived alone but under the same roof. Oh, it was all too long ago and nothing could be changed. It was a poor sort of marriage, but without it there would have been no Jeanne and no Lizzie. He had never really thought about having children, it was just the natural way of things. If he had given it consideration he would have dreamed of sons not daughters. It could not, would not be that he should never see his little girls again. They had lost one parent already to lose another at such a tender age, God would surely not be that cruel.

"Why did you marry Tamsin, John?"

"You know why."

"You owed her nothing and took on another man's child. She's not even pretty. Sorry, that sounded rude, but she is a funny looking thing."

"That's true, I know. I just liked her spirit and I felt sorry for her. I can't imagine what it would be like to have no one, absolutely no one. She needed me and she did not know it, or admit to it, but she really needed me. Pretty girls lose their looks soon enough but Tamsin will always be a scrappy little fighter. And my Luisa, what father would not want such a beautiful child." John started to cry.

"John, I'm sorry to have made you think of them—"

"—I want to think of them, I miss them, I want to hug my little girl and sing her lullabies. I want to hear my wife scolding me, she is a terrible nag, a terrible nag." He was both crying and laughing now.

"Do you think Alice loves me more than she loved William?"

"Well that's a question and a half, Diccon, William being my brother and all. They were both young when they wed. Alice was sixteen I think and Will twenty-one, it was young love. I don't think either of them knew what they were really doing. Will was green. He had never been with a woman before, he told me that the night before the wedding and then boxed my ears to make sure I never told anyone. I think Alice scared him, she was lusty, I mean she was a virgin but I think the Ferry girls all know what's what, with so many living in such cramped spaces. I think they both had an itch but you know Alice needed to have a ring." John paused for a moment, "I was shocked when she told me she was expecting Tom."

"I think she was drunk. She is a different woman when she drinks too much, she doesn't do it too often and it catches her by surprise. I just don't know why she pushed me away."

"Well I think she shocked herself, she doesn't approve of fornication ironically. She tried to get rid, but it didn't take."

Richard was stunned, he had no idea.

"And then you pushed off and married someone else. She was devastated, you can be such a prick at times, Diccon."

"Just because we are prisoners and likely to die doesn't give you the right to tell me exactly what you think of me."

John laughed softly, "But I love you, despite all your faults and so does Alice, and yes she loves you more than she loved William."

★

"What are they saying, Diccon?"

"They have finished with us."

"Are we to be freed?"

"No."

"Are we to die?"

"No."

"Then what?"

"They are turning us over to the Inquisition."

They did not know the nature of the offence for which they had been accused. It was enough that they were Protestants from England in Catholic Spain. The secrecy with which it worked made the Inquisition an organisation to be feared. It was how they exercised power and reduced victims to panic. They left it to the imagination of their captives to conjure up what torture awaited, the fear this engendered itself produced the effect the Inquisitors were trying to achieve.

"I have no feelings in my limbs or joints," rasped John, blood and water dribbling from his mouth. Richard held him in his arms, he was too weak and feeble to take any sustenance by himself so Richard fed him what scraps there were. They had put John on the rack.

Chapter Thirty-Seven

John was gone. They came and took him away. Richard just thought it was for another round of torture but they never brought him back. It was some while before he realised John was not going to return and the panic had risen like bile. He had screamed and yelled. He begged them to tell him what had happened. Had he died on the table? Had he been burnt? Had he perhaps been released and gone home? No reply, there was never any reply. They were masterful at cruelty.

He had to lay on his stomach because his back was red raw. For a long time he could not think of anything except the pain but he fought to put something else in his mind. He went over the things he had done in his life. He knew he was not good but did not believe himself to be bad either, he thought he was like most people trying to survive, trying to make his way. He supposed now he would have the opportunity to confess his sins and be forgiven, to have the slate wiped clean. Would his inquisitors pray for him or say a mass? They might, that would be ironic, but it was a comfort to know that someone, anyone, might intercede for him.

He made himself think of Alice, it was important that every day he remembered her face. One, two, no three days ago he had woken in a terror as he couldn't remember what she looked like, he could still feel the hysteria building within him. He had made himself breathe slowly and then started to put her face together one bit at a time. What was the colour of her hair? It was fair-brown. Was it fine or thick? Ah that was a trick question, it was finely made but there was a lot of it so it looked very thick. And her eyes? Grey, they were grey. Her lashes were not over long but again thick. Her nose, she did not like her nose and thought it too big but he told her it gave her face character. She accused him of saying she was plain. She was not plain, her face was strong and attractive. She was proud of her fine wide forehead, many women were jealous of it. Her mouth was wide also but her teeth were quite delicate in comparison and had small gaps between them, like children's teeth. She was well formed, neither slender nor plump, and strong, she had worked hard all her life, physical work. He thought about her strong thighs and suddenly in his mind he could see her naked body. He didn't want to think about that, it made the longing too great, he pushed his raw back against the wall and made himself scream. Now he would think about the little ones, they were too young to know him. They would not miss him at all.

The water torture was the worst.

He wanted his mother. All the memories of her had come flooding back, in random, bright, colourful pictures. His mother had taught him to sing, she had the most beautiful voice. His father loved to hear her it. He said that he fell in love with her hearing her sing whilst she milked her mother's cow. Richard did not want to think about his father. His mother had taught him to dance. She was the most wonderful dancer, his father used to twirl her round the kitchen and say that it was how they had danced on their wedding day. Richard did not want to think about his father. His mother used to love him unreservedly, she loved to ruffle his hair and chuckle his chin. His father used to get jealous and say she loved him more than her husband. Richard did not want to think about his father.

They brought him back and threw him in the cell. He had soiled himself and was ashamed. He was frightened. He didn't want to die, he was certain of that and he decided that no matter how he was brutalised or what he had to say or do, he was going to stay alive and get back to his family. He didn't think God cared about the nuances of belief. Wasn't belief itself enough? If not, when he got home he could be vilified by his countrymen but he would deal with that when it happened. He knew that many people had suffered torture or gone to the flames for their beliefs on both sides but that was not what he wanted to die for. He would die to protect Alice, he would die to protect his children but not for this, this would be pointless and he would be condemning those he loved as well to a life of poverty if he did not return to them.

They had brought him into a small crowded room, but it had windows, he could see a sunlit square. There were hundreds of people milling about and seats set out for some entertainment. It was like a fiesta and Richard half smiled. He wished he was among that crowd. And then he saw why they had come. In the centre but nearer to the building were the stakes and pyres, it was an auto de fe. He glanced at the other people in the room. Were they all victims, was that why he was here? To be tormented before his gruesome death? No, that did not make sense. The other people were not bound like him, their clothes not in tatters, their feet not bare, they had no lice in their hair, their bodies were not harvests for insects. Some were chatting earnestly, some laughed and joked, there were officers, officials, priests.

He made himself look out of the window again. The seats were beginning to fill up, there was a tension and expectation in the air. He noticed a beautiful woman in a red dress sat right in the centre of the crowd, she had thick dark hair, piled high, her cheeks and lips were reddened. She was not a queen of the stews, she was surrounded by admirers, all out for the day, looking for enjoyment. She put back her head and laughed, he was too far away to hear the noise of the laugh but imagined it tinkled. It was as if they were out at the playhouse not come to watch a real life tragedy.

There was a collective sigh from the crowd as the victims were brought out. Incense drifted up to his window and he wanted to cough but was too scared in case it made them notice him and realise he should be down with the other prisoners. Most looked resigned, some were scared and even begged, a few stood tall as if they welcomed their fate. He had never seen a burning. He had witnessed a hanging and had helped pull on the man's legs to hasten his death and shorten his suffocation. He had seen men shot and drown and blown to pieces but they had all had something of a chance in the battle. Not like this. The screams, the smell of burning flesh and hiss of melting fat became etched in his memory. There was an explosion! The crowd screamed and then they yelled. Of course, someone had managed to smuggle a small bag of gunpowder to a loved one to make the death fast and quick rather than long and agonising as flames licked toes and legs and shins.

They had made their point.

★

Richard was beginning to lose track of time. He had no window, heard no sound except for an occasional scream. He missed John more than he felt he could possibly bear. He was worried that his wounds would fester, and if he had survived so much agony, only to end up dying of a fever or gangrene. He was light-headed for want of food, just enough to keep him breathing was pushed through the little shuttered door of his cell and the length of his chains meant he had to strain to reach it, the pain almost unbearable. He quite enjoyed the dizziness, it helped his thoughts and imagination fly. He wondered if he was delirious but he did not mind, in his delirium he was home and he was cuddling his children and Alice was stroking his hair and scolding him for being away so long. Would he go mad, deprived of human contact? He had always been solitary and liked his own company, but that was when he had his books to read and study, or fine food and wine to taste, or his home to keep clean and he knew that there were companions and even family close by if he needed them. He almost longed for the torturer to return and beat him so he could feel human contact. He had sold his soul for a chance of freedom, was it all for nothing?

He thought about the Queen, she had found herself in the Tower when not much more than a girl and must have been certain that she would die. Everyone thought Mary would send her to the axe. Where had she got her strength from to live? She must have been haunted by the ghost of her mother who had been shut up in the same place; she had lost her head. Richard had never troubled himself to consider the truth in stories told

245

of Anne Boleyn's licentiousness. When you were a prisoner with all the state railed against you, you had not a chance. He should have stayed true to his faith, playing false just for the hope of life it was the coward's way.

The Queen was there in his cell with him. He tried to stand so that he might bow but his legs collapsed. The Queen was kindness itself, she bade him to sit. She said she had heard how he was a prisoner in her service, but she had been annoyed that Richard had taken her favourite Essex away and placed him in such danger. Richard begged forgiveness, saying that the Earl had only wanted to serve her. Richard hoped he had returned safely to England. The Queen told him he had. She let him kiss her hand and said that she would do her utmost to free him but he must remember, he was an Englishman. Richard had felt like crying but had no tears, he confessed to Her Majesty that he was a poor excuse for an Englishman. He had not betrayed Her but she must understand, he had turned from Her church to save himself from the flames. She was most kind and sympathetic, she said it would be their secret. She had made the same choices once and Richard said that is why he knew that she would realise that in his heart his love of Her Church was unchanged. She told him to sleep with a clear conscience. She could see into his soul and knew the truth of it. Then she stroked his hair and told him she would sit and wait until he fell asleep.

Chapter Thirty-Eight

He was being dragged from the cell, the guards held him under his arms as he struggled to make his feet work. He blinked furiously in the light. The gaoler was yelling at him and pointing and waving papers. Richard could not follow what was being said and assumed it was a letter about his execution. He thought he would not mind so much to be hung, shot or even beheaded but he was scared of the flames or being drawn and quartered. They took off his manacles. What was left of his skin was red and raw. He lent against the rough stone wall and was surprised no one insisted he straighten up.

"So the tables are turned. You do not resemble much the man who made threats to me."

Richard tried to focus his eyes, a figure swam before them. He concentrated harder and the shape took form.

"Luis de la Castro?" His voice did not sound like him, it was cracked and hoarse.

"Well done, Mr Mudford."

"Why? What?"

"For amusement." Richard did not know if he meant his capture or his release.

Castro clicked his fingers and other hands gripped his arms

and helped him along. He was put into a cart with other goods and chattels and was next bumping across the cobbles and if he did not mistake it, away from the gaol. Surely, he thought, if he was being taken to the auto de fe he would not have been thrown into a cart with bags of flour and sacks of oranges.

The cart pulled into a courtyard perfumed with flowers and fruit. He was hauled out and taken to a small room off the kitchen and dumped on a cot. He passed out. When he regained consciousness a man was examining his arm.

"Who are you?"

"I am Dr Lopez."

"You look like a Jew."

"My ancestors were Jewish. I am a convert."

As am I thought Richard.

"Your body is in very bad shape, especially your arm."

"Will I lose it? I have a family I need to get home to. I am no use to them with one arm."

"I can promise nothing, it does not look good but I will do what I can."

"What is the date?"

"17th November"

"That is a very lucky day, I know you will save my arm. What is the year?"

"1590!"

Only a year.

"Will he live?" It was Luis's voice, "He cost me money, I want a return on my investment."

"He has been brutalised, has prison fever, but his constitution is I think strong and his willpower stronger." Richard could hear the doctor speaking.

"I am going away on business and will be in the country for Christmas. I want him well when I return or the Inquisition can have him back."

That settled it thought Richard, he would get well.

He was still a prisoner. His room was locked from the outside but it had a window, even if it was barred, and he had decent food. He had not been able to stomach much at first, could not keep it down. Slowly he had begun to eat a bit more each day and as he got stronger he started to make himself walk. Although his room was very small the first time he had tried to make a circuit he had collapsed in a sweat, but he needed to move his limbs. The doctor had saved his arm but it hung limp and withered. The room was actually a store and he used the pots and bags as weights. When he was stronger he did press-ups and sit-ups and exercises the doctor had shown him to help get back the movement in his hand and arm.

The doctor was the only relatively friendly face. A servant came with a guard to bring him food, though he did not have the energy to escape. They were not happy to have an Englishman in the house but they did not torture him. He tried to engage the doctor in conversation, for companionship and to improve his Spanish, which he thought would be a help for when he did have the strength to escape.

One day a priest came. Richard felt terrified, he was just starting to regain some strength. What would this devil in a dress do? The priest talked to him kindly, but Richard knew it was a trick and that he was only after his soul. The priest then came every day and brought Richard fruit and wine and spoke to him slowly in heavily accented broken English. Richard knew he was trying to catch him out and he was determined not to be caught. Sometimes the doctor and the priest came together and outwardly their visits seemed innocuous, but Richard knew they were playing with his mind. He would outwit them, he would let them think he was taken in, he would have their food and medicine and mimic their Spanish. He was becoming fluent, maybe one day he would be able to fool enough people to escape.

Part Six

1591

Chapter Thirty-Nine

"You are looking a lot better than when I saw you last, Ricardo," Castro remarked.

"That would not be difficult. And you are looking finer and more Spanish," Richard replied. He was still underweight but his muscles were becoming defined once again and he felt more supple.

"It does to know when to cut one's losses. Sadly for my poor country Dom Antonio was no heroic prince. So now I think what is best for myself and my family."

"Well that I can understand well. What do you want of me?"

"Believe it or not I do have a shred of humanity. I don't care for the Inquisition – but this I will only admit to between ourselves of course, they have agents everywhere. I recognised you, I saw you at a gathering for an auto de fe – one has to be seen at these things you know, although I usually find an excuse to be somewhere else at the appropriate moment. Anyway, I thought you might be of some use to me."

"How?" Richard was at a loss to know what he could offer Castro.

"You had an excellent reputation as an officer of your town, you have experience of privateering which might be useful and you know about deals and cargoes and how to drill men. And You know about guns too of course."

"Guns?"

"Please come."

Since Castro had returned home Richard enjoyed a limited amount of freedom as long as he did not attempt to leave the confines of the house and grounds. Richard had no intention of leaving just yet. He was not strong enough, had not any money and did not know the layout of the town. All this might come to him if he could do some small service for Castro.

Castro took him to a warehouse at the back of the house. It was locked and guarded and it seemed Castro had the only key. Inside he pulled back a cloth to display a Spanish canon and other small arms.

"Tell me what is wrong with this gun. Why are your English guns better?"

Richard gave the gun some attention, "It is the way it is made."

Castro sighed heavily.

"That cannon is individually made and has its foibles, so when you have a ship which has a dozen individual cannons you cannot have a fusillade you are able to rely on. The carriage does not make it easy to quickly reload either. On English ships we use four wheel carriages, it makes the guns easier to handle and reload. An English gun can fire ten to twelve shots an hour."

Luis frowned.

"Look, look here," Richard pointed, "it has been bored awry. It's Crooked, full of honeycombs and flaws. It is likely to break or split. Spanish iron is of poor quality – that is why so much English iron was traded from Southampton."

"And English cannon?"

"Are all made from the same cast."

"And your ships?"

"They're faster and swifter, easier to move, with experienced crews. The guns have a longer reach, a mile. At a hundred yards they can penetrate oak, travel right across the deck and out the other side."

"So what can be done?"

"What your master is doing already, heavy convoys." Richard did not think he had said anything that most people could not have worked out for themselves.

"Do you know how to make an English cannon?"

"Sorry no, if that is what you hoped for you have made a bad bargain."

"But you know how to make a gun crew work better?"

"That I can do." What else could he say? Castro had probably seen him at the muster. Though he doubted whether Spaniards would want to take lessons from an Englishman.

Castro then took him to a room which operated as some sort of office.

"I am not a man of paper, I am sure I am being cheated by everyone because they know I am rich."

"And are you?"

"I have been successful since I gave up on heroics."

Richard looked through the mess of papers, there was no system.

"My written Spanish is shaky, some things I know from goods traded through the port."

"The priest will help you." Richard wasn't happy about that.

"Do these tasks for me and if your ransom can be found, I will free you."

"Why are you willing to trust me with this?"

"You have everything to gain from aiding me. I'm not plotting an armada, its just trade. I think we understand one another."

"Well I had better get started then."

The priest came every day and helped Richard understand what the papers said. Luis was right, he was being cheated by all and sundry. It took several weeks to get things into any sort of order. Luis then took him and the small, elderly priest to his warehouse on the Cadiz dock. He wanted Richard to reconcile what was in there with the paperwork. It was a thankless task and Richard's eyes and muscles ached at the end of the day. He still was not as strong as he used to be, but he was getting there.

He wished the priest was not so pleasant, he sometimes forgot to hate him. Through him Richard learnt what was going on and the layout of the town. Initially Richard was under guard as he was taken here and there on his tasks but as he made no move to escape and was careful to let his captors know where he was going in advance, things were relaxed. He even confided to Luis that he had no desire to risk everything on a fleeting chance of escape – there was no the point if he would soon be ransomed. Of course he was lying.

Silently he made plans to leave. Each day he knew more about the geography of Cadiz. Each night he would draw a plot, memorize it and then destroy the evidence so none would know what he was about. One day the priest took him to see the four hundred year old Cathedral. It had been built by some king called Alfonso. There were as many King Alfonsos as there were King Henrys. Richard had no idea who this one was but he found the building interesting enough. He had to go to mass of course, go to confession and take communion. He pretended he was Edward Alleyn acting a part.

Richard started to teach himself to play the guitar, the house had several and the doctor told him it would help give exercise to his fingers and hands. One of the stable boys was a gypsy and a very talented guitarist. He was suspicious of Richard at first but could not resist displaying his skills and in the end would show Richard chords and teach him tunes at the close of the day as the sun went down.

Richard wondered what had happened to Luis to turn him from the idealistic young man who had come to Southampton not so many years ago with dreams of freeing Portugal from Spanish domination. He had inherited property from his Spanish step-father, recently deceased, perhaps money was enough to turn his loyalties. But it was a fleeting thought. Luis may have broken dreams but to Richard he was just another gaoler. Castro was not a cruel master, most of the time he was pleasant enough, Richard decided to take a chance.

"When I was taken there was another with me."

Castro raised an eyebrow and frowned disinterest.

"A man called John Dypere. I don't know what happened to him."

"And you want me to find out?" Castro was incredulous. "And I should care because?"

"You owe him more than you know."

"What do you mean?"

"He has raised your daughter."

Castro's eyes flickered, not understanding what Richard was saying.

"Don't you remember having some fun with a young girl you were in prison with?"

He looked blank for a while and then a memory pushed to the surface. "Scrawny wench. I don't remember her name."

"She remembers yours."

Castro shrugged carelessly.

"Luisa, your daughter's name is Luisa."

"And I should care?"

"All I ask is to know if John lives or is no more."

"Get on with your work."

The priest asked him to help improve his English. Richard told him some foul swear words were a friendly greeting. When the priest found out he was upset and sorrowful and Richard felt strangely rotten. The priest decided Richard's cruelty had just been a little joke but he did not come so often after that. The doctor did not visit much either, he said that he had done all he could for Richard it was now down to him. Luis was pleased with him, as well he might be. Richard was saving him a fortune. He felt uneasy drilling the men to be better soldiers and sailors for the protection of his ships but he told himself he had little choice.

Luis had become very, very rich. As he placed more and more trust in Richard, Richard began to know more of his business. Luis was obviously in a place of trust and involved with the transport of King Philip's vast hoards of treasure. Richard had not believed the wealth he had seen when he had ventured briefly into privateering but this was something else entirely. It was also very clear to him that as much as Luis had been cheated by others, he was also creaming off plenty of gold and jewels himself which should have gone to El Escorial. Richard was not averse to relieving wealthy men or impersonal governments of some of their money. He had not been Alderman Crooke's best apprentice for nothing, and the less money Philip had the less he would have to spend on Armadas. Yet Richard worried how little England could ever defeat a foe with such unlimited resource. Richard would have liked the opportunity to relieve Luis of some of his gold and silver, and not just the stuffing of some jewels in his pocket. If he ever gained his freedom he would give thought to how he might gain some of this treasure for himself. He practised his understanding of written Spanish by translating some of the books on the new world in Luis's library, Monardes' *Joyfull Newes out of the New-Found Worlde* and Gomara's *Pleasant Historie of the Conquest of the West Indies.*

Luis's sister was coming to stay. Initially Richard could not quite understand what the servant girl was saying, she came from a different part of Spain and spoke an almost incomprehensible dialect, but slowly Richard pieced together that Señora Jacinta Gomez was a half-sister of Luis, the last remaining member of his family and that they were very close. The house was cleaned from top to bottom. The Señora was very demanding. Richard kept out of sight when she finally arrived two days later than expected but managed to spy on her and her entourage. She was in her twenties with masses of dark hair, unnaturally red lips, cheeks rouged with water of alum with a touch of basil, thick shaped brows over brown eyes and with a gap between her front teeth that made Richard think of Alice. She had an undulating figure that caused Richard some unexpected reactions.

He thought he had seen her before but it took him a long while to realize it was at the auto de fe. She went down quickly in his estimation after that. She was, as the servant girl said, demanding, as well as being rude, spiteful and cruel. She had the servant girl sacked and thrown out into the street for some minor indiscretion around the cleaning of shoes. She and Luis enjoyed many intimate suppers. She was apparently married but there was no sign of her husband. Richard thought she was trouble and wished he was not thinking of her at all. She was like the sun, everything revolved around her.

Richard was working in Luis's office one afternoon reconciling some bills when she marched into the room looking for her brother.

"Where is Luis?" she demanded.

"I believe he went out hunting this morning."

"Why did he not wake me? I love to hunt! He knows I love to hunt!" She did not seem to want an answer so Richard gave none. She started to root away amongst Luis's papers upsetting Richard's system. He bit his tongue as he tried to rescue the parchments.

"So you are the English prisoner?"

"Yes, my Lady."

"You're very polite in your words but not your manner."

"Really? I am sorry to have offended you my lady."

"You are not the least bit sorry."

"I think I hear your brother's horse in the courtyard." She gave him a dark look and flounced out.

From then on she tried to find reasons to be in his company. It clearly made him uncomfortable, but that just spurred her on. She used him as a servant, sending him on silly errands. Richard complained to Luis that it was taking him away from his work, Luis just laughed. She walked too close to him, brushed up against him in the corridor and berated him for the insult. When he felt her eyes upon him and turned to look she would run her tongue over her full lips and he found he had to relieve himself as his frustration built up. He found amusement in telling the priest in confession of his thoughts of fornication and how he pleasured himself. He needed to get out of Cadiz.

When he was next in the warehouse he paid special attention to the port, it was the headquarters of the Spanish treasure fleet which meant it was tempting for Barbary pirates as well Drake. If he could get his hands on some money he could, he felt sure, bribe a vessel to carry him out of town. Maybe during the week long carnival was a good time. It had processions, costumes, music, was said to be modelled on the carnivals of Venice. Venetian ships still traded into Cadiz, not as they had once, but he knew a bit of Italian and could perhaps make it to Venice. From there he could get a ship bound for London.

Luis had guests staying leading up to the carnival and his house like the rest of the town was buzzing. Richard thought he might be able to pick the lock of the money chest. In it would be enough money for a bribe, surely?

"You are to go to the dining hall." A supercilious servant summoned Richard. He could not think why he had been called. Luis was away for several days but his sister was still in residence and had a few of her friends to dinner. When he entered the room he recognised some of the people who had been with Jacinta at the auto de fe. They were flaccid and had been drinking heavily, one farted loudly as he came in.

"So this is your English monkey."

"Ugly devil."

"More like a bear!"

"A dancing bear."

"Can you dance, bear?" They thought themselves incredible witty. Richard could imagine what was going to come next.

"Come on dance! Entertain us!"

They started to throw bread at him along with insults. He sighed to himself. He looked around. There were only half a dozen of them plus Jacinta. He fantasised briefly about killing them all.

They were jeering in unison now. "Dance! Dance!"

"You hear my friends, we want entertainment." She had been drinking too but was not drunk. She looked at him, sly and amused. Her ruby lips supped at a goblet of wine. "Now!" she snapped.

Fantasy over, Richard made a bow. He smirked inwardly. In fact he didn't mind dancing at all. He walked over to the musicians in the corner and whispered to them what he wanted them to play. They looked surprised and glanced at Jacinta.

"Play!" she spat.

He had asked for a galliard. He marched to the wife of the most obnoxious of the men sat around the table. She feigned shock but looked delighted to have been chosen to do something so dangerous. He danced high as the Queen preferred. Her Majesty's delight in dance was often remarked upon. When Richard was young he applied himself to learning to dance as it was the mark of a gentleman and he had thought one day he might be asked to dance by the Queen. The woman shrieked as he lifted her high in the air and twisted her around. The other women were shrieking also, the men were dumbfounded and then outraged. Luckily they had left their swords at the door.

"Stop playing," demanded Jacinta and the music ended mid chord. Richard led his partner to her seat, bowed and left. The room exploded behind him.

As he expected after the guests left, he was sent for. He went to her private apartments. He knocked and went in. Jacinta was waiting for him. She raised her riding whip and struck Richard across the cheek.

"How dare you embarrass me in that way!"

Richard raised his eyebrows in question, which infuriated Jacinta further and she lifted her stick again. Richard finally lost his patience and easily disarmed her. She flew at him but he side stepped her and as she dashed by he struck her on her backside with the whip-stick.

"How dare you!" He dared and thrashed her again.

She ran at him her nails like claws, he dropped the stick and grabbed her wrists instead, she writhed and kicked and spat. He threw her onto the day bed and straddled her trying to contain her twisting and turning. Her gown tore and he caught a glimpse of a nipple. He felt excitement rising in him, she could see it in his eyes and stopped struggling, licking her lips instead, he ripped her gown open nearly to her waist. She had the most enticing body he had ever seen. He was breathing deeply and controlled himself with difficulty. He got off of her.

"I'm sorry, my lady." He was going to swing for this. He turned to leave, he could feel blood dripping from his cheek.

"Don't be."

When he turned back she had sloughed off her ruined gown and sat on the edge of the daybed, thrusting her chest forward. He hesitated but only for a moment.

It was like making love to a tigress, she scratched and howled, and pounced and rode him. She licked and sucked and did many other things not even seen in a whorehouse. They did not leave the room for three days. At first Richard was completely carried away with the sheer physical release. It had been two years since he had known a woman. But he tired of the brutality of her passion, he didn't want tricks, he did not want sex without feeling, and longing for Alice, reached for the door

"Where are you going? I have not given you leave." She grasped him and bit his shoulder.

"I, unlike you my lady have work, and your brother will be home soon."

"What do I care for him?" She pinched his nipple.

When the next evening came she sought him clutching a mask. "It's carnival, here, I have a costume."

"What?" Richard was irritated he needed to plan his escape. Then it dawned on him that perhaps this would be of assistance.

"Get changed!"

He did as he was bid and put on the mask. Jacinta was wearing hers and she took his hand. They ran into the streets. It was madness, wonderful madness, the Spanish often so sombre, drank the cup of carnival and embraced it. They slaked their thirst with wine that ran from the fountains and paused in alleys to kiss and fondle. Richard felt light-headed, as if he was in some drug-induced dream.

They danced and laughed and drank. He pushed her into the doorway of a church and nuzzled her neck, sucking to deliberately leave a bruise, his brand on her. He pulled up her skirts as she unlaced his hose and soon they were rutting like a queen and her customer.

"Luis's spy is looking shocked."

"What did you say?"

"Luis, he has spies who follow me and spies who follow you. They are over there is the shadows, taking notes. Don't stop." He tried not to but suddenly his mind was whirling. Ah, he had not been trusted after all. His plans were only in his head so he thought Luis might not know what he had hoped to do, but had they told them how he walked the narrow alleyways and piazzas of the walled city learning each twist and turn? Had they told him the interest he took in the ships of the port?

"Will anything happen to you?"

"Don't be ridiculous. Luis loves to hear about my adventures."

"Even when he finds out those adventurers are with me."

"Especially with you." Richard was tidying himself.

"What is the matter, you were so keen before."

"I was drunk and more than a little mad. We should go back to the house."

"You go if you want to. I am going to enjoy the carnival."

Chapter Forty

He didn't see her for a few days but she turned up one evening when he was sat on the roof playing the guitar. She purposefully scratched his face as she went to kiss him.

"Just stop! What is wrong with you?"

She was shocked at his aggression.

"I'm sorry but you do not seem to know how to be tender."

"Tender? What are you some milksop?"

"No, I am a man who misses his wife and his children, who is lost in a foreign land."

"How poetic." She flung back and laughed. He got up to leave.

"When you have been used as I have been, tenderness is not a feeling you understand."

He sat down again beside her, pushed her hair from her face and gently brushed her lips with a kiss.

"Is that supposed to transform me? I was married at fourteen to a lecherous pervert. By the time I was fifteen there was no depravity he had not subjected me to. At sixteen he sent me to seduce a man he needed a favour from. I was his mistress for two years until my dear husband had a fit, his body became useless and he could command and threaten me and control me no longer. I have had my revenge, he is trapped in his useless body but his mind is still sharp and I torment him with tales of my infidelity with stable boys and bullfighters and now with English prisoners."

"And you are as bitter and miserable as he."

"Well it seems it was a match made in hell."

"You don't have to live like this. You can change, your husband will not live forever."

"You may leave now." He didn't move so she marched across the terrace and into the house, slamming the door behind.

Richard went back to his quarters, washed and changed to try to purge her smell from his body so he would not be distracted. He avoided Jacinta until Luis returned. She was obviously avoiding him as well. It was insanity. How could he say that he loved his wife and longed to hold his children when all he could think of was a Spanish virago? He was losing his mind.

Luis had sent for him. Richard thought he was going to be returned into the arms of the Inquisition. He was such a fool risking everything and for what? Luis said nothing, only asking for a report on his business dealings. Richard wondered if he was being toyed with. It was a few days later that Luis suddenly spoke about Jacinta.

"My sister is in the foulest of moods. Have you slept with her yet?"

Richard said nothing.

"I can't decide if she is angry because you have slept with her or because you have not."

If he had spies then he would know that he had slept with his sister. Had Jacinta lied about the spies? Had he lost his best chance of escape? He should have checked, challenged the men.

"I have seen how she looks at you, I know that look. I just ask for discretion. My sister has had a very unhappy life, there was nothing I could do to prevent it, so now I indulge her."

Richard was feeling uncomfortable.

"You need to sign these, sir."

Luis chuckled and reached for the bills.

★

Richard lay on his truckle bed and thought about Jacinta. He had been living the life of a monk until she had appeared. Now she had awakened something in him and he found the longing almost unbearable, especially in the night. He felt guilty as well. He had betrayed Alice and realised that recently he had gone for days not thinking about her. He wanted to be home, to be with her, to hug his children. These feelings never changed, never went away. He had been extraordinarily lucky to have been saved by Luis and although this was not the life he would have chosen it was a million times better than the one he had been living a year ago. What if this was it? What if he was never ransomed? What if he was doomed to end his days in Spain?

He got up, it was the early hours of the morning and the house was asleep. He crept along the dark corridors till he reached Jacinta's door. He opened it slowly and carefully and slipped into the outer room and padded across to the bedchamber. He opened the door quickly and hurried to the side of the bed. She must have been a light sleeper for she awoke with a start and went to call out.

"Don't say anything, don't do anything!"

"Why are you here?"

"I'm going to make love to you."

She shrugged, "I'm tired, I do not want you here, you bore me."

He took her in his arms and kissed her passionately.

"I told you to say nothing and do nothing."

He woke in the morning to see Jacinta stretching like a cat. She was almost purring.

"Thank you."

He was astounded. He didn't think Jacinta knew those two words.

"It was entirely my pleasure." He kissed her and stroked her magnificent body. He didn't tell her that this time when he held her in his arms he had imagined she was Alice.

"Why?"

"It seemed to be something that you needed and I needed it too."

"I shall take you for my lover."

"Till I am ransomed?"

"Or till I tire of you."

Richard wondered which would come first.

Richard thought he was becoming too comfortable in this warm and scented land. He was sat on the flat roof in the midday sun, gazing out across the walled city of Cadiz. Most of the household was sleeping but he liked the quiet of that part of the day. He could sit and reflect and think of the damp and misty island of England, the showers of rain, the cool blast of the sea winds. He thought about the fruits of England, apricots, muskmelons, apples, pears, cherries, plums and of laurel and rosemary that flourished, even in winter. He imagined boats and ships coming into Southampton harbour, bringing not gold and silver but tin and lead. He thought of sea-coal and iron, wool and English beer made of barley and hops. He thought of the birds: crows, ravens and kites. Crows stopped worms eating the corn the old men of the land had told him, and in the town kites and ravens could not be killed because they ate the filth that accumulated in the streets. He thought of the plentiful fish, oysters, mackerel and herring.

"Daydreaming about my sister?" Richard started. He had not heard Luis approach.

"She has been much calmer since she took you to her bed." Richard was uncomfortable with this sort of conversation.

"I can understand her anger after the life she has been forced to live, to be married to someone so perverted when she was so young."

"Is that what she told you?" Luis was amused and Richard felt uneasy, "I am very fond of Jacinta but she makes things up."

"She was not married off to an old man?"

"In that she told the truth. Dom Miguel was a friend of my stepfather. Richard I am fond of you, I took to you even back in Southampton so heed what I will tell you. My sister did have a harsh life. My mother was a religious fanatic and she kept Jacinta hidden away, women in this country do not have the same freedom of women in England. It is more like the Moorish kingdom of old. My mother was fearful of Jacinta's beauty, even as a child she was – well let us say she was truly a daughter of Eve in the way she tempted. My mother thought to entomb her in a closed order."

"Make of her a nun?"

"Unbelievable, yes? Jacinta managed to escape and ran away with an unsuitable young man. She was brought back, deflowered and of no value. The boy disappeared. My mother beat her so soundly she nearly died. However, Dom Miguel took pity on her. He was many years a widower and wanted someone to warm his life. He was old but not unkind. Jacinta married him. It was that or a life of scourging and repentance. But she soon made him a cuckold."

"She said she had been forced to become the mistress of an evil man."

"There was no force involved, but her lover Don Carlos was cruel and depraved. Eventually his wickedness caught up with him. He had a massive fit and became a drivelling wreck. Jacinta slunk back to Dom Miguel and he took her in again."

"And this is true?"

"It is the truth as I know it, Ricardo. She is playing at being the tender lover but she will tire of you and you will find yourself sent to the galleys to join your compatriot."

"My compatriot?"

"I meant to tell you, I made a few enquiries. Your friend was not sent to the fire but to the galleys, that is all I know. It is a harsh environment who knows if he yet lives."

Richard felt a fool, he was Jacinta's dupe and he had betrayed Alice for nothing. He went to the church where the priest served. He confessed he had betrayed his wife and his country, he had been guilty of fornication. This time there was real pain in his voice and the priest was lenient with him. Richard wanted a harsher punishment. Afterwards when Richard was sat in the square in front of the church the priest came and found him.

"Do you like Spain?"

"No."

The priest looked sad.

"There are some good things about Spain but it's not my country, it's not my home."

"Are you sure you want to go home to England?"

"Of course, there is nothing I want more."

"There have been enquiries about you."

"Enquiries?" Excitement filled Richard's breast.

"An envoy who has come to ransom English prisoners."

"Ransom!" Richard sat bolt upright, "When? How? Does Luis know? He has said nothing."

"You are too valuable to him, Ricardo."

"You mean he has deliberately kept this from me? He has not told the consul of me?"

"That is what I have heard. The doctor knows more than I."

"How can I find him? I need to speak to him."

The priest gave him directions. He lived not far from the church. Richard ran to the house and knocked the door. The doctor did not invite him in but they went and sat at a little tavern opposite.

"The priest should have kept his council."

"No, he did the right thing. Tell me, tell me about the envoy."

"He is a merchant man. Apparently he has done much to rescue Englishmen from slavery in Turkey and now is helping to free English prisoners here. His name is Cotton, Edward Cotton."

"I know him, if it is the same Edward Cotton. He was a merchant in my home town of Southampton. I need to meet with him."

"You cannot it is too dangerous. Luis still has you followed." The doctor glanced at an innocent looking passerby standing in the doorway of a shop looking at baskets.

"How did I not notice? I have fallen asleep, forgotten what I should be about. I need to get a message to Cotton. Will you help me?"

"I will see what I can do. I promise nothing you understand. Here take this unction. If Luis enquires you can say you came for a consultation."

"Thank you, thank you."

"I have done nothing yet, and may do nothing in the future. Good day to you."

Richard was finding it difficult to concentrate. Every day he thought Cotton might come or there would be a message. He worried he was going insane. How could he have let these weeks turn into months having a stupid reckless affair, helping Luis de la Castro get richer, sitting around learning to play the guitar and talking Spanish like a native? He should have escaped, he could have if he had really wanted to. He could have overpowered a few spies.

★

"Come with me," said Luis, "I have something to show you." He was excited.

Richard thought for a moment he was going to tell him Cotton was here to negotiate his release but no, he took Richard to the store at the back of the house where he kept his armaments. Inside he pulled back a canvas cover to display an English cannon. Not just any cannon but one of the new breed that Elizabeth had commissioned.

"Where did you get this?"

"From the *Revenge*."

"The *Revenge*? Sir Richard Greville's ship?"

"He bravely but foolhardy took on superior Spanish forces when he should have cut and run. And this was part of the booty," said Luis. "I should like to know more about English guns, why they are so superior to our own."

"I'm not much of a gunner, more a small arms man." Richard caressed the cannon. Why Greville had not sent his own ship to the bottom rather than let the enemy take such a prize was a mystery.

"Well we shall see. I am happy as you know to consider a ransom for your eventual freedom, but in the meantime I must insist you make yourself useful." You lying bastard thought Richard.

"I want to be useful. I don't like to be idle."

"So you will show me how best to use this and perhaps we will be able to make more, based on this design." Richard nodded and wondered how best to sabotage the gun.

★

Cotton came at last in the company of the priest and an official from the Spanish judiciary. They arrived at a time of day when there were witnesses and Richard was working with Luis in his warehouse. Luis could no longer hide Richard's existence.

"Well it seems that you have friends Ricardo."

Richard had wanted to embrace Cotton but bowed. Cotton seemed surprised to find Richard not bound and starved but working for a wealthy minor noble.

"I know you sir, I thought when I was given your name that I should remember you but could not bring your face to mind but now I see you I know you. I am glad to be able to assist a Southampton man."

"Not as glad as I am, Mr Cotton."

"Have you gone native, Mr Mudford?" he muttered under his breath, "I have seen that with some of the Turkey slaves, they have prospered so much in their captivity they have taken to following the ways of the infidels and wearing turbans."

"Part of the condition of my release from hellish captivity was that I should work as an assistant to Señor de la Castro, nobles here do not like to muddy their hands with trade."

"Mmm, he has set a heavy ransom for you."

"I have friends sir, I have connections."

"Yes, I have been given suitable sums."

"Just get me free, sir. Whatever it costs I will repay with interest."

★

Mr Cotton was handing over the final instalment of his ransom. Soon he would be going home. Richard walked into the courtyard and took a deep breath, closing his eyes so he would better remember the smells of bougainvillea and orange blossom. He felt the warmth of the sun on his face.

"So, you are really to leave?" It was Jacinta. She had been tearful, then angry, then vicious when she had first found out and Richard bolted his door and barricaded it at night in case she sent men to kill him or take him to the galleys.

"You are already becoming bored with me. I don't really

273

want to find myself castrated and sold into slavery to some Turkey lord."

"Luis has been telling tales again." She wrapped her arms around his neck, "has it all been so bad?"

"Not at all, you are incredibly beautiful, and full of life and passion. If things were different I might even have fallen in love with you," Richard lied.

"How different?"

"Were I not married and in love with my wife. If I did not have children growing up without knowing who their father is."

"I don't want you to leave." She kissed him, biting his lip so he could taste the blood.

"Only because you want to show you have the power to make me stay. You will find another lover, you could try living with your husband for a while."

"I shall have to visit him and feel the touch of his desiccated skin, his touch makes my flesh crawl and his manhood is a pinched and shrivelled thing. He is near five and seventy, did I tell you that?"

"You did."

"He should have had the grace to die ten years ago. I was a child when I married him. Our wedding night disgusts me even now. He was so red in the face I felt sure he would collapse and die, that his heart would give out at his exertions. Still I have had my revenge many, many times since and now will be the sweetest of all."

"Why what are you planning?"

"To present him at last with an heir, to make him believe his watery ejaculation could make a child, to put a cuckoo in his noble nest. I am carrying your English bastard, Richard."

"You're lying."

"Why would I do that?"

"So that I will stay with you."

"I am resigned to your going and I could not carry this child if you remained. But I should thank you, I thought I was barren, as did my husband. He thought his estate would go to a hated cousin."

"What will a child do with a mother like you, Jacinta?"

"It is no matter, the child will have servants enough to raise him."

"So it is going to be a boy?"

"Of course! Otherwise what is the point? Now come behind the pillar, we should bid farewell properly."

"So Ricardo," said Luis, "your ransom is paid, and you are to leave us at last. I am loathed to let you go. Your services have helped my business grow efficiently."

"I wish I could say I was glad to be of service, but you know it was just self-preservation that made me work hard," replied Richard.

"Of course. But you may still be here for a while, Señor Cotton has other business I think."

"No, I am taking passage with a Dutch merchantman, I cannot wait another minute."

Luis pulled on his ear, "There are no hard feelings, I trust. I did after all preserve your life." He held out his hand to shake Richard's.

"Even if it was for your own ends." Richard took the proffered hand and was surprised to feel something small palmed into his.

"Does my daughter resemble me?"

"From what I remember, her hair is dark and curls like yours, her skin is fair, her eyes blue and I think she will grow up to be well-shaped like Jacinta but without her temperament."

"Well let's thank God for that." He moved away.

The business done Richard left with Mr Cotton, a small bundle of clothes under his arm, a guitar slung across his back and a diamond and pearl earring hidden in his shoe.

Part Seven

1592

Chapter Forty-One

The white cliffs of Dover were barely visible through the drizzling rain. There was no ball of sun in the sky, only a watery light struggling through the grubby clouds. Richard wasn't sure if the reason his stomach turned and dipped was because of the waves or his apprehension. He wondered what was wrong with him that he felt some longing for the warmth of the Spanish sun, that he missed the colours and the smells. The little ship lurched again as she struggled to make port. It took two more hours before she was safely in the haven. Richard shakily climbed down into the lighter. He felt shocked to hear people around him talking in his native tongue, he was still getting used to speaking English again. He thanked the men who helped him onto the dock and looked about him wondering what to do next. He had no money, save for the hidden jewel and it would not do him any good to pass that around, it would cause suspicion and be confiscated. He would end up in prison or worse. He tried to brush himself down, straighten his clothes and look as respectable as possible and then asked where he might find the town's Mayor.

He had to wait in line, he was faint with hunger and thirst was overpowering him. He did not know how long he waited but eventually he was before the town's leader, who looked at him scornfully and sniffed.

"Well, what kind of vagabond are you?"

Richard was expecting this, he had been party to such interviews from the other side of the table, he knew it would do him no good at all to rail or protest. He must keep his temper, be polite and respectful and show due deference and gratitude.

"Thank you for seeing me, Mr Mayor. My name is Richard Mudford of Southampton." He heard a scribe scratching away as he spoke, "I am a man of some position in that town." The Mayor looked sceptical. "But I have been these last two years a prisoner in Spain until I was recently ransomed."

"Spain you say? How did you come to be prisoner?"

"I was with General Norreys' army that went into Portugal. I was with the rear-guard and was captured."

"You look healthy enough for someone who has been under the Inquisition for two years."

"I had some luck sir, a Portuguese merchant I once knew in Southampton managed to save me from the galleys, I made myself useful–"

"–turned traitor?"

"No sir! I am a true and loyal subject of Her Majesty, I merely meant in the general business of trade but I was still a prisoner, I had no freedom, I still felt the lash and knew chains. It was thus, Mr Cotton found me."

"Cotton, I have heard that he labours to free good Englishmen from Spanish captivity."

"He is a noble gentleman, sir, and acted on behalf of my family to gain my freedom. Here, I have a letter, I was anxious to be home or would have travelled with him. Unfortunately I could not get direct passage to Southampton and so sir, I find myself here in Dover."

"And what do you want of me!"

"A passport that I might travel onto Southampton," the

Mayor seemed relieved that Richard intended to leave, "and a few pence for the journey, sir," the Mayor was less pleased to hear this. "As I say I am a man of some standing in my home town sir, I can repay any small amount that you might see fit to give me."

It was a small amount, 4d. If he was careful it might feed him for a week but Richard felt he would do better to get a good meal and a night's rest. He needed to try to keep himself neat and tidy so that he might present a good picture to the other men he would come before on his journey home. He found a room at a small, clean inn which served wholesome food and the next day headed out on the coast road towards Southampton. Some were kind to him on his journey, wanting to ask him about his imprisonment but most begrudged him, there had been too many poor soldiers and sailors on the roads. He learnt that the Queen was focusing her foreign policy on the Netherlands and aligning herself with the rebels. General Norreys had been leading her armies there.

As he crept closer to home he wondered what he would find. Did they know he was alive or had Alice just hoped, how was he going to answer their questions about John? Would they know him? Had he changed? He was thinner he thought, he was still strong, his skin tanned by the Spanish sun, his hair was longer and bleached even fairer. He had been forced to sell his guitar as he could get more money for it than he could by singing for farthings. He felt sick with worry and as he reached Itchen Ferry with the walls of Southampton spread in front of him he threw up. He kept his head down, he didn't want to be recognised. He wanted no questions until he had them from his family. He had saved a ha'penny for the fare. It was one of the younger Parker boys who rowed him across, and he was not recognised.

He joined the trickle of people toiling up the path to the East Gate. No one paid him much heed. As he marched quickly along East Street, across English Street down to Brewhouse

Lane, over French Street, and down Vyse Lane some people stared at him but as he did not speak or greet them they shook their heads and moved on; and there it was, the Angel inn. He stopped for a moment and looked at it. The sign needed repainting, the windows were dusty and it didn't seem busy. Richard looked up at the sun, it was still early. He went through the door. Someone he didn't know was on the other side of the bar. He was slovenly and unkempt, clothes stained, hair greasy, carrying too much weight, a suspicious look in his eye.

"We're not open."

"I'm looking for Mrs Mudford."

"Who?"

"Mrs Mudford, the owner of this inn."

The man looked Richard up and down and spat on the ground, "I'm the owner of this inn."

Before Richard could recover his shock, the back door opened and a thin boy struggled to push a barrel through.

"Watch what you're doing with that you clumsy wastrel."

The boy looked up with a terrified glance, flinching as if from remembered beatings.

"Jacket!"

The boy turned around and rubbed his eyes in disbelief. Suddenly his face lit up, he abandoned his unequal struggle with the barrel and dodged around the bar throwing himself at Richard.

"Come back here you have work to do, or I'll dock your wages and you'll get a beating–"

"This is my father!" said Jacket in triumph.

The man stared at Richard. He judged rightly that Richard knew how to handle himself in a fight and Richard gave him his hardest look, the one that made prisoners quake with fear and dread.

"I'll not pay you for time lost," he said and stamped out into the back room. Richard pulled Jacket down onto a bench.

"Jacket what's happened? Where is Alice, is she all right, she's not dead?"

"No, Father, she is not dead." He hugged Richard again.

"Jacket, tell me please where I might find her. Why is she not here and who is that blackguard?"

"Father, things have not gone well for us whilst you were gone." Richard felt a pain in his heart. "Mr Biston, he evicted us and put his own man in charge."

"What? I don't understand."

"Mother will be able to explain sir, something went wrong, Mr Biston was very angry at being arrested and although he managed to get free he blamed you sir, for what had happened."

"Me? I didn't report on his misjudged words, but I don't understand, our loan was with Alderman Crooke—"

"—Alderman Crooke is not what he once was, sir. It seems he owed too much money and then he had grave losses as sea. Mr Biston demanded back money he was owed and when it could not be paid took the Alderman's notes – Mother begged and pleaded but he would have none of it."

Richard sat back in shock. Jacket went and got him a jug of beer.

"Here Father, drink and then I will take you to Mother."

Richard did as he was bid and then stopped himself, "I have no money to pay, your new master will not be happy."

"It doesn't matter, Father, he beats me for much less, and now you are back soon all will be better. I have done my best and give all my wages to Mother."

Richard hugged the boy and kissed his head. "So Jacket, where is Alice?"

"Mother is back at the tippling house, everyone lives there with Aunt Tamsin."

He had walked straight past and not felt her presence so close.

"I'll go there right now."

"She will be so happy, Father, she prays for your safety all the time." Jacket looked nervously at the door to the back room, "I should stay here and finish my work but perhaps I may leave here soon. Maybe we will all come to live here once more."

"We'll see."

Richard helped Jacket move the barrel and when the innkeeper returned he whispered in the man's ear, "You may tell your master I am back and I will make him sorry but if you lay a hand on my boy again, I will kill you."

He went back outside and retraced his steps, this time he did not bow his head because he was oblivious to everything and everyone. His legs were like jelly, he did not know how he found himself back at the tippling house. The brush of twigs was above the door. He went in. A couple of men were drinking in a corner and calling out for more, banging their tankards on the table. There was a swish of a curtain and Alice came through carrying more ale. She put it on the table and the men tried to grab and fondle her but she pushed them aside before Richard could step forward. As she turned he was in her path. She stopped dead, there was a sharp intake of breath and then it seemed she stopped breathing altogether. She let out something between a cry and a sob, her hands reached out to touch him as if to check he really was there.

"It's me, love, I have come home."

Like Jacket she flung herself into his arms, kissing and hugging and crying.

"Is it you? Is it really you?" There were deep shadows under her eyes, a touch of grey in her hair. She was thin and sallow.

He embraced her again, "It is me, I am home, I'm home." He pulled her into a corner seat.

"You look well." She seemed confused by this, "So many of the men that come back are broken."

"I was lucky."

"John? Where is John?"

"I don't know, we were captured together, but got separated, I tried to find out where he was, but failed."

Alice nodded, she was still looking strangely at him, "And you must find us greatly changed."

"What has happened? I saw Jacket, he said the Alderman is ruined by Biston, and that he also took away the inn."

"He always was a cruel and bitter man but how he could see his own father-in-law put in prison. Without his protection we had no one"

Richard blushed with shame, "The Mayor promised to look after you."

"He did his best but he left office. No one in the town is greater now than Biston."

"What of Jack?"

"He has been gone almost as long as you, sailing off over the horizon in search of treasure."

"What of his house, his money?"

"All left in Joannie's care and she has taken up with William Biston. Alderman Biston took her into his household. She hopes for marriage but Biston is holding out to see if Jack returns with more treasure. If not he will find a better match for William."

The world was tilting on its axis.

"What money we could scrape together went towards ransoms."

"Oh love, what has my folly cost us?"

"A lot more than money, Richard."

"What? No, no don't tell me something has happened to the children?" She did not speak for the longest while and Richard could not press her.

"Tamsin and I tried to make a go at the tippling house, but it's been hard, unseen hands against us." Unseen but not unknown thought Richard. "There were too many mouths to feed. Your girls are with their grandparents." Richard was relieved he had thought much worse.

285

"William and Tom live over with John's mother in the village, with Tamsin's Lawrence. George Parker has taken Will on his fishing boat...only Luisa and Little John are here."

Richard did a calculation in his head, "And what of Christian?"

Tears appeared in Alice's eyes. "Oh no, love don't, don't tell me—"

"She was taken, this last winter, the influenza, there were so many sick people in the town...and there is something else."

He didn't think he could bear to hear any more distressing news but then thought himself a churl. He had suffered little compared to his wife.

"I was pregnant when you left, but I lost the baby. She lived just a few hours."

They both clung together and wept.

There was a noise on the stairs, Richard looked up. Tamsin was walking down buttoning her bodice. As she came a man trailed after her. He grabbed her at the bottom, one hand fumbling for her breast, the other for her crotch. She shoved him away.

"You've had all you paid for."

He made for the door. As he brushed past Tamsin's eyes flicked around the room and stopped when she saw Richard. She blushed furiously and looked around. Richard realised she was searching for John, afraid he might have seen her shame.

"Where's John, where's John?"

"I'm sorry, Tamsin, I'm alone."

"Alone! You promised to bring him back. Where is he?"

"I don't know, we were separated. But as far as I know he lives."

"As far as you know? What kind of answer is that?" She was furious, almost a madness in her eyes.

"Mama, I'm hungry." A little girl had appeared and from her dark hair and eyes Richard guessed it was Luisa.

"Not now."

"Yeh, not now," said one of the men who had been sat at the other table. "Your Mama is busy." He made a grab at Tamsin but she pushed him away.

"I've finished for the day, go find some other whore."

"I've been waiting this half hour bitch and I'm going to get what I came for," he lunged at Tamsin but with a practised move she stepped aside and then pushed him, he fell across the furniture onto the floor. He got up cursing and swearing, his drinking companion laughed and pointed at him, which made him even more angry.

"Well if I can't get it from you, the daughter of a whore will do." He grabbed at Luisa who screamed in terror.

"Put her down, she's not more than a baby."

"I like 'em young."

Richard's fist struck him full in the face, he let go of Luisa and Richard took the opportunity to knee the man in the groin Richard grabbed his collar and thrust him out of the door and then turned to his companion, who held up his hands in surrender, grabbed his hat and ran out after his friend.

"So what do you want a round of applause? I can handle the customers." Tamsin spat.

"Why are you so angry with me?"

"Because you are here and John's not!"

"That doesn't make sense."

"Doesn't it? Well while you have been adventuring we have been living in the gutter."

"Adventuring? I have been a prisoner—"

"You don't look like any prisoner I know, no prison pallor, your clothes are travel stained but they are good. What kind of prison treats you like that?"

"Would you rather I was broken on the rack or burnt for a heretic?"

Tamsin looked as if that was exactly what she would have liked.

"Tamsin, go and feed Luisa. It's not Richard's fault he is here and John is not."

Tamsin did not look convinced but grabbed the child and went out back. Richard sat down and sucked his sore knuckles.

"She is angry at the world."

"Alice, you have not had to...that is...you...?"

"Tamsin is the only prostitute in our household if that is what you are asking."

"I did not mean to suggest anything. Whatever you have had to do to stay alive, I would never question. I've done things I am ashamed of, so that I might live."

"Such as?"

"I made myself useful to my captors in ways of business so that I did not have to suffer the brutality meted to others. I was saved from death by Luisa's father."

"What?"

"He abandoned Dom Antonio, sold honour for money."

"And you?"

"I don't believe I betrayed the Queen or England."

"And me?"

"What do you mean, Alice? Everything I have done these two years has been solely for the purpose of reuniting myself with you. My love I cannot bring back the dead. I cannot imagine what you have gone through. But I will spend the rest of my life making it up to you."

"We have no money, no prospects, no friends."

"We don't need friends, we have each other and although I don't have ready money I know how to get it. I will rebuild our prospects."

He laid Luis de la Castro's jewelled earring on the table.

Chapter Forty-Two

Somehow it felt unnatural lying in a bed with his wife. So much had happened in his absence, he was not the same man. He done things and said things and experienced things that had changed him forever. Was he being truthful when he said all his actions had been a means to an end; to return to his wife and family? That is how things had begun but was it how they had ended? Alice had been his perfect woman but he scarcely recognised the person who lay by his side with the one he had held in his memory during his captivity. Had she changed so much, or had she always had the look of a peasant? He broke out in a cold sweat, he was callous and shallow, he must put from this mind perfumed air and hot breath, tomorrow he would reclaim what was his.

He breakfasted on horse loaf and ale to the angry stare of Tamsin and the perplexed look of Alice.

"I am going to see the Sohiers and get back my girls."

As he left the tippling house he bumped into George Parker. He gasped to see Richard and dropped a packet of fish he had with him. Richard nodded briefly and Parker nodded back, he picked up the fish and muttered that it was for Alice. She came to the door and thanked Parker for the gift he pressed into her hands. "How is Will?" she asked.

"He caught them for you," muttered Parker as he turned on his heel and walked back towards the ferry.

Alice looked a little uneasy, "Well we can't afford to be proud," she said clutching the fish as she went back inside.

Richard left for the Sohiers but went first to the goldsmith shop to arrange for the sale of the jewelled earring. He found his way to Mr Darvolle. The man looked at him with suspicion and why would he not? He did not look like a man who would own such a jewel.

"How did you come by this?"

"It is mine, payment for two year's captivity in Spain."

The goldsmith seemed surprised and then studied Richard's face more carefully.

"I know you, I think I know you."

"I am Richard Mudford."

"Of course, you were town sergeant, you sailed with Norreys. Everyone thought you dead."

"I very nearly was."

He examined the jewel closely, "It is a very fine piece."

"I know. And I know what it is worth."

"It's worth what I can get for it, I'm not sure there is a suitable customer here, there aren't the men of wealth that once there were." He sighed and gnawed his lip, "It would go better in London."

"You have contacts, you will receive a good commission. I just would like something on account, to show good faith."

They agreed a price, less than it was worth but more than Darvolle had wanted to pay. Next he would go to the Sohiers, he had promised himself not to touch the dowry money that had come with his disastrous first marriage, and to pass it on intact to the girls, but needs must and he would earn them a new dowry. He headed down to the French Quarter, the Sohiers still lived in the same relatively modest house where he had come to court Jeannot. He wrapped on the harke ring and a dourly dressed young woman came to the door.

"Is your master at home?"

"My master and my mistress are at their prayers."

"I'll come in and wait." Richard pushed past the astonished girl. "Tell them Mr Mudford wishes to meet with them."

The girl scurried away, he heard raised voices, a scream and then Madame Sohier appeared in the hallway, her husband at her heels. Richard made a low bow. Madame looked as one might if a ghost had shimmered into the house. Monsieur Sohier looked unbelieving. He also appeared to be ill, he was bent over now, his hair thin, his skin showed no colour.

"Richard, my boy, is that you?"

"Yes, sir, I am come home." The older man shuffled across the hall and embraced him, Richard could feel his bones.

"We thought you dead," said Madame Sohier. Wished more like thought Richard.

"I have come for my girls."

"They, they are about their business, it would not be good for them to have this sprung on them, they would be upset."

"About their business? They are small children. As for a surprise, they will not remember me, they were babes in arms when I sailed. But nevertheless I am their father and I will see them."

"My dear, he is right we cannot deny him," said his father-in-law.

With bad grace Madame ushered him into the great hall where a small red-headed child was playing with a cup and ball in the company of her nurse. "Jeanne dear, put that away and come here." Madame Sohier spoke to the child in French. Jeanne was obedient and did not make a murmur of dissent. She was dressed in black like a little bird, a little Huguenot bird. "Jeanne, this is your papa, he has come back to us." The little girl tilted her head and looked up at Richard with pale green eyes. Richard knelt down to her level.

"Bonjour Jeanne, je suis votre papa." Jeanne did not seem

very impressed and looked back longingly at her cup and ball.

"And where is Lizzie?" The Sohiers became embarrassed. Monsieur Sohier glanced at his wife, leaving her to make explanations.

"She is about her chores, she helps out–"

"Helps out? What do you mean?"

They said nothing, then Madame Sohier signalled to the nurse, "Take Monsieur to Miss Elizabeth." The woman bobbed and gestured to Richard to follow. She took him away from the family rooms and through to the kitchens. A small golden haired child was stood tiptoe on a chair so that she could reach into sink full of dirty plates.

"Lizzie!" The little girl turned around and smiled. "I'm Lizzie." She spoke in French also.

"Lizzie, stop doing that."

"Oh I cannot, Monsieur, my Grand-mère would be very unhappy."

Richard lifted the little girl down. "Elizabeth Mudford, I am your papa, and I do not wish to see you cleaning dishes."

The girl's deep blue eyes opened very wide and when she smiled her cheeks were dimpled. "Are you really my papa?"

"Yes, really."

"You are very fine."

"Thank you, Lizzie, and you are very pretty." She held up her arms to be picked up and he obliged. He was becoming angry as he saw her patched clothes and bare feet and that her curls were tangled. He marched back to the hall. The Sohiers were huddled together for support.

"Richard, you must understand–"

"I need to understand nothing, except that you are cruel and unfeeling. Jeanne come here."

His other daughter looked confused and then ran to her grandmother. "Jeanne, do as you are told."

"You cannot mean to take her from us?" said Madame Sohier.

292

"I mean exactly that." He strode across the room and pulled Jeanne away from her grandmother's skirts, she began to cry. "Stop that Jeanne." She looked up at him and gulped.

"It's Papa, Jeanne," said Lizzie. Jeanne did not look convinced but allowed Richard to pick her up in his other arm and as they left the hall, Madame Sohier called after them.

"Do not take her, you have no home. What will become of Jeanne? She is better with us, do you hear me? She should be with us." Monsieur Sohier said nothing.

As he walked out of Winkle Street he knew that what Madame Sohier said was true. He doubted they would hand over the dowry now and he could not afford to take them to court. He walked out onto the town quay trying to gather his thoughts and found himself outside his brother's house. To his surprise the door opened and Mrs Lister's daughter Annie came out.

"Annie, Annie Lister." The girl turned to hear her name and then screamed at the sight of him, before blinking her cow-like eyes and squealing, "Mr Mudford! Mr Mudford! Mr Mudford!"

"Yes it's Mr Mudford. Annie, Annie please be quiet for a moment."

"I don't think I can sir, I am that overcome, I thought you dead, I thought you a ghost but then it's the middle of the day and everyone knows ghosts only come out at night. So you must be alive."

"Yes very good, well-reasoned. Annie, what were you doing at Mr Jack's?"

"Well Mr Jack asked me to help out when he went to sea and then after Miss Joan went to Alderman Biston's she asked me to mind the house so I come and give it a dust every now and then, make sure all is well."

"So you have the key?"

"Of course I do, Mr Mudford, or how would I get in."

"Annie, I have come back to find that the Angel inn has

been cheated from my family, and my children have been spread to the four corners."

"And a terrible thing it was, I loved looking after your little ones. And look at them now quite little ladies."

"Annie do you not think Mr Jack would like to see his brother with a roof over his head?"

Annie considered this for a while, "I believe he would sir, he was very fond of you was Mr Jack."

"So Annie, we know what we must do."

"Do we, sir?"

"Yes, Annie, you must give me the key to Mr Jack's house and then you must look after Miss Lizzie and Miss Jeanne for me whilst I fetch Mrs Mudford."

Annie didn't seem at all sure but allowed herself to be ushered back into the house. It was small and compact but well-furnished and a much better prospect than the tippling house. He left Annie with the girls and hurried back to the tippling house. Alice was sweeping the floor half-heartedly.

"Get your things together, we are moving."

"What do you mean?"

"We are going to live at Jack's house."

"We can't do that."

"Why not? I am his brother, his elder brother, he is God knows where, I am the guardian of his estate. Come on, see I have money."

"What about Tamsin?"

"One thing at a time. I will leave some money for her and the children, so she won't need to do... other things, and once Mr Darvolle has sold the jewel there will be more. But first I need to see you safe, the boys returned and we must make our plans. I will get the Angel back and we will begin our life again. You trust me Alice don't you?"

Alice looked as if she was trying very hard to. "I'll go and tell Tamsin to explain. Give me the money. I will pack a few things."

Richard heard them arguing as he waited out on the street but in a short while Alice joined him, her worldly possessions tied in a bundle. She presented him with a battered wooden box.

"Here are your treasures. I sold the chest and some of your keepsakes too but there are a few things left."

He kissed her, "You are wonderful Alice. I love you." He thought he meant it.

He left her for a moment at the corner of Brewhouse Lane as he ran to the Angel he opened the door and whistled, "Jacket!"

The boy's head appeared above the bar.

"Come on you're leaving."

He didn't need to be asked twice but shot out clutching Richard's arm. "We are going to Mr Jack's house, I want all my family around me again."

Chapter Forty-Three

Within a couple of days the house was stocked with food and Tom and Will had been brought back from Itchen Ferry. The girls and Annie had taken over Joannie's room, Richard and Alice had Jack's and the boys crowded into the third tiny box room. It was shortly after that Alderman Biston came to call. Richard expected him earlier but had heard he was away from the town on business. He didn't bother to knock but walked in on the family as they dined, he had young William and Joannie in tow.

"I see your manners have not improved Mr Biston."

"How dare you! What are you doing in this house? It is the property of my son's betrothed?"

"And who betrothed them?"

"What do you mean?"

"Has my brother given his blessing? I thought not, how could he? He is away. And would he give his consent if he was here to his only child marrying into the family of the man who has tried to ruin his?"

"I don't know what you are talking about. You deserted your family and left them no means to pay the loans they owed, their plight is on your head."

With difficulty Richard stopped himself from sticking his kidney knife into the spot where Biston should have had a heart.

"Nevertheless, I am head of the Mudford family, in my brother's absence I am responsible for Joannie and I do not give my consent to her betrothal." Joannie burst into tears.

"You cannot do this."

"Oh I think you will find that I can. Now, Alderman, my family is at supper, if you will excuse us."

He left with bad grace and the ringing of laughter in his ears.

"You should be careful about antagonizing Biston further, Richard," murmured Alice.

"After what he has done to my family, why should I care about what he thinks?"

"He does not play straight, Richard, one of the reasons Tamsin is so angry is that we found out that it had been Bart Biston who had been pressed. He sent a message to his father begging him to be freed Margaret did not want to lose another son at sea. Biston got him out by finding another to take his place."

"John?"

"John. Tamsin is convinced he was chosen deliberately because he was your friend."

"He is a bitter man."

"And malicious, but he has also lost a son."

"And that he lays at my door as well?" Alice shrugged. Richard could not cope with Biston and his devious revenge, not right now, there were more pressing matters.

"I should seek out Alderman Crooke. Alice, do you know what has happened to him?"

"Since his wife died and he lost his money he stays at a room in the Dolphin, he is not the man you remember Richard."

Nothing is as I remember, thought Richard.

"And there is something else, Richard." What more? "Your pa."

"What of him?"

"He's sick"

"Oh."

"He is at the alms-house, I don't think he has long."

"You cannot be too sure, he has fooled us before."

"Richard!"

"All right, I will seek him out. Now children, we are all together again and our first job is to fatten up your dear Mama." They started to giggle, "Your Mama has worked very hard to look after you all whilst I was in Spain and now we must look after her." He raised his cup to Alice who looked wearily back at him.

"Why can't I live at the Ferry with Gran?" William was a stocky lad built like his father but with his mother's colouring.

"Why don't you want to be with your brothers and sisters?" asked Richard. William looked around at the children at the table, "My sister's dead."

"William!" said Alice.

"It's true, and at the village I can fish and sail with George."

"Go to your room" snapped Alice. "In fact it is time you were all in bed, Annie can you help please." Lizzie and Jeanne looked puzzled. They had heard so little English in the last two years they could scarcely follow any conversation. Jeanne started to cry for her grandmother.

Richard went outside to the quay, he gazed out across the water. Alice came and stood beside him.

"It's not their fault, they have all had so many changes."

"I know. I was a fool to think I could just turn up and everyone would rejoice to see me and we would be as once we were."

"It will just take a little time."

Richard looked down at her hand, "Where is your wedding band?"

She covered her bare finger, "I had to sell it." She started to cry.

"Love." He put his arm around her shoulder, "It will get better."

"Promise."

"Promise."

"Do you really think I am too skinny?"

"No love, I just want to look after you, put the roses back in your cheeks."

"I'd like to be as I once was."

He kissed the top of her head, "Tomorrow I will look for work, we need to have a steady income whilst I consider our next move. The money from the jewel will be useful but I need to make sure Tamsin and John's family are all right."

"And he might still be alive and a prisoner, we have to save for a ransom."

Richard could think of nothing to say, their problems were many.

Richard left the house early the next morning. He found Joannie waiting for him.

"Joannie."

"Miss Joan."

"Ah." he started to walk away.

"This is my house, my money."

"This is your father's house, your father's money."

"It's my dowry."

"Joannie, why do you want to marry William Biston."

"He's nice to me."

"His father is a shit face."

"He is my protector."

"Joannie, his only interest in you is how many Spanish ducats your father might be worth."

"It's Joan," she screamed, "And why would he not like me for myself."

Richard thought it best not to answer.

"Joan how could you not help your Aunt Alice and your cousins?"

"Why should I? No one ever helped me."

"I watched out for you when I could."

"You still owe me twelve silver cups!" She flounced off.

Richard went first to see the new Mayor of Southampton. Richard did not know Mr Holmes, so had made a few enquiries and found he was from Salisbury. He had been made Searcher of the Port back in 1570 and had been a free burgess since 1560 but he had never held minor office and he and Richard had not moved in the same circles. He was an elderly man, well dressed, wealthy. He looked Richard up and down.

"You were an apprentice of Mr Crooke. He was once a man of good wealth and trade, sadly decayed by losses at sea," he said wearily, as if it was bound to happen. Crooke had flown too high, got above himself.

"So I understand Mr Holmes, I regret my imprisonment meant I was not here to support him as he long supported me."

"I think nothing could have saved him, he over-reached himself. So you are looking for some position?"

"Yes, sir, I was once Senior Sergeant. I spent many years serving the town. Mr Bullackre, the former Mayor, when he asked me to serve General Norreys said he would look after my family and that my place would be kept for me."

"I'm sure Mr Bullackre, had no thought of you being away so long."

"I had not thought it either."

"You look remarkably well for two years in prison."

"So I have been told, I have a good constitution." Richard tried to keep the bitterness out of his voice.

"That's as maybe. We have no need of any sergeants, the positions are all full. And we have many soldiers and sailors coming back from Spain and elsewhere who are a drain on our resources. Still as a former servant of the town..."

Richard waited scarcely able to breathe.

"...there is a building project?"

"Building?"

"Yes, we require labourers to work on the repairs to the waterworks."

"Labourers!" Richard caught himself and tried to stay controlled, "Thank you, Mr Mayor, I will of course be happy to—"

"—if you have a boy, he could be useful as well."

Richard felt miserable as he went back into the street. He wasn't afraid of hard work but the pay would not be much and he could barely stand to face his enemies gloating at his position. He found himself near to the Dolphin and went inside. He looked for the ostler and asked after Mr Crooke, he found him sat in a dark corner, he was surrounded by ledgers and accounts, paper and parchment, his fingers were ink stained. He was adding up columns of figures.

"Mr Crooke, sir?" He was older now, with a large bald patch in the centre of his head and a straggly crown of hair around. His clothes once grand, were stained and torn. He looked at Richard without recognition, his eyes had lost their sparkle and colour.

"Mr Crooke, it's me, Richard Mudford, your former 'prentice." Richard had felt Mr Crooke might live in the past.

"Richard, my boy, where have you been, nose stuck in a book again? All that study will make you dull, business Richard, business is all."

Richard sat down opposite his former mentor.

"How are you, sir?"

"Well, my boy, lots of schemes, but say nothing we don't want others to know what we are about."

"No sir."

"Have you had your supper? I will ask Margery–" Richard knew Margery Crooke had perished of the same sickness that had taken Christian.

"I have had my supper, sir. I have come to give you this, sir."

"What, what is that, my boy?"

Richard put some coins on the table, "One of your creditors, sir, gave me this to pass onto you."

Crooke counted the money carefully and then made a note on a parchment already much covered in figures. "Well done, my boy, now off to your bed, there is much business to do tomorrow."

Richard was sad to see how his former mentor and been broken in his mind due to his reverse of fortune and was determined not to follow the same fate.

Chapter Forty-Four

It was back breaking work, digging out a channel in the dry compacted roadway. There was a regular gang working, William Brewer, John Singleton, Arnold James, William and John Crocker, Henry Foster and his boy. The waterworks ran from Hill a couple of miles outside the town, down to Water Lane and the Conduit House about halfway along and then onto the old friary before spreading out its clay pipe work around to the churches and also some private dwellings about the town. The pipes had been laid hundreds of years earlier and had been patched and mended over the centuries but now had become so bad with leaks and blockages that they were digging up the whole length. Work had already been going on for some months.

Richard's experience meant that after several weeks the Mayor started to employ him more as a foreman. He arranged for lime bricks to be made and brought to site and he was even sent into Dorset to commission new pipes from Robert Syms the potter. This failed to make him popular with the rest of the workers but he didn't care. Jacket worked alongside him and sometimes William, who was much stronger than the older boy. One day when Alice came to bring them some beer, the gang was a man short and Alice jumped into the ditch, grabbed a shovel and worked as hard as any of the men. The boys were amazed to see their mother as strong as they, laughing and joking with the other workers.

There was one friendly face, Foxe still a town sergeant, who was employed to use his cart to help move materials.

"Diccon Mudford, never thought to see you alive and breathing," he spat out a thick juice.

"What is wrong with your lung?" asked Richard.

"It's tobacco. Want some?" He chomped down on the leaves, "I tell you it's bloody marvellous stuff for clearing blockages"

"No thanks, I'll manage."

"Can't understand them wasting you out here, you were the best sergeant they ever had."

"Good of you to say Sergeant."

"Bloody true, what a way to thank a man who's fought in Spain and been enslaved."

"Well I'm just one of many."

"That's the truth, lost count of how many we've moved on, lots coming out of Brittany now."

"General Norreys is out there fighting I think."

Richard did not like to beg but he knew he had no choice, you could not eat pride and Darvolle had still not turned a profit on the earring. There was a potential buyer but it was not straightforward. Darvolle had asked Richard if there was a mate to the earring. Richard had shaken his head and suggested that it might be better if he found a different go-between. Darvolle had advanced him a little more money.

"If you hear of any other work...." Richard picked up his shovel.

"I'll let you know. The Mayor employs a Hollander for a sergeant you know, a bloody Hollander. Still I thought you might have gone to see the Lord Treasurer." Another spurt of tobacco juice hit the ground.

"Why would you say that?"

"When the Chimney sweeper's son came out from Spain he was taken to see him as they thought he might have useful knowledge, but he wasn't in Spain as long as you. Might be some reward to be had, for useful information."

"Thanks." Richard pondered it for a while, Lord Burghley was the Queen's oldest and most trusted advisor. Perhaps there was something to be done.

"Are you going to do any digging today?" Henry Foster called out. Richard jumped back into the ditch. Foster was a hellier, he would earn 5s for five day's work, Richard would only earn half that. Foxe would earn 2s 8d. just for one day with his cart. Maybe he should invest in a cart.

"Tamsin is in trouble."

"What do you mean?"

"That fellow you beat up has accused her of whoredom, she is going to be ducked."

"The ducking stool?"

"Yes, into the filthy ditches."

"I'll go and see the Mayor, we must be able to pay a fine, we can plead for her, accuse him of unnatural practices. We are not powerless anymore."

"Yes, I'm sure you will be able to fix everything."

Richard bit his tongue at Alice's sarcasm and hurried out to the town ditches outside the north walls. A crowd had gathered, anxious to see the sport. The ducking stool was in position and Mr Holmes was in discussion with the crier. Tamsin stood defiant her hands bound. Richard was horrified to see Luisa tucked in close to her mother's skirts and struggling to hold onto Little John. He went over.

"Tamsin." Close up he could see where tears had coursed down her cheeks and now left dirt-stained rivulets.

"I don't need your help. I don't need anyone."

"Mama," Luisa's lips were quivering, "why have they tied you? Why can't we go home?"

Tamsin looked down at the little girl and her baby, she pursed her lips and then glared at Richard. "If you want to do something useful take the children away."

Richard with difficulty prised Little John from Luisa but when he tried to take the little girl's hand she just clung on harder.

"Luisa, let go this minute and stop that crying, you must never let people see you cry. Go, go with Richard." Luisa wiped her face with her sleeve and held out her hand to Richard. He took it and went over to the Mayor.

"Mr Holmes, sir."

"What? Mudford? What do you want? I am busy."

"The ducking, sir."

"What of it?" Holmes was irritated. He didn't like to spend time amongst the common folk of the town.

"I know this woman, sir, she is a good woman, her husband fought for the town, fought for the Queen and is still a prisoner in Spain."

"What is that to me, sir? She has been found guilty of fornication." His nostrils flared whether at the stench of sin or the foul water in the ditches was not clear.

"Who has accused her?" Richard asked as his eyes raked over the crowd. Little John was starting to grizzle.

The Mayor looked around impatiently, "That fellow yonder."

It was indeed the man from the tippling house. He was sporting two black eyes from having his nose broken.

"That man sir, is a base liar. I can attest that he acts from malice."

The crier was tying Tamsin to the stool and manoeuvring it into place above the filthy, stinking ditch. Luisa was whimpering, trying not to cry.

"There has been a lot of talk about the lewd acts carried out by her, Mudford," Holmes argued.

"Idle gossip sir, not to be believed in a court of law. And as I say I know that the witness has been motivated by revenge."

"Revenge, sir?"

"Aye, I came across him in the tippling house Mrs Dypere runs with my wife. He was threatening to have his way with this child, sir." Richard nodded towards Luisa.

Mr Holmes looked shocked, "Is this true, sir? It is an unnatural act to accuse a man of. I cannot believe anyone could be that corrupt." He seemed genuinely appalled.

The man had become suddenly aware of Richard and his conversation with the Mayor and began to look uneasy, hopping from foot to foot. The crowd was getting restless demanding their sport.

"Did you not notice the bruise on his face, Mr Holmes? It was from my fist as I rescued the child."

"Fighting, I could fine you for that Mudford." Richard fought to remain calm.

"Defending the defenceless, women and children, harassed by villains."

Mr Holmes looked down at Luisa. "Child!" she jumped and moved closer to Richard, the baby started to cry again and Richard's arm was getting numb, "Child, did that man try to hurt you?"

Luisa's eyes got rounder and she said nothing. "Luisa, tell Mr Mayor—"

"That is enough, Mudford, the child needs to speak for herself."

Richard turned at the creaking of the stool as it was being lowered towards the fetid water, again the crowd jeered and Luisa looked terrified. The man was edging back into the throng.

"He hurt me! He hurt Mama! Richard saved us. Don't let them hurt my Mama."

Mr Holmes looked irritable, the stool was on top of the water, the crowd were screaming for Tamsin to be ducked, calling her names and spitting, those who had known her intimately yelling loudest, her hair was already in the water.

"Pull it up, there is a new witness." The crowd turned on the Mayor, angry to have lost their entertainment. Mr Holmes indicated to the sergeants and the watch that it was their job to quiet them. "Van der Plank, find the man, the accuser, he can take the woman's place."

The crowd thought this fine sport and decided to help Van der Plank in his task. They only had the vaguest idea who they were looking for and thrust forward several unfortunates, the real quarry having slipped away.

Tamsin rubbed her wrists and straightened her clothes. She took Little John from Richard without a word, and Luisa grabbed her mother's hand.

"Do not think that I am unaware how you earn your living, Madam. Next time it won't be the ducking stool it will be the branding iron." Mr Holmes strode away.

"Tamsin," said Richard but she walked off without acknowledging him.

Chapter Forty-Five

Alice was starting to regain her former curves. She was more relaxed and although she did not yet have her old energy, Richard thought it would return. After all she was still mourning the death of her child, her two children. Richard wondered about his lost baby and the other baby far away over the sea. He decided it would be better to push such thoughts from his mind forever. Biston had complained to the Mayor about Richard taking over his brother's house but as the brothers had left legal instructions in the event of one of them dying or being away for a long periods, for once Biston could not twist the law to his own ends. Richard had used a lawyer who was a friend of Queen's College who owned much property in the town and who had their own dispute with Biston, so he worked extra hard on Richard's behalf. Richard did an inventory of the house and decided what could be sold if needed and asked the lawyer to look into how he might get back the Angel inn.

He also put aside time to make sure his daughters had a command of the Queen's English. They were still young enough to learn quickly and soon were chattering away to Annie and Tommy in a slightly accented but understandable tongue. He thought it would help if he also taught them their letters and he found time to sit with them most days. Of course it made sense to teach Tommy also and then Jacket asked if he could learn too. William felt left out so grumpily sat down to join them and sometimes Tamsin would leave Luisa also – or rather dump her and her baby brothers on drawstrings. Thus Richard found himself a schoolteacher with children fluttering around him like pigeons; Alice did not approve of education as she thought it gave people ideas above their station but sometimes even she would recite her ABC.

He decided to write to Lord Burghley and tell him something of his sojourn in Cadiz and offer his services to the Queen. He also had a message from Darvolle to say a buyer had been found for the earring. Sergeant Foxe was as good as his word and used Richard on town business where he could. So Richard found himself as one of three men employed to cut up a giant wherpool fish that some fisherman had dragged up and which was deemed to be the property of the town. He was wondering if the 9d he would receive was worth the stench but thought he might end up with a small bag of fish to take home for soup.

He was only vaguely aware of the other activity around the quay. Cutting up the fish was hot work and he sent Jacket off to get some beer for him and the other men. A ship was coming into harbour, Richard glanced up briefly as he took a draught from the jug Jacket brought him and which he passed to the others. There was something familiar about the way the ship handled. He could scarcely believe his eyes. It was the *Magpie*.

Richard's knees almost gave way underneath him. He watched, heart pounding as the ship was tied up, he strained his eyes sweeping the vessel looking desperately for his brother, he prayed he was alive, prayed harder he had come back with booty. There, there he was as jaunty as ever scrambling over the side.

Richard started to run, shouting, "Jack, Jack!"

His brother's blond tousled head turned, searching for

whoever it was that had called his name. He looked shocked and amazed to see Richard. He jumped onto the quay and started to run as well. The men fell into one another's arms.

"Diccon, I thought you must be dead!"

"And I thought the same of you."

"We hoped you'd been taken a prisoner – so that there was a chance of life!"

"And I was, I have only been back these six months. Where the hell were you, Jack? Everything has turned to ashes."

"I went off to kill some Spaniards of course, they took my brother." They hugged again and walked arm in arm up the quay.

"We're all squatting in your house, Jack."

"Why? What happened?"

"I'll explain later, it's a long story – but you can't have been chasing Spanish treasure ships for two years and more."

"We had some luck, helped to take the *Madre de Dios* stuffed full of gold, then I kept sailing, I didn't know what else to do. I sailed round the world Diccon, I sailed right around the world."

Richard was dumbstruck, he grasped his brother to him again. They were at the door of Jack's house, Alice opened the door, her eyes opened so far, it was a miracle they didn't fall out. Jacket and William emerged from behind her, also incredulous.

"Look, Alice, look who is back."

"Where have you been, Jack Mudford?" she clipped him round the ear.

"Give me a kiss, sister."

They all crowded into the hall and sat around the table. Annie brought beer.

"So tell me what has happened?" asked Jack.

"For now Jack all you need to know is that Alderman Biston took advantage of our both being away to steal the Angel inn and put my family and John's into penury."

"Where is John?" Alice peered into her beer and Richard felt a little embarrassed.

"As far as we know still a prisoner. We were captured together and at first kept together but then I was lucky, a merchant who had known me in the past recognised me and my situation improved. I tried to get John out too but by the time I had any influence he had disappeared onto the galleys. There has been no news since. Six months ago I was ransomed and found my way home."

Jack spoke a little of his adventures. The boys were on the edge of their seats, firing questions. Richard knew the tales were probably embellished but were none the worse for that, and he was sure Jack glossed over the deprivations, dangers and fears. Those stories were for late at night between the two of them, as were some of Richard's truths.

"I spent a little time in the Americas trading, plenty of work for the Mudford Brothers Company."

"So the voyage has been a success, we can start to claw our way out of all this–?

"Success? Diccon, sorry I should have said straight away."

Richard's heart sank.

"We don't have to claw brother, we can leap. Ten thousand ducats, I have ten thousand ducats."

There was another stunned silence and then Richard and Alice started to laugh and clasped Jack to them again.

"Not such a wastrel now."

"No Jack, you've come good."

"Thanks, Diccon."

There was a knock on the door, Alice called for whoever it was to come in.

A sailor from Jack's ship entered.

"Captain Jack, I have the woman."

"Christ, almost forgot!" Jack leapt up and went out and came back in with the strangest creature Richard had ever seen.

She was yellow skinned, with high cheekbones and slanted eyes, she had black hair and wore a long dress of skins, beads and feathers and a band decorated with coral around her head.

"Er," said Jack, "this is Saskatan. She's my wife."

Alice sat down with a bump.

★

Richard helped Jack to secure the *Magpie* and their cargo. No one was renting the Pigeon House so they managed to re-let it and they went to see Darvolle about the golden ducats. They also visited their lawyer. They finished by having a drink at the Angel.

"Well it's not what it was when Alice ran it," remarked Jack. The innkeeper gave them a malevolent look and served them with bad grace.

"I'd like to get it back for Alice, she needs something. She loved it here."

"I'm sorry about Christian, she was a sweet little girl." The men were reflective for a moment.

Jack broke the silence. "We have enough money, Alice doesn't have to work."

"She needs to."

"Seems I must go and see Biston and that brat of a child. I told you Joannie was no child of mine. How could she not offer Alice a home"

"She doesn't feel like she owes us anything."

"Well she's probably right, but if she thinks she is getting a dowry out of me she's mistaken."

"Would it be so bad? She seems to want young William Biston, and she would be out of your hair."

"True brother, the voice of sense as usual." Jack snorted and tool a swig of his ale, wincing at its poor taste, "There is something you haven't been telling me about Spain."

Richard looked into his empty cup, "It was hell at first, and I was always aware that death could come at any time but once I had Castro as something of a 'patron' for want of a better word. As long as I was useful to him I got well fed, I slept in a bed. And later I slept in another bed."

"There was a woman?"

"A relative of Castro. There was something devilish about her, the temptation was certainly great. And I do believe if I had not succumbed her vengeance would have been terrible. But after a while...I'm a man and I'm a Mudford."

"Don't be too hard on yourself, Diccon, I would have done the same – and I do know that's no comfort – but you have lived to fight another day and came back to your family, ransom or not. I imagine you could have stayed."

"She said she was pregnant when I left."

"Jesu, I don't know how you do it. The old King would have loved to know your secret."

"Shut up, Jack. What about your wife?"

"Not quite sure how it happened, was doing some trading, but her father made it pretty clear if I didn't take his daughter I wouldn't live too long. She's not so bad, got a lot of useful skills, and she doesn't smell now I have stopped her putting bear fat on her hair. They don't age well though."

"Jack!"

"Well it true."

"Jack, Pa is in the alms-house, he's supposed to be sick, likely to die."

"You haven't been to see him then?"

"No."

"We can go together."

"I suppose we must."

"No one should die alone, Diccon, not even that old bastard. He'll burn in hell soon enough."

"Maybe."

"God I'm tired, Diccon—"

"You must be, we'll move out of your room, give you and Saskatan some privacy."

"Don't you worry about that, I don't intend to sleep at home tonight. I need a plump English girl. Sasky'll be happy on the floor – what? Don't look at me like that, I didn't want to get married, she's a good girl but not my type. She's used to sleeping on the ground."

"Jack."

But there was no moving Jack.

Word had spread like wild fire about the Mudfords' good luck and those shopkeepers who a day before would not extend Richard credit now beat down his door.

Chapter Forty-Six

"Alice, love, you know our fortune is made." She was scrubbing down the table after an orgy of baking.

"What does that mean?" She didn't pause in her task.

"The boys can go to school. We will get back the Angel inn, if you want it, we can enlarge it or lease a house for us to live in. We can have servants and help."

"Everything is fine then." She hadn't even flickered for a moment in her concentration on cleaning the table top.

"No, Alice, I don't mean that all that has past has been swept away, but perhaps we can create something new. Love you wanted to build a business, you were so happy before."

"I had a daughter back then."

Richard took her in his arms but she pushed him away.

"What is the matter with you? Why are you so angry with me? Are you sorry I came back? Are you sorry I am not broken?" Desperation crept into his voice.

"Yes, no, I don't know. I feel you have kept something back from me."

Well he had, of course.

"What? Do you want to know how I was tortured? Do you want to know the guilt I feel that John was left behind? He was my friend I miss him too. I go over and over all that happened in my head and wonder if could I have done more. Would it have been better for him if I had let him drown when our boat was sunk?"

She sank down on a seat. "I don't know what is wrong with me, don't hate me."

"Love, I don't hate you, but I have lost my Alice, my brave, feisty, wildcat. I just want her back."

"I'll try," she said in a small voice.

The children were sat in a circle around Saskatan, they were not sure what or who she was, they poked her and pinched her, and tugged her hair. Saskatan put up with this ill treatment without a murmur, the only interest she showed in anything was the door; each time it opened she looked up looking for Jack. Jack had not been seen for three days. This time when the door opened it was Joannie.

"So it is true. My Pa has come back with a savage!"

"Joannie, don't screech." said Alice calmly, "Come and meet your stepmother."

Richard smiled as he watched the look of horror that crept over Joannie's face.

"Stepmother? He cannot have done this, has he done this to spite me?"

"Why would that be Joannie?" sighed Alice.

"My name is Joan. And he would do anything to ruin my chances."

"I happen to know that he intends to speak to Alderman Biston about your engagement," said Richard.

"Speak to him?" Joannie was suspicious.

"He wants you to be happy Joannie, and so will get you William Biston if that is what you want."

Joannie snorted with derision, "He has never cared about my happiness, I don't believe you."

"As you will."

"Anyway, the Bistons would not want to join with a family that contains her!" She pointed at Saskatan, who flicked a look at Joannie and then took her focus back to the door.

"Ah well that's that then." said Richard reasonably.

Joannie stamped in frustration, "Where is my father?"

"Out."

She banged the door loudly as she left.

"Do you think she understands anything?" said Alice looking at Saskatan.

"Jack says she has a few words of English but mainly they use signs."

"I can't imagine being taken across the ocean away from everything you know."

"Perhaps you could help her out?"

"How?"

"Get her some other clothes, dress her hair, make it so she does not stand out so much."

"Would she want that?"

"I guess that it might make her more attractive to Jack and God knows why but I think she would like that."

Alice kissed Richard's cheek. It was the first unsolicited show of affection she had made since he had come home. It stirred his heart.

Jack had done a deal with Biston.

"I've promised an indecent dowry for Joannie, and that she will have my fortune when I die – probably at the end of a hangman's noose apparently."

Richard snorted. They were sat around the fire at Jacks house. Saskatan was curled like a cat at his feet and he stroked her hair absent-mindedly. Alice was half listening as she tidied away the empty plates.

"Anyway, these are for you." He handed over the promissory

notes to his brother. Richard scanned them, "They are for the Angel."

"That's right she's back where she belongs, free and clear."

"Alice, do you hear, we have our old home back."

Alice came and sat next to Richard and gazed at the papers in his hand.

"Jack, you did not have to promise that bastard too much did you?"

"Only not to have more children. But as I said to him, I have fucked half the women in the town and only have Joannie to show for it, I have the reproductive power of a Tudor. Told him all the fertility lay with my brother." Richard shot Jack a glance but Alice just laughed.

"You are a terrible man, Jack Mudford."

"Thank you I take that as a compliment. So do I get to use the bed tonight? I think Sasky wants a poke."

"Of course take it," said Alice, "I'll sleep in with the girls and Richard can have Jacket's bed, he can share with Will and Tom."

"Wife! Come and do your duty." Saskatan padded obediently after her lord and master.

Alice sighed.

"What is it, love? Aren't you happy?"

"I'm not sure I can do it."

"What do you mean?"

"Live back at the Angel, there are so many memories."

Richard was a little angry and frustrated. He had thought this would make Alice happy.

"Well we can let the inn, rent somewhere else."

"I'm not being ungrateful, truly. Perhaps it will be fine."

"No, love, I understand." They sat for a while watching the flames till they guttered and died.

"Alice what if, what if we leased a house, a new house with no memories, for us and the children and moved Tamsin and

319

her brood to the Angel. If you wanted you could work on it as a business and if not let Tamsin. You could start brewing, you were keen to do that once."

Alice thought for several minutes, "That is a good plan, Richard."

Richard found himself grinning widely and glad it was dark and that Alice could not see, he gave her a squeeze and tried to fondle her but she pulled away.

"I'm tired, I'm going to go up. I'll see you in the morning."

Richard sat in the chilling air and felt uncomfortable that he could not release the hardness in his crotch. He glanced across the room to where Annie was snoring gently on her truckle bed. He mentally traced her wide hips and thought about her udder-like breasts but shook his head, adjusted his clothes and went upstairs.

Richard and Jack were walking over the causeway outside East Street and were heading towards St Mary's Church, Richard walked reluctantly, Jack whistled. They stopped in front of the alms-houses. There were twenty-five years old now, some 120 feet long and finely built, the town coat of arms stood proudly over the door.

"Needs a lick of paint," said Jack

"Let's go." Richard turned away.

"Diccon, he's our Pa."

"Not much of one."

"I know how he used to beat you, Diccon, I know you stopped him doing the same to me."

Richard hadn't realised his younger brother had known so much, but he still didn't know it all. Still he pushed open the door and they went in. Some of the less frail inmates were sat at the long table spooning porridge. They looked up, any

320

visitor was a subject of interest. The Warden came out from the kitchen with a basket of apples and put them on the table.

"Gentlemen, you don't seem poor enough or sick enough to be in need of alms."

Jack looked at Richard but he didn't speak.

"We have come in search of our father; we have both been at the wars. Our Pa was taken sick and brought here."

"Name?"

"Mudford."

"Ah, you are barely in time gentlemen. I am sorry to say he has not long left in this world, in fact I believe all that has held him here is the hope of seeing his sons one more time."

Jack looked uncomfortable and glanced at Richard but his brother's face was impervious. The Warden led them upstairs, there were twelve beds, most occupied and the Warden called out the unfortunates' symptoms as they passed by.

"Canker of the throat, the surgeon has operated but we have little hope, broken back the bone-setter has done all that can be done, sweating sickness, old age, recently delivered of a bastard child, childbed fever. Ah here we are. Lungs have gone." He stopped at the foot of a bed. A skeletal figure with rasping breath lay in the bed.

"Pa? Pa. It's Jack and Diccon."

With a great effort the old man prised open his eyes and tried to focus, the Warden beckoned them to go nearer. Richard didn't move so Jack grabbed him and pulled him around to the side of the bed and made him kneel so they were on a level with their father.

"Boys, my boys are back." The effort was great and he coughed and wheezed. Jack patted his hand.

"I'm dying boys; old Nick sits on the end of my bed."

The Warden tutted and walked off.

"He knows his own," said Richard.

"Diccon!"

"It's all right, Jack, Diccon never will forgive his poor Pa."

"Why should I?"

"I saved your life, Diccon, you must grant me that." Richard said nothing.

"Come on, Diccon, make your peace whilst there is still time," Jack pleaded.

"And you, Pa? Have you made your peace?" Richard asked pointedly.

"I regret nothing in my life, Diccon. Can you say the same?" He coughed pitifully.

"Nothing? What about my sister?" the old man looked shifty and Jack was bemused.

"Sister? What sister is that, Diccon?"

"Nothing, Jack, forget I said anything." Jack looked from his brother to his father.

"I don't like secrets."

"Pa?" The old man closed his eyes and turned his head. Richard stood up, "I truly hope God can forgive you, I cannot."

He strode away. He waited outside for Jack to rejoin him.

"What is that all about? We should stay; the Warden said he won't last the night."

"I will pray for him."

"Diccon!" Richard walked away and went and stood inside St Mary's Church. He stood for a long while, remembering the events of his childhood. He went and lit three candles, one each for his mother, his father and his lost sister. When he came out Jack was sitting on a wall waiting for him.

"He's gone."

"He lived his life for himself alone."

"Don't we all?" Richard went to walk home but Jack grabbed his arm, "Not so fast. Tell me. Tell me!" His fingers dug into Richard's flesh.

"Are you sure you want to know?"

Jack stared at him.

"Do you remember when Mother died?"

"I remember her loss, not the act of her dying, I was sent from the house, I remember that."

"She died in childbed, like the girl in the alms-house, she got the fever."

"Lots of women do."

"She was delivered of a daughter."

"I didn't know, so we had a stillborn sister."

"She wasn't stillborn."

"What do you mean?"

"Ma was delivered of a healthy child, but then Ma got the fever. I was taken into see her just before she died. She gave me her blessing and told me to look after you and our sister. The baby was crying as if she knew she was going to lose her mama. I was sent outside and Pa went in. Ma died soon after and a little time after that the baby stopped crying."

"What do you mean?" Jack stared at Richard, "No you can't be saying... he wouldn't have done that, not even Pa."

"It was another mouth to feed. I asked him why the baby stopped crying. He wouldn't answer me and when I said I wanted to see her he beat me, I thought he was going to kill me."

"He really was a bastard." Jack thought for a while, "Will you see him in a pauper's pit?"

"Yes I would but he was right, he did save my life, one good deed in a sea of wickedness, so we will do more for him than he did for our mother and our sister."

"If that is what you want, Diccon, then I am agreed."

There was something else Richard wanted to do to ease his conscience, perhaps or because he felt a bond to all the ragged and bedraggled fighting men who limped back to Southampton en-route to who knows where. Some were surely knaves but most had served their country well fighting against all the odds. Richard knew that Hawkins had set up a chest at Chatham so money could be collected to look after the welfare of those who had served in the Navy but who had now fallen on hard times. He went to the smith and had a strong metal chest made with a stout lock and metal bands and then he went to see the vicar of St Michael's to ask him if he would hold the chest in the church so that on hearing God's word, men might be moved to charity.

"Say it is Philip of Spain's chest and here is a donation from that King." Richard tossed in some Spanish ducats.

"That is very generous of you, Mr Mudford." The vicar's eyes lit up.

"And the money is for poor, sick and wounded sailors only." The vicar said this as a statement, and he was dejected by the thought but could do nothing but acquiesce.

Part Eight

1593

Chapter Forty-Seven

Richard had been glad of all the activity. He and Alice had taken back the Angel and had it cleaned, repaired and painted. He had purchased a licence to brew and restored the equipment long left to dust and rot. Tamsin, though still cool towards him, was glad to move to the inn with her three children. Annie's younger sister Dowsabell had been employed as a general servant. They converted one of the rooms into guest room so they might put up visitors and their old back room became a private parlour for those wanting more privacy than the bar allowed. For his own family Richard rented a magnificent corner tenement on the edge of St Michael's Square opposite the old Lord Chief Justice's house. It had a great barrel vault beneath and was spread over three floors. Jacket had his own small room, as did Annie and the two younger boys and the 'twins' shared a larger room each. Richard and Alice had a graciously appointed bedroom with a private solar and downstairs even had room for an office for Richard. There was also a courtyard, buttery and kitchen and other working rooms, and more that might later be brought back into use.

Alice thought it too large and expensive, she feared they were stepping above themselves for the house was fit for a mayor. Richard hushed her with a kiss, she would get used to luxury. She pulled away still wearing a worried frown. Richard was saddened at her obvious discomfort, as if she felt she did not deserve to live so well and she seemed uncertain as to whether to unpack their meagre belongings. Richard told her they could furnish the house new but Alice wanted to wait awhile, afraid it seemed that they might yet be evicted. There were odd bits of furniture left by the previous tenant and Alice said they would do for the time being. Some of the pieces were good and sturdy albeit dating from a much earlier age, but Richard wanted to make sure there were good beds at least and had a quiet word with one of the town carpenters.

Jack said he had no need for a bigger home and he and Saskatan stayed on at Quay House. Well that was to say the house had Jack's name on the lease, but he was seldom there. His poor lonely wife sat for days alone in the hall watching the door until Alice could bear it no more and installed her in the room she had set aside for guests. Saskatan became her devoted follower, trailing around until Alice was fit to scream. She did discover that Saskatan could do beautiful beadwork, making hangings for knives and pretty purses. Alice saw an opportunity to make trifles and trinkets for sweethearts. So each day Saskatan would go with her to the inn and sit outside in good weather or in the corner by the fire in bad and work away making her wares. The Mayor was unsure if this was in breach of some town ordnance but Richard quieted him with a small craft fine. Saskatan even learnt some English and would tell the children of her homeland. Their chatter became speckled with native words as they invented their own private language. Every now and then Jack would appear and lift up Saskatan and swirl her around. Her eyes would shine and they would spend a little time as husband and wife till he went off on another adventure and she returned to pining for him.

Jack decided to invest his money in the expensive repairs

that were needed to make the *Magpie* seaworthy again and had her moved around to West Quay just along from the Pigeon House. He would often take William to see the men work on the ship, which the boy adored and it helped him forget his misery. He had threatened to run away to the Ferry village after he was enrolled along with young Tom at King Edward's free grammar school in Winkle Street. He hated it, Tom loved it. The school consisted of a large room and three smaller ones over the town stable. The boys started their day at six in the morning and did not finish till five o'clock at night, although there was a two hour break in the middle of the day.

William could not fathom why they were expected to learn Latin and speak it to one another at all times. He struggled and his parents thought in the end if he could master reading, writing and some arithmetic they would think his stay a success. Tom, though very young, was according to the Master, a born scholar who would go far, perhaps as far as university. Richard dreamed that his son might even gain a post at Court as other graduates of King Edward's school had done. He asked Alice again if they could properly acknowledge Tom as their very own boy, sprung from their love and loins and not a merely a charity foundling, but still Alice baulked. She also continued to spurn any advance he made to her, so Richard was glad of the activity around the house and warehouse. He spent more time at target practice and turned once more to tennis; it burnt off his energy and stopped him lusting after other women.

Richard was in his office auditing accounts. They had spent a great deal of their booty money, and Richard had snuck so many pieces into their house that the furnishings were now very fine. Alice thought it wasteful to have their plate engraved with their initials but Richard felt the need for some display. He was only too aware of the baseness of their background but knew if you had talent and made money you could get to the top of town society that was what he wanted for his children. Many of the town burgesses and their wives were not impressed or taken in by fancy crockery and Alice complained about their sour looks and unfriendliness; Richard said they would come around. Jack felt they needed a new ship, the *Magpie* was getting old and he was keen they had more than one vessel at their disposal. There was always a danger of losses at sea but he argued if they had one ship for local trade and one that could venture further afield there would be even more profit. Richard looked up as Alice came in. She was in a beautiful russet gown, which she thought ostentatious, but she looked so very fetching in it that she was eventually won over.

"You will never believe who has just come to the inn."

"You are looking very lovely, Mrs Mudford." She blushed and waved him away.

"Guess?"

"Philip of Spain."

"Don't be an idiot. It was Bart Biston come to ask if he could have his old job back." She was barely able to keep the incredulity from her voice.

"He's not made his peace with his father then?"

"Seemingly not. His life is beginning to show in his face." Richard made no comment but Alice carried on, "He is becoming jowly, eyes bloodshot. I always wonder how Jack can live a life of debauchery and still look like an angel."

"Does Jack look like an angel?"

"I remember when I was young there was a window of stained glass, it pictured the Angel Gabriel visiting Our Lady. I cried so much when the reformers came and smashed it to pieces, I kept a sliver of the glass for years. Anyway, I always thought the angel looked like Jack."

"Sure it wasn't depicting the serpent and Eve?"

Alice focused back on the here and now. "So what are we to do about Bart?"

"We?"

"Should we take him back?"

"Do you need more help?" Richard wasn't keen on Bart and thought there were plenty of other labourers to be had in the town.

"Jacket does what he can, but he is still a puny boy and Bart is strong."

"And lazy as I remember."

"True, well maybe I'll just give him a trial, no promises."

"Well I'm glad *we* sorted that out." Alice did not notice the irony. She lingered.

"I thought I would have an evening off from the inn, we could go for a stroll, the cherry trees are in bloom in the orchards."

Richard looked up in surprise, "Yes, I would like that."

"Good. I will go and make sure Annie sees to the children."

Richard hummed a tune to himself as he finished his paper work. There was a tap on the door.

"May I come in father?"

"Yes, Jacket, but I only have a moment; Alice and I are going out for a stroll."

"Father..." The boy looked embarrassed.

"What? Speak up, boy." Richard was keen to be gone.

"I wonder if I might have an allowance, father?"

"An allowance?"

"You are very generous and I have all my needs for clothes and food and the like met, and I do get some tips at the inn."

Richard smiled to himself, "So what pray tell would you spend an allowance on?"

"There are many things sir – that is I would not waste it, but I should like to put my own penny in the collection at church, and I saw a pretty ribbon that would match Mother's gown. I want to give Alderman Crooke some recompense too." He was breathless after his speech.

Richard was now totally bemused "Why do you need to recompense Alderman Crooke? I have already arranged a small pension for him."

"He has been kind to me."

"How?"

Jacket breathed in, "I know, Father, how he took you as an apprentice and taught you many things and I thought that if I had more learning I could be of more help, so I go when I can to Alderman Crooke. He helps me with my letters, talks to me of business and tells me tales of when you were his apprentice."

Richard felt a lump in his throat. "Jacket, you are right to admonish me—"

"No, Father, I would never, never do that." Jacket shuffled his feet.

"Come here. See this book, I shall call it Jacket's book and I will use it to record the wages you will receive to do with what you will."

"Wages! I don't need wages. How could I take wages? It would not be right."

"Of course, I am stupid, no one pays wages to their children, I meant to say allowance. And I hope to see that you have used it wisely."

"I will, Father." He hugged Richard warmly, "I am helping at the inn tonight, I must hurry or Aunt Tamsin will not be happy." He scampered out and Richard was lost in thought till Alice returned.

They strolled across the square, bell-ringers were practising and washerwomen were hanging out laundry, gossips sat in front of their houses chattering and children played with hoops and balls in the street. People bowed and curtseyed as they swayed by. They went past their old haunts in East Street, out of the gate and in a few minutes were amidst the town orchards all in bloom, pear trees and apple trees as well as cherry, so very beautiful. Alice had slipped her arm through his as they left the house and they felt companionable, an old married couple. They sat under the shade of a tree and listened to the birdsong.

"I like to hear you sing," she said.

"I don't sing."

"Yes you do, I hear you when you are in your office, or if you are in the brewery."

Richard said nothing.

"You have been very patient with me." She said at last as she picked falling blossom off her dress and blew it from her fingers.

"Have I?"

"I know I have pushed you away. I have not done my duty."

"I don't want you to be dutiful." She picked a daisy and another and began to make a chain.

"Richard, I want a baby, I want you to fill my belly."

He sat up with a start from where he had stretched himself on the grass.

"A baby, just as the children are growing enough not to need our attention every minute of the day?"

"Please, Richard, please I want to feel a baby growing inside me, I miss my lost children."

Her eyes pleaded with him.

"You have suffered in the past—"

"—I know what I have suffered."

"And you will only sleep with me to make babies?"

"No, of course not, I long for our former closeness and to be joined to you, but since I lost our daughter I have felt such sadness as I have never known before when I miscarried. And there is such an emptiness where Christian used to live."

Richard plucked a piece of clover, it had four leaves. He tossed it away.

"I had better get to work then." He slipped his hand under her gown.

"What here? Out in the open, with people wandering by?"

"I bet behind every tree there are lovers rolling in the grass."

His hand had reached the top of her thigh, he realised she was no longer wearing the amulet filled with God knows what designed to ward off conception. He moved on in his exploration and his hand slipped down between her legs, "As desperate as you are for a baby I am just as desperate to be inside you again." His breath was becoming heavy, she lay back on the grass and he moved on top of her as she spread her legs wide.

"See, despite our fine clothes we are still peasants at heart," she said in some triumph.

"Don't you believe it, the nobility rut like pigs."

It took him a couple of attempts to thrust inside her and he sighed in relief, she wrapped her legs around him and he felt her muscles squeeze him as if she was determined not to lose any of the precious liquid that would bring her a child.

Chapter Forty-Eight

The Queen was coming to Southampton. The news spread quicker than the plague around the town, a great progress, with lords and knights, a great honour to the town, a great expense to the town.

"I'm so excited," said Alice. She was happier now and at ease with Richard again, she was not yet with child but he was enjoying the trying and if the truth be known was relieved each time her mensis flowed.

"Are you, love, I can feel the need for a new gown."

"You are a man of wealth in the town, we could be presented, I would not let you down. The girls too, they might be asked to give the Queen flowers or some such, they are quite the prettiest girls in the town."

"I think so."

"And the boys, they should have matching doublets, they would look so fine, like pages." Richard was pleased, perhaps as last Alice was becoming at ease with being a merchant's wife.

"Mmm and what should I look like?"

"A hero, a merchant, a privateer–"

"–I'll leave the last to Jack."

"The Queen will love Jack, she loves a rogue."

"It's said she is besotted with that arrogant young Lord of Essex."

"What was he like when you were with him in Spain?"

"A braggart, full of the surety of youth, spoilt but charming, handsome I suppose."

"Will he be with her?"

"Maybe, she will travel with most of her Court, and I dare say stay with the Earl of Southampton, another pretty boy and a close intimate of my Lord of Essex." Alice was enthralled, she loved gossip, especially about the great people.

"How do you know such things?"

"From the burgesses and traders from London. I expect most of it is just stories, but you know I like to hear tales of the Queen," admitted Richard.

"If she has a great train with her, they will need lodgings; they will need to refresh themselves." Alice's eyes lit up.

"And they will want it all for nothing." Richard hated to deflate her.

"Really?"

"Would you send the Queen a bill?"

"But to say the Queen visited our inn, it would be a great inducement to others."

"I would have thought she would stay in her castle."

"That draughty old place, it's hardly grand enough for Her Majesty."

Richard looked out of their chamber window; he could see the keep thrusting into the sky overlooking the whole town.

"Come away from the window, I don't want everyone to see my husband naked."

Richard smiled and came back into the room. Alice was straightening the bedclothes. She still had a well fashioned figure, there were fine stretch lines and the heaviness of her breasts had made them droop a little but the physical work she had always done meant her arms were defined and her waist slim. She was as yet only twenty-seven. She straightened up and surveyed her work.

"I still feel there is something wicked about being abed in the middle of the day."

"It's not as if we were sleeping."

"I think that maybe this time." She smoothed her belly. Richard came across the room and took her in his arms and kissed her long and tenderly.

"We could try again, just to make sure." He slid his hands down to her buttocks.

"I have work to do, Mr Mudford, and so do you. If we are to have more children you must make another fortune."

"Just how many more children are you planning?"

She tilted her head as she considered, "Perhaps three."

"Three?" It was Richard's turn to consider, "Alice, how many children do you have?"

She looked quizzically at him. "I have two children living."

"Ah."

"And two stepdaughters of course," she added hurriedly.

"And Jacket?"

"He is Thomasina's boy, you should not have encouraged him to think we are his parents. We have looked after him but he should not think it is more than that."

"That's a bit harsh, Alice, we are all he has."

"You have changed your tune; you were always at me to put him out." She was a little snappish.

"I know."

"Just because he clings to you and calls you father." She disentangled herself from his grasp and started to dress, "I will always keep my promise to his mother. I will give him a home till he is grown but in a couple of years he will be sixteen and should make his own way in the world. We must look to our actual children." She turned her back to Richard so he could lace her into her dress. Attired, she stood on tiptoes and kissed

337

his nose. "Now I must go and chivvy that new maid, her idea of polishing and mine are far, far apart."

The door banged behind her and Richard dressed slowly. When he was done he left the house and walked down the street to the Angel. Inside he found Bart Biston spread out on the settle watching Jacket sweep and clean the bar to get it ready for business. Richard pushed his feet off the furniture and Bart tumbled to the ground with a curse.

"If you want to keep this job, Bart, then you should try doing it." With bad grace and no apology he grabbed the broom from Jacket and started to push dust around the room. Richard signalled Jacket to come outside with him. They sat on a bench, it was a bright day but not yet warm.

"Do you like the brewery trade, Jacket?"

The boy looked confused, "Erm, I am trying my hardest–"

"–that's not what I asked. Truth now boy."

"I like it well enough. I like to help out, to be useful." He wasn't sure if this was the right answer.

"Jacket, you will soon be a man." Looking at his small frame it was hard to believe, "You must have a trade."

The boy swung his legs, scuffing his boots, "I don't think I want to be a brewer. The barrels are so heavy and I don't like it when people get drunk."

"Then what would you be?"

"If I could be anything in the world I would like to be a merchant, like you, Father."

Richard was afraid he would say that. "Very well Jacket, then we should give you a trial and see if you have any skill. You will come to my office every morning and I will teach you what I can, what Alderman Crooke taught me. I am still learning myself of course. Mostly I have just traded little things, took parts of deals Alderman Crooke had made, or side deals that could be done when you were a town official. It has only been since we chanced our luck at privateering that I have traded big cargoes, butter, fish, Spanish wine, and that disgusting tobacco weed."

Saskatan was sat on a barrel outside the inn, chewing on a knot of tobacco as her fingers worked tirelessly.

"Good morrow, Sasky." She gave him a nod.

"Look at my bracelet, Saskatan made it for me." Jacket held out his thin arm, brightly coloured beads circled his bony wrist.

"Fine work, Sasky." Richard thought again, "I will talk to the muster captain as well, Jacket, we need to build you up, and you need to learn how to use a gun, being a merchant has its dangers too."

"Guns!" His eyes lit up. "William will get jealous; he loves to shoot guns and arrows."

Richard thought about the target William had set up in the yard to practise, they had nearly lost a good servant in the process.

"Tom wants to be a knight and learn the sword."

"A sword won't help you much against a stone cannonball."

"He says it is a skill any actor will need, like dancing and singing and tumbling."

"He seems to know a lot about play acting." Richard's eyes narrowed.

"The schoolmaster is writing a play for the scholars and Tom has a part."

"Ah." His children had an entire life he knew nothing of. "I always liked plays; I expect there will be plays and other entertainments when the Queen comes."

"I long to see the Queen."

Jacket, like many others thought of their Queen like a fairy princess and she encouraged it. Richard knew she was a woman of near sixty and wondered how she would hide the wrinkles and thinning hair.

They were shopping for material, as were half the burgesses' wives of Southampton. Richard had never seen so much cloth in one place, buckram, fustian, grogram, Holland cloth, Norwich worsted, broad and narrow russells, white kerseys, red kerseys such as that he used to wear for his livery as town sergeant, but this was of course not fine enough for a visit from the Queen. Taffeta, tufted taffeta, taffeta sarsenet, broad taffeta, narrow taffeta, Levant taffeta, corded sarcenet, Bruges satin, carrel, Venetian camlet, damask, velvets, fine broad cloth, crimson silk, russet silk, collared silk, silk mockado double and single, and even silk sackcloth. And then there were all the necessaries, Guernsey gloves, furred gloves, Scotch caps, gold lace, lace in chains, lace in openwork, crown lace, biliment lace to ornament the neck and face, partlet, passement lace of gold and silver, girdles, buttons, handkerchief buttons, sisters thread and Spanish thread, crewel work, gartering.

The boys were getting bored and causing a nuisance, the girls were squealing with delight at the pretty ribbons and all things that sparkled. Alice and Annie were pouring over materials in deep discussion with the merchant shopkeeper, who was recommending a good tailor. Alice and Annie were good enough needlewomen but not able to do the fine work needed for such rich fabrics.

"I wish Tamsin would have come," said Alice, "I am going to get this blue taffeta for Luisa, she will look beautiful in it and this for Tamsin. I will get enough extra of the boy's material to make matching outfits for Lawrence and Little John. Jacket, come here and let me see this against you. No, the colour makes you look too sallow."

The merchant pulled out more bales, "How about these mistress? And if I may say, the tailor could make some clever additions to give the young man more shape." Alice was keen to learn more.

Richard drifted towards the door grabbing his two younger boys and took them outside. Some other children were kicking a ball around the street and Richard motioned to Will and Tom to join them. They whooped off, glad to be free.

"Try not to get too dirty or to come back with too many cuts and bruises."

"Children, it is difficult to believe we were all once so lively."

"Mr Payneton."

Richard bowed to the Mayor. He was an aesthetic looking fellow, very measured in his gestures and in his words. He was of country gentry and learned, an attorney by profession. He had acted for the town in its long-running dispute with the Lord Admiral.

"I'm glad to see you prospering again, Mudford." It irked Richard that he had not seen fit to call him Mr Mudford, but his words were soft and kindly spoken.

"I am not sure I have enough money for all the cloth my wife is presently buying."

"Such frenzied activity, the Queen's visit is provoking much excitement."

"I'm sure Her Majesty would not approve of such ostentatious display," said Mr Pett, the preacher and mayor's chaplain. He had tucked himself away behind the Mayor and Richard had not noticed him at first.

Richard and Payneton exchanged glances; ostentatious display was exactly what the Queen would expect.

"Have you seen the Queen before, Mud– Perhaps I might call you Richard? We are both merchants of standing now but I have some year's advantage I think."

"Thank you, Mr Payneton, please do. I was fortunate to see the Queen when she visited here, back in '69 was it? I was just a lad but the Queen had a special connection to me, which she was of course oblivious of – I was born on her Coronation Day."

Payneton clapped Richard gently on the back and smiled. "Special indeed. We must get you more involved in the town affairs. I remember you as an excellent sergeant; I thought you might have tried for other office."

"My time with the Queen's ships and in captivity cut short any hopes I had of that preferment."

"Nonsense, you are still a young man, well set up. In fact I am pleased to run into you as I was going to ask a boon for the Queen's visit."

Richard held his breath worried at what might be coming next.

"I have seen the wonderful work created by your brother's... er..."

"Wife."

"Ah just so, just so. As you are aware it is traditional to give Her Majesty a small gift of money when she visits, back in '69 a purse was brought in London to contain it, and was finished by a local woman. On this occasion however, I thought Her Majesty might appreciate something more exotic that has connections with Her Majesty's colonies in the New World."

"You would like Saskatan to make a purse for the Queen?"

"Just so." Payneton looked as if he was waiting for a rebuke, for a legal precedent to be flung at him that would make him look a fool.

"Mr Mayor, I will speak to my sister-in-law but I am sure she would be delighted to make the present." Richard was relieved he had though he was going to be asked to fill the purse with money.

"This is excellent news–"

"–Mr Mayor, if I may?" interjected the preacher.

"Yes, Mr Pett?"

"I am just wondering about the appropriateness of commissioning a..." He struggled to find an appropriate description, "A...native to provide an offering of such importance to Her Majesty?"

"How so?"

"The woman is a savage sir, not one of God's creatures. Her Majesty as head of our church–"

"Her Majesty has graciously consented to be the Queen of all the strange creatures that are to be found in the northern shores of the Americas."

"Mr Pett, if you would like to make the purse yourself I am sure it will be as nothing to Saskatan. She is a placid, easy-going woman who puts up patiently with the effects of her presence in Southampton," snarled Richard.

"Richard, Mr Pett is over anxious, I am keen to commission the work and the Council is in full support. Perhaps, Mr Pett, you might seek out this Saskatan and assure yourself that she has a soul to be saved and is a good servant to the Queen."

Richard did not know who was most shocked, himself or Mr Pett.

"And, Richard, we must talk more, about salt." Payneton bowed his head and moved on. Richard knew he was a major trader in salt and felt pleased.

The door of the shop opened and Annie popped her head out, "The mistress asks if you would come, sir, she has found the most perfect material for your doublet."

Chapter Forty-Nine

Richard was in his counting house trying to decide about investing in another vessel. He and Jack had decided that they did not want to have other partners if they could avoid it. It increased the chance of profit but also increased the risk. Jack had taken the *Magpie* out for a sea trial. Richard thought he was making for Meadhole a notorious centre for privateers and pirates, a black market for hardwoods, hides, sugar, salt, iron, corn, wine, salt fish and even olives. Jack would feel very much at home. Alice brought him in a mug of ale.

"Thanks, love, figure work is more thirst-making than cutting up fish."

"We are not short of money are we?" She still worried.

"No, love, we are well set up and the inn is prospering, earning, more than enough to look after the Dyperes and give us a healthy profit – must be your beer, you have a natural skill."

"I do, don't I? I was talking to a Flemish merchant the other evening. His family have been brewing for generations and he said they would be glad to serve my beer."

Richard pulled Alice onto his lap, "My clever girl." He kissed her deeply. However could he have regretted returning to her? The heat of the sun must have sent him mad.

"Want to go and make babies?"

"We cannot, that preacher is here again."

"What?"

"I don't know what he thinks he is doing. He sits for hours, reading the Bible to Saskatan, talking theology, I'm sure she doesn't understand a word. He seems to think she will be ready to be baptised very soon."

"I don't suppose it will do any harm and it might be good for Sasky, to be seen as one of the flock. At least it gives her something else to do besides sewing beads."

"Jack is so cruel to her and she is so devoted to him."

"He's not going to change alas and at least he doesn't beat her."

Annie knocked at the door, "Sir, you have a visitor."

"Who is it?"

"It's Mr So-ear."

"Who?"

"The old gentleman who is grandpa to Miss Jeanne and Miss Lizzie."

Alice slipped off his lap and smoothed her dress, "What can he want?"

Richard shrugged. "Show him into the hall Annie and bring us some wine and spiced biscuits."

Annie bobbed and went out.

"I'll leave you to it Richard, the Sohiers always make me feel wanting."

"Love, this is your house, it is they who should feel ill at ease."

She kissed him, "Nevertheless they are your former in-laws," and she swept out.

Richard went into the hall, he was glad to see the old man was alone. He had become very bent over and his breath rattled in his chest.

"Sir, sit please." Richard ushered him to a seat near the brazier that warmed the large hall.

"It is good to see you sir, it has been a very long time."

"Indeed, not since your return." The old man raised his hand, "I know the cause of that is at our own door. My wife misses our daughter, as do I. She blames herself for what happened, although it may seem she takes it out on others."

Richard did not want to rake up the past again. "What can I do for you, sir?"

Annie came in with wine and biscuits and Richard poured for his guest. He noticed how the old man's hand shook as he took the glass to his cracked lips.

"I wondered if you might intercede for us?"

"Us?"

"The Communion, we would like to make a presentation of thanks to the Queen."

"I'm sorry, I don't understand. What you are asking me to do?"

"The Queen has been most generous to the Communion, allowing refugees from persecution to live under her protection here in England. By letting us have use of the Chapel of Saint Julien to worship in the way that ensures our salvation, the Queen has been most gracious, and she continues to support our brethren in the Low Countries and France. We merely wish to thank Her Majesty. We made a petition but have had no success."

"I'm sorry but I don't know what I can do. I neither have Her Majesty's ear or the Council's. I am just an ordinary citizen."

"I had heard you are organising the Queen's gift, and our intelligence has told us..."

"Told you what?"

"Nothing, I am sorry I mistook your position." The old man went to rise but fell back down.

"Sir, are you ill?"

"Old age and I have a canker eating away at my insides. I will be fine in a moment, if I might just rest a while."

"Of course. Would you like to see Jeanne...and Lizzie?"

The old man became quite animated. "Thank you, thank you, Richard, I must admit I had hoped that I might catch a glimpse."

Richard went out to the back parlour. The girls were sat at the virginals he had recently purchased. Their feet did not touch the ground and their faces were screwed up with concentration as they tried to make something that resembled a tune. They would be six years old at the end of the year. Lizzie's hair was still golden blond, with mad, tight curls, her cheeks dimpled and she was carrying a little baby fat. Jeanne was solemn and had the palest skin, the envy of any aristocratic lady, her health had improved somewhat but she still had a fragility about her.

"Girls."

"Yes, Papa." They spoke in chorus without the trace of any accent.

"Your Grand-père is here and wishes to see you."

They looked at each other and clapped their hands. "Grand-père" again unison.

"Come." Richard took their hands, one on each side, and walked back to the hall. When Monsieur Sohier saw them he held his arms wide open. The girls looked up at their papa.

"Off you go." They ran across the room and into his embrace and they all chattered at once in a mixture of French and English.

When it became time to leave Richard walked the old man to the door, his daughters asking him to come again soon. He said nothing but waved and blew kisses. At the door Richard stopped him.

"I've been thinking about your problem. The Queen will arrive by the Bargate. It's a narrow gate designed to cause people to stop, to file across singly. Even the Queen will be forced to move slowly and not be over pressed by her courtiers. If you position yourself outside the gate, away from the notice of the burgesses, you should be in a position to attract the Queen's attention."

"Thank you my boy, thank you. I will make your suggestion to the Communion."

★

Saskatan was being baptised. The church of St Michael was packed as news had got around. It seemed to Richard that the whole town was there except for Jack. Alice had dressed Saskatan up like the finest lady, Richard did not think the outfit suited her, she was short and squat and her face alien to European eyes. Mr Pett was entirely pleased with himself, he beamed at everyone, he hugged a bemused Saskatan and introduced her to the congregation who stared at her. Richard was sure they wanted to prod and poke her as his children had done when she arrived. They were at the front of the church whilst Mr Pett conducted the service and made his overly long and self-congratulatory sermon, before they marched down to the back of the church to the font where Richard had baptised his girls an age ago. Mr Pett stood godparent himself along with Alice. He had painstakingly taught Saskatan responses by rote and nodded encouragingly as he led her through the baptism. She was not impressed to be splashed lavishly with water, especially as it stained her new gown. The service had just completed when the door of the Church burst open and Jack stormed in his face like thunder. He took in the scene, grabbed Saskatan by the arm and yanked her away.

"Sir, what do you think you are doing? This is a house of God, this woman has just been received into the Church."

"How dare you!" stormed Jack, his hand was on his sword which was still at his side. "And as for you, brother, how could you take part in this charade?"

Richard felt his face go the brightest red.

"Jack!" exclaimed Alice.

"Don't say a word, don't say a word." He pulled Saskatan

out of the church and everyone started talking at once. Alice came and threw her arms around Richard.

"I'm glad we decided not to bring the children. Why is Jack so angry?"

"I think I can guess. He does have his own twisted form of honour. He thinks we have abused Sasky."

"He's a fine one to talk. Doesn't he want her to go to heaven?"

Richard waited for a few hours. Jack had a hot temper but it cooled just as quickly. He went down to the little house on the quay. Lights were shining in every window of the house. He didn't bother to knock the harke ring but just went straight in. Jack was sat at the table, he'd obviously had a lot to drink. He was looking at a mouse snatch that had caught a small grey animal in its teeth. He pushed a flagon of wine towards Richard, who poured himself a draft and sat down.

"Sorry, Jack, I thought there was no harm."

"Sasky's furious with me."

Richard was staggered.

"It seems she is very fond of Mr Pett and interested to hear about Jesus. She has taken him a hanging she has made by way of an apology. I told her he won't want anything that is beautiful and brings joy. He is a black-hearted Puritan." Jack sank another cup of wine.

"She was my little savage, wild and new. No one should have tried to turn her into a fake English woman."

"She has her own mind, Jack, she probably wants to fit in, most do."

"Not me. I think we should go back to America but Sasky wants to meet the Queen." He swore and cursed and Richard was glad there were no servants around to eavesdrop.

Chapter Fifty

The Queen's procession was sending up a cloud of dust that could be seen miles away. The town had been dressed, the lions, unicorns and vanes all newly painted. A portrait of the Queen had been placed above the Bargate's main arch, between the paintings of Bevis and Ascupart . The streets had been swept and the walls cleaned, flags hung everywhere about the town. No one was at work that day but instead lined the main street down as far as the entrance to the Castle. Castle Green had been cleared, ready to take the tents and baggage and horses and other paraphernalia. The bell ringers had been practising since dawn, the singers were in voice, the Morris Men set to dance, the waits ready to play. The watch were keeping the crowd in check but everyone was in a merry mood. The Mayor had provided just enough free ale and there would be many parties and feasts that evening.

The town guns had all been brought out of the store and were put above the Bargate ready to salute Her Majesty. The cooks had been at work since before sunrise preparing the Queen's feast. New rushes had been laid in all the civic buildings. Armies of women and men had been pressed into service to help make the castle ready for its owner. Tapestries had been hung to keep out draughts and hide what should not be seen, chimneys had been swept and fires laid, the Queen's plate and her home comforts had arrived before her and were placed in her private chambers. Bakers were baking on extra days, the best wine had been made available from the merchants' vaults, bucks had been sent from noble patrons. Children had been scrubbed clean and were getting tired and fractious trying to remain that way through the long wait. The burgesses and their wives were in gorgeous array and would put many a courtier to shame. The Mayor said he hoped it would not make the Queen or her officials think the town had more wealth than they pretended.

The Queen would be in the town for three days before continuing across the Itchen to travel down to Netley to stay with the Marquis of Winchester, thence moving onto Tichfield the country seat of the Earl of Southampton. It was rumoured that when the Queen reached Itchen Ferry she would plant a pear tree, which induced much excitement. Alice had made arrangements with her former in-laws for them all to be taken across the water to see the great event. Richard and Jack had hired a room in the Crown inn overlooking the main street so they could have an unrestricted view of the royal procession. Saskatan asked if she herself would get to present the Queen with her purse and was disappointed to know that it would be presented, along with its contents of hard money, by the Mayor. The children asked every few minutes when the Queen would arrive and had worked themselves into a pitch of excitement made worse by too many sugary comfits.

"I thought as we had some position in the town we would have been part of the Mayor's party," said Alice, although she would actually have hated to be in their company.

"We are not nearly good enough for that," muttered Tamsin.

She had become increasingly bitter, despite all Richard had done to make life easier for her and her children. She looked much older than her years and her soul was older yet. Her boys were set to be boisterous tearaways as she seldom checked them. That job was left to Luisa, who had grown into a pretty little girl with thick lustrous dark hair and large blue eyes, very much her father's daughter in look but with a placid, friendly nature that could have been John's. Richard wondered what she had inherited from her mother.

"I intend to toss a rose into the Queen's lap. When she looks up I will blow her a kiss. She will become entirely enamoured of me and I will be knighted on the spot," laughed Jack. Richard thought this could be entirely possible.

A huge cry went up as cannon fired, the Royal Procession was at the gate! There were speeches, the presentation was made. Jack had brought a perspective glass along and they took turns to look. The Queen was invited to enter the town, which invitation she graciously accepted. Then the progress continued. Knights and footmen led with tabors and drummers, which clashed with the town's musicians and the din from the townspeople.

The Queen was carried in a golden litter, her dress was of cloth of gold, dressed in rubies and pearls, it dazzled and blinded. Jack nudged Richard and passed him the glass and Richard looked upon his monarch's face. A white mask and painted lips, bewigged with russet hair, her powdered breasts still thrust upward like a virgin girl's. Glorianna. She was not the woman Richard remembered from his youth, but she did not disappoint. It took a good couple of hours for the procession to slowly pass by and disappear into the gates of the castle. Then the festivities began. It was a wonderful day like the celebrations Richard remembered as a boy. There were many invitations to dinners and suppers and Jack and Saskatan disappeared into the crowd. Sasky had become a celebrity due to the story of her purse and many ladies wanted one similar for themselves. Tamsin stomped off back to the Angel, determined to open up and make some money. Annie, Dowsabelle and Jacket went with her to help out.

"Should I go too?" asked Alice.

"Bart's due to turn in isn't he?"

"Supposedly."

"Let's both go and see how things are after we have taken the children home."

"I've given all the servants the night off."

"Well let's tuck them in with Tamsin's little ones, they will be fine."

The inn was heaving; Bart did eventually arrive but was drinking as much as he was serving. Richard took off his fine new doublet so it wouldn't get ruined and Alice tied a large apron over her beautiful gown, looking ruefully at her husband. The exchanged a long kiss before going into the bar. They had been working away for an hour and were all ruddy and sweaty, when a young man in the Queen's livery forced his way through the crowd, losing his hat in the process. It was kicked around the room to the amusement of customers whilst he tried to retrieve it. Alice went and grabbed it, dusting it off and giving it back to the youth.

"Thank you, ma'am. I wonder if you might help me? I am looking for Mr Richard Mudford, I have searched all over and was told he might be here." Alice stood for a while with her mouth open like the village idiot. "That is my husband, he is Mr Mudford, is he in trouble?"

She called Richard over.

"Not that I know of, Mrs Mudford, I have just been sent to find him. The Queen wishes an audience."

The whole bar, which had been listening in intently, fell silent.

"I had better not keep Her Majesty waiting," said Richard, sounding more confident than he felt and reaching for his doublet.

Alice looked fearful. Richard kissed her cheek, told her

not to worry and followed the boy out into the night air. They walked up Bull Street and went in through the castle postern, once they had satisfied the guard. Richard was taken into the Castle Hall, a well-proportioned but old chamber, he knew it was near the private apartments. It was crowded with courtiers, no familiar face anywhere, all looked down their noses at him. He was sure he smelt of stale ale. He waited a very long time, he legs were starting to ache and he was thirsty. Eventually another liveried youth appeared and directed him into a small antechamber, where a small hunchbacked man was sifting through papers. He did not look up for a long while; Richard assumed to make him nervous, and he was nervous but determined not to show it.

"Are you Richard Mudford?"

"Yes, sir."

"I have here a letter you sent to the Lord Treasurer." He waved the paper that Richard had despatched to Lord Burghley some time previously. Richard said nothing.

"It says you have been in Spain." Richard remained silent.

"It says you are very familiar with the town of Cadiz." Again Richard kept his peace.

"And you thought it might be of interest to Her Majesty, why?"

"I had heard that Her Majesty was keen on any intelligence about her enemies. I thought what I knew might have some use, that is all."

"And?"

"I could draw a plot of the town, the harbour, the position of guns, the weak points and where treasure might be found."

"How did you come by such knowledge?"

"As I made clear in my letter, when serving with General Norreys I was taken prisoner. However, I managed to gain a little freedom as a former business associate, a Portuguese gentlemen, took a little pity on me for past favours."

"This would not be Luis de la Castro, sometime agent for Dom Antonio?"

"You obviously have other intelligence."

"How did you get into such a position of trust to gain this information?"

"I don't think I was trusted. I was useful, I kept my head down but my eyes and ears open."

"And how do we know that you are not a secret agent for Spain?"

Richard became immediately worried and uncomfortable. If he was thought to be a spy he could find himself being tortured in the Tower, or worse.

"I have nothing but my career of service to put before you. I was, I think, of some help during the Armada. I felt I needed to do more and so served the General in what was a difficult campaign. I was with the rear-guard and helped to save those that had survived. I was captured and in fear of my life but had one small stroke of good fortune, yet I was away from my family for two years and thought only of how to stay alive and get home. Mr Cotton helped to ransom me and I came home to find my family in desperate straits. I have spent the time since in trying to recover my position."

"And you feel bitter?"

"A little, and sad. I lost my stepdaughter and a baby I never knew whilst I was away. But my anger is against Spain. I know Her Majesty did not want conflict and all she has done has been to protect this realm."

"Your rehabilitation was funded by a jewel brought back from Spain."

Richard wondered how he could've known so much. "I felt I was owed something for my captivity. I took an earring and managed to smuggle it out of the country. I used it to rebuild my fortunes."

"I understand your fortune is based on piracy."

"My brother has Letters of Marque and uses his skill as a privateer to strike blows at Her Majesty's enemies and to accord tribute to the Queen."

"Letters from Justin of Nassau I believe?"

Richard remained quiet.

"Yes, we know well the dubious nature of the men of Southampton, the way they make themselves rich to the detriment of the Lord Admiral and thus the Queen."

"I cannot answer for anyone else, only myself."

"You are an associate of Alderman Biston I understand?"

"Hardly, he has tried to ruin my family."

"Yes he complained bitterly about you too when questioned."

"He thought I had given evidence against him."

"And did you?"

"You know I did not but I would like to shake the hand of the man who did."

"Mr Biston's son works for you does he not?" Of course! Richard was tired of being played with.

"I wrote to my Lord Burghley in good faith, I did not do so to seek reward or favour–"

"Then you are unique amongst our countrymen."

"–and I certainly am not a spy."

"As it happens I believe you Mr Mudford, you do have friends at Court."

It was the first Richard knew of this and he assumed that perhaps Norreys, Hawkins or even Drake must have mentioned his name favourably.

"The Queen was most interested in your intelligence."

"Thank you, sir, and to Her Majesty."

"There are some advisers around the Queen who think another attempt should be made on Spain, but one more focused, something that will make the Spanish think again about another attack, or at least slow them up. Perhaps more akin to the raids Sir Francis undertook in the past. Can we rely on you?"

"Of course, Mr Secretary." The man's eyes flickered, he had not given his name.

"The Queen has graciously agreed to grant you an audience, you may bring your wife and the native woman who made the Queen's gift, she is keen to see one of her subjects from the New World. Come tomorrow." He waved Richard out.

Having left the interrogation Richard realised he had come over in a cold sweat and his hands were trembling. He took a breath, raised his head and tried to walk with something like a swagger. By the time he returned home he had regained his composure. The house was silent and dark, Alice must still be at the inn. He did not know how long he sat, he thought himself a fool for writing the letter, at the time he had hoped it might bring him some reward to help get him started. The door banged and he heard Alice's purposeful step across the hall.

"Richard? Richard are you here?"

"I'm in here."

She came in still holding the small lanthorn that had guided her home.

"Why are you in the dark? Has something happened? What did they want? I thought perhaps you had been arrested as they did with Biston."

Richard got up and lit the candles.

"It was fine, nothing to worry about; they wanted to hear about my exploits in Spain."

"Spain? Why?"

"I have a lot of useful knowledge it seems. Still that is not the best news."

"Why? What do you mean?"

"We are invited to an audience before the Queen; we are to bring Sasky also."

Richard thought Alice was going to faint and caught hold of her. Her musky perfume was mixed with the smell of hops.

"An audience? I have nothing to wear."

Richard laughed out loud.

"I am serious, I wore my new gown today, if I had known I would have saved it, and there is no time to make another."

"Wear the velvet, it's practically new, and you could dress it up with jewels."

Alice did not look convinced. "And a gift, we will have to take a gift. What can we possibly give?" "We will have to send a message to Jack to come here at daybreak so we can form a plan," Richard suggested. She was still in his arms. "And in the meantime, we are alone in the house, with no children to disturb us."

"Is that all you think about, Richard?"

"No, but I do think about it quite often, you are just too tempting." He nuzzled her hair, and she pressed herself against him.

"Perhaps this will be the time; the Queen's visit is a good omen."

"Mmmm." He was kissing her neck and squeezing her breast.

"Come, let us go to the bedchamber, I don't want you messing up my new gown."

"Wife, you are devoid of romance."

"But I have boundless energy."

They were sat around the hall table trying to decide what would be an appropriate gift.

"Why did Her Majesty not invite me?" asked Jack.

"I don't know, I don't know why she invited me."

"I am Sasky's husband after all, I'm going to come anyway."

"As you will, but don't blame me if they turn you away at the gate."

"I'm the only one who has a suitable gift."

"What Jack?" said Alice.

"I have a pair of the softest leather gloves, Spanish leather that I acquired on a trip. I was told the Queen believes her hands her finest feature and she adores gloves."

"Who told you that?" asked Richard.

"I can't remember, some fellow in a tavern I expect."

"What kind of recommendation is that?"

"Can you come up with anything better?"

"No."

"Well shut up then. I'll go and get them wrapped and we'll make ourselves fit to see the Queen."

"The audiences start in an hour's time, we just have to go to the hall and wait our turn, it could take a long time." Richard replied.

"Well I better make sure I have something to eat and have a piss first," said Jack as he got up.

Saskatan looked exotic, having added elements of her traditional costume to her formal clothes. Jack of course was dashing and handsome, Alice was neat, with clothes of good quality but that were not overly showy, Richard hoped he looked fit to meet a queen. Jack talked his way through the gates and they then spent several hours waiting in the draughty castle hall. It looked out over the Royal Quay at Castle Water Gate and was next to the Royal cesspit, so the air was unpleasant despite the newly laid rushes and other perfumes that choked the air.

Sasky was stoical, Jack amused himself by flirting and gossiping, Alice was at first overawed and then became bored and tired and rested her head on Richard's shoulder. He was bored too, he didn't know how courtiers could bear the endless waiting, he was getting cramp, wanted to relief himself and his stomach was starting to grumble. And then suddenly a liveried servant was before them and they were taken to the presence chamber. When they reached the door, they were informed of the etiquette, not to speak unless spoken to, to bow and curtsey low and not rise till indicated, to stand back until called forward. And then in they went. Alice curtsied low pulling Saskatan down with her, the surprise almost causing them both to topple. Jack's obsequiousness was, of course, perfect as if he spent all his days in the company of princes. Richard thought he made a fairly good fist of it and managed to glance at the Queen through his lashes as he bowed.

"You may rise." Her voice was strong with the weight of thirty-five years of autocratic rule, "Mr Richard Mudford, come forward, so I may see you." She emphasised the 'Richard' and Richard felt his brother's frustration. The nerves fluttered. He knew she was not as tall as she appeared but the Queen was famed for her performance of monarchy. Yes, she was much older than the striking woman he had seen so many years before, and there was a touch of the sadness of old age about her but the veiled eyes showed she was still a woman of power and intelligence. He glanced at her hands and she with a movement of consummate grace offered him one to kiss. He bowed again and kissed her ring.

"Mr Mudford." She glanced up "And your family."

"Majesty." His voice sounded funny and he tried to clear his throat.

"So you think you may be of service to your Queen?"

"I have always hoped that, Majesty, and strived to serve my Queen."

"I understand you are a very good shot, Mr Mudford." She said it as a statement of fact and Richard did not quite know what to say.

"I...er...I had some luck during the recent wars, Majesty."

"I received a good report of you from the Lord Admiral at the time of the great threat to our reign."

"I am flattered the Lord Admiral noticed my small part."

"Especially as you have conspired to deny him his rights to pirates goods, along with the rest of the burgesses of Southampton."

"Er, there is a case to be made on both sides, I am not informed enough in the law to say who is in the right, but I hope I have done nothing to offend the Lord Admiral or Your Majesty."

"Never trust lawyers, Mr Mudford." She twisted a small ring on her long finger.

"And you have been a prisoner?" She asked this as a question, but Richard knew she already knew the answer and more.

"Yes, Majesty, I was held captive in Spain for nearly two years until ransomed by my family." He bit his lip, the Queen might think this a criticism of her and her policies.

"Mr Cotton does much to retrieve our subjects who have been unlawfully taken."

"He works tirelessly, Majesty."

"General Norreys was sorry to lose you."

"It was good of him to say so, I have great respect for him as a commander."

"As do I, Mr Mudford."

She looked at him, and he could not work out what she might be thinking.

"When your letter arrived before the Council, there was much discussion about your motives."

Richard opened his mouth to protest but the Queen held up her hand.

"You do not have to defend yourself, Mr Mudford, there were others who did that more eloquently."

Richard obviously looked bemused.

"My Lord of Essex, Mr Mudford, is quite your champion."

"Again, Majesty, I am overcome to be noticed by such an elevated gentleman."

"Come, you are too modest."

Richard just felt out of his depth. "Majesty, I am sorry if I have offended you in any way. I'm just a common man from a small town. When my Queen asked for men to serve I answered that call like many, many others. I just wish I had done better."

"There, there, Mr Mudford. You did well, I have done teasing you." She leaned forward and he saw her teeth were blackened and how the white paint creased into her wrinkles. "We shall call upon you again. We are about to embark on an enterprise to strike at our enemies. We will call upon you." This was almost in a whisper, and then she raised her voice, "You must be Mrs Mudford and this, our subject from the Americas, who is a fine needlewoman." Alice and Saskatan came forward, Alice bobbed again and Sasky followed her lead. She then tried to reach out to touch the Queen, with whom she was obviously fascinated, but Alice grabbed her hand. "I see you are as intrigued by me as I am of you. I should like to hear more of the Americas." The Queen turned to Alice, "Mrs Mudford, you have a handsome and brave husband." Richard blushed and Alice looked at him as if he was a stranger.

"Yes, Majesty, we are all very proud of him. He is a good husband and father."

"How many children do you have, Mrs Mudford?"

"I have two boys and my husband has two girls from his first marriage."

"Did you cast off your first wife Mr Mudford?"

"No, Majesty. My first wife died in childbed."

"Ah, a hazard women have to bear." The Queen was obviously thinking of someone else. "It is a sorrow to me that I have no children."

"Your Majesty's subjects are all your children," said Alice, Richard was proud of her.

"What you say is true." The Queen motioned to a servant who gave her a small purse. "You must buy some comfits for your children."

"Your Majesty is too kind." Jack could not restrain himself any longer.

"And who is this? I did not expect a fourth."

"This is my brother, Majesty, the husband of Saskatan."

Jack stepped forward and bowed, flashing his blue eyes at the Queen, "Forgive my impertinence, Majesty, but I could not forgo the chance of a moment in your presence, even if it caused me to be clapped in irons."

"Really? I understand being clapped in irons is where many people feel you belong."

"I am the subject of great jealousy, Majesty. Something I know Your Majesty will understand too well."

"Hmmph. Why are all my sailors such flatterers? Who teaches them such sweet ways with words when they are most times at sea surrounded by base men?"

"It runs through our veins as does the salt water."

"I understand you have been most successful as a privateer Captain Mudford."

"Moderately so. If I had a bigger ship or more than one I would be able to give even greater tribute to Your Majesty."

"And do you have any tribute for me today, Black Jack?" She was flirting with him, he knew it and loved it and returned her looks in kind.

"I am overcome that Her Majesty has the time to know my name. Sadly I have been confined to port in recent months making repairs and other business but will sail shortly, for the benefit of my Queen. I have, however, brought Your Majesty a modest favour from the Mudford family."

He withdrew from his doublet a packet wrapped in silk and tied with a knotted string that was obviously Saskatan's workmanship. The Queen hesitated a moment and took the proffered gift and passed it to a white-clad lady-in-waiting. The servant glanced at the Queen who nodded subtly to indicate it might be unwrapped. Inside lay a beautiful pair of soft gloves in Spanish leather, trimmed with gold fringes and edged with tiny seed pearls embroidered on the cuff. Her thin lips formed into a smile, her dark eyes softened.

"I thank you all, they are fine gloves indeed. Good day to

you Mr Mudford, I thank you for your service and for bringing your family to meet with me." Richard bowed his head with a jerk as he caught sight of the Queen's earrings. He recognised the jewels. They were a matching pair to the earring Richard had smuggled back to England from Spain. The Queen's hand fluttered to her ears.

"Part of the crown jewels of Portugal, given in thanks by Dom Antonio for our support. For several years I could not wear them as one had gone missing. Dom Antonio did not know how but miraculously they were recently reunited." Richard blinked.

"They suit Your Majesty exceedingly, no ears could do them more justice, no jewels could have a better setting."

"Very good, Mr Mudford, very good indeed."

She indicated they should now leave, and they bowed as they walked backwards out of the chamber. Jack was ecstatic.

"Did you hear that? She knew my name. I knew she wanted me to come. Did you see that jewel at her breast? A pelican. That is what I am going to name our new ship Diccon, the *Pelican*, in honour of the Queen, the mother of us all."

"She still has her breasts uncovered like a young virgin girl," said Alice, obviously somewhat shocked.

"The Queen is unmarried, it is her right." Richard always leapt to the Queen's defence.

"She was a little heavy with the rouge I thought," Alice muttered.

"Ssh wait will we are outside" said Richard, he was still convinced he was about to be arrested.

As they walked back to their house Alice continued to comment on the Queen's wig, the jewels, the embroidery on her gown, the height and stiffness of her ruff, the tiny crown headpiece in her hair, the smallness of her hands, the length of her fingers, the sturdiness of her body for one of her age, the strings of pearls about her neck, the width of her farthingale, the magnificence of her sleeves, her kindness to think of the children, her ladies all in white. She asked if she had disported herself appropriately, about the depth of her curtsy, the meanness of her gown, her lack of fine jewels, whether she should cut and curl her hair. She gloated at the thought of all the proud women of the town who would be beside themselves with envy. Richard nodded and grunted in what he hoped were the right places. Jack hugged and kissed Sasky, praising her needlework. Sasky was happy to have met the Queen who looked like a great warrior and chief. Yet Richard cursed that he had ever written to the Council, he was certain he would before long find himself on a ship back to Spain.

Chapter Fifty-One

They were all down on the shore of the River Itchen. For hours the Queen's baggage and household had been ferried across the water and a small encampment had set itself up on the Ferry village side. The horses and courtiers would be next and only at the last would the Queen herself come to be rowed across. That honour had been given to George Parker. Richard's party were to be taken across by young Mark Dypere a cousin of John's. He was barely into his teens but already broad and strong from rowing, and nimble and lithe from scampering around the little ferry boats.

The boy cast an eye over Alice, the children, Annie, Tamsin and her brood, old Alderman Crooke, who Richard felt had earned the right to see his Queen one last time as he had masterminded her last visit to the town at a cost of over two hundred pounds. Then there was Jack and Saskatan. "It will probably take two trips, Aunt Alice."

"I'll help row," said Will, leaping into the boat despite a cry from his mother. Richard helped Alice into the boat and lifted the girls in after her, Jeanne was nervous of the water but Lizzie leaned over the side until Mark told her to sit still. Annie clutched at Mark like a wrestler until she was seated safely in the centre of the boat. Tamsin passed her Little John and then went aboard with Lawrence in her arms.

"Jacket, you go with them and help out on the other side." The boy went and sat next to Tamsin. Will and Mark took the oars and Richard pushed them off.

"Luisa! Where is Luisa?" Tamsin looked around her.

"I am here, Mama, with Tom." The little girl took Tom's hand and held it tight as he tried to pull it away and complained to Richard.

"Tom, stop whining, in a short while you will be begging girls to hold your hand." Tom looked dubious and called out to Will to encourage him to pull faster.

On the bank Sasky squatted down, looking at all the activity around her. Alderman Crooke nodded, called out and pointed as if he were still Mayor and in control of all.

"Jesu, what a palaver," said Jack.

"Unbelievable," agreed Richard, "I'm sure the chaos must be organised."

They heard someone calling them and turned to see Alderman Biston, Margaret, young William and Joannie pushing through the crowd.

"Do you have a boat?" Biston took rudeness to a new level.

"We are waiting for Mark Dypere to come back." Richard pointed to the little ferry boat about half way across the river.

"You must let us go first."

"Why?"

"I am senior burgess, I need to attend the ceremony."

"You should have planned better," said Jack.

"I don't need a pirate to tell me what to do."

"Privateer!"

Biston snorted. "Under letters from a Dutch sea beggar."

"Under letters from the Queen."

Jack took even more pleasure than was strictly necessary in withdrawing from his doublet the Letter of Marque he had received from the Queen that morning. Biston snatched it away and read it greedily, his eyes and mouth widening with each word. He thrust the letter back at Jack, who folded it neatly and put it away.

"Her Majesty must be losing her faculties," Biston muttered.

"Careful Alderman, remember what happened last time you made comment on the Queen," said Jack.

Biston turned from crimson red to palest green. "You have promised me dowry money, think of that when you go off on your adventuring."

"Do you hear that, Joannie? Your future father-in-law won't take you without a large bag of money."

Joannie burst into tears, Margaret tried to comfort her, William Biston thrust out his lower lip trying to think of some suitable riposte.

"Why you make your daughter cry?" Saskatan poked Jack.

"Joannie, don't take on so, I will buy young Biston for you, I promised. Now come and greet your stepmother."

Joannie stopped crying abruptly and began to scream. "I will not, she is no mother of mine, she is a savage." Jack went to strike his daughter but she dodged his blow and ran back towards the town.

Saskatan showed no emotion but just returned her attention to the river.

"William, go after her," said Margaret.

"No, I want to go to see the Queen."

"Biston, speak to your son."

"Leave him be, Margaret, the girl will be there tomorrow, the Queen will not."

"Margaret, my dear girl." It was Alderman Crooke, back from ordering the Queen's packers around.

"Father?" Margaret looked embarrassed. Richard knew she had not been near her father for many months and could not forgive her, even though he felt sure she had been stayed by Biston.

"See, see how busy your father is? There is so much to do, the Queen does us such an honour. She is a grand girl, her father's daughter."

"God spare us," muttered Biston. "Boy, over here!" he gestured to Mark who was just pulling up on the shore. Before anyone could say anything Biston was clambering aboard beckoning his wife and son after. Mark wasn't happy but Richard tipped him a wink and tossed him a coin. Much to Biston's fury he helped Alderman Crooke and Saskatan into the boat also.

"There is no room, we will capsize!" yelled Biston. Jack shoved the boat away. The brothers laughed as they watched Mark row as badly as he could to make Biston's journey both long and tortuous.

"There's the Queen!" Luisa started to pull Tom after her and towards the gloriously presented Elizabeth. The largest vessel possible had been put at the Queen's disposal, but only after it had been repainted, lined with cushions and other necessaries. Richard and Jack caught up with the children close to where the Queen was being helped into her boat. Luisa and Tom were calling out at the top of their lungs. The Queen turned and nodded in their direction and then caught sight of Richard and Jack.

"Yours, Mr Mudford?"

"The boy, Majesty, the girl is the daughter of John Dypere, my former comrade still imprisoned in Spain."

The Queen stopped for a moment and then stepped aboard. A moment later one of her ladies was instructing the boat captain to bring Richard, Jack and the children on board.

"Your Majesty's thoughtfulness and kindness is boundless," said Jack.

"Her Majesty is the most thoughtful of sovereigns," said her pretty young lady-in-waiting.

The Queen was surrounded by her closest circle so they were prevented from any further conversation but Jack lifted up Luisa and Richard did the same for Tom so they could ogle the Queen and store away the memory for their grandchildren. The Queen's boat made land before Mark Dypere's but that boat was close enough for Biston to stare astounded as Richard and Jack disembarked in the Queen's entourage. The Queen was whisked away up towards the green where she was going to plant a pear tree. Richard couldn't see the rest of his party and assumed they had already gone on to secure a good vantage point. Jack said he would wait for Saskatan and Alderman Crooke who were just coming into land, so Richard took Tom and Luisa by the hand, told them to hold tight as they were in danger of getting lost in the crowd, or being trampled under a horse's hoof.

"I have never seen so many people, Pa, not even at Trinity Fair," said Tom.

"You will probably never see anything of the like in your life again Tom. Take it all in, I'm sure your masters will be asking you to write about this day in your lesson."

Tom groaned, "But they will want it in Latin. I shall write a poem for myself and our family in the English tongue."

"Sounds an excellent idea, Tom. I believe there will be some performance on the green."

"Do you mean a play?" Tom could hardly contain his excitement. Luisa cried out as a horseman galloped too close and Richard caught her up in his arms, and then grabbing firmly hold of Tom again carried on up the hill.

"Yes a play, two of the greatest acting companies in the land have come together and lately arrived, I think the Mayor has asked them to contribute to the festivities." Tom started jumping up and down.

"What will they do? What will they do?"

"Don't know Tom, we will have to wait and see. Look, look over there, your mother has secured us the best of views."

They elbowed their way through the crowd and seated themselves on the hastily erected seats that had been put around the green, which formed a natural amphitheatre with the backdrop of the river and town of Southampton in the distance. There were stalls and tents and tumblers and jugglers, minstrels and singers. Richard also saw that some of the town guns had been dragged across the river ready to make a salute to the Queen when she finally departed. Will begged to go and see them at closer quarters so Richard agreed to take him. Jack arrived with the others, the Alderman slowing their progress by shaking hands and clapping them on their backs. Biston and his family had thankfully disappeared. Annie and Tamsin came back from the tented village laden with toffee apples, pies and flagons of ale. Everyone was laughing and enjoying the day. Richard would remember that later. He took Will across to where Gilbert Clement, blacksmith and recently appointed town gunner, was ordering his labourers and gunners as they manoeuvred the guns into position so they would loose their shot out over the water.

"Not there, you will take the mast off that ship." He had laid out bags of powder, match and rammers. Richard could tell he was looking to produce lots of impressive smoke and noise rather than cause any damage.

"Gilbert!"

"Come to give us a hand, Diccon?"

"I was always more a handgun man, you know that."

"These guns have seen their best, Diccon, I just hope they don't blow up in our faces. But I have something else planned too." Richard raised his eyebrow.

Gilbert took him to one side, "See here, fireworks, the Queen will well remember her visit to Hampton."

"Fireworks," yelled Will.

"Hush boy, it's a secret."

"Pa, can I stay here and help, can I? Please."

"Gilbert?"

"As long as you follow my every order, this is every order, these aren't your wooden toys."

"Will, hear what Gilbert says and obey him."

"Yes, yes, anything."

"Gilbert, any trouble and you have my permission to give him a clout around the ear and you can put him in stocks. I'll come back and give you a hand later."

Richard rejoined Alice, who was terrified for her eldest boy. Richard gave her a cuddle and kiss and chucked her under the chin. "He is a boy, he likes to do boy's things, he goes to the muster this year, and soon will be a man."

"He is still my baby."

"I know love. He'll be fine, I'll be with him when the fun starts."

"Pa, Pa, the actors are over there. Can we go?" Richard sighed and protested but was secretly happy to have an excuse to visit the actors' tent, he loved the plays as much as Tom.

"See the fellow doing the jig, that's Will Kemp. He is one of the greatest clowns in the country. Those boys there, they are young actors who take the part of female characters in the plays."

"Boys playing women?" Tom was bemused.

"Well it would not be seemly for women to be on the stage, it's barely respectable for men."

"Why?"

"Er, well I...woman should be modest and virtuous and er.."

Luckily for Richard Tom had lost interest, distracted by a couple of actors practising stage fights. Richard searched through the throng as they limbered up for their Royal performance; he recognised several faces from previous visits to the town. One who stood apart from the rest, gathering his thoughts and quietly mouthing his lines, seemed familiar but it took Richard some moments before he bought his name to mind.

"Mr Alleyn!" Richard had not thought to say the name out loud it just sprang out of his mouth. The young man looked cross to have his concentration broken. "I'm sorry, I did not mean to disturb you, I just recognised you, forgive me."

The young man frowned, "I am used to it, strangers who have seen me on the stage think they know me personally."

"Ahh yes, I can understand how that would be." Richard almost turned and walked away, but found himself adding, "But we have met, you toured here, with your brother...Tamburlaine."

The actor looked at Richard carefully, "I recall now, you were assistant to the Mayor, wouldn't pay us anything on account."

Richard smiled, "That would be me."

"I can see the years have treated you well."

"Richard, Richard Mudford. Overall, I have prospered as have you, Mr Alleyn."

"You said I would go far. I took you at your word and here I am."

"The greatest actor of the age."

"Mr Burbage might disagree."

"Pa, Pa, you should have watched the fight, it looked so real."

"Hush Tom. Mr Alleyn, this is my boy Tom. Tom, Mr Alleyn is the leader of this troupe, he will be the main player, the hero."

"Master Tom."

Tom went shy all of a sudden.

"Tom, loves poetry Mr Alleyn. I think he dreams of a life on the stage."

"Ah Tom don't be taken in by fake glamour and pretend fights. Do you love our language and to tell a tale?"

"Yes sir, I do. I think my real father might have been a travelling actor. I dream that one day he might come back and find me."

Alleyn looked strangely at Richard and back at the boy. Richard forced himself to speak.

"Tom, was a foundling baby taken in by my wife and I."

"Well he's a good match, sir."

"And what are you playing for the Queen, Mr Alleyn?"

"A popular piece, *The Seven Deadly Sins*, always goes down well in the pit but encourages overacting. We will be in town for another few days presenting work from a new writer. If you like language and poetry young Tom you could do worse than listen to the words of Master Shakespeare, as you once said of me Richard, he will go far."

The Queen had finished the lavish banquet laid on by the Mayor. She declared herself delighted at the performances and displays put on for her benefit, she announced herself touched by the love of her people of Southampton. Her Majesty graciously took the silver spade and made to break the ground, which had been prepared earlier. The pear tree was placed in the earth and all applauded. Then the Royal progress began its stately move onto the next gracious host. Gilbert Clement, aided by Richard, Jack, and the other gunners let loose a volley of cannon and then as the Queen made to leave and dusk was falling the fireworks were ignited. Will was beside himself as he was allowed to light the touch rope with Clement's ornately carved linstock. It had the face of a dragon and the rope formed its tongue, when it was lit the flames and sparks brought the stick to life. Then all there was left was smoke from the gunpowder and dust from the hooves of many horses. The tents were dismantled and the seats broken up. Townspeople trailed down to the shore and queued for the ferry boats. Alice gathered everyone together and they walked as far as the Ferry inn and John's mother, where they were staying the night. When the day dawned there were still stragglers wandering down to the shore but George Parker called Alice forward and they all clambered onto the Queen's barge, which was now looking worn and dirty again and soon found themselves back on the Southampton shore.

Part Nine

1594

Chapter Fifty-Two

Alice was pregnant. She confessed to Richard after they spent a vigorous night celebrating the recent visit of the Queen and the honour it had brought to the family. She did not want anyone else to know until she was absolutely certain but she was sufficiently late to be confident. She placed Richard's hand on her stomach and pulled it back went he went to venture elsewhere. She worried a little that she had been too carried away with their successes and disported herself too rigorously in their marriage bed. She declared that they should perhaps abstain till she was sure of the baby. The thought did not make Richard happy but he knew how much it meant to Alice so contented himself with the memory of how the baby had been conceived. Besides, there was always tennis.

Jack had heard of a ship for sale that he thought would suit their plans to expand the Mudford Brothers' business and had gone off to give the *Ayd* the once over. Richard and Jacket were in the Pigeon House going over their stock, woad, cloth, soap, currants, raisins, oakum, wax, salt. Fish was, as Jack had predicted, a staple and a good source of money.

"This is all to go to the Soke at Winchester, the carter

should be here soon, Jacket. I'd like you to travel with him. The merchant is a good customer of ours, make yourself known."

"Yes, Father. I have a note here of outstanding debts, one or two from notable burgesses."

"Mmm, some are starting to struggle a little in the town."

"There are so many incomers, Father, I heard some of the porters complaining about the number of poor people coming into the town. They say the town is over-pressed."

"It's a true observation but I know better than most how easy it can be to slip into poverty, we should not harden our hearts."

"Few wanted to help Mother when you were in Spain."

"But we should perhaps try to behave better than they, once our own family is safe and not hungry."

"Thank you for taking me in, I thank God every day."

"You have repaid us Jacket, I would not be without you."

The boy coloured and gave an embarrassed smile.

The cart, with Jacket alongside the carter, creaked as it moved slowly up the incline away from the West Gate. Richard locked the Pigeon House and walked down the outside staircase. A dark-clad figure was hovering at the bottom of the steps.

"Monsieur Mudford?"

"Who is asking?"

"Arnold le Clerque, I am in the household of Walerland Sohier. My master is dead, Mr Mudford and his widow, my mistress, asks if you will come."

Richard was a little sad, he had thought the old man sick when he saw him last, he had the mark of death upon him. He wondered why his former mother-in-law had sent for him but he followed le Clerque back to Winkle Street. There were many figures in the hall and a Huguenot minister brushed past Richard on his way in. He waited while le Clerque sought out his mistress and in a few minutes was taken into a private chamber where he was not pleased to see Walerland laid out on a trestle table. His wife sat, her head in her hand, gazing at the waxen figure.

"It was good of you to come, Richard."

"I was sorry to hear, a great loss to you and to his community."

"We have been together since I was sixteen, not a day spent apart in all those years. But I have not asked you here to be sentimental. You should know my husband's will makes provision for our grandchild. Jeanne is well-endowed, she is a wealthy young girl. You must beware of fortune hunters. I have had some thoughts on a suitable husband–"

"She's seven years old!"

"My marriage was arranged in the cradle."

"And Lizzie? Has she been mentioned?"

She looked at Richard as if he were simple minded.

"We have protected Lizzie with our name and honour that must be enough."

"Why are you so cruel?"

Again she stared at Richard as if he was talking in tongues.

"I owe Lizzie nothing, she is not of my blood."

"She doesn't know that, she thinks you are her grandmother and that Walerland was her grandfather."

"She should know the truth, it does no one any good to lie, it's against the law of God."

"It suited you to lie when it saved your daughter and your precious reputation."

The old woman said nothing. She pursed her lips and closed her eyes.

"I will not accept the money."

"Don't be ridiculous. It's not your choice, the legacy belongs to Jeanne."

"She is my daughter and I control what is hers and what is not."

"You are so self-righteous. You drove my daughter away,

you slept with her maid, you fathered a bastard and favour her over your legitimate child."

"I have always treated my daughters exactly the same." Richard knew this was not strictly true but it should be, "And you have twisted the past into your own version." This was going nowhere, they had been having the same argument for years. He paced up and down the room for several minutes.

"Stop that you are making me feel like screaming!"

Richard was amazed at so much passion coming from the dried and desiccated widow.

"Wauldure."

She was affronted that he had used her personal name. So he used it again.

"Wauldure, we are not so very different, you want what's best for Jeanne, as do I – I just don't want it at the expense of Lizzie, the girls love each other, they are as close as sisters can be. Jeanne relies on Lizzie, Lizzie is strong and when they were tiny I believe Lizzie willed Jeanne to live during her many ailments. Listen, all I am asking is that you let it be thought the girls have a good dower and I will find the money for Lizzie. If you do this I will welcome you into our family. The girls both need you, just a little compassion, Wauldure that is all I ask. You don't have to love Lizzie just tolerate her for Jeanne's sake till they are a little older."

"I don't understand you."

"Well that makes two of us." He sat down beside her and they stayed in silent vigil with Walerland through the night. An uneasy truce had been reached.

Madame Sohier made a bargain. She would hold the money in trust for Jeanne, it would be their secret as to the disbursements of the will and Richard invited his former mother-in-law to dine with the family after a period of mourning had elapsed. He also stood as chief mourner at Walerland's funeral.

★

"Was it really necessary for you to invite her here?" asked Alice. Her pregnancy was not agreeing with her and she was tired and fractious, "She looks down on me. I am not a worthy stepmother for her grandchildren I am not the lady that the sainted Jeannot was."

"Jeannot wasn't the sainted lady that Jeannot was."

"It's not funny."

"I'm not laughing but please keep your voice down, I don't want the girls hearing you speak of their mother like that."

"Oh I'm sorry, of course it would upset them to know their mother tried to poison their father and lived an unnatural life."

"Don't be sarcastic."

"Why shouldn't I be? It's me that has raised those girls whilst my own daughter lies in a cold grave."

"Alice, don't please don't start again—"

"—start what? Remembering my daughter? I'm the only one that does, no one else ever speaks her name."

"I don't know what to say to you when you are like this."

"Like what? Like what, Richard?" Her voice was getting louder. Richard turned away.

"Don't walk away from me!"

"I'm trying not to." She started to cry and he felt like a monster.

"Ssh ssh, love, I'm sorry, I know what you have done for my girls." He cradled her in his arms, "I know you miss Christian, I do too, she was a beautiful, loving child. I hope that the baby you are carrying will be a daughter for us."

Alice muttered something into his shirt that he could not understand but he stroked her hair and kissed the top of her head. She raised a tear-stained face.

"I don't know why I am such a scold. I am finding carrying

381

this child so hard, I don't understand it. We live so well, it should be easier."

"Why don't you go and lie down? I'll get Annie to bring you a posset and I'll put off Wauldure."

"No, don't do that I was being mean, but I will go and lie down. Ask Annie to bring some lavender water for my forehead."

She went upstairs and Richard sent Annie up after her. He felt like he needed fresh air and went out onto Bull Street meaning to walk down to the quay. As he passed the Angel, Tamsin came out.

"I haven't seen Saskatan for a few days Richard. Has she been at your house?"

"No, she's probably pining for Jack, I'm walking down to the quay I'll call in and see if she's there."

Tamsin gave him an odd look, her features were becoming harsher the longer she was parted from John. Richard didn't think she liked running the inn, she only did just enough to keep the business ticking over and without Alice he felt sure it would have foundered. Lawrence was turning into a tearaway and Luisa looked after Little John far more than Tamsin did.

"What's wrong with you?" Tamsin asked him. He felt caught out by the question, especially because of the way his own thoughts had been running.

"Er, nothing, just a bit worried about Alice, the pregnancy, she's not felt well since she conceived."

"She's strong but she has lost more babies than she's delivered."

"Thanks, Tamsin, I feel so much better."

She scowled. There were deep lines around her mouth.

Richard was surprised, Quay House looked as if it was sleeping. He knocked on the door but there was no answer. The door was unlocked and he went in, calling out as he did. There was no answer and the house looked uncared for, there was no sign of the two servants Jack had employed when Annie had re-joined Richard's family, and dust had started to gather on the furniture. It only took a few minutes to search through the downstairs quarters and Richard mounted the stairs and went to the main bedchamber. He knocked again on the closed door and this time heard a moan from within. The room was gloomy as the heavy curtains were drawn. Richard threw them open and then turned to the bed. Saskatan lay in the centre of the bed, she looked dreadful and there were tears in her eyes.

Richard sat on the edge of the bed and felt her forehead. She was hot and the sheets were damp.

"Sasky, it's me, Richard."

She nodded, "Where Jack?"

"He's still away, Sasky, looking for another ship. He wrote to me to say the one he had found wasn't seaworthy but he has news of another and also has some potential business. Sorry Sasky, he probably will be away a little longer. I'll send Jacket and a servant to try and track him down."

Sasky nodded.

"Where are the servants?"

She shrugged, "Run way."

"Have you eaten?" She shook her head, "Thirsty."

The jug by the side of the bed was empty.

"Tell me how you feel."

"Head pain, back pain, here hurt." She stroked her throat.

"Sasky, I am going to get you some water and some broth and make you a bit more comfortable. Then I will get the apothecary and fetch Annie to sit with you."

She smiled weakly, "You nicer than Jack."

"If Jack knew you were sick he would come running, Sasky, he would."

Richard went down to the kitchen and found a bone that would make a broth and put a pot on the fire. He fetched water to drink and warmed some more to bathe Saskatan. He went back to the bedroom and found a new nightgown and sheets. He gave Saskatan a drink first and then he helped her to sit up and carried her to a chair. He bathed her down as best as modesty would permit. he turned away as she slowly changed her nightgown and then wrapped her in a blanket. He stripped the bed and remade it and lifted her back in. He went and fetched the weak broth. Sasky did not want to eat but he managed to get her to take a few mouthfuls.

"Feel a little better?"

She nodded but then started to cough. Richard wondered if she had the influenza.

"I'll be back soon." She nodded and closed her eyes. Richard hurried home.

Back at his house he found Alice sat with the girls. They were all working at some embroidery. She looked up with a smile.

"How are you feeling, love?"

"Much better, I had a sleep, it has restored me. Where did you get to?"

"I went for a walk but Tamsin saw me, she was worried about Saskatan." Richard related what had happened next.

"I'll go to her."

"Do you think you should love, in your condition?"

She hesitated for a moment "We are her only family and Jack is away."

She called Annie and started to give orders for what they would take, food and herbs. Richard sent for Jacket and one of the man servants. He gave them details of Jack's last known whereabouts. They had their own horses now although they were still kept at the Winkle Street stables and Richard thanked heavens that all the boys had been taught to ride. He gave Jacket money, a hand gun and sword. He still wasn't an expert with weapons but was now handy enough. He gave the servant a bill and crossbow.

"You know what you have to do, Jacket?" The boy gulped

and nodded. "Do the best you can. Jack may be at sea but I think we should try to find him. I know when I was in Spain they would talk about how the Indians could not cope with illnesses, I don't want to think the worst but..."

He then went to the apothecary and asked him to visit his sister-in-law and arrange a nurse. He then went back to Quay House. Alice and Annie were cleaning.

"How is she?"

"She seems to have rallied. We have given her an infusion – I hope it is just a slight fever. She brightened when she saw the girls."

"The girls are here too?" Richard tried not to show his concern.

"They insisted on coming, they are very fond of Sasky, they are fussing and nursing her–"

"–but you know how prone Jeanne is to catching every ailment."

Alice gave him a black look but went to the stair and called out, "Jeanne, Lizzie, come down, your father is here."

The girls clattered down the stairs.

"We have been looking after Aunt Sasky, Pa," said Lizzie, "Jeanne has been nurse and I have been the entertainer."

"Well done, girls, I am proud of you, but I think that we should let Aunt Sasky rest now, the apothecary will be here soon."

On cue the man appeared with an experienced nurse called Bridget. Alice took them upstairs.

"Poor Mrs Jack," said Annie

"Indeed. Please will you take the girls home."

Richard went upstairs and hovered by the bedroom door. Alice came and joined him.

"It's difficult to know exactly what ails her, it could be a fever, flu or something worse," the apothecary pronounced.

"That's comforting," muttered Richard and Alice elbowed him in the ribs.

The apothecary mixed up a few potions and gave instructions to the nurse. There seemed to be nothing more that Richard and Alice could do so they walked slowly back to their own house.

"I have sent Jacket and a man to try and track down Jack but I doubt they will have much success."

"Do you think it is that serious?"

"I don't know it's just I have heard native women succumb easily."

"To be that far from home, it's so sad. What is it?"

"Pardon?"

"You have a distant look in your eye."

"Ah, sorry, Alice, I was just thinking about John."

"I didn't know you still thought of him"

"Of course I do, almost every day."

"But you never speak of him."

"What would be the point of that?"

She squeezed his arm.

The next day the apothecary sent good news, he thought Sasky much improved following his ministrations and said rest and quiet would be her best medicine. Alice decided they should continue with their plans to welcome Madame Sohier to dinner.

Chapter Fifty-Three

"Jeanne would you like some neats' tongues?"

"Oui, Papa"

It was a small family supper. Richard, Alice, Jeanne and Lizzie, William looking uncomfortable in his formal clothes, young Tom looking like a miniature version of his Uncle Jack. The family likeness was so strong Richard felt sure Madame Sohier must have been drawing conclusions.

"I am glad Jeanne is keeping up her mother's language" said Madame Sohier, as she picked at her plate.

"Je parle francais aussi, Grand-mère," piped up Lizzie her golden curls bobbing. Madame Sohier nodded her head in acknowledgement.

"Would you like some meats?" asked Alice a nervousness in her voice made it sound sharper than usual. Madame Sohier had confined herself to a small pigeon although the sideboard groaned with beef, calf, lamb, bacon, chicken, rabbit. The air was heavy with the scent of cloves, cinnamon, saffron and orange. She was about to refuse but saw Richard glowering at her.

"Perhaps some rabbit, I have a weakness for rabbit."

Alice breathed a sigh of evident relief.

"Well I would like more meat!" declared Will, who had been told to hold back.

Richard laughed and started to carve large slices, the family began to relax and slip back into their usual behaviour which was robust, talking over one another, laughing and jostling. Madame Sohier looked horrified at first but started to weaken at the onslaught of care and fuss made of her by Jeanne and Lizzie. William grilled her about sea beggars and the Spanish invasion. Tom told her how much he liked the singing that came from the French Church that he could hear whilst at school. After the meal Madame Sohier was escorted to the best chair and entertained by the children, the girls played the virginals, Tom sang with his father, William danced a jig. Alice made sure she was not in a draft and that she had plenty of watered wine. It had less water in it than Madame Sohier was accustomed to, her cheeks became flushed and she almost giggled. At the end of the evening the boys practised their bows and the girls their curtseys but could not resist giving the old woman a hug. Richard then escorted her to her door. She was a little unsteady on her feet and to his discomfort, she started to softly cry.

"There was one Christmas, we had not been married many years. Jeannot was a baby and two of our older children were still living, just toddlers. We had such a happy time. To have a house full of children is a blessing from God."

"You are always welcome with us, Wauldure. We desire nothing from you but to be a grandmother to all our children."

She gave a slight nod, Richard did not know what this might mean but hoped at last they had reached a rapprochement and he let her servant help her into her house.

The supper was, Alice considered, a success. She had a little headache herself the next day having taken more Dutch courage than had been strictly necessary. They all slept in and did not go to morning service. There was no news from Jacket or from Jack himself. Alice or Annie called in to see how Sasky fared most days, there did not seem to be much change. Her coughs, sneezes and sore throat seemed to indicate a severe cold or flu but the fever had worsened and the apothecary was concerned.

It was some ten days after Richard had first visited Saskatan that Alice hurried into his counting house. She was pale and shaking. "Richard!" She could say no more and sank into a chair. Richard went to her side and kneeled by the seat.

"What? What?"

"I have been to Quay House, Bridget was just sending for the apothecary. Sasky has a rash on her face, arms, legs, the palms of her hands, the soles of her feet."

The terror in her eyes was palpable, her breath was shallow.

"Smallpox," said Richard almost in a whisper. He had heard talk around the town of others falling ill and had not wanted to believe.

"I'll go and see—"

"—be careful."

"I think I'll be all right. When I was child we suffered a mild dose of cowpox, I don't know why but we never got the pox after that."

He put his hand on Alice's stomach. "I know." She started to cry, she knew the danger.

"Have you had any symptoms, Alice, anything?"

"I don't think so, I don't know."

"Perhaps you should go across the water?"

"Maybe, I don't know. I can't think at the moment."

"Look, pack some things together. If there is going to be a serious outbreak I want you safe."

She nodded. Richard was scared but he made himself go back to see Saskatan. When he got there the apothecary was already arrived.

"I have ordered Bridget to begin the red treatment, it is most important the patient is entirely enveloped in red. The curtains at the window and around the bed, she must be wrapped in red flannel cloths and kept in a hot room, I have sent Bridget to buy red flannel in your name."

"Yes, yes of course whatever is necessary."

"I suggest she should be bled and purged." Richard nodded.

When Bridget returned laden down with yards of red flannel he helped her nail it at the window. He ripped down the curtains around the bed and replaced them with the red flannel. Richard chopped plenty of wood and stoked up the fire. They heated sheets of flannel which they were to wrap Saskatan in. The room was soon stifling, Richard took off his doublet and worked just in his shirt, when the flannel was thought warm enough they carefully lifted Sasky from the bed. The pustules on her body had begun to run together and her skin was starting to get dry and flaky. She was stoical but Richard could tell she was in agony. The bleeding and purging seemed in his eyes to be making her weaker but he was not a medical man. When all that could be had been done Richard wearily made his way back home after agreeing another nurse could be employed to give Bridget a break. The apothecary hurried off, he had other patients, it seemed there was a severe outbreak about the town.

When he arrived at the house hours later he found Alice sat in the hall, her bags packed. She looked very pale and drawn.

"It's as bad as it could be, love, it's definitely smallpox. Sasky is very, very sick." He explained the treatment that was being given and Alice began to shake.

"You must take the children and go over to the Ferry village." She nodded.

"I kept the boys from school they are playing in their rooms."

"I'll go and fetch them – Annie! Annie!" The girl appeared.

"Annie, go down to the inn and tell Tamsin to shut up shop, tell her to get some things together and that she and the children should come here. You are all going over to Itchen Ferry, quickly now."

Richard went to his counting house to get a money bag for Alice. He called up the stairs to Will who came clattering down, Tom at his heels.

"Boys, I need you do something for me."

"Yes, Pa," they chorused.

"You are all going with your mother and Aunt Tamsin across to the Ferry village and you are to stay there until you get a message from me."

The boys looked at one another in surprise and then back to their father.

"Will, run down to the Cross House and send a message across to your grandma to say you are coming and make sure there is a boat ready to take everyone. Tom, go down to the quay and ask one of the carters to come back here with their cart, to carry everyone down to the hard – get John Major's cart if you can if not Goodman Maddocks." He gave the boys some coins to help smooth the way. "Good boys, off you go."

They tore out of the house. Richard went back to the hall. He smoothed Alice's hair and kissed the top of her head.

"Try not to worry, you are strong, you are my brave girl."

"Why is life so hard, Richard?"

"Part of God's great plan, to make sure we will be grateful when we get to heaven."

"Richard don't blaspheme so, not now, we need to pray."

"Sorry, sorry, I should not rail against things I don't understand." He sat down beside her and put his arm around her. "I love you more than life itself, you know that don't you?"

"In truth, sometimes I'm not sure."

He took her face in his hand. "I think a marriage is like a story, a play, there are moments of drama, moments of misunderstanding and mistake but when people are meant to be together, like you and I we will find our way through."

"Will we have a happy ending?"

"We are own authors, Alice." He kissed her lips.

The door burst open and Tamsin came into the hall, holding a shawl with a few essentials and Little John on her hip. Annie was behind her with another bundle and Luisa struggled with a third, dragging a complaining Lawrence.

Richard got to his feet, "Lawrence Hush! Behave for your sister." He heard wheels bumping along the cobbled street and looked out of the door. Tom was sat on John Major's cart as the carter guided the vehicle past foot passengers and other traffic.

"What's going on?" asked Tamsin. "Annie came with a garbled message, said we had to leave urgently go across the Ferry."

Richard lowered his voice, "Saskatan has the smallpox. With Alice in her condition I would just be happier if you were all across the water." He felt eyes upon him and looked down at Luisa whose grave face and wide eyes were gazing up at him. "You are all going on a holiday for a while." The little girl did not seem convinced. The cart pulled up. Richard stowed all the belongings on board and helped Alice up next to the carter.

"I'll go and get the girls," he said, "I thought with all this noise they would be down by now. The carter helped Annie and Tamsin into the cart and lifted Tamsin's two little boys in after them. Tom and Luisa lingered on the pavement. Richard ran up the stairs calling the girls' names but they didn't come running. When he got to their room he flung open the door without ceremony.

"Didn't you hear me call you? You need to stop playing and come with me."

Lizzie was lying on the bed and Jeanne was sat at her feet, she turned her pale face to Richard.

"Papa, Lizzie doesn't feel well."

Richard's heart skipped a beat, he hurried to the bedside and bent over his daughter.

"Lizzie, its Papa. What's the matter? Eaten too many sweetmeats?"

Lizzie opened her blue eyes, "My head hurts and my throat is sore."

"Ssh, close your eyes, try to sleep. Jeanne, are you all right?"

"Yes Papa, I feel well, I have been trying to look after Lizzie. I put lavender on a kerchief and laid it on her forehead."

"Good girl, you did very well. You need to come with me now and go with your Ma, and let Papa look after Lizzie."

"Can't I stay here, Papa? I want to be with Lizzie, I always stay with Lizzie."

"I know, sweetheart, but not today. I will bring Lizzie to join you in a little while, when her headache is gone away." He picked Jeanne up and she wrapped her arms around his neck and he kissed her head.

"Bye Lizzie, see you soon." Lizzie murmured a farewell.

"Papa will be back in a minute, Lizzie." He carried Jeanne down the stairs, feeling his way as his eyes were full of tears. When he got outside all the others were in the cart and ready to go, sitting on their bundles.

"Where is Lizzie?" Alice was a little impatient till she saw Richard's face, "Richard—"

His look stayed her, and he watched the colour drain from her face, she shook her head. She went to get down from the cart.

"Alice, no. It will serve nothing, I need to know you are safe. I will send word."

She sat back down. When Richard went to put Jeanne in the cart she would not lose her hold on him.

"I want to stay with you, Papa, and Lizzie, please, please let me stay with you, please, Papa, please." He prised her hands away, she was sobbing now.

"Jeanne, come sit with me." It was Luisa, she held out her own small arms and Jeanne fell into them. "I will look after Jeanne for you, till Lizzie comes."

"Thank you,"said Richard, "To the hard, my boy Will'll be waiting there for you with a boat." He slapped the horse's rump and they moved away. Alice gazed back at him till they turned the corner down Vyse Lane. Richard fell to his knees and wept, he did not care what people thought as they scurried by. After a few minutes he pulled himself together and wiped his face with a sleeve. He called out for the kitchen maid.

"Go and buy me as much red flannel as you can find." He pushed coins into her hand and the girl ran off. He went back into the house and up to Lizzie's room. He went and sat on the bed and smoothed her damp curls.

"Hello Lizzie, it's Papa, we are going to have a fine old time together, just you and me."

Lizzie's symptoms worsened and she started to get a fever. Richard decked the room out in red and sent for the apothecary. He refused to let Lizzie be bled or purged, she was just a small girl and he could not believe her constitution would stand it.

"Very well, if you go against my advice I will not be answerable but at the very least boil this alkanet root in beer, it will turn the liquid red and give it to her to drink. Dress Lizzie only in red, including a red hat, and only give her red food to eat. She must only play with red toys, this is most important."

Richard nodded. "How is Saskatan?"

"I fear for her life. I have done all I can, I have dosed her with mercury and spirits of hartshorn but already the pustules have run together and her skin has almost all flaked off, even the lining of her mouth and throat. I do not think she will last much longer. This child will not reach crisis for a day or two."

Richard nodded again. When the man left he went down to the kitchen searching for food that was red. Red apples? Did they count? What about colouring food? He was an idiot he should have asked the apothecary more. He went to the market and bought a red bonnet more red material to make a nightshirt. He found a red cloth lion that made him think of the puppets and porcupine seen all those years ago, before Lizzie was even conceived. He bought food dye, beetroot, radishes and red tomatoes, he was becoming frantic.

"Richard?" It was Madame Sohier, she looked at all his purchases.

"Is it Jeanne?"

"No, Jeanne is safe, I have sent her away over the water, it's Lizzie." He knew he was crying again.

"Come, come, let me take some of these things, girl help here," she gestured to her servant. "It's all right, Richard, I will come back with you."

Richard was too exhausted to protest. The little party trailed back to the house laden with their red purchases. Madame Sohier sent her servant girl into the kitchen with instructions on what to prepare and then went with Richard to the red bedroom.

"Wipe your face, don't let her see you are afraid!"

They went into the room, a maid was moping Lizzie's face, red blemishes were starting to appear.

"Let me do that," said Madame, taking the red cloth and sitting beside the bed.

Lizzie opened her eyes, "Grand-mère is that you?"

"Yes dearest, I am here, I have come to help your papa make you well."

"Thank you, Grand-mère, poor Papa, he is so worried." Madame Sohier looked up at Richard.

"You should go and get some rest, I will be at hand."

"Thank you, Wauldure. I should go to Saskatan, she is sick also and Jack is still away." Madame Sohier nodded and turned her attention back to Lizzie, showing her the red lion Richard had bought.

Quay House had a horrible rancid smell about the place. Richard went up to the other red bedroom. The nurse was nodding asleep and woke with a start as he came in. She looked guilty but Richard could not blame her for taking rest, she had nursed her charge around the clock.

"She is drifting in and out of consciousness, sir. She has suffered terribly, it has reached her bowels and she was screaming in pain. I gave her some sheep's dung in poppy juice."

"Thank you, Bridget."

Richard went across to the bed, the creature lying hardly resembled anything human, her face was riven with pustules, there was no skin to be seen. As he sat on the bed Saskatan opened her eyes, they were barely a slit and she attempted a brave smile. She gestured to the drawer in the little cupboard by the bed. Richard opened it, there was a beautiful embroidered beaded bracelet, she signalled him to put it on.

"For me?" there was a hint of a nod. "It is very lovely," he put it around his wrist. "I will wear it always." She gestured again, there was a companion in the draw. "Is this for Jack?" he guessed. Again that infinitesimal nod. "I will put it around his wrist and he will wear it always." She closed her eyes and died. Richard had no tears left but he felt unutterably sad, the poor creature was so far from home and from the arms of the man she'd loved most in all the world.

"Bridget, your charge does not need you anymore." The woman gave a sigh. Richard pulled coins out of his purse and gave them to her. "Thank you for what you have done. If you will do something more for me. See the house tidy, burn all the bedding and the flannel, and ask the priest at St Michael's to arrange the funeral. My daughter is sick, or I would see to this. If you need more money, seek me out."

He left the house and went back up Bull Street. "Please God, don't let Lizzie suffer like this, if you must take her, then take her though it will break my heart, but don't let her suffer, don't let her suffer."

Richard and Madame Sohier took it in turns to stay with Lizzie. The pustules showed themselves on the parts of the body that were exposed, but they did not join together and this the apothecary said was a positive sign, giving cause for some hope. Lizzie cried out over and over for her mother. Richard did not know if this was for Alice or for the woman Lizzie believed to have been her birth mother. When he thought he sent messages across the river but he heard nothing back and he could only assume that the rest of his family had not fallen ill. Richard heard that Bridget also took sick and died, as did several members of her family. Richard felt overcome with guilt but the apothecary told him the woman had disobeyed his orders and had kept the red flannel for herself, taking it home instead of burning it and thereby bringing death into her own house. Madame Sohier had no fear of the pox, she had lost some of her children to the disease but had always escaped herself by some fluke of nature. Besides, she said she was old and if her time had come she was ready. She sang French lullabies and Richard found members of the Communion praying in his hall, jostling with the vicar of St Michael, who when he heard, felt Lizzie's soul belonged to him.

It was six weeks before they all were ready to believe that Lizzie would not die. The pustules eventually dried and flaked off, those on the souls of her feet being the last to go. Her beautiful creamy complexion was scarred but Madame Sohier thought the scars would fade, hopefully to almost nothing. Richard remembered that when he was a little boy the Queen had had smallpox and almost died. There was a great deal of consternation even in poor houses like his home, about what would happen when there was no obvious heir to succeed her. He assumed that the Queen's use of white paint on her face was to disguise the pock marks left by the disease. Lizzie was playing with her red lion,

"Pa, when can I go and be with Jeanne? I miss her."

"So do I, sweetheart. Now you are stronger I will go to Itchen Ferry and tell them all the good news. I think the town will be free of the outbreak soon and they can all come home."

Jack and Jacket arrived home first. They sailed in on the *Pelican* and Jack finding his home locked up, feared the worst and came to find his brother.

"I'm sorry, Jack. I did what I could and I was with her at the end."

"Poor old Sasky." Jack turned the embroidered bracelet between his fingers. "I was fond of her and she never did anyone any harm."

"She loved you."

"I know."

Jacket came down the stairs, he had been up visiting Lizzie.

"How's my girl?" said Richard.

"She is fine, Pa, but her pretty face is ruined." he began to cry.

"Don't let Lizzie see you like this. You must not let her know that we find her changed."

The boy sniffed. "No, Pa."

"I've let the business go to the devil these past weeks."

"That all right Richard, Jacket and I will see to it. I didn't bring just the ship back but picked up some cargoes on the way."

"Are you sure, Jack? You don't want a bit of time—"

"What, to mourn? Not my style, Diccon, you know that."

"Right, well I'm going to go over to Itchen Ferry first thing tomorrow."

It was barely first light when he went across the water. There was a chill in the air and he wrapped his cloak around him. He jumped from the boat before it had reached the beach and his boots splashed in the water and crunched up the gravel. They were just stirring at the inn. Annie and Tamsin were helping John's mother to make porridge for breakfast. Tom and Will had gone out fishing with some of their cousins. Jeanne and Luisa were laying the table. Richard hoisted his elder daughter into the air.

"Our Lizzie is recovered, Jeanne. She is well."

"I prayed every day, twice a day sometimes more."

"You see, your prayers were answered my lovely, beautiful Jeanne." He put her down and asked where Alice was.

"She's abed," said Tamsin pointing above her head. Richard dived up the stairs and tracked down the right room. Alice was lying in what must have been John's mothers bed. She was pale and wan. When Richard came in she opened her arms and he gathered her in his.

"I lost the baby. I lost the baby."

Part Ten

1595

Chapter Fifty-Four

Joannie was getting married. Alderman Biston tactfully conceded that now her unfortunate 'stepmother' had died there was no further impediment to the marriage. Biston had no idea how close he had come to death. When he had come to meet with Jack to make final arrangements for the dowry he had almost rejoiced that Saskatan was in her grave and not proving an annoyance to his plans. Jack stayed very cool and leaned back on his chair, rocking it too and fro as he made to clean his fingernails with his tooled Spanish knife, but Richard could see how his blue eyes glistened as if embedded with diamonds. He knew his brother was a killer and had ended life with far less provocation. He had laid a hand softly on his brother's arm, to stay his hand.

"Don't worry, Richard, not in your house." He leapt to his feet and clasped Alderman Biston to him.

"So we are family at last." Biston wriggled free as best he could, he didn't trust Jack but he trusted gold. Jack refused to give Joannie away and went privateering instead leaving Richard to guide his niece up the aisle. Joannie had never seemed to grow very much, perhaps she really didn't ever get enough to eat, and so looked always like a small child wearing her mother's clothes.

As they waited outside the church of All Saints, Joannie paced up and down impatient for her moment in the light.

"Joannie, I have a present for you," said Richard.

"I like presents."

Richard took a small packet out of his pocket and Joannie looked unimpressed at its size. She tore open the packet to reveal a charming silver bracelet from which dangled twelve silver cups.

"I suppose you think this amusing?"

"Yes, I do actually," said Richard as he secured the bracelet around her bony wrist.

"I shall be a grand lady now. I will have nothing to do with my father or his family once I am Mrs Biston."

"I can understand that, Joannie, and I am sure the family will reciprocate."

She narrowed her eyes, not sure if she had been insulted.

"You should try not to be too bitter, Joannie. I grant your life has not been easy and your father is a knave but in the end it was his money that got you what you wanted."

"Only because it suited him to be rid of me."

"Perhaps you are right. I hope you will be happy, Joan."

She gave a thin smile that he had used her proper name.

"Happiness means nothing to me. I will have a fine husband who will buy me dresses and I will be able to eat as much as I want, eat until I make myself sick. People will have to curtsey to me and I will have servants to beat."

"An interesting life you will lead."

"Can we go in now?"

"It doesn't do to look too eager."

"What do I care for that? I just want to be married and free from my former life."

Richard gave her his arm and they walked up the aisle. The wedding feast was a mean affair. Biston was puffed up and Margaret looked on edge, her eldest son had been invited to the feast but was not at the top table and her father was not there at all. Bart Biston sat in the corner and drank himself stupid. Joan and William barely looked at one another and never exchanged a word. Richard was also not given a seat on the top table, for which he was glad, but sat with Alice and the children; none of the guests spoke to them. Lizzie had started to go out in public again now her scars were not so red but she was very conscious of her face and bowed her head and tried to twist her curls to cover some of the marks. Her sister and step brothers were very protective and Will had blacked a few eyes of thoughtless children who had made cruel taunts.

"This meat is tough," said Alice pushing it to the side of her plate. "How soon can we leave without looking rude?"

"Oh I'm not worried about looking rude," Richard replied. Tom was banging his heels in boredom. Jacket and Will were playing cards under the table. "I think there will be some dancing soon, we could slip out then."

"I suppose it won't be many years before we will be planning weddings too."

Richard looked appalled.

"Don't look so shocked. Jacket is coming up seventeen, Will, thirteen–"

"I don't think any of the boys should marry before they are 25 and can earn their way in the world." said Richard as if that ended the matter.

"And what of the girls? How old should they be?"

"They, I am sorry to say, will never marry as there will never be any young men good enough." He pulled a face at his daughters.

"Papa!" squealed Jeanne.

"Its true sweetheart, you will have to live in a tower like a fairy-tale princess and I shall sit at the bottom with my gun."

"You won't need a gun for me, Pa." said Lizzie.

"Are you so sure, my Lizzie? You are still the most beautiful girl in Southampton."

"Oh Pa." she reached over and gave him a kiss.

"Where has Annie gone?" asked Alice. She had come along to the feast to help Alice with the children.

"She went to get a bowl of pudding," said Richard as he pulled Lizzie's curls teasingly.

"Can you go and find her and say we will be leaving soon."

"Would you like some warmed mead before we go?"

"Mmm, that sounds nice, and might take the taste of the food away!"

Richard skirted around the room chatting to a few people on the way, he sent a servant over to Alice to fill their mugs and asked if the girl had seen anything of Annie. She looked a bit uneasy and glanced over to a side room. Richard walked across the darkened hall to where a door was ajar. He stopped as he heard noises. His heart sank, he was pretty sure he knew what was going on inside. Annie was bent across the table and Bart Biston, his hose around his ankles, was stood behind her, his grimy hands clasped on her hips as he thrust like a dog inside her.

"Annie!" the girl coloured, looked confused and then burst into tears.

"For Christ's sake, Bart, she's just a silly girl, she knows little of the ways of the world."

Bart didn't stop, he slapped her buttocks, "stop squirming, Annie." The girl kept crying and Bart swore and pulled himself free, hoisting up his hose. "Stop looking at me like that, we've been fucking for years, haven't we Annie? She's my sweetheart." He grasped her round the waist, nuzzling her neck.

"Is that true, Annie?" Richard knew Alice would be furious if it was so; the girl kept grizzling, she looked more bovine than ever. "Your mother would expect me to keep better control of you than this."

"I told you we are sweethearts. Since we worked back in the inn." Richard looked at Bart with disgust. If what he said was true Annie was but twelve back then.

"Then why are you still spreading your favours all over the town, Bart?" Richard curled his lip. Annie stopped squawking for a minute. "What do you mean, sir? One day we are to be married, Bart would not go with other women."

"Annie, you are a very foolish girl. You may thank God that you are not pregnant." Richard replied with a sigh, she started to cry again.

"Shut up, Annie," yelled Bart.

"Annie your mistress needs you, tidy yourself up and go back to your duties." She scurried from the room wiping her nose on her sleeve.

"Are you really intending to marry her, Bart?"

"Don't be stupid! Common little tart."

"She is only what you made her."

Bart shrugged.

"You have ruined her Bart."

"It's just a bit of fun. Don't tell me you haven't ever had any yourself. Look, I like her well enough, she's plump and willing but my Pa will never take me back if I married her."

"Then leave her be."

"I have tried that before but she weeps and begs, it's just easier and more pleasant to keep her happy." He winked, "It's nice to have a willing dog to wag a stick at."

Richard raised his eyes heavenward and went back to Alice. Annie sat sullen with Lizzie dozing on her lap.

"Richard, what is wrong with Annie? Every time I try to speak to her she starts crying," hissed Alice.

"It seems she fancies herself in love with Bart Biston and thinks he returns her affections."

"No don't tell me—"

"—it seems he has been having her for years."

"Years! She will have to be dismissed."

"She is a good-natured girl, but not very clever. If you dismiss her she will indeed be ruined."

"I cannot have a fornicator in my house looking after my children."

"Send her back to work with Tamsin in the inn."

"And where Bart can pray on her?"

"Whatever we do that could still happen. I think he might steer clear for a while, he has hopes of returning to the fold."

"I'll send her there for a while till I decide what to do. Perhaps we can find her a husband." Alice didn't sound if she had much hope of that.

"I am not sure she will take anyone else whilst she has hopes of Bart."

"Why are women so stupid about men?"

"Well I am glad you were stupid about me." Richard picked up the sleeping Jeanne from Alice's lap.

"Let's go home."

Chapter Fifty-Five

Richard had been summoned by Mr Davison the schoolmaster of the free grammar school.

"It will not do, Mr Mudford, it will not do. Young William is missing more often than he is here, and when he is here he hardly applies himself, his letters would not be recognisable as a language known to man. His Latin in unintelligible, he is disruptive. Tom, Tom has promise but he is led astray by his elder brother. I have tried Mr Mudford but even the sternest discipline has no effect on the boy, he is a lost cause. I will persevere with Tom but William is, I fear, as I say, a lost cause."

"I think you too harsh, Mr Davison, Will can apply himself when his interest is engaged."

"Sadly the only thing that engages him is fish. Tides, nets, sails, these are not the stuff of a scholar, but of a labouring man, a common man, Will cannot overcome his beginnings I would say."

Richard was finding it difficult to overcome his own beginnings, which were prompting him to punch Mr Davison on the nose.

"Thank you, Mr Davison, I will speak to Will."

Richard left the master's room, Will and Tom were on a bench outside and looked nervous. Richard towered over them.

"Do you think I have nothing better to do than be hauled here to have your master berate me about my misbegotten children? There are plenty of boys out there who would give anything to be in this school."

"Then they can have my place," muttered Will.

"Fine. Tom, go back to your class, I will speak to you further this evening, Will, come with me." Will was not sure whether to whoop with joy or feel concerned that he was about to get a beating.

They walked outside of the school and down to the Water Gate which was busy with carts and pack horses taking goods to and from the town quay. Richard waved to one of the porters lounging by the gate waiting for a job. He went to the Virginie inn next to the Custom House, bought a couple of pots of weak ale and he and Will sat down on a bench outside to drink. Will had relaxed a little he felt he was on holiday and was smiling as he took in all the activity around the port. Then he looked at Richard who was grim and displeased.

"So you have no interest in learning, Will?"

Will decided his best defence was to be belligerent in his reply, "Not in learning Latin. How is that going to help me?"

"It means you could become a cleric, a lawyer, a secretary."

"But I don't want to be any of those things." Will scoffed, his stepfather did not know him at all.

"So what do you want, Will? You can't live off your mother and I forever. How will you provide for your future family?"

Will had never really thought about the time he would have to stand on his own two feet, feed himself and maybe others, he shrugged a little discomforted, "I could be a fisherman, a ferryman like my father."

"I knew your father well, we were friends and he would have told you what I am going to say. Your father could not make ends meet, he was fed up with being hungry. That is why he moved to the town and took a position in the watch before he died." Richard paused a moment as he saw a flicker of pain in the boy's eyes, "He had not been able to put enough aside to look after his family."

Will complained, "It's all right for Tom, he's clever, he finds it easy, he knows more than that old fraud who calls himself a teacher. But I'm not Tom, I'm stupid and the only thing I'm good at is fishing." His bravado was slipping.

"You're not stupid, Will, you have many skills and your father would want you to do better than him to make the most of your chances. That's what I would like for you too, Will,"

"How can I be better? I heard old Davison, I'm only fit to be a labourer." Will thrust out his lower lip.

"How would you like to become an apprentice to a seafaring man?"

Will took a second to process the proposal, he saw a lifeline.

"Do you mean Uncle Jack?" Will looked excited.

"I most certainly do not mean Uncle Jack," said Richard firmly, "but I could speak to Captain Prowse. We sailed together in the Armada campaign and I hear he is moving to Southampton permanently. He is a good mariner, he taught Jack plenty."

Will considered his options, and as if he was doing Richard the greatest favour replied "Yes, I think I would like to be an apprentice with Captain Prowse if he will take me," but he had a smile that he could not control.

"Now, how are we going to tell your mother?" said Richard.

Alice was not happy.

"Your brother is not a man to be trusted with the well-being of a boy."

"I grant you he has a chequered past but since he took up privateering he has changed."

"He hasn't changed at all, he has just found an occupation that suits his devious nature."

"That is a little harsh." Alice gave him a long stare. "Besides which if you let me finish, I was not intending to apprentice Will to Jack but to Lawrence Prowse."

Alice was a little mollified and whilst she digested what Richard said he tried to ram his point home.

"And what is Will to do otherwise? He has no aptitude for book learning."

"He can fish and sail."

"Exactly, but if he does it alone he will struggle to make a living, you know that, Alice, but under Lawrence's tutelage he could become a master of his own ship. Instead of fishing just for his dinner and in the hope of selling a few on at market, he could make big catches off Newfoundland."

"Newfoundland! That is on the other side of the ocean, anything could happen to him."

"Alice, the truth be told he could drown on the Itchen, ferry boats go down in rough weather just as easily. You know Lawrence, he is a good sort."

Alice sipped at the ale she had been brewing and smacked her lips together, "Mmm, not at all bad Mrs Mudford, do you think one of your children might want to be a brewer?"

"Perhaps the next one." Richard patted her stomach, Alice was a few days late.

"Very well, but only if Lawrence says Will is good enough."

Richard decided to strike before Alice changed her mind, so dressed Will up in his best and they went to Prowse's house on English Street. They were shown into the hall and Lawrence appeared himself a few minutes later.

"Richard, how are you? I have been meaning to call but it has been all business and I'm trying to get the house ready for my family. Not a good enough excuse but that's all I have."

"I should have called earlier myself and invited you to dinner, and in fact let me do that now, if you are free next week?"

"Yes, Tuesday – no Wednesday, Wednesday would be excellent."

"I'm afraid my call is not just social Lawrence, I have a boon to ask of you."

Lawrence raised an eyebrow.

"This is my stepson, Will Dypere." Will stepped out from behind Richard and gave a stiff bow.

Lawrence gave a graceful nod in return.

"The thing is, Will shows great promise as a sailor and I hoped you might think to try him as an apprentice."

Lawrence was a little taken aback and scratched his head. "An apprentice? Never had one of those before, don't quite know what to say."

"You are a fine man of the sea, Lawrence, you would be able to show Will not just the practical things but the characteristics he will have to develop to become the captain of a ship."

"So Will, you want a life at sea?" Lawrence looked Will up and down apprising his potential.

"Oh yes, sir, more than anything."

"I know, Richard, that you would not put Will forward if you did not think he had what is required. I'll tell you what I will do, I am shipping out on a short voyage next weekend. I will take you, Will, and let's see how we get along."

Will's eyes were out on stalks, "Thank you, sir."

"Will, why don't you go down to the kitchen and ask cook for a biscuit, I need to have a word with your pa." Will trotted off and Richard looked quizzically at Lawrence.

"I've been up at Court as you know, well on the edge shall we say. There is something afoot, another attack on Spain and it seems you are involved."

"Hardly. I thought I might do myself some good to tell what I know of Cadiz but I did not think to precipitate an invasion."

413

"Well suffice to say I have been sounded out about taking a ship. I think the town will be asked to provide one, like they did before. Will, you come along?"

"I don't think I will have much of a choice," said Richard grimly.

Will was, Lawrence said with no trace of irony, the best apprentice he ever had. The boy was formerly articled to Captain Prowse and began his training immediately. Alice was still cross at Richard for taking her firstborn from her and showed her displeasure by denying him marital rights for several weeks. It was only her ongoing desire for another baby that eventually caused her to relent, when her mensis dashed hopes that she was with child. Richard was heartily glad as he was but a man and found his major contentment in work and bed.

Chapter Fifty-Six

A letter came that had the insignia of the Earl of Essex and requested Richard's company in the Earl's London house. Richard knew the word request was politeness only, he had no choice but to pack a bag and make plans to visit the capital. He disguised the visit somewhat from Alice, wrapping it up with business matters but Alice was deeply suspicious.

"And why would my Lord of Essex want to do business with you? You should not involve yourself with your betters."

"Thank you, wife, for having such faith in my business acumen. Although the Earl is rich and favoured he is always looking at ways to expand his fortune. He knows we have interests and plans to exploit the Americas, he may put money into the scheme."

"You said he was a spoilt boy."

"Indeed he is but he is also the Earl of Essex and the Queen's favourite, if he calls I have to go running."

The journey to London was a trial, the weather was appalling as were the roads. It was becoming a concern to Richard and other merchants as a poor road network made it difficult to move goods about the country. He made such slow progress he had to make more overnight stops on the way than he had planned and many of the inns were overflowing with others in the same situation. He had taken to travelling with his own linen to protect himself from the worst of the bedbugs but he hated sharing rooms with strangers. These days he drew the line at sharing a bed so had taken the precaution of packing his hammock as well, which caused interest and amusement amongst his fellow travellers. He was not in a very good mood by the time he reached London but managed to get a room at The Swan in Holborn having sent a message before him. He knew the inn well as it was often used by officers of the town who came up to London on official business. He visited a bathhouse to get rid of most of the dirt of the road and had his hair barbered but refused the other services on offer.

London was a large and mighty city of business, trading with almost every corner of the world. On the river were ships from France, the Netherlands, Sweden, Denmark, Hamburg and other kingdoms. The streets were so thronged with people Richard could scarcely pass along them. The noise was incredible with carts and coaches thundering by and at every corner men, women and children converged like shoals of fish. Hammers were beating, tubs being hooped, porters swearing, chapmen skipping in and out of shops. The inhabitants were magnificently apparelled, even wearing velvet in the street. The houses were very narrow onto the street with most of the frontages being shops, they stood five and six roofs high. Most were made of timber and clay with plaster but on the river there were many grand and showy palaces built by nobles using brick and freestone. The Queen's palaces were magnificent with gardens and fountains: Hampton Court, Richmond, Greenwich, Nonsuch, Oatlands, Sheen, Windsor and Whitehall.

Richard visited a stationer to see what books were to be had, below the shop window the stall-board was covered in the title pages of books that could be found inside. Richard wetted his lips in anticipation. The shop in St Paul's churchyard was four stories high, plus garrets and was more than forty feet deep, it had books printed in roman and blackletter, bound and unbound, pamphlets and even plays, ballads and jest books. He spent much longer there than he intended and after picking up a basic Latin school text, *Lily's Grammar* he purchased three more books before taking himself off for dinner: *Aesop's Fables,* Malory's *Le Morte d'Arthur* and the works of Chaucer. He also bought a selection of songs by composers including Morely, Dowland and Campion.

He decided to make the most of his time in London and pay a visit to the theatre. He studied the handbills posted around the town to decide which play to go and see. He thought a comedy would best lighten his mood and decided on *A Midsummer Night's Dream* because he remembered Mr Alleyn mentioning the name of Shakespeare. He checked the name of the theatre, asked for directions and took a boat down the river.

He still couldn't believe there were actual structures purpose-built just for the showing of plays. He was early and spent time admiring the construction; the frame of the building was three stories in height, he estimated the first to be about twelve feet, the second maybe a foot shorter and the upper being about nine foot. Within the galleries were divided into rooms for gentlemen and two-penny rooms for lesser mortals. Richard had already decided to purchase a two-penny ticket rather than stand in the pit which was open to the elements. The stage was over forty foot long and jutted out into the middle of the yard. Made of good English oak, it was overlooked by the tiring house which had glazed windows. The building was covered with a tiled roof and had lead gutters to carry water away from the performance area. The entire frame was enclosed with a mixture of lathe, lime and hair.

The theatre was starting to fill up and Richard hurried to find himself a seat with the best view of the stage. He was amused to see so many young men coming first into the pit and scouring the audience for the prettiest girl and then jostling and pulling and pushing to try and be seated next to her. There was chatter and card playing, Richard bought a pie to eat and apples. Everyone was dressed up like a festival day. Richard leaned forward to see who else was sat around the playhouse and nearly fell off his seat when he spied the Earls of Essex and Southampton along with their other intimates in the lords' boxes. He ducked back and cursed that he had found himself a such a prominent position, he did not think the Earl would be amused that Richard had put players before his Lordship's needs. Richard thought about leaving, but he had paid his two-pence and longed to see the play and as the Earl obviously wished to view the performance as well Richard concluded there was nothing to be done but to sit back and enjoy the show.

"So how did you enjoy the entertainment, Mr Mudford?"

Richard cursed as he recognised the courtly drawl and turned to meet the Earl of Essex's gaze.

"Gentlemen, this fellow was with me in Spain and comes to London at my summons, yet he thinks it best to loiter and enjoy the delights of the playhouse rather than concern himself with the security of England."

This was too much, "Sadly, although I was indeed with my Lord in Spain, I was not able to return to England with him. But my two years as a prisoner will, I hope, provide intelligence for Her Majesty in her struggle against our enemies. I was on my way to Your Lordship's home when I heard that you were making for the theatre, so followed on. I would not presume to interrupt Your Lordship at leisure. As to the play, I am not one for fairies and magic potions but I recognised most of the rude mechanicals as neighbours of mine in Southampton." He made a good bow.

Essex paused a while before laughing and clapping Richard on his back, "Southampton, this is one of your flock. Do you know Mr Mudford here?"

The young Earl squinted, he was the worse for drink and

saw at least two of Richard. "He looks somewhat familiar. Do I know you, sir?"

"Not formally, my Lord, but when I was town sergeant I was often detailed to carry the town's New Year's gift to Your Lordship and to return to the town with bucks for the feasting days."

"Fine fellow, he's a fine fellow," he clapped Richard also. "Now I am going to be sick." He weaved away.

"I am dining at Court this evening, come to my town house at ten of the clock tomorrow."

"My Lord." Richard bowed low again.

Richard was at the Earl's townhouse by a quarter to ten and the Earl appeared at eleven.

"Ah we were at our revels last night Mr Mudford." He always made Richard's name sound like an insult. "You know why I sent for you?"

"I can hazard a guess."

"Hazard away."

"You were thwarted in your ambitions in Portugal and are looking for another Spanish adventure. You have seen my letter to the Queen, you know I have good knowledge of Cadiz and I think you are after singeing the King of Spain's beard."

"You are an arrogant knave, Mudford."

"So I have been told." The Earl laughed again.

"But I have a liking for you and you did me a favour at Lisbon and I do not forget such things. You are right, we have persuaded the Queen that she should support a strike into the heart of Spain, but the Queen hesitates. The Queen always hesitates, it is her nature. She is worried about costs." The Earl shook his head, more in sorrow than anger.

"But you think you will carry the day?"

"The Queen, the Queen holds me high favour, I am not sure if it is because of my stepfather or myself. Be that as it may I think that Her Majesty will agree and we will have to move quickly before she changes her mind back again."

The Earl spread a plot of Cadiz on the table, "I need you to tell me all you know, it is my intention to be in charge of this campaign. The last venture failed due to Drake's avarice and Norreys' lack of ...well shall we say commitment, no, too harsh, his cautiousness."

"Do you think there will be others vying for position?"

"My Lord Howard for one and Sir Walter for another."

"Raleigh?"

"You know him?"

"He has often been in Southampton, he brought in three prize ships whilst I was town sergeant and I helped him dispose of some of the goods. He was also Governor of Jersey and the town has many links there."

"And what do you make of him?"

"Like most of the freebooters he thinks much of himself, but he is a much better sailor than his brother."

"Carew?"

"No, my Lord, I refer to his stepbrother, Sir Humphrey Gilbert. The town helped to finance his voyage to the Americas and he and Sir Walter were made burgesses. It was a disaster and Sir Humphrey was lost at sea."

"Yes, I remember he was not known for his abilities as a sailor. The Queen has a fondness for Sir Walter, just like the rest of her common sea dogs. I am an Earl by blood and birth, it is my right to command. Still, Mr Mudford, I must load the dice. Tell me, what you know of Cadiz?"

Richard studied the plot and made amendments and additions, he pointed out what he had perceived to be weaknesses in the defences.

"My Lord, do you mean to bombard the town and then withdraw?"

"I should like to do a bit more than that. There is gold and silver to be had I want to take the town and return with enough booty to bring a smile to the Queen's face. Where do I find it Mr Mudford?"

Richard had no intention of telling him all he knew, but gave him some information where booty might be had.

"If treasure is the main aim it would be sensible to wait until the bullion fleet is in harbour. It will come in here and it should be possible to seize the cargo."

"You will of course accompany me." Richard had been expecting this and saw no way out.

"As Your Lordship commands."

"My Lord of Southampton and others of my supporters will be joining us later. We will talk more of our plans."

They kept Richard in town for three further days. When he finally got back to Southampton he sent for Jack and they both met with Lawrence Prowse.

"It is going to happen. Word will come soon about making ships ready."

"I am going to command the *Elizabeth*," said Prowse. The *Elizabeth* was a ship of some 140 tons.

"Jack, which of our vessels should go?"

"*The Pelican*, she is a younger ship, bigger, more fire power and more room for booty."

"What I am suggesting, Lawrence, is that when the town is secure, I take a contingent of men and secure for us some Spanish treasure. Jack will have another contingent to keep our line of communication to the ships."

"I am with you, boys."

"We will see you and all the men receive a good reward but the Mudford Brothers will be the largest sharers."

"I am content, Richard, it is your knowledge that will hopefully make us all rich. I am not greedy – well yes I am pretty greedy – but I am realistic" They shook hands and agreed on dispositions and what should be put in place for to their families if they did not make it back alive.

Chapter Fifty-Seven

"Why do you have to go with them? Remember what happened last time. What will become of us if you are taken prisoner?" Alice was beside herself.

"I don't actually have a choice, I have been ordered, I won't lie to you it is still dangerous but I think the plan and the fleet is better, there will be more an element of surprise. I am also older and wiser and we are in a much better position than when I went last time, no one will be able to take anything away and I have put things in place." Richard tried to sound more confident than he felt.

"I don't want you to go. We have been apart almost as long as we have been together–" she pleaded, Richard could feel himself weakening and was saved by the arrival of a servant.

"Sir, I am sorry to disturb, there is someone to see you."

"You should not interrupt, girl!" shouted Alice.

"Alice, please, who is it?" Richard was glad of a diversion so he could gather his arguments.

"She said her name was Mary, she is a common woman, sir, but said she knows you."

Richard looked blank, "Alice, let me take care of this and then we will talk further."

Alice was furious and slammed out.

"Or I could put this Mary off?" Richard called after her.

He went into the hall. A poorly dressed woman, grimy and careworn, stood in the hall, obviously nervous and wringing her hands.

"Mary! Mary Smith, come in, come in – girl bring us some ale and biscuits. Mary come and sit yourself down. Is everything all right?"

The woman looked relieved that she was obviously not going to be put out onto the street.

"Richard, it is good to see you again, you have done wonderfully well for yourself. How are your girls?"

"Flourishing, Mary, and your children?" She lowered her eyes, and bit her lip. Mary Smith had been one of his neighbours in Silkshop Yard, he remembered her as a happy woman with a lively family of four, no five children and a good-hearted husband, who perhaps was a little too fond of drink. She had been one of the ringleaders of the gaggle of women who had rallied round when he found himself a widower with two tiny babies.

"Richard, you must know I would never have bothered you, you are such an important man now, but the truth is I am desperate and have nowhere else to go. It has cost me a lot to come a-knocking at your door but my children's faces spurred me on."

The sustenance arrived and Richard noticed that Mary palmed a biscuit into her pocket as she took a long and welcome draft of her drink.

"Mary, please, we are old friends. What is it?"

"We are starving, Richard, we eat grass, rats. My Roger went off looking for work, there is nothing to be had here, too many people now in the town. It has been many weeks since I saw him. I appealed to the Mayor, but he wanted to know where my husband was, he thinks he has abandoned us so that we will be a drain on the town. We are Southampton born and bred, we have a right to be here. I thought perhaps, you must have shirts that need laundering, I used to do your shirts before, you remember, anything so that I may earn a few coins. I cannot go to anyone else in the Yard, they are all in the same way. Children are dying, and the old people–"

"Mary, you should have come to me sooner! I curse I did not think to visit you this long while, I have been so concerned with my own cares."

"I know you were prisoner, Richard, and that your family struggled, but you have clawed your way back, I just need a hand, I–"

"No say no more. I am in your debt. Come, come now to the kitchen you will take food for the whole yard. I promise you and yours will not starve, Mary. I promise."

They went down to the kitchen and Richard found a couple of sacks and started to fill them with food to the astonishment of the kitchen maid. She scuttled off and moments later Alice was in the kitchen.

"What are you about, Richard? This food is for our dinner."

"Alice, my former friends at Silkshop Yard are starving, we have plenty."

"We have enough but you should put your own family foremost–" hissed Alice.

"Excuse us a moment, Mary," Richard took Alice's elbow and walked her into the hallway. "Alice, please, I need to help, they came to my aid in times past."

"There are so many poor people about the town. The preacher last Sunday, said many were beggars, idle and not wanting to work."

"Have you forgotten so soon that we were once close to poverty ourselves?"

"No I don't forget, but I remember none came to our aid,

we had only ourselves to rely on." Richard's pleading eyes at last won her round.

"Take it! But only for Southampton folk, not incomers."

Richard went back to the kitchen and picked up the sacks and helped Mary carry the food to the Yard. It was strange walking again that once so familiar route. The Yard looked smaller and more cramped than he remembered. His old cottage had lost its thatched roof and now was patched with timbers, the paint had peeled off most of the buildings and the Yard ran with muck and worse. Three or four times as many people were now living in the same tumbled rooms. Eyes looked at him from every corner and when they learnt he had food they crushed about him.

"Stand back, stand back or I will hit you with the flat of my sword! You will all get a share, but only if you wait your turn." They forced their way to Mary's cottage, and set up shop there, portioning out the food as best they could. Word rapidly spread through the nearby yards and alleys and soon even more people crowded into the Yard.

"I'm sorry but this food is for Silkshop Yard people only!" Richard was forced to be harsh but he knew he did not have enough to go around. "I will speak to the Mayor about poor relief for the rest of you, I promise." They looked mutinous and Richard feared that there might be a riot, but he was strong, armed and spoke with authority. After a moment on the brink, he carried the day.

"Dear God, Mary, I had no idea. Food scraps aren't going to help."

"The harvests have been poor and so many are coming here from the country."

"I don't know what to do or say, I will speak to the Mayor."

"It's work we need."

"I know. I know."

He was utterly dejected when he reached home.

"What's the matter?" asked Alice, she had found something else to feed the family for supper and the children were all tucking in to a tasty repast.

"We are so lucky. I have never known such poverty. Their faces, children with swollen bellies, I'm sorry, Alice, I find I have no appetite."

He went and sat in his counting house and in a little while Alice came in, she sat on his lap, and he held her close, burying his face in her chest.

"Poor Richard, you can't save the whole world."

"I know, but maybe just a few people from Silkshop. Surely I can manage that, can't I?"

A couple of days later and he found himself outside Madame Sohier's house. He knocked and was admitted and went to the old woman's solar. She was dozing in her chair and woke with a start when he came in.

"Sorry, Wauldure, I did not know you were resting."

"Just my eyes, I was not sleeping."

"Of course. May I sit awhile?"

She gestured for him to join her.

"To what do I owe this singular pleasure?"

"A favour I am afraid."

"It was too much to expect that you would seek out my company for its own pleasure."

"You know that I like to talk with you, but today I need something else." Richard told her about his old friends in Silkshop Yard and the dire straits that they found themselves in.

"Are you wanting alms, Richard? The Communion usually look after their own first but I will see what assistance can be given."

"No, it is more than that, Wauldure. I'd like you to help me set up a cloth making business using the skills I know are still held by the people of the Yard."

"What? What are you saying?" Wauldure sat up straight.

426

"The Yard used to be a centre for the making of silk tassels and fancy goods in the days when the Italians were much in the town. When they stopped coming work dried up, but the skills are still there. I thought that Walerland used to have some dealings with serge making and the new draperies that the communion introduced to the town."

"That is so, but since his death much of his business interests have lapsed. I am no business woman, just a poor widow."

Richard laughed out loud, "There is nothing poor about you and you were much involved in many of your husband's dealings, some said you had the sharper brain for business."

Madame Sohier feigned shock.

"Do you want to slumber away the rest of your days?"

"Enough! You have not earned the right to talk to me in that way."

"I apologise."

"Go away now I need to think. I will send for you when I have decided what to do."

Richard thought that a victory had been won and left her staring into the distance, her brain obviously whirling.

Chapter Fifty-Eight

He received a missive from the Earl of Essex, the Queen had been persuaded to support the planned attack on Cadiz. Reading between the lines he gathered that speed and haste were the order of the day, not just for secrecy but in case the Queen changed her mind. He did not have a lot of time to try and help the poor of Silkshop Yard but luckily Madame Sohier was one who made quick decisions and sent a note to say she wanted to visit the Yard with him the next day. In the meantime Richard had found the Mayor and argued with him long and hard about increasing the poor relief. The Mayor retorted that the usual collection had been made and dispersed. Richard told him it was not enough as the need was too great. Mayor Ellyott was a candlemaker by profession and had served as town steward. He had owned a few small barques but was not a great trader like so many of the former mayors. He had been in constant trouble early in his career not keeping up his end of his contract to make candles for the town, so that he lost it due to the amount of complaints received. Back in '76 he had also been imprisoned by the order of the Privy Council on suspicion of spreading seditious rumours, being released because he was thought to not be right in the head. Yet ten years later he was climbing the offices of the town.

"What you must understand, Mudford, is that we are over pressed with the poor in this town. People are flooding in from the county and I fear many are just idle and probably have criminal intentions. If we let them see there are easy pickings to be had here, more will come."

"Sir, I am not asking you to support the incomers but to help good, honest Southampton folk who have through no fault of their own lost work, or had their pay cut and see the price of wheat soar due to the bad harvests. Here, I will put my marker down first, I am sure others will follow your lead, Mr Mayor." He had succeeded in blackmailing the Mayor into action. He did understand how difficult it was for the Mayor the population of the town had doubled in the last few years. At the same time as the town's trade was suffering but there were still wealthy men in the town and they should not be allowed to avert their eyes as he had almost done.

The next day Richard met with Madame Sohier and took her to Silkshop Yard. He had asked Mary to gather the best weavers and makers into her small cottage. The Yard people and Madame eyed each other suspiciously. The Communion was notorious for keeping themselves to themselves, yet they were hard-working and skilful, had been successful in their own land and had bought those abilities to Southampton. Local people blamed them for taking work away from those they thought of as true Southampton people.

"My son-in-law tells me that you have talents that could be applied to weaving." No one said anything. "My family have some interest in the making of serge, mainly broad serge used to weave cloaks." Still silence. "However, this needs a double loom for two people to operate, and I think until we see what skills there are, that it is too big an investment. I do think there is room in the market for the production of the coarser pinion serge though and perhaps stammet, there is not much of this as yet produced in the town." The yarn for this had to be scoured to make it finer.

"What of silk weaving?" asked Mary, "We used to produce silk goods."

"But you were never permitted to weave the silk yourself."

"No, but we wanted to but the Italians protected the trade."

"I think you would be better employed in spinning yarn. It will save on importing it from the Netherlands and it would be easy to set up a spinning wheel in each cottage. My son-in-law has trade contacts in Oxfordshire where we can source the warp and we can use Hampshire wool for the weft, or Devonshire if we can get it."

"How many could be employed as spinners?" Mary asked again, as the appointed spokesperson for the neighbourhood.

"For fine serge a weaver will require ten spinners." This time there were murmurs people were starting to become interested. "There is the preparation work as well, the wool will need to be carded and greased before it is ready to be spun.

"Where will we get the spinning wheels? We have no money."

"Myself and my son-in-law will supply the initial capital, and you will pay us back over time once you start producing the yarn. I am also willing to take a couple of boys to be apprenticed as weavers. I have looms in my yard. They have been idle a while but one of my relatives is willing to get them into working order and train the boys."

"What is in it for you?" said someone in the back of the crowded room.

"I wish to turn an honest profit, of course, but not an unfair one. I am doing this because Richard asked me, for no other reason."

"And what of the dying of the cloth?"

"The Communion has a dye house out at Hill and if there is demand it may be that another will be opened in the town itself, at West Hall."

"The Mayor won't like that very much, the stench and all," said another.

"That is for the dyer to sort out. But you have my offer, take it or leave it, for my part I will need to know that those we take on have sufficient skill and are reliable."

There was muttering and discussion but the answer was forgone, hunger overcame any prejudice about working for an incomer. Madame Sohier arranged for the first set of spinners to visit her so that she might test their skills before she invested in them.

"Thank you, Richard, it is a good thing you do for us," said Mary

"It is Madame Sohier you need to thank, Mary, without her skills, contacts and money this would not be possible."

"Well if I must."

"You must."

"I meant what I said Richard, if they have no skill or are lazy and unreliable they will not be kept on," said Wauldure as they walked back to her residence.

"I understand, you are quite right to demand these things. We have given them a chance of a better life. It is up to them now."

Richard put down Hakluyt's *Principles of Navigations*, his orders had arrived. He was bound again for Spain.

Part Eleven

1596

Chapter Fifty-Nine

As he walked up the street to the house of Luis de la Castro, his heart was pounding, and not through fear of ambush. All sorts of images were rushing into his brain, the moment he almost let John drown to escape himself, the fear he felt being in the hands of the Inquisition, having to hide his true feelings – betraying himself at his core – in order to placate Luis de la Castro so that he might be free of torture and have hope of life, and then that worse betrayal as he got used to feeling the sun on his back and became comfortable of his life in Spain, and finally the destructive relationship with Jacinta, beautiful, wild, cruel and heartless. Jacinta who was more alive than anyone else he knew.

He signalled the men to follow him carefully into the courtyard of the place of his former residence. They fanned out, the house seemed to be empty and there were signs of packing that had been disturbed. Richard was pleased to see the cases and boxes already full with treasures, it would make their task easier. One of the men his eyes wide with greed, forgot to move stealthily and went to rummage in a box. A shot ran out and he fell a trickle of blood running down his forehead. Richard glanced up whilst ordering his men to get down. There

435

on the upper gallery stood Jacinta in a flaming red dress with a smoking gun in her hand.

"Jacinta!"

She was shocked to hear her name, her eyes surveyed the courtyard.

"Jacinta, you are outnumbered, I don't want to have to shoot you," Richard called out in Spanish

She saw him and raised her gun, "Richard Mudford, it would give me pleasure to die in your company. We can go to Hell together."

"There is no reason for either of us to go anywhere quite so unpleasant. I came here to find you. Cadiz is a dangerous place at the moment. I hoped you might have left the city."

"My servants fled, for which I will take delight in flaying them alive. Come up, Richard, I don't want to keep shouting, it is so unladylike."

Richard worked out the risk and decided it was worth the gamble. He told his men to hold their fire unless he was betrayed, then they could shoot Jacinta dead. He scaled the marbled steps until they were eye to eye. She was still as beautiful as he remembered, no he did her an injustice, she was more beautiful. Her eyes were flashing and her breasts heaved, trying to break free from her very tight bodice. Defiantly she wore jewels in her hair, ears and around her neck, her face was subtlety painted to enhance the fullness of her mouth and the wideness of her eyes, her brows were black and arched. She dropped the spent gun but clutched the handgun as she stepped forward and kissed him full on the mouth.

"I knew you would come back, once a man has tasted me he is mine forever."

He kissed her back, it was intoxicating.

"What are you still doing in the city? Dressed like a queen? You are courting a horrible death or something worse."

"I could not leave without my money, you should know

436

that, but the servants were fearful. Even when I threatened to kill them myself they were still more frightened of the sons of Drake. But God has sent me you instead." She kissed him again and pressed herself against him.

"You are pleased to see me as well!"

Richard drank in her scent and remembered the brutal sex that he had been swept up in the madness of. It was a drug which he was powerfully tempted to take again.

"You have enough men, we could take the money and smuggle it from the city. My dear husband has thankfully joined his ancestors but I still have his country estate mortgaged though it is, the bastard, we can wait there till it is safe."

"And what of my men?"

"We can kill them once they have served their purpose."

"Seems to be a plan."

"We can leave by the postern gate in the eastern walls."

"I remember it. There is so much chaos." He kissed her again.

She put her hand down his breeches and squeezed him almost too hard.

"Jacinta, we don't have much time." She pouted but she loved money more and withdrew her hand. Richard ordered the men to fill the packing cases with the rest of the gold and silver, paintings and other items of worth.

"Where is the money, Jacinta?"

"Can I trust you?"

"I came back for you didn't I? I betrayed my Captain and my Queen. Instead of fighting for the Reformation I am here squeezing your breasts and putting my tongue in your mouth."

"I don't have a lot of choice do I?"

"No, I could use gunpowder and blow the place apart until I find the treasury but that might alert others to what we are about, which would not be good for you as I would have to kill you to save myself."

"You are making me moist with desire." Her voice was husky.

With great effort Richard ignored this. "Where is the treasure?"

She took him to a room with a hidden door which when sprung revealed more gold and silver than Richard could have ever imagined. He tried not to show his shock.

"Luis's treasure is here too, we were gathering money together for a scheme he was hatching."

"That's good for us. Where is Luis? Is he still in the town?"

"He does not visit here very often, he hides himself away in the family castle. I act as his agent."

Richard was bemused. Jacinta read his face, "There was an accident, with the guns, he was always playing with those stupid guns."

"Accident?" a twinge of guilt caught at him.

"He lost a hand and his manhood, he is horribly disfigured. He sees no one if he can avoid it. If he cannot the room is draped and all is darkness." She lost interest in her sibling's suffering.

Jacinta pulled Richard to her again kissing him and began loosening his clothes.

"Jacinta, there is no time."

"There is always time, tell me you are not hungry for me." He pushed her roughly against the wall, hoisting her skirts, she wrapped her legs around him, her nails dug into his shoulders. He heard his name being called, he pulled himself away breathless and sweating. "I have to go."

The courtyard was full of so much treasure and booty Richard wondered how they were going to take it all.

"Looks like you might need some help, Diccon." Jack appeared in the gateway with another cohort of men.

"Jack, thank God, I thought we were going to have to leave some behind and it would have broken my heart."

They started to organise the men and at that moment Jacinta re-appeared.

"Who is this? What is happening?" She spat, her eyes flashed and sparked as she realised that she had been betrayed.

"Jacinta, please meet my brother Jack." Richard saw the understanding that passed between them. They were kindred spirits and recognised one another immediately.

"This is the whore who kept you in Spain so long," muttered Jack as he looked her up and down, undressing her on the way.

"What is he doing here? This is not part of the plan!" She spoke to Richard but her eyes did not leave Jack and she wetted her lips.

"It's part of my plan, Jacinta." Richard felt calm but also strangely jealous.

"What do you mean, you bastard?"

"Language."

She pulled her attention away from Jack and ran at Richard, her hands like claws and murder in her eyes. Jack caught her before she scratched Richard's eyes out. She fought like a hellcat.

"I see she doesn't know you are taking her treasure to England."

Richard shrugged and went back to ordering the men.

"If you are done with her now, do you mind?" Richard shrugged again and Jack carried her upstairs and into one of the upper chambers.

The slow movement of treasure began. Richard tried to focus on that, but his eyes flicked too often upstairs. While working Richard received a message from Prowse on the progress of the battle, the town was secured and he reckoned they could hold out for several days, maybe even a couple of weeks. Richard was pleased as it would mean they could get most of the treasure back to the ships. He sent a message back to say all was going well his end and asked Prowse to keep Will safe for him. Jack re-appeared some hours later.

"How's it going?"

"Fine. Where's Jacinta?"

"I locked her in a cupboard. She is wild." Jack's face was covered in scratches and Richard thought the rest of his body probably was too. "She likes to play rough, doesn't she?" he looked quizzically at his brother. Richard was unable to talk he was feeling sick. He pulled himself together and changed the subject.

"We need to keep working, I'm going to the kitchens to see if there is any food. The men will need sustenance to keep them working at this pace, these chests are as heavy as original sin."

Richard found bread, cheese and fruit. He piled it all onto the table. He would let the men come down in pairs so as not to break the rhythm of the transportation. He became aware of noise. Every nerve told him someone else was in the room. Behind the water barrel? There wasn't much room, perhaps it was just a rat. He moved quickly across the room, his gun ready to fire. He pulled the barrel aside, crouched in the corner trying to make himself invisible was a small boy of three or four at most. He was richly dressed and obviously no servant. He was also absolutely terrified. Richard put down his gun and knelt beside the boy who tried to push himself through the wall.

"Don't be afraid." The child started to cry. Richard realised he was speaking English and switched to Spanish, "Don't be afraid, I will not hurt you I promise. What is your name?" The boy said nothing. Richard decided to gamble, "Your mother sent me to look for you, Jacinta, your mother, I am her friend." Now the small boy seemed completely confused but he did react to Jacinta's name. Richard grabbed some fruit off the table and came and sat. He started to eat a pomegranate and then passed one to the boy.

"I expect you are hungry. You must have been hiding here a long while. It was very clever of you to hide yourself like that. I used to live here once too." The boy started to eat the pomegranate, "I had a room behind the kitchen. I worked here first helping out and then for your Uncle Luis. I had to go away but came back to look for you and for your mother."

"You came to look for me?" The boy stared hard.

"I did. My name is Richard."

"Are you the English Devil?"

"I expect I might be, but I am more English than I am a devil. What do they call you?"

"Antonio."

"Hello Antonio, I am pleased to meet you at last."

"Where is my mother?"

"She is fine, in fact I came to get her some food. Perhaps you can tell me what she likes to eat."

"She loves pomegranates too."

"Then that is what she will have."

Antonio allowed Richard to pick him up and carry him upstairs.

"Well," said Jack "who have we got here?"

"This is Antonio, Jacinta is his mother." Jack considered this information and looked more carefully at the boy. His skin was paler than most Spaniards he had known, his hair was also fairer but it tumbled in curls. He was well formed and stared at Jack with hazel eyes.

"Jack, look after him for me, I want to go and talk to his mother."

Upstairs Jacinta was banging on the cupboard door. Richard unlocked it and she scrambled out cursing. Her hair and clothes were dishevelled.

"Your brother has ravished me! He is a brute and a pig."

"Yes he is, but I have never known him to take a woman who did not want to be taken."

"He has abused me! You did nothing."

"Jacinta, I saw the looks that passed between you. I know

441

you. If I thought you did not want him I would have stopped him."

"Really?

He passed her the pomegranates and she devoured them, the juice running down her chin and dripping onto her breasts.

"He is much better in bed than you."

"I don't doubt it."

"And does he have a muling, puking, little wife at home?"

"No."

She looked at him for the longest time.

"Jacinta, I mean you no harm, I will help you escape—"

"—without my money I do not think so." She tossed the fruit onto the floor.

"The money is coming to England with me. I am sure you have other resources."

"My husband lied to me about mortgaging the estate, it was mostly taken by creditors. We have been taxed to the hilt for Armadas and wars in foreign lands. Besides, much of this money belongs to Luis. He will kill me when he finds out."

"Well he won't find out your part, it's not your fault the servants ran off."

"He won't see it like that."

"So what is your plan?" She would have a plan, she always had a plan.

"What? You think I will tell you?"

"Jacinta, the boy..."

"What boy?" she tossed her head in disinterest.

"Antonio...your son." He could see her calculating what to say to him.

"What of him?"

She seemed disinterested. "I found him hiding in the kitchen. Weren't you worried about him at all?"

"He is well is he not?" She sounded bemused.

"Yes, I won't let anything happen to him."

"How touching." She held his stare.

Richard locked her back in the cupboard. He heard a ruckus downstairs and hurried back to the courtyard. Bart Biston was holding Antonio up by the ankles and was swinging him to and fro, threatening to dash his head against a marble pillar. Richard jumped over the balustrade, landing and rolling, coming to his feet again by Bart. He grabbed Antonio in one hand and put a stranglehold around Bart's neck with his other. Bart's face started to turn red as he kicked out trying to get Richard to break his grip. Richard knew he would not be able to hold Bart long with a screaming child in his arm so he kneed Bart in the groin and was pleased to see him collapse to the ground.

"Fuck you! We don't go around terrifying children."

"The little bastard is Spanish, what does it matter?" wheezed Bart as he cradled his privates.

Richard kicked him in the face to shut him up. He looked around for Jack, who came running in from the outer courtyard.

"Fuck you, Jack, I told you to look after him, Bart was about to dash his brains out."

"Sorry I left him for a moment, there has been another message from Lawrence. Will's been wounded."

"What? How?" Richard blinked several times he could not take in what Jack was saying.

"I don't know. Look, he's not dead, it's a wound to his leg."

"I should go to him." Will must be the priority now.

"He is being taken down to the port to the makeshift hospital, they will patch him up and then he'll be put on board ship."

"Fuck, fuck, I must go and see him. Alice will kill me, fuck. It's not good to get wounded Jack you know that." The harshness in Richard's voice was making Antonio wriggle and squirm, trying to free himself from Richard's grasp.

"Leave Antonio with me." Jack held out his arms, Richard was unconvinced. "I promise I will keep a better eye on him.

Go and see if you can find out more about Will. I'll get things moving a bit faster here. If we need to pull out sooner, we will. Trust me – I swear I will shoot anyone who threatens the boy." Reluctantly, Richard handed Antonio over.

Richard went with the next team of men who were taking booty back to the ship along the route secured by Jack. When he got to the port he looked around for the hospital tent. It was full of groaning men and dead bodies. It reminded him of the aftermath of the Armada and the men they had tried to help in Margate. He found an orderly who directed him to a billet in the corner. The surgeon was pulling a cover over the head of the boy who lay there. Richard thought he was going to be sick, he pulled the cover back. It wasn't Will. He cast about him frantically.

"Pa, Pa!"

He saw Will on the other side of the tent.

"What the hell of you been doing Will? I told you to stay out of trouble."

"Sorry Pa, tried my best." The boy's face creased with pain.

"Don't talk, let me have a look." Richard examined him carefully. The leg wound was a mess from below the knee, blood and bone exposed. He got Will some water and cursed that he did not have his own medicine chest with him, it was still on board.

"It does not look good Will, but your heart beats strongly and you have no fever. This place is filthy, will you be able to stand it if I move you? I want to take you to where I can look after you better." The boy nodded.

Richard searched around and found some clean bandages and bound up his leg. He wrapped him in a blanket and despite the protests of the surgeon carried him out and back to the Castro house. There he commandeered a room, washed and bathed the wound. He found the family's medicine chest and did his best to make Will comfortable, but he didn't like the look of his leg one little bit. Neither did Jack.

"It's going to have to come off Diccon, you know that don't you?"

"Damn, I thought if I cleaned it up it wouldn't look so bad."

Richard let Jacinta back out of the cupboard, "I need to find a surgeon, a good surgeon. Is the Jewish doctor still living here?"

"There are no Jews in Spain."

"You know who I mean, stop playing games!"

"Or what? You will beat me? Rape me? Steal my money? Oh no you have done all that already."

"Jacinta, please, my stepson needs a surgeon."

"The son of the milksop you married? How every interesting! If the doctor hasn't run off, he is still in the same place. He patched you up well I remember after your disagreement with the Inquisition." Richard went to put her back into the cupboard. "Enough! I will behave, I will go and sit with your son."

Richard hesitated for a while, Jacinta shrugged her beautiful shoulders. He led her to where Will lay. Antonio was there too and ran to his mother who fussed him in an abstracted way and then she sat down by the bed and started to bathe William's forehead.

"How touching," said Jack.

★

He took a few wrong turns and was beside himself with frustration by the time he finally found himself in a square he recognised. At the centre was the small church that had been the sinecure of the priest who had tried to save his soul. Richard let out a cry. Dangling from the large wooden cross that stood outside the church was a body, a makeshift noose around its neck. Richard hoped he was wrong but he knew he was not. It was the small form of the priest. He managed to clamber up

445

the cross and clamping his legs around its trunk and leaning his arms over the cross piece he took out his knife and started to cut through the rope. He slid with the body to the ground, pricking himself with splinters as he did so.

The man was long dead, there was no saving him. Richard cut the knot of the noose which was embedded in his neck and removed the rope. He picked the priest up and went inside the church. It had been ransacked, the statues of the saints smashed along with the stained glass. The font was overturned and the altar desecrated. They had tried to burn it but the fire had not taken. Richard laid the body down in front of the altar. He straightened the limbs and folded the arms across the priest's narrow chest. He tried to remember a prayer for the dead and muttered what he could in Latin crossing himself at the end. He heard a noise to his right and stealthily put his hand on the hilt of his sword, he pulled it out in a flash as he sprang to his feet, reaching for his handgun. An elderly nun shrunk back into the shadows. Richard put up his weapons and told her in Spanish that he would not harm her. She hesitated for a while before coming slowly into the light. She gasped at the sight of the priest and fell to her knees in prayer.

"I'm sorry." said Richard.

"For what? You did not kill him. I saw the men who did, whilst I hid like a coward."

"It would have done you no good to come out, they would have killed you too."

Richard dropped to his knees again beside the body.

"I did what I could, I could not remember the rites."

"You are a Catholic?"

"I used to be, for a while."

She looked at him strangely, not quite understanding.

"He was trying to help the injured and was giving comfort to a dying English soldier when they came upon him. They

446

thought he had harmed their fellow. He tried to speak to them in English but they did not understand him."

"He had a terrible accent," said Richard.

"You knew him?!"

"A little a long time ago, I should have tried to know him better. I am sorry I cannot stay longer, you should hide yourself. We will be gone in a few days. I cannot help you bury him. I am sorry, I have to go, my son is injured and I am looking for a doctor."

"There is a novice here with me. We will take him down to the crypt where we have been hiding.

Tell me, which doctor do you seek?"

"Dr Lopez, he lives near here but I cannot find the way."

"I know him. Take the path on the far side of the church till you see a yellow house on the corner, turn right there and just after the basket maker's you will find the courtyard."

"Of course, yes I thank you, sister."

She pressed the priest's rosary into his hands.

"I can't take this!"

"Father Ricardo has no need of it now. Perhaps it will help you find your way back."

Father Ricardo! They shared the same name. Richard nodded in thanks and hid the rosary away as he hurried from the church. Soon he was standing outside the familiar tenement. Doctor Lopez was barricaded inside. It was not a wealthy part of town and was receiving little interest from the English. Richard called out and made himself known. The doctor stuck his head nervously out of an upstairs window. He was astounded to see Richard below and looked around quickly to see if there were others with him.

"Ricardo? What are you doing here? Are you with those devils who are burning the city?"

"I am afraid so Dr Lopez. We are at war and the Spanish army would do worse to us if they could."

447

"That does not make it right."

"You should be safe here sir, there is nothing to tempt them hither. But you are right to stay out of sight," called Richard. He also looked around, worried he might be set upon by the inhabitants cowering behind the walls and doors.

"I was about to say it is good to see you, and that you are looking well but that would be ridiculous under the circumstances. And you have obviously not come here to pass the time."

"No sir, you shame me but it is so. I have come in search of your medical skills."

Lopez cocked his head to one side like a sparrow.

"My stepson Will is with me but he has been grievously wounded. His leg has been smashed, I fear it must come off, I need a good surgeon."

Dr Lopez did not hesitate, he was a physician first and foremost. He gathered his instruments together and bade his wife and children not to worry. Richard had never thought of him as a family man before, but then he had never bothered to ask. The children looked terrified about having an Englishman in their midst.

"Did anyone see you come?" asked Lopez.

"I don't believe so."

"If it is found out that I have helped the invaders, it will be the worse for me."

"I understand, thank you, sir."

They strapped Will down on the bed. Richard gave him an infusion of poppy juice to help with the pain but the screams were still gut-wrenching. Dr Lopez's knives were sharp and he worked well with Ned, one of the crew who had gained much experience over the years of cauterizing wounds from amputated limbs. Uncharacteristically kind, Jacinta stroked Will's forehead and sang to him softly. It seemed to comfort the boy. Will fell into a sleep and they tidied the bloodied room and disposed of the mangled leg.

"I have done all I can, Ricardo, I hope it was enough. I have used comfy and goosegrease and anointed with styptic. Check it in a week, if the pus is yellow and has no smell it is a good sign. I am glad to have seen you again, even in these conditions," said Dr Lopez as he cleaned his hands.

Richard thanked the doctor and led him safely back to his home, whereupon he gave the doctor a bag of gold coins. Dr Lopez raised his brows.

"I do not understand what is going on any more," he said as he took the bag.

"Neither do I, but I thank you for your humanity to Will. I can tell you we will be withdrawing in a little while. Do you have enough food and water to last?"

"Sufficient if, as you say, it will not be too long. I did manage to stockpile some goods and water, we can last another couple of weeks at least. I hope your boy makes it, he did not die of shock on the table, the cut was clean and the wound cauterised. He is young and strong. Remember that positive thoughts and a will to live make all the difference."

"Thank you, Doctor Lopez, I am again in your debt."

"I may perhaps offer another service?"

"Yes?"

"There are English prisoners being kept in the old gaol. Do you know it? You were brought there when you first came to Cadiz."

"I could never forget, thank you again Doctor, I will free them and we will take them back to England with us." He embraced the man and then hurried back to the Castro house.

★

"Why did they have to take off my leg? What will become of me now?" Will asked. He had awoken confused, demanding to know what had become of his leg.

"Don't worry, Will. Although I would never have wished this upon you, many men have managed very well with just one leg." Richard tried to think of something positive to say, he remembered how he had felt when he thought he might lose his arm, he sounded more cheery than he felt. "Oliver Lambert for instance, he is from Southampton, you know him don't you? He is here on this campaign. Oliver has served the Queen in Ireland and the Netherlands with great success and courage. You would never know he had only one leg. I could ask him to meet with you if you would like?"

"Maybe, I don't know. Whatever will Ma say?" He cried a little, and then slept again. Richard felt like crying too, knowing he would have to face Alice.

"He is a handsome boy, it's a shame he has been maimed so," said Jacinta.

"Don't let him know you pity him."

"Will he live?" She stroked his forehead.

"I am hopeful. Lopez was quick, he's not lost too much blood and has no signs of fever yet," said Richard, sending up a silent prayer.

Chapter Sixty

"Diccon, another message from Lawrence, they are going to start falling back to the ships tomorrow. Lawrence said he will sweep around and pick us up if he can, but if not we should make our own way to the ships," said Jack.

"I'm worried about Will. He should not be moved so soon."

"We have no choice Diccon. The good news is the booty is all on board."

"Excellent. Now there is just one more thing we must do."

"What?" said Jack impatiently.

"I have heard there are English prisoners held at the old gaol. I am going to break them out."

Jack rolled his eyes.

"Jack!"

"Fine." Jack didn't seem fine. With his hands on his hips, his mouth turned down, and his shirt open at the neck stained and dirty, he looked every inch a brigand.

"In the morning we'll take Will on a stretcher and then I'll take a few men and make for the gaol." Jack shrugged, he just wanted to get out to sea. He narrowed his eyes and looked at Richard, he knew there was more.

"Jack, what am I going to do about Antonio?" Richard ran his fingers through his hair and sat down on a nearby barrel.

"Do you want him back in England?" Jack sat down beside him.

"I don't know. I'm not even sure he is my son, he could belong to Jacinta's husband. I am sure that is what everyone was told, but she could have had any number of lovers. I even wondered about her and Luis."

"That's sick." Jack pulled a face.

"They are only half brother and sister." Even to his own ears that sounded ridiculous.

"Well that's half as sick then."

"But I shouldn't take him away from his mother and the only life he knows."

"I don't get the impression she cares that much for him."

"He cares for her, but if I leave him, anything could happen in this turmoil."

"Granted, but what would Jacinta say?" Jack reached for a bottle of wine and pulled out the stopper, took a draught and passed the bottle to his brother. Richard drank deeply.

"I'm not sure. She is plotting something, she won't give up her money easily."

"She is a devil in bed, almost broke my back."

"Jack for God's sake!" Richard stood up abruptly, uncomfortable at the thought of them together.

"Sorry, didn't think you cared."

"I don't, but she does get under your skin."

"Like poison." Jack drained the bottle.

"I thought there might have been something between you Jack, more than just a good fuck." Did Richard really want to know? What answer would be worse?

"She is glorious and I have never met a woman so beautiful, but she's hard work, Diccon, and I can't be doing with a woman who needs constant attention." Jack rummaged around for more wine.

"I'm going to go and sit with Will."

"You better make up your mind about Antonio soon," Jack called after him.

★

"You have to be brave, Will, we must leave Cadiz, and the journey back to the ship will not be pleasant."

"I will bear it, Pa."

"Good boy. Jack is going to look after you, and I would like you to take this back for me."

"What is it Pa?"

"A guitar, I learned to play a bit when I was here. I'll teach you when we get home, now though I have to go and break some English prisoners out of gaol and then I will meet you at the ship."

"Is that little boy coming too?" Will nodded to where Antonio was sat playing in the corner. God knows where Jacinta was, probably in bed with Jack.

"I don't know, Will, I am worried about him. It's not safe here and his mother is only concerned for herself."

"You were here before weren't you, Pa?"

Richard took a deep breath, "Yes, after I escaped from the Inquisition, still a prisoner but in slightly better conditions."

"That woman, you knew her too?"

"Yes I did."

"Ma, thought there was someone."

"What are you talking about?"

"We heard some of the arguments you and Ma had."

Richard winced. "When you get older you will understand more."

"I understand a bit about girls, the scullery maid let me

453

touch her paps and showed me her hairy bits." said Will in an attempt at manly conversation.

"Her what?" Dear God this was no time to have a father and son chat.

"Ma won't like it if you bring Antonio back."

"I know."

"But I would hate to think he might get killed."

"Me too."

"Jack, I'm moving out. Any sign of Lawrence?"

"No I have sent him a message and told him to meet us at the square. If we aren't there when he arrives he'll go straight for the ships."

"Look, give Jacinta some money. Get her to hide some of her jewels – the ones you haven't stolen – and then drop her and the boy off at the postern gate. She is resourceful, she will survive."

"Sure?"

"What else can I do?"

Richard took his band of men and moved quickly towards the old prison. They could hear the gunfire getting stronger, the counter-attack must have begun and there wasn't much time. Thankfully the prison guards had fled as had most of the prisoners, but down in the pit Richard could hear groans and men calling out for food and water. His blood had turned ice cold and he thought he might faint with the memories that came flooding back.

"What now, sir?" asked one of the men.

"What? Oh...er...this way, this way. He found a torch, lit it and took them down to the fetid, stinking pit that had once been his prison. He shot the lock off the door and wrenched it open.

The stench was almost unbearable; the pit was full to

bursting with prisoners. Richard cursed that he had not thought to come here sooner. He saw a water barrel in the corner outside the door. He thrust the torch inside the cell. Men were groaning, unkempt, unshaven, lying in their own shit, clothes in rags, bones sticking out.

"I am Richard Mudford, I am come from England. The Queen has sent us to rescue you, but there is little time. I beg you to gather what strength you have left, there is water out here to drink, and then follow my men down to the port. There are ships there boys, bound for England."

For a moment nobody moved or said a word. Richard thought they might be too far gone to have understood him. Then they were scrabbling for the door, pushing past him, making for the water, some blessing and thanking him. He ordered his men to start leading them out. The men helped those who were too weak to walk unaided. Somewhere inside them the desire to get home was such that even those who a moment before had lain in misery were on their feet and scurrying like rats down to the port. The pit was empty, Richard looked around there was a bundle of rags in the corner.

"Too late for him," a toothless man said as he staggered by. Richard hesitated for a moment and then went over and kicked gently at the bundle.

"You need to stand; if you can't stand we can't take you."

There was no sound. Richard turned to go and as he did the bundle made a noise. Richard strained to hear, his heart nearly stopped when the bundle said his name. Richard went down on his knees and rolled the heap over. He knew it was a human being though his eyes told him otherwise as he looked at flesh so thin and shrunken.

"Diccon, I stayed alive," a voice barely rasped.

"Oh my God, John? John!" He was a mere shadow of his former self. He looked as if he had been broken, shattered into small pieces and pasted back together by someone who had never seen the original.

"Sir! Sir, we must go, the Spanish have broken through, there is no time!" one of his men called.

Richard gathered John up in his arms and slung him over his shoulder.

"Hang on, John, I'm taking you home, just hang on."

They were running, there was smoke and noise and shells exploding. Everywhere was ablaze, the ancient and glorious cathedral, the treasure fleet in the harbour. Richard's eyes stung and his muscles ached, he moved John further over his shoulder and willed himself to keep running. It was becoming hard to breathe. In the distance he could see the masts of the ships, then Jack and Lawrence Prowse were running towards him.

"Christ, Diccon, what are you doing? We need to get out of here, everyone else is on board," yelled Jack.

"It's John, it's John."

"Jesu, here let me help." They slung John between them and with Prowse and a few other men giving covering fire made it down to the dock. Richard passed John into the first boat. To his surprise he saw young Lawrence Dypere sitting on an oar.

"Lawrie!"

"Yes, Uncle Mudford. Lawrie, look after this man, it's your father." The boy's jaw dropped open but he scrambled forward and took John's head and laid it on his lap.

The other men were scrambling into the ships.

"Is Will aboard?"

"He's on the *Elizabeth*," called Jack.

"I'll go with Lawrence then." He pushed Jack off in the first boat. Lawrence was getting into the other boat, the last left at the dock.

"Come on, Richard." Richard looked around to make sure that no one was left behind, he heard crying.

456

"Richard, for Christ sake come on, I'm casting off, jump for God's sake," bellowed Prowse

Richard was searching amongst the debris on the dock. He found the boy Antonio screaming in terror, lost and alone. He looked around for Jacinta, she was nowhere to be seen. He grabbed the boy, ran to the edge of the dock and leapt across the few feet of water, landing on top of Bart Biston.

"Get off me you bastard!"

"Stop whining Biston and pull on those oars," yelled Prowse.

Chapter Sixty-One

They weren't far from Southampton. Richard was sat with Will making sure he ate all the stew the cook had prepared. The boy Antonio had shared Will's billet all the voyage back, he seemed to have realised that they were connected. For his part Will appeared to be happy to have something to think about other than the loss of his leg. Many of the men on board were unhappy about having a Spaniard on board, even if he was just a little child. Richard suspected Bart Biston was stirring up trouble, Prowse kept the men busy, putting in extra drills and practice in case they were chased by any Spanish ships. He also didn't want the men to get too many ideas about the booty they were carrying, he could not believe the amount of treasure in his hold and knew that the *Pelican* held even more.

"This will set me up in business in Southampton. And you, Richard, will be the richest man in Hampshire!" Lawrence was grinning, standing up on his toes as he imagined his future life.

"Maybe, money isn't everything I now discover."

"Are you thinking about the boy?" Lawrence clasped Richard around the shoulders.

"I'm thinking about what Alice will say."

"Can't you just say he stowed away or something?"

"And if she tells me to send him back to Spain or put him in the alms house? She always suspected I didn't tell her everything about my time in Spain." Richard hung his head.

"I can't imagine what you endured, looking at some of the prisoners and hearing their tales, and horror stories about the Inquisition."

"Fear and mystery were their main weapons. You spent your time worrying what might happen to you – they didn't really need actual torture though they used it well enough. Working on the galleys as John did was more horrible, being treated worse than slaves, year in year out, I don't know how he survived. He was determined to see his family again I suppose. He was braver than I, hung onto his ideals."

"What do you mean?" Lawrence was suspicious.

"Nothing. I just have a bad feeling that my luck has run out."

"How is Will?"

"He is doing remarkably well, he had a good surgeon and he is a strong boy." Richard gnawed his lip, "He loved to sail, play football. What will his life be like now?"

"There are plenty of men who have lost legs and arms and still scoot up the rigging."

"I got Oliver Lambert to speak to him–"

"Well there you go, he is a great soldier, Ireland, the Netherlands and now Spain, nothing held him back." He clapped Richard's back.

The lookout called out "land ahoy."

The *Elizabeth* and the *Pelican* had shadowed each other all the way home and now tied up next to each other at town quay. Richard nearly fell overboard when he saw Jacinta, strolling around the deck of the *Pelican*. He picked up Antonio and went across to the other ship. The little boy ran to his mother who patted his head as if he had just been out playing.

"You left him on the dock, Jacinta, you abandoned him."

Richard was coldly furious and wanted to wring Jacinta's neck.

"He ran off, I looked for him, I could not find him. What was I to do?" She shrugged her pretty shoulders and chuckled her son under his chin. He leaned against her leg.

"What were you doing on the dock in the first place? I left orders for you to be taken to the postern gate."

"She bribed her escort and smuggled herself on board," said Jack joining them, "She loves money even more than I do."

"You shouldn't have brought her here, Jack!"

"What would you have me do throw her overboard? I didn't even know she was on the ship till we were well out to sea. She said she had sent the boy to her country estate."

"This is a nightmare. Look you are going to have to keep her out of sight for a while."

"I don't see how," said Jack wanting to wash his hands of the problem.

"Think of something. I need to take Will home and explain to his mother how he came to be maimed. Now is not the time for her to discover my former mistress and my probable bastard are in town."

"I will do what I can, but hiding a Spanish noble woman might be a bit difficult, it will be all over the town once the crew goes ashore."

This was a nightmare, Richard remembered there was more.

"Do what you can, what of John? Did he survive the journey, Jack?"

"He did, God only knows how, sheer bloody mindedness. I would never have recognised him. I don't know how his family will cope. Lawrie couldn't handle it, decided John wasn't, couldn't be his father. Didn't want anything to do with him, I had to threaten him with the yard arm."

"Jack!"

"Don't Jack me! I had a hysterical woman, a hysterical boy

460

and John, waking up in the night screaming from nightmares. I barely held the crew together."

"Sorry, I'm sorry."

"You know what her plan is don't you?" said Jack he nodded towards Jacinta as she watched some of the cargo going ashore.

"Who? What plan?" asked Richard momentarily confused.

"Jacinta."

"I'm sure it includes several people ending up dead and her finding great wealth."

"Apparently I am to cut your throat and then we are to sail off into the sunset. There were days when I was sorely tempted."

Richard embraced his brother, "I can't work all this out at the moment, all I can be is practical. Lock Jacinta up in the brig for the time being. Then work with Lawrence to get the booty stowed. Post guards. Put the most valuable things in my counting house, it is a strong room and beneath I have secured the old vault. The rest will have to go to the warehouse. Arrange for the men to come there in a couple of days to sign off and get their share. Then we can best decide on how to dispose of our goods. Keep John on board a while, I will take Will home and then go and tell Tamsin."

"Sounds like a plan," Jack said nodding. "Diccon, I could dispose of her, wouldn't that be easier?"

"Probably but she is still Antonio's mother."

"I'm glad I don't have your conscience."

Richard sighed and went back to find Will. He was carried on a litter up Bull Street to the corner tenement where he and Alice lived. They went into the hall and put Will's litter down on the floor. Annie appeared and screamed.

"Shut up, Annie, I see your mistress has taken you back!" said Richard. "Where is Alice?"

The girl pointed towards the kitchen just as Alice appeared wiping her hands on her apron. Alice took one look at Will and also screamed, she ran to his side, kneeling and asking him if he was all right, kissing him and smoothing his hair. It took some minutes before she discovered the true nature of his disability. She wailed and cried and then it was Will who comforted her. Alice's eyes were like fury as she turned her attention at last to Richard.

"You! You were supposed to protect him. How could you let this happen?"

"I didn't let anything happen, it was a battle Alice, men die, they get wounded."

"My son has lost his leg and you stand there without a scratch on your body!"

"Alice, I am so sorry."

"I don't want your mealy-mouthed words." She fussed over Will and got him carried to his room.

Richard knew she would be busy for a while. He found Jacket and told him about Will and John and that he should prepare for the receipt of the booty from Jack. He also asked Jacket to approach the Mayor for money, food, shelter and passports for the released English prisoners. He then went to the Angel, the inn was already busy. Many of the men from their ships and others that had made for Southampton harbour were celebrating their victory and were lauding the feats of the Earl of Essex. Tamsin was carrying six mugs of ale at a time and still could not keep up with demand.

"Tamsin."

"Not now Richard, I have thirsty men to serve." A cheer arose. Richard decided just to come right out and tell her.

"Tamsin, I have John with me." She stopped dead and stared at him as if he was speaking in tongues.

"What are you saying?"

"John is alive."

She faltered for a moment but did not fall, she delivered the ale to her customers and wiped her hands on her apron.

"Where is he?"

"He is still on board the *Pelican* – he is much changed Tamsin. He has been a slave on the galleys all these years, he has suffered but he is alive. He stayed alive for you."

She undid her apron and smoothed her hair.

"Take me to him."

"Mama, what is it?" Luisa had appeared carrying more ale.

"Look after the inn, I have to go out."

"Mama?"

"Just do as you are bid." She snapped as she signalled for Richard and they walked out onto Bull Street.

"Are you going to be all right, Tamsin?"

"I don't know. I had given up. I used to think that someday one of the soldiers or sailors who passed through the town would be him, later I thought one of them might say they knew of him and that he had died. In my head he is buried."

"If there is anything I can do Tamsin tell me. He will need care and nursing. I have his share of booty so you will have no worries on that score."

"Well that is something." They were at the quay. "I need to do this alone." Richard called one of his men and told him to take Tamsin to John.

Much later Alice sought out Richard. He was lying on their bed staring at the ceiling. He guessed things were going to get a lot worse.

"I have known nothing but misery since I married you," was her opening gambit.

"You are being unreasonable."

"I was happy in my tippling house with my children. Now my daughter is dead and my son only half a man and all you give me is dead babies."

"Alice, I know you are upset and angry, but you speak as if I have deliberately set about hurting you. All I have done is love you and tried to do the best for you."

"How is he to live now? Will he marry and have children?"

"He's lost a leg, Alice, not his manhood." She looked daggers.

"Alice, I have also brought back enough treasure that Will can live like a gentleman—"

"—that is not who Will is, that is not who I am, we work and earn our living honestly, we don't steal."

"I was about the Queen's business," Richard said firmly, he would not lose his temper.

"Don't tell me how you and Bess are intertwined, it's like a story from one of your stupid books, it's not real and the only business you and your brother are about is your own. You have always been the same, all those shady deals with Alderman Crooke, that earring you somehow smuggled from Spain. I am too weary to talk to you. I am going to look after my son." She banged the door on the way out and Richard fell back onto the bed. He didn't even have a chance to tell her John was home.

That night when they finally went to bed they both kept as far apart as possible. Richard could not sleep worrying about Jacinta and how he would explain Antonio.

"Richard!" Alice's was sat up and her voice sounded strange. Richard lit a candle.

"What is it?" he said wearily, expecting more arguments. The bed linen was soaked with blood. Alice had miscarried again.

Alice was left very weak and ordered to stay in bed. It gave Richard some respite, Alice was in no condition to hear the news. He made sure she would not be disturbed. John was bedridden also and his family were in a state of shock. Only Will was eager to be up and around. Richard arranged for the finest carpenter to fashion him crutches, he also talked to the man about a wooden leg for Will. His stump was healing well and the amputation had been smoothly done at the knee. Will was actually very keen to be involved in making his leg himself. He had good skills with a knife and had made many toys, whistles and other items. Tom and Jacket would sit with him working on designs and encouraged him in the use of his crutches. Will's upper body strength was such that he could easily support himself but his balance and clumsiness did hold him back. Mostly though he laughed when his attempts went awry, although when he was alone Richard sometimes found him crying and would sit and hold him till he wiped his eyes in his shirt and shook Richard off. Will asked about Antonio.

"I don't think he has any friends, Pa, he seems so lonely. What will become of him?"

"I don't know, Will, to be brutally honest. As you rightly said, your mother would not be happy to have him here and I do not think he would want to be parted from his mother."

"I don't like her."

"There is not much to like."

"If you had not been ransomed, would you have been content to stay in Spain?"

"I don't think content is the right word. I was resigned and you learn to adapt Will, a bit like you with your new leg. There will be times you forget what your old leg was like. That is how it was, there is much to love about Spain, the warm winds, the wines, the music. But I missed my family Will and that never went away, never."

He went down to the family vault, it was full to the barrel vaulted roof with booty. Jacket was still trying to do a proper inventory. They had paid the men from the money chests and Lawrence had taken his share from there as well.

"Father, we must be as rich as the Queen."

"There are plenty of jewels here but I think Bess could still out do us."

Jacket was laughing, "I just can't believe it, I just can't believe it."

"What's that, young Jacket?"

465

"All this booty, Uncle Jack." Jack loped down the stairs into the vault.

"You should see the warehouse."

"Have you decided on any pieces you want to keep, Jack?"

"You know me, anything gaudy. But I'd rather turn it into another ship."

"Of course, Jack, have two if you would like."

"I have heard there is vessel designed by Matthew Baker to be had."

"Admiral Hawkins designer? That won't be cheap."

Jack gave him a long look.

"Sorry, still coming to terms with us being beyond wealthy," Richard managed a grin, "A racing ship, eh?"

"Longer in the keel, seasoned timber not green, hull ribs clad in a double layer of oak plank. The cavity filled with tar and animal hair, helps preserve it from rot."

"Very poetic, Jack."

Jack narrowed his eyes and Richard clapped him on the back.

"Like I said, get two. We ought to siphon off some booty for the Queen before too many questions are asked." Richard turned over the emeralds, gold chains and rings.

"All in good time, we have more pressing matters now, Diccon."

"Of course." Of course, no time to thank God for their good fortune and enjoy it. "Carry on here, Jacket." They left him chuckling to himself as he undid more boxes.

"Diccon, you have got to do something with that woman or I will strangle her with my bare hands."

"I thought you and she were well suited."

"Up to a point. I found her exciting in the bedchamber but enough is enough, she is a wild cat, I just want a woman with a bit of flesh, compliant and undemanding. She thinks we should marry, I don't know if she is serious or just sees it as a way to get back at you and gain some liberty. And the boy Diccon, now you know I am the world's worst father but she would not notice if Antonio starved. He is a winning little fellow but I only have a sea dog's Spanish."

"Let us go and see her."

Jack had moved Jacinta and Antonio into the Quay House but only after he had fixed strong locks on the doors and windows. When they arrived she was pacing the main room and threw a pewter tankard at them along with a torrent of Spanish that would have made any pirate blush.

"Jacinta, be quiet and sit down or we will leave and throw away the key," said Richard in much more refined courtly Spanish. She sat down and began to sob.

"What is to become of me in a land of heathens, with no money, no protection?"

"You should have stayed in Spain."

She pouted.

"Look we are where we are and it is a mess. I am happy to send you on a ship to the Netherlands, you will have money enough and we will engage a trustworthy entourage. From there it will be easy to find your way back to Spain."

"And Jack? Will you not come with me?" She fluttered her eyelashes and bent her head to one side.

"And how would that work Jacinta? Good day King Philip, yes I am Black Jack Mudford, yes the very same man who plundered your ships these many years and recently helped burn your city."

"I have nothing, I am dishonoured." She shed some crocodile tears, "I shall stay and marry Jack and we will all be merry together."

"I am not the marrying kind, and you may not have noticed but Spaniards are not much welcomed here, they are as popular as we heretics are in Spain."

"So I am to be burnt!" for the first time Jacinta seemed genuinely fearful.

467

"It could happen, Jacinta, this is not a safe place for you," said Richard.

"But I could become Protestant! Richard turned Catholic. What is the difference?"

"You did what?" said Jack.

"I didn't want to die a horrible death for some strange reason." Richard said with heavy sarcasm, "Jacinta, it would not work, please go to the Netherlands."

Then she laid her trap. "I'll leave only if I can meet your wife first."

"Don't be ridiculous," snapped Richard.

"How is it ridiculous? You preferred her to me, I want to know why. I will behave and play the unfortunate victim, a prisoner longing for ransom. Grant me this and I will go quietly. I do not like your country, it is too cold and too damp."

Chapter Sixty-Two

"I don't trust her at all," said Richard.

"Neither do I but what are we to do?" replied Jack. "You won't let me kill her."

"It seems we have no option. Let's go over our story. So, she was a hostage but she got caught in the wrong place as the town was evacuated. There were several Spanish prisoners taken by my Lord of Essex for ransom and we thought to follow suit. You are arranging a passage for her – how soon?"

"Almost immediately. One of Justin's men is in town, his ship is getting some repairs. I have already spoken to him."

"It is not fitting that she should be left in the hands of a single man like you with such a reputation, and so needs somewhere to stay."

"Might work." Jack did not sound convinced.

"How are you, love?" Alice was pale and her eyes shadowed.

"Why can't I carry a baby to its full term now?"

"I don't know, love, I wish I could give you what you desire," he said honestly.

"How is Will?"

"He is well, Alice, truly he is a resilient boy. I did everything

I could to save him. I thought he was far enough from the front line. I would never have put him deliberately in harm's way."

"He is like his father, he will not hold back."

"Shall I fetch him to sit with you awhile?"

"In a moment. I'm sorry I was so harsh Richard, I should not have lashed out at you."

"And who else? Believe me I've berated myself much worse." He bent and kissed her forehead.

"You look tired, Richard."

"There has been such a lot to do with the booty, signing off the crew, John—"

"—John?"

"Oh dear God, I forgot, you were so angry with me and then losing the child. Alice, I found John alive."

Alice dashed her hands to her face, incredulous. "Tell me, tell me how?"

"When we were parted he was taken as a slave on the galleys that is where he spent most of his time. I don't know how he mustered the strength to survive but he did. Eventually his health broke down and he found himself a prisoner back in Cadiz. Someone I knew from before, a friend, a doctor, in fact the doctor who helped to save Will, told me about the English prisoners. I managed just before we had to leave to break open the prison and there he was."

"Oh Richard." She held out her arms and he embraced her, "You are so brave, I am sorry to have been such a scold, and Tamsin, how did she take it?"

"I'm not sure love, if I am honest. John is not how we remember him. He has come back an old man, he is sick. Tamsin nurses him, I have offered any help, but I don't know."

"I must go to her."

"No, first you must gain your strength. I don't want anything to happen to you." He kissed her forehead again.

"Alice, I need to ask you something, a great favour. I don't know what else to do."

"Tell me." Her eyes were wide and trusting.

"When we went to take the treasure the house we found it in was not empty, Luis de la Castro's sister and child were there. Jack had to take them under his protection, there were some who would have slaughtered them. When we left for the ships we thought to take them somewhere safe but in the confusion, it was not possible. I was fighting my way from the prison, Jack took them onto his ship, he thought he could look to ransom them."

Alice furrowed her brow trying to follow what he was saying. He did not know he was such an accomplished liar.

"The situation is that he finds himself with two Spanish... prisoners...casualties of war...I don't know what to call them. We haven't the energy to think about ransom now, and we have already confiscated much of Luis's wealth. Jack is trying to arrange passage over to the Netherlands, it will be easier then to get them back to Spain, but he doesn't want to keep them at the Quay House. He wanted me to ask if they could stay here just for a few days. It's up to you."

"No, it's perfectly all right. Luis's sister?" She said after a moment.

"Well I think more a half-sister."

"What is her name?"

"Jacinta, Jacinta Gomez."

"It sounds so exotic. What is she like?"

Richard shrugged, "Spanish, a woman, I don't know what else to say."

"Is she pretty?"

"Yes."

"And you knew her before?"

"Only vaguely. I was in Luis's household and his sister would stay there whilst in the city."

"What of her husband?"

"I don't really know, he lived always in the country, she said he is now dead."

"So you have spoken to her?"

"A little, in Spanish."

"Of course. Tell Jack we will take her in but he must arrange quick passage."

Richard kissed her on her forehead for the third time, "You are kind and gracious, Alice, I will send Will in for a while so you may see how well he does, and then you must rest."

He started to leave.

"You said there was a child?"

"Yes she has a son."

"How old?"

"Three or four I would guess."

He left the room in a cold sweat.

Alice rose from her bed the next day. She sent a message to Tamsin offering assistance and then she prepared for her guests. Richard was overcome with worry. When Jack arrived with Jacinta and Antonio he thought he would be sick. Jacinta had obviously decided to amuse herself by playing the poor widow. She was dressed immaculately, she must have persuaded Jack to clothe her. She was all in black lace, her face bare of her usual potions. Antonio clung to her skirts, shy and nervous.

"Señora, welcome to our home," said Alice, "I am sorry that you have found yourself in such a strange and frightening position. I have prepared a room for you and your son."

Richard translated and Jacinta nodded demurely. He knew she had some English but he hoped she would keep quiet or just speak in Spanish. She stepped forward, clasped Alice's hand and murmured in Spanish, what Alice thought was thanks. "I am disappointed, Richard, she has no real beauty, pasty faced in that unpleasant English way. She must be good in bed." She curtsied very low.

472

"Hello Antonio," greeted Will. He offered the boy a wooden toy. Antonio hesitated for a moment and then took it. Alice stared at the boy long and hard. Richard hastily called for a servant who took them to their room.

"Well Jack, another mess you have landed us in," said Alice.

"What can I say, sister? Mud sticks to me, you know that!"

Just three days, then Jacinta would be gone, and all would be well.

★

Terrible screams were coming from the kitchen. Richard flew down the hall, Alice behind him. A horrific sight awaited them. Annie was shrieking in agony, her face, neck and chest a livid red where a steaming pot of hot water had been thrown over her. Jack stood petrified with shock and Jacinta, breathing heavily after her exertion, held the empty pot in her hand. She let it clatter to the ground, which awoke Jack from his stupor. He flew across the kitchen and wrapped his hands about her neck. Annie ran into the yard and plunged herself into the water butt. Alice screamed and ran after her yelling that the shock might kill her. Richard managed to pry Jack's hands away with difficulty and Jacinta coughed and wheezed.

"Jack, what happened?"

"She is the Devil and I will kill her!"

Alice brought the dripping Annie in, she was indeed going into shock. Alice started to plaster her with butter, yelling for a servant to fetch the doctor.

"Why?" Richard was shouting now at Jacinta, "Was it an accident?"

"Of course it was no accident," muttered Jack.

"It was his fault," spat Jacinta in heavily accented English, pointing at Jack. Alice stared at her.

"What is going on?"

"I found them." Jacinta looked oddly triumphant. "He was rutting with the kitchen maid. You were mine Jack, you do not go from me to that, not without my permission. What is it with Mudford men that they would rather lie in the gutter?"

"Were you and Jack lovers?" Alice asked astonished, but momentarily relieved.

"Not just Jack," purred Jacinta.

Annie was moaning. "Sorry, mistress."

"Silly, silly girl." Alice glowered at Richard. He felt as if a black ox had trod upon his foot.

Richard grabbed Jacinta and took her into the hall where he tied her to a chair. Jack had turned his attention back to Annie, talking softly, trying to get her to be calm. The doctor arrived and Annie was carried to a bedroom still crying.

"You knew her, knew her body?" Alice was coldly calm.

"Alice, don't start, you don't understand–" began Jack.

"I am talking to my husband."

"He knew my body, many, many times," sighed Jacinta, her voice hoarse due to Jack's ministrations.

"Let me finish throttling her," said Jack.

"What good would that do?" Richard asked wearily, "What happened with Annie?"

"We were having a bit of fun, she's made for fun," said Jack. "You don't own me!" He said to Jacinta, "No one owns me. She found us and threw the boiling water over poor Annie."

"Do we call the watch?" Richard asked.

"And have everyone know what a fool you have made of me?" retorted Alice.

"Annie might die."

"She is just a servant, a nobody." Jacinta said with ease.

Alice punched her in the face. Jacinta screamed and tried to work her arms free as her legs kicked out at Alice. Alice pulled her hair and the chair went over. Jacinta managed to wriggle free and the two women began to wrestle on the ground gouging, scratching and biting. Jack looked on in glee. Richard tried to grab one, then the other, yelling at Jack to lend a hand. Eventually Jack caught hold of Jacinta by the hair and dragged her off. Richard held Alice in his arms. She screamed abuse relentlessly and only paused when Richard saw blood running down her legs.

"Alice, stop. You are bleeding again." She became hysterical and it was with difficulty that Richard carried her upstairs. As he did Jacinta dealt her death blow. "I did not lose the baby he planted in me. Our son Antonio is strong and healthy."

It seemed Alice had been carrying two babies. Whether she would have lost the second anyway or whether it was the result of a blow from Jacinta could not be known, but Alice knew her longed-for child had been killed by her husband's whore, the whore with whom he had had a son.

Annie was very, very ill. The doctor felt she would live but would be heavily scarred. Jack had her carried to Quay House as soon as she was strong enough. Jacinta was locked in a cellar until her passage was assured out of the town. Alice, driven mad by grief and anger, had to be sedated.

"Antonio, you are to go back to Spain with your mother."

"Why is she locked away?"

"She has been...naughty. Antonio I have a little present for you."

Richard pinned a brooch to his jacket, it was the one Alice had given him on their wedding.

"If you ever need me Antonio, just send this brooch to me and I will come." He was not sure the little boy understood but he seemed to like the gift and polished it with his sleeve.

The Dutch ship eased out of the harbour, the pilot boat guiding it into the channel. Jacinta stood on the deck with Antonio in her arms. Richard felt different emotions sweep over him, anger, hatred, sorrow, love. He remembered the look on Alice's face as she realised the truth, had her suspicions confirmed. Could they find their way back from this? How could he ever make her understand what had happened in Spain? Or was he just making excuses for his cowardice and the way he had given into his baser emotions? Jacinta was smiling. Perhaps she had forgiven him now that she had had her revenge. She raised her hand and waved at him, and he waved back. And then all at once she let Antonio fall from her grasp and he tumbled into the sea.

Richard blinked several times. He could not believe what he had seen. Jacinta was still smiling, making no attempt to call for help from the crew, who themselves had been too busy to notice what had happened. He pulled off his doublet and kicked off his shoes, stepped back to get a better run up, leapt to the side of the boat and dived into the water. He had always been a strong swimmer. The water was choppy but not like the open sea. He could hear men calling and yelling from the pilot boat and he struck out. Antonio struggled and then disappeared from sight. Richard took in a large painful breath, his lungs burned. He could see nothing, the water was too dark. Up to the surface he rose for a breath and down again. He thought he saw a glint, the brooch he had given Antonio. He reached and grabbed hold of a body and kicked again for the surface. The pilot boat had come up close and hands were pulling them aboard. The boy was blue and not breathing. One of the men, a seasoned sailor, held him upside down and thumped his back, then lay him down and pressed on his chest. Water sputtered from the boy's mouth and he was coughing, then he began to cry. Richard found something warm to wrap him in. He was aware of the sailors' incredulity all around.

When they landed Richard carried Antonio back to the house, he was still dripping wet himself. He went into the hall and stood making puddles on the floor. Alice stared at them in disgust. She said nothing, turned on her heel, marched up the stairs and Richard heard the banging of a door.

Part Twelve

1597

Chapter Sixty-Three

She would not see Richard, would not speak to him. He knelt outside her door pleading with her and praying to God, neither heeded him. She would not share a room with him. If he entered a room she left, she moved his things into another room so he had to sleep there. Everyone picked up the atmosphere and crept around, and the house operated in almost total silence. Silence was where Antonio hid himself. He had not spoken since the near fatal drowning. He followed Richard around like a lap dog, sat at his feet and slept in his bed but never uttered a word. Everyone in the house moved in concentric circles around and about one another but never together. Richard buried himself in paperwork but did not visit the warehouse, the ships or any merchants. He saw no visitors, not even Jack.

After nearly three weeks Alice suddenly appeared in his counting house. She looked sleep-ravaged and had no care for herself, but she her eyes were of steel. She was ready for an argument.

"I told you I wanted your whore and your bastard out of my house and you think so little of me you flaunt your by blow in my face."

"His mother abandoned him. She threw him into the sea and if I had not intervened he would have drowned."

"Perhaps that would have been better."

"Alice, I cannot believe that you mean that."

"Why? Why would I not mean what I say? Do you expect me to just put up and shut up and take in any child you decide to father with other women?"

"It was not as simple as that."

"Really? It's as simple as rolling in the grass."

"What do you want me to do?"

"Get rid of him."

Antonio did not understand what she said but he understood her anger and pressed himself closer to Richard's leg.

"You speak of him like an unwanted kitten that can be put in a sack and thrown down a well."

"Get rid of him."

"Don't be ridiculous. He is alone and frightened, and I am his father."

"So you admit that at last."

"None of this was done to hurt you, I made a foolish mistake when I was far away from home."

"I never made a 'mistake' when I sat here waiting and worrying, saving every penny for a ransom."

"You are a better person than I, I think that is established."

"If you do not get rid of him, I am leaving."

"Don't be ridiculous."

"Stop telling me I am ridiculous," she was screeching now, "if I am ridiculous it is because you have made me an object of ridicule. I cannot set foot in to a shop or at the market without people talking and sneering. I have had years of those merchant wives looking down their noses at me and now they are sniggering and they think me more of a fool than ever. I can't do this anymore."

Richard was starting to become worried for her sanity and appalled he had brought her to this. He had begun to see that she had been unhappy for some time in their grand house and now she had had misery heaped upon her yet again. He tried to reach Alice, his wife and lover. "The boy is young and in shock, I cannot turn him out. Perhaps if you give me time I can find a suitable household for him to be brought up in—"

"There is no more time, I cannot live with your falsehoods. You deceived me with that woman and concealed it from me, you made up a packet of lies to sneak her into my home. You are an adulterer, you are corrupt and you expect me to forgive all and welcome the child you fathered with her into my family. All my dead babies, all I have suffered, and now you want me to raise another woman's child, a woman you slept with and caressed whilst your family starved. Tell me how can we survive this?"

"I don't know what to say." He was worried that he might push her to the brink with a wrongly placed word.

"You had plenty to say when you were weaving your lies and conceit."

"It was wrong, I was trying to save you from pain and I made everything so much worse. I am sorry."

"What do I care for your sorrow?" And then she struck, laying down her plan before him, "I am leaving and I am taking Will and Tom with me."

"You cannot!" Alice was being irrational. A wife could not desert her husband. A wife did not have control of the children.

"Cannot? And how will you stop me? Command me as your wife? And when I tell everyone how I have been abused, and mark me I will tell everyone, you will never be able to raise your head in this town again. No you will let me leave and we will quietly live separate lives."

"No I will not, I cannot. I love you Alice."

"I don't love you. You have killed my love."

He had thought if he gave in to her she would calm down like before. He was frightened that if he tried to restrain her she might be lost to herself and to him forever. He was as crippled as she. He had thought that with enough money and a grand house his family would be safe and looked after, that all would be well. How had it all gone so wrong, so terribly wrong?

She packed up the things she wanted and ordered a cart. Will and Tom seemed as bewildered as Jeanne and Lizzie but none dared to ask for an explanation. They were all in the hall.

"Where will you go?" Richard was weary from pleading with Alice to change her mind.

"To the Ferry village." She herself seemed much calmer now that she was going back to the village. She had cleaned and tidied herself. She looked the very inch a merchant's wife, a sombre matron, except for the exhaustion in her face.

"What about Tom's schooling?"

"He can row across to the school."

"When will I see him and Will?"

"I do not think it will be helpful for you to see them, not for a while."

"And can they not see their sisters?"

"Jeanne and Lizzie are your daughters, we should end this pretence of brothers and sisters and families."

"Alice, don't punish the children."

"They will come to understand." She fixed her wide mouth into a thin smile.

"Mother, what am I to do?" asked Jacket. Her eyes flashed cruelly.

"I am not your mother. You are eighteen years old and need to stand on your own two feet."

"Alice, stop this," said Richard as Jacket crumpled looking once more like a rat-faced boy.

"You have made me like this!" Her control was slipping, but within her she still had the core of steel that Richard had always admired. She gathered up her bundles. "Will, Tom, get into the cart now." Will shifted uncomfortably on his crutches as Alice hustled them out of the house.

Jacket was sobbing. Jeanne and Lizzie wrapped their arms about him.

"Stay with us, Jacket, we'd love you stay with us," said Lizzie.

Richard encircled all three, "Don't cry Jacket, you still have me, poor father that I am. You will always have me."

"Oh Papa." Jeanne began to cry and then Lizzie. Richard looked over their heads to where Antonio sat on the stairs, peering at them all through the railings.

"Is it because of that boy, Papa?" asked Lizzie.

"No Lizzie, it is because of me," said Richard.

Chapter Sixty-Four

Now the house was even quieter except for crying. Eyes were red and skin pale, food was pushed around plates. No laughter could be heard. In the evenings Richard sat staring at the fire, Antonio at his feet like a cat. Jeanne and Lizzie would bring him food but he put aside and they would curl up beside him and stare at the fire also. Jacket moved about like a ghost, aimlessly at first and then he fixed himself on the work of the Mudford Brothers Company. It was if he could keep the company going there was hope for the family, that it might become right. More weeks passed and Richard lost track of time. He was becoming unkempt, he was losing weight, he was losing his mind. He drank, and then he drank more.

A pitcher of icy cold water hit him full in the face. He woke with a shock and a curse and tried to focus his eyes. Jack was stood in front of him with the empty jug and in the company of Madame Sohier.

"For Christ's sake, Jack, you could've have just given me a prod."

"Tried that, you were dead drunk and nothing would wake you."

"Why are you here, why are you both here?"

"Because your children are worried about you, when it is you who should be worried about them!" said Madame Sohier sharply.

"They are perfectly fine, we have servants aplenty."

"Your daughters are ten years old. And this little boy is your son? He is not much more than a baby, he is lost and confused whilst you just wallow in self-pity."

"Thank you for your concern Wauldure, it is touching and unusual."

"That's enough, Diccon!" snapped Jack. "Besides it's not fair on me and Jacket, trying to run the business, I should be at sea but I can't leave him to cope. What the hell is wrong with you?"

"You know what is wrong, Alice, has left me, she is gone."

"Then go and get her back again if you miss her so much!"

"It's not that easy. She was right to leave. I betrayed her and I can never make amends."

"You watch too many plays. This isn't some huge tragedy, you fathered a bastard. Well so have half the men in this town and the other half are bringing up someone else's kid as their own. It's the way of the world, not the end of it."

"It's not the way you treat someone you are supposed to love."

"And are her actions those of a Christian woman?"

"By the Church and the law you could command her to return" interjected Madame Sohier.

"I don't want her to come back because I command it, or some sour-faced preacher demands it."

"Diccon, she is never going to come back if you carry on like this! You stink, you look like a beggar and you are not behaving as a man should."

Richard held his head in his hands. He knew what his brother said was right, it was wrong of him to wallow, neglect his duties.

"I am sorry Jeanne, I am sorry Lizzie."

"That's all right, Papa, we just don't want you to be sad," said Jeanne.

"I won't be sad any more. Thank you for looking after Antonio."

"Oh Papa, he cries so at night and we don't know how to talk to him, he only knows Spanish," complained Lizzie.

"Antonio," said Richard in Spanish, "I am sorry I left you alone, I have not been well. I am your real papa and these are your sisters. We want you to stay here with us. Would you like that?"

The boy spoke for the first time since his ordeal, "Where is my Mama? When will she be back?"

"What did he say?" asked Madame Sohier.

"He wants his mama."

Madame Sohier knelt and smoothed Antonio's hair. "I don't know where your mama is or how she could leave you little man, but I am your grandmother," she kissed his cheek, "and I am going to stay here and look after you, look after you all." She stared pointedly at Richard.

"Let's get you to the bathhouse brother, and then Wauldure, if you would oblige, we shall all sit down for a proper dinner together and we can plan what we do next."

It was hard to carry on as if nothing had happened but when he felt himself sliding back into misery Richard remembered his children. He was aware they all watched him with concern and he could not bear to see worry on their faces so he tried hard to be as he once was. There was much still to do to sort out how best to use their booty money and there was John and Tamsin to consider as well, John would never be as he once was but he had recovered some strength and become something of a celebrity. Visitors came to hear tales of his ordeal. John made it sound an adventure, telling of how he tricked and played the

Spanish, but Richard knew it was all a lie, the truth too horrible. The boys did not react well to having a strange man presented as their father and railed against his authority. Luisa, however, loved her Pa and fussed over him, making sure he was warm and had the best of the food. She would let him lean on her like a crutch when he was feeling up to taking a turn around the square. They were sorry to learn that Alice had moved out of the house and Tamsin worried how she would manage the Angel without her. Of course she blamed Richard entirely, John was more sympathetic.

"It is so hard to make people understand what it is like to be a prisoner, that you would do anything to gain freedom."

"You didn't though John, you stuck to your principles, you never gave in, never took the easy way."

"And I was an utter fool."

"Don't say that."

"It is the truth, I have missed my sons' childhood, I placed my wife and daughter into poverty and worse and for what? No, given my time again, I would have compromised every belief and fathered a dozen bastards to be home a day earlier."

"I think you are trying to make me feel better and I thank you for that."

"They fed us on a diet of pulses and grains, bread and water, they thought meat and wine would spoil our condition. We rowed seated on straw-filled cushions, wearing fetters and chained to the benches. We slept, vomited and shat at our oars and hoped if the galley went down someone would remember to free us."

Richard did not know what to say, he patted John's arm and John nodded.

"And I thank you for watching over my family whilst I was away, you did not have to."

"Of course I did, for friendship as well as conscience."

"Surely Alice will come back, once she has calmed down."

"It's been nearly three months, not a word, not a sign."

"You should go and see her."

"Yes I will, soon. She should come and visit her friends and not be banished from them just because she does not want to be near me."

"We have some good news that might tempt her."

"What is that?"

"Tamsin is with child!"

"John, that is marvellous."

"It's good to know something still works, it's early days yet but I hope to have one child whose growing up I can enjoy. How is Antonio faring?"

"Good, John, good. I have taught the girls some words of Spanish and Luisa has come and played with him, she has picked up the language well from you. And Antonio has started to understand and speak English. He has a natural ear for language I think. Wauldure has been our saviour. Who would have thought that? Antonio has formed such a bond with her, made stronger by the sweetmeats she feeds him."

"And you have heard nothing of Jacinta?"

"I am sure she is flourishing, people like her always survive, more than survive. Jack would strangle her with his bare hands if he could. Did you hear what happened with Annie?"

"Jack told me."

"Jack has had her living at his home, under the care of a nurse. She is horribly scarred, but is recovering. We will have to do something for her."

When Richard got home he found Antonio sitting alone on the stair. He went and sat next to him, ruffled his tousled hair and kissed the top of his head.

"Why do people keep kissing me?" the boy asked.

"Because we love you and we want you to know how much."

"But you are English devils, you eat children. How do I know you are not tasting me?"

490

"Ah, good point. Well, as a rule, we don't eat children. I think perhaps in Spain children are told that to stop them from being naughty." Richard shuddered as he remembered tales he had heard of when famine was so desperate children had been eaten.

"Antonio, you realise that you are half English?" Antonio's eyes were like platters.

"Who was the old man in the country?" Richard guessed he meant Jacinta's husband. Poor Antonio, there was too much confusion for so young a child to understand, but Richard hoped that like many children he would just accept the world as presented to him by the adults who cared for him.

"I think he was your mother's husband and while I was away he looked after you for me."

"He was not very good. If you paid him you should ask for your money back."

"I'm sorry, Antonio, I did not know that."

"The lady who left, why didn't she like me?"

"She liked you well enough, Antonio, but she didn't like me."

"It is too difficult, it gives me a pain in my head."

"I know how you feel. Would a spiced biscuit help?" Antonio nodded, Richard took his hand and they went in search of comfort.

Chapter Sixty-Five

Richard dressed with care, nothing too expressive; Alice did not like frippery, but enough so she would see he had made an effort. Mark Dypere rowed him across, he looked a bit embarrassed. When he reached the other side he made for the inn run by John's mother as he assumed Alice would have gone there, or if not the old woman would know where she was. He saw Will and Tom first working on fishing nets.

"Boys!" They looked up and seemed glad to see him, but then bent their heads back to their work, obviously confused as to how they should feel. "How are you, Will?"

"Good, sir, I think I will soon be ready to try my new leg soon."

Richard was hurt to be called 'Sir' but made no comment. "I am glad to hear it. And Tom, how is school?"

"It is well, when I can get there."

"How so?"

"Sometimes it's too rough on the water and I am late, the Master is not happy with me then and gives me a hiding. Sometimes I have to help out..."

This was not right, Alice should not punish the boys, he had sent money regularly although it had not been asked for, to make sure they all had enough to keep themselves comfortable.

"Your Uncle John sends his love, Will. He is doing well and longs to see you. You should visit him, come with your grandma if your mother is...too busy."

Will nodded and looked uneasy. Richard decided not to make the boys feel worse and started for the house.

"It is good to see you, Pa," said Tom.

Alice was baking and covered in flour. She was looking restored, even if there was a new hardness about her that Richard did not recognise. John's mother sat in the corner supervising. Alice looked up at his entrance and then carried on with her task. Richard sat awhile with the old woman to give her news of her son. Presently, she took a clay pipe and went outside.

"Alice, we need to talk."

"I am done with talk, you should not have come."

"You are my wife."

"It's a bit late to realise that."

"Alice, please, I must talk with you." She banged down the bowl she was using and wiped her hands. She ripped off her apron and strode past him.

"Come on then if you must talk, let us go somewhere more private."

As they went out George Parker came in, his eyes slid from one to the other.

"Is all well, Alice?"

"Of course," she snapped.

They walked up to the green and sat looking over at Southampton.

"Why did you bring us here?" asked Richard.

"Not a good memory?"

"It was the best day of my life, the best day."

"And mine too."

"Then why did it go so wrong?"

493

"Because we want different things. You were different back then. You hardly ever spoke, were quiet, restrained, contained. You had a nice home and a good steady job. My head told me I was not ready to remarry but my heart spoke of something else. I imagined we would have a life where you went to work and came home and we would talk of the day, we would have children and then grandchildren, and there would be a rhythm. But then you went a-soldiering, and mixed with earls, met the Queen and sent ships around the world and you had affairs with beautiful, tempestuous, fine-born women."

"One affair, if that is the word you would use, not done to hurt you but because I was missing you, the touch of you, the smell of you, you, Alice. I worked to make us safe and secure. Do you know how many people are starving and dying from bad harvests, poor weather, and the war, even on the streets of Southampton? I could have been injured or even killed as a town sergeant. When I got too old, then what? Poor relief? I'd not have been able to provide for you."

"You're eloquent now. Richard, I was so very angry with you when I left, but these past weeks I have made peace with myself and maybe it was my actions that led us to where we are, that meant I couldn't have children with you."

"We have Tom."

"Our bastard. But there are no children of our marriage, perhaps God is giving us a message."

"I doubt if God has time for us."

"Don't blaspheme."

"Many people lose children, it's not as if we have none."

They had been gazing out over the water to Southampton, afraid to look at one another but now she turned and stared at him until he was forced to seek out her fine grey eyes. She was appraising him as one would a stranger.

"You could go back to Spain," she suggested, though she did not sound convinced, even to herself.

"I can't do that even if I wanted to, I have responsibilities."

She snorted and then fell silent again. He felt she was making a decision, her jaw became tense.

"I think we should divorce."

"What!" His heart was stopping.

"So we can both start again."

"The only person permitted to divorce in this country was the old King."

"There are ways, and you have money."

"Acts of Parliament are involved are they not?" He turned away from her again. He could not bear her look upon him, "Besides I don't want a divorce, I came here to tell you I want you to come home. I will change, I will leave the business, we can − buy a farm in the country, or move to another town and set up an inn..."

"I'm too weary, Richard, too weary. Let us remember the good years and forget the rest, I have spoken discreetly to a priest."

"How could you! How can you throw us away?" He was angry now.

"With your adultery, your bastard and other things, our living apart−"

"Other things? What other things?"

"How was it that you did not end up in the galleys like John?"

"I told you, Luis de la Castro interceded for me."

"Is that all?"

"So you are determined to blacken my character, do anything to be rid of me."

"In the end it will probably be my character that is called into question."

"Stop speaking in riddles. It may be unjust but no court will penalise me for adultery, only for violence and I have never been violent to you Alice, you cannot accuse me of that."

495

"Let us leave things where they are for the moment, I think that would be best." Alice was finished so of course all discussion was over.

"And you get to decide?"

"I do."

"I could go to the church court, they would command you to come back."

"Don't do that, Richard, it would hurt a lot of people beside us."

"We are not hurting them now? And the boys, am I never to see them?"

"I think it would be better for Will to remain here for now, Tom may visit after school."

"That is big of you."

"Don't be so petulant."

"You are ruining my life and breaking my heart. I think I can be a bit petulant, don't you?"

She leaned forward and kissed his cheek and then she was gone. He sat there till the sun went down and the air become cool.

Richard was in his library, he had various religious works spread on the table before him. His books were an eclectic mix, some he bought because he was interested in the subject, some texts from religious houses he had purloined whilst town sergeant to stop them being cut up for tapers, occasionally there was a book in the goods of thieves and murderers. Now he had money he could buy books new but he loved his old battered books from his Silkshop Yard days the best. Jack put his head around the door.

"I've seen a ship, I think we should buy it."

"Mmmm."

"More tonnage, I shall call it the *Swan*. What are you doing?"

"Looking up the reasons which might allow divorce."

"The meeting with Alice did not go well then?"

"She is determined that we live apart, and would like to be free. She's has talked to a cleric and seems to think there are grounds, but I don't know how that would be. It says here bigamy, pre-contract, non-consummation, forced marriage or minority of one the partners might in rare occasions be seen as reason for the court to grant divorce. But none of these apply."

"If you start stirring things up you might well be ordered to live together again, which even though you want Alice back, would not work." Jack plucked the *Mariner's Mirror* off the shelf and idly skimmed the pages until Richard glared at him.

Richard banged the books shut, "Perhaps she is planning adultery to give me cause?"

"That seems a bit extreme. Alice was always a moral woman."

"I don't understand why she is doing this, was I that bad a husband?"

"You had your faults but compared to me, you were, are, a paragon. If you don't mind me saying, and even if you do, Alice hasn't been happy for a while. This longing for a baby and the loss of them has dragged her down. Having a child became more important than your marriage. I think if the business with Jacinta had not happened there would have been something else."

"You are talking nonsense."

"Probably. Now, what do you make of the *Swan*?"

★

It became clear what Alice's plan was. She had a scribe write to him. The letter said that their marriage was not a marriage. She was sorry to have deceived him but it was caused by her ignorance of God's laws. She maintained that during the time of his betrothal and marriage to Jeannot, she had herself pre-contracted to marry George Parker – George Parker! Richard was incredulous, George would have been but a green boy then. When Richard had become free on the death of his wife, Alice had put aside her plans to marry Parker. She had now realised that she'd broken God's laws and had in fact committed bigamy. She felt that God had chosen to punish them by taking away their children. She had been tormented and had driven Richard into the arms of another, but as he was technically free there was no fault on his side. God has shown this by granting him a son. She had testimony from George Parker and many witnesses in the Ferry village and even a record from the now elderly priest who had overseen the pre-contract. Parker had not sued her for adultery as he wanted her to return to him. She begged Richard to support her cause and to provide the financial means to help them through the courts. Thereafter she would expect nothing further from him.

Richard was convinced she had gone quite mad.

Chapter Sixty-Six

"Diccon, I want to make a longer voyage to the Americas," said Jack, "I've been thinking more and more about opportunities around colonies, increasing our portion of the fishing trade, and keeping open the options for privateering of course."

"Do you have to go now?"

"Please don't tell me you need me, Diccon, it makes me uncomfortable. I don't know why you keep moping after Alice, if she wants to go let her, move on. There are plenty of other women Diccon, plenty."

Richard didn't bother to answer.

"I want to take all the ships."

"All of them? That's a big risk. How do we continue our local trade?"

"The bigger the risk, the bigger the reward. If I take all the ships we can carry more goods, plain and simple."

"One storm and we could lose everything."

"That's true up to a point, Diccon. We are lucky we still have plenty of ready cash, we have the other business interests and we could rent or buy a smaller vessel to move things around the coast."

"Well I did notice a little coastal vessel, it caught my eye because it was called *The Swallow*."

"Fate!" pronounced Jack. "I take three ships with me, we keep one in readiness in the Americas, one trading, keeping a watch out for opportunities, one bringing goods back. I think we should set up a trading post on the mainland, we are known enough now, and I could look out how we might encourage some colonists. We could have our own people out there, growing tobacco, starting a market for goods from England. The natives have no interest in farming or setting up businesses, they are free spirits."

"Like you used to be?"

"No nothing like I used to be. Come on, Diccon, have something else to occupy your mind. Maybe if Alice sees that you are carrying on without her, she will wake up and come running back!"

"You think so?"

"I don't know, I am just saying anything to get you out of this torpor, but I might be right for all that."

Antonio was having nightmares. Richard feared for him and did not know what to do other than hold him tight. Then he started having tantrums during the day, screaming hysterically and kicking and punching anyone who tried to comfort him. Again, all Richard could think to do was encase him in his arms till he tired of the struggle.

"Please, Antonio, tell me what is wrong?" he whispered when the boy had gone quiet and limp after a particularly violent outburst.

"I want my Mama, I want to go home."

"Antonio, it is too dangerous for you to go to Spain, but when you are older if you wish I will take you there."

"It is not safe here either, everyone hates me."

"No, that is not true! I don't hate you, neither does Jacket or Jeanne or Lizzie or Grand-mère Sohier and there is Uncle Jack."

"I'm scared of him."

"He is fearsome, Antonio, but not to those he cares about, and he cares about you," said Richard somewhat hopefully.

"The girl with the freckles, she hates me." Richard struggled to think who he meant and then thought it could be Dowsabelle. Annie's sister had been helping in the house whilst Annie was convalescing and she had a sprinkling of freckles over her nose.

"Do you mean the servant girl, Dowsabelle?" Antonio nodded.

"What has she done to make you think she hates you?"

"When no one looks she pinches me and spits at me and calls me names and says if I tell she will..." He drew his dimpled hand, which still was pudgy with baby fat across his throat.

"She is a wicked girl and she will leave here immediately. She is spiteful and mean but she will not harm you Antonio, she knows it will be worse for her if she does."

"I wish my Mama would come."

"I know, but she has gone away for a long time Antonio. I don't say this to upset you but because I do not want you to wait for her return. I am sorry. Antonio, I think it would be good for you to have lessons to help you learn English properly and you should go to church with your sisters. You will make friends and I hope in time you will be happy here."

Antonio said nothing.

Dowsabelle burst into tears and called Antonio a liar but Richard was unmoved. He thought her a stupid lazy girl, not kind and helpful like her sister. Yet he felt she had probably been put up to the malicious treatment of Antonio and could not think by whom. Distracted by more pressing matters he soon stopped worrying.

Richard went to see his lawyer.

"I wish to get a divorce."

The laugh the lawyer let out did not fill Richard with confidence. "I have discovered that the woman I took to wife was pre-contracted to another. Here are statements made, she has confessed to me."

"But you and Alice have been married these, what, eight years? No one need know of this, forget about it, tear up the statements."

"I cannot and you will see my wife, that is the woman Alice, is convinced our marriage has been without children because of her sin. I am convinced of it also. She has gone back to her... husband? So whatever way you look at it she has given me cause."

"I thought your marriage was a happy one."

"It was no marriage."

The lawyer looked uncomfortable, "Even with these proofs it will be difficult."

"That is what I am paying you for."

Alderman Biston was to be Mayor again. Richard found the news most depressing. He wanted to be somewhere else.

Tamsin gave birth to another son and John decided to call him Philip. Richard thought he was being perverse. He was furious with him when he asked Richard to be godparent, because he had asked Alice as well. She was subdued at the service.

"Do you think as a fallen woman who has lived with a man

502

to whom she was not truly married for eight years that you are a good role model for your godson?"

Alice had the grace to colour the brightest red. "I wanted to thank you, for helping to achieve a divorce."

"It's not achieved yet, there will be many lawyer's bills and it will need the consent of Parliament."

"Parliament?"

"You know how the Queen feels about divorce."

"Is it a divorce if there was no real marriage?"

"God knows, in fact God does know, Alice." She coloured again.

"Was there really a contract?"

"There was an understanding. When I went back to the village, I was pregnant and miserable, you were marrying another. George has always been fond of me, more than fond."

"Spare me the details please."

"He was there when you were not."

Now it was Richard's turn to colour.

"He kept asking me...I weakened...George had talked to the priest, there was a question of consanguinity, cousins of cousins..."

"Don't go saying things like that it will undermine everything."

She looked miserable.

"There is time, please change your mind. I still love you."

"And I also care for you, but I am so tired, so very tired. I want to go home, I want to be with my people. I want a simple life and life with you is anything but simple. I tried Richard, I tried for almost ten years."

"But we were happy, weren't we happy?"

"I was happy on our wedding day."

"Was that all?"

"Please stop talking at me."

He looked at her. He thought he had known her so well,

503

she had been everything to him for nearly fifteen years but now she was a stranger. He made a decision. "I love you so much that I will give you what you want. It is my gift to you, Alice, the ultimate sacrifice that I can make to prove to you how very much I love you."

Part Thirteen

1598

Chapter Sixty-Seven

He felt like a hollow man, completely empty. He felt eyes upon him as he tried to go about his business. His servants whispered in corners. It was shocking for a wife to live apart from her husband, it was a scandal, an affront to God. It was not enough that she did not want him, wanted to be away from him but to go straight to another? He tried not to think of Parker but he kept forcing himself into Richard's consciousness. He was personable enough, though he stank of fish most of the time. He made a reasonable living, had a couple of small boats but nothing to compare to the *Magpie*, the *Pelican* and the *Swan* or even to the *Swallow*. He was taciturn and Richard thought there was a surliness in his look, but then plenty of people said the same about him.

What did Alice see in him? Was he just a prop? Was he just not Richard? Parker had always been there on the horizon, in the corner of your eye, a face in the crowd, waiting, looking as if he knew that one day Richard would make an error, a mistake he would not recover from. Richard was wealthy now. He could use his resources to crush Parker as Biston had once endeavoured to crush him. But he was not that man. Parker had not won Alice, Richard had lost her. He had to put that memory away in his box alongside his other mementos of the past. He didn't know what to do. He had spent all his effort on becoming wealthy so he could give security to his family, but half his family was now estranged from him. He must focus on those that remained, but he did not feel up to the task. He was restless, he could not settle.

Then there was Antonio, an embodiment of his conscience, following him around with that piercing stare. His tantrums had expressed the screams in Richard's own head. Richard was worried that it wasn't Alice going mad but himself. But when Antonio slipped his small hand in Richard's as they walked to church or to the market, he knew he could not have abandoned him. They would walk together down to the quay and visit the ships. Richard would time the walks to coincide with the dinner break of the grammar school so they could bump into Tom, and if he did not have to dash back to the Ferry to do some chore or other Richard would take the boys on a picnic. It gave him good heart to see how the unknown brothers bonded with one another. Even though Tom thought himself much too old to play with Antonio, they still ended up kicking around a football, or running here and there at hide-and-go-seek. Sometimes Will would sneak across with a rowing boat and they would go up the river to Bitterne, where they could see the Bishop of Winchester's grand house. It was a guilty pleasure and Richard did not like to think that Alice would disapprove.

He tried not to neglect his daughters either but worried they had no mother figure now, he didn't know what little girls thought, he wanted them to be well mannered and ladylike but roared with laughter when he caught Lizzie sliding down the banisters into the hall. He tried to be interested in Jeanne's cat, Mrs. Stuart, at the same time suggesting that cats were flea-bitten, only useful as mousers and therefore should be in the yard. But Jeanne still dressed Mrs Stuart in dolls clothes and carried her around in a basket.

For all that, time dragged and nothing inspired and motivated him. He needed something else.

★

"Wauldure, I am thinking of going away for a while."

"What do you mean? To London?" Madame Sohier was trying to embroider a sampler but her arthritis made it difficult. She put it aside and started to look at work samples from the latest Silkshop Yard spinners.

"No, to the Americas."

Madame's head shot up, "The Americas! You are not privateering again?"

"No, Jack and I have been thinking for some time about setting up a company to encourage colonies. The Earl of Southampton is interested, as is my Lord of Essex." Richard's speech was rehearsed.

Madame sniffed, unimpressed, "They are interested in any scheme that will make them money. They are almost on the point of ruin, despite the Queen's favour."

The noble lords' financial problems were many and the courtly gossip had even reached Southampton.

"It doesn't mean the scheme is a bad one."

"But I don't understand why you feel the need to go, your brother knows those lands well." There was a hint of impatience in Madame Sohier's voice.

"I think I should see them myself, to better be able to encourage others."

"And is that the only reason?" She knew of course, she could see right through him. Richard hung his head in shame but he could not let himself be beaten.

"No. I shall go mad if I stay here, mad from anger, mad from grief, mad from despair. I will just be gone for a few months, I need to get away."

"And your children, what is to become of them?" Madame Sohier knew what was right, she thought Richard wallowed and neglected his responsibilities.

"Tom will continue to live with his mother and I have a promise that he will follow his studies. But I am hoping that I might persuade you to come and live in Bull Street permanently and watch over the girls...and Antonio of course." This was his trump card, he felt sure it was what Madame Sohier longed for.

"You know I am always happy to look after Jeanne and Lizzie, I was going to talk to you anyway about their education, I want to teach them things they will need to know when they are married and will have to run a house. But Antonio, he is still so young and so troubled. He needs you, not a crabbed old woman like me."

"I know I should not leave him but it is too dangerous for me to take him. Yet if I do not get away for a while I will not be of use to him or to any of them. There is more I need to ask of you."

Madame raised her untidy grey brows.

"With Jack and I both away, we need someone to oversee the business."

"You want me to look after your family *and* run your business?"

"You are more than capable, if you need support Lawrence Prowse can give advice." He was sure he had thought of everything.

"And if you die whilst on this journey?"

"I have made provision, you and Lawrence will be guardians."

"I may die before you."

"Well you can't." Richard sounded fractious, even to himself, "The children will have goodly inheritances but they will need guidance and to be kept from those who might seek to separate them from it."

Madame sorted through a few more samples, tutting with disapproval or clucking if her standards were met.

"You should know Richard that I have altered my will." She spoke as if she was commenting on the weather.

"How? Why?"

"Jeanne as you know is well provided for, but I have monies of my own and they will come to Lizzie."

"Lizzie! Bless you, oh bless you." Richard embraced her.

"Stop that, you know I do not like to be handled so."

"Forgive me, but I am so overcome."

"That is as maybe, but I want you to consider further this foolish scheme of yours."

"I will think again but I do not imagine I will change my mind."

"And what of Jacket?"

"He will be given a portion in my will."

"I meant if you go away."

"I don't know, he is grown he could look after himself. He might wish me to establish him in his own business."

"I doubt that."

"Why?"

"He idolises you, Richard, even more so now he separated from Alice. It was mean spirited of her not to take him."

"I don't know why she did not, she knew I would provide, I wondered if she was already thinking of Parker and he had forbidden it. She has become bitter thinking of other women's children that flourish when hers did not."

"Give him a bit of your attention, Richard, I know you think he is grown but show him a little kindness. I speak as one who has not been kind in my life and have suffered because of it."

"You do yourself a disservice, Wauldure, you have had to bend firmly held principles and beliefs, I admire your courage." He went to go but returned, "Wauldure...Jeannot...I did not

511

knowingly betray her...they bound my eyes...she was so shy...I thought if it would help her…"

Wauldure was focused on the swatches of cloth, as if she was not listening, but he knew she was.

"I should have tried harder…I'm sorry I made her unhappy." She still said nothing but cleared her throat as if there was a lump in it.

Chapter Sixty-Eight

Annie was getting married to Bart Biston. Her face was heavily scarred and she wore a veil as she was still too embarrassed to be seen in public. Some of the scars on her neck and chest were visible but people pretended not to notice. The wedding party was at the Angel. There were about thirty guests and it was a jolly enough day. The Bistons did not attend of course but Richard fetched old Alderman Crooke, who sat in the corner nodding and smiling and not really knowing that his grandson was the groom. Bart drank too much and largely ignored his bride, who in turn looked at him adoringly.

"Oh Mr Mudford, I am the happiest girl. I could not believe it when Bart said he wanted us to wed, he said I was still the same under the sheets. I think if he had not gone off and left me, I might not have needed to go to Mr Jack's bed and I might still have my old face – but then Bart might not have come back, so maybe it was all meant to be." It amazed Richard that Annie always managed to find the positive in any situation. He resolved to try that himself.

Richard nodded in reply, but Annie did not know he had paid Bart to marry the girl he had first despoiled and then abandoned. If Annie had been persuaded to marry someone else Richard thought she would have had more of a chance to be happy but Bart was who she wanted. Richard wondered where Bart had gone, he had disappeared from the party, but he was distracted by John asking if he would help fetch another barrel. Richard went around the back of the inn and there also found the errant bride groom against the wall with his new wife's sister, her skirts around her waist and her bodice undone. Bart caught Richard's eye and without losing his rhythm gave him a sly smile. Richard grabbed the barrel of beer and went back to the party.

"Jacket."

"Yes, Father?" The boy looked worried.

"I need to talk to you of your future."

"My future?" The boy was terrified at the thought.

"Your mother, that is to say Alice, was right when she said that you are growing up. And I think it is time to talk about what you might want to do."

Jacket looked utterly miserable, "I thought I could just keep helping you, especially now Will and Tom have gone away...I thought that as I was the only one...that maybe...but of course now Antonio ...if you wish me to leave, I will go gladly, you have been very good to take me in, sir."

"Take you in? Jacket you mistake me, I don't want you to go anywhere, I just wanted to be sure that you are happy to be part of Mudford Brothers and live in this house."

The relief on the boy's face was obvious, "Of course, Father, of course, I love working with you and I think I am good at it. Do you think I am good at business?"

"Yes, Jacket you are a born merchant. I am glad you want to continue your apprenticeship because I have been considering making a trip."

"A trip?"

"Yes, I think it would be appropriate and useful to go to the Americas to judge if Jack's plans for the expansion of business are sound."

"I think that too, Father. It is exciting but frightening too. When do we leave?"

"We? Er, that is, I hope passage can be secured within the month."

"And who will look after things whilst we are away?"

"Erm...well...that is I hope that Wauldure and Lawrence Prowse will act for us."

"I will start to make a plan, the things we need to take. May I borrow the book you were reading?"

"Which?"

"The one on the voyages of Captain Fenton, there might be useful things for me to know and can I borrow your maps as well and *The Seaman's Secrets*."

"Er yes that would be sensible." Richard was unable to fathom how he came to be taking his eighteen year old foster son with him on his voyage to find himself.

Jack was already in the Americas with what he grandly called the Mudford Fleet so Richard had to look for another ship to give Jacket and himself passage. He went to see the captain of the *Hopewell*, a ninety foot vessel of 180 tons, a typical ship designed with a cod's head and a mackerel's tail. Designed so that the ship would not heel over too far under full sail. The ship carried three boats, a skiff, longboat and shallop. The longboat was giving service as a coop for rabbits and poultry. The captain was pleased to show Richard around his ship, the main place for passengers to sleep was the great cabin, Richard had to stoop as he was above the five foot height of the below deck space. There would only be the space the size of grave to sleep, eat, store personnel belongings, change clothes, keep clean and prepare food for several months.

The captain was loading up with trading goods to tempt the natives, bracelets of beads and metal, rings and knives, pins, needles, scissors, copper chains, bells, red and blue cloth, small looking glasses and cheap glass earrings. Richard recognised the items he and Jack had stowed on their own ships, in fact he knew the captain had purchased goods from the Mudford stores. Boxes of smoked herring, dried ox tongues, sacks of turnips, parsnips, onions, beans, cabbage, spiced and salt beef, salt pork, peas and pease pudding, hogsheads of oatmeal and rye meal, wheat flour and Spanish rusk, tubs of pickled eggs and firkins of butter were loaded. Again the Mudfords had helped provision the ship, and the captain was grateful for the good deal he had managed to get. There was also dried salt cod, smoked beef and pork, lemon juice, and spices, ginger, pepper, cinnamon, mace, nutmeg, wormwood, and green ginger, conserves of roses and clove gilliflowers, sugar, raisins, currants, spiced wine and salt. Gin, brandy, beer and wine were also brought aboard. The ship was commissioned to undertake exploration and trade.

The Mudfords were not the only ones to wanting to discover the potential of American colonies, the past failures of Gilbert, Raleigh and others did not daunt the explorers, there was too much possibility of reward. Richard had met John White when he landed back in Southampton just prior to the Spanish Armada. They had spent a night drinking and telling tales. It was White that told him stories of Virginia and New England and shown him drawings of the strange things he had seen. Richard just listened, not expecting that ten years later he would be making his own voyage. Richard was not the only one to be inspired by White, a generation of explorers followed in his footsteps.

The Captain's name was Jurd. He hailed originally from the

Ferry village, his mother had been an aunt of George Parker, Richard tried not to hold it against him. He was also related to John, there were only four or five families in the village everyone was related to everyone else.

Stone ballast was being laid down, it was better than the sand and gravel, which held sewage and became sloppier as the voyage progressed. Richard could smell vinegar which indicated the vessel had only recently been cleaned and re-ballasted. The ship's cat wound around his legs, tired of chasing rats. It found a warm spot on the deck and curled up for a snooze. Richard vaguely recognised several of the crew, the Captain had returned to his home village to recruit men he knew and could rely on. He nodded to Ned Dible who sometimes shipped out with the *Pelican* but had been sick when Jack left port. He was shipping out as bosun.

"Ned! You are looking better."

Ned had few words but gave a brief nod and then scurried barefoot up a rope to check the rigging. Like many of his fellows he usually wore filthy clothes, but having been home a while he looked cleaner than usual. Richard wondered how much Jurd was paying the crew, 10s a month was the usual rate. The Mudfords also included some clothes, providing a loose blue serge coat with hoods for use during wet or cold weather. Richard had them made by the workers in Silkshop Yard.

Jurd offered Richard use of an officer's bunk for the voyage but Richard thought he might pack his hammock. He was still a poor sailor but found some comfort in the way the hammock moved in tune with the ship. He thought he could even ask Jurd to construct a temporary cabin to provide some limited privacy, depending on where it could be built. He did not want to be between decks as water would too easily be let in.

Chapter Sixty-Nine

Luisa Dypere knocked quietly on the door to his counting house. Richard had been trying to work on some accounts but really he had just been staring at the figures, his mind already drifting away across the sea to the Americas.

"What?" He looked up expecting a servant and for a moment couldn't think who the young girl was at his door. "Sorry Luisa, what is it?"

"Papa wondered if you would come to the inn?"

Richard felt a pang of guilt, the inn had not being doing so well since Alice had moved away. She had decided that the Angel was too close to her old haunts and she had plans to set up a new inn herself. The small tippling house ran by John's mother she judged not big enough to serve all the traffic travelling the coast road to Southampton and beyond. Tamsin was not as good a brewer as Alice, she was competent but had no love for the task and you could tell that in the taste of the ale.

Richard scooped up his papers and locked them in a chest and after securing the counting house walked with Luisa along to the inn.

"Is your Pa well, Luisa?"

"As well as ever he is thank you, sir."

Richard could think of nothing else to say so it was a mercy the inn was just a few steps away. He drew up a stool opposite John, who had a cup of strong beer waiting.

"Double beer?" he said raising his brows as he downed his own cup. Richard nearly gagged on the brew but hid it well.

"It's certainly strong."

"You drink too much fine wine these days."

"Maybe so."

"Sorry to call you out, you must have many preparations." John did not approve of his intended adventure.

"Well, you know."

Richard looked round the inn, it wasn't bustling but it was busy enough. Luisa had joined her mother behind the bar but Richard couldn't see any other helpers. John must have read his mind.

"We are a bit short of servants."

"I'm sorry about Alice, you know I am."

"No, no you mistake me. Dowsabelle has run off." The girl had returned to the inn after Richard let her go.

"I thought it was a mistake to take her back."

"Needs must. Bart is missing as well."

"Bart? You don't think they are together?" John shrugged.

"I thought you would want to know." Richard sighed, another problem.

"Are you going to take on anyone else?"

"We'll see, Little John is getting bigger and helps out. Luisa works herself to the bone. It's not what I would wish for her."

"There are plenty looking for work, John."

"The inn is not making as much money as it used to."

"Granted but it still does good enough business." Richard did the accounts. "If Bart has run off maybe Annie would come back?"

"Don't think she would be good for business." John gestured at his face.

"Perhaps not. What about Mary Smith's husband? He is back."

"I know he drinks here, too much."

Richard was losing patience.

"Don't worry, Diccon, I will put the word around, we will get more help, I really just wanted to let you know about Bart."

"Thanks John, I'll call around to see Annie now."

Annie and Bart lived in a small cottage Richard had rented for them off Half-knight Lane, Richard tapped on the door and went in. Annie was baking in a desultory way, her eyes were red and swollen from crying. She was heavily pregnant. She looked up expectantly at Richard's arrival but he could see her hopes were dashed.

"Mr Mudford, sir, come in, I was not expecting company." She dusted off a chair and gestured to Richard who sat down.

"How are you, Annie?"

"I do well, sir, as you can see. I helped my mother deliver many babies so I know how things go."

"I expect Bart is pleased."

She bit her lip and made a show of clearing away the pastry, "Oh yes, sir, he cannot wait."

Richard noticed that her right eye, her good eye not disfigured with scars, as well as being puffy from crying also showed faded bruising.

"Annie, Mr John has told me that Bart is run off."

"No sir, no Bart would not, it chafes him to be confined in such a small place, he is used to better sir, you know that. He is just about his business, he will be back, sir, he always comes back."

"Annie, has Bart taken the money I gave for your dowry?"

She could not, would not look at him, "He is my husband, he has every right, every right."

"Of course, sorry, I didn't mean anything. Annie, how will you manage if Bart is not back when the baby is born?"

"Well, sir, I have been thinking about the future, how I can make things better for Bart. I am to follow my mother, sir, as a midwife. When the babe is born I can also wet nurse. I also thought to sell pastries, I like to bake. I like to do that." She began to sob.

Richard stood up and tried to offer some comfort. "Ssh Annie, you shall have a pension and Mr Jack and I will help your business venture."

"Sir, I cannot, you have done so much for me and I always let you down."

"I do not think I did so well promoting this marriage Annie. If Bart does come back, you should not let him—" Richard gestured at her eye and Annie's hand went involuntarily to her face.

"It's not his fault sir, he has been disappointed. He can't handle drink and I am so clumsy, I dropped the ale bottle, he struck out sir, it was nothing." Her hand went to her belly. Bart had kicked their unborn child, Richard was sure of it.

"But he is so loving sir, and barely mentions my face, he makes me sit just so." She laughed turning her good side to Richard, "There he says, there Annie, come sideways into a room and none will be the wiser! He is such a joker."

"Annie, I will be away for a little while but if you need anything ask Madame Sohier—" Annie looked terrified at the prospect, "Or Mr John."

"I will, sir. Look what Miss Luisa has made for the baby." She fetched a tiny nightshirt, "I wish I could stitch as delicately."

"It is indeed a fine garment. Now remember what I said." Richard went back into the lane, stepping over the gutter which ran with muck and sewage.

Chapter Seventy

Richard waited in Winkle Street leaning against the wall of St Julien's chapel, when Tom appeared he whistled and called him over. Tom looked around obviously expecting Antonio.

"Where's the brat?"

"Tom!" the boy shrugged but did not say sorry.

"I thought we would go to the Dolphin today, have a good meal, there is fish stew on the board."

Tom looked suspicious but fell into step beside him.

"You should not blame Antonio."

"Why not? It's his fault."

"No it's not. If anyone is to blame it's me." Tom said nothing.

"I thought you got on well enough with him?"

Tom kicked at a stone, "He's all right, I just wish he wasn't here, everything has changed."

"Are you unhappy at the village?"

"I don't have my own room." Richard did not know what to say about that.

"I think your mother may be setting up an inn, it will have more space."

"So we won't be coming home then?"

"Not at the moment," Richard said quietly.

"Who decided?"

"Who decided what?" Richard guided Tom into a quiet corner in the inn.

"Who lived where."

Richard ordered the food.

"Well Alice, wanted to go back to the Ferry for a while. Jeanne and Lizzie are my natural children so had to stay with me."

"And Will is Alice's, but Jacket is an orphan and I am a foundling, so why did she take me and not him?"

Hell's teeth. "Jacket is grown, and I know you think you are grown Tom but to us you are still our little boy, foundling or no, and Alice would not be parted from you."

Tom tucked into the fish stew, Richard thought this was a good sign and that he was not too unhappy.

"Tom, I wanted to speak with you." Tom looked up with his Mudford eyes. "I am going away on a trip, a long trip, to the Americas, Jacket as well."

"For how long?"

"Some months, maybe six, so long but not forever."

Tom ate more of the stew, tearing off lumps of whitened bread.

"Tom, if you are really unhappy at the Ferry..."

He shrugged, "It's not too bad, I like being with Will, I just miss home. I wish we could all be together again."

"So do I, Tom, so do I."

"Perhaps Mother will miss you when you are gone and want to come home."

"Well I have a hope of that myself, but I think Tom we may both be disappointed. Your mother has an allowance for you, for books and school and other necessaries. If there is anything else you should go to Madame Sohier."

"I don't think Mother would like that." Tom mopped his plate.

"True, and I doubt you will have the need but just in case, just in case."

Tom nodded, "You won't get yourself into any trouble in the Americas will you?"

"I will try not to Tom." Richard gave him a hug.

"I have an errand to run for Mother." Tom stood. Richard gave him a purse of pennies.

"Try and find time to see Jeanne and Lizzie, they will be lonely." Tom nodded.

"Bye then."

"Goodbye." Richard gave a small wave.

"The old lady said you are going away." Antonio looked at him gravely.

"I have to go on a voyage, Antonio, I will not be so very long." They were sat side by side on the stairs.

"What will happen to me?" Antonio was trying very hard to keep the fear from his voice. Richard tried to sound light-hearted, thinking it would help reassure the boy.

"Happen? Well you will stay here with your sisters and your grandmother. You like Madame Sohier, don't you?"

Antonio considered "She gives me nice things to eat." He still spoke English with the trace of a Spanish accent, though in dress and looks he grew more English.

"There you are then. She does that only to those she likes very much."

"Does she give you nice things to eat?"

"Never."

There was a pause as Antonio digested this piece of news. He mimicked how Richard was sat, his hands on his knees. "Are you going to look for my mother?" Oh how he hoped still, Richard drew in a breath.

"No, I am sorry, Antonio."

Antonio nodded, he had not really believed it could happen. His little body seemed to sag

"I am carrying a great burden."

Richard lifted Antonio onto his lap. "A burden, Antonio? You are too little to be weighed down so, you must give it to me."

Antonio swung his legs back and forward.

"My mother went and away, and the other lady went away and she was a mother too."

"And you think this is your fault?" Antonio nodded and leaned his head on Richard's shoulder.

"Now you are going away." Richard gently rocked him.

"But I am not going away from you, I would never go away from you. It is my work, I have to work to buy sweetmeats to feed you."

"I will stop eating sweetmeats and then you can stay at home." The little boy clung to him.

"Oh Antonio, you break my heart."

"I am sorry...Papa." It was the first time he had called Richard that. Richard kissed his curly hair.

"You must not be sorry. It is my wish to give you my heart, even though it will break to be away from you. It will be mended when I came back and we are together again."

"You will come back?"

"On my oath."

Part Fourteen

1599

Chapter Seventy-One

It was April when they set sail, they sailed passed the Canaries and on to the West Indies. There was much sickness on the boat. Some of the crew had gone down with scurvy, getting progressively weaker and more tired, the worst had swollen black limbs. Old scars opened up again, old fractures broke once more. Teeth fell out, blood trickled constantly from nostrils and eyes. Richard had brought on extra rations for himself and Jacket. Luckily few had a taste for Spanish fruit and delicacies, preferring salty meat and mouldy bread. Thankfully he and Jacket had maintained reasonable health. Jack had told tales of ghost ships where all the crew had died from scurvy, dysentery and typhus. Richard hoped they would make land soon to take on supplies. He passed the time reading Sir Walter Raleigh's essay, *The Last Fight of the Revenge*. Raleigh had made a foolish action sound like an act of heroism. Richard thought about Luis de la Castro and wondered whether he had tried to fire the gun from the *Revenge* he had somehow purloined. Richard was fairly sure the sabotage he had carried out would have made it blow up when shot. It may have been this accident that had injured Luis.

They fell into stormy weather. Richard was on deck where

he felt marginally less sick. The *Hopewell* suddenly pitched violently and before he knew what was happening Richard was thrown overboard. He sailed out over the side with nothing between him and the plunging sea. He did not know what sense of self-preservation made him catch hold of one on the topsail halyards which hung over the side. The rope cut into his hands and the salt made them sting but he knew he had to hang on. He swung like a hung man in a gale for what seemed like eternity, his arms nearly wrenched from their sockets. He was scarcely able to breathe as he choked on seawater. His luck held. Several of the men had seen the accident and rushed to grab hold of the rope. As the ship righted itself they managed to pull him up. Ned Dible fixed a boat-hook into Richard's belt and tugged him aboard, dripping and spewing up water. He retched, trying to get his breath. For a few days he was very sick. Jacket sat by his side looking pale and frightened. Richard heard him praying earnestly not to let his father die. Richard thought how his girls had cried and clung to him when he had left to board the ship and felt guilty that his latest adventuring could leave them orphans. He would try not to be so foolhardy in future.

Richard's near drowning was not the only mishap. *Hopewell* sprang a leak which was so bad that the watch had to pump at five hundred strokes. The leak was only stopped by shifting the ballast till the hole came out of the water and they could fix it. Sailors were superstitious and murmurs circulated about the voyage being unlucky. They were probably right, Jacket reported to him that the main beam amidships had been bent with the strain of the storm and a crack had appeared. Richard was enough of a sailor to know this was very bad indeed, it was only the fact that they were nearer to the Americas than to England that encouraged the captain to press on. The ship's carpenter managed to carry out a makeshift repair on the ship so it was hoped that with God's will they would make land. Water ingress was dealt with by packing the joints with dried meat.

It was exhausting to be always wet and cold, chilled through to the bone. Jacket complained about his soaked boots and the growing stench on board the ship.

At the beginning of July they fell in with the coast of Florida in shoal water, where a sweet smell wafted across the decks, though they saw nowhere to land. The captain was having difficulty finding a harbour. Another storm sprang up, the ship began to leak once more and they lost a water barrel overboard. Being calmer the next day, it was decided to put a boat over to see where they might make land. Richard was itching for something to do so he went, along with Jacket and Ned Dible and some twenty others, in the long boat. They found the storm had done them a service and run them near to land. When they ran the boat ashore they left some of the company to look after the vessel, whilst the rest of the party struck inland looking for fresh water to replenish the ship. Ned thought they were close to where they intended to be. He had made several voyages across the ocean and knew more about the New World than any other who sailed with the *Hopewell*. He and Richard went to higher ground and Ned declared the next cove was the site of the trading post established by the Mudford Company. Richard's heart leapt at the thought of being so close to seeing Jack again.

They were unprepared for the attack even though they had posted lookouts. The natives were stealthy, painted savages in the skins of strange beasts, armed with spears and flint arrows. They outnumbered the scouting party and were not so well armed but were a terrifying sight up close. Richard led the retreat back to the shore but was horrified to see that their boat was gone, the rest of the party turning tail, pursued by other natives in dugout canoes. Richard led the men, who were becoming downcast, to higher ground that they might defend more easily. They had already lost half their number. He looked around for Jacket who, though frightened, was keeping his head. At just that moment the boy was struck by an arrow. Richard grabbed him and managed to pull him behind an outcrop, which he used as a natural barricade. Down in number, the natives retreated for a while. Richard ordered Ned to pick up the guns from men who had fallen.

"Jacket, Jacket!"

The boy opened his eyes. "I am shot, Father, it hurts."

"It would, be brave, let me see." He peered at the wound. It lay in a dangerous place near the boy's heart.

"Don't try to take the arrow head out," said Ned as he broke off the shaft, "Not here, it will jag the flesh and cause more damage." Richard nodded.

"See what you can do, Ned, I need to check what powder and shot we have."

He went round all the men and tried to buck their spirits. He told them not to fire until they were sure of their mark. He held out little hope, they had a fair amount of ammunition but no food or water. In the distance he saw Captain Jurd taking on board the men from the long boat and giving orders for the anchor to be raised. The natives in the canoes threw a few futile spears, like Essex had done outside the walls of Lisbon, and then retreated. Once again the natives on land attacked Richard's party and were beaten back. Two more men were grievously wounded. Jacket was as pale as death.

"Father, am I going to die?"

"Certainly not."

"Will the natives overrun us?"

"Not if I can do anything about it. We are the better armed."

Richard and Ned assessed the situation.

"There is nowhere to run or hide. We must trust that Jurd will return when he learns we are left behind, there are enough to see off our attackers."

"I wouldn't count on it," said Ned with a pessimism born of many travails. "The boy is in a bad way."

"I know."

"If they overrun us, keep a shot to see him off." Richard looked at Ned a while and nodded his head.

"Pa, Pa."

"I'm here Jacket."

"Tell Mother—"

"Stop say no more. Jacket Hall, I am telling you, you'll live to see your mother again. I will not let you make a liar of me."

"No, Father. I am awful thirsty."

"As we all are. Be a man, Jacket."

"Yes, Father." He passed out.

Two more attacks came, the defenders were dwindling. Ned did his best to patch them up. Richard fought hand-to-hand with two of their enemies who had breached their meagre defences. He had managed to kill them both but had also been cut himself.

"One more and we are done for Ned. I have no more shot."

"It's been good sailing with you, Diccon."

"And with you."

Richard wiped the dirt and sweat from his eyes and wondered when he should end Jacket's life. He heard new whoops and screams. He took a breath and looked at where the next descent was coming from. A fresh band of natives appeared over on their flank.

"Sweet Jesus." He started to mouth a prayer asking God to forgive his sins and take the souls of him and his men into His merciful arms. Then he was astounded. The new batch of natives did not attack his beleaguered position but fell instead on their attackers.

"They are another tribe," said Ned. "See, their dress and markings are different and also the way they wear their hair. I bet these others are raiding territory that is not their own."

"Is that good for us?"

"Who knows, they might turn on us when they have run off these others."

The new group was so great in number that the original natives soon ran off. Richard and his surviving compatriots were then surrounded. The new bunch of natives looked even more fearsome than the first. Richard hauled himself to his feet and went to stand in front of the man he thought to be the leader, who had a band of white coral around his forehead. He bowed, the man stroked his head and breast and Richard thought this a sign that he meant no harm. He pointed to Saskatan's bracelet, which Richard had around his wrist, and then to one of a similar design that he wore himself. Richard's spirits slightly rose at the possibility that the man was from the same tribe. The leader gave orders to his men who went and helped the wounded. They made a makeshift stretcher for Jacket, although Richard inferred from the leader's gestures that he thought Jacket unlikely to live. They had no choice but to follow the natives. Richard scoured the horizon but could see nothing of Jurd and the *Hopewell*.

They were nearing a settlement. It was obviously native from the construction of the dwellings and Richard brought to mind the drawings of John White, and Tom Hariot's descriptions of Indian villages from his writings on the new found land of Virginia. The leader of their party directed them to the edge of the village where a little way apart was a rough dwelling that bore some resemblance to a single storey house. Outside sat a man dressed in skins but fair of skin and hair.

"Hello Diccon. What are you doing here?"

"Jack!" His hair was much longer and his beard bushy but it was most certainly his brother. He got up and spoke to the native leader in his own language.

"Diccon, let me introduce Saskatan's father."

Everything fell into place. Richard made a deep bow as Jack explained who he was. The Chief embraced Richard and uttered something unintelligible.

"Jack, Jacket is badly wounded. We were attacked and most

of our fellows killed, except for the few you see here. We thought we were done for till the chief turned up."

"We had heard a ship was on the coast."

"We were on it and we'd been blown off course. We came ashore to search for water but ended up marooned. The captain was either a coward or a knave."

Jack was looking at Jacket, who was thankfully still unconscious.

"Berta!" He called back at the house and a little while after a tall Negro woman emerged. "Berta, my nephew, sick, wounded, help please." She came by, sashaying slowly. There was something very calm about her. She looked at Jacket and made some assessment and then directed the stretcher to be carried into the house.

"Who is that?" asked Richard. Jack looked shifty.

"Long story, I'll tell you later, let's get everyone sorted." Richard sat outside Jack's house whilst he arranged for the remnants of the landing party to be fed, watered and looked after. Richard went inside to see how Jacket was faring. He was laid on a cot and Berta, Ned, a couple of native women and a man who was obviously some kind of elder, cut away his clothes and were examining the wound.

"Not good," said Berta.

"You speak the truth" said Ned. "I did what I could, in a life of fighting battles you learn a bit about wounds. But we need to get that arrowhead out"

"You did well. The elder here knows much about such injuries." She spoke to the women, who went out on an errand. The wise man was chanting incantations over the prone body of Jacket.

"What's he doing?" asked Richard suspiciously.

"Some spell or other," said Ned. "Don't imagine it will do any harm and this is their land, they know things we don't."

"Berta? Do I have your name right?"

"Yes, that is what I am called here."

"Can you help my boy?"

"He is your son."

"My adopted son, yes my son."

Berta stroked the boy's forehead, "He has a fever." She shrugged. "I will do what I can, we all will."

"I'll stay and help," said Ned.

Richard went outside he thought about Will. Would he bring Jacket back home broken or not at all? A long time later, Ned came out wiping his bloodied hands.

"Ned, you should go and get some food, you must be exhausted."

"And you are not?"

"I will stay here a while till Jack gets back."

Ned went out and Richard found a seat. He sat down to watch over Jacket, but soon his head nodded and he fell asleep. He awoke when Jack shook his shoulder.

"Come on, Diccon, food is on the table. Jacket is sleeping and she will watch him." A pretty little native girl was sat on the floor beside him.

Richard hauled himself off and joined Jack and Berta at the table. He wasn't quite sure what he was eating but it tasted good. He drank water flavoured with sassafras and other herbs.

"Tell me, why are you here?" asked Jack as he spooned more corn porridge onto his plate.

"I needed to get away, and wanted to understand more of what we were becoming involved with here."

"So you and Alice, it's all over finally?"

Richard didn't answer.

"Who is looking after things at home?"

"Wauldure and Lawrence."

"How long are you planning on staying?"

"Don't know, not long it's not fair on the children."

"You have other children?" enquired Berta.

"Yes, yes I do, a son Tom, two daughters Jeanne and Elizabeth and a younger child another boy, Antonio and there is my stepson Will of course."

Berta rolled her eyes and said something in a strange dialect.

"Talk English Berta," said Jack. She was the most graceful person Richard had ever seen and he found her quite mesmerizing to watch.

"Berta comes from Africa, Diccon. We are married." Before Richard finished reeling from the shock a child started crying in the side room, "And that's my son, Samuel." Jack got up from where he was sitting cross-legged on the floor and went to fetch a black skinned baby whom he brought back and sat on his knee and began to feed from his plate.

"Jack?"

They were sat outside and Jack pulled on a pipe. Richard was listening to the strange night time noises.

"I picked her up in the Caribbean. She was a slave being bartered for gold, sugar, hides. They had her in chains and were selling her like she was a cow. Men were poking and squeezing and looking at her teeth. But she held herself proud as if they were the prisoners, and she the master. Anyway I bid for her, I had more money than anyone else so I got her. I thought she would be grateful! I was going to take her to bed, she was so beautiful. She looked at me as if I was shit on her shoe. So I said I would free her and take her back to Africa as soon as I was able."

"I am sure it was all more complicated than that."

"Possibly."

"But you said you are married, there is a child."

"It's simple, Diccon, whilst I was repairing my ship and deciding what to do I fell in love with her, and in the end I think she fell in love with me too. She chose, not me, and now I am a father. There is no doubt Sam is mine. Who would have thought it, Diccon?"

"Not me that is for sure."

Berta came out and sat with them. "He has told you how he wooed me?"

"It didn't sound very romantic, Berta, but then the Mudfords have never been ones for romance."

"I hated him so much, so very much. I thought I would cut his throat as he slept but I could not. He is so white." She stroked Jack's arm. "I did not know that eyes could be so blue."

They all sat in silence for a while.

"You have a fine son Berta," said Richard. She nodded, "I think the crisis will come for your son tonight. I will sit with him."

"I will sit with him, Berta."

"We will both sit with him."

Jacket survived the night but he was still very, very sick and everyone except Richard was convinced he would die.

"Diccon, you need to prepare yourself," said Jack.

"For what?"

"The boy will not make it."

"That's not true."

"Diccon, for God's sake."

"He is not going to die!" Richard was getting angry.

"Why are you so sure?"

"Because I told him not to."

"And who are you, the Almighty?"

"Jacket will do whatever he needs to please me. I am his anchor, if there is just the smallest fragment of hope he will hang on, he has lived this long after all."

"Whatever you say, Diccon, whatever you say."

Chapter Seventy-Two

In the evenings Berta would talk about her home on the west coast of Africa, a place of gold, ivory and pepper and Jack would talk about the Caribbean islands and the possibility of them setting up their own sugar plantation. Richard marvelled at how big the world was and how little he knew. They spoke of trading with Muscovy and China and India, there was no limit to the possibilities. Richard wondered how big the Americas were, it seemed never-ending.

It was three months before Jacket fully started to recover but Richard was right about his will and his determination. After the first month Richard began to relax enough to discuss with Jack the probabilities of them setting up a formal colony in the Americas.

"Grenville and Raleighs' efforts failed," said Jack.

"And we must learn from them. Supplies were a problem and the land was not as hospitable as the colonists were led to believe. We need a plan to make sure we have the resources to support any colony over a long period."

"It could be expensive, even for us."

"We need other backers to spread the risk, increase the fleet, and recruit the right type of colonists that have skill and staying power. What of the natives?"

"Bit unpredictable. My dear old father-in-law is a solid sort."

Richard had been amazed to see a painting of Queen Elizabeth hung in the Chief's hut. Jack had presented it to him and told him she was queen of them all, and that his daughter had met and impressed her. He embellished the truth, saying that the painting was a personal gift from Elizabeth to the Chief and his subjects. The Chief had been in awe and like many men before him, had fallen under Elizabeth's spell.

"The thing is," Jack added, "He is getting old now, there are younger men and they don't all take his view. They put up with me and we do good trading and get some protection, but that might change if there was a new chief."

"So guns and cannon as well as ploughs and seed."

"There are other options to consider as well."

"Like what?"

"Such as surveying the land here about. I have been mapping islands in the Caribbean, there are some rich and lush uninhabited ones with good harbours and they would be a good base en-route to the mainland. We could set up there, they look good for sugar."

Richard smiled, "I'm proud of you little brother, growing up at last."

Jack pulled a face. Richard continued, "What of slaves, Jack? Hawkins is getting heavily involved in it, attracted by the rich pickings and cheap labour."

"You know me, Diccon, I'm not known for my morals and if it wasn't for Berta I would probably say let's go for it. There is certainly plenty of money to be made."

"Yet I was little better than a slave in Spain and I wouldn't wish that on anyone."

Jack considered briefly, "So no slaves…not unless we have to!"

"Jack!"

"Options need to be kept open, Diccon."

"I really like Berta, she is so" Richard searched for the right word, "calming, and she seems to move so slowly and elegantly but gets such a lot done! And her English is marvellous."

"I believe she picked it up on the ship coming over and then made me work really hard teaching her more. She saw it as a weapon I think."

"What a terrible and terrifying adventure to happen to a woman."

"She had some luck, if you can call it that. The man that took her knew she would be worth more over here if she was in health and a virgin. She was sold by a relative! Can you believe it?"

"I assumed she had been seized."

"Some are, others have been enslaved by rival tribes and sold on." Jack shrugged, "That has always been the way of the world, even in the Bible."

"I didn't know you read the Bible Jack?"

"All sailors know the Bible, besides we had the same god-fearing mother, Richard."

"I think she may have been a Catholic in her heart."

"Really? What makes you think that?"

"When she was dying, she was sad that there could be no mass said for her soul to help her out of purgatory."

"I doubt if she would spend much time in purgatory, she was too good."

"She was good."

"I was jealous of you," said Jack.

"Why?"

"You know why. You were her favourite."

"She loved us both. I just caused her less worry."

"Maybe so. Tell me, are you still a Protestant?"

"Of course I am, like all good Englishmen," retorted Richard.

"I know you are a good Englishman, Diccon."

"And what are you going to do?" Richard asked, changing the subject.

"What do you mean?"

"Are you going to stay here?"

"What, forever? God no, I like it well enough but I miss the alehouses and whorehouses. No I'm coming home, I've been talking to Ned Dible, he's a good man and I think we should offer him a position. He may be happy to stay here awhile, keep an eye on things."

"Sounds like a plan, he is a good sort and has lots of useful experience. What of Berta and Sam?"

"They will come with me of course." Jack looked surprised that Richard would think otherwise.

"Well I suppose your neighbours did get used to Sasky, and there have always been blackamores in the town."

"Berta and I will cope. I am worried about Sam though. If anything happens to me Diccon you will look out for him, won't you?"

"Of course Jack. How could you think otherwise?"

"I just wanted to make sure that's all. I think we should go exploring. We could visit the traps, look at sites and then go and see how the repairs are progressing on the Mudford fleet."

"I think it will be safe to leave Jacket awhile, let's go tomorrow."

They passed by the sea towards the top of the next range of hills, from which the water was visible on both sides. The valley was full of tall red cedars. There were pines, cypresses, sassafras and lentisks, all of excellent smell and quality. When they made an undue noise a flock of cranes, mostly white, took flight crying like an army of men all shouting together. The woods were full of deer, conies and fowl of all kinds. Jack pointed out melons, walnuts, cucumbers, peas and other roots and corn, which he said grew three times in five months. The soil seemed to have something magical about it. Peas could be put in the ground and grow fourteen inches high within ten days. They took crossbows with them and shot at partridge and pheasant. They ate wild strawberries.

They went down to the natural harbour where men were working on repairs to their vessels. Some were curing long strips of meat on a barbecue over a slow fire of dung and wood chips.

"We learnt this from the Indians, the smoked meat means it is preserved for ages, good for taking on voyages or to get through the winter. Could be another commodity for us, Diccon."

"What are they doing to the *Magpie*?"

"Coating her hull with tallow. If you go cruising in the warm water around the tropics you have to be beware of the teredo worm, they have teeth like saws and love wooden ships. They are fertile bastards as well, lay eggs in their millions. Can turn a hull into a honeycomb in no time. That's why double planked ships are best with tar and felt laid in between. It's a bugger to careen the ships and dangerous too."

"I see you have taken off the guns." Richard nodded to where they were mounted on improvised earthworks commanding the entrance to the bay.

"What I'm looking at is replacing some timbers with cedar, there is plenty around here and the worms don't like it. I'm going to ship some home for trade as well."

"Another thing we need to make sure we have a good supply of is mosquito nets."

"Nasty little brutes aren't they?"

The old *Magpie* was making the next voyage back to Southampton. Richard stood supervising the stores and the trade goods going on board: fish, skins from beavers, otters and seals. He looked at where fish was drying out after being soaked, gutted, split and washed in brine, and spread on homemade flakes or wooden racks to be cured in the sun. Stockfish was delicious when it was soaked and properly cooked. They had seen nothing more of the *Hopewell* since their arrival at Jack's camp and Richard wondered if the vessel had made land or if the ship had eventually foundered. If he got back to Southampton and found it there he would make the captain sorry.

Ned Dible had taken himself a native wife to go with the one he had back at Itchen Ferry, something that happened a lot. The young girl who nursed Jacket had made it very clear that she was interested in knowing him better. Jacket had been embarrassed but Jack filled him with Dutch courage, sent him out into the woods and told him not to come back until he was a man. Jacket found to his surprise that he enjoyed very much becoming a man and practised a lot with several other maidens. Richard was worried he might end up married or that the natives would be angry that their young women had been used so. Jack laughed and explained that morality was different out here and encouraged him to sample it himself. The girls were pretty and willing but Richard found he could not.

He wondered what would happen when they arrived home. Would Alice have realised her mistake? It was probably too late if she had, with all the lawyers and arguments involved in first obtaining their right to separate and finally the great financial and emotional cost of achieving an annulment. But they could come out *here* where there were no priests or lawyers to tell them how to live. Alice wanted a simple life, well it would be simple with everything fresh and new. They could be like Adam and Eve, except George Parker was the serpent in the garden.

Richard enjoyed his stay in the Americas, like Jacket he became stronger also. He voyaged along the islands with Jack awhile and they made many plans. He liked to sit at night around the native camp-fires and he learnt a little of their language, many of them had some words of English also. He played with Sam and thought about his own children at home. He watched Jack squeeze Berta and felt lonely. Jacket picked up many skills from the natives, both men and women. It would have been easy to stay but he was a man of responsibilities. He borrowed a slop chest to hold canvas breeches, doublets, petticoats, a rug and long woollen stockings, changes of clothes for the journey back to England. So he boarded the *Magpie*, hugged his brother and wished him home soon. With Jacket beside him they set sail, spooming before the wind as they scudded over the sea and back home.

Part Fifteen

1600

Chapter Seventy-Three

He was back home. Southampton seemed so small compared to the vast oceans of the Atlantic and the wide landscapes of the Americas. He felt deflated and let down. When did everything become so grey? Was it his imagination or did the port seem much less busy? It was the new century, time to look forward but the town appeared as if its great days were in the past. Richard glanced at Jacket. The boy was smiling and his eyes shone.

"I'm so longing to see Will and Tom, and the girls of course. May I go and visit moth...Aunt Alice?"

"Of course, Jacket, let's go to the house first and make sure everyone is well and prospering but tomorrow go and visit your brothers."

They would notice a change in Jacket. For years he had been puny and hardly grew but it seemed his body had just been biding its time. He was now taller than Richard and his days of hunting and exploring with the natives had broadened his shoulders and thickened his thighs. His nights with the Indian girls had made him a man. He now had a neatly trimmed beard, he looked fit and tanned. Richard clasped him around the shoulders.

"Jacket, you have made me very proud this last year, you

have become a man and I thank God for giving me such a fine son."

Jacket looked astounded and his eyes glinted with tears. He grasped Richard close, unable to speak.

"Come, let's go home."

The girls were watching from the window, Richard had sent a message before him so they were expected. A respectful servant gave them entrance indicating Wauldure's influence.

"Papa, Papa." The girls had forgotten all decorum and had sped down the stairs to encircle him. How different from the time he had come back before and they had not even known him.

"Jeanne, Lizzie! Remember you are young ladies! Don't let your papa think I have been raising you like savages." Madame Sohier was more stooped, she used a stick now and her knuckles were swollen.

"Wauldure! It is good to see you, you all look so well," beamed Richard.

"My joints plague me, this country has a disgusting climate. But you are looking tanned and fit. Surely this cannot be little Jacket?"

"No longer so little Grand-mère," Jacket kissed her on both cheeks.

"You are grown so tall, Jacket, and broad," Lizzie was agog.

"I know, it must be something in the air of the Americas."

"You have been gone such a long time, Papa," complained Jeanne.

"I have, sweetheart, much longer than I intended and wanted."

"You must blame me Jeanne," said Jacket, "I was ill."

"Ill?" Jeanne looked concerned.

"It was a bit more than that, Jacket." Richard explained, "He was grievously wounded, our ship ran into problems and we put ashore in search of fresh water, then we were attacked by natives."

"Attacked?" Lizzie squealed.

"I am recovered as you can see but Father is right, I was sick for a long time and he would not leave me."

"As it should be," said Madame. "And you see we have managed very well whilst you were away."

"I can see and I thank you."

"The business thrives as well, so you could have stayed away even longer."

Richard smiled, "No, I could not I missed my girls, and there was someone else I wanted to be with. Where is Antonio?"

The mopped head of Antonio peeped from behind Madame Sohier's skirts. "Come out from behind me little man, see, here is your papa."

He was still a little boy but he had changed more than any of them Richard knelt and held out his arms. Antonio hesitated until Madame Sohier pushed him forward into his father's embrace. "Oh my son, I have missed you so much. I promise I will never leave you alone like this again." Richard picked him up and carried him into the hall, ushering and half hugging Jeanne and Lizzie with his spare arm as if there were a gaggle of unruly geese.

Madame began ordering servants to stow away baggage and shooed everyone into the dining hall.

"I did not know if you would be hungry, but I can imagine sea rations are not very edible."

"This looks wonderful, Wauldure, and far better than dried meat and weevilled biscuit. I did not think I was hungry but now my insides beg for good English food."

"Well come sit, eat, and get to know your children again. Tomorrow is soon enough to catch up on other things."

"I thought Tom might be here, even Will."

"We see little enough of either of them, especially now that Tom has been removed from school."

"Removed? How so? I know he had trouble sometimes getting to the classes. Has he lost interest in study?"

"I think not. It is more to do with his stepfather."

"What are you saying?"

"Tomorrow, we will talk of this tomorrow," said Madame with a note of finality. But she squeezed his hand to show him that she was also happy to have him home.

That night Richard lay in his bed. He could not sleep, it seemed strange not to feel the rocking of the ship, plus he was concerned about Tom, and he worried about seeing Alice again. What would be worse, if she missed him or if she did not? The door of his chamber opened and the small figure of Antonio stood there. He looked awhile and then came into the room, he reached out and touched Richard as if to reassure himself he was really there.

"Would you like to stay here with me tonight Antonio?" The little boy said nothing but clambered into the big bed. Richard tucked the coverlets around him, and kissed his forehead and they both slept.

The next day he made the trip over to the Ferry village. Here it was as it had always been except the village had a new inn called The Ferry, which he assumed must be Alice's. It was too early for the inn to be open. He knocked on the door and to both their surprise, Alice opened it.

"Hello."

"So you are back."

"As you see."

"What are you doing here?"

"I came to see you."

"Why? We have nothing to say to one another."

"You may have little to say to me, I on the other hand have much to say to you."

She folded her arms across her chest and looked hostile.

"Why has Tom been taken out of school?" Alice had the grace to blush.

"He was required elsewhere."

"Elsewhere?"

"George needed him on the fishing boat. Everyone has to contribute."

"I believe I have contributed so that Tom may finish his studies."

She went into the house and came back a moment later with a money bag.

"We do not want or need your money. We get by good honest toil."

"Alice, if that is how you want to live your life it is your choice. If that is what you want for Will, likewise that is your decision. But Tom is my son and it is not the life I want for him. I only agreed that you could take him if he continued at school. You have broken the bargain."

"Bargain? We had no bargain! My son is not a sack of wheat to be fought over."

"Your son does not even know he is of your body and mine." Now she went pale.

"Why did you come back?"

"This is my home, my family are here."

"My husband will be home soon, he would not want to see you."

"So you married him?"

"The courts decided we had always been married, you know that."

"You may delude yourself, Alice, but you and I know the truth of the matter."

"I want you to go."

"What you want is of no interest to me anymore."

She banged the door shut and Richard sat himself down on

the bench outside and waited. He guessed Parker was still out with his fishing boat and had the boys with him. It was nearly an hour before he appeared lugging a wicker basket full of fish. Will and Tom followed on carrying another behind him.

He did not acknowledge Richard. He banged on the door and demanded entrance. Alice opened it and he went inside, she looked surprised to see Richard still sat there.

"Tom, sit with me awhile." Tom glanced at Alice. She made no sign one way or another so he decided to sit. Will went on into the house.

"When did you get back?"

"Yesterday."

"Oh. You were gone a long time."

"Longer than I meant to be. Jacket was wounded and almost died." Tom looked up, shocked. "He is well now and none the worse for his ordeal, but for many months he could not be moved. I'm sorry I have not been here. Tom, why have stopped your studies?"

The boy squirmed, "I needed to work, to earn my place at the table." Richard tried not to let the anger show on his face.

"Would you rather be in school?"

Tom looked uneasy and did not want to reply.

"Tom, you will not be disloyal to Alice or your stepfather if you tell me the truth."

"I hate fishing. I hate George Parker. I hate the village. I want to be in school, I want to study."

There was such vehemence in Tom's voice that Richard felt sure the boy had been suffering greatly. He wondered if the fact that Tom had the look of the Mudfords made Parker dislike and distrust him.

"Then you must come and live with me."

"Will Mother be angry?"

"No, she might be a little cross but knows deep down that you are a scholar and not a fisherman."

"Then I would like to come home."

"Is there anything you want to bring from here?"

"No."

"Let's go."

"Perhaps, perhaps I should say goodbye, to Will and to Mother."

He went back in. Richard heard Parker shouting and Alice weeping. Tom came out a little while later very subdued.

"Your mother will get over this, and you can come and visit often."

"I know, can we go now please?"

When they got back to the house everyone was happy to have Tom with them, except perhaps Antonio who was not sure about there being another boy in the house and where he fitted into the strange family. Jacket wanted to know why Richard had gone to Itchen Ferry without him.

"I thought there might be some problem because of Tom and did not want you involved, to seem to be on my side even. You go on over, take some gifts. Tell of your adventures, Will is bound to be envious."

"He will be amazed to see I am now so grown, I must be taller than him at last."

Richard spent the rest of the day in business with Madame Sohier and Lawrence Prowse who was equally glad to see him home. They told him that business had been doing so well they had taken the opportunity to rent another building: the old wool warehouse adjacent to Jack's house on the quay.

"It may be old Richard, but it is still sturdy," said Lawrence as he unlocked the large double doors.

The warehouse had been built more than a hundred and fifty years before on the order of the monks of Beaulieu Abbey, who ran large flocks of sheep and needed somewhere to store the wool whilst they waited for the Italian galley fleets to arrive. Of course, the wool trade had been devastated by Henry VIII when he forbade its export but the warehouse was still a magnificent building, with a hammer beam roof and stone built with tiles on the roof. Richard gazed up at the high ceiling.

"It's a goodly space, I wonder at the town having no use for it," he said.

"Alas, trade is not what it was – in general terms," Lawrence added hastily. "The Americas are where the money is to be made, you and Jack were right there. Even privateering is not bringing the rewards it once did."

"It was always high risk, we were very lucky when we started," said Richard he gazed around the warehouse which was about half full of goods in transit. "We'll need do even better if we are to fill this place to the rafters."

"I was worried you were lost till we received word when the *Pelican* docked." Lawrence looked a little embarrassed, not wanting to show that he had been sorrowed by the thought of losing his friend.

"The voyage out was rough, I thought at times we would not make it, but for all that it was worth the trip."

"You are making me keen to visit the Americas too," said Lawrence. They had spent a good few hours discussing Richard's adventure over a fine meal prepared by Madame Sohier.

"You should go, it's such a vast land, it is past all imagining," said Richard.

Richard asked about the Silkshop Yard venture and was pleasantly surprised to hear it too prospered and the cloth now being produced was much sought after. The operation had been expanded as a result. It seemed to Richard that he was lucky in business if in nothing else.

"Thank you both for looking after my money and my children."

"Well Richard," concluded Lawrence, "I turned a healthy profit into the bargain. Your former mother-in-law is a wily woman in business."

Tom settled back in school. Having quickly caught up with his studies, he soon started to stride ahead again. Antonio had also begun at the school. He complained bitterly about having to go but Tom would take his hand and trot him down the road.

Chapter Seventy-Four

"Papa?"

"Yes, Lizzie?" Richard was reading in the solar.

"Why can't I go to school with Tom?"

"Because you are a girl and schools are for boys."

"Why?"

"It is the way of things. Girls do not need great learning, your Grand-mère has taught you the things young ladies must know."

"But I like learning."

"Er yes, I know you like books, Lizzie."

"I think I could be as clever as Tom if I could go to school."

"But what would you do with the learning? You cannot be a cleric or a lawyer or a teacher, it would be a waste."

"Did the Queen go to school?"

"No Lizzie, she was a princess. Princesses don't go to school."

"But you said she was very clever."

"Yes, the Queen is most clever, she is a great ruler."

"How did she learn these things?"

By now Richard was feeling very uncomfortable, "Well she had tutors."

"And what did they teach her?"

"Er, Latin and other classical things, but like you she was also taught needlework and music and dancing." Lizzie was giving him a long hard stare. "Languages, I believe the Queen also knows Greek and Italian and French. She has a fine writing hand and is also bookish..."

Lizzie still stared at him.

"Run along now, I am busy."

The next day Richard went down to the grammar school to see the Master. Mr Davison agreed to a meeting with bad grace. He was a man with many duties and seeing parents was not one of them. Richard explained that he was looking for tutor for his daughters – he got no as further the schoolmaster guffawed out loud.

"You seek to educate your daughters as if they were boys? That is arrant nonsense sir, and I will not countenance it, you waste my time, sir. No man will want to marry an educated woman."

Richard felt grieved at his treatment and marked the schoolmaster down as someone he would make sure got his comeuppance. He went back into Winkle Street to ponder his next move. Perhaps he should write to The Queen's College, Oxford and ask if there was a young graduate looking for a position.

"Sir?"

He turned and saw a whey-faced young man in a shiny gown, too big for him.

"Yes, do I know you?"

"I am under usher at the school, sir."

"Oh and how do you like that position?"

"Not so much if truth be told. The Master is not the best, and neither is the usher, I think they do the school a disservice."

"Do you think you should talk of your employers in such a way?"

"Probably not, sir, but they pay me a pittance, I don't get enough to eat and there are not many books to enjoy."

"What do you want with me?" asked Richard, although he had a fair idea.

"I am an Oxford man, sir. I did well in my studies but my widowed mother had little enough money and no connections. So I am here sir, but I hope for improvement, I overheard, I did not mean to listen but I was clearing away in the next room, and I overheard you are looking for a tutor for your daughters."

"Mmmm."

"I should like to apply for the position. I have recommendations sir, from my old tutor and also from a gentleman whose children I schooled whilst I was studying, to help me to live, sir." He rummaged in the pocket of his gown and thrust papers at Richard, who felt disinclined to take them but the young man looked so desperate. They were fine testimonials to the young man's scholarship, work ethic, he was god-fearing, not a drunkard, firm but fair with his charges.

"What is your name, sir?"

"Mr Dutton, see it is writ there, sir."

"Come tomorrow morning and we will see if my daughters approve of you."

"Thank you sir, I will, I will."

He came the next day, his gown shinier than ever. He had tried to comb his wavy hair into some sort of style and he had cleaned his nails, but his fingers were still ink stained. His clothes were clean but over-mended. His shoe had a hole in the sole.

"Mr Dutton, these are my daughters Miss Jeanne and Miss Elizabeth." The girls curtsied very prettily. Jeanne looked dubious, Lizzie could barely contain herself. "I suggest, sir that you give the girls their lesson and I will assess how you do."

Mr Dutton swallowed hard and his Adam's apple bobbed. He stood and almost lost his balance.

"Forgive me, sir, I am a little light-headed."

"Have you eaten, Mr Dutton?"

"Not since yesterday, sir, or the day before."

"Then I think you should go to the kitchen first and get some breakfast. It would not do for you to faint before you have had chance to educate my daughters."

Madame Sohier sat in the back of the lesson to assess whether Mr Dutton was worthy of the education of her grandchildren.

She reported back to Richard, "He was exceedingly nervous."

"So would I be if you were sat at the back of the room, glowering."

"I wonder if he will be able to control the girls."

"The girls have wonderful, even temperaments, for which I thank you. If he had the care of Antonio I would understand your concern."

"It seems as if you have decided already."

"I did ask around a little about the boy. He is of a good family but poor, he sends most of his pittance to his mother and he sleeps in the schoolroom so that he may save on lodgings to send more to her. It's true I want to give him a chance, as long as the girls are happy."

They were. Richard hoped that it wasn't because Mr Dutton was just a handful of years older than them and had the romantic look of a poet. He offered Mr Dutton a salary equivalent of half that of the headmaster of the free school, which was much more than he would earn as an under-usher or indeed an usher, with the promise of an increase if his charges progressed well. He told Mr Dutton he would also expect him to take on some small secretarial tasks also. He included the feeding of the under-nourished Mr Dutton. Richard thought he might be less romantic if he was fatter.

"Thank you sir, thank you. I will not let you down." Mr Dutton hesitated to leave, "Sir, I do not like to ask but I wonder if I might have an advance?"

"On your wages?"

"Yes, sir, when I give up my position at the school I lose my lodgings as well. I need to find somewhere to live and I fear any landlord will want money on account. I do not like to ask sir, in fact wipe it from your mind, I am sure I can manage something. Thank you again sir, for this opportunity."

"Wait," said Richard with a sigh. "Come with me." He took him to a small storeroom over the buttery. It was warm had a small window overlooking the courtyard and currently was full of broken furniture and chipped pots.

"If you want to clear this space out you may have it for your lodging, there will be no charge. I'm sure we can find a truckle bed and some of these bits of furniture may be saveable, it might do till you can afford better."

Richard thought for a moment the young man would hug him. But he clutched his cap and bobbed several times in something like a bow.

"Come, I want to show you the books we have in the house. You must let me know if you need to purchase others. I have no primers except what Tom has discarded. It is an eclectic mix, just volumes I picked up over the years that caught my eye."

The young man was very impressed by the collection and Richard found himself swelling up with pride. They shook on their contract, Richard would get his lawyers to write it up later and his girls began their formal education as little princesses.

Chapter Seventy-Five

Old Alderman Crooke was dead. He passed in his sleep. The nurse Richard had lately employed to watch over the old man when his mind started to wander too much, sent a message. When he reached the small room at the Dolphin, which had been Crooke's home since his fortunes failed, the women were already there preparing the body. Richard asked them to leave for a moment so he could be alone to say his farewells. Before Crooke fell ill his mind had been sharp. He was a man of business, making deals, expanding trade. Of course not all of these actions had been legal, in fact, during the early days most of them were not, but he could be generous as well. He had been a devoted husband and father and he was very good to Richard, giving him a chance where there had been no necessity on his part to do so. He recognised Richard had promise and as Crooke had climbed he took Richard with him. He was more of a father figure to Richard than his real father.

Richard decided he would make sure the Alderman had a fine canopied tomb, not a pauper's grave. He would be given his due as a man who had been mayor on more than one occasion, who had shouldered responsibility and helped the town stave off its economic slide. In fact, it was only when Crooke was

563

no longer there as a powerful burgess that the town's fortunes began to dip. He should have gone at the peak of his powers, he would have had a grand funeral then, with all the burgesses and town officers parading behind him. Richard stroked his hair, kissed his forehead and whispered goodbye. He knelt by the bed and prayed for his soul, he hoped God would look in his great book and see that on balance there was more in the column for good than that for bad.

Jack was home at last. He had sent the small boat on ahead to warn Richard and Jacket to prepare the warehouse and to open up and air the Quay House. They had been looking out for his ship for the last two days. As soon as she was tied up it was all business as the porters got to work taking the goods from the ship into Wool House.

"Well that makes life easier!" said Jack. He had shaved and trimmed his hair and was wearing a costly doublet. He clasped Richard and Jacket.

"Glad you are looking so well. Your return journey was not so adventurous as the outbound?"

"No, Uncle Jack."

"You are taller still, I am sure Jacket."

"Is Berta with you and Sam?" Jacket strained to see the deck of the ship.

"Yes, of course," said Jack, "I wanted to make sure the house was ready first."

"Yes, come," said Richard. They went to the Quay House and were met by Jeanne and Lizzie and Madame Sohier along with servants Richard had engaged. Annie was there as well.

"Annie! Is that you girl?" asked Jack. She had part of her face covered and was holding her child.

Jack lifted her veil and kissed her full and long on the lips. "How are you, Annie?" She squealed with delight whilst protesting she was a married woman.

"I do well, Master Jack. I am married and have a son." She didn't say that Bart had run off with her sister Dowsabelle.

"He's a bonny boy. Have you come back to run my house?"

"No sir, just to wish you well. I have my own little cottage and a small little pastry shop. I brought you some pies and have put them in your kitchen. I am now a midwife as well, my life is good sir."

"I am pleased to hear it Annie, you're a good girl." Annie took her leave.

"Is she really managing, Diccon?"

"She is doing well. Bart was a complete bastard of course and has gone off who knows where, taking the money I gave him to support his wife. But Annie works hard and I keep an eye on her. I eat a lot of pies!"

"Jeanne! Lizzie!"

"Uncle Jack!"

"Madame Sohier!"

Madame Sohier nodded, she could not bring herself to approve of Jack, but she did appreciate him.

"This is marvellous. Is this little Antonio?" Antonio could not answer as his mouth was full of pie.

Quay House shone and smelt of fresh herbs. A fire had been lit, candles were in the sconces and the scent of baking wafted through the hall. "I will go and fetch your Aunt."

Richard had forewarned his family as tactfully as possible about Jack's latest choice of a bride. Jeanne and Lizzie were jumping up and down trying to get a view of her before she arrived until they were admonished by Madame Sohier, who Richard noticed was on tip-toe herself. It was like the Red Sea parting as Berta with Sam in her arms strode along beside Jack. Men stopped working, passers-by froze in their tracks.

"Berta, this is my family. Richard you know of course and Jacket." Richard bowed and Jacket stepped forward to kiss his Aunt. "This is Madame Sohier, Richard's former mother-in-law and these are his other children, Jeanne, Lizzie and Antonio. There is another, where is Tom?"

"He is still at school, where Antonio should be but he complained so loudly about bellyache that he's here." Antonio did not look chastised.

"Uncle Jack, is this your little boy?" cooed Lizzie.

"This is Samuel." The girls crowded around.

"Girls, let your Aunt have space," said Madame Sohier, "Come into the house, you must be weary after your journey." Berta stepped into the house and looked around amazed.

"Husband, is this grand place yours?"

"It is nothing, wait until you see Richard's tenement."

"Tomorrow we will have a welcome feast at my home." said Richard, "I hope this house is as you would like it, Berta. The girls and their grandmother have toiled very hard to make it ready."

"It is wonderful. Thank you brother Richard."

"Shall we show you around?" asked Jeanne, her eyes blinking as she got used to the look of Berta.

"We have made a nursery for Samuel."

"Thank you...Jeanne is it? You are very kind."

"Berta is a funny name," said Antonio.

"It is my English name. The man who took me was called Bert." All went quiet.

"Pies?" asked Richard. "A neighbour brought them."

"Berta, this is Tom, you did not get to meet him yesterday." Tom had composed a welcome poem, which he read very solemnly. Berta was richly caparisoned, bedecked with jewels.

"This is Mr Dutton, my daughters' tutor." Mr Dutton stammered and stuttered and apologised. "Everyone else you know. I thought to keep the party small, just family. There will be time enough to meet our wider circle when you are settled," said Richard.

"We have had many visitors already. I am a curiosity I think. Is this my husband's first wife?"

She had alighted upon a small painting of Saskatan in her mix of Indian and English dress.

"Yes, it is not done from life, but I tried to describe her look to the artist."

"He did well, Diccon," said Jack.

"So I am not so strange then, husband?"

"I am the strange one my love," said Jack.

Berta had bought Sam with her. Madame did not approve of toddlers at the table but Berta could not be persuaded to leave him behind in a strange house in a strange land. The girls were already in love with Sam.

"Papa, if you have more children will you have a little black boy like Sam?" asked Lizzie.

"I don't think that is a conversation for the table Elizabeth."

"I am rebuked," she muttered to Jeanne who suppressed a laugh.

"Mr Dutton, my daughters are becoming uncontrollable and have views not fit for young ladies of gentle birth."

Mr Dutton crumpled, "Sir, that is I, their youthful exuberance, I...well...I try, I did not want to dampen but I see I was mistaken, my charges before were boys, that is, I...".

"Papa, take pity on poor Mr Dutton, he does not know you jest, you are scaring him," said Lizzie

"Eat up, Mr Dutton, you are not nearly fat enough yet."

Mr Dutton picked up his spoon. He was not sure he wanted to be fat but neither did he want to displease his benefactor.

"So you have no other relatives, my husband?"

"Our parents are dead, as are our various stepmothers," muttered Jack.

"What about Joannie?" said Jacket.

"Who is Joannie?" asked Berta as Jack scowled at Jacket.

"Some people say she is my daughter."

"Daughter! Did you and Sasky have a child?"

"No," said Jack and helped himself to a savoury pudding.

"Jack was a wayward youth," said Richard to put Berta out of her misery. "He had a child out of wedlock, which he maintained he might not be the father of but he has brought her up after a fashion and now she is married into a fine Southampton family."

"Why was she not invited here?"

"Because she is unpleasant, almost as bad as her pig-headed husband and her butcher-faced father-in-law. She has grown very grand and forgotten she was born in a gutter with a whore for a mother."

"Jack Mudford!" Madame Sohier banged down her spoon, "You are not in an alehouse now."

"My apologies to you all."

"My niece has cut herself off from her family," said Richard. "I am not sure she will welcome you."

Berta shrugged, "I am not sorry for myself but am sad Samuel will not know his sister."

Jack and Richard looked at one another. Joannie would be beside herself with fury. They both started to laugh.

Mr Dutton was proving a great success. Richard was astounded to one day go into the classroom and find not only his daughters, but Tom, Antonio and Madame Sohier also listening enraptured as Mr Dutton declaimed in Latin the exploits of Julius Caesar. He was dressed in an improvised toga for the occasion and had deemed it necessary to stand on a chair. He nearly fell off when he realised Richard was in the room.

"Sir." He bowed low, "I was just, that is I..."

"Trouble yourself not, Mr Dutton, if you can make Antonio pay attention to Latin you are a great teacher."

"Papa, I can pay attention when it is interesting," said Antonio in surprise.

"Mr Dutton is a vast improvement on Mr Davison, Pa," said Tom. "I scarcely learn anything from him now."

Richard made enquiries and found many who had complained about the schoolmaster and the usher. Numerous presentments had been made to the Mayor. After speaking further to Tom, Richard added his weight to the clamour to have the schoolmaster removed. He also involved himself in the approval of the new appointment, a Mr Bathe. He was about thirty years of age, and had a halo of brown curls and hands too big for the rest of his body that he curled in strange shapes around his head as he considered matters of philosophy or mathematics. He was slightly absent-minded, devoted to education and a goodly scholar. He often forgot to eat or ate strange combinations of food, mixing whatever he happened to find first, but he was devoted to his charges and Tom's education accelerated again. In fact, it was not long before Mr Bathe came to see Richard to tell him he felt Tom was more than ready to take the Oxford entrance exam. Richard was overcome with pride.

Chapter Seventy-Six

Joannie was more than furious when she learned of her new stepmother and even worse when she realised she had a half-brother. She forced herself to seek her father out at the Wool House to vent her spleen.

"Why do you do this? Do you hate me so much you think to destroy me?"

"Oh please Joannie, I don't think of you at all so I certainly have no great plan for your destruction."

"Why can't you marry an ordinary person?"

"Ordinary? Like William Biston?"

"My father-in-law has a blackamore servant."

"And I have a white servant."

"How can I raise my head high in society?"

"Leave Biston."

She threw her pomander at her father.

"You asked me to broker your marriage, which I did. I gave you an excellent dowry and you will still inherit a good portion on my death."

"Something which cannot come soon enough!"

"Why don't you meet your little brother? He is a dear fellow and I guarantee you will love him like I do."

"You love him?" She screamed, "I will never forgive you."
Jack sighed when she stormed off.

"You could have been more tactful, Jack," said Richard.

"What do you mean?"

"You have never shown an ounce of affection for Joan."

"Because I feel none. That's the way it is, Diccon. That's the way it is."

Richard made his way to the Angel inn. It was Philip's naming day and Richard had a present for his godson. When he arrived he saw Alice sitting in the inglenook with John. He should have expected it of course, they were both Philip's godparents, but it was still a shock. He took a deep breath and willed his legs to take the last few steps over to join them.

"Richard." John coughed and Richard spent a few seconds patting his back and settling him down again.

"How are you today, John?"

"Ah, I am perfect, perfect, it is good to see you. Come, let us go through. Tamsin has laid out some food."

Richard nodded at Alice and they went into the back room. Tamsin was stood supping a pot of ale watching Luisa as she flew around laying the table whilst holding her youngest brother on her hip. Lawrie and Little John were having a mock battle. John tried to calm the boys with little success. Alice took hold of baby Philip and Luisa got her younger brothers under control.

"Mama! The pastries!" Luisa ran to the bread oven and rescued the fancy tarts just before they burnt, blowing on her fingers as she tried to slide them onto a pewter plate and stop her brothers eating them before they reached the table.

"Drink?" asked Tamsin as she banged down the ale cup. The rest of the visit was as chaotic and Richard took a minute to chuckle Philip under the chin.

"I wonder if he will survive to maturity," muttered Alice.

"His brothers managed to scrabble along," replied Richard.

"I don't know why Tamsin keeps having children, she doesn't really like them." There was a hint of bitterness in her voice.

"That's a bit harsh."

Alice ignored the rebuke.

"Alice, Tom has done remarkably well in his studies." She seemed disinterested. "Next year he is to go to Oxford."

"Oxford!" she exclaimed as if he had told her he was bound for the moon.

"Queen's College. It was useful to have connections there, through our, my, lawyer."

"So you are determined to turn him in a soft-handed gentleman?"

"No, I am determined that he reach his potential. You should be proud, Alice, it is a great achievement."

"Proud my boy will be so far away, mixing with drunkards and lechers? You know what students are."

"I know what all young men are like, but there will be many opportunities to learn and meet like-minded people."

She gave him a piteous look. "And now you are about filling Jeanne and Lizzie's heads with all sorts of nonsense that will be of no use to them in finding husbands."

"What do you mean? They are keen to learn and pointed out the Queen's erudition."

"The Queen is an unmarried virgin."

"Only by choice. There are many who would marry her."

"For the Crown, not for her education. You should not indulge the girls so, if you had their best interests at heart you would teach them how to run a household."

Richard was subdued, "I would value a woman who was well-read and had a love of poetry and learning," muttered Richard. Alice rolled her eyes.

"Spiced wine?" They had not noticed Luisa hovering nearby with a flagon.

"Thank you, Luisa." Richard offered his cup.

"Not for me. You have done well organising this celebration," Alice said pointedly. "You will make a goodly housewife one day."

"Thank you, I hope I may...but I love books too," she said under her breath and then coloured, realising it seemed she had been listening to a private conversation. She scurried off.

"Wipe that smug look off your face. Luisa is growing into a pretty girl, that is all she will need to get a husband," muttered Alice.

"I don't want that for my girls."

"Well I hope you know what you are doing."

"You are an intelligent woman Alice, you run a business."

"That is no different to running a house. I don't sit around with my nose in a book."

Richard changed the subject, "How is Will doing?" They had hardly seen anything of him since he had moved to the Ferry with his mother.

"Marvellously well. He takes the boat out and is a better sailor than many who...who are whole."

"He has a great strength of character, just like his mother." She smiled.

"And how do you do?" he asked.

"I? What are you asking?"

"I was just making conversation."

"I am fine. The tippling house is prosperous. It is well placed for those coming from Portsmouth or the Hamble Valley to rest in while waiting for their crossing."

"And I know your various cousins will make the wait for the ferry longer to help lighten their pockets." Alice gave him a black look. "It was just a joke Alice, I am sure it is the taste of your beer alone that makes them linger. I am glad you prosper."

She looked peeved, calling out to Tamsin to give herself an excuse to leave his side. Soon afterwards she left.

Chapter Seventy-Seven

"Papa?"

"Yes Jeanne."

"May Luisa take lessons with us?"

"Luisa?"

"Yes Papa, I think she wants to learn. She loiters when we go to class and is always borrowing books."

"Loiters?"

"Yes Papa, you know." Jeanne stood in imitation, her head to one side, gazing longingly as she sighed.

"I have no objection if Mr Dutton does not, but another pupil won't mean a higher wage."

"No Papa, I'm sure Mr Dutton will find it acceptable. He likes it here very much and his little room."

"Is he still sleeping in the store house? Has he not found lodgings yet?"

"No Papa, he cannot waste money on lodgings and has to send all his money to his poor mama, who scrimped and saved so that he might have a start in the world."

"Is that so Jeanne?"

"Yes Papa, Mr Dutton loves his mama very much."

"So we must leave him in the store room."

"I think so Papa."

★

Jack was back to his old ways. Richard did not doubt his love for Berta and Sam but it was too much of a struggle for him to stay faithful. Richard was pretty sure he was sleeping with Annie, partly out of guilt and partly because he liked plump, pliant women. He had another mistress, the widow of a merchant, a sluttish woman who had married above her station to a misguided old man. Richard did not know if Berta realised, if she did she kept her council. She did not go outside much as she found the climate too cold and Richard assumed she was happy to stay in and look after Samuel. She would visit with her new nieces and occasionally went to the Prowse's but her circle of friends did not grow any further.

And so he settled back into the rhythm of life of the town. He went from warehouse to warehouse, from ship to shore, to the spinners and weavers. He accompanied Jacket on trips to London, Oxford, Newbury and Winchester doing business. He thought more about colonies. It seemed that the best way to go about these would be through a joint stock company, chartered by the Crown, whereby any land grant became incontrovertible. They had to give incentives to settlers, the chance to own land themselves. In Virginia the land which was open, had slow moving rivers, mild winters and hot summers and lent itself to the plantation system. There was also plenty of opportunity to move westward. Further north the winters were colder, there were forests and the rivers flowed fast, the landscape was made for smaller communities and townships but you could still move westward. Crops would grow.

Richard dined with Ferdinando Gorges one evening. Gorges was also interested in developing plantations and he had connections; by marriage he was linked to the Raleighs. He had been a prisoner of the Spanish as well, he had been taken in Flanders and then was exchanged for a prisoner of equal rank. He had fought with the Earl of Essex so the two men had much in common, except that he was far more enamoured of the Earl than Richard. Gorges offered to broker with the Earl the possibility of them working together on a new colonial expedition.

★

"Papa, can you come? Luisa is not well, she has terrible pains in her stomach."

"Luisa? What are you talking about Lizzie?"

"After we finished our lessons Luisa came over faint. Hurry, Papa, Jeanne is sat with her."

Richard sighed and trailed after Lizzie. Jeanne looked up as Richard came into the room. She had her arm around Luisa, who looked appalled at the sight of Richard.

"What's this, Luisa? Lizzie says you have pains in the stomach. Have you eaten something?"

"It is nothing. Lizzie, you should not have!" Luisa was as pale as parchment and clutched her stomach wincing. "I am sorry to have taken you from your business, I am a little unwell but I assure you it is nothing of concern." She would not look him in the face and seemed worn out.

Richard thought he knew what the problem was.

"Girls, I think Luisa will be recovered in a little while but in the meantime help her to your room, she just needs to rest. Go on, I will be up in an instant."

He went to the kitchen and filled a stone water bottle with hot water. He found a diaper cloth to wrap around it and look some liquorice off the shelf. He cursed all the while. There weren't enough women in this house. He would have to employ some more house servants. He took the stairs two at a time and strode along to the girls' room.

Luisa was curled up on the bed. Richard proffered the water

bottle, "Here hold this against your stomach or your back, wherever the ache is worst. And take some of this." He held out the liquorice, "Alice swore by it."

Luisa looked utterly embarrassed but took the water bottle and the liquorice.

"Try and have a sleep, it will pass in a while. Girls, let Luisa have some peace."

Outside Lizzie and Jeanne looked up him enquiringly, "Will Luisa be well, Papa?"

"Yes Lizzie, she is just...well most women...on occasion... Girls, have Alice or your grandmother spoken to you about... well when girls grow up they change a bit...their shape changes outside...and inside..."

The girls looked blank.

"Never mind, I will ask your grandmother to speak to you."

Richard slammed the ball. Tom slithered and stretched but over-balanced and crashed to the ground. The girls clapped and cheered. Will groaned and denounced Tom's tactics. Richard bent down, gave Tom his hand and hauled him to his feet.

"Good play, Tom!"

"I still lost!" Tom's hair was plastered with sweat and droplets splashed to the ground as he shook his head in despair, "Will I never beat you, Pa?"

"Not for a while." Richard winked as he pulled off his sodden shirt and wiped himself down with it. He tried not to let Tom see that he was almost at the end of his strength. He had already played and beaten Jacket, but he wasn't as fast as he used to be and had to rely more on guile and experience. Tom had a quick brain and good co-ordination, he just needed to get stronger.

"Well played Father, bad luck Tom." Jacket clapped Tom on the back. He was still damp and red from his own exertions.

"Tom, you were an idiot!" yelled Will. "You let Pa trick you into a foolish play. I could have done better than that." Will banged his wooden leg on the floor.

Jeanne, Lizzie and Luisa clattered down the stairway, "You are still king of the court, Papa!"

"Thank you, Lizzie. Run and fetch our fresh shirts, sweetheart." Tom and Jacket pulled off their damp clothes, they were both well-muscled but Tom still had the skinny frame of youth and Richard recalled he had once been the same.

"Has anyone ever beaten you, Papa?" asked Jeanne as she and Luisa passed out oranges to the players and Will grabbed one as well.

"Your Uncle Jack."

"That's because he cheats, Pa," said Tom as he ripped the skin off his orange

"I wish I could still play." Will had been a brutish player, crashing around the court, but he had enjoyed any form of physical activity.

"Perhaps we could try bowls?" offered Richard. Will scowled.

"Boys, dry yourselves off and get dressed before you catch a chill!!" It was Alice, she had Tamsin in tow and they had been to market together. Jeanne handed the boys cloths and Lizzie reappeared with clean linen. Alice shook her head and gave Richard a black look.

"What are you doing here, Luisa?" asked Tamsin, her voice sharp, her lips pinched.

"I was just visiting...I..."

"Prancing around in your best dress, you should be at the inn, there is work to be done."

"Sorry Mama, ... I was just..." Tamsin stood hands on hips, unimpressed.

"You are not a lady who can sit around all day without a care."

"Tamsin, it was just an hour–" said Richard.

"This is nothing to do with you, Richard. You may raise your girls as you please. Luisa, get back to the inn." Richard smiled ruefully as he pulled on his clean shirt.

"Come William, we need to get back to the village." Will sighed and trailed after his mother.

"Rematch, Pa?" asked Tom.

Part Sixteen

1601

Chapter Seventy-Eight

The Earl of Southampton was in town for a fleeting visit on Twelfth Night and requested to see Richard. They met at Bull Hall, the Earl's town residence.

"We met at the playhouse, did we not?"

"Yes, my Lord."

"Not that I remember, but my Lord of Essex reminded me. Anyway enough pleasantries, I have called you here over a matter of business."

Richard waited for him to continue.

"I have heard talk that you are looking for potential investors for a joint stock company and that you mean to petition the Queen about a licence to develop a colony."

"It is an idea nothing more, we think there are opportunities—"

"Indeed, some of my friends share the same thoughts. What I propose is that we petition the Queen. She is very fond of my Lord Essex, although she keeps him short of money. We will then engage you and your ships to transport the colonists. A fair exchange."

"I don't think so... my Lord."

"You are impertinent, sir!"

Richard said nothing. The Earl could not bear the silence.

"What is your price?"

"We would want to be partners, to have more of an interest in the colony and receive a better return by being shareholders."

"You have money?" The Earl licked his lips and Richard knew that for all his title and lands he had no ready cash.

"We have some funds, sir." Richard thought they had more chance of getting a return from the colonists and having land themselves than unpaid bills for voyages, with little chance of extracting money from impoverished nobles.

"I will speak again to my compatriots." The young Earl gave Richard a long look, "You were a sniper were you not, an expert in guns?"

"Hardly my Lord. I made a few lucky shots, I'm a bit out of practice."

"I have to return to London. You like the theatre do you not? You should come with me, the Earl of Essex has commissioned the players at the Globe to make a special performance of *Richard II* and I am a patron of the author."

"I am sorely tempted my Lord but cannot leave my business at present, mayhap I can join you shortly." The young Earl was displeased at the refusal, especially as he thought he was showing much favour.

"I am sure that you might leave aside your business dealings for a short while. It may be there is another service you can do for my Lord of Essex."

"I cannot think there is anything that I can provide for such a noble Lord."

Southampton almost pouted like a girl. "You shall travel with me tomorrow, for now you are dismissed."

Richard could not fathom why the Earl was so keen to take him to London but at the very least it would be an opportunity to talk directly to potential patrons of his enterprise. The Earl was jittery on their journey, which they covered at a great pace. When the Earl did speak to him it was either about money or his military prowess. Richard wondered whether the Earl was on the verge of insolvency and if that was true, how he intended to get monies to back any scheme, let alone colonies. He doubted Essex and their fellows would have any ready cash. Credit and the kudos of their names were likely to be all they brought to the table. Richard knew that the Earl of Essex was in dire financial straits, because his grant for sweet wines that he had bought from the town had not been renewed on orders of the Queen. It was believed this was a way of Elizabeth teaching the Earl a lesson as after he had defied her authority and left Ireland against her command. It was said he had even forced his way into the Queen's private chambers. Many had expected him to be thrown into the Tower and be put on trial and the Earl took to his bed, ill with worry. The Queen's resolve weakened and she had sent him her physician.

When they reached Essex House it was full of his supporters. It was clear that Essex was not happy about Richard's presence. He dragged the Earl of Southampton into a corner and berated him. Richard felt uneasy, there was something else in the air and he was fairly sure he did want to be a part of it. During discussions he was excluded from the inner circle, but he did overhear protestations about Essex's exclusion from the leadership of the country The Earl of Essex was after all deemed to be the most popular man in England.

They went to the Globe to see the history play of *Richard II* and there, Richard's suspicions almost overpowered him. He had known nothing of the play or indeed the long ago king. At first he was mesmerized by the language and the poet's vision of England but as the performance unfolded he realised a political point was being made and that it was no accident that this play had been selected. Could the Earl be considering revolt? Surely not? But Essex had a fever about him. He certainly felt himself badly done by. Richard knew the Earl believed that his rightful place was at head of the Queen's Council but did he want more?

Was he considering deposing the Queen, ruling himself like the over-throwers of Richard II?

Richard felt sick, he could not breathe. He forced himself back through the crowd and slipped away from the theatre before the plays end. What should he do? If he just went home without warning the Queen of his thoughts would he not be culpable? It could be enough to send him to a traitor's death. How could he warn the Queen? What actual proof did he have? A performance of a play? Jack always said his imagination was too riotous.

He found himself making for the Palace of Whitehall. The Queen's standard was flying. Richard felt nauseous. He couldn't just roll up to the Queen's apartment and accuse her favourite of such a heinous crime, but also he could not return to Southampton without sharing his fears. He threw up. He hovered outside the great gallery where Vroom's tapestries of the Armada battles blazed. Finally he reached a decision and sent a note to Mr Secretary Cecil, who he had met briefly all those years ago at Southampton Castle. He paced for nearly two hours before Cecil appeared with some retainers. Richard went pale but Cecil told them to stand off.

"Thank you for seeing me, sir, I know it was presumptuous to ask."

"Yes it was." Cecil raised his eyebrows.

"I...that is I..."

Cecil sighed impatiently.

"I was ordered by my Lord of Southampton to accompany him to London."

Cecil's eyes narrowed just a flicker.

"My Lord has been at Essex House."

Cecil took Richard's arm and guided him away from his servants.

"Why did he bring you? What do you know?"

"I know nothing sir that is the trouble."

"But you are here, you sent for me?"

"I have been at the theatre."

Again came the raised eyebrow, the hint of impatience.

"My Lord Essex, he commissioned a special performance, sir."

"Special?"

"The play was the tragedy of *Richard II*."

Cecil digested this information, "And?"

"That is all, sir."

"All?"

"Sir, I've felt uncomfortable at Essex House since arriving and watching the story it seemed plain to me that something is afoot there. But maybe I am over wrought. I am common man who knows little of lords and princes."

"Oh please stop the false modesty!" Richard gathered his courage.

"My opinion is that my Lord of Essex has been overtaken with some madness. He feels himself unhappy with his lot and his friends do not dissuade him. In fact, they encourage his fantasies."

"Sir John Harrington has told me he is appalled by the state my Lord of Essex's mind." Richard relaxed a little, glad he was not alone in his concerns.

"Can he be reasoned with?" asked Cecil.

"I know not sir. He is like Icarus he believes himself invincible."

"And what do you think, Mr Mudford?"

"I think the Queen is the sun."

"Will you openly accuse Essex? Give witness?"

"Accuse of what? Being a patron of the theatre? Sir, I hope with all my heart I have merely been swept along by the playwright's skill. If I knew anything with certainty I would lay that before Her Majesty. The Earl of Essex has always treated me with great civility and even kindness for one so lofty. I would not denounce him on a feeling."

"But you come here, you sought me out?"

"Because I would not be able to live with myself if I said nothing and Her Majesty suffered because of it. You are a man of politics, sir, you will know what to do, I do not."

"And what will you do now?"

"I just want to go home to my family, sir."

Cecil considered his request for a moment.

"Then do that, Mr. Mudford, I thank you for your service."

Along with everyone else in the town, Richard was shocked to learn that the Earl of Southampton had been a major conspirator with the Earl of Essex in a plot to seize the Queen's person, possibly to assassinate her and give Essex the power he felt should be his. Richard thanked God he had left London before news of the rebellion had broken. He hoped there were none of his papers that could be misconstrued in the Earl's possession. The Mudford Brothers' plans for colonies needed to be shelved for a while. This time there was no exile from Court. No pleading letter, no illness real or feigned that could save Essex. The Queen signed the Earl's death warrant and on Shrove Tuesday, he was executed.

Chapter Seventy-Nine

Tom was stretched out on the stone bench in the courtyard, waving about a clay pipe as he emphasised his point. Jacket, holding Antonio on his lap, sat on the water barrel whilst Mr Dutton leant on the sundial nodding, waiting for an opportunity to riposte.

"Good evening boys." It was a warm summer day, a lazy day made for talking and philosophising. Mr Dutton jumped and tried to stand up straight but caught the arm of his gown on the point of the sundial. Richard moved Tom's feet and sat on the edge of the bench, and breathed in the scent of roses, apothecary's, damask, and of course eglantine. He scowled at Tom who hid his pipe away under the bench.

"Mr Dutton has been telling us about his plans to start a school," said Jacket.

"Dreams. Dreams only, and not my own I confess." Mr Dutton's brow was dewy with perspiration.

"Then whose?" asked Richard.

"Sir Humphrey Gilbert's, Pa," said Tom propping himself up on his elbow.

"The unfortunate explorer." murmured Richard. At the boys' quizzical looks he continued, "When I was young,

589

I remember the great excitement in the town when many merchants backed Sir Humphrey's voyage. He was trying to discover the fabled land of Norumbega."

"Fabled? Does it not exist them?" asked Jacket.

"Maybe it is just well hidden. Men have searched for years and some like Sir Humphrey died in the attempt."

"Was he not a good sailor, Papa?" asked Antonio.

"Not the best, he was a man of the Court rather than the sea. When the Queen was a princess in a parlous situation, he was in her household. She favoured him thereafter, she values loyalty. But, Mr Dutton, what has Sir Humphrey to do with schools?"

"He had plans for a school, sir, an alternative to the old universities, designed for practical men of action."

"It sounds fun, Pa, I wish it existed," Tom sighed.

"Sir Humphrey wanted to train a new breed of men, sir, to lead Her Majesty's new empire. His curriculum included mathematics, both theoretical and practical, ballistics, navigation, naval architecture, enough law to enable men to serve as Justices, modern as well as ancient languages, equitation, swordplay, dancing and music." Mr Dutton became eloquent when enthusiastic about his subject.

"It does sound fun Tom," Richard agreed.

"You are a man such as Sir Humphrey wished to design, Pa," said Jacket. Richard looked at him questioningly.

"Jacket is right, Pa, you have figures and know of guns. You know your way around a ship and have a grasp of Latin but can speak Spanish and French. You dance and sing, though granted your horsemanship needs work."

Richard smiled and gave Tom a gentle cuff, "My learning has been in the hard school of experience, and the more I read, the more I realise how little I know. I envy you all your education. I wish you well in your dreams, Mr Dutton, they are grand ones to have."

Richard lived quietly these days. He found enjoyment in musical evenings with his children. Antonio now managed to pluck something that sounded like a tune from Richard's guitar, it had taken weeks of practice to get him that far. One such night he had played and Tom had sung, doing his best to accommodate Antonio's erratic melody.

"That was a fine song Tom. Will you not sing one of your own composing?" said Luisa.

She had started to spend more time with Jeanne and Lizzie of late. Madame Sohier said she thought the poor girl was trying to improve her manners and education. Madame Sohier did not approve of Tamsin and what she felt was the slovenly way she ran her home and neglected her children. Luisa was fortunate to have a natural grace and temperament and Richard wondered if that had been inherited from the man who had fathered her. After blushing and much protestation, Tom had sung a handsome ditty that he had been working on. Lizzie was next on the virginals, she played with such verve and gusto that she was easily forgiven for the randomness of some of her notes but Jeanne had Tom's gift for music and played like an angel. Mr Dutton was of the party and turned the music encouraging Jeanne on in her efforts.

"Well done, Jeanne that was truly wonderful."

"Really, Papa?" Jeanne never could quite believe a complement was hers only, she hid in her sister's bright shadow.

"Really, come and sit here and let me give you a hug for being so clever." Jeanne ran to Richard's side both glowing with pleasure and nervous at receiving such praise. Madame Sohier caught Richard's eye and nodded.

"Where did you get such skill, such lightness of touch? You could perform at Court."

"Oh Papa, you just say that because I am your daughter."

"Nonsense, I say that because I am proud to have such a talented daughter."

"Did my mother play music, Papa?"

Richard's heart skipped a beat for a moment, "Sadly Jeanne I never heard your mama play..."

"Your mama loved to listen to the music in church," said Madame Sohier.

"What was she like, Papa? Am I like her?"

Richard wondered where this had come from, he had not thought of Jeannot for years. He considered for a while and was aware of all eyes being upon him, he drew in a breath, "Your mother was a very pious woman, she loved God very much, she was tall like your grandmother and indeed she had your colouring Jeanne, the same lovely red hair. She was quiet, even you might say shy."

"Am I like her in anyway, Papa?" asked Lizzie.

Richard gulped, "Sorry, Lizzie, you got a poor bargain, you are entirely your papa's child."

Lizzie laughed and Richard gave Jeanne a squeeze. He was saved from saying anything further by the arrival of the Mayor John Major at the same time as Jack and his family, who had come to supper.

The Mayor asked to see Richard in private and Richard directed him into a side chamber along with Jack, who had no understanding of the word private.

"This is a very difficult subject Mr Mudford." Richard said nothing, the Mayor was uneasy and perspiring.

"We have received a missive from Her Majesty touching on the recent troubles."

Richard glanced at Jack, the Mayor could only have meant one thing the abortive rebellion of the Earl of Essex.

"As you are no doubt aware my Lord of, that is our Lord, that is the Earl of Southampton has been arrested and is being held in the Tower for his support to the traitor Essex. May I?" The Mayor gestured to the wine on the sideboard.

"Of course, Mr Mayor, forgive my lack of manners. Your

visit caught me by surprise and in fact, I am still in that state."
Richard poured wine into three glasses.

"The Earl's misfortune reflects badly on the town, and we
have troubles enough of our own. We don't know if we'll get
paid the fee farm for the sweet wines that we are owed from the
late Earl of Essex."

"You mean he did not settle his account before he went to
the block?" asked Jack. The Mayor squinted not sure if Jack was
making fun of him.

"As I say, we have received this missive and to cut straight
to the point, we have been directed by Her Majesty to make an
inventory of all the goods in the Earl of Southampton's townhouse, Bull Hall. Her Majesty has particularly asked you to
undertake the inventory."

"Me?!"

"Yes, see it is writ here." Richard took the letter bearing
the Royal Seal that the Mayor thrust at him. It was true. Her
Majesty asked her devoted servant Richard Mudford to take
on the task of listing all the items that had recently come to
the Crown on the forfeiture of the Earl of Southampton's
lands and properties. Whether the young Earl would follow in
Essex's footsteps to the block was still in the balance. There was
nothing Richard could do but accept the request and he agreed
to start the task tomorrow. Jack volunteered to help purely out
of morbid interest in the contents of the Earl's house.

It took them several days to go through all the rooms in the
large tenement house at the bottom of Bull Street. Bull Hall
took its name from the Earl's device of a Bull which could be
found embroidered, embossed and carved around the house.
Richard was most interested in the books. The nobleman was a
lover of the arts and a great patron.

"Do you have to open every book, Diccon? Can't you just
measure them by the yard?"

"I wish I had a library like this."

"You have plenty of books. I don't know how you find the time to read them all."

"Jack, put that back." His brother had secreted a bauble in his pocket.

"Don't we get to keep anything for our trouble?"

"No." A piece of paper fluttered out of one of the books. Richard picked it up and studied it.

"What's that?"

"A sonnet."

"What?" asked Jack.

"A sonnet, a poem. It doesn't look like it is the Earl's work. It's not in his hand writing."

"What are you doing now?"

"I'm copying the lines, they are beautiful."

"Why don't you just keep the original? No one would know!"

"I would know. The Queen has entrusted this work to us Jack, we should go about our task honourably. Look, I am finished, it's done." Richard blew on the ink and then replaced the original back inside the book from which it fell.

"This isn't even his main residence," said Jack, who was being less than helpful.

"Well let's just be thankful we don't have to do the others. We've got to deliver the inventory ourselves, straight to the Queen."

"Really? You don't think we will be arrested or anything, do you?"

"I should hope not, we weren't involved in the plot."

"But we had business dealings – and our proposed partnership to develop colonies–"

"–there isn't anything treasonable in that, quite the contrary."

"Ah but we don't know if the Earl was really planning on setting up a kingdom for himself in the Americas."

"Let's secure the property and tomorrow we travel to London."

They made good progress despite the uneven weather and presented themselves at Court. Richard was even more overawed then when the court had visited Southampton and he had been presented to Her Majesty for the first time. He half expected to just meet with a secretary, so was amazed to be taken before the Queen herself, in her presence chamber. She looked old and tired. Many said she still mourned for Essex but perhaps it was just the strain of reigning for over forty years. Her skin was papery, her eyes more sunken and the slender fingers of which she had been so proud were mottled with age spots and swollen at the joints. She had lost some of her teeth and when she spoke it was difficult to understand her.

"Richard Mudford and the disreputable Captain Jack." The brothers bowed very low.

"I thank you for doing this small service for me."

"It was a pleasure to be of assistance to Your Majesty."

Elizabeth did not even glance at the inventory, just passing it onto a courtier.

"I do have an ulterior motive for enticing you here of course." Richard's stomach fluttered and he was sure he had gone very pale.

"Majesty?"

"Don't look so worried, I wanted to thank you."

Richard thought to speak but his mouth was too dry and he thought he must look like an imbecile.

"Over the years you have served me well, the Armada, Counter Armada, the attack on Cadiz and you have always shared your bounty with your Queen."

"As is only right and proper, Majesty."

"You would think so, wouldn't you?" She knows how much we kept back, he thought.

"I had intended to reward you properly after Cadiz but you

ran away to the Americas, yet I made a promise to someone that I would recognise your loyal service. Kneel."

Richard saw a cushion at the Queen's feet. He felt a bit awkward but kneeled as commanded, trying to think what could be coming next. He fixed his eyes on the hem of the Queen's gown embroidered in white and silver. He almost jumped out of his skin when he felt the touch of steel on his shoulder and barely stopped himself from lunging at the Queen in an attempt to disarm her.

"Arise, Sir Richard Mudford." Richard didn't rise, he was stuck to the spot. He thought he must have drifted off to sleep and dreamt the Queen had just knighted him.

"You can get up now," the great Elizabeth, his guide, his lodestone, said to him. He scrambled to his feet.

"Majesty forgive me, I am utterly overcome, I do not deserve…that Your Majesty should notice me is enough, thank you." Richard could feel tears pricking his eyes. His mother would have been so proud. There was a ripple of polite applause.

"Majesty, if I might?" interjected Jack. "Please accept this small token, we did not wish to come into your presence empty-handed." He gave the Queen a small, exquisitely tooled Spanish paring knife.

"Captain Jack, if you weren't quite so notorious we would perhaps have knighted you too but we are trying to make friends abroad at present."

"Majesty, I would have to become respectable, which is beyond me for now, but when I am as old as my brother I will turn over a new leaf and perhaps become a pirate catcher for Your Majesty."

"Then your knighthood would be secured also."

They were outside, Richard clutching the official papers which confirmed he really was Sir Richard Mudford. "I am sorry Jack, you are entitled as much as me. You are the one who sailed around the world."

"But it was just for my own amusement. I am pleased for you Richard and there is plenty of mileage for me in being the brother of a knight. Who would have thought it? We're just two boys from the Shambles. We are going to celebrate."

"A trip to the theatre, supper?"

"I was thinking more of a couple of whores and plenty of wine."

"Perhaps we can do both."

"Whatever you command, Sir Richard."

Chapter Eighty

Richard sucked on his pen, he had the blank parchment in front of him and the scrawled note he had made at Bull Hall. It was the anniversary of his wedding day to Alice. Usually on that day he would shut himself away, or take himself off somewhere to be alone with his thoughts and memories. He drew in a long breath and with a slightly unsteady hand began to copy the words of the sonnet he had found between the leaves of the Earl of Southampton's book.

O! never say that I was false of heart,
Though absence seem'd my flame to qualify.
As easy might I from myself depart
As from my soul, which in thy breast doth lie:
That is my home of love: if I have ranged,
Like him that travels. I return again,
Just to the time, not with the time exchanged,
So that myself bring water for my stain.
Never believe, though in my nature reign'd
All frailties that besiege all kinds of blood,
That it could so preposterously be stain'd,
To leave for nothing all the sum of good;

For nothing this wide universe I call,
Save thou, my rose; in it thou art my all.

He sealed the document and marked it for Alice's eyes. He could not bear to write Parker on the note and dared not put Mudford, so settled instead for Dypere. He was a fool he knew but still he entrusted it to a reliable servant and made sure they understood they were to wait till they found Alice alone and then give her the note.

He could hear music, squeals and laughter. He went to the gallery and found dancing in progress. Mr Dutton was playing the virginals and a young man Richard did not recognise was leading out Lizzie, calling steps and directing Tom who partnered Jeanne. Luisa was dancing alone. Mr Dutton looked up, saw Richard and stopped in mid-phrase. The other, berated him. "Don't stop Nicholas! We almost had it that time."

Mr Dutton cleared his throat and scrambled to his feet. The dancers turned and saw Richard. After a moment's awkwardness, the other young man made a deep bow.

"Sir Richard! I, that is we, this is my friend Mr Davenant, he was visiting nearby and thought to–"

"Papa, Mr Davenant is teaching us the latest dance! All the ladies at the court dance in this way."

"Is that so Lizzie?" Richard circled around the young people as they nervously awaited his response.

"A pavan, Mr Davenant?" Richard arrived next to Luisa made a deep bow and took her hand. "Play on Mr Dutton, play on." Lizzie shrieked in a most unladylike way and the music began again. They were agog at Richard's prowess. They knew he liked to dance, they had played at snake dances and the like when they were younger, but he outshone them all. As the music died away he made a bow to his partner and strolled from the room. When he was out of sight he heard an eruption behind him and smiled to himself, it was fun showing up his children.

★

He was in the Pigeon House. It was the end of the day, and he was alone. He poured himself a glass of sac and sat down to enjoy it in the quiet. He heard a step on the stairs and Alice's head appeared.

"Good evening. Would you like a glass of wine?"

She nodded as she came in and sat next to him. She sipped the wine and gazed out of the little window that overlooked the West Quay. She reached into her pocket and took out the poem and handed it back to him.

"You should not have sent this."

"I know."

"Then why?"

"Because it sums up how I feel in words I could never find. I just wanted you to know."

Tears began to trickle down her face.

"How did we come to this?"

"I don't know. I thought we were meant to be together forever."

"So did I."

"Will you come back to me?" She did not reply. Richard found a little corner of hope in that silence. She wiped her face with her hands.

"Tamsin said you were called to London on business for the Queen. That must have pleased you."

"It was an honour. I was asked to inventory the Earl of Southampton's house."

"Is he to be executed?"

"I don't know, he is still in the Tower but it is said the Queen has lost the taste for blood after Essex."

"You are doing well for yourself, Richard."

"Even more than you know."

"What do you mean?"

"The Queen has made me a knight."

Alice stared at him as if she could not make sense of the words, "A knight?"

"Yes. You see before you Sir Richard Mudford."

She made a funny little noise, not quite a laugh, and her hand went to her mouth as if to catch it.

"I cannot believe it."

"Neither can I, though I would forswear the title for you, Alice."

"I would not let you. It was a beautiful poem."

"I confess it was not my work. But it was how I felt, how I feel."

She got up to leave and he stood also. She did not move and he took hold of her hands.

"At least tell me you have forgiven me my mistake."

"I do. At last I do. We had some happy times. We made Tom."

He held her close and she rested her head on his shoulder.

"If only we could have stayed at the Angel inn. That was the best time," she said.

"It was."

"I said some terrible things about Antonio."

"You were hurt, you were suffering."

"I did not really wish him dead."

"I know."

"You must not write to me again. I cannot bear it."

"I know."

He raised her chin. She pressed her lips to his and they kissed with passion. She let his hands fondle her body.

"We cannot do this," she said at last.

"Just once more."

"It is wrong, it's sinful."

"I could fetch a priest to argue it is not."

Part Seventeen

1602

Chapter Eighty-One

Richard sat down by the fire at the Angel opposite John. His friend scarcely stirred much these days, his body was racked with arthritis and he was still skin and bone. In youth he had been lithe and wiry, whereas years of starvation had now made him skeletal and despite now having plenty available to eat he nibbled like a mouse. He had taken also to smoking tobacco, which was supposed to be a remedy for congestion but seemed to have only given John a hacking cough.

"You should give up the tobacco, John, I don't think it is good for you."

"It calms me and I have a craving for it. Let me have my small pleasure."

"How do you keep?"

"Well enough. I can't help as much in the inn as I would like. It's not the fine place it was in your day." That was true enough, it looked shabby and careworn.

"I could get a painter to come in?" offered Richard.

"No don't bother, it will do well enough, it only needs my girl to brighten the place up." He nodded to where Luisa was polishing the bar and chatting to the regular customers.

Richard stared, "Is that Bart Biston back again?"

605

"Bad pennies and all that. He has made up with his father again, I gather when he left Annie he took all her money and somehow managed to invest it well. God knows how, he never had a head for business. He has bought his way back into Biston's good books."

"What happened to Annie's sister, the one he ran off with?" asked Richard.

"No one knows. Abandoned somewhere, I imagine."

Bart was whispering in Luisa's ear and she coloured bright red, he made a lunge for her but she avoided him and dashed back to the kitchen bumping into her mother on the way.

"She's so pretty my girl, I'm concerned for her with lechers like Bart about. I did hear some talk that he made his money as a bawd up in Southwark, pimping out Dowsabelle and other silly girls who'd fallen for his charms" John began to cough violently.

"Richard."

"Tamsin."

"We haven't seen much of you here lately."

"Business, Tamsin, it takes a lot of my time."

"When will Jack be back? I want to see Lawrie."

"A good few weeks yet, Tamsin, the boy is doing well for himself."

"Too much adventuring."

"How is Little John, has he got the makings of a brewer?"

"He seems to like it well enough."

"And my godson?"

"I don't know where Philip is. He roams the street like a feral animal."

"Tamsin, you are too unkind, he is just being a boy," said John. Luisa returned to the bar and came and sat with her father. "How's my girl today?"

"Well, Pa. I just brought this book back, I borrowed it from the library." She looked shyly at Richard too nervous to say his name. He took the book from her.

"Herodotus. I didn't know you liked history, Luisa."

"I like it very much, I like all books, you have a fine library."

"You know you can borrow whatever you want. Perhaps you can try and get Antonio interested?"

Luisa kissed John and went back to her duties.

"I know I should not have favourites," said John, "but I love my girl the best, I do."

"You spoil her," said Tamsin, "telling her how pretty she is, turning her head."

"You spoil her too," said John.

"I worry about her," countered Tamsin.

"How so?" said Richard.

"Because she is a pretty girl and an innocent one, too often in the way of men like Bart Biston."

"She would never have her head turned by the likes of him," exclaimed John. Tamsin said nothing but pursed her lips.

"I should go" said Richard.

"Don't leave it so long," said John. Richard walked outside to the sunlight and paused a while blinking in the brightness of the day.

"Richard!" called Tamsin, who had followed him out. "I would like to talk to you, but not here, let's walk to the square." Richard was surprised. Tamsin never sought out his company. They strolled to St Michael's Square and sat on a seat near the fish market.

"God this place stinks, they ought to move the market elsewhere," muttered Richard.

"Have to keep your fine glass windows shut?" said Tamsin with a smile.

"What do you want?"

"Have you thought of marrying again?"

Richard was taken aback, "No, not that it is any business of yours."

"Why not?" she asked undaunted.

"I don't know there is any particular reason. I have been married twice, or once depending on which cleric you talk to, and I have no reason to think well of marriage."

"You are rich and successful, you should marry again."

"You sound like my mother."

"I think you should marry Luisa." Tamsin spoke very quickly and started to brush down her apron as if she had just remarked upon the weather.

"I'm sorry, I think you just said I should marry your sixteen year old daughter."

"She will be seventeen soon and getting past marriageable age."

"Perfect. I won't see forty again."

"You could pass for thirty."

Richard shook his head in disbelief, "I am not having this conversation with you."

"Think about it, it would solve all our problems."

"I don't have any problems."

"Luisa is pretty, she has a good temperament, she deports herself well, and thanks to you she has a fair education."

"Enough, Tamsin, I am not marrying your daughter, it's a mad idea. I bounced her on my knee when she was a baby for Christ's sake."

"She needs to be married. I have seen how the men who come into the inn look at her, lust after her. I fear for her, I worry she will be taken advantage of."

"I can see you might like to see her wed and I am happy to find a husband for her, provide her with a dowry."

"What decent man would take her? Too many people know me, what I have done."

"Money solves many things, Tamsin."

"But I want her to be happy, not to be bought and sold like a heifer."

"What on God's good earth makes you think she would be happy married to me?"

"You have a grand house, you have a title. No one would look down on her if she were Lady Mudford and she would be provided for."

"I am too old for her."

"It is the way of things."

"What are you talking about?"

"A young man marries first for money to give himself a start in life, often a rich widow. Jeannot was not young when you married her. Then when his wife dies he marries a young girl to keep him warm in his old age. When you die, Luisa will still be a young woman, but she will be a wealthy young woman, and with a title she will have her pick of young men."

"That is marvellous, everyone ends up happy. Except I will never marry Luisa, even if she was the only single woman left in the town, all the whores had been transported to the Americas and I was desperate for a fuck."

"You are a foul-mouthed shitface."

"And you speak like a Duchess." Tamsin stormed away. Richard found he was in need of a drink but went to the Crown in search of peace and quiet.

Tamsin would not let it rest, she haunted his footsteps and she put herself in his way. He could not go to his favourite places. If Richard saw her coming he would dodge up alleys or dive into shops, anything to avoid her. He was walking one day with Madame Sohier and saw Tamsin in the distance. He dragged a shocked Madame into the Dolphin.

"Richard, what are you doing? You nearly knocked me over."

"I'm sorry, sit here, I will get us something to drink."

"I don't want anything to drink, and why are you staring out of the window?"

"I'm trying to avoid Tamsin."

"I am not over enamoured of her company but this is somewhat extreme."

Richard sat down and signalled to the server to bring some refreshment anyway.

"She keeps pestering me."

"How so?"

Richard fidgeted and felt embarrassed, "She has got it into her head that I should marry her daughter."

"Luisa?"

"That's the only daughter she has. Sorry, I did not mean to be rude, but it's such a ridiculous suggestion."

"And why's that?"

Richard stared at his former mother-in-law, "Well isn't it obvious?"

"I have a fondness and admiration for Luisa. She has risen above her background, which I grant you has little to recommend it. She has educated herself, has refined manners, which I take some responsibility for, she is kind and loving. Of course, if you are in the market for a marriage partner I am sure that there are several women who would be excellent candidates, and could bring with them power, influence, connections and money."

"I don't want to have power or be close to it, it's a dangerous position, I have connections enough and if I need more I will marry my children off. As for money, I have plenty, and apart from all this I have no desire to marry again. It is not something that I have done very well."

"There is truth in that, but if you are not looking for a marriage that will give you advantage, then you had just as well marry someone like Luisa."

"I don't want to marry Luisa or someone like her. I have no need of marriage."

"Alice will never come back, and I don't know why you would want her to. She is a judgemental woman."

"Don't speak like that, I wronged her."

"You did what men always do."

"Did your husband sleep with another woman, father a child?"

"Yes."

Richard knocked over his glass and spent some time while mopping up the debris.

"But he was such a god-fearing man."

"What has that to do with anything? Our parents arranged the marriage when he was in love with someone else. I spent so much of my time pregnant and sickly, he was young and lusty. Do not mistake me, it made me unhappy at first, but when I knew he would never leave me I got used to it."

"What happened?"

"We left and came here. I don't know if he tried to keep in contact, I never asked."

Richard embraced the old woman and kissed her cheek.

"Enough, enough it was long ago. When you were in Spain the choices you made had huge consequences, but I admired you for acknowledging Antonio."

"I felt the disgrace but what could I do? It was not his fault. Alice never understood that it changed nothing about what I felt for her. Perhaps if we had had more children of our own it would not have mattered so much."

"You have punished yourself enough. You do not have to live alone now."

"I am not alone, I have my children and I have you."

She patted his hand.

Richard decided he needed to go and talk to John, the situation was becoming too embarrassing and he did not want to lose his friendship. John as usual was sat by the fireside, he never could get quite warm enough these days.

"I told you not to be a stranger, Diccon."

"Sorry, John, I have been wrestling with a problem. Can I talk to you?"

"Of course, sit down – Luisa, please bring Diccon a mug of ale."

Richard felt himself colour as the girl brought the frothing cup and smiled shyly at him. He wondered how much she knew of her mother's plans and prayed she was unaware. As she bent forward to put the cup on the table Richard's eyes went involuntarily to her chest and he blushed even more. Thankfully John did not seem to notice but Richard was fairly sure Luisa did as her cheeks too flushed pink.

"So what is this great problem that has vexed you these last weeks?"

"Has, er that is, has Tamsin spoken to you about, well, about her plans?"

"We don't have plans, Diccon, just every day as it comes."

"Oh Tamsin has plans John!" Richard took a long draft. "Look, I don't know how to say this so I will just blurt it right out." But he didn't, he took another draft, looked at the fire, and twiddled a loose button on his doublet.

"Diccon, what is it? We have been friends most of our lives, we shared many deep secrets in our prison."

"Tamsin has this ridiculous notion that I should marry Luisa." The words tumbled out of his mouth. "There I have said it and I promise you John, I have had no hand in this matter, none." Richard drained his glass.

"Is my girl not well favoured?"

Richard did not answer for a while, "She is very pretty John, very well favoured and any man would be pleased to wed her."

"But not you?"

"No of course not, we both know that would be inappropriate, if not actually immoral, in the eyes of the church."

"Didn't think morals or the church meant that much to you Diccon?"

"That is unfair, John, I have made my peace with God for my actions. I trust Him to be more forgiving than some of my countrymen."

"Sorry, Diccon. In the great scheme of things I think you made the better choice."

"Then why attack me now?"

"Why do you hide behind pretending you cannot remarry when everyone else has accepted the invalidity of your union with Alice? You are a lucky man to have been able to 'divorce'. There are so many that are forced to stay in bad marriages or suffer torment in the afterlife by committing bigamy."

"I am not here to discuss the legalities or otherwise of my previous marriage. I just wanted you to have a word with Tamsin and ask her to stop pressing this, this other matter."

"My daughter is just a matter?"

"No, you are twisting my words. I thought you would be as horrified as me at the suggestion."

It was John's turn to look into the fire, to take a long drink.

"I will die soon, Diccon, I wonder how I make it through each day. What is to become of my girl, Diccon?"

"Tamsin will look after her, I will look after her, John, I have always looked out for your family. I hope you know that."

"I think the world of Tamsin, but she is not really cut out to be a mother. She does her best but she knows her reputation does nothing to protect our girl. Once I am gone Luisa will be preyed on, she is too beautiful for it to be otherwise."

"If anything happens to you I will take Luisa into my care and protection. I'll find her a good husband who will care for her and look after her."

"Will he have a title and be a gentleman? She is like a cuckoo in our nest, she should have been well born. She has the manners and gentleness of a fine lady."

"I may have a title and that might mean I can call myself gentleman, but you are more deserving of that title than I and there are many fine-born ladies who have neither grace nor manners."

"Just tell me Diccon, is she not good enough for you?"

"Luisa is more than good but I never thought to remarry John, that is the length and breadth of it and to me she is still a child. There are too many years between us."

"I see. Well if that is how it is, I will speak to Tamsin."

"Thank you John."

Chapter Eighty-Two

Tamsin made her displeasure felt in as many ways as possible and although Richard still visited the Angel to sit with John and talk of times gone by he felt awkward. It seemed to him, although he had not paid much attention to Luisa over the years, that she also was more withdrawn in his presence and he worried that she may indeed have had some knowledge of what her mother was about and felt spurned or appalled. One day he came to the inn and John was not in his place. A fear encircled him. He could not see Tamsin either but Luisa was in the bar so Richard forced himself to speak to her.

"Luisa, your Pa is not at his post. Is all well?"

She cast her eyes down and would not look directly at him.

"He is not so well today and could not leave his bed."

"Does he need a doctor? The apothecary? Is there anything I can do?"

"Mama is with him. He is just tired to death."

She carried on about her tasks.

"She has filled out," It was Bart.

"What?" said Richard.

"She has curves that weren't there when I went away." Bart cupped his hands over his chest to illustrate his observation.

"Why are you back, Bart?"

"I wanted a reconciliation with my family."

"I hope Annie is well." said Richard as he went and sat at his normal place. He was dismayed when Bart followed him obviously looking for company.

"I meant to patch things up with my father. I can see no good of seeing Annie again."

"Other than she is your wife and the mother of your son."

"I wanted to ask you about that. How did you manage to dissolve your marriage to Alice?" the coldness in Richard's eyes made Bart change tack.

"Now Luisa, she always had a soft spot for me."

"Really? I thought that was Dowsabelle."

"Dowsabelle? I haven't thought about her for a while, she was fun though."

"What happened to her?" Bart shrugged.

"I heard you had turned to bawdry and made of her a queen."

Bart thrust out his lower lip, "I don't know who would say such a thing! If Dowsabelle went bad, it was her own doing not mine."

Richard was getting tired of Bart and wished he would go away.

"Luisa, she could make a fortune on her back."

"What did you say?"

"If Luisa took to whoring she would make a fortune, though some say she has already offered her favours around the boys of the town. She still plays the innocent. Maybe she needs a man to see to her."

Richard grabbed hold of Bart's shirt front and dragged him across the table. "You go anywhere near her and I will cut off your balls myself."

"Sorry, didn't know you wanted first dibs." Richard raised his fist to smash Bart's nose, he cowered away and Richard decided he wasn't worth the bruised knuckles. He threw him back in his seat and went to leave. Tamsin was stood behind the bar looking at him, he knew she had heard every word.

She came to see him at the warehouse as he knew that she would. He was just unpacking some books recently sent by his London bookseller, Isidore's *Etymologiae* and Breydenbach's *Pilgrimage*, plus a copy of Ptolemy's *Geographia* which he had been trying to find for some time.

"Don't start this again, Tamsin, the answer is still no."

"But you saw, you heard."

"It was just Bart, he would say the same about any woman."

"It wasn't any woman it was Luisa. And look, look at this!" She thrust a rough drawing into his hand, "This was nailed on the door of the inn." It was a crude drawing of a mermaid, the commonly understood symbol of prostitution.

"What do you want me to say?"

"That you will give Luisa what is her due."

"You make it sound as if I owe her something."

"And don't you?" Tamsin stared at him.

"I do not understand your meaning."

"Alice told me that when you came back from Spain the first time you had a jewelled earring, you were given it by Luis."

"And?"

"Why would he give you a jewel?"

"He owed me a favour."

"Did you tell him?"

"Tell him what?" he knew what was coming.

"That he had a daughter?" Richard didn't answer.

"I will take that as a yes. Did he intend that jewel for her?"

"He did give it to me, but asked me a favour that I should look after Luisa. And I did that, in fact I did more than that, I looked after you, Lawrence and Little John, and now John and Philip also."

"You should have given the jewel to me to use for Luisa

617

alone! We could have moved from here, had a good home, she could have had fine dresses and maids. Not have to wait on men like Bart."

"Tamsin, the reality is you would have probably been arrested for possessing a jewel considered too rich at item to be owned by a common-born woman. You have no business head, you would soon have been back on the street but this time with Luisa as well. The Angel is a fine house and a fine business for your family. It is yours and worth far more than an earring."

"You always twist things to suit your own ends."

"Then why, by God and his saints, do you want your daughter to have anything to do with me?"

"Because you were born under a lucky star Richard Mudford, you and yours will always do well.

Do you not love your girls, Richard?"

"Of course I do, they mean the world to me."

"And you would do anything to protect them?"

"Without a doubt."

"Then I ask you to think again."

"And why would I want to do that?"

"I know your secrets, Richard, and not just about the poison, Jeannot's murderous intentions or her unnatural friendship with Elizabeth. I know you slept with both mistress and maid. Did Elizabeth cut her throat because you had forced her, because she was overcome with guilt at carrying your bastard or did you cut her throat to keep her quiet?"

Richard's blood had run cold. John must have told her what he had seen.

"Say one more word and I will strike you down where you stand."

"No you won't. You just have to understand that I would do anything, anything to protect my daughter. I know you will do the same for yours."

Luisa was in her Sunday best, they had all just come from Church and she was lingering in the square talking to her friends.

"Luisa." She looked at him in answer before dropping her eyes to the ground, "Walk with me a while." She fell into step beside him. "Your parents desire that we marry Luisa. What is your wish?"

"I am content with my parents' choice," she said quietly, still not looking at him.

"But what of your choice? If you do not want this it does not have to happen. I am happy to provide you with a dower that would attract many suitors."

"I am content with my parents' choice."

"Well then, it seems we are to marry." He strode off and left her standing alone in the middle of the square.

He had to tell his children he was getting married. How was he to do that? He hardly said a word through supper. Tom was away at university but Jacket, Jeanne, Lizzie and Antonio were all around the table along with Madame Sohier.

"Children, I have something important to tell you." Four pairs of eyes were upon him. Madame Sohier also looked intrigued but tried to hide it.

"I have decided that it is time I remarried."

There was a moment's silence, broken only by Antonio cracking a walnut.

"I am pleased, Father," said Jacket. "It is good for a man to be married."

"Who is it to be, Papa?" asked Jeanne.

"Is it the Widow Harrison? She always simpers when you are around her shop," suggested Lizzie.

"Simpers? What nonsense is that? No, it is not her." The Widow was ten years older than Richard.

"Do we know her, Papa?" asked Jeanne.

"Is it Jane Bryant? I have heard she is expecting to marry soon."

"No, it is not Jane Bryant!" Jane Bryant was extremely plump and had an unattractive mole on her chin.

"I think Father can do better than Jane Bryant," said Jacket. "Ah, I have it, that silk merchant's daughter we met in London last winter. She was very taken with you, Pa, asked me all sorts of questions about your situation."

"You didn't tell me that. But it isn't her either. I am to marry Luisa Dypere."

This time the silence was stunned, there were three mouths wide open. Only Antonio took the news more nonchalantly.

"She is very pretty, Pa."

"Thank you, Antonio."

"Aren't you too old to be getting married?"

"Thank you again, Antonio."

"Papa isn't so very old, Antonio," said Jeanne.

"And now I think of it, Luisa has always been taken with Papa," said Lizzie with distaste.

"Yes, she has always been most interested in Papa and solicitous of him," said Jeanne.

"And always turning our conversation around to him!" said Lizzie.

"Is Luisa happy, Father?" asked Jacket with concern in his voice.

"It is her choice. I am not forcing her, John and Tamsin have promoted this match. It won't change things between us all, there will just be someone else living here."

"What about Tom?" asked Jeanne.

"I will write to Tom and tell him also." Jeanne looked at Lizzie who nodded at her.

"Papa, Tom likes Luisa, he has written poems and has hopes."

Part Eighteen

1603

Chapter Eighty-Three

Everyone else had left for the church, Richard lingered in the house, not sure what he was doing. He didn't want to get married again, to many in the eyes of God he was still married to Alice. Would Tamsin have really brought up the past and hurt Lizzie and Jeanne? He roamed from room to room, perhaps he should just go to the stables get a horse and ride away. He heard the door click and wondered if a servant had returned or someone had come to find him. With no enthusiasm he walked back to the hall. A woman stood there, it took his a few moments to realise who it was.

"Alice?" She looked up at him.

"Hello Richard."

"What are you doing here?"

"I felt the need to see you."

"Well here I am." He was stood very close to her now. He studied her face, the wide forehead, slightly long nose and strong mouth were still the same, just a few more lines. Maybe the skin around her chin was not so firm or perhaps it was just a trick of the light. As a married woman her breasts were covered over but he could tell they were as big and pendulous as he remembered.

"What are you thinking?"

"I was remembering what your breasts looked like."

"Don't be coarse."

Richard shrugged, he was so far removed from wanting to be pleasant.

"What are you after, Alice? I am leaving for the church soon."

"So you intend to go through with this mockery?"

"Mockery?"

"Marrying a child, it's disgusting."

"She is seventeen and old for her years, I am told I am still a fine figure of manhood."

"You always could delude yourself."

"And how many years older than George Parker are you?"

She looked at him malevolently. "I just think you are making a mistake."

"How so?"

"If you wanted to marry, as someone in your position you could marry an heiress, a woman with an estate, someone more mature."

"I don't need any more money and as you know I have a taste for the gutter." She struck him hard across the face.

"I will grant you that blow Alice, for past wrongs but you have no right to dictate to me anymore. You chose your course. You are back at the Ferry with your friends and family around you. Parker is a good worker and strikes me a lusty fellow, so who does it matter who I share my bed with?"

Her eyes welled with tears and he felt like a churl.

"Alice, whatever is the matter?"

She raised her face to his and briefly kissed his lips. Richard was now in total confusion. He thought for a second and then roughly took her in his arms and kissed her much more forcibly. She kissed him back, thrusting her hips forward so their bodies rubbed against one another. He pulled away from her and questioned her with a look. She wetted her lips and then turned her back to him so that he might unlace her dress. He hesitated briefly, but then fumbling like a schoolboy undid it. Her dress slipped to the floor, she turned again so he could undo her stays and pull down her petticoats.

She stood before him naked in a sea of satin. She ran her fingers over her breasts and then reached out to unbutton his doublet. He stood there immobile and let her undress him. She knelt down in front of him and started to suck him. He suddenly woke up as if he had been in a dream. He grabbed her by the hair and pulled her to her feet, she wrapped her arms around his neck and he clutched at her buttocks, lifting her up as her legs came around him. He staggered to the table and spread her like a feast upon it, climbing onto and inside her, thrusting and pumping. She was moaning and screaming, urging him to thrust harder. He collapsed on top of her.

"My God that was incredible, Alice. I don't remember our lovemaking being that passionate, or is it something Parker taught you?"

"Don't be uncouth. George is like William, climbs on top each Saturday night for a few minutes whilst I plan what to cook for dinner. " She laughed, "It's never been that important."

"Liar. You can't pretend you don't care after what's just happened. God I have missed you, Alice."

"Don't get sentimental."

"It's true, we were always so right for each other."

She pushed him off her and went and started picking up her clothes.

"What are you doing? Let's go to the bedchamber."

"Someone could come in at any minute." She was lacing her stays, "Get dressed."

Richard reluctantly did as he was bid.

"I never understood how one minute you could romp like a queen of the stews and the next be a prim and proper housewife worrying over the neighbours."

"Well we agreed some time ago that you did not understand me. There, am I respectable?"

He didn't reply to that question, "So what now?"

"Whatever do you mean?"

"Will you leave Parker? Or do you want to be just my mistress?"

"Neither."

"We could leave the town, start somewhere else afresh, I have the funds."

"I could never leave here, it's my home."

"It took such an effort to obtain a divorce it will be impossible to overturn it now."

"I will not divorce George, he has been through too much to be with me."

"What of me? What I have been through to be with you and without you?"

She said nothing and went to go.

"Alice, what the fuck is going on? Are we to be together again?"

"That would never work."

"Then what was this all about? A fond farewell before I wed someone else?"

"Surely you are not going to go through with that sham now?" Alice was incredulous.

Richard was even more so. "So this was to stop me marrying Luisa? To show me what I am missing, you dangle yourself before me like a whore, out of spite? Am I never to be a husband again? I am never to have someone to share my life with? I just have to sit here in this house and mourn your going, is that it?"

"If you were really interested in marrying Tamsin's by blow you would not have made love to me quite so easily."

"Believe me, Alice, love had nothing to do with it."

"Really? Yet you would run off with me without a second thought!"

"I ask you again, why did you come?"

"To talk sense into you."

"We didn't do much talking that I can recall."

"Go on then, marry that little slut and turn a barmaid into Lady Mudford."

"Oh I see, it's not about me, it's about a stupid title. You are more of a slut than Luisa would ever be."

"Just try and remember to call out the right name when you bed her." She slammed the door behind her. Richard sank to the ground, his head was literally spinning. The door banged again.

"Alice?"

"No it's me," said Jack, "What's going on? Why aren't you at the church?"

"I'm not going."

"Don't be a prick. Everyone is there."

"What do I care?"

"Why did you think I was Alice?"

"She was here, we just, you know." It took a few seconds for Jack to comprehend.

"You just fucked Alice on your way to the altar? Are you completely insane?"

"Shut up, Jack."

"The fuck I will. Why did she come here and more to the point, why did she lift her skirts?"

"To stop me getting married."

"She wants you back?"

"No, most definitely not. She just doesn't want me to marry Luisa."

"Well then I can't think of a better reason for doing just that. Straighten yourself up."

Richard started crying.

"For God's sake, stop behaving like a girl."

"I only ever wanted Alice."

627

"Well you can't have her, so you can sit here blubbering like a lovesick schoolboy or you can move on. If you don't marry Luisa she will be devastated and it will kill John. You know that, don't you?"

Richard wiped his face with his sleeve.

"Shit, shit, shit."

He was walking up the aisle. At least he thought he was, it was like he was in someone else's body. He almost stopped altogether when he saw Alice sitting prim and proper next to George Parker but Jack pulled him along. Madame Sohier and the boys were sat in the front pew, Tom was scowling. The church was absolutely heaving, a world away from the quiet wedding he'd envisaged. He heard music playing and assumed Luisa must be on her way on John's arm. He did not turn and look.

When they were next to him, John leaned across. "Look after my girl Diccon, she is the light of my life." Richard could not speak, he thought he might have nodded his head.

The service was a blur. He knew he mumbled his responses and Luisa spoke so softly he could not tell if she had taken her vows at all. They walked back down the aisle man and wife, her arm rested so lightly on his he could have shaken it off like a stray leaf. There was plenty of feasting. He didn't eat but he drank a lot. He declined to make any kind of speech. After the meal he pretended to circulate meeting guests but he only said the minimum. John had tears in his eyes and Luisa's attention was diverted to her papa.

"Richard!"

"Tamsin."

"It was a grand wedding."

"Mmm."

"Luisa looked like a princess." Richard was unmoved.

"I need to speak to you."

"I think you have said enough to me Tamsin. You have had your way, your daughter is Lady Mudford."

"She is so young."

"I told you that but you disagreed."

"I think you should wait."

"What?"

"I think you should wait, before you consummate the marriage."

Richard couldn't understand what she was saying and tried to focus, "I don't understand you."

"I simply mean that there is no need to rush into the physical act. You have taken your vows, there is plenty of time to do other things."

"I am sorry? When did you decide all this?"

"I was just thinking, and I asked Alice–"

"–you did what?"

"She knows what Luisa might be made to do."

"Made to do? Do you think me such a brute?"

"Stop raising your voice, people will hear. It is not long until her eighteenth birthday, perhaps you could wait till then. So we are agreed?"

Richard said nothing, he thought again about saddling a horse and riding off into the night.

"See, that was not so bad," said Jack later. "And look at her, she is so pretty and ripe."

"Hmm! Tamsin has forbidden me the marriage bed till Luisa turns eighteen."

"What! She can't do that."

"It doesn't matter and I don't care. If I don't consummate the marriage it can be annulled."

"I give up," muttered Jack.

"Get me another drink."

Richard walked up the stairs to the bedchamber. He hesitated at the door, perhaps he should just go back down and let his new wife work out for herself that their marriage would remain unconsummated for the foreseeable future. He knocked gently and went in. Luisa was sat in the centre of the bed, her hair cascading down over her shoulders that were half bare as her delicately laced nightgown was provocatively slipping down. She looked a little nervous but smiled widely as he came in. He sat down in a chair and stared at her, gnawing the inside of his cheek and wondering how to begin.

"Luisa."

"Yes!" she was slightly breathless.

"It seems to me that perhaps it would be more seemly if we did not sleep together-" he got no further.

"What do you mean? Tonight is our wedding night!"

"Yes but you are still very young and–"

"I am old enough to marry, the vicar gave me instruction as to my wifely duty. I am ready!"

"Have you ever slept with a man before?"

"No! How could you suggest such a thing, has something been said? People sometimes assume, because, because of my upbringing–" she was getting distressed.

"No, no nothing has been said, I am not putting this too well, for a young girl to ...to be penetrated by a man, and a much older man, might be er...well suffice it to say, there is no hurry."

"But it is my wedding night. I want to be joined with my husband."

This was not going as it should. He had assumed that because of Tamsin's forceful views, Luisa would be only too delighted to turn over and go to sleep with her maidenhead intact. He said nothing for a few minutes. She was very lovely and it seemed there were full breasts beneath the gown.

"Come here."

She padded out of the bed and stood in front of him.

"Take off the gown."

She reached down and drew the gown up and over her

head. As she did so she revealed creamy thighs and a thick and curling bush of hair, hips curving into a waist, and breasts if not entirely formed, more than a handful, round and pert, the nipples already raised. She tossed the nightgown on the floor. Her breathing was shallower now. Richard reached out and touched the coarse, curling hair, she gasped sharply and trembled. He slipped his fingers between her thighs and felt she was already wet with anticipation.

"Go and lie on the bed."

She did as she was bid and slowly he removed his own clothes. Turning and facing her, he was already erect. Her eyes widened in surprise.

"Don't pretend you have never seen a cock before, Luisa, you have three brothers."

He lay down beside her wondering what the hell he was doing, he squeezed her left breast but quickly changed his mind and eased her legs apart.

"The first time usually hurts a bit." He decided just to be quick and get it over with, he had no interest in the idea of deflowering virgins. He rolled on top of her and as he thrust inside her he felt her hymen break. She sharply took in a breath. He waited for a moment so she could get used to the feeling of him and then began to move rhythmically. He put his hand beneath her buttocks, encouraging her to move with him. His thoughts drifted away back to Alice and he could feel his anger rising again. Why did she think she could use him in such a way, that she could control him by flashing her privates at him? He realised that he was moving fiercely, thrusting deeper and deeper. Luisa was moaning but he wasn't sure if it was from enjoyment. He decided to release and rolled away from her. He found a cool spot in the bed and closed his eyes.

"You might want to clean yourself, there will probably be blood," he murmured.

He was aware of her slipping out of the bed and going over

to the ewer and basin. He heard water being poured and then he must have drifted off to sleep. He didn't know how long he slept but when he awoke it was still dark and he was still alone in the bed. He felt a little drunk and disorientated and then with horror remembered what had happened, he looked over to the basin. Luisa was sat in the chair by the little cupboard, she looked like a marble statue in the moonlight, she was shivering and he thought her cheeks were tear-stained.

"What are you doing sat there? You will catch your death, come back to bed." She obeyed him but with some reluctance, slipping beneath the sheet and lying on her back staring at the ceiling. She pulled the coverlet up to her chin.

Richard propped himself up on his elbow feeling mildly irritated.

"You are frozen." He rubbed her feet with his own. "Have you been crying? I'm sorry, I told you it might hurt, I hope it was not too much, I could have been gentler."

"It did hurt a little down there but it hurt more here, she placed her hand on her breast– do I repel you? Is that why you did not want to sleep with me?"

"Repel me? What on earth gave you that idea?"

"You...you never kissed me, not once."

Richard lay back he thought about their courtship, their wedding, their wedding feast, the consummation, he had sleepwalked into marriage. She was right, he had never kissed her. She was sobbing now, it was a soft noise not a wail, but all the more heart-breaking for that. He should have listened to Tamsin, he should have drunk less and been more thoughtful.

Richard turned back to Luisa and gently wiped the tears from her cheeks. "Luisa, Luisa, I am sorry, I have been self-absorbed and thoughtless, you have married a cruel man." He hesitated for a moment and then started to kiss the tears away, her cheeks, her lashes and finally her rosebud mouth which tasted of sandalwood. It was soft and moist and her breath was sweet, and made him think of fennel and lovage. She responded and began to kiss him back, her tongue was tender, she wrapped her arms around his neck and twirled her fingers through his hair. He held her close and she pushed herself against him, he could feel himself getting excited and a warm glow crept over his body. It had been so very long since he had held someone in his arms who wanted to be there who was urging him to love them. His hands expertly explored her body and hers, hesitant and trembling but insistent, explored his. He broke away for a moment, properly looking at her for the first time. She was his wife, this was probably the most important day of her life and he had made vows before God. Her irises were huge dark pools. Did she want this? She gave the briefest nod as if she had read his thoughts. He kissed her again, their tongues played and teased and then his ability for rational thought was gone.

A long time later and they dozed, lying twisted up in the sheets, her head was resting on his abdomen and he stroked her hair. Their bodies were slippery with sweat and the whole room reeked of love-making.

"Did I do better that time, Luisa?"

He felt her smile on his skin.

"You did very well, just as I dreamed it would be."

"You dreamt of this night?"

"Many times, since I was a young girl."

"you are barely a woman now."

"Oh Richard, for a clever man you are very dense."

"Well I won't dispute that especially where women are concerned."

"I knew, I always knew, and after we danced...I just hoped you would not re-marry but wait for me... I think we could be happy Richard, if you let us."

He squeezed her buttock gently, what else could he say?

"You may be right, I would like to try."

"Really?" She looked up at him, her eyes shining with happiness. He felt uneasy.

"I am sorry about before, can you forgive me?"

In answer her hand slipped down and she gently caressed his private parts. He groaned and she pulled her hand away but he caught it and took it back with his own, showing her how to arouse him. After they made love again Richard insisted they should sleep.

"I need to be up early and check Jack has not forgotten he is to oversee our latest cargoes. You will be sore enough tomorrow."

She cuddled into him and was asleep in an instant. It felt strange to hold a woman in his arms after so long, he always forgot how soft a woman's skin was, her hair smelt of dried roses and spices. He lay there much longer thinking of his previous wives. Most people married two or three times, death often took away spouses before a marriage had time to go sour. He thought of Jeannot and how repulsed she had been by the act of marriage and the coldness of their marriage bed. Alice, Alice for most part had been earthy and lusty matching his own appetites till she tired of him. There had been other women in his life notably Jacinta, she had been a cruel lover, in fact love had nothing to do with it. Luisa, Luisa was so tender, so passionate and she seemed to adore him. He had no idea why and that disconcerted him but he was glad to have someone warm his bed. Then he remembered Tamsin.

Chapter Eighty-Four

He hummed as he marched down the street, he knew he was smiling like an idiot but he could not help himself. When he got to the quay he found it all activity, he could have stayed in bed.

"Hey!" called Jack. "You don't trust me do you?"

"Of course not. How's it going?"

"Everything is fine but I have a cursed headache, I can't drink wine like I used to, I will have to add more water."

Jack narrowed his eyes and stared at him." You're looking very pleased with yourself. You had her didn't you?"

Richard blushed crimson, "She wanted it, she practically begged me."

"Fine, I wasn't the one telling you not to consummate your marriage. In fact, I would have been more surprised if you hadn't, she's a beautiful girl."

"But that's the point, she is just a girl. And what am I? An old man."

"Don't be ridiculous. The one thing about the Mudfords is that they age well. You could pass for ten years younger, you have your own hair and teeth and you haven't run to fat."

"Even so."

"If you weren't so unobservant you would have noticed that

Luisa is utterly in love with you. God knows why, you are such a miserable bastard, but she always has been. You should see the way she looks at you."

"Really?" Richard was not entirely convinced.

"Really, Diccon, you know I would not lie to you. You deserve some happiness, I always liked Alice but she wasn't right for you."

Richard stared at him.

"She wasn't, her focus was always too narrow. She was happiest being a ferry girl but you, you were always meant for a wider stage."

"Really?" he said again.

"Really, anyway what was she like, Luisa?"

Richard mumbled something inaudible as he went crimson again.

Jack clapped him on the back, "Good for you, you have lived like a monk for too longer. Indeed, from what I have heard of monks, they've had more women than you. I'm surprised your cock didn't fall off from lack of use."

"Shut up, Jack."

Jack turned and waved at his wife who was watching Sam and Antonio playing at football.

"Antonio!" called Richard.

"Yes, Pa?" He ran across to Richard.

"Are you behaving yourself?" Antonio rolled his eyes at being called over to answer such a question.

"The porters are baking potatoes in their brazier. Can I have some money Pa? I'm hungry."

"So your Aunt Berta has not fed you this morning?"

"Yes, but I'm hungry now."

Richard fished some coins out of a pocket, "Get one for Sam too."

Antonio gave a backward wave. He was already running back across the quay and down Porters Lane hallooing Sam to follow.

"If all is right here Jack, I need to go buy some rolls. I'll see you tomorrow when you bring back Antonio."

Jack clasped Richard to him and clapped his back. "Enjoy this marriage Richard, let yourself enjoy it."

Richard marched back up Bull Street swinging the bag of rolls. He didn't see Tamsin coming out of his house till she was almost upon him, her face was like fury. She caught sight of him at the same time, marched up to him and slapped him right across the face.

"What—"

"You promised!"

"No I didn't."

"It's always about you, isn't it? What you want? What your needs are? She is just a girl!"

"A girl that you badgered me to marry."

She struck him again.

"I'm warning you, Tamsin."

"Warn away you complete bastard."

"I didn't force her. You were the one who said she was ready to marry, that you would worry she would toss away her virtue on some callow youth." All the same he felt a twinge of guilt.

"I wanted her protected."

"I haven't beaten her! I just slept with my own wife."

She went to hit him again, but this time Richard grabbed her arm, dropping the white rolls in the process and they fell from the bag and into the gutter.

"Have you spoken to her?"

Tamsin did not answer.

"You must have done to know how I spent my wedding night. Is she unhappy? Is she crying that I raped her?"

Still Tamsin remained silent.

"No, she didn't did she? I expect she was smiling and as happy as she was when I left her."

"She doesn't understand. She thinks only of her duty."

"No, Tamsin, you were right the first time. She was ready and if I had turned from her last night I dare say I would soon have found myself a cuckold. Now stay out of my marriage or you will not be welcome in my house."

She wrenched her arm away and stormed back to the Angel.

Richard slammed the door. Luisa appeared from the hall, she looked very pretty and a little flushed. She could immediately see something was wrong and became nervous, trying to work out what might have happened.

"I take it your mother has been here."

"Yes, she came to see how I was, if I, that is if we, how it was..." She was by now blushing furiously, "I told her you were gentle and solicitous."

"Which we both know isn't true!"

"Richard, what is the matter? What have I done? You seemed so happy this morning."

Richard calmed down; it wasn't after all Luisa's fault.

"I'm sorry." He took her hands and felt a bit sheepish, "Your Ma accosted me in the street, for deflowering her daughter."

Luisa was shocked, her large eyes even bigger. "She did what? I gave her no cause, please believe me."

He took her into his arms. "I know, but from now on just remember you are my wife first and Tamsin's daughter second."

He went into his counting house and sat down, wondering if he had made yet another mistake in his marriage. Luisa came in a few minutes later, twisting her hands. She looked scared and even trembled slightly.

"Luisa, are you frightened of me?"

"A little, I don't want to do the wrong thing."

"Luisa, I don't want a wife who lives in fear, I want a partner in my life."

Richard's mind flicked briefly back to Alice. Then he stared deep into Luisa's eyes, her lips were slightly parted and he suddenly wondered why he had never really noticed how heart-stoppingly lovely she was. In a moment they were in each other's arms, tearing at their clothes, overcome with passion. The table crashed over and Richard's counters spun in all directions but he didn't even notice.

The midday sun was warming their bodies.

"It looks like I have been robbed," said Richard looking around the room.

Luisa was removing a quill that had been prodding her back.

"Is this how you usually behave, husband?"

"I'm generally very restrained and boring, do my counting in my counting house and my fucking in my bedchamber – sorry, sorry, sometimes my manners are still of the gutter." He kissed her nipple and she stroked his hair. "I'm afraid when the children get back tomorrow we will have to be more respectable."

"It's going to be strange being a stepmother."

"Mmmm." He nuzzled her breasts. "My poor children are pretty confused about their parentage as it is, but it will be good for them to have a woman about the house again. Luisa, Tom, well Tom has been a bit upset about us getting wed."

"Why? Does he think I am not worthy to be your wife?"

"God no! He likes you Luisa, he likes you very much. I didn't know myself till a short while ago and we are a little estranged at the moment. He is going back to Oxford and I am hoping distance will heal the wounds."

"I had no idea, we have always been more like brother and sister, I never gave him cause."

"Luisa, I am afraid men would not need a lot of cause around you."

"What do you mean?"

"You are a very pretty girl and you have no idea how lovely you are. It is very appealing."

"Does it appeal to you?"

"Oh I think I have shown you how it appeals to me."

"Will you show me again?"

Chapter Eighty-Five

Tom slammed into the house and disappeared up to his room. There was a lot of banging of doors and cupboards and Richard thought he was making a show of packing. Madame Sohier brought the girls back a little while later; they all tiptoed into the hall. Richard came out of his counting house and watched them for a moment.

"What are you doing?" The all jumped guiltily.

"We were not sure if we were expected, we did not want to disturb," said Madame Sohier.

"Disturb what, Wauldure?"

Madame Sohier, pursed her lips and drew herself up to her full height. "Well my dears, I will be off, be good for your papa and, and his wife." She kissed both girls and strode out. They looked around them.

"Go and get ready for supper."

"Yes, Papa," they chorused, and he could hear them whispering all the way up the stairs.

There was another crashing of the door. "Antonio! Can't you enter a room more quietly?"

Antonio looked nonplussed. "Is it time for supper? I am starved."

"Come here and give your Pa a hug." The boy ran to him and squeezed him round the waist.

"Aunt Berta is so strict, she said you don't beat me enough."

"That is probably true, I'm a terrible father." Richard ruffled his hair. "Try and be well behaved tonight."

Antonio sighed deeply, "I always try Pa but it's difficult." He stomped up the stairs.

The evening meal was very quiet. Luisa was a bundle of nerves and kept squeezing his hand under the table for comfort and reassurance. Jeanne and Lizzie kept stealing glances under their lashes and exchanging looks, Tom pushed his food around his plate, Antonio was completely oblivious and gorged himself as if to make up for Tom.

"Are you travelling back to Oxford tomorrow Tom?" asked Richard.

Tom muttered something unintelligible "Does your manservant know? Is all prepared?"

"And what are we supposed to call you?" spat out Tom, glaring at Luisa.

"Tom!" Richard was annoyed at his boy whilst he could understand his pain.

"Its reasonable question, is she to be our mother? If we are to call her Ma, what do we call Alice? Not that Alice is actually our real mother either. Jeanne and Lizzie's mother is dead and we never had chance to call her anything. Antonio's mother is probably dead and as for mine, who knows where she is."

"That's enough, Tom!"

"Shut up, Tom, don't speak about my mother." Antonio hurled a piece of bread at Tom

Jeanne started to cry.

"Tom, I'm sorry I have upset you," said Luisa. Tom stormed out of the room. Luisa's lip trembled but she gulped back her tears and addressed the other children. "I'm not your mother;

I am just Luisa, the same as I have always been. Please just call me Luisa."

"Why did you marry our Pa?" there was no harshness in Antonio's voice, just a vague curiosity.

"Because I love your Pa very much and I was honoured that he would want me to be his wife and to let me come here and help look after you all."

"You won't beat me will you? Even if I am bad?"

"No Antonio that would not be my place."

"No Antonio, that pleasure remains mine," said Richard and his younger son scowled and dished himself some jelly. "I had better go see Tom."

Tom was lying on his bed in the darkness.

"Tom, Tom," said Richard softly.

"Go away."

"Can't do that, I'm your Pa and I can't bear to see my boy unhappy." He sat on the bed and put his hand on Tom's shoulder but he shrugged it away.

"I didn't know how you felt Tom."

"But when you found out you still married her anyway."

"I made a promise. It's difficult to explain but I felt I owed it to Tamsin and to John."

"What about me?"

"Luisa would not have married you."

"You don't know that."

"Yes I do. Tom you are young, and you will love again. And you may not believe me but the girl you love at sixteen is not the girl you will love at twenty, you will change so much in the next few years as you grow to be a man. Tom you are very clever, you will achieve great things and you will break many, many hearts. I know you hate me now but I will always love you and always be your father and Alice will always be your mother."

"Oh Pa, I'm so miserable."

"I know Tom." He smoothed his hair.

The next day Tom returned to Oxford. He was pale and the shadows were deep under his eyes through lack of sleep but he was civil to Luisa and his father, and he kissed both his sisters who cried to see him go and he had a mock fight with Antonio who asked if he could have Tom's room. Richard gave him an extra allowance, told him to look after himself and study hard and said they would be lonely without him till he returned home for the holidays.

Chapter Eighty-Six

Richard stabled his horse leaving his manservant to unsaddle and cool the animal along with the stable boy who had woken sleepily at their knock. Richard gave the boy a coin for his trouble and the disturbance of his sleep. It was cold and he was glad he had worn his cloak with the white weasel collar. He ached, it had taken longer to return from Winchester than it should have done, he had left too late but the merchant he had come to meet had insisted on a leisurely meal. Richard wanted to sink into his bed and sleep. He soon was back on Bull Street, he glanced across at Bull Hall shrouded in darkness, a few drinkers stumbled out of the Angel. He looked inside as the door was closing and saw Tamsin pouring ale for others who had no homes to go to.

The lanthorn above the door of his house glowed in welcome. Richard fumbled for his key, expecting the door to be fastened but it was unlocked, he went inside and secured the door behind him. Luisa was sitting in the hall where she had been stitching by the light of half a dozen candles. Her face shone as she saw him, it made him uncomfortable that he had the power to engender such emotion. He took off his cloak and flung it on the settle.

645

"It's late; you should not have waited up." He felt edgy; the candlelight made her hair shine.

"I was engrossed in my stitching; you said you would return this evening. Are you thirsty? Hungry? Can I get you some food? Wine?" Her smile was broad, her voice eager.

"No, I don't want anything, you should go to bed," he rubbed his eyes.

She looked unsure, "Should I await your coming?"

"What?"

"Will you wish to lie with me tonight?"

Richard felt tired and irritable, "You sound like a brothel keeper." He cursed as the words were out of his mouth.

She blushed crimson and bit her lip.

"I'm sorry, Luisa, that was uncalled for."

She turned and started to mount the stair, "I'm just trying to find my place. I know I bring nothing to this marriage, no money, no connections. If I am not allowed to look after and care for you what else is there?" She ran up the stairs.

Richard walked over to her needlework, he held it up, it was a finely embroidered shirt and from the size he guessed she was making it for him. He blew out the candles, mounted the staircase quickly and went to their chamber. She was sat in the window seat her knees under chin, she was unhappy. Richard went and sat beside her.

"Are you making this for me?" She nodded.

"It's beautiful work." He wasn't sure how to go on, "Luisa, I'm finding it hard to remember what it's like to be married." She wouldn't look at him. "I don't need money and connections. And I am out of practice in letting someone look after me. It makes me uncomfortable."

She looked up at him with sad eyes.

"But I can get used to it."

"Do you really think me a queen of the stews?"

"Dear God no, you could not be further removed."

"Am I too eager when we..." He realised she was terrified that somehow she might have awakened in herself something that would condemn her as a common woman, her mother's daughter.

Richard swallowed, "No, no you are as any man would desire his wife to be."

"Why did you...? I have never known you to speak so unkindly...not to anyone."

"I'm sorry I was irritable, I was angry at myself and lashed out at you. I'm very tired." He felt himself to be pathetic, it wasn't tiredness, he had blamed Luisa for his own thoughts and needs.

She moved so that she could massage his neck and shoulders. "You work so hard for us all; I did not want you to return home to a house in darkness with no one to greet you. I am your wife, I should welcome you home. I only have my body with which to honour you." Honour, the word hung in the air. How could he explain that he was struggling with a sense of disloyalty?

"I travelled through the night to come home," he confessed. It had been a mad thing to do, why had he pushed himself so?

She wrapped her arms around his neck, "You will look well in your shirt." He pulled her round till she was on his lap and kissed her, "Come it's late we should sleep."

She struggled trying to unlace her robe, Richard helped her, he was aware of his heart beating faster, her shoulders were beautiful. It was late and the room was chilly. The fair hair on her arm stood on end, her skin was goosey, her nipples were proud. She folded her clothes and shimmied into a diaphanous nightgown which left little to the imagination and could hardly provide any warmth. At supper with the Winchester merchant he had been served pomegranates. As he had sucked the flesh he had thought of the taste of Luisa and became eager to be home. He had ridden through the night, bouncing on his horse he had throbbed, ashamed at his lustful thoughts.

647

He pulled himself together, he considered that maybe they should have separate chambers; would not that be more seemly? He realised she was talking to him. "Sorry, what?"

"You were lost in thought; I only said my feet are cold." She hurried into the bed and shivered. Richard splashed cold water on his face and pulled off his clothes. He snuffed out the candles. He warmed her feet and of course one thing led to another.

The next morning he was up early leaving Luisa in a deep sleep. It was a cold, bright day but his cloak was thick and his boots sturdy. He went first to meet with Lawrence Prowse and then to pay off a ship's crew, he mused that Mudford Brothers must be one of the main employers in the town these days. He went up French Street from the warehouse to the town Weigh House where a shipment of iron was due to be weighed for custom duties. It took longer than he would have liked but he didn't trust that he would not be overcharged in his absence. Then he cut through to Silkshop Yard to visit the spinners. Every cottage was now involved in the weaving business and the evidence of its success could be seen in the repairs done to the houses and the chubbiness of the babies. A few houses in the neighbouring yards had also been taken on but Silkshop was the hub of the enterprise. He took a cup of ale with Mary, her husband was back and she was pregnant but still the main breadwinner and continued to oversee the rest of the workers.

Next Richard went to the Audit House and paid his contribution to the Poor Relief fund, chatting for a while to other merchants and burgesses who wandered in and out of the building. From the window he gazed down at the butter market and saw Luisa wandering around the stalls buying food, which she stowed in a large wicker basket. She was plainly dressed and had no servant with her. The wife of an alderman, strode through the market, Richard recognised Margaret Biston, she had not aged well, the result of a life spent in the house of Alderman Biston no doubt. Her way intersected with Luisa's and his wife dropped a curtsey which Margaret ignored as she pushed past her and on her way. Luisa glanced around embarrassed, worried that others might have seen, and then began to pay rapt attention to the purchases in her basket. Richard was angry, he was not one to stand on ceremony but Luisa, as his wife, took precedence over the wife of an alderman and she should have received the deference. He ran down the outside staircase and came up behind her.

"May I carry your basket, my lady?"

"Richard!" She looked delighted to see him, "I did not hear you leave this morning."

"You were dead to the world!"

She blushed.

Richard dropped his voice, "I hope I was not, er, too... rough? He whispered and would not look at her.

"You were just passionate," she whispered back, he knew she was staring up at him.

"Er...I'm sorry about your gown."

"It can be mended."

"My trip away...I...missed..."

"I missed you too."

He felt embarrassed, "Have you more shopping?"

"No, no I have done enough," she muttered.

"I'll walk back with you, then I have to meet with a couple of carriers." He took the basket and gave her his arm, "You could have sent a servant to do the marketing."

"I wanted to choose the best myself."

"You should still take a servant with you, as befits a lady."

The realisation that her position in life had changed and certain things were to be expected, dawned on her face, "Oh yes of course, I did not think, and they were all about their chores."

"We should get you a lady's maid."

"A lady's maid!" She was incredulous. "What would she do?"

"Help unlace your dresses."

"I have someone to do that already." She smiled.

"I'll speak to Wauldure, get her to find some suitable girls to consider." They were near to a merchant's shop that was displaying beautiful materials. "Dresses, you probably need more, new fashions, order what you will."

"I don't know that I need–"

"Order what you will." He handed back the basket and kissed her cheek, "I will be back by sunset."

Gradually the atmosphere relaxed in the house, Tasmin never visited whilst Richard was at home and Madame Sohier said she felt she ought to let Luisa find her place, which she would not be able to do if Richard's former mother-in-law was looking over her shoulder. Jeanne and Lizzie found having a mother not much older than they gained them great sympathy in issues of new dresses, dancing lessons and gossiping. Richard noticed with horror that his two daughters were starting to be interested in young men and would sit in the oriel window with their books or needlework to better notice and be noticed by the young men who strode across the square, he wished they had not closed the nunneries.

Luisa had taken to bringing Richard a drink and spiced biscuits if he was working in his counting house so she could sit for a while and ask him about the running of his household or the welfare of his children.

"Perhaps we might have some entertainment one evening and invite some of our friends and neighbours," suggested Luisa. She bit on her lip waiting for his answer.

"And would that include the young parson who spends so much time walking up and down practising his sermons outside his church rather than inside?"

Luisa ignored her husband's remark, "I have been studying the household account book." She had been pink with pleasure when Richard suggested she might want to take over the accounts for the house.

"I believe our cook to be robbing us!"

"Yes I know." Richard was trying to add up a column of figures.

"You know?"

"She has a large, extended and poverty-stricken family but is very proud and would not except a handout from me. However, she gets great pleasure from duping me out of vegetables and the scrag end of meat." He initialled a set of accounts.

Luisa was shocked. "And then there is the payment to Annie's boy who arrives every day and sweeps leaves in the courtyard and eats all his meals with the servants."

"He's a bit simple, and since Bart ran off."

Luisa nodded and muttered "Of course," under her breath

"The child is also unfailingly happy and smiling and helps polish things," continued Richard as he put to one side bills due to be sent out.

"Helps polish things?" Luisa came and sat on his lap and kissed him.

"What have I done to deserve that?"

"Absolutely nothing."

"Please don't distract me; I am trying to finish these bills." He didn't sound at all concerned about being distracted.

"Richard, may I change some things?"

"Change?"

"The house is, well it's just like it was when Alice lived here."

"I never really considered it but you are right. Change whatever you want Luisa, you are the lady of the house now."

Her eyes gleamed with excitement.

"Ah, I can see my money chest will be emptied."

651

Chapter Eighty-Seven

They were having a small party for the Coronation Day, a good banquet, games and music. Richard however, felt the need to be alone. Today was his day, when he would reflect on his life. This year, he felt something was not quite right. There were rumours about the Queen's health and a sense of latent excitement as if something was about to happen. He went and sat on the stone seat in the courtyard bower. He thought about Alice, about the arc of his life. He heard a step on the flagstones and felt annoyed. He wanted to be by himself.

"Richard? Is all well?" It was Luisa, he tried not to let his irritation show.

"All is well; I just want a moment of quiet," he said pointedly.

"Should I shoo our guests on their way?"

"No, I will be in shortly. You should go in yourself, you will get shrammed out here, it's a cold night." She looked abashed.

"Or course," she went to go but turned back. Richard sighed. She rummaged in her pocket.

"For your naming day," she said and handed him a small packet.

"I didn't know you knew." Now he felt guilty.

"It was always a little joke; someone said that you were the Queen's own child."

"Treason!" He turned the packet over in his hand.

"It is only a little thing, it's not even new, second-hand. I did not use my allowance but some pennies I had saved."

He felt churlish as he opened the packet. It was a book, well more correctly it was a play, dog-eared it was true, printed in 1598, *Love's Labour Lost*, the frontispiece proclaimed the writer as William Shakespeare.

"Thank you Luisa, it was very kind and thoughtful, thank you." She turned to go and he caught her arm. When they returned to their guests they were a little flushed.

The entertainment became entertainments. There were many people who wanted to associate with Sir Richard Mudford, eager to peer around his house. There were also many potential suitors for his daughters, though Richard insisted they were much too young to even consider such possibilities. The Mayor and burgesses were keen to try and persuade him to take more of an interest in town affairs and politics. Richard liked it best when he had his real friends and family about him, when there was singing, dancing, acting and stories around the fire about fighting the Spanish or discovering new lands. He realised he was content, and might even be happy.

Over the next few weeks Richard gradually noticed things altering around him. The house smelt of beeswax polish, there were flowers, tapestries were changed, cleaned or dispensed of, glassware and silver stowed away was polished and displayed, a turkey carpet appeared in the hall. New bedding and curtains arrived, a side room became a music room, books were proudly displayed, and the paintings of Richard and his children were placed prominently in the hall, which prompted him to commission one of his new wife. A mappa mundi appeared on the wall of his counting house showing the Americas along with a beautiful new cabinet to display his treasures. He did not realise Luisa was aware of his collection of memories but she helped him place them in the cabinet and made him tell her the stories behind them: the cutler's knife, the picture of the Ronceval, the bracelet from Saskatan, now so worn it could not safely remain on his wrist, the story of Bevis, a small piece of Venetian glass one of his first trades, the arrowhead dug out of Jacket, Lizzie's old red lion, the Spanish priest's rosary.

"I fear I have overspent, Richard." Luisa bit her lip as she sat down opposite him, "We have entertained greatly these last few weeks, and I could not resist the pretty baubles for the girls, and Antonio is growing so quickly."

Richard gravely took her account book and shook his head, she looked so solemn he did not like to tell her she could overspend twenty times and it would not make a dent in their finances.

"This is tragic indeed."

"Oh, perhaps I can make savings in the coming weeks to balance things out."

"The tragedy is, my dear Luisa, that you have shown me up to be a skinflint, dressing my children like paupers, entertaining my neighbours in a paltry fashion. Thank you my dear I will increase your allowance immediately." She looked at him primly.

"You are making fun of me."

"Only a little, we are making more of a show in the world now Luisa, and I should not expect you to manage on accounts designed for quiet living."

"Do you want to be in the world more, Richard?"

"Now I do," he reached for her hand and turned it over so that he could kiss her wrist. She lifted her hand and delicately traced the pattern of his lips.

Chapter Eighty-Eight

"Pa what has happened to the house?"

Jacket had just returned from business in Winchester and London. He had become quite the gentleman, his American adventure had turned him into a man. He was an excellent merchant and businessman, negotiating tight deals for Mudford Brothers now known as Merchant Venturers. Now that he had well-cut outfits, neatly trimmed hair and had honed his manners, he was an excellent ambassador for the company.

"Luisa has been having a change around. Don't you like it?"

"I do, I never realised we lived somewhere so fine."

"How did things go in London?"

"Well, well, I did a good deal on the gunpowder; we should make a good profit on what we don't need for ourselves. I was also invited to dinner by one of Lord de la Ware's men. His Lordship is interested in our joint stock venture for the colonies."

Jacket entered a record of his business dealings in the account book.

"I bought these in London, Pa." He fished a pair of pearl earrings out of his pocket.

"Very good quality. Do you have a sweetheart, Jacket?"

"No, Pa, I bought them for you to give to Luisa as a belated wedding present."

Richard rolled the earrings in his hand, "What a state that I have come to that I need to be tutored by my children. Thank you Jacket, it was very thoughtful of you."

"Well I guessed you might be a bit out of practice. I'm glad you have found someone at last."

"You don't think she is a bit young for me?"

"If she doesn't care I don't know why you should. You ought to see some of the old men in town married to girls straight out of the schoolroom."

"Thank you Jacket, I think I feel better." Jacket was oblivious to the irony.

Jacket embraced him as he had always done since he was a young boy, "I'm glad to be home, Pa."

Richard gave Luisa the earrings that evening. She was delighted, holding them to her ears and moving her head first one way and then another.

"They are so beautiful, thank you, thank you."

She embraced him and he felt guilty, but not guilty enough that he shirked from asking her to pleasure him. She looked nervous and uneasy but he thought it due to her innocence and lack of knowledge. She bent her long neck and hesitated for a moment before encircling his member with her lips. Richard breathed deeply, he gently stroked her head hoping to encourage her to take more of him. Suddenly she pulled away and within seconds had become hysterical.

"What is it? Luisa, calm down, it's nothing, don't worry, it doesn't matter."

She curled up childlike on her side away from him, shaking and sobbing. He tried to calm her but she shrugged him off.

"Luisa, please, I'm sorry I should not have asked you, some women don't mind, it's not important please."

Her sobs subsided and she let him hold her.

"Luisa...did anyone hurt you or make you do something?"

"No...no I'm sorry...it just brought it all back, it was so horrible."

"Tell me, I might be able to help."

"It was a long time ago, it doesn't matter."

"It obviously does" There was a long silence. She rolled over and lay her head on his chest.

"It was when you and Pa were in Spain. Life got very hard and Mama had to do things to make sure we had enough to eat. She would put me behind the curtain and tell me I had to be very quiet, but there was a hole in the material and I would watch the men come."

Richard held her more tightly. "One man, he, he wanted Mama to do...to do that to him and Mama knelt down before him...he was facing me and I could see the expression on his face...and he kept telling Mama to eat more and calling her horrible names and he pushed her head and she was choking and struggling and I could not keep quiet and I ran out and told him to stop hurting her. He was very angry and started to yell and Mama was telling me it was all right and to go back behind the curtain...and then he started to hit her...and didn't stop till Alice and some of the men in the bar came up...he knocked out a tooth...and it was weeks before she could go out..."

"Ssh, ssh, it's all right, I am so sorry to have caused you to remember such a horrible thing."

"You were not to know, I never told anyone before."

"I'm glad you told me, and if there is ever anything you do not want to do, if you would rather just roll over and go to sleep, you just need to say so."

"But the priest told me I must never refuse my husband, I must do anything that is asked of me."

"Really? It never bothered my other wives. Look, he has been a widower these last twenty years, he knows nothing about the marriage bed."

"But I can never imagine wanting to roll over and sleep."

"Believe me, you will." He kissed her shoulder and smoothed her hair till she slept and he was left alone in the night with his thoughts.

The next day he decided he should broach to Luisa the idea of separate bedchambers. Her eyes widened with consternation.

"It would mean you could have your own space." Her eyes were welling up. "Your sleep would not be disturbed." Her bottom lip trembled and she tried to brush away an errant tear so he would not see. "I just thought you might want your own chamber. I understand it is most common amongst the gentry."

"But, I just want to be with you." She came and buried her head in his shirt, making it damp.

"It was just an idea, only an idea."

"Did you have separate chambers when you were married before?"

"Er, no...but both Jeannot and Alice threw me out of the marital bed."

Luisa pulled away, "Really? But why?"

"I, that is, they weren't very happy with me." Richard grimaced.

"I am very happy with you," said Luisa simply.

"Well think no more of it, but tell me if you change your mind." She shook her head.

Richard went to visit Madame Sohier, he felt uneasy that the old woman who ran his household for several years had now been, to all intents and purposes, banished back to her own home. She was sat in the window where the weak sunshine could give some warmth to her arthritic limbs. A servant girl massaged oil into her wrists and fingers, the old woman winced and told her to have more care. Curled up like a cat and sound asleep on the window seat was Antonio. Madame Sohier brought a bent finger to her lips to hush Richard so he would not disturb the boy. They moved over to the fireplace and Richard banked it up with logs.

"I hope my boy is not causing a nuisance?"

"He comes here in his school break most days, for his dinner."

"Is that before or after he has had his dinner at home?"

"He is a growing lad."

"I wonder he is not the shape of a barrel," smiled Richard.

"Nervous energy, and he has a stocky build, he is fine Richard."

"I'm glad he comes to visit you, I hope not just for cupboard love, I was worried you might be lonely."

"Lonely? I barely have a minute's peace!" Madame Sohier rolled her eyes in mock irritation. "Lawrence calls several times a week."

"Lawrence Prowse?"

"We do business together, we worked well whilst you were in the Americas."

Richard didn't know his mother-in-law had business deals which did not include the Mudford Brothers.

She must have read his thoughts, "I still have my own interests, Richard, worry not it will all come to you one day."

Richard smiled again, "The girls visit regularly I hope?"

"Nearly every day, showing off what young Mr Dutton has taught them. I think Jeanne might be a little smitten."

"That is what I was worried about, he is like a lost puppy, I think Jeanne sees him as a replacement for her cat Mrs Stuart."

"Let her have her romance, it will help her confidence. I would not have her shy and withdrawn." She stopped, they both thought a moment of Jeannot.

"And I visit, my friends in the communion, Berta–"

"–Berta?"

"She goes abroad little, and as for that scrapegrace brother of yours."

"Are you trying to convert her?"

Madame Sohier ignored this remark and stretched out her fingers as much as she could in front of the fire.

"Your wife is a regular visitor too."

"Luisa?"

"Of course, she wants my advice on household matters, on manners, on you."

"Me?"

"She wants you to love her so she wants to make you happy."

Richard poked at the logs making sparks fly.

"You do not realise how your family wishes to please you, do you?"

Richard pulled a face.

"It's true! You make them feel safe and cared for. Luisa has been put upon and abused most of her life–"

Richard went to protest but Madame Sohier raised her hand, "I don't mean she has been beaten or not loved but she has been a prop to her mother since she was in drawstrings and she was in danger of being preyed upon by unscrupulous men."

"I think I may be one of their number," Richard said to himself.

Antonio stirred, it was almost time to return to school. "Papa?" he said sleepily, a little confused that he may have fallen asleep in one house and woken in another.

"What is this I hear that you are eating your grandmother out of house and home?"

Antonio sighed deeply, "Papa, if I come to eat, then Grand-mère will eat also, old people forget to eat."

"Ah, that is very selfless of you Antonio." The little boy bowed and came and kissed Madame Sohier on the cheek clasping her tightly around the neck, Richard thought the old lady in danger of suffocation.

"Come, Antonio, I will walk you back to school."

"He thinks I will not go," Antonio confided in Madame.

"Off you go, I'll see you tomorrow." She embraced the boy again and kissed his cheek.

★

They had been invited to a dinner with many of the senior burgesses and their wives at the Audit House. Luisa was nervous but dressed with care and wore her pearl earrings, Lizzie and Jeanne teased her hair into the latest fashion. Richard told her not to worry, that these occasions were remarkably dull, but she wanted him to be proud of her, wanted to disport herself like the wife of a prominent citizen. The evening was not quite so dull as usual and it was because Richard and Luisa were the centre of much attention and whispering. The men made inappropriate comments to Richard and nodded and winked like lechers, the women were cool and aloof to Luisa, making sure she realised she was not one of them in ways subtle and cruel. Luisa held her head high, was unfailingly courteous to everyone, made intelligent remarks when she was given the opportunity and let no one see that she was hurt by their barbs and slights. As they walked slowly home on a startlingly clear night, the moon hanging large and low in the sky, Richard told her how well she had done.

"But they did not like me Richard, and I don't know why, I have never done anything against them."

"Well I saw this evening how small most of them are, how provincial our town has become. When I was a young man the burgesses were larger than life characters, they loved the town, they loved to trade. I didn't realise how things had changed. It has happened slowly but I'm sad to say Southampton is not what it once was. You should care nothing for their opinions Luisa, you are better than them."

"Thank you Richard, I know you did not want to marry me but you are so good and kind, I am glad you did."

"Well I think it might have been one of my better decisions."
She laughed and smiled up at him.

"Perhaps we should widen our horizons for the benefit of
the children," she said. "The girls will have good dowries, they
have been educated as ladies, Tom is so clever and handsome,
and Jacket is kind and diligent and good at business."

"And Antonio?"

"Oh I fear he may be a lost cause." They laughed together.

"So, what do you propose?" asked Richard.

"I think we should introduce them to men of letters and
culture, perhaps we should visit London or even consider a
house in the country."

Richard stood stock still, "You have given this a lot of
thought in such a short time."

"Have I overstepped? I meant nothing, I was just
daydreaming when all those women were being so mean." She
was cross with herself, "I am sorry if I have over-reached, I just
thought if we were somewhere else, where people did not know
me, know I am the bastard child of, of a woman, of woman
who..."

"Of a woman who loves you more than anything in the
world, who would do anything, anything to be able to provide
for you."

"Oh you make me feel so ashamed." She lowered her eyes.
"I just don't want you to regret that you married me."

"Luisa, you don't have to try so hard. I know our marriage
is one of convenience but I think we rub along very well."

"It's more than that to me," she said in a small voice. "I love
you."

"Oh Luisa, I wish I was worthy."

Chapter Eighty-Nine

The Queen was dead. Richard was numb with shock. He had been at a mayoral banquet where he knew they would be asking him to help pay the town fee farm again. The pursuivant had arrived to say that his beloved Bess was dead and James VI of Scotland was to be the new King. Richard had never known any other monarch than Elizabeth, she was his Queen, she was special to him and whilst her star had ascended so had his. His parents had known many reigns born under the terrible tyrant that Henry VIII had become, the fabric of their lives had turned upside down. They had known the austerity of Edward, the flames of Mary and then Elizabeth the Virgin Queen had come and made a contract with her people. She would devote her life to them if they would be faithful in return. Richard had been faithful to his red-headed princess, he had loved and worshipped her, he had been born on her day when her reign had begun and God had dedicated him to her. While Bess lived all would be well. What would happen to him now?

He travelled to London for her state funeral, he could not do otherwise. They brought her body by water from Richmond to Whitehall and then onto Westminster Abbey for her interment. The procession was sombre, the chariot drawn by four horses, the coffin was covered with purple velvet and upon that the representation of the Queen looking so lifelike, fully dressed and bearing the royal regalia. The canopy was borne by six knights and Richard wished he could have been one of them. The horses and the knights, the footmen and all the other supporters were dressed all in black. As it passed people sighed, and groaned and wept, the grief was universal and it was said there had never been such lamentations for the death of a sovereign. James was already in England, lurking till he could take possession of Whitehall.

Chapter Ninety

They had had much fun at the May Day revels, morris men, singers and ringers, mummers in disguising apparel telling the tale of Saint George, the Turk and the doctor. Richard shifted the weight of Antonio is his arms. Jacket walked a little ahead with Luisa, Richard looked behind.

"Girls, keep up."

Dusk was falling and the cutpurses and thieves would be out in the crowds. They crossed the square and turned the corner to the front door of the house. A parchment fluttered in the wind where it had been secured beneath the harke ring.

"What's this?" said Jacket as he pulled it from the door. Richard glanced over his shoulder and saw the crudely drawn picture of a mermaid. The others had seen it too.

"What a funny thing, Papa! What does it mean?" asked Lizzie.

"Nothing, Jacket give me that and take Antonio please." Richard crumpled the paper and hurried the party into the house, by the time all had been stowed away and he turned to look for Luisa she had disappeared. He went to their chamber, it smelt of her but she was not there. Likewise the family rooms showed no sign, the kitchen, buttery, the garden all were empty.

Richard felt a twinge of worry. He didn't know what made him go into the scullery but he found her there in the corner of the cupboard-room, she pressed herself against the wall as he entered. He folded his arms as he lent against the shelves crowded with jars, boxes and foodstuffs.

"You know I can still see you, don't you?"

She gnawed her lip, her eyes fluttered downward.

"It is nothing, just a prank," he said.

He saw her breasts rise and fall as she sighed, "I have brought shame into your house."

"And how precisely did you do that?" She turned away picking at a splinter on the shelf.

"You must think of Jeanne and Lizzie, their reputations."

"Their grandmother is a pillar of the French church, I think their reputations are secure."

"Oh Richard, I wanted to marry you so much, I did not think what that would mean for you and your family. I have dishonoured your name."

"That's nonsense." What was it with women and reputations? Had Alice been right, was it all they had to stand between themselves and destruction? He walked the few steps to the far end of the scullery. He stood very close to her, she tried again to push herself through the wall. He held out his hand.

"Sweetheart." She looked up at him, touched by the endearment, not sure she had heard correctly.

"Sweetheart." He said softly as he proffered his hand again and slowly she placed her hand in his. He led her out of the servants' quarters to the door to the family quarters.

"You will not mention this, you will put it from your mind, as if it never was."

★

"Papa, Luisa will not be down for breakfast, she is feeling sick again."

"Ah, thank you Jeanne, let's join the others."

"Do I have to go to school, Papa?"

"Of course Antonio, how else will you learn to be a gentleman?"

"I am of noble blood, I do not have to learn."

"It takes more than that to be a gentleman," said Jacket.

"Mr Bathe tries to put too many things in my head, I have no room for thinking my own thoughts."

"Shall I take something up to Luisa, Papa?"

"No that's all right, Lizzie, I will go and see her. Jacket, make sure Antonio is not late for the schoolroom."

"Yes, Father."

Antonio groaned at the injustice of his life. Richard went up to the bedchamber he and Luisa shared. He sat on the bed.

"How are you feeling, sweetheart?"

"I feel better now, I just felt so sick this morning."

"Like yesterday."

"Yes, perhaps you should send for the apothecary."

"Mmm, perhaps... Luisa, do you think you might be with child?"

She looked at him blankly, "But, I...I am only just a wife... With child?"

"Well, you haven't bled recently, you are young and healthy and we have been joined many times."

She tried to digest the thoughts he had put in her head.

"It's too soon, I am just learning how to be married..."

"I should have considered, we could have taken some precautions."

"I just never thought, I'm not ready, oh Richard, I'm not ready." She looked terrified.

Richard rubbed his jaw considering his words, "Luisa, if you really don't want to have a baby, you are not that far gone, there are herbs you can take."

"Herbs?"

"They will make your stomach ache and it will be like a bad mensis, but then there will be no baby."

She considered for a while, "What would you do, do you want a child?"

"I have a house full of children, for which I thank God. If you do not want the baby I'll understand, there is still time when you are ready."

She placed her hand on her stomach. "I cannot get used to the thought."

"The other thing to consider is that I am likely to die long before any child we have comes of age, you would have to raise them alone, till you remarry."

"No! No do not say such things, you are strong and healthy. Why should you die so soon?"

"Well maybe I won't but I have already lived a good span."

Luisa covered her ears.

"You do not have to decide anything for a week or two but if you want to use the herbs it must be soon. In the meantime perhaps I should send for Annie, she is the best midwife in the town, just to make sure."

Luisa barely nodded.

Annie was sure that Luisa was indeed with child. Richard asked her to say nothing, he said they wanted to wait until Luisa was a little further along before telling people. He knew that if Luisa decided to abort the baby that Annie would know what potion to brew, perhaps penny royal tea. She had quietly helped many women of the town who had too many mouths to feed, or who did not have a husband to support them. If found out she would have been heavily punished of course. It was late one night a week afterwards that Richard was sat reading by the light of the fire, or rather he was trying to read but his thoughts kept being distracted by the firelight. He heard a rustle of silk and Luisa came and sat at his feet and leant her head on his knee. She said nothing for a long time, hypnotised by the flames.

"I am going to have the baby. I thought about it and I can't kill it. If you should leave me I don't think I could bear it, but if I had your child it would be a comfort, not a burden."

"If that is what you desire, then that is what we shall do."

"I am scared."

"Come sit by me." She curled up beside him on the settle, her head in his lap as he stroked her hair.

"We will all look after you, you will have the best of care."

The weeks passed and Luisa stopped being sick and regained her usual rosy complexion. She was not yet showing so they had still kept the news to themselves but Richard knew he would have to tell the children they were going to have a new sibling and let Tamsin know she would be a grandmother.

"You tell the children and I'll talk to my mother."

"I'm sure the children will be appalled now they are old enough to understand how babies are made and your mother will come after me with a knife to remove my manhood."

"You have fought the Spanish, been a privateer and survived an attack by Indians but you are afraid of a tiny woman."

"But she is fierce, you know she is fierce."

He gathered the children together. Tom he would have to write to, he did not want him to get a shock when he arrived back at the end of the term.

"There is something I need to tell you."

"You are not going away again are you, Papa?" Jeanne looked upset.

"No, no not at all. I just wanted to let you know that you are, God willing, going to have a little brother or sister." He waited for a reaction. Antonio looked as if he could not quite follow the logic before screwing his face into a look of both surprise and disgust.

"Oh we know, Papa," said Jeanne

669

"You do?"

"Yes, Luisa is going to have a baby that is why she was so sick in the mornings. Didn't you realise, Papa?" said Lizzie

"Well I was not sure."

"Oh Papa," the girls sighed and shook their heads in despair.

"So you must not feel that any new baby will make me love you, any of you, the less."

"We know you love us all, Father," said Jacket, "even Antonio."

"Why would he not love me?" demanded Antonio

"Jacket, don't tease," said Richard as he lifted up his youngest boy, "You are really my favourite, Antonio, don't tell your brothers and sisters," he said in a stage whisper.

Chapter Ninety-One

Richard decided he should go and tell Tom in person. It would not be long before he came down for the long vacation and Richard thought they could travel back together, spending some time healing the rift between them. Jacket and two servants travelled with him as the company had some business interests in the Midlands and then Richard would travel back with Tom and his manservant. Jack wasn't at sea and agreed to watch out for his affairs whilst they were away. One thing he was concerned about was that there was no one yet who he felt could take over the running of their ships and Richard thought he should try and broach with Alice about William returning to the sea. The boy was still a great sailor despite his infirmity and longed to be at sea but he was confined to offshore fishing by his mother and new stepfather. Jack had taken on Luisa's younger brother Lawrence as an apprentice but he was a hothead and Jack complained about him vigorously. Richard was amused by this as he thought Lawrence had a lot of Jack's own characteristics.

The ride to Oxford was thankfully uneventful and Richard bade goodbye to Jacket at the gates of Queen's College.

"Normally I would suggest we all have dinner and a reunion Jacket but I need to be with Tom alone."

"I understand, Father, I'll see plenty of Tom over the summer. I have already told him he should stop moping and channel his heartbreak into his poetry, give him my love and best wishes."

Richard was enquiring from the college students where he might find his son when the college bursar sought him out and asked him to walk in the quadrangle for a moment.

"I take it Tom is in some sort of trouble?" Richard asked.

"Why would you think that?"

"You are a busy man, I'm sure you have better things to do with your time than take a stroll with the parent of one of your students."

"I have a pastoral interest in all my charges but you are right, I am concerned with Tom and he has been in some trouble this term."

Richard looked enquiringly.

"I am realistic, I know to have so many young men together without the influence of their families will inevitably lead to pranks. They tend to drink too much, are rowdy and upset the townspeople. But Tom although not an angel, he had a thirst for knowledge that meant his studies always came first. I have given him latitude because of his many talents but I worry about the path he is on. I have seen it in others who lose themselves in debauchery and waste what God has given them."

"Debauchery?!"

"Perhaps I over-egg the pudding, Sir Richard, but Tom is more often drunk in his lectures these days than he is sober, he had been caught in flagrante with unsuitable women of the town, he spends money like water on people who only pretend to be his friends and who will disappear when his purse is empty. It is such a marked change Sir Richard, I wondered if there was some underlying cause?"

Richard was embarrassed to have to speak of matters he thought private and personal, "Tom has been unsettled because of my recent marriage. That is why I have come here today, I thought we had overcome our difficulties but I had no idea how bad things were. His servant is meant to keep me informed of Tom's welfare but I have heard nothing of this."

"The man is very loyal to your boy. Tom is much loved by his true friends. Tell me, is this new wife worth the loss of your son?"

"You overstep yourself, sir. If you would direct me to Tom's lodgings–"

An usher took him to Tom's room, there was no answer to his knock but the door was not locked and Richard went in. The room was stale, curtains when drawn back revealed a rat's nest of books, clothes, upturned furniture, empty wine bottles, spilt ink, half-eaten meals. He eventually found Tom in a drunken stupor, his clothes stained with wine, food and vomit. A door opened behind him and Tom's manservant appeared carrying bread and other consumables. His jaw dropped and he turned pale at seeing Richard.

"Sir, we were not expecting–"

"Get this place cleaned up and open those windows." Richard found a pitcher of water and threw it over his son who woke with a start, spluttering and cursing till he saw his father.

"What are you doing here?"

"I have come for you and not a moment too soon. Get up and tidy yourself, you look like a vagrant who has spent all his time among the piss pots."

"Why do you care what I look like?"

"Oh no Tom, don't try that with me, I didn't bring you up to wallow in self-pity. Now clean yourself up, you are coming back to Southampton."

"And if I refuse to come?"

"I will truss you like a chicken and throw you over my horse for all your new friends to see."

"It's just like you to use force to get what you want."

"Well it's stood me in good stead all these years."

Tom stomped off and Richard turned back to the servant who was so completely intimidated he had lost all rational thought and was wandering around the room picking things up and putting them back down again.

"What are you doing? Put the dirty clothes in a pile there and get the laundry woman to have them cleaned. Throw all food and bottles into the waste pit, stand the furniture upright and when you can see what you are doing clean the place up. Where is Master Tom's trunk?"

The boy pointed to the corner where the trunk was hidden by discarded clothing. Richard pulled the trunk out and started to fill it with Tom's books and unsoiled clothes. Tom came back smelling fresher, with damp hair and a clean shirt and breeches.

"Don't blame Peter, Pa, he did his best."

"He should be dismissed." Peter sniffed loudly.

"He is his family's only breadwinner."

"Then perhaps he will learn to follow his orders in future." The boy dropped the boots and clothes he had been gathering. "Stop snivelling Peter, I am not going to dismiss you this time but take this as your one and only chance."

"Yes sir, thank you, sir."

They all worked to restore the room to order in silence. Richard then sent the boy to see to the horses, he wanted to be on the road quickly and take Tom somewhere else to talk to him. They travelled for a few hours to an inn on the Newbury Road and after they had eaten Richard took a deep breath and decided it was now he should speak to Tom.

"What happened, Tom? I thought you were reconciled."

"You were wrong."

"Tom, you must not let this ruin your life, you have so much to be thankful for."

"I don't see that."

674

"Tom, I would do anything to put this right. Would it help if you moved to another university or travelled to Europe?"

"There is only one thing that would help me."

"And what is that?"

"Give Luisa up."

"What?"

"Give her up."

"She would not turn to you, you know that."

"That doesn't matter, at least she would not be with you."

"Tom, you are being unreasonable."

"You keep saying how much you love me and that you consider yourself my father, so choose, her or me."

Richard said nothing for several minutes. "Very well, Tom, I choose you."

"What?"

"You heard me."

"You are just saying that to make me forgive you."

"I don't need your forgiveness, Tom, but if the only way I can have you back is to send Luisa away then that is what I will do. We will speak no more of this matter."

Richard got up and retired for the night.

The journey back to Southampton was too quick. Richard felt sick to his stomach but Tom was special to him, he could not tell him he was his real father because of the ancient oath he had made to Alice. For that reason he had always held back from showing his affections in case others might guess that Tom was his natural son. Sometimes he worried that Tom might have felt neglected so this was a grand gesture so he could show him how important he was to Richard. But what of that other child not yet born. What of Luisa? Their marriage was a mere arrangement but she did not deserve to be put aside like a worn out shoe. Perhaps he could buy a country house and install Luisa there. It was not unusual for husbands and wives to live apart in that way, if the husband had business in town and if the family were of the gentry. She would be taken care of, he could not visit of course, that would be his punishment. Perhaps in time Tom would come around. They had sent Peter on ahead so they were expected. There were hugs and greetings but Richard could not bear to continue the pretence. He sent everyone away except himself Tom and Luisa.

"Sweetheart, I need to speak to you. Tom has been very unhappy and I have promised him things will change."

"They will change, Tom, I promise," said Luisa. "We were always such great friends and I miss that so, I do understand how you feel truly I do, I know we cannot choose who we love."

"Why did you choose him?" Tom was sulky and it disfigured his handsome face.

"He is my hero."

"Because he fought the Spanish?"

"That is no small thing, Tom, but no, it is because he always looked out for me. He defended me against a man who threatened me when I was a child, he snatched me from beneath the hooves of a horse, when my Pa was a prisoner he just gathered us all up and looked after us, he did not have to and he went back to Spain to rescue my Pa—"

"Luisa, please, I am not a hero, nothing like—" Richard had not realized the impact of his actions so carelessly done.

"You are to me and more, my heart turns somersaults when you come into a room and it is as if all the air has been sucked out. I love it that you share with me the stories of your life, and when I am in your arms – I'm sorry Tom to cause you further pain but I ache for Richard in every possible way—"

"—Luisa, please, please say no more," Richard was finding it difficult to breathe. "Luisa, there is something I must do for Tom, he is my son..." Luisa looked confused and her hands went to her stomach, as the material from her dress was smoothed the gentle bump of her pregnancy became obvious.

"What is it, Richard?" There was fear in her eyes.

Just as Richard opened his mouth, Tom interjected, "Pa has agreed to help me, I want to, to turn some of his adventures into a play and it will mean he will have to spend more time with me and he was concerned...er ...that in your condition you might feel he should be at your side!" Tom finished in a rush, pleased at the quickness of his brain.

"Tom, that is wonderful." Luisa was embracing him, Tom was staring at his father over her shoulder and Richard was shaking his head at a loss at what to do or say, "Of course you must spend time with your father, it is a wonderful idea, you could present a masque as part of the festivities for the coronation. I could help with costumes if you would let me, I am so happy, I have been miserable at the pain I caused you." There were tears in her eyes.

"Oh don't worry yourself, there were plenty of girls in Oxford to take my mind from you," Luisa pulled away looking both shocked and eager for gossip.

"I should go and say a proper hello to Jeanne and Lizzie and throw Antonio out of my room." He moved away and Richard went after him to the foot of the stairs.

"Why didn't you tell me she was pregnant?"

"That was the main reason for my visit to Oxford, but when I found you in such despair how could I?"

"Would you really have left her for me?"

"Yes."

"You don't deserve her."

"No."

Tom ran up the stairs.

Chapter Ninety-Two

It was a gloriously sunny day and the town was alive with people out walking, market stalls heaved with produce, and everyone getting ready to celebrate the Coronation, it was if the whole country had breathed a huge sigh of relief. The shock of the Queen's death, the anticipation of a new reign for a new century, the worry about squabbles over succession leading to civil war, but in the end it had all been so smooth and easy and life went on as before. This was the day Luisa was finally confiding in her parents her happy news. They were all sat outside Richard's house in the sunshine. He had wandered into the square waiting for Luisa's sign that he should re-join them. The fish market was teeming with people and suddenly Richard found himself face to face with Alice. Of course she was bound to be there, George Parker was a main supplier of fish. It was the first time he had seen her since his wedding day.

"Alice, you are looking well."

"As are you, Richard, all puffed up and strolling around like a gentleman surveying his serfs."

"Don't be like that."

Alice shrugged and Richard glanced over to Luisa, her dark head was bent forward in close conversation. Alice was still stood in front of him, staring at him.

"It was well that we met, Alice, I wanted to talk to you about Will."

Her face turned to stone, "Will is no concern of yours."

"For ten years I was his father."

"George Parker is Will's father now."

"And I am sure he is a good one but I am still interested in him and his welfare."

Alice was livid and then on cue Will himself arrived, "Pa, I mean, er you are looking well." Richard clasped Will to him, "So are you, Will." He could feel the power in Will's arms. He was still the same sturdy, stocky boy he had known all these years. Richard stepped back and looked at him. "How is the leg, Will?" He tapped the wooden stump on the ground.

"It is well, I can do much everything, though these cobbles can be a bit of a devil."

"Your Uncle Jack and I were talking of you only recently, you should come for a visit. We have another ship—"

"—you do?" Will's eyes lit up

"The *Phoenix*—"

"Will, you should be helping out on the stall" Will was abashed.

"Sorry Mother, it was good to see you." He and Richard clasped one another again, ignoring Alice's obvious displeasure. Will hurried off at such a speed it was remarkable to know he had just one good leg.

"Don't you dare!"

"What?"

"Think to take him off to sea again, I will not have more harm come to my children because of you."

"That is unfair, Alice."

"Is it? How is Tom?" There was a nasty hint of smugness in her voice, "I see Luisa is blooming."

Richard glanced again at his wife who was nodding that he should join her.

"She is with child."

"I know. We will be able to share many intimate conversations about childbed."

"What do you mean?"

"I am with child also." She looked up at him in defiance.

Richard was concerned, "Is that a good idea?"

"What do you mean? Do you think me too old? Well perhaps I am compared to your child bride."

Richard ignored her barb, "It's just you have suffered so much and not had a healthy baby since Tom."

"Whose fault is that? Your bride wants you." She turned on her heel and strode off leaving Richard feeling he was, as always, in the wrong. He put back his shoulders and walked across to join Luisa and her parents.

"Good news, Diccon, I did not think to live to see my grandchildren!" John stood unsteadily and looking at his frail body Richard fervently prayed he would be around when Luisa delivered.

"I'm glad you are pleased John, we were a little shocked ourselves at first, but are very happy." He helped John to sit back down.

"Shocked?" said Tamsin. "Have you yet not learned how babies are conceived?"

"Keep forgetting, must be old age. So shall I get us some wine to toast health to our baby and my beautiful wife?"

"Mr Bathe!" Richard called out from the oriel window as the schoolmaster scurried beneath.

"Ah Sir Richard, good day to you, good day."

"Mr Bathe, could you spare a moment?" The schoolmaster hesitated for an instant but replied he could. Richard came down and met him in the hall and led him into an antechamber.

"Thank you Mr Bathe, I have been wanting to speak to you."

"Is it about Antonio?" Mr Bathe winced, "I try my utmost Sir Richard, I assure you I do."

"No it's not Antonio Mr Bathe, its Tom."

"Tom?" Mr Bathe looked concerned.

"He has not had a good term at Oxford, barely survived being sent down. I fear he has found my new marriage unsettling. To be truthful, he had a fondness for Luisa, my wife, himself, that neither of us were aware of until the moment of our marriage. I am sure you remember Mr Bathe what it was like to be sixteen and in love."

Mr Bathe did not look like he remembered any such thing. "The young take these things so seriously. I remember when I was in London a few years ago I went to see a new play, by a protégé of the Earl in fact, *Romeo and Juliet*. You would not believe how an affair of the heart could lead to such tragedy – and of course if they had waited they would no doubt have soon had their ardour tamed by the realities of marriage and in fact–"

"–Mr Bathe, if we may, Tom–"

"–Yes of course, forgive me."

"Mr Bathe, he always thought very highly of you as a teacher. I wondered whether you had some time to tutor him during the holidays, involve him in one of your plays–"

"Actually, I am preparing something for the Coronation celebrations."

"Excellent, Tom is out at present helping his brother Jacket at our warehouse on West Quay."

"Well I could go that way en route to my lodgings and engineer a meeting."

"Thank you Mr Bathe, I would appreciate it greatly."

They went back in the hall where he could hear a jabber of voices.

"Do you have foreigners in the house, Sir Richard?"

"No, that would be more peaceful, it is my children and indeed my wife."

"It is wonderful to have a house full of young people and laughter."

"They play a game where Luisa and Antonio speak only in Spanish and my girls reply in French and vice a versa, apparently it is utterly hilarious."

"If only Antonio would apply himself with such diligence to his Latin."

"Indeed it is a trial, Mr Bathe. Thank you again."

It was late, Richard stretched and rubbed his tired eyes, even with young Mr Dutton's help there was always so much paperwork, so much correspondence and Richard had to think carefully about words and his hand. He heard the front door bang and went to his office door, it was Tom. Luisa must have heard him also and came from the hall where she had been reading by the fire.

"You are late, Tom, you missed supper."

Tom gave Luisa a peck on the cheek, Richard was glad to see they were friends again, "Rehearsing, I want the play to be perfect, the topic is a bit dull and preachy but I have persuaded Mr Bathe to let me polish it a little."

"Tom, what are you up to?"

"You will have to wait for the Coronation Day celebrations to find out. Anyway, shouldn't you be resting, in your condition and everything?"

Luisa clasped her stomach; it was still impossible for most people to see she was pregnant, "I find I have boundless energy now the sickness is past."

"Are you happy to be …" Tom gestured at her belly.

"Well it did take me a little by surprise but I am happy, yes."

"Surprise? Luisa, you and Pa are like a pair of rabbits!"

There was a momentary silence. Richard his hand still on the handle of the door took a moment to react by which time Luisa had burst into laughter and Tom had joined her.

She hugged Tom, "You are wicked Tom. What can I say? We enjoy the married state."

"So you are glad that he and you…are together."

"I adore being married, your Pa is a wonderful man Tom, please forgive him."

Tom looked uneasy.

"You are both so alike."

"I don't know why, he is not my real father."

"But he raised you, Tom that counts for everything."

Tom did not want to have this discussion and abruptly changed the subject, "Did you save me any supper?"

"Of course, come."

Richard softly closed the door so they would not know they were overheard.

Later he mounted the stair to their chamber, he kept remembering Tom's comments about rabbits. Perhaps he was too demanding, feasting after years of famine, pleasuring himself, giving into his urges. Well what was wrong with that after all? Maybe he should teach his wife some of the tricks Jacinta had taught him. He thought about her hard, almost black eyes, the way she had writhed and scratched. He hadn't wanted to be married when all was said and done, so what was wrong getting some reward?

Luisa looked up as he came in, she was removing her pearl earrings. Her large, soft eyes almost melted with the love that shone out of them. She smiled, "Come and sit down Richard, let me help you out of your shoes, you must be weary, you have worked away for hours."

"I'm not a scholar; it takes me longer than most."

"You should have called Mr Dutton."

"He's more worn out than me most of the time, educating my girls is exhausting it seems."

"You should allow me to help you more, I have a good hand." Richard nodded.

"Is Tom home?"

"Yes, I saved his supper, I'm surprised you did not hear us laughing, I can barely repeat what he said!" She leaned close to him and whispered in Richard's ear.

"Rabbits!"

Luisa laughed again; she was knelt at his feet pulling off his shoes. "I am so embarrassed!"

Richard pulled her towards him, he was almost swept away with feelings of tenderness. She was no Jacinta to be used as a toy, if only she could have been Alice. "Rabbits."

"Rabbits."

Chapter Ninety-Three

Richard was working down at the store house with Jacket, Mudford Brothers was as busy as ever but more and more of their business was now based in London.

"We should set up a London office, Pa, Southampton is no longer the place to expand our enterprises."

"I know, I have been thinking the same, and you have to spend so much time on the road."

"I don't mind that but it would be a better use of my time if I had a proper base in the capital."

"Let's sort something out."

"Pa, is that Antonio?"

Antonio was running like the hounds of hell were behind him and arrived breathless at his father's side.

"Why aren't you at school?"

"Because it's over for the day, Pa! I was there all day!" Antonio spoke as if this was a great sacrifice. "I just got home and was going down to the kitchen when I heard Luisa calling for me."

"What?"

"She is locked in your counting house and said you must come, you alone."

Richard was confused but he took Antonio by the hand and they hurried back to the house.

"Go down to the kitchen, I'll see what is wrong." He knocked on the fastened door.

"Luisa, are you in there? Open up, it's Richard."

"Are you alone?"

"Of course, what's wrong?"

He heard the lock turn but the door did not open so he stepped forward and turned the handle himself. When he got into the room he found Luisa sat on the floor, her hair was dishevelled, her dress ripped to shreds and when she looked up at him he saw blood and bruising around her eyes and her lip was swollen.

"Dear God!" He shut the door behind him and knelt down at her side. She grasped hold of him.

"Richard, oh Richard, I am so glad you are come home."

"Sweetheart? What happened? Who did this to you?"

She swallowed hard and pulled away from him, he saw her dress had been cut from top to bottom and she clasped it trying to hide her modesty.

"It was Bart, Bart Biston."

Richard couldn't take in what she was saying, "Do you mean he attacked you?"

"He had been drinking; I don't think he quite knew what he was doing."

Feared gripped Richard, "Tell me what happened, no I need to get the physician–"

"No, you must not, I am bruised but that is all I am sure, I don't want anyone to know, please Richard, please."

"Tell me then briefly so I may decide what best to do."

"I was alone in the house, the servants were out about their work, Antonio was at school and Tom had gone to help Mr Bathe, the girls were with their grandmother. I was about my duties and he just appeared, he probably followed me home,

I had been to see my mother, perhaps I did not fully close the door. He started to confess his love for me, said he knew I felt the same – I don't, I have never given cause, never – I could tell he was worse for drink, I asked him to go but he would not."

Her voice was very low and she would not look at him. "And then he grabbed me and tried to kiss me and his hands touched me. I fought, I did fight him truly, but he hit me and I fell to the ground and he kicked me and I feared for the baby I curled up and begged him, I told him I was with child. He wouldn't listen, he called me a whore like my mother, said I led him on." She was crying now and Richard took her in his arms and tried to soothe her. He was deadly calm.

"I thought I must submit to stop the blows. He seemed to think that I wished him to …to…he cut my dress, he uncovered me, he got on top of me. He was trying to …. he was cursing ... I tried to blot it out, I turned my head away and I saw the logs by the fire, I stretched my fingers and grabbed one and I hit him on the side of the head. He rolled off but he was just stunned. I tried to think what to do, then I remembered the counting house had a strong door and lock – I ran in here – he followed me and banged and banged on the door – it went quiet and I heard nothing till Antonio came." She stopped and looked at him begging him to forgive her.

"I can't take this in – Luisa, has there been any blood, have you had pains in your stomach?"

"No, I think the baby is safe, that is the only reason I let him, I would have rather died otherwise."

"Ssh, ssh, you did well sweetheart, but you must let me fetch a doctor or the midwife–"

"No please, I don't want anyone else to know they will judge me. Can't you look after me Richard, please, please?" He didn't know what to do but she was so obviously terrified of anyone finding out what had happened.

"I need to take you upstairs and see what your injuries are, but if I judge they are beyond me I will send for help." She nodded.

Richard pulled her tattered clothes around her, picked her up and carried her to their bedchamber. He stoked up the fire before peeling off the remnants of her dress and sitting her on a stool in front of the flames. Besides the cuts and bruises to her face, there was bruising around her neck and bite marks on her breasts, the mark of a boot could be clearly seen on her hip and there was more bruising around her wrists. Her thighs were also bruised. Richard wet his lips which were suddenly very dry.

"Luisa, sweetheart, did he, did he penetrate you?" He held his breath; God only knew what whorehouse diseases Bart was riddled with. She shook her head and he let his breath out slowly.

"He was very ...small and bent and he couldn't...and he was trying...and that's when I hit him with the log." Part of Richard wanted to laugh.

"You are the bravest girl."

She broke down, "He kept calling me vile names, he said I encouraged him, please you have to believe me, he said I had been with many men, it's not true, it's not, please forgive me."

"I know, I know, I know you were innocent when you came to me, I know I was your first and that you have been faithful, I'm sorry I did not protect you, it is you who should forgive me." She became calm and he wrapped her in a blanket, he fetched his medicine box and used his skills with cuts and bruises to mix unguents, which he carefully rubbed into her skin. He also concocted a mild sleeping draft, made her drink it and then carried her to the bed.

"I can walk, Richard, really."

"I don't want you to. I want you to try and sleep. I will fetch a maid to sleep by the door and you must call her if you are in any pain—"

"Where will you be?"

"I am going to have Bart arrested and hung."

"No you can't! I would have to be examined, there will be witnesses called, they will point to my mother and say I am like her, I cannot bear the shame!" Her eyes pleaded with him and weakened his resolve.

"Sleep, no one will know what he has done, but I swear he will be punished."

Richard left the room and sent for the maid. He then fetched his outside cloak.

"What has happened, Father?" asked Jacket, who had been waiting for him.

"Bart Biston attacked Luisa."

"What? Why?"

"He doesn't need a reason, he is a nasty drunk."

"Where are you going? What will you do?"

"I am going to kill Bart Biston." Richard strode out of the door.

He went first to the Alderman's house. Since he had had some sort of reconciliation with his son born from booty, Bart had been taken back into the household. Richard thumped on the door demanding admittance. When the servant arrived to explain the family were at supper and not receiving guests, Richard just pushed him to one side and made for the hall. He kicked open the door. The family were like a frozen tableau, the Alderman held a chicken leg to his mouth, the grease oozing down his chin, Margaret was flustered and had dropped her spoon and William was mopping himself with his napkin, having dropped food in his lap in surprise at the intrusion. Only Joannie kept calmly picking at her food.

"Where is he?"

"How dare you burst in here like a ruffian!" exploded Biston.

"Where is he?"

"I don't know who you are talking about."

Richard strode to the table, picked up a fifth plate and threw it hard at the wall. It chipped the wall painting and clattered to the floor.

"I said, where is he?"

"Richard, please." Margaret's voice wavered and she was close to tears.

"Not this time, where is Bart?"

"He's not here."

"Liar!"

"How dare you speak to my wife like that you knave! Do you think I would pass up my son to you, you who corrupted him, you who forced him to marry a whore—"

"No, I am the person who took your son in when you disowned him. I offered him a trade and a home and rich dowry, it was me that provided him with the booty which restored him to your favour. Now where the hell is he?"

"Get out of here, I will have you arrested!"

"If anyone is to be arrested it will be Bart, and he will be hung."

Margaret screamed and Joannie smiled. Richard saw her eyes flick towards an arras. Richard marched across the room and tore it down, to reveal Bart cowering behind it. He scrambled across the floor, trying to reach Margaret..

"Come here you coward!" Richard drew his sword, "Do you want me to run you through whilst you snivel behind your mother's skirts." Margaret was by now hysterical; William had run to his father's side yelling at him to do something. His father told him to shut up.

"It is you who will hang, Mudford."

"As long as I take you all with me, I don't care."

Bart tried to make a run for the door but Joannie tripped him up. Richard threw down his sword so he could grab Bart by the collar and pound his fist into his face, breaking his nose and letting lose a spray of blood. Someone else ran into the hall and grabbed Richard. He thought it was one of the servants and went to shake him off, but stopped when he realised it was Jack.

"Let go of me, I need to kill Bart."

"Diccon, stop, he is not worth it."

"That may be your view but it's not mine."

"Your brother has gone insane! He broke in here and is intent on murdering us all."

"Don't be so bloody stupid Biston." Jack had Richard in a vice-like grip. "Help me get him out of here or I will kill you all myself." Servants had arrived and they handled Richard out of the banqueting hall. He was fighting like a madman.

"I will call the watch!" screamed the Alderman.

"You are a fool if you do. Bart has gone too far this time; it will be the gallows for him."

"I don't believe anything you have to say, Jack Mudford."

"As you will. So don't believe this, it was Bart who betrayed you to the Queen all those years ago, not Richard or me, and the proof is with Mr Secretary Cecil if you want to see it."

Alderman Biston was struggling to speak, he was spluttering and confused. Richard tried to break free once more hoping to take the moment to finish Bart off. Jack punched him in the face and everything went dark.

He came to in the Grave Maurice. He could feel his nose was swollen.

"Why did you stop me?"

"Didn't want to see you hung."

"How did you know where I was?"

"Jacket fetched me."

"I am going to disown that boy."

"He did the right thing; he said something about Bart attacking Luisa?"

"Oh God, Jack," Richard swallowed back a tear, "that poor girl, I have bought her nothing but misery, it is like all my past sins have come back to haunt me but she is the one being punished. He tried to rape her Jack,"

"Shit, did he...?"

"Couldn't get it up thank God. I shouldn't have married her, she has seen terrible things in her life and now this. She's seventeen, married to a man who doesn't love her but just uses her for his pleasure and she's pregnant."

"For Christ sake, Diccon, you think too much. There are plenty of girls in the town much younger than Luisa walking around with a full belly. It's a woman's lot. She's not starving like most and God knows why but she is happy with you, and you think more of her than you pretend."

"I need to go and kill Bart."

Jack put his hand on Richard's arm, "Leave it to me."

"What?"

"You heard me, stay out of it."

"It's for me to sort out."

"And it will be sorted out, I'm better at this stuff than you." Richard went to speak. "Leave it, Diccon."

It was just before dawn by the time he returned home. A sleepy doorman let him in; Jacket must have instigated more security for the house. He walked slowly through the hall and sat on the stairs uncertain what to do; he felt rather than heard someone approach him.

"Father!" Jacket was worried and Richard thought he saw in his face the little rat-faced boy he had once known.

"It's all right, Jacket."

"Father, you have not...that is... Bart..."

"He breathes still, if with difficulty. Don't worry, I just broke his nose your and Uncle Jack prevented me from going further."

Jacket sighed in relief.

"You should have not sent for him, Jacket."

"No Father, I did the right thing. If you had killed Bart – as you had the right to do – the Alderman would have twisted things and you would have ended on the gallows. He is a conniving man, he manipulates the law to his own ways, it has always been like that. I remember."

"You are probably right, go and get some sleep now, I promise I won't fetch my gun and Uncle Jack kept my sword, and say nothing about what has happened this day!"

Jacket nodded and wearily climbed the steps, "And you should sleep too, Father."

Before Richard could think of that he needed to check his family were all safe. He went first to the girls' room and gently opened the door. They were cuddled together in the large canopied bed, their room smelt sweet and was full of the trinkets girls loved, Antonio's room looked as if it was lived in by wolves, Tom's desk was strewn with papers and ink and quills, clothes tossed here and there, books all over the floor. The maid stirred as he reached the bedchamber he shared with Luisa.

"It's only me Peg, go back to sleep." He eased open the door, Luisa was still sleeping soundly, her lovely face discoloured with bruising. Richard undressed and lay on the bed. What would he do if Luisa's ordeal meant she could no longer enjoy their former intimacy? Would he turn eventually to others for comfort? He was a shit; he could not protect his own wife and was already dreaming of bedding whores. He slept fitfully. It was mid-morning when he awoke and he was alone in the bed. He reached for a gown, stumbled onto the landing and bumped into Peg.

"Where is your mistress?"

"She wanted to bathe." Peg obviously did not approve. "I have filled the tub in the antechamber and she is soothing herself." Richard was worried Peg might have thought he had beaten Luisa; it was after all something the Church preached men should do.

"You must take care of your mistress; she had a nasty fall yesterday whilst she was alone in the house." Peg looked guilty, thinking Richard was remonstrating with her for leaving Luisa alone.

"Don't be worried, Peg, it was not your fault. I just ask you watch over her for me when I am at my work."

"Yes, sir."

Richard knocked softly on the door to the antechamber.

"Luisa? It's Richard may I come in?"

"Yes of course."

She lay in the wooden tub that was lined with fine linen; Richard could smell the aroma of violets. He went and kissed her damp hair it smelt of broom and lavender. Oats in muslin bags floated in the water to soften the skin.

"How is my girl this morning?"

"I am feeling better Richard; I just had an overwhelming need to scrub myself clean."

He drew his finger around the line of her chin.

"You have the most gloriously black eye; Peg almost accused me of beating you."

"No! I did not think—"

"—don't worry, I told her you had had a fall and that in future she must keep a better eye on you."

"Poor Peg."

"Your lip is still swollen but I don't think there will be a scar, the marks will start to fade soon. Are there scars I can't treat, Luisa?"

"I am not going to let Bart ruin things for me or for us, Richard. I decided that last night. Richard, you did not do anything rash did you?"

He stood up and paced a while, "I meant to kill him, I thought it through quite calmly, it was the obvious thing to do but Jack of all people stopped me."

"I'm glad. I would not want to be the cause of you having blood on your hands."

"He deserves death, Luisa, that is all there is too it. However, I promise you it will not be by my hand."

She shifted slightly, "Will you help me out of the tub please?"

He offered his hand and she rose out of the tub. Despite the marks and wheals on her skin she looked like Aphrodite rising from the waves.

"God, you are beautiful. I would like to have you painted, just like this," Richard blurted out.

"Naked!" Luisa was visibly shocked.

"For my eyes only of course."

"Why would you want a painting when you have the real thing?"

"That is true," he said as he wrapped her in a sheet.

"He uncovered my nakedness." Her voice shook, she could scarcely believe that such a thing happened.

"I know, sweetheart."

"He saw what only my husband should see." Her head was bowed and she clutched at the sheet.

"Luisa, look at me." She slowly raised her head, "He did not see what I see, do you understand what I say?"

She smiled faintly and sighed as she continued to gaze into his eyes. "Make love to me," she asked in a whisper, so uncertain was she of his response.

"Are you sure, sweetheart?"

"All I can think about is the weight of his body upon me. I don't want to have that feeling; it's you I want to feel."

"Oh sweetheart, I was fearful that after your ordeal you would not want to lie with me again."

"I was just so scared you would turn from me because I had been used by another man." They both knew that he would not have been judged if he had turned her out of the house. He kissed the tip of her nose and held her very close.

He was as kind and gentle as he knew how to be, and although it was hard for him he spoke to her and told her what he saw, his dear wife, who showed him such tenderness, whose trust and innocence almost overpowered him. She winced at his touch, though she tried to hide it.

"Please Luisa, I can't, I'm hurting you, I can't even kiss you for fear of bruising your lips still further." She looked distraught. "Here I will kiss your neck here, that special spot that only I know makes you tingle. And I will hold you close, and when you are healed I promise I will come to you. I promise." She nodded and began to cry like her heart was breaking until she was exhausted and fell asleep. Whilst she slept he slipped away and gathered the children and told them the tale of the fall and the bruises received, which they pretended to believe. Antonio went and curled up with Luisa, he was forgiven school. When she woke at midday he had the servants make her favourites, frumenty and syllabub, and Richard read to her and showed her card tricks learnt long ago from his father. Luisa insisted that on the morrow all should return to normal, but she jumped at any noise and was fearful that Bart would have boasted of his deed, twisting the truth. Richard knew she was torturing herself with the thought that she had let another man see her body, that what had happened was a mockery of what occurred between her and husband.

Chapter Ninety-Four

She was sat on a bench in the courtyard, a faraway look on her face; her arms cradled her stomach as if she was trying to comfort her unborn child. Richard went and sat behind her, straddling the stone bench so that he could wrap his arms around her and place his hands over hers.

"I think the baby is safe, no I'm sure, everything feels the same, I would know."

"Of course, sweetheart." He kissed her temple and tried not to think of Annie's boy, a simpleton, whose problems, Richard thought, must have been caused by the beatings Bart had given Annie when she was pregnant.

"I was wondering if there was anything I did, that made him think, unknowingly—"

He held her face in his hand. "I will never forgive myself that you were alone and unprotected in your own home. You have nothing to reproach yourself with. Nothing."

"I thought it would be all right to let myself be pretty once I was married, I tried to hide myself before but I wanted to be pretty for you. But...but... I am a daughter of Eve—"

"Luisa, I do not understand all this arguing about religion, all the interpretations men put on God's word, but I do understand men, and their urges. Some try to blame women for them, most of us try to, well, take our pleasures but what Bart did was wrong, and you are not to blame."

"Did I wish for too much? To rise above my base origins? I wish I was more worthy, Richard, a woman of quality."

"You have many qualities, sweetheart, you have noble blood coursing through your veins." He traced the blue vein that ran across her wrist. "I'm just a poor boy from the Shambles." He rocked her gently. "And you are beautiful and please my eyes."

"My tears have cleansed me, I will be well now, I promise." She said as she leant against him, sinking deeper into his arms. "And you did protect me, if I had still been at the inn, I would have been ruined."

Richard delicately rubbed more of the salve into Luisa's bruises. Outwardly she seemed to be coping well but he knew she worried about the thought of leaving the house. She was frightened of coming face to face with Bart, she worried what he may have said about her around the town, so she hid herself away and Richard wondered if he would ever persuade her to step outside.

"They are coming out sweetheart, it may appear unpleasant but that is a good thing." He looked steadily into her face. "Luisa, I'm...I'm not much for reflection, and mostly worry about what is good for me, but I have been thinking, I er, I did not treat you much better than Biston on our wedding night."

She went to speak and he gently put a finger to her lips. "I just was concerned with my own feelings and bruised ego and gave no thought to you at all, no thought. It is not in my power to turn back time. I wish I could give you a potion to make you forget so I could come to you again and...I just wanted you to know."

"I do. I put myself there, Richard, you did not force me, you are not Bart. You did realise and have been most tender and caring of me since that night."

"You are too understanding, Luisa, but I thank you." She leaned in closer to him and spoke almost in a whisper he could barely hear her.

"When I was growing up I could not understand why women would spit at my mother in the street, why children would call me names. When I got older I didn't like the way some men looked at me licking their lips and asking if my mother had schooled me in her skills. When I was at market men would press themselves against me in the crowd, one of the men who came to the inn would expose himself when no one else could see but I. But you always treated me like I was a lady, you made me feel I could be a lady."

"Ssh don't talk of those things," Richard was appalled. "I'm sorry, you should have spoken to me when you were being tormented so, I could have done something."

"No I could not; I did not want you to look upon me differently." Richard bit his lip, hadn't he, hadn't he used her? She must have read something in his face.

"Richard you have made me a lady and a woman I don't want to be anywhere else."

He met Jack at the Grave Maurice. They sat hunched over their mugs of beer, speaking in whispers, eyes darting about, their body language making it clear none should sit too close.

"I had a message from Joannie," said Jack.

"Joannie?"

"She is perhaps my girl after all, looking after number one."

"What do you mean?"

"Well with Bart reconciled with his father, young William would have had to share the inheritance. Joannie wants Bart out of the way just as much as you."

"And?"

"He has been given money and smuggled out of the town, he is going to Poole."

"Poole?" Richard thought for a while, "Of course, Margaret has family connections there, old Alderman Crooke was from Poole."

"So, we should wait awhile, let them think all if forgotten if not forgiven. I don't want any fingers pointed at us and after your little display the other night–"

"If you say so."

"I do."

"At least Luisa will be relieved, she has been so afraid of seeing Bart again. She worried going about the town in case their paths crossed and she was a-feared that he would speak of what happened."

"Luckily he is a coward. I have heard of no boasts he has made." Richard nodded, he knew his brother would make sure Bart never had the chance to besmirch Luisa's reputation in the way he had her body.

"Right, I need to go and see John and Tamsin." Richard stood.

"Why?"

"They will wonder why Luisa hasn't been to see them and I don't want Tamsin to come storming in, see the state of her daughter and shoot me."

"How much are you going to tell them?"

"Don't know." Richard clasped his brother to him and then made his way out of the inn.

Richard was in his counting house, moving his counters across his board, quickly flicking them as he made his calculations. He picked up his pen and dipped it in the ink and scratched the numbers in his ledger. He heard raised voices in the hall and his heart sank as he recognised one as Tamsin. She wrenched open the door of his office and strode into the room. She stopped before his desk her legs planted astride and hands firmly planted on her waist, waiting for him to look up and acknowledge her presence. Richard's pen moved down the column of figures and he initialled the account, he just stopped himself cursing out loud as the ink blotted on the page.

"Can I help you Tamsin?" he asked without looking up but turning the page of the ledger.

"What happened to Luisa?"

"Did I not tell you? Did she not explain? She tripped and had a nasty fall. It shook her up, frightened her, but did no serious damage. She has just to rest-"

"-a fall? Do you think I of all people would not recognise the mark of a man's fist?"

Richard said nothing for a while, running over his options. It was clear Luisa did not want her mother to know the truth about her injuries. She was probably correct, Tamsin would undoubtedly storm across to Biston's house yelling and causing a scene, exactly the opposite of what Luisa wanted. She would do more harm than good. Richard put down his pen and reached for his blotter and started to clean the nib.

"Luisa had a bad fall. She was shaken, she is bruised but she will recover. There is nothing more that I can tell you Tamsin." He could feel her displeasure.

"I know what you have done. You will pay for this." She swept his inkpot off the table and marched out.

Chapter Ninety-Five

"Luisa, I have been thinking about the future."

Luisa was lying on the couch on plumped up cushions and Richard was rubbing her swollen ankles. Jeanne sat in the oriel window stitching at a christening robe for the awaited new baby. Lizzie was reading one of Richard's battered books, Grafton's *Chronicles of England.* Copies of Cicero and Homer lay at her feet. Sun was streaming through the windows catching floating dust in the beams.

"The future?"

"I realised that if you were to deliver of a son he would be my only legitimate male heir."

"I don't understand."

"Jacket was taken in by Alice and I became his father by default, there is Will of course who is my stepson. I am probably Antonio's father but it's just as likely that I am not, and in either case was never married to his mother, but on the other hand most of my money was rescued from his mother. The girls are all mine of course and besides what I will leave them, they will have their own inheritance."

"And Tom?"

"He, well everyone knows he was a foundling," Richard muttered.

"Richard, I know Tom is your son," Luisa said in a whisper.

"What?!" The girls looked up and Richard lowered his voice, "What?"

"People would say things around me when I was child, I was quiet and most of the time I think they would forget I was there. So I know Alice is really Tom's mother and you are his father. I have never understood why Alice would not recognise him."

"I wanted to, do you know that?"

She nodded, "Alice and her reputation. It is so sad. It would make all the difference in the world for Tom to know."

"It's probably too late now."

"I still don't understand what you are saying Richard."

"Should I leave the bulk of my estate to the child who in law will be my legitimate heir?" He stroked her belly.

Luisa considered his words and her brow furrowed, "That is not right, Richard, it is your money to do with as you will, but if I hold any sway with you I would say treat them all the same."

"You amaze me, Luisa. Many women would fight for their own."

"I know what it is like to be abandoned by my father and be brought up by someone else who loved me as a parent should and never treated me different from his own."

"There is something else you should know. The founding of my fortune was based on a jewel given to me by your real father. It was his intention I should look after you, though I am not sure this is what he had in mind."

"You knew my real father?" Luisa felt a thrill of excitement.

"Yes, I thought you realised."

"No, that was one thing that was never talked of. Will you tell me about him?"

"If you wish."

"He will not take Pa's place of course but I am happy to

think he may have cared for me, even just a little. And I do mean what I said, all the same...besides we may have a little girl."

"No please! I am in torment about all the young men circling around Lizzie and Jeanne, I could not do that again!"

They were interrupted as Antonio, Sam and Tom burst into the room.

"Antonio! That is my best dress!" screamed Lizzie.

"I had to wear something, I am to be the Fair Josian."

"And I am to be Ascupart," said Sam.

"Ascupart is thirty feet tall," argued Lizzie.

"But he comes from the East and so does Sam," said Antonio.

"Sam was born in the West in the Americas," put in Jeanne, "and Ascupart was from the Turkish lands, everyone knows that."

"Well I am writing this play," said Tom, "and all actors can convince their audience that they are from China if they're any good."

"I am going to tie barrels to my feet," said Sam.

"Now be quiet everyone. I am taking the role of Sir Bevis and we shall act for you the story of how Bevis vanquished Ascupart and won the hand of the Fair Josian."

Sam complained about being vanquished when he was a giant and Antonio swirled around in Lizzie's dress trying to look coy.

"Why can't I play Josian?" said Lizzie.

"Because you are a girl, now be quiet," retorted Tom.

"I hope you don't want any more children," muttered Richard and he kissed Luisa's ankle.

Richard was at the loft in Pigeon House. He was daydreaming rather than working thinking of Luisa. He had lived alone for so long and had never thought to be a husband again, to share a bed with someone every night. It felt strange because in so many ways he still considered himself married to Alice, but she had another completely different life across the river with another man, in another house. Parker was ten years younger than Alice but she was a good catch for him, still a handsome woman, shrewd at business, fruitful, and with a good dower thanks to him.

"Am I interrupting?"

"Joannie!" Richard almost tumbled off his chair as he had leant back precariously whilst his thoughts had jumped about. "What brings you here?"

He never saw Joannie, she was not one to visit.

"Am I not to be offered a seat?"

Richard leapt up and removed some boxes from the chair usually occupied by Jacket. "Wine?"

She nodded, he dusted off two glasses and poured a glass of sac for them both.

"It is a pleasure to see you Joannie."

"No it isn't, I am just here on a matter of business that concerns us both."

Richard waited for her to continue. She sipped the wine and nodded approvingly, her tastes must have improved somewhat during her time with the Bistons.

"I am in mourning."

She didn't look very sad, "Has something happened to William?"

"Don't be so dense. My dearest brother-in-law is dead."

"Bart!" Richard felt a tingle up his spine.

"Oh please don't feign surprise."

"What happened?"

"He was at an inn, drinking, playing cards, well to be more accurate cheating at cards, one of his companions objected to being duped, there was a brawl and poor, dear Bart was stabbed in the eye. Fatally." Joannie finished her wine and delicately

705

mopped her mouth with a kerchief. She rose and made to leave. "The Bistons are not a pleasant family but Bart was the worst. My regards to your wife." And with that she left the loft.

The news did not make much of a ripple in the town; Bart was known to be a bad lot, always destined for a sorry end. His parents were deserving of pity. Thank the Lord that William was such a credit to his family. Luisa confessed herself to be relieved but felt guilty about rejoicing in the death of another. Only Annie cried. She always thought Bart would come back, any knowledge she had of his evil ways was immediately forgotten and thereafter she always spoke of him as a fallen hero.

Richard and Jack took a drink in the Grave Maurice. "I thought you would like the poetic nature of his demise," said Jack and they raised their glasses.

Chapter Ninety-Six

"Mr Dutton? How may I help you?"

"I thought, sir, you may wish for me to report Sir, that is, on the progress of Miss Jeanne and Miss Elizabeth."

"They progress do they, Mr Dutton?"

"Oh yes, sir, I say this not to puff up myself, I hope you... That is I would not want... Miss Jeanne does wonderfully well in her studies of divinity, her composition of prayers – she has a fine hand – and she is most excellent at mathematical problems – I think her love of music. And Miss Elizabeth is voracious in the study of history, she is a prodigious reader. They both excel in Latin and Miss Elizabeth is making strides in Greek and Lady Mudford–"

"–Lady Mudford?"

"Er, yes that is, her Ladyship still joins us that is, when she can and she begs me for work to study privately."

"I see, and what is her Ladyship's forte?"

"She is most interested in the study of geography and the foreign lands, poetry and the drama, she wishes to have more conversation, that is she, er she er, wishes to be...that is an ornament to your household."

"Ah, well I see I shall have to take lessons myself, Mr Dutton, or all my girls will have the besting of me and then I shall be lost."

Mr Dutton gave a nervous laugh.

"Mr Dutton, you may purchase some books for me on the history of Spain and Portugal, any philosophical or poetical writings that you think relevant. My wife has both Portuguese and Spanish relatives, as does my son Antonio, and I would like them to know something of those lands – other than what is commonly talked of."

"Yes, Sir Richard, and perhaps I could purchase some music books, Miss Jeanne needs more of a challenge."

Richard nodded and wondered if Mr Dutton was becoming a little partial to Miss Jeanne.

Richard clapped John on the back as he coughed and wheezed.

"Not so heavy, you will break a rib," John spluttered.

"There's a fug in here. Why don't we sit outside in the sunshine?"

"I still feel a chill in the air, I would rather be by the fire."

John hunched over and started to stuff more tobacco weed into his long-stemmed pipe. Richard looked up as he heard Luisa laugh, she was in the backroom with her mother and brothers, he wished she would hurry so they could leave.

"My girl's blooming," rasped John, "growing a child in her belly suits her."

"She carries it well," muttered Richard studying his boots, he was uneasy having these conversations with John.

"You marrying her was the right thing to do, she was born to be a lady. She tells me you are good to her."

"I try my best." Richard stared at the curtained opening, willing Luisa to come through it.

"And she? Does she service your needs?"

"For God's sake John, she's not a horse. Let's talk of something else."

"I just know how it was with you and Alice."

"What do you mean 'how it was'?"

"Well you were so in love with her and something in you died when she left. I know it isn't the same – you and Luisa – but at least if you are compatible beneath the sheets–"

"Enough!" Richard went to the bar, refilled his cup and drank off a draught. "I was thinking perhaps Philip should go to school."

"What will he need with school?"

. "He seems bright enough. Lawrence will make his way at sea and Little John seems to enjoy learning about beer brewing. So how will Philip find his way in the world?"

"He is barely out of his toddler's bands."

"He is running around with his own little gang of ruffians, if he filches something off the wrong market stall he will find himself in the stocks or worse."

"I think Luisa has all the cleverness in the family, things have gone a bit awry since she isn't here to manage them. I can't see school quietening down Philip, perhaps I'll send him back to Itchen Ferry."

"To be a fisherman or a smuggler?" John merely smiled.

Luisa emerged shortly after and they strolled out of the Angel. "It's such a lovely evening would you like to step out?" Richard asked his wife.

"Oh yes."

They walked to the quay, arm in arm and looked at the ships, they sat awhile with Berta and Sam watching the activity on the dock and Richard pointed out the different vessels and where they were from. They called in at the warehouse and Jacket showed them their latest goods, Luisa chose some Dutch tiles to decorate the kitchen. They went out of the little Friary Gate, past the bowling green and paused to greet Lawrence,

Richard promising him a game of tennis on the morrow. They wandered through the meadows and orchards and spoke of poetry, they walked by the river where the ferry boats bobbed, and Richard told her how his father had taught him to swim by throwing him into the river and not letting him out till he learnt.

"Richard, my mother–" he groaned, "–don't!" she said giving him a gentle pinch. "She has been preparing me for the months ahead."

"She hasn't been frightening you, has she?"

"No she said ignorance was a blessing, but she did tell me that when I get too large, which will be soon, that you might wish to, that is if you need to, if you have needs, then I will understand."

Richard didn't say anything for a while as they continued to stroll, "Do you think that little of me?"

"No! No of course not but I know that I am not very tutored in the ways of the world."

"And how would you really feel if I left the side of my pregnant wife and took my solace elsewhere?"

It was her turn to walk for a while before she spoke. "I would be heartbroken."

"Then it is just as well that you have spoilt me for anyone else." She stood stock still.

"Are you making fun of me?"

"No." She smiled and they walked on.

They organised a great party for the coronation but only invited the people they liked, Jack and Berta of course and John and Tamsin and their children, Lawrence Prowse and his wife and family, Mr Bathe, the young chaplain, Mr Dutton, Madame Sohier and other Sohier relatives, Alice and George Parker so that Will might attend, and John's ancient mother along with a few of her more respectable relations. There were also some of the burgesses and gentlemen of the town who had not been unpleasant to Luisa, the old sergeant Foxe, captains of their ships, their lawyer, the goldsmith and apothecary, and merchants and traders with whom they did business. In the courtyard they laid out food and provided entertainment for servants past and present, Annie came with her boy, along with some of Richard's old neighbours from the Silkshop Yard days.

Tom was their Master of the Revels and had all the daughters of the town swooning after him. Jacket used the occasion to cement business deals old and new. Jack continued to drink his wine without water and Berta looked down loftily at the people of the town. Antonio made himself captain of the younger children and organised raids on the food and stole wine out of glasses temporarily abandoned by their owners. Jack was dancing with Luisa, they were smiling and laughing, others clapped and cheered them on. Luisa was radiant, dressed in a new gown that contrasted yet complemented the new gowns it was essential for Jeanne and Lizzie to have. Alice on the other hand was obviously having a bad pregnancy. She sat in the corner until she could excuse herself and leave, she was pale and her eyes were shadowed, her lips had no colour. Richard watched her studying Luisa, she must have felt his eyes upon her and she stared at him raising her chin in challenge. He strolled over to where she sat.

"How are you, Alice?"

Her eyes flicked again to Luisa "I cannot compete with the child bride. Did I ever have that much energy when I was with child?"

Richard ignored her barb, "All women are different." She gave him a look as if to say he would know. "Some need to rest and care for themselves."

"Are you suggesting I am not cared for?"

"No, I'm sorry I should not have come over, I just hoped.... The children are pleased to see you."

She sighed, "George is fetching my cloak, it is a grand celebration but I should go home."

"Of course, I am pleased that you came...and George of course," he lied deftly.

"I barely recognise the house."

"Well, I wanted Luisa to feel that this was truly her home too."

Her eyes flashed and he saw the Alice of old for a brief moment, then Parker appeared. Richard bowed, he did not think it appropriate to kiss Alice's cheek.

Jack was at his side. "I remember Alice when we were growing up, paddling in the river, making eyes at William Dypere." Richard looked at him, Jack did not do sentiment. "We have all changed so much since then. Alice stayed the same."

"What's your point Jack? Is this about Luisa?" Richard sighed, took a draft of wine and wished people would stop interfering in his life. Luisa was dancing with Tom. They made an attractive couple, surely that was the match that should have been made.

"I have a good feeling about this new reign, Diccon, new opportunities for the Mudford boys," said Jack, his face a bit flushed.

"I think you may be right but I still miss old Bess. I know I'm a fool but I always thought our fate was intertwined and I feel a bit lost without her."

"You are a fool, but I still love you best in all the world."

"More than Sam?"

"Mmm, low blow brother, you share my affections. I'm thinking maybe I should go to Africa, let Sam meet his relatives."

"Sam knows nothing of Africa, accept what his ma tells him."

"But I worry what will happen to him if we stay here, or rather if I should die. I don't trust his sister not to steal his inheritance and turn out her stepmother."

"You're right there. I was thinking what would happen to my brood if I went. Jacket is a good steady boy and would look out for them but he's not ruthless like you and I, Jack, they are all so young."

"Well we have good lawyers and let's hope one of us sees them through to their majority, that's all we can hope for." Jack raised his glass, "To King James."

"King James."

It was the early hours of the morning after the guests had left, the house a swirl of debris and chaos. Luisa glided through exuding calm and charm, supervising the servants about what was to be done now and what could be left till the morrow. Everyone was merry having enjoyed the celebrations despite all the work. Luisa had ensured the servants received a gift of money to thank them for their extra efforts and some food to take home to their families to spread the commemorations further.

Richard sat by the embers of the fire, draining his glass. He saw Luisa walk by. "Come sit with me, you should not tire yourself."

She came and sat by his side. She was dressed in gorgeous shade of light blue and silver that suited her dark colouring and accentuated her eyes. "I'm not tired really, it was such a wonderful evening. I am so happy."

"Are you, sweetheart? Are you truly happy?"

"Of course, how can you doubt it?" She kissed him briefly on the cheek and sat back putting her beautifully shaped feet in their embroidered slippers, onto a footstool.

"What did you hope for from life, Luisa?"

She looked at him strangely for a while trying to understand his meaning, "When I young, I hoped I would not know hunger, that I would have a roof over my head and clothes on my back. I hoped that I would marry a kind man who would not beat me and we would be happy."

"It seems a small thing to want."

"It is what most people wish for. But I have been very lucky

713

and have lived a much better life than many. I've not had to work myself into an early grave, I have been given the gift of reading and writing and tried to use those to make myself a more educated woman. And I am thankful for the goodness of others to me and hope to follow their example and do good turns for others, but I could never have believed I would be so, so blessed to have you as my husband."

"You shame me, Luisa, I am not such a great catch."

"How can you speak of yourself so? You know I think you handsome, and you are strong, brave and hard working. You have made your own place in this world, you are a cultured man and you have done all these things yourself. And more importantly, you are so kind and so caring, looking after your friends and family. You were the only one who helped Alderman Crooke—"

"He was very good to me, I would be nothing without him."

"And you paid him back; you never forgot your friends from the Yard."

"They helped me when I had need, what else would anyone do?"

"Oh Richard," she laid her head on his shoulder.

"I have not been so good to the women in my life, Luisa. My first wife loathed me and wished me dead, my second would rather imperil her immortal soul than live with me and my lover hated me so much she sacrificed our son. What will I do to you, Luisa?"

"Nothing, nothing, you have honoured me by sharing your life and your home, you could have chosen anyone and you took me." Of course he had not chosen.

"You don't owe me anything Luisa." She gazed at him with such love in her eyes that he had to look away. She did not profess her love in words anymore because she knew it made him uneasy, but it was so clear to see it gave him a physical pain in his heart.

"But I hope I may give you something, help you to open up to life once more, you are so dashing when you smile and when you laugh!" she said.

Richard smiled, "And you have the most lovely dimples," he leaned in close and whispered, "on all your cheeks." She blushed prettily. "So you say you are not too tired?"

"No I am not tired at all," she said.

Chapter Ninety-Seven

"Papa?" said Jeanne, Lizzie hovering behind her.

"Yes, Jeanne?"

"I have written this prayer, Mr Dutton thinks it is well done. I thought I might copy it out in my best hand and give it as a New Year present to Grand-mère."

"May I read it?"

Jeanne nodded and Richard glanced quickly over the work, it was neat and well phrased.

"It seems Mr Dutton is earning his salary Jeanne, this is very fine and your grandmother will appreciate it greatly."

"Thank you, Papa."

"Jeanne is becoming so studious, Papa, she will have to start wearing glasses," exclaimed Lizzie.

"Papa has been good to give us a tutor and we must repay him by studying hard."

"I do not think you find it hard being in Mr Dutton's company."

"Mr Dutton is very kind and a good teacher." Jeanne was blushing and becoming tearful.

"Lizzie don't tease," said Richard, pulling her ringlets, "I hope you are doing as well as your sister."

"Better, Papa!" laughed Lizzie, "I am reading Greek now as well as Latin."

"So I understand," said Richard.

"Here, Papa, let me show you."

Richard and Lizzie poured over her books. Richard was envious of his daughter. He would have liked to have been able to read Greek. He looked up to say something to Jeanne but she had disappeared, leaving the copy of her prayer where it had fallen on the floor.

Richard caught Luisa looking at herself in the glass hung on the wall of their bedchamber, she was stood sideways studying the size of her bump and pouting.

"You are so lovely, even more so with our child inside you. Here, I will rub your skin with oils, it will help where it is stretched." He reached for his medicine box and mixed some oils together. He lifted her shift and gently rubbed in the oils and soon found himself distracted. They broke apart from their embrace. Richard reached for the oils and began again to smooth them into Luisa's skin.

"How did you learn?"

"Learn what?"

"To give a woman...pleasure."

"Well I have been married three times!" Richard murmured and flexed his muscles.

"I don't think all men are the same."

"Do you not wife? And how pray do you know that?" He raised his brows dramatically.

"When I chat with my gossips—"

"You talk of me? Of us?" Richard was shocked. He stopped his task and stared at her.

"Only in a general way, but some of the women.... Well

717

I think I am luckier than most." She indicated that he should carry on.

He kissed her gently, "I am pleased to hear it." She was still looking at him questioning.

"When I was young, still a boy in fact, I knew a girl, she was older than I and earned her living..."

He paused but Luisa nodded in understanding. Richard put away the bottle and thought backwards.

"She was my first...I think she felt sorry for me... Well the first time we...I had a grand time but she was not so impressed," he grimaced.

"Don't be embarrassed."

"It was embarrassing, more so when I think of it now. Anyway, she taught me a few things so that I would be popular... with women..." he shrugged and winked.

"Well I thank her. What became of her?" Luisa sat up and wound her arms around his neck.

"She died. Was killed." Richard had not thought of those days for so long. He remembered how angry and jealous he had been at those who had used and abused poor Martina, men like Biston.

Luisa pulled away eyes wide, "Do you mean murdered?"

Richard nodded. "I was distraught. It was rumoured to be one of her clients, she was only your age."

"Poor girl."

"I thought I could bring the man who did it to justice, but there is little to be had when you are poor and lowly. It spurred me on to better myself, to get enough money and influence to protect me and mine, even if I had to bend the law to do it."

"I have heard tell you were a reckless youth, Alderman Crooke's henchman."

"I can see I will have to ban your gossips from the house, I did not realise I was such a topic of interest." Richard was genuinely bemused.

"I like to hear stories about you."

"Mmmm." Richard thought the whole truth would be much more shocking.

Richard wandered around the hall looking at the paintings of his children and planning where to put Luisa's. God willing there would soon be another to place. He realised how quickly his children were growing and how they were no longer the little people in the paintings but now on the verge of adulthood.

"Papa, what is that tune you were humming?" asked Jeanne.

"Was I humming Jeanne? I did not realise."

"It was something like this," and Jeanne repeated the notes.

"Ah that was a song I used to hear in Spain," and he sang a few words. "I can't remember exactly how it went on."

"Papa, might you teach me the guitar?"

"The guitar?" It had lain silent for a while as Richard had not been able to stir enough interest in Antonio.

"If you are not working this morning, I could fetch it, Papa."

Richard hesitated for a moment, "Very well, Jeanne. Where is your sister?"

"She is in the courtyard," said Jeanne the happy lilt in her voice vanishing.

"If you want to call her and fetch the guitar we will begin our lesson."

Jeanne went to say something but hesitated and turned away, slowly walking towards the courtyard.

Richard kicked himself for being such an idiot, "Jeanne!"

"Yes, Papa?"

"Would you mind very much if it was just you and I to have the guitar lesson? Lizzie is not as musical as we are and I fear she might hold us back."

"Well there is that, Papa, I don't think Lizzie would mind, she would rather read a book."

719

"You are right of course Jeanne. Quick now, fetch the guitar."

"Yes, Papa!" Jeanne beamed and ran off.

They sat in the oriel window and Richard showed his elder daughter how to place her fingers. She picked up the basics very quickly.

"Jeanne, you will soon pass me by, I shall have to find you a proper teacher!"

Jeanne produced a wrong note, "Oh no Papa, see, I have a long way to go, I think we shall have to have many lessons before I am ready for that."

Richard smiled silently, "Well it does no good to rush these things. We must work on some pieces that we can play for the new baby, as a present from their very clever sister."

Jeanne blushed, "Thank you for helping me Papa, I know you are so very busy."

"Jeanne, I will never be too busy to sit awhile with my eldest daughter."

"Shall we try these chords again?"

They practised for nearly an hour, until Richard was sent for to deal with some issues over a new order with the Silkshop weavers.

Richard's muscles ached but satisfyingly, muscles that reminded him he had done a good day's work. He had been helping to load a ship. He enjoyed getting his hands dirty and the men kept up their spirits making lewd jokes, saying he need to keep in shape with his new young wife. He laughed along with them and wondered if in part they were right. He came home to scrub himself clean before supper.

"I love your body, it's like a map with secrets to explore, here the wound from your battle with the Spanish off the Isle of Wight, there the mark of an Indian's knife, a dagger tattoo." Luisa's finger gently traced the lines on his back. "When will you tell me the story of these scars?"

"I don't want to talk of them."

"Are they from the Inquisition?"

He stopped washing but would not look at her.

"I'm sorry I should not have spoken."

He turned and looked at her at last, "I cannot speak of them."

She reached up and kissed him. "You need never explain."

That night he had a nightmare, the like of which he had not known for many a year. He sat bolt upright and in a cold sweat.

"Richard, what is it?" She was sat up also, stroking his hair, he took him some time to realise she was speaking to him.

"Nothing, just a bad dream, nothing."

"Papa has nightmares, he wakes up screaming."

Richard moped his brow with the back of his hand.

"It is my fault I stirred the memories." She was hugging him now.

"It's not your fault. I have to keep some thoughts buried very deep, it is the only way I can go on living."

"Oh my love." She clasped him to her and made him lie back and rest his head on her chest. His arm lay across her belly.

"I can feel the child move Luisa."

"Your son is very lively, I think he likes to play football."

"So it is to be a boy?"

"I think so and Annie says the way the way the baby lies means it will be a boy."

"I am glad you wanted to keep him Luisa."

"So am I dearest, so am I." This time she comforted him until he felt asleep

Chapter Ninety-Eight

Mr Dutton tapped nervously on Richard's door.

"Come in, sir, do not hover."

Mr Dutton entered gingerly. He had his cap in his hand, twisting it out of shape, he was gnawing his lip.

"Do you wish to speak to me?"

"Yes, no, yes." Richard raised his eyebrow.

"I can see you are busy sir, I will return—"

"Have my girls been giving you trouble, Mr Dutton?"

"Not at all sir, they are wonderful young ladies and very scholarly, better than many boys I know."

"I am pleased to hear it. Do you think they will be too scholarly to get themselves husbands?"

"Not if those husbands are decent men. I myself would— that is, not that I would presume but hypothetically, I would.... Yes."

Richard looked confused. "So it is not about my daughters."

"I hate to presume sir, it's just that – it's my mother."

"Your mother? Mr Dutton please come right into the room and sit yourself down."

He perched so far on the edge of the chair Richard put more attention as to whether he would slip off than to what

722

the young man was saying. Eventually he got to the nub of the matter.

"My mother is very sick, the priest writes that she is likely to die."

"I am very sorry to hear that, Mr Dutton, very sorry, I know you are very close to your mother."

"I am, sir, though I have not seen her for near two years."

"Then why are you not there now, sir?"

"That is why I am here, sir, to ask if I many take a little time – if I could hire a horse, I could be there in a day, I could see my mother and be back the next day or at the latest the day after."

"Mr Dutton, you mother is sick, likely to die. You must spend more time with her than a few moments and if God forfend that she is taken, there will be arrangements to be made."

The young man looked miserable, "You have been very good to me, sir, I do not want to let you down."

Richard patted the young man on the shoulder, "I am more than pleased that you are a boy who loves his mother. Go, take one of our horses, take a manservant with you for safety's sake. And I have been meaning to give you this bonus, take it now in case it is needed." The boy was swallowing back tears of gratitude and sorrow. "Thank you, sir," he said softly.

"Now go Mr Dutton, my wife will see that Jeanne and Lizzie do not neglect their studies during your absence."

He went upstairs to find Luisa. She was sat on the seat in the oriel window, her eyes were closed and she was asleep. Her cheeks were pink and her breasts rose up and down slowly, around her were many packages, she had been out shopping for the baby again. Richard wondered how something so little could need so much. He sat down and rummaged through some of the opened items, he found a delightful little silver rattle which he couldn't resist shaking.

"You look very sweet," she murmured and sighed.

"Sorry, it was thoughtless, I did not mean to wake you." He bent over and kissed her stomach.

"I can't believe I get so tired!"

"Shopping can do that to you."

She laughed and leant her head on his shoulder, "I couldn't resist, I'm sorry."

"I know what you mean," said Richard and pulled his own package out. Luisa gave a little squeal.

"Show me, show me." Richard tore apart the wrapping to reveal a little mechanical bird with a moving tongue.

"I know the baby won't appreciate it for a while, but it is so clever!" and he released the mechanism so the bird trilled and Luisa clapped at its trick. "I was thinking that I really didn't get to enjoy my other babies. By the time Jeannot became pregnant we were long estranged, then I was very sick for a long while, Tom was fully formed before I knew of his existence and Antonio likewise."

"But you looked after the girls all alone after they were born."

"Indeed and I have to tell you I am an expert in the putting on of napkins. But it has been something special to see our child grow within you."

She kissed his cheek.

"Luisa, I marvel at you, I do, the way you have made yourself lady of this house. Alice never liked living here, I think she felt a servant in her own home but you are like to the manner born. You grace my table and enchant our guests and take an interest in my work. I forget you are but eighteen."

"It is good of you to say, Richard, but all I want is to be a wife to you. Do I perform those duties well?" Richard tried very hard not to smile but failed.

"Adequate my dear, adequate."

She punched his arm.

"Are you sure you are able to go to the fair?" Richard looked at Luisa, she seemed happy and glowing enough but she was now very large and waddled like a little duckling.

"I am bored with being inside. I feel well, the baby is not due for a few more weeks and Lizzie and Jeanne will be with me."

"Take a manservant and have him bring the cart in case you are tired. If I can get this cargo moving I will come and join you, it's just that with Jacket away and Jack at sea, I must attend to it. Is Tom still studying?"

"Yes, don't disturb him, it is wonderful he is writing again. He is working on a book."

"A book?"

"Yes, he is writing about Jack."

"Jack?"

"It is called I think *The Fabulous Voyages of Captain Black Jack Mudford.*"

"Well that might get Jack his own knighthood. I'm glad you and Tom are as you once were, he is still a little cool with me."

"You are both too alike, you find it hard to speak of your emotions, but at least Tom can pour his into his writing."

"Mmm." Richard did not know what to say, which rather proved Luisa's point. "So you will take care?"

"I will be well looked after. We will probably see Berta there, she said she was going to take Sam and Antonio, and there will be others we know. Don't worry."

"Sorry, can't do that." He kissed the tip of her nose and made sure she had money in her purse.

A few hours later he was just finishing up his work. It had become very humid and he thought there would be a storm later. He saw Lizzie running about the quay obviously looking for him, she seemed distraught.

"Lizzie, Lizzie, here. What is the matter? Is something wrong?"
"Oh Pa you must come quick, it's Luisa—"

"Dear God, is it the baby? It's too soon!"

"No, no but something happened at the fair."

"What? Wait, catch your breath and tell me."

"I will but you must come now."

Richard put away his bills of fare and locked the warehouse.

"We were just walking around the fair and having a wonderful time, we were all so happy and laughing," Lizzie told him as they rushed home. "Jeanne and I went off to buy some toffee apples and left Luisa talking to Alice."

A coldness gripped Richard's heart.

"I don't know what was said Pa but Luisa suddenly became hysterical, Alice walked away and left her and we struggled to get her home. She ran up to her bedchamber and locked the door and will not come out or let anyone in, but she is crying so hard I fear for her and the baby."

Richard was running now, Lizzie hoicked up her skirts and scurried after him. As they reached the door of the house there was a huge clap of thunder. He took the stairs three at a time and when he reached the door he found it still locked. He hammered at it with his fists.

"Open this door, Luisa, or I swear I will fetch an axe and chop it down."

He heard her get off the bed and come and withdraw the bolt. He burst into the room. He had barely got inside before she flew at him with her fists beating him on the chest.

"For God's sake, Luisa, stop this! What is wrong?"

"You slept with her. You slept with her on our wedding day."

"Who?" questioned Richard, although he knew the answer already.

"Alice. Don't try to deny it, she told me herself."

"I don't intend to deny it." Luisa stopped her in her tracks, her hand went to her mouth as if to stop herself from being sick.

"But it was our wedding day, our wedding day."

"She came to see me before I left for the church."

"And? You both slipped off to bed? Was it here in this chamber?"

"No."

She looked at him.

"She came to see me, to dissuade me from marrying you. I thought she wanted us to get back together. I made love to her and then found I was mistaken."

"And if you had not been 'mistaken'?"

"I would have left you at the altar and gone off with Alice."

She sank to the ground, he tried to catch her.

"You have to understand—"

"No, no I don't."

"Alice was the love of my life. I did not leave her, she left me and I think I did not remarry in case she came back. You know, you have always known, that ours was a marriage of convenience but once I put a ring on your finger I have been faithful to you alone."

"That was magnanimous of you. She told me you are the father of her baby."

"What? That's ridiculous."

"Is it? Is it? If you sleep with someone it happens. Get away from me, get away from me." She was crying again.

"I cannot deal with you like this, Luisa, please stop crying and talk to me." She just kept sobbing.

Richard could feel his anger rising. He got up and ran back down the stairs and out of the house. The rain was pelting down, great drops crashed to the ground. He barely noticed, he looked around trying to decide a course of action and then started to run towards the Cross House. Down Vyse Lane, across French Street, down Brewhouse Lane and across the High Street, along a tiny alley till he came out not far from the old friary, out of Friary Gate and across the ditches, over the fields to the shore where the tiny Cross House provided shelter for passengers waiting for the ferry boats. The rain was so heavy it was getting into his eyes and he could barely see. He was almost at the Cross House before he recognised Alice's back, draped around with a green cloak.

"Alice!" She turned her head slightly but did not answer him. He grabbed her elbow and swung her round.

"Let go of me."

"Why did you do it?"

She stared at him defiantly. "Because she was so happy."

"What? What hurt has she ever done to you? If it's me you were angry with then take it out on me." The water was getting in his mouth and his clothes were soaked. He pushed her further under the roof of the Cross House so he could get out of the rain.

"I ask you again, why did you do it?"

"And I answer you the same, because she was so happy, because she kept telling me how wonderful you were and how she had worried about having a baby but how you supported her and how perfect your life was."

"She's just a young girl who has never been anything but kind and for some reason thinks well of me, or used to. Why did you have to hurt her so?"

"I just told her the truth that is all, she wasn't living in the real world."

"It was real to her. What good will come of it?"

"You are so naïve Richard, you think her so innocent. She was always hanging around, inveigling herself into our household—"

"Our household? You left. You didn't want me, you chose George Parker."

"You never fought for me. Why did you never fight for me?"

"I begged you to stay. You were the one who split up the family and decided who went where. You were the one who wanted me out of the town."

"But you came back."

"Was I never to see my children again? Alice, this all happened so long ago. Why now for God's sake?"

"Because she has everything and I have nothing."

"That is not true."

"She has my house, my son, my husband."

"You threw it all away and even then I would not have married Luisa if you would had come away with me."

"You always sleep with whoever is closest, don't you?"

"I don't even know what you are talking about any more. I made one mistake, I thought I was a prisoner forever. I was lonely, I was weak, I thought it might make my chance of escape better."

"But you enjoyed it didn't you? You and your Spanish whore, and then you bring her back to my house and her bastard with her. I've done Luisa a favour, it is right that she should know what is in store for her."

"It was cruelly done, Alice, cruelly done." She looked at him with fire in her eyes and then as if a red mist had lifted, her composure cracked, she gave a moan and convulsed as if to retch. "Oh my God what have I done? What have I become? Nothing but a bitter and twisted woman. Oh God I am so sorry." She laid her head on his shoulder and he knew he should have thrust her away but he comforted her till the ferry boat crunched on the shore.

"You know it was only because I realised I had lost you and would never have you back again."

"I know. I'm sorry, Alice, our moment has passed."

She nodded and he helped her into the boat. She looked back at him as it pulled away and they gazed at each other until she reached the further shore and the rain had blurred their images. Richard stood for a long time before he turned and walked slowly back to St Michael's Square. His clothes were plastered against his body, his stomach was turning in somersaults, he kept going over and over his conversation with Alice. He realised he had been standing outside his own front door for several minutes. He opened the door to find Tom, Lizzie, Jeanne and Antonio sitting on the settle obviously waiting for him. They stood up as he came in, he patted their heads as he went by but could not bring himself to speak and they were silent also.

He walked wearily up the staircase and opened the door to the bedchamber. Luisa was pacing up and down and turned to look at him, her eyes were puffy and red and her face streaked with the trail of tears. She set her jaw firmly expecting him to speak, apologise, say something. But he didn't. He walked to the linen press and threw open the doors pulling out clean, dry clothes. He peeled off his wet garments and left them piled on the floor. Luisa could keep her silence no longer.

"Where have you been?"

"I went to speak to Alice," he said flatly.

"Alice! You went to her, I am your wife not her, not her!" Her voice was getting higher and wavering.

"Please, Luisa, I cannot do this right now."

"Cannot? Will not! I don't know you anymore."

"Of course you don't know me!" he snapped. "I lived a whole lifetime before you were born."

"Why did you marry me?"

"You know why."

"Convenience? Why was it convenient?"

Richard was pulling on the clean clothes. He stopped and turned slowly to her, "Because your mother blackmailed me."

Luisa looked as if her world was collapsing, "How? What could you have done that she holds such power over you? Please, I need to understand."

"It is better you don't know."

"No, please, I don't understand what is happening."

"It was a long time ago, it concerns Lizzie and I had to protect her."

"Lizzie?"

"I'm not going to say more Luisa, I married you so I would not have to speak of it or have it spoken about."

"But I love you and I would never have done anything to harm you."

"You don't know what you are talking about. People who love you always hurt you the most."

"What makes you say such a thing? I'm not Alice."

"No, you are not."

"Our marriage has been built on lies and deceit."

"Don't pretend you didn't know that and besides you did quite well with fine clothes, jewels, a title." He wished he could just stop talking but he didn't seem to be able to, he knew his words were causing more pain than if he had struck her with his fists.

"What am I do now?"

"I don't know, do what you will. If you want to leave, leave, go back to serving at the inn, I don't know and at the moment I don't care."

She was crying again and he finished dressing. He was trying to get his thoughts together, he held tightly to the door of the linen press, he had a raging headache and he suddenly felt his years as if all his injuries and bruises from all his fights and battles had started hurting at once. He realised Luisa had gone completely silent. He turned around. She was absolutely still, her face ashen and she clutched the bedpost. She was staring down at the floor. Richard followed her line of vision and saw a pool of water. He rushed to her side, his anger vanished.

"Luisa, look at me." She raised eyes so full of hurt, pain, despair and now shock.

"Luisa, your waters have broken, the baby is coming."

"It's too soon." Her voice was so quiet he could barely hear her.

"Luisa, listen to me, let go of the post and come and sit on the bed." She looked at her hands as if they did not belong to her but loosened her grip and let herself be led to the bed. Richard knelt in front of her.

"Luisa, I know I have no right to ask anything of you, but I need you to try and put aside what has happened today and to think only of yourself and of the baby. Please tell me you will do that." He smoothed her brow, she seemed to be in a trance. "I am going to get the midwife and fetch Tamsin."

Luisa seemed to come alive again at the mention of her mother's name, "I want my mother, I want my mother."

"She will be here in a few minutes."

Richard got up and walked to the door, he rubbed his hand around his face, this was not a nightmare it was real. He glanced back at Luisa she was sat on the bed, her arms cradling her stomach. She looked so young and so alone. Richard pulled himself together and went back down to the hall, the children were still sat there.

"The baby is coming Jeanne, run to the Angel and fetch Tamsin. Lizzie, take Antonio to your Uncle Jack's and ask if he can stay with them till the baby has come." For once Antonio did not argue. "Tom, run to Annie and ask her to come immediately. Lizzie, when you return get the servants to organise hot water and clean linen."

He ran up the stairs. When he went into the chamber Luisa turned, a pleading look in her eyes.

"Is my mother here? Is she coming?"

He went to her side, "Just a few minutes, be brave."

"I will be brave for my baby, my baby is all I have now."

Richard went to speak, to tell her she still had him, but the door flew open and in burst Tamsin.

"Mama, Mama," Luisa opened her arms.

"Mama is here. Richard, you should leave, it is no place for you."

As he left there was a flurry of activity around him, women running up and down the stairs.

Chapter Ninety-Nine

He was sat in his counting house. The house was relatively quiet, Annie had said it would be some time before the baby made an appearance. He heard a rapping on the front door, loud and insistent. Where were all the servants? He got up and went to answer it himself, the knocking was getting louder and more frantic. He opened the door, it was still raining and the bedraggled figure of Will stood on the step.

"Will? What is it? Come in boy you are drenched."

Will tumbled into the hall and threw himself into Richard's arms. "Pa, Pa."

"I'm here, what is it, Will?"

"It's Ma, it's Ma."

"Alice? What has happened?" Richard remembered how strained she had looked, how weary.

"The baby came, a girl, but something went wrong, there was too much blood.... Ma is dying...she's dying...she wants you to come and to bring Tom." Richard had turned to stone.

"Pa, please, please, we must go, we must go now, she might even be dead as we stand here."

Richard woke up and roared Tom's name. He came running down the stairs, Jacket behind him.

"Will take off those wet things."

"There is no time."

"There is go and grab something of Jacket's and get a cloak."

"What is happening?" asked Jacket as Will tore past him.

"Tom, go and get your cloak, we have to go across to the village, your mother is very, very ill, she wants you to come." Tom looked confused but dashed up the stairs after his brother.

"And me? Did she send for me also?" asked Jacket. Richard pulled himself together.

He placed his hand on Jacket's shoulder, "Yes of course, I just wanted your brothers out of the way for a moment. Alice is going to die Jacket, and I need you to be a man for me. The family is falling apart and I don't know if I can save it. I can say no more but I need to rely on you."

Jacket was pale, "Yes Father, I will fetch my cloak also."

As they went through the door Richard heard a terrifying scream, Luisa was going into labour. He hesitated for a few seconds and then banged the door shut behind them. They hurried down the streets that were running with streams of water.

"I have a boat waiting," called Will as they skittered across the cobbles. He slipped and almost fell but pushed away Tom's proffered arm. They clambered into the boat and all took a place at the oars and pulled together. Despite the choppiness of the waters they made a great pace across the river. The bottom of the boat was full of water and it soaked into their boots. At the shore they jumped out and ran the boat up the shingle. They could see the house above them where Alice lived with George Parker. There were lights in the windows and the shadows of people moving about.

On entering the house they found various women sat about. George Parker was in the corner, his head in his hands. John's mother came out of the room where Alice lay. She hugged them all and then ushered them in. The room was quite bare, there were candles guttering in holders and a mean fire was fluttering in the grate. The centre of the room was dominated by a bed and on it lay Alice, her hair damp and limp and her skin waxy. Richard could see her chest gently rising so knew she still lived but it was the only sign, there was no colour to her cheeks and lips. Her eyelids fluttered open.

"My boys, all my boys." They crowded around the bed. She looked at them one by one as if she was determined to remember their faces.

"Will, you must look after your Pa for me." Will glanced at Richard. "George will need you, he won't find it easy with the new baby." Richard realised there was a cradle next to the bed and a tiny baby wriggled inside.

"Jacket, did I keep my promise to Thomasina, well?"

"Yes, Mother."

Alice closed her eyes again.

"Mama!" cried Tom, anxious not to go without his final blessing.

"Lean close Tom, I am losing my strength." The boy moved forward and Alice whispered something into his ear. He pulled away.

"Boys, let me speak to Richard for a moment." They went and huddled in the corner. Richard bent in close so their faces were just inches apart.

"I'm sorry, Richard, for everything."

"No you have nothing to be sorry for, love."

"I did love you. I do love you."

"Alice, don't go, please don't go."

"Hush, its better that I do."

She reached up and touched his face and he bent down and brushed his lips against hers. He stood up and the boys came one by one and kissed their mother goodbye. Parker was standing in the doorway, he stared at Richard with anger and bitterness. Richard guided the crying boys out of the room and Parker closed the door behind them. They went and waited in the living room with all the others. A few moments later Parker came back out, sunk to his knees and howled. The rest of the room fell silent for a moment and then the sobs began.

Richard took Jacket to one side, "I need to go back, Luisa..."

"I know, Father."

"Tom," the boy looked up with a strange light in his eyes, "I have to go back to Southampton."

"I'm staying here with Will."

"Of course." Richard turned back to Jacket, "Wait with them and send for me for the burial." Jacket nodded.

Richard went back outside. It was still raining, though not quite so heavily, all greyness and drizzle. He retrieved the boat and pushed it back into the water. Every muscle ached as he pulled on the oars, he thought about giving up the struggle and letting himself be swept out to sea but kept rolling back on the oars. Eventually he reached the Southampton shore, tied up the boat and hurried home.

The house was completely quiet. Richard was filled with horror. "God no!" He ran up the stairs. Tamsin was coming out of the bedchamber, shutting the door quietly.

"Where have you been?"

"Luisa, is she all right?"

"What would you care?"

"Just don't, Tamsin, don't. Tell me."

"She sleeping, she was delivered of a boy child." Tamsin glowered at him.

"And? For the love of God Tamsin please, I am begging you."

"The child is well, Luisa is well. She is exhausted, you need to let her sleep."

Richard sunk down to the floor, "I've made a mess of things Tamsin."

"You make it sound as if that is something unusual." Richard let her gloat for a moment.

"Alice is dead."

"What!" Tamsin sunk to the floor beside him.

"What has Luisa told you?"

"Nothing much, she is very loyal to you Richard. She said that she had disappointed you and that she thought the marriage was over."

Richard groaned.

"I should not have left her but Alice sent for me and Tom. I knew she was dying, I could do nothing to help Luisa, she was with you."

"Did she tell Tom?"

"By the way he looked at me, I think so."

"I will miss her, she was my best friend."

Richard hauled himself up and walked down to his counting house, locked the door behind him, sat down at his desk, put his head on his arms and wept. The house went into mourning, the burial was arranged for the next day. Richard did not visit Luisa at all, he felt embarrassed and guilty. Once he went to the door and Tamsin had brought the tiny bundle that was his new son out to him. He kissed the baby on the forehead and the infant had promptly cried.

Richard made his way to St Mary's Church under a lowering sky. It was damp and he pulled his cloak around him. A group of cloaked mourners stood around the church, he saw Jacket and Will but not Tom.

"He was too upset, he wouldn't come," said Jacket. "He hasn't come out of his room."

The service was dull and Richard wasn't really listening. Instead he was thinking about Alice, as a girl, as the wife of his best friend, rolling around with him on the Green, their marriage, the pain he felt when she left him, which was nothing to the pain he felt now when it was all too late. The hole in the ground was sticky and waterlogged and her shrouded body looked like an old bundle of rubbish. Richard reached into his money purse without thinking to give a few coins to the pit man but Parker growled at him. It was not Richard's place to make such a gesture, the right belonged to her husband. Parker smelt of drink.

Jacket came back with him after the funeral. "Father, I'll look after things for a while. You should spend some time with Luisa and the new baby."

"I think I am the last person Luisa wants to spend time with at the moment."

Tamsin had gone back home to get some rest herself, but Annie had stayed to look after Luisa. She told Richard that his wife was doing very well, as was the baby, and his sisters were fussing around him and their stepmother. Richard called into Jack's house to ask him if Antonio could stay a little longer and to tell his brother a little of what had happened.

"I'm sorry that Alice is dead, but don't die with her, Diccon."

"I'm exhausted, Jack, I don't want any more crying and screaming, I just want quiet."

"We are not made for quiet lives, and it seems to me Luisa has the right to scream a bit. Don't blame her for the mess you and Alice made."

Richard went back home. It was raining again. He went up to the bedchamber and knocked softly on the door.

"Come in," came Luisa's voice, but she was obviously not expecting him. She looked around as if for a means to escape.

"I won't stay if you want me to go."

"I want you to go."

He started to close the door.

"Do you care nothing for me?"

"You are utterly precious to me." he said.

She turned away and buried her head in the pillow and began to cry.

Chapter One Hundred

Richard spent all his time in his counting house, staring at his treasures, the markers of his life. Perhaps he should be like Old Bess, sit on cushions and fade away. He sat one night a few days later, the house in darkness. He didn't know what the time was but imagined it must be the hours after midnight. He sat down at his desk and put his head in his hands, he wished it would just stop raining. He gradually became aware of a noise and it took him some moments to realise that it was a baby crying. But there was something wrong, it was not coming from the chamber above. Richard went out into the hall and thought for a moment he must be going mad. The crying was coming from outside. What would a baby being doing out on the street at this time of night and in this weather?

He shook his head but went to the front door and unbolted it all the same. He could not believe his eyes, on the step was a straw basket and the crying was coming from within, he knelt down and peered in. A new-born baby lay there wrapped in a loose cloth. He touched the child's skin, it was freezing, he grabbed the basket and brought it into the hall. He lifted the baby out and started to gently rub it. The baby screamed even louder, he tried to shush the infant in a futile attempt not to wake the house. Within a few minutes figures carrying candles were coming down the stairs.

"Papa? Is that the baby? Why is the baby down here?" asked Jeanne.

"It's not our baby, Jeanne, I found it."

"What is going on, Father?"

"I know not, Jacket, I heard crying and opened the door and there was the baby."

"But who would leave a baby on our doorstep?" Lizzie was at his side peering at the crying child, "It's very cold, Papa."

"I know, Jacket stoke up the fire."

Richard laid the infant on the turkey carpet in front of the warmth.

"I think it might be hungry, it's so little, just born," said Jeanne as they all crowded round.

"Papa, do you think it will die?"

"I don't know, I should get a wet nurse. Why did Annie go home?"

"Let me have the child." They all turned, Luisa was stood on the stairs looking down at them.

"Luisa, you should not be up, go back to bed." Richard begged.

"Give the baby to me." There was something about her voice that silenced all argument. Jeanne picked up the infant and took her to Luisa, who gathered the child to her.

"Luisa, we don't know whose baby it is and where it has come from," said Richard.

"Oh I think we do," she said. She turned and went up the stairs and closed the door of her bedchamber behind her.

"What did Luisa mean, Papa?"

"I don't know, Lizzie, go back to bed all of you, we will sort this out tomorrow."

The candles disappeared but Jacket still stood beside him in the hall.

"It's Alice's baby isn't it?"

Richard shrugged, "I don't know, perhaps, probably."

"Why would it be left here? It doesn't make sense.... Unless..."

"That's enough, Jacket, go to your room."

Richard stalked back to the counting house and crashed the door behind him. He dozed, daylight creeping up the wall when he finally woke. He splashed water on his face from a jug on the side table. There was someone at the door, he groaned, the banging was desperate but soon faded. Richard sat back down and his eyes started to close.

A few minutes later and the servant Peter burst in to tell him he was needed urgently. Richard went to the door. Slumped in the porch was the bruised and bloodied body of Will.

"Sweet Jesu," Richard was wide awake now and on his knees. Will's eyes flickered open. "Thank God, I thought for a moment...Christ and his saints what happened?"

"The baby, the baby is gone, I came back from fishing and the cradle was empty." Will was clawing at Richard's shirt, "I kept asking him where the baby was, he was drunk he wouldn't tell me. I grabbed at him, trying to shake it out of him. He went mad, he just started beating me. Ma made me promise to look after the baby and I've failed her."

"Will, Will, listen it's all right, the baby is here, the baby is here."

"Really? Really?"

"Yes, it's all right, you are safe now, the baby is safe." Richard was lifting him up and calling for Peter to help. Richard checked Will over, he thought a rib was broken as was his nose, his eyes were nearly closed, boot marks were on his back.

"I shall kill him for this, I shall kill him."

"No Pa, it's all right, I'm all right really, he was drunk. He's been drunk since Ma died, he's mad with grief, he didn't know what he was doing."

"He knew enough to leave a baby to freeze and starve on my doorstep and to beat the son of the woman he supposedly loved to a pulp."

Jacket appeared and Jeanne beside him, who screamed at the sight of Will.

"Jacket, let's get Will up to Tom's room – dear god Tom! Will, is Tom still there?"

"No, no he's not there."

"Where is he?" Will looked sheepish. "Will?"

"I'm sorry he made me promise not to tell...he went to London, the day after Ma died."

"What?"

"He said he didn't know who he was any more that he wanted to get away from us. I'm sorry."

"It's not your fault Will, let's get you upstairs."

He told the servant to fetch the apothecary and the bone setter. They made Will more comfortable and both Lizzie and Jeanne sat with him, trying to soothe him.

"What is happening, Father? It seems only a moment ago we were all happy and merry and now all is misery."

"I think I must have angered God, Jacket. I did try to do the best thing, but I am full of human frailty."

"I know you do the best for us Father."

"I shall have to go to London, try to find Tom, and if he won't come back at least make sure he is safe and well. Look after Will, tell Luisa.... I don't know.... Something."

"You should speak to her yourself Father."

"I know, but I find I cannot."

Richard journeyed to London via Alton, stopping at the George inn on the way, then onto Guildford and Kingston. When he got to Lambeth he took a boat into the city and found a room at the Cross Keys inn. He visited his London lawyer and factor to replenish his purse and to see if Tom had been in touch with them for money. Nothing had been heard. It seemed to Richard that the best place to start was at the theatres, poetry and plays were Tom's passion. If he was to make his way in London he might hope to do that via his pen or take up an actor's life. He visited the Globe, the Bear, the Fortune but saw no sign of Tom, and met no one who professed to have seen him, but he sensed that even if there was news it would not be divulged. He decided he needed help and by note, asked the actor Edward Alleyn to dinner.

"Mr Alleyn, it is very gracious of you to find time to see me."

"You were my early supporter, Mr Mudford, come sit."

"I see you prosper, sir."

"I do well enough, not all actors are drunkards and villains, though I grant you they are in the majority."

Richard sat and broke bread, "Mr Alleyn, I have to confess I have renewed our slight acquaintance as I hope you might be of help to me."

"How so?"

"I am searching for my son, Tom. I brought him to meet you when you were in Southampton performing during the Queen's visit."

"On the green! There was a tree planting I recall!"

"Yes – you gave a wonderful performance on that day, I remember it vividly."

The actor nodded in acknowledgement.

"And so what were you saying about your boy?"

"Not to put too fine a point on it, he has run away from home. His mother recently died and he has been unhappy with me for some time. He found out that I was his real father and is angry that I did not acknowledge it, though I wished to do that with all my heart, all my heart."

"A sad tale, but I don't see how I can help."

"His brother confessed that Tom had come to London and I believe he might mean to try and make his way as an actor, he has some talent his tutors tell me. I have spent several days wandering around the various playhouses and can find no trace of him, but it would be easy for him to hide away. I thought that if you let it be known you were looking for a new talent to join your company – a boy of around sixteen – he might be tempted along and I could have a chance at reconciliation. I would, of course, recompense you for your time and trouble."

Alleyn considered it for a while, "Well we do hold auditions from time to time and it is always a good idea to keep an eye on talent. I will assist you Mr Mudford, and perhaps in return you will let me persuade you to be an angel for one of our new productions."

"You want me to become a supporter of your company?"

"Sorry I can never resist the opportunity, it was importunate of me."

"No, not at all. I love the theatre Mr Alleyn, I have some funds and you find me now 'Sir Richard Mudford'," Richard said, a little embarrassed, "and if you will assist me with my boy I should be proud and honoured to support your company."

Alleyn arranged for flyers to be placed all around the theatre district announcing auditions for his company. Richard was beside himself and fretted until the hour for the auditions came.

He hid himself away in the tiring house, in an upper chamber with a window overlooking the stage so that he could espy on the aspiring actors. The flyers had had more than the desired effect, hopeful young men and boys were queuing right around the theatre. The day wore on as more and more hopefuls traipsed onto the stage. Many were utterly deluded, some had promise. Richard was beginning to the think his plan had failed. The light was starting to fade and he felt his eyes dropping. Then he was suddenly wide awake, Tom was walking purposefully onto the stage. He looked well, his clothes were a little travel-stained but he had made a go of tidying himself up.

He was smoothing down his hair as he found the centre of the stage.

"And who do we have here?" asked Alleyn.

"Tom, sir, Tom Foundling."

"Foundling? That is an unusual name."

"It is the only one I own, sir."

"So, Tom Foundling, what pieces have you prepared for me today?"

"As suggested, I have two contrasting pieces. I intend to do a speech from Tamburlaine." There was uproar around the theatre.

"You do know that is one of my best known triumphs do you not, young Tom?"

"Yes sir, my Fa– friend saw you perform it some years since and talks of it still."

"And the other piece?"

"Well, sir, I thought I should show that I could also play the dame, so I have a piece from something of my own that I was writing–"

"Something of your own? Is there no end to your arrogance, Master Tom?"

"I suppose not sir, but I hope that if I have the good fortune to become one of your company I might have the opportunity to write as well as perform. Is that wrong of me, sir? I have nothing else prepared."

"And what is this piece?"

"I have been minded to create something of the story of Bevis of Hampton, my home– a place I once lived. I shall play the Fair Josian."

"Go to then, Master Tom Foundling."

A quiet descended on the theatre as Tom gathered his thoughts about him and transformed himself first into the great Tamburlaine. He performed with great physicality, and had chosen well, something from the warrior's early days when he was a boy with all his conquests in front of him. Richard felt he acquitted himself more than well, even with his bias, he looked at Alleyn and his coterie who were listening intently and nodding. Tom came to an end. He stopped awhile, not sure if there would be comment or even applause. There was neither. He composed himself again and took upon the features and gesture of a young girl, a girl who loved the enslaved Bevis, who should have been her mortal enemy but for the love of whom she would leave her father and travel to strange lands, cutting herself off from all she had known. The poetry has full of meaning and pathos, his acting tender, fearful, passionate. He ended by falling to his knees and weeping for a father lost, never to be seen again. Richard had to stop himself from rushing to the stage and comforting the boy. The moment held for a few seconds and then Alleyn began to clap.

"Well performed, Mr Foundling, well written, young Tom."

Tom leapt to his feet, a smile dazzling his face.

"Go to my room, you will be shown where, there are things to be discussed."

Tom scurried off not knowing he would soon find himself in front of Richard. When he entered the room he almost turned on his heel and left.

"It was a fine performance, Tom, you have it in you to be a good actor and great playwright."

Tom hesitated.

"What would you know of the drama?"

"I have seen many fine players and heard many fine words over the years. Mr Alleyn would not have praised you so if it were not true."

"Did you arrange this?"

"Yes."

"Why?"

"I was desperate to find you, Tom, to know you were safe and well."

"As you can see I am both."

"And in your heart and your soul?"

"What do you care?"

"I care, Tom, I always cared."

"You have a funny way of showing it, you never even let it be known you were my father."

"It was not my secret to tell."

"Then whose?"

"Your mother's. And if you had waited till after the funeral I was ready to acknowledge you. The papers have been drawn up since I first knew of your existence."

"Even though I was born of sin?"

"Sin? What do you mean, Tom?"

"You know, you know!" He was shaking, angry and upset. Richard stepped across the room and held Tom in his arms. Tom fought at first, punching and kicking but Richard was unmoved and then he began to cry and held onto Richard like a raft in a fast flowing river. He finally sank to the ground unable to stand, all his strength and energy gone and Richard sank with him, still holding onto him.

"Tom, do you think you might be able to tell me what Alice said to you?"

"That she was my mother and you were my father that I was born of sin and she had carried that sin with her, but that she'd been happy to do so because she loved me."

"Well that is one thing that we can agree on. She loved you and I loved you and it is ironic Tom that you are the only child I have that was born of love, and you are the one I am separated from."

"Don't you love Jeanne and Lizzie or Antonio?"

"Oh yes, Tom, I love them very much, more than I ever thought possible. But when I married Jeannot it was well, a business arrangement, everyone advised me it was the thing to do, what most people do. I thought I had lost Alice so I didn't care, I had no idea she was carrying you or I would never have left her side, no matter how often she sent me away. Antonio was born out of loneliness and stupidity and venality and yet somehow he is so dear and wonderful."

"Why didn't my mother want to acknowledge me after you were married?"

"I don't know, she felt her reputation keenly and maybe she was worried even then about the pre-contract and what would happen if that all came out. I don't know Tom, truly I don't but I had to stand by her decision, I did not feel I could do otherwise. Tom, please come home, please I beg you."

"All my life I wished you were my real father."

"I'm sorry I let you down Tom. I hope you will in time be glad your wish was answered."

"What will everyone say?"

"All the people who care about you only want you home. I think many may have guessed the truth already."

"How?"

"Can you not see when you look in the mirror?" Tom thought for a while, he was still finding it hard to comprehend all that had happened, so he fixed on what he could understand.

"Then Mr Alleyn lied when he said my performance was fine and that I could be a great playwright?"

"No, Tom, not at all, that was Mr Alleyn's true opinion, nothing I put him up to."

"Really?"

"Really, Tom, I have only ever lied to you over one thing Tom, which I greatly regret, but not over this. And Tom, if this is where your dream lies I will support you in it. But I need you to come home now, things are not well there. You told me once I did not deserve Luisa and I have proved you right."

"No Pa, don't say that. I was wrong, I should not have made you choose and I have wanted to tell you many times that my heart is mended. When I see you and Luisa together and so happy I understand, it was churlish of me Pa."

"You are a better man than I, Tom."

"All heroes are flawed, Pa, you should know that."

"I am not a hero Tom, I am a common man caught up in uncommon times."

"So am I Tom Mudford now?"

"I would be honoured, Tom, if you would take my name. I will speak to my lawyers, have you declared legitimate, my first-born."

"It's all right, Pa, I don't want the fuss, it would stir things up and my mother would not have wanted that." Richard nodded though it was a great sadness to him.

"I should like to come home, Pa, I have been a bit scared."

"London is a scary place, but I think we will be having a home here Tom, so you will have more chance to find out if the theatre is the place for you."

"Does Luisa want to live in London?"

"We spoke of it, but I think Luisa will probably not want to live anywhere I am."

"I can't believe that is so, Pa."

There was a knock on the door. Richard and Tom leapt to their feet, embarrassed at their sentimentality. It was Mr Alleyn.

"Do I intrude?"

"No, Mr Alleyn, come in. I am most grateful to you, through your good offices Tom and I have reconciled, I hope."

"So you intend to steal my best new actor from me!"

"For a short while sir, Tom has not finished at Oxford and his family are not quite ready to give him up."

They dined with Mr Alleyn and Richard signed papers promising money for the upcoming production. They saw a play the next day and then took the road for Southampton and Richard told Tom of the recent events which had led to his half-sister being taken in by Richard.

Chapter One Hundred and One

When they got home they found a house in mourning for happy times past. They also found Tamsin.

"So you show your face at last!"

"I am pleased to see you, Tamsin, how does Luisa do? And the baby?"

"Which baby?"

"My son," said Richard flatly.

"How dare you! How could you bring your by blow into the house whilst your wife is still in her childbed?"

"The infant is not mine and I only brought it in to prevent its death."

"Even after all you did to her, Luisa screamed for you in the agony of her labour."

"I did not know that."

"No, you were too busy chasing after another woman."

"You know Alice was dying, that is the only reason I went."

"Really? All the servants are talking."

"Let them, if they don't want to be here they can find work elsewhere."

"The child is Alice's and you are the father!"

"The child is Alice's but I am not the father."

"My poor girl, she is petting that baby because she believes that is what you want, that you will expect it."

"I never asked her to. I will not see the infant starve for Alice's sake, but I would never expect Luisa to care for her."

"Why not? You expected Alice to take in your other bastards."

"What passed between Alice and I is no concern of yours."

"I am going to take Luisa home, it is what she wants, I will not have her abused. What next? Will you sleep with her maid?"

"Tamsin, John is my best friend and I love him, and for that reason I have always given you great latitude but you overstep yourself."

"Overstep the great Sir Richard, begetter of bastards, whoremonger to his wives?"

"Papa, what is the matter?" Lizzie and Jeanne had appeared from the music room where they had been entertaining their grandmother; Tamsin had been shouting.

"I was just talking to your pa about twins and how they are made in this house."

"Don't, Tamsin, don't, it will achieve nothing."

The girls started to cry, sensing something was very wrong. Richard sprang to their side and took them in his arms.

"Ssh, ssh, all is well, Papa is here and nothing will harm you, Papa loves you." He kissed their heads, and looked at Tamsin pleadingly.

"What is it like having a cuckoo in the nest, Lizzie?" Lizzie's blond head jerked up looking first at Tamsin then at her father.

"Get out of this house!" shouted Madame Sohier. "You heard me, you are not welcome here."

Tamsin hesitated for a moment, then she spat in Richard's face before clattering down the stairs and out of the door.

"What did she mean, Papa?" Richard could not speak, there was too big a lump in his throat.

"Am I a cuckoo, Papa?" Lizzie hiccupped.

"Do not be so foolish Elizabeth Mudford!" declared Madame Sohier. "I was there at your birth, both of your births, it was the saddest and happiest day of my life! And your papa, although he was very, very sick, dragged himself to your mother's side and claimed his girls while everyone was telling him to put you out to nurse or be fostered! Now enough of this nonsense, you are upsetting your papa, go and wash your faces." She peeled them from Richard and tried to shoo them along, but they ran back to him and kissed him, and Richard in turn kissed Wauldure full on the lips.

"Enough of this nonsense, come."

"Pa?" It was Tom, Richard had forgotten that he was there.

"Oh Tom. Why is it when I try to do the best, it always turns out for the worse?"

"Pa, I know Parker is the father of my new sister, I will make sure everyone knows, so shall Will. We could take her and start our own establishment, we are strong and can work."

"Bless you Tom, but my shoulders are broad and the only thing that matters is my children know I love them, nothing else."

"Oh Pa, we have all been such a trial to you."

"Never! Now we have had a long trip, go and clean yourself up and visit Will. He is sharing your room. He has suffered greatly, he needs you."

"It makes a change from Antonio camping in my room! How is Antonio? Is he all right, Papa?"

"Yes, he has been staying with your Uncle Jack, he is too young to be involved in all this upset."

"I'll go and visit him after I have seen Will, and Jacket as well."

"Jacket has been a great strength to me, doing what he always does, quietly working away for the benefit of the Mudford Brothers so that none of us starve!"

★

There was a step on the boards and for a moment he thought Luisa was coming to him and he was surprized his heart skipped a beat. He heard a scuffle outside his door and whispered voices, and then the door opened and Lizzie was thrust in by unseen hands. He looked up at her.

"Papa, Luisa is getting ready to leave."

"Lizzie, I cannot in good conscience blame her. I have made a terrible mess of everything, Lizzie, I'm sorry."

"How can you say that, Papa, when you look after us all? You could have abandoned us but you didn't." She came and wrapped her arms around Richard, "Don't give up Pa, you can't just let her go, when you love her so."

Richard looked strangely at his younger daughter and then slowly rose. Richard stood once more outside the bedchamber, thought to tap on the door but changed his mind and just walked straight in as if it was the most natural thing in the world.

"Richard!" Luisa was startled, there were a few belongings strewn about the room.

"I will be returning to the inn, I will not take the many kind gifts you have given me. I am sure the gowns can be altered for Jeanne and Lizzie, but I should like to keep the pearl earrings." She looked so pale, the spark had gone from her.

He said nothing.

"Before I go, I do have a confession to make, I have spent a long time here alone, thinking. You did not lie to me, Richard. I was foolish and arrogant believing I could make you love me because I wished it. It was my idea to marry you, I planted the seed in my mother's head and she thought it her own. I was so jealous of Alice and on that day I did flaunt my happiness in her face, I wanted her to think that you were utterly mine and she had no more chance of you. I've learnt that you can't choose who you fall in love with, for you it was Alice, for me it was you."

"I see, and when you go, Luisa, what will become of my son?"

She was thinking hard, "I thought, I hoped that I might take him with me, he is so tiny, he needs me." Her voice fell away.

"I cannot allow that, Luisa. The boy is my son, in law I have control of him." He didn't know why he said that, it was cruel. "So you intend to leave this house and make me the butt of gossip?"

"No, no that is not my intent, it's just that I can't go on like this, I just can't." She was clenching her fists so hard her nails must have been digging into her flesh.

"I told you once that you would not be happy with me that you would leave like the others. You said you just wanted to be with me." It was a bitter triumph.

"Nothing has changed and everything has changed." her voice wavered. He found himself marching about the room not able to find the rights words, his pride getting in the way of him begging her to stay. "I could go to the church court they would order you back to fulfil your wifely duties!"

"You want me to do my duty?" She flung herself down on the bed, "Well here I am, use me as you did on our wedding night!" Richard felt the colour drain from his face. Luisa bit her lip.

"I didn't mean…" She took a gulp of air as if she was finding it difficult to breathe.

"Well then go, if you care nothing for me, cannot bear to be with me, it is best." He threw himself down on the chest at the end of their bed.

"Care nothing? Care nothing? You are right I cannot bear to be with you." she muttered and he snorted taking some delight in being proved right.

"I cannot bear to be in the same room with you and not touch you. I cannot bear that we share this house but no longer share a bed. I miss your breath on my neck, I miss the weight of your arm across my body. I long for you to look up at me and smile. I want to hear your voice reading me poetry, and hear you humming a song as you dress in the morning. I want to watch as you stretch your muscles when you come from work, I want to straighten your ruff before we go out to the theatre and for you to bend and kiss the tip of my nose. I want you to rub my feet when they are cold. I want to feel you inside me. I thought I could stay here and be a maid or do your laundry so I could just be near you, smell you, touch the things you have touched but I can't, I can't, I am in agony and despair, it is a physical pain in my heart." She pounded her fist on her chest.

Richard was in shock he moved his mouth to try and form words, any words, "Why? Why did you not come to me? Tell me?"

"I could not come to you, not this time."

"But why?"

"Because you do not want me. You chose her." her voice was raised up like an animal caught in a trap.

"No, no you are wrong, when I went to her, when I went to Alice, it was to tell her she could have no more of me that I was yours!" Luisa looked at him in disbelief then exhausted came and sat beside him. Looking at him straight in his eyes she asked, "Then what happened?"

He looked away, moistening his lips he replied, "She died."

"Oh Richard, I could not compete with her alive, how am I to do it now she is dead?"

"There is not a competition Luisa."

The door of bedroom swung open and they were disturbed by the arrival of the wet nurse who seemed displeased to find the mistress and master together. She carried a tiny baby.

"Ah, perhaps I should make myself scarce," said Richard.

"No stay, please." She was so desperate, afraid if he went he would not come back. Richard nodded and went and stood in the corner. Luisa made herself comfortable, loosening her gown to expose her full breast she took the baby and began to feed him. "Do you not think your son the most beautiful child?" She asked as if she thought he might disagree.

Richard stared at the infant's downy head. "As beautiful as his mother, thank God."

He wanted to kiss Luisa's neck as she bent over the baby's head, he thought the wet nurse must have read his thoughts as a scowl crossed her face as she swept out of the room.

"She's fierce."

"But she has rich, sweet milk." Luisa looked at him quickly but then turned away.

A moment later the woman came back into the room and sat in the nursing chair and began to feed the other baby. Richard was mesmerized, he did not know what to say or think. When the time came for Luisa to change breasts she exchanged babies also. He stepped towards her and put his lips to her ear.

"Luisa, what are you doing?" he muttered in a low whisper so the wet nurse hopefully would not hear.

"Feeding our babies."

"She is not ours, you do not have to do this."

"God gave her to us to look after, Richard."

He bit his tongue until the babies were fed and the nurse had left. "It's not right, Luisa, you should not have to do this, you are not the baby's mother and I am not its father."

"Alice thought you were."

"It may have been what she wished, she had longed for a child for so many years but to put it crudely, the dates don't fit. I doubt I will get Parker to believe me but, ridiculous as it sounds after all I have done, I would not want you to think that I fathered a child with someone else during our marriage. I swear on the heads of my children I have not known another woman since I knew you. I know my past might make you doubt it."

"I do believe you Richard, but what was I to do?" Luisa mopped her breasts and re-laced her gown. "I admit at first

I wanted to hate her, when I saw her cradled in your arms–but that was base of me. She is Will and Tom's sister, she was abandoned and you loved Alice. So I had to take her into our home. It was the right thing to do."

"I have treated you so badly and you always forgive me." Richard muttered. She was so close to him he could smell the scent of gentian, berberis and cardamom flowers on her hair. He sat down beside her.

"I told you on our wedding night I was cruel but even I did not know how cruel I could be."

"No, you were not cruel, you were honest and that was what was so painful."

"I am truly sorry to have hurt you. I just do not understand how you could love me."

She sighed "God made Richard Mudford a good man."

"But I am not a perfect man."

"I would not want to be with a perfect man." He could tell she was almost exasperated with him.

"Sweetheart, I have no gift for using the right words, I don't know how to do this, what to say."

"Well it is time you learned." Richard was taken aback at the iron in her voice and he had to hold back a smile. He drew breath.

"I will not stop you leaving if that is what you want, and I would never remove your baby from you, I don't know what made me say such an awful thing other than to force you to stay. But you should know I am going to fight for you Luisa, I shall come to your parents' inn every day and go down on my knee and beg you to come home." He went to get up but his legs would not move. He sat on the edge of the chest and began to pray as he had never prayed before.

"Every day?" Her voice was soft but he was sure he had not imagined it.

"Every day."

"And you bear me no resentment?" she asked.

"Resentment? I have never resented you." He turned to look at her in surprise. Her hair was cascading over her shoulders. She had lost weight and her cheek bones caught the light. His heart almost stopped and he realised he was not breathing.

"My mother should not have threatened you."

"She did me a favour. I was angry I cannot deny that, but then I have been angry most of my life. I convinced myself that this was to be another marriage of convenience. That I would occasionally do my duty. That resolution did not even survive our wedding night."

Her eyes searched his face, she went to speak but changed her mind, and stood up walking over to the window.

"Don't go." he said.

She hesitated again, then took a breath, "Richard, did you sleep with my mother?"

"What!" he roared, he felt anger rising through him, tasted bile in his mouth, "Is that what she told you? Shall I tell you how I met your mother? Arrested for sucking cock, arrested as common drab. Even when she was in prison – that is where you were conceived! Carted and banished but I took pity, thought I could save her, found her a home. I know she blames me for John being pressed, I blame myself but I did all could, looked after his children and in the end I found him and brought him home. She forced me into marrying you and I let her do it and I let her think it was me who beat you!" He realised he was shouting and brought himself under control. Luisa looked distraught. He reached out and put his arm round her waist and pulled her closer till she was just inches away.

"I did not love you when we wed, I cannot even say I loved you when I planted my seed in your belly." She swallowed and shuddered, "But when I came home that day and found you broken and beaten and so scared I knew deep, deep down I knew, and I knew I had been no husband to you, I was ashamed." He planted a kiss on her forehead.

"Have you grown to care for me?"

"I think about you all the time."

"What are you thinking now?"

"I am thinking that as you were sat here longing for me, I was down below missing you. Every time I heard a step in the hall, I hoped it was yours, that you would come in like times past, bringing me a glass, sitting at your accounts with your brow furrowed in concentration. Copying letters for me, chatting about my children. I thought about your laugh when we watched a comedy or when you play with Antonio in the garden and that my poor damaged Antonio at last had the mother he deserves. I remember how you carried my son with joy in your belly even though you were frightened ...I think about the hollow of your neck, the curve of your lips and how much I want to kiss you all over your body." He did not think he had ever made such a speech, "I'm sorry I can't make the words."

"Just three Richard."

He swallowed, wet his dry lips, he had to make her believe, "I...love...you. I love you."

He could scarcely believe when she leant forward and her lips found his. He wanted to take her in his arms with such passion but pulled away.

"I took advantage of your innocence Luisa."

"And did I not want to be taken?"

"I was overcome with lust."

"Is it wrong to lust after your wife?"

"You always think the best of me."

"And why should I not? You are my husband, the father of my child."

"How can you forgive me?"

"Because I love you. When we were married it was the

romantic love of a silly girl but now, after all that has happened, it is a woman's love. I know you hold back from me but in your eyes, your eyes made me hope."

"I'm so sorry, I'm so very sorry." He held close. Her body was tense, it was soft and familiar but also so strange. He just held her, remembering every curve, the softness of her skin, the taste of her, he felt her gradually relax sinking into him.

"All I have wanted was for you to take me in your arms and tell me all would be well, I was so frightened I had lost you." She whispered into his ear.

She clung to him and began to cry.

"Please don't cry, sweetheart, please don't cry."

"I have been so lonely, I felt I had lost my only true friend... my lover. I could not sleep without your arms around me. I never felt safe before we wed. It terrifies me how much I want and need you, how at your touch I am lost in you."

"I have longed for you. I curse that I was such a coward, hovering outside this door and afraid to come in case I was sent away again."

"You came to the door?"

"Often, I was told you did not want to see me, and when I did see you I made you cry."

"I didn't know, I thought you had turned from me...and our child."

"Our child? How could I do that? When he was put in my arms, when he was just a few hours old, he took his place in my heart alongside the rest of my children."

She was crying again, "Why did no one tell me?"

"Ssh, ssh,, to protect you I am sure, and I cannot lay blame after how I spoke to you, treated you."

She reached out and stayed his words. Her fingers were so soft and gentle as they brushed against his lips and almost gathered away his breath.

"You really love me?"

"Love you? I am mad for you, I thought you knew."

She was laughing and crying and softly. "You love me."

★

He held her hand, looking at her wedding ring, it was a mean thing, and had become lose on her finger, he twisted it round her finger, turning her hand over he kissed her wrist.

"We must never quarrel again. I cannot bear it, I had such a pain in my heart I thought I would die of it," she said.

"Oh sweetheart, I still don't understand why you chose me."

"Because you shone more brilliantly in my eyes, more than anyone else I have ever known."

He stood up.

"Where are you going?" There was a hint of panic in her voice.

"I, that is I, I did not want to presume but if you want me to stay with you tonight, I will tell the servants we are not to be disturbed." She nodded her head

★

They lay together side by side, both staring at the ceiling. He could feel the soft fluff of hair on her arm alongside him.

"Was I really conceived in a prison?" He turned on his side propped up on his arm.

"I don't know, it is likely, it doesn't matter. I'm just glad you were born at all."

"I love you," he said. She smiled.

"And so, you manipulated your mother and me to engineer this marriage."

"I did what I had to, to achieve my desire."

"And I desire you," he murmured.

"I have been churched, whilst you were in London."

"Are you sure, sweetheart? I don't want to cause you pain, I can wait." Though he knew it would kill him if he could not pour himself into her.

"Oh Richard," She smiled again, "I cannot."

★

He watched her sleeping, so soundly now, her dark hair spread across the pillow, he thanked God for being given this gift, a second chance to love and be loved. Alice would always be his first love but to know he would not have to live the rest of his life alone was indeed a blessing. He remembered reading in a pamphlet that the Queen of Scots had said on the eve of her execution, that the theatre of the world was more than the realm of England. He had seen more of the world than he could ever have imagined, but he knew that he could hold his own whole wide world in his arms, his wife and his children.

Her eyes slowly opened and she broke into a smile when she realised he was gazing down at her.

"I'm so glad it was not a dream."

"I'm the one living in a beautiful dream." Richard blushed, "I wish I was more of a poet."

"I love you being a man of action." He raised his eyebrows and grinned.

"Richard, may we have a supper with all the children, they have been so worried about us, about what might happen to them and it is Christmas, and the anniversary of our union."

He had completely forgotten. "Dear God, I did not think, or remember. I have been living such a nightmare."

"You need do nothing, don't worry, and let me do this for us, for our family, please, please say yes."

And nothing he did. He went to Church and gave thanks to God properly. He bathed, dressed with care in his best clothes, cut in the latest fashion, he had his hair trimmed and put in an earring, and he whitened his teeth with burnt white marble and pumice and chewed on parsley to sweeten his breath. He woke up Darvolle the goldsmith and demanded to see the best golden ring in his shop. He strolled down to the Quay House to bring Antonio home.

Jack punched his arm, "About time you recognised what was under your nose!"

"I love her, Jack." He was sheepish.

"Of course you do, sweet Jesus, she is beautiful, clever, dotes on you and is a loving bedfellow."

"Jack!"

"Well I'm glad I didn't have to give you another punch to bring you to your senses."

"That was a lucky blow. Will you come join our Christmas celebrations?"

"Of course."

"Where is Antonio, I thought he would have heard me?"

Jack pointed to the quay where Antonio was sat on a coil of rope watching the ships. Richard crossed the quay.

"Antonio, you have no cloak, here, share mine." He said as he sat beside the boy.

Antonio blinked and stared at him in that intense way he had.

"Why did you send me away, Papa?"

"What? I just wanted to make sure you were safe and looked after, there was so much happening, I'm sorry if you have felt neglected."

"I just wondered why it was only me."

"Because the others are older and I'm sorry, but you are my little boy and I wanted to protect you from death and misery." Richard kissed the top of his head.

"I am quite grown, Papa."

"Yes, perhaps you are, Antonio. I should not treat you like

a baby." They sat for a while watching the ships creaking and gently swaying. "Do you come here often, Antonio?"

"Sometimes, I used to come and look for a ship from Spain."

"Ah."

"Why did my mother throw me away?" Richard was dismayed. He thought Antonio had no memory of what had happened.

"I think, I think that she knew how much I wanted you to stay and at the last moment she could not bear to take you from me. She was always impulsive, so she let you stay in the most dramatic way she knew."

The little boy looked again with that penetrating stare. "It's all right, Papa. I am glad to be here, you don't need to make up a story."

"Are you really glad?"

"I like having brothers and sisters. Even if the girls are very silly at times and are always trying to pet me. I like it when Jacket gives me pennies for buns, and Will makes me things with his knife. Tom pretends to fight with me when I follow him around but gives me hug and helps me at school. And I like it when we walk around the town together and you tell everyone I am your son."

Richard kissed the top of his head again.

"And I like Luisa being my mother. She reads me stories and talks to me about Spain and dresses me in fine clothes. Will she still do that now she has her own baby?"

"Of course she will. She has been a little tired these last few weeks, it is a great thing to give birth. But she is preparing an entertainment for us all tonight and sent me to bring you home."

"I am not the youngest anymore."

"Indeed not, and when he gets a little older your baby brother will look up to you and follow you around and you will pretend to be annoyed but love him like Tom loves you."

"And we can still go to Spain when I have grown a bit more?"

"Yes we will." Richard gave him his hand and they walked up the street. He was proud of his little boy and hoped he had done right by him, carrying him away to Southampton.

Somehow by evening the halls were decked with rosemary, holly and ivy and the yule log burned in the hearth. The best plate was laid, glasses from Murano striped with fine white paint lined the table and the sideboard heaved with riches, the air was heavy with spices. Seated around Richard and Luisa were all his children, Jack and his family and Madame Sohier. Mr Dutton had returned that afternoon, his mother he declared was much improved and it was thought she would indeed live. He believed, as did she, that his visit had entirely revived her spirits. He thanked his master and mistress profusely and had bought back new sheet music with Christmas songs for them to all enjoy. They feasted and drank and danced. They performed the story of Prince Christmas with his attendants Mince Pie and Mulled Wine. They paraded the boar's head, they presented Richard with the spiced soaked bread at the bottom of the Wassail cup and sang his favourite carols: 'I saw three ships' and 'Tomorrow will be my dancing day'.

They talked of the ships they would buy, of a grand house in London and another in the country. Somehow Luisa had found gifts for all and Richard spun the terrestrial globe she had given him in wonder.

Richard twisted the ring he bought for her in his hand, "And you sweetheart, what would you like?"

She gazed into his eyes.

"I should like you to live to be a very old man," she replied, and Richard promised he would.

Glossary

alderman	former mayors were given the title alderman
arras	heavy wall hanging
argosy	large ship
assize	the size and weight of bread was monitored by the council
bearward	bear-baiting was a popular sport, the bearward was the keeper of bears
billman	town watchman, who carried a bill, an axe with a long wooden handle
burgesses	senior merchants of the town
caliver	type of light musket
cap paper	used to ignite powder in a gun
conies	rabbits
Coronation Day	of Elizabeth I, 15th January 1559
Coronation Day	of James I 25th July 1603
corslettes	breastplates of leather or steel
crewel work	fine worsted yarn
the counter	the prison at the Bargate
cucking stool	ducking stool which dipped victims into water

culverin	field gun
cutler	maker of knives
cutted thorn	ancient meeting place in Southampton since Saxon times
disguising apparel	mummers costume
farm of sweet wines	annual rent paid to the town in return for taking customs of wine
farthingale	petticoat held out by cane hoops
fee farm	annual rent payable to the monarch by chartered boroughs
firkin	small cask
flyboat	small 3 masted flat bottom boat
fowlers	gun used for hunting fowl
frumenty	hulled wheat boiled in milk
gambion	bottomless basket of earth used in fortifications
harke rings	door knockers
hellier	tile maker
homen wood	shot designed for fowler guns
horse loaf	cheapest type of bread made from beans
jakes	public latrines
lanthorn	lantern
mappa mundi	map of the known world
letters of marque	letters of authorisation for privateers
liveries	uniforms
mazer	plate
mensis	month
muster	compulsory military exercises for all men
neats tongue	ox tongue
okam	fibre created from old rope used to caulk ships
ordnance	cannon
perspective glass	early type of spyglass
posset	hot milk, curdled with ale, or wine

	with sugar and spices
pursuivant	royal messenger
queen	prostitute
sac	Spanish wine
sea beggar	Dutch privateers
skelling	lean-to
skiff	small boat
stamell	type of woollen cloth, usually dyed red
the stews	a brothel
sweating sickness	inflammatory fever
tabor	small drum played with a stick
tester	canopy over a bed
tippling house	house which sold ale and beer
touch hole	firing pin on a gun
trochisk	pastille or lozenge
truckle bed	a low bed that fits underneath another bed
waits	musicians and watchmen
Wallons	French speaking protestants
wantcatcher	mole catcher
wherlpool	huge whale-like sea monster

Author's Note

Many of the incidents and characters in this novel are based on reality, and are detailed in the records kept by the Mayors of Southampton in their record books known as *The Book of Fines*. Alderman Crooke and his son-in-law did exist and the latter actually did ruin his father-in-law and disinherit his eldest sons. Richard Mudford was Crooke's apprentice and rose to be senior town sergeant thanks to Crooke's patronage, he also had a disreputable brother called John, referred to as Jack in the book. Richard did live in a thatched cottage within the walls but the rest of his life as described in this book is imagined or created from fragments of other lives lived during the period. Southampton did supply the *Angel*, captained by Lawrence Prowse and used by Drake as a fire ship. Prowse also commanded the *Elizabeth* during the attack on Cadiz and made enough money to eventually become mayor of Southampton. Southampton was a centre for privateering and voyages of exploration throughout the sixteenth century. Edward Alleyn did visit the town with his company of actors on a number of occasions and went on to be made a town burgess. Southampton was also a place of refuge for Protestants fleeing persecution in the Low Countries and France.

Minor characters, the various mayors and sergeants, apothecaries and members of the French communion and the Ferry village are also real. Alice Dypere, widow of William, lived in East Street and did look after the orphan child of Thomasina Hall. Portuguese merchants like Manual Diaz traded in the town and supported Don Antonio, who visited the town at the time of the Counter Armada.

Many of the buildings and places of interest in the novel survive today and the walls and gates can still be walked. The Sohiers' Chapel of Saint Julien and Richard and Jeanne's house on French Street still exists. The Angel inn is now the Duke of Wellington. St Michael's Church is still a place of worship, as is St Mary's, though it is not the building known to Richard. Holy Rood is a ruin and St Lawrence is just marked by a few stones. All Saints has gone completely, as has much of the Ferry village, bombed during the Second World War. A few stones and bricks mark the site of Bull Hall now a small park not far from the Wool House. The Pigeon House was the sixteenth century name for West Gate which still stands. The building that housed King Edward VI school survives and bowls are still played on the old bowling green outside the site of the Friary. Silkshop Yard did exist until it was swept away as part of slum clearances in the late nineteenth century. The trade of Silk women was highly praised and had been supported by Italian merchants. Hampton serges were a new cloth developed in the town by the French-speaking Protestants.

Southampton had been one of the wealthiest towns in England throughout the middle ages and even into the sixteenth century. But by the reign of Elizabeth it was beginning to struggle economically both due to the decline of its trade and the rapid increase in the population. The town had a brief respite from its financial woes when it became a centre for privateering, some might also say piracy. It was involved in a long running court case with the Lord Admiral over the ownership of seized pirates' goods. When peace came with Spain the town no longer flourished and became a back water for nearly two centuries when it re-invented itself first as a Spa town and then as a passenger port for those travelling to America.